A Shade of Darkness & Deception

Book 2 in the Power and Promise Series

Jordan A. Day

KINGDOMS OF DISPARYA

CAELUM
ELEMENTAL MAGIC

UNDA: WATER AND ICE
IGNISIAN: FIRE AND HEAT
AERIAN: WEATHER MANIPULATION

MINISTRO
ANATOMICAL MAGIC

MEDICUS: HEALER
EMPATHI: EMOTION MANIPULATION
IMPERIUM: ANATOMICAL MANIPULATION

AGNITIO
INTELLECTUAL MAGIC

SEER: CLAIRVOYANCE
VERUS: TRUTH TELLER
MAGUSIER: MAGIC AND BOND DETECTION

VENATOR
STEALTH MAGIC

OCULI: PRETERNATURAL VISION
SONOR: PRETERNATURAL HEARING
VENARI: PRETERNATURAL TRACKING

TENEBRAE
DARK MAGIC

TREMO: FEAR INDUCER
SHADOW SHIFTER: DARKNESS MANIPULATION
ILLUSIO: ILLUSIONISTS

DISPARYA
VENATOR
TENEBRAE
AGNITIO
ARCANUS
MINISTRO
CAELUM
THE SOUTHERN SEA
N
E
S
W

PRONUNCIATION GUIDE

CHARACTERS

AINSLEY: AYNZ - LEE
FELIX: FEE - LICKS
DASHIELL: DASH - EEL

EVANDER: EH - VAN - DER
OLIVIER: AH - LIH - VEER
MARCELINE: MARSA - LEAN
LIA: LEE - UH
CALIDORE: CAL - EH - DOOR

TALLIS: TAL - LIS
JAHIER: JUH - HEAR
SIRONA: SIH - RONA
IMOGEN: IH - MUH - GIN
PERCEVAL: PUR - SUH - VL
BRANDLE: BRAN - DLE
ELENORA: ELL - EH - NORA

PRONUNCIATION GUIDE

PLACES

DISPARYA:	DIS – PAR – YUH
CAELUM:	KAY – LOOM
MINISTRO:	MIN – EE – STROW
AGNITIO:	AGNEE – SHE – OH
VENATOR:	VEN – AH – TOUR
TENEBRAE:	TEN - EE – BRAY
VORSUTOS:	VOR – SUE – TOWS
PRAVUS:	PRA – VUS

MAGIC

UNDA:	OO – N – DA
IGNISIAN:	IG – NISS – EE – AN
AERIAN:	AIR – EE – AN
MEDICUS:	MED – EE – CUSS
EMPATHI:	EM – PATH – EE
IMPERIUM:	IHM – PEER – IUM
TREMO:	TREM – OH
ILLUSIO:	ILL – OO – SEE – OH
MAGUSIER:	MAG – OO – SEER
VERUS:	VER – US
SEER:	SEE – ER
OCULI:	OC – YOU – LIE
SONOR:	SO – NOR
VENARI:	VEN – ARY

Ripple Recap

You know how shows always have that "Last time, on XYZ" (and usually it doesn't matter because it's not like you didn't just binge 30 episodes of the same series so everything is still fresh in your mind)? Well, we all know that with books our brain works a bit differently. As soon as I pick up a new story, my previous read vacates the premises as quickly as a man getting called out on BookTok for trying to gain clout without doing the work. I think you see what I'm getting at. I firmly believe that all fantasy books should have a recap in the beginning to refresh our depresso espresso little brains. So that's what this is. And who better to recap Ripple, than fan-favorite Felix?

When Jordan first asked me to do this recap, I thought about turning her down, (we all know that's a lie) but decided it was in the best interest of the people that I carry out this task. We're all aware of just how mediocre her writing is and that her storytelling leaves much to be desired, so this arrangement is probably for the best (I'm only slightly kidding, Jordan. Please don't kill me off).

A Ripple of Power & Promise starts out with a bang (quite literally). We're introduced to our female main character (and my future best friend), Ainsley. She hadn't had the greatest life growing up. Her parents were slaughtered shortly after her birth, and she was raised by two caregivers who hated her with a passion. Before my future best friend was born, her parents made a deal with King Perceval of Caelum, arranging the marriage between their daughter and his son, Prince Dashiell. In this world, women are sought after for marriage solely because of the magic they possess—and Ainsley's bloodline was said to have a lot of it. Upon marrying Dash (my other best friend), she would have to forfeit some of her magic to him. As much as I'd like to say, 'fuck the patriarchy,' I'm not in a position to do so without bringing about my death... And I rather like my life.

Despite hating Dash and me when she first arrived at the palace, she is unable to resist my charms for long and falls prey to my plan of making her my new best friend—and I guess Dash's too. She also gets closer to her maiden, Imogen. I can't help but love their mother/daughter relationship. But as our little trio starts to enjoy our new normal, a dark presence makes its way into the palace, attempting to kidnap and hurt Ainsley at every turn. Given the clues, we're convinced the King of Tenebrae is trying to capture Ainsley and use the power that she may one day possess, for his own gain. Not cool.

Eventually, I get to witness Dash and Ainsley fall in love (despite cockblocking them at every turn for my own amusement.) Just when I think everything is perfect, Dash starts acting like a dick and ignoring Ainsley. Again, not cool. Following her twenty-first birthday (when she becomes immortal), she takes a trip to a nearby orchard to clear her head and is attacked by evil men from Tenebrae. They fail in their kidnapping attempt thanks to Dash, but Ainsley is nearly killed. Luckily, she heals quickly but Dash is *not* happy over the whole ordeal. He calls a meeting consisting of the Five Kings of Disparya, to put an end to the attacks on Ainsley's life and formally accuse King Evander of Tenebrae.

Some time passes, and Ainsley and Dash get back on track and fall deeper in love, but she starts to become disappointed that even though she turned twenty-one, she doesn't seem to possess any magic. As usual, we try to comfort her the best we can. During the meeting, while Dash and I are trying to get to the bottom of what's been going on, Ainsley is chatting it up with a stranger in a room she wasn't supposed to be in. We get nowhere with our accusations and the meeting ends on shaky terms. Later, we came to the conclusion that she was speaking with Brandle—one of the Princes of Ministro (and a total prick). Shortly after that, King Perceval announces that he is moving up Ainsley and Dash's wedding to take place in two days' time. Ainsley is a little freaked out by the news, but she loves Dash and wants to marry him.

The day before their wedding, I decide that I need attention and take Ainsley out for a special Delicious Duo date. We travel to a spot that has meant so much to me over the years, but Ainsley can't enjoy it fully because she starts to feel sick. I give her a tonic that Imogen provided me, in hopes it'll help, and take her to a nearby stream for some rest. And that's when they showed up…

A group from Tenebrae surrounded us, and though I instructed Ainsley not to fight, she didn't listen (as usual). Due to her sickness, she was weak and exhausted. She expelled the last of her strength and passed out. When she awoke in Tenebrae, she recognized a voice from a nearby conversation—Brandle. But it wasn't Brandle. It was King Evander of Tenebrae THE WHOLE TIME *gasp*…

He tells Ainsley that she possesses magic and that King Perceval has been keeping it dormant by giving her suppressants in her tea. He also explains that the king wanted to Entwine her and Dash together so he could drain all her magic and give it to his son. At first, she denies the claim but then amends it to say that Dash doesn't know. And that's where I had to break her heart and tell her that he *did* know… That we both did. Ainsley is understandably upset, and in her rage, her magic breaks through. But it wasn't magic from Caelum as she always thought. Ainsley possessed shadows. Shadows from another kingdom. Shadows from Tenebrae. She was now home. What. The. Fuck.

1.

For three days I didn't move. I sat at a window and just stared at the unfamiliar mountainous landscape of Tenebrae, watching day turn into night over and over again. Birds chirped and flew past the window each morning. Leaves, already turning shades of orange and red for autumn, danced along the wind. People strolled through the grounds, deep in conversation and laughing endlessly. It was odd to see such joy coming from a kingdom known for its dark magic and ill intent. But I knew better than anyone that just because things seemed one way on the surface didn't mean there weren't dark secrets lurking beneath.

Despair, anguish, and a never-ending wave of doubt filled me until I was nothing more than an empty shell of who I once was. Each morning, afternoon, and night a tray of food and water was brought to my room, but I didn't touch it. It wasn't that I believed it was dangerous to consume. I just physically couldn't eat. I felt numb and heavy and lifeless. I refused to cry, think, or speak. I didn't so much as move except to tend to my personal needs. I couldn't do anything other than sit and stare out that window.

Three days. It had been three days since I learned of the betrayal from the two men I had trusted and given myself to. Felix, the first person I had ever let into my life, had lied to me for weeks, keeping the secret of who I was from me. Dashiell, the prince of Caelum, and my fiancé, whom I had fallen irrevocably in love with, had plotted to drain me of the magic I didn't even know was running through my veins.

I cringed as I thought of the shadows that expelled from my hands while screaming at Felix once I had learned the truth. I wasn't from the Kingdom of Caelum as I had always believed, and I didn't possess their elemental magic.

Instead, I had darkness swirling inside me. I was the product of the Kingdom of Tenebrae—The Dark Kingdom, as Dash had once called it.

That day, after the shadows disappeared from my hands and Felix was hauled away, Evander, the King of Tenebrae and the bane of my existence, smiled as he studied me from head to toe. Typically, I would have fought back and told him to fuck off, but I felt so numb and dead inside—not to mention I was still in shock after what I had learned.

Thankfully, he seemed to recognize for once that I was in no mood for his arrogance, and he called forth two names I hadn't yet heard. I watched as the golden-eyed man who helped kidnap me from Caelum came forward with a beautiful woman at his side. She was tall, and her long red hair flowed down her back in voluminous waves. She seemed slightly overdressed compared to everyone else, wearing a vibrant formfitting golden dress that hugged her curves in all the right places.

Evander introduced the two as Ophelia and Calidore before instructing them to take me to a room so I could *relax*. I don't know why I went with them. It wasn't like me not to put up a fight against doing something I didn't want to, but maybe I just didn't care anymore. Perhaps I was too broken now.

For three days, Ophelia came to see me. Sometimes it was just to take away my untouched food and replace it with a fresh tray. Sometimes she'd try to strike up a conversation, though I'd never say a word in response. She was kind and I was being rude, but I couldn't find it in myself to care. I didn't want the company. I wanted to be left alone. Occasionally, Calidore would show up with her. He never tried to speak to me, and I had the sense he was only there because he happened to be in her company at the time. Judging by the quick kisses he would steal from her, I could assume they were a couple. I always looked away from their intimacy, not wanting to relive the moments I had done the same with the man I loved. When I'd stare at their exchange for too long, my heart would start to break, and I'd have to will my mind not to go there, not to think of Dash.

I hadn't allowed my thoughts to travel to him since I'd learned what he was planning to do. I was barely holding myself together, and I knew that if I pictured his deep teal and navy eyes, the way he'd kiss me tenderly, or how good it felt to be in his arms, I'd shatter and crumble completely. So instead, I focused on anything else.

For three days.

I only knew how long it had been because I was told.

"It's been three days," a voice said, and I turned my attention from the view of the snowcapped mountains to *him*.

When I heard the door creak open, I assumed it was Ophelia with breakfast, but it was none other than Evander holding her usual tray. I held his gaze for a moment longer before directing my eyes back to the window without a word.

"You need to eat something, Ainsley," he said. He was met with silence. "King Tallis is waiting to speak to us in the study, so you need to get up and follow me."

His demand had me twisting to look at him. I was so freaking sick and tired of everyone determining my *needs*. I didn't respond as I chewed on his words. I had heard the name 'Tallis' before when the five kings of Disparya met in Caelum. King Tallis had stopped Dash in the hall, disrupting our plan, and Felix had to take me on another route to safety. Why was he here now, and what did he want to say to me? When I didn't move, Evander spoke again.

"You need to get your ass up and follow me."

His command set my blood on fire, causing me to feel for the first time since I arrived in this room.

"The only thing I *need* to do is tell you to shut the hell up and get the fuck out of my face, Evander," I spat, my voice cracking and horse from not speaking in days. He grinned at my insult, and I shoved down the darkness I felt creeping up.

"We have important matters to discuss, so you *need* to come with me," he replied.

"I'm not going anywhere with you," I told him, crossing my arms and settling in.

"Fine," he said as he walked over to the empty chair on the other side of the room and sat down, crossing his arms over his chest to mimic me. He was such a prick, and he knew it.

"Fine," I replied as we stared each other down, neither of us moving nor speaking again.

Minutes passed, and finally, Evander broke my gaze, closing his eyes as he tilted his head back like he was about to go to sleep. I watched him with strange curiosity until he lowered his head. When his eyes fluttered open, wickedness was dancing within, and a sly crooked smile crept up his face. I had no idea what brought about the change in him, but something told me I wasn't going to like it.

A gentle knock sounded moments later, and a tall man with deep olive skin and stark white hair appeared in my doorway. My breathing hitched as I realized it was the same man I had seen from my window the day the kings departed Caelum. When our eyes met that day, he had placed his hand over his heart as he bowed before mounting his horse and riding away. Was he one of Evander's advisors that were in the meeting?

"Hello, Ainsley; it's so nice to meet you finally. My name is Tallis," he said before stepping further into the room. "Sorry to keep you waiting, but Evander just informed me that you would rather discuss our business here rather than in the study." I turned to Evander, and my mouth dropped open as he smiled widely, his face full of amusement.

"But you were here, so how did you..." I asked, unable to form a complete sentence. Evander winked at me as he stretched his long legs and gestured for Tallis to take the empty chair beside him.

"As I said, we have important matters to discuss, and I wasn't going to let your temper deter us," he replied, and I rolled my eyes. If he wanted to see my temper, I'd gladly show him the extent of it. I opened my mouth to retort, but he waved his hand at me absentmindedly like I was a gnat in his face. Oh, *fuck him*. "Go ahead, Tallis."

"Ainsley," King Tallis started, "As you are now well aware, you possess shadow magic. Your mother was born here in Tenebrae, but your father was not." His declaration stopped all visions I was currently having of murdering Evander, and I abruptly turned my attention to him. King Tallis sat forward, resting his forearms on his knees as he spoke. "He was born in Ministro, and because of that, you also possess the Gift of—"

I sat straight, pressing my back hard into the window behind me as my heart hammered in my chest. If my parents were from two different kingdoms and I had a Gift from each, then my very existence was against Disparya's most sacred law. Combining two kingdoms' magic, also known as Conjoining, was not only illegal but punishable by death. I gripped the cushion beneath me and worked to control my breathing as my eyes darted between the kings before me, terrified that they would breed or kill me. King Tallis held up his hands, and his light brown eyes were calm and pleading.

"It's okay, Ainsley; no one here will hurt you," he said carefully, and I looked to Evander to find him nodding along, his grey eyes warm for the first time since I met him all those weeks ago.

"You're safe here, love," Evander added. Though I didn't fully trust him or his motives, I believed that fact alone. Since arriving in Tenebrae, I developed a strange sense of calm that I had never experienced. The magic inside me stretched and curled around, slumbering like a cat on a sunny day; finally content to be *home*.

My head spun as I tried to comprehend what King Tallis had told me. Could I trust what he was saying? Would there be any reason he or Evander would lie about my Gifts or parentage? I didn't know what or who I could believe in this new kingdom. If I was going to survive, there was one person I had to see.

"I need to speak to Felix," I said. King Tallis looked at Evander questioningly.

"King Perceval's advisor is here?" he asked incredulously.

"Not by choice," Evander replied flatly, disdain for Felix coating every word.

"So then why would you—"

"I need to speak to Felix," I demanded again, not caring if I was being rude in the presence of royalty. I could tell Evander was about to argue, so I cut him off. "I won't discuss anything further until I see my friend." Did I even consider him my friend anymore after his heartbreaking betrayal?

"Marceline," Evander called. A woman appeared immediately in the doorway as if she had been standing right outside it, waiting for an order. It was the same woman that helped capture me from Caelum days ago. "Take Ainsley to the dungeons to see Felix." Not expecting him to give in so quickly, I climbed off the bench and made my way to the exit before he had a chance to change his mind. "When you're finished, find me in the dining room. Marceline will point it out to you," Evander instructed.

Marceline didn't speak as she led me through the palace, only pointing at the open door with several dining tables beyond it. She walked gracefully yet with an air that suggested she was deadly to anyone that wished her harm. I was in awe and couldn't help but stare at her beauty. She had dark blonde hair that was tightly curled and bounced as she moved, and her deep golden ebony skin made her turquoise eyes stand out.

"Are you and Olivier related?" I asked tentatively, remembering the name Evander called the leader of the group that took me. He and Marceline looked so much alike that I couldn't imagine they weren't.

"We're twins," she replied as we turned the corner to the dungeons. "He's in the last one on the right." She pointed down the dimly lit corridor before walking away.

"Wait, I don't have a key!" I yelled after her.

"You'll be able to open it," she called over her shoulder as she rounded the corner from which we came, leaving me to face Felix alone.

2.

I made my way down the stone hallway, and as I observed my surroundings, I was surprised at what I found. I had expected the dungeons to be a cold, damp part of the palace, filled with chains and torture devices depicted in many of the novels I had read, but it seemed to be the opposite here in Tenebrae. Behind the bars of each cell was a small bed in one corner and a toilet in the other with a curtain hung around it for privacy. Most of the cells were empty, with only a few occupied by prisoners. As I passed, they looked up from their books or the paper they were writing on and waved or bowed, always with a friendly smile.

I stopped before reaching the last cell on the right, taking a long deep breath as I readied myself to see Felix for the first time in days—for the first time since I had learned of his betrayal. He had been my closest friend, but after he learned that Dash had been instructed to drain me of my magic completely, he chose to keep it a secret from me. His choice was devastating, and I wasn't sure if I could ever truly grant him my forgiveness.

But right now, I needed him.

I was not only in the foreign kingdom that I had been told for months wanted to enslave and breed me, but I was surrounded by strangers and new magic. I didn't know who or what I could believe. Even though I was still angry and hurt by him, having my friend by my side during a time like this was crucial. But before I could tell him that, I needed to hear exactly what happened when he found out about me all those weeks ago.

I peered between the bars to find Felix sitting crossed-legged on his bed, his back pressed into the stone wall behind him and his head tilted up as he stared at the ceiling. Though his cell was the same setup as the others, it seemed darker and colder. There weren't any books or paper or anything to occupy his time while imprisoned.

"Hi, Felix," I said cautiously, and his stare shot to me the instant his name left my mouth.

He looked exhausted and worn down, his amber eyes dull beneath the dim lighting. He stood and rushed for me, stretching out his hand to hold mine through the bars. Instinctively I stepped back, pulling away from him. I hated that my body did that. I hated that I had to be cautious of my friend and needed to protect myself from him. The agony in his eyes as he dropped his arm to his side fractured my heart, and I fought the desire to explain myself and comfort him. It had always hurt me to see Felix upset, and I felt this protective need to be there for him. But he had been the one to cause me pain, and I couldn't allow myself to forget that. I had to put my own feelings first.

"I'm sorry," he said, stepping back from the bars and returning to his bed.

Once he was seated, I grabbed the handle of the cell door, and just as Marceline promised, it opened for me. I stepped through and rested my back against the bars as we stared at each other. Felix's face was pale, and his hair was unkempt and unbound as it rested on his shoulders. He looked terrible, as if he hadn't slept since arriving in Tenebrae days ago.

"King Tallis and Evander came to see me this morning," I said, though I wasn't sure if that was where I should have begun. "They told me that my mother was from Tenebrae and my father from Ministro; as such, I am a product of Conjoining. Apparently, my Gifts come from both kingdoms." I watched him wring his fingers in his lap, refusing to make eye contact.

"They're telling you the truth," he said quietly, closing his eyes as he took a deep breath before twisting to face me. When his eyes fluttered open, they were misted over, and the emotion was clear on his face. "As we both know, you possess shadow magic from Tenebrae, but you are also an Empathi. Like me."

"Is that what Dash told you?" I couldn't hide the skepticism in my voice.

"No. I felt it," Felix replied, and his answer had me crossing the room to sit next to him on the bed, though I kept a large gap between us.

"When?"

"The day you told me you were in love with Dash, and I hugged you. I felt you exploring my feelings. It rattled me, but I chalked it up to pushing myself onto you without realizing I was doing it."

I closed my eyes and visualized that evening, remembering the sense of joy and longing I had felt from Felix. I had assumed he had shared those emotions with me willingly.

"You said that you had found out about Dash and King Perceval's plans for me the night of my birthday, but the exchange you're referring to happened days prior," I explained, trying to understand precisely when Felix had known about my Gift.

"As I said before, I wasn't sure what I had felt and assumed it was my Gift allowing you in. When I spoke to Dash on your birthday, he wasn't sure what magic you possessed and only knew that you were a product of two kingdoms. My suspicions were confirmed after King Perceval informed us that your wedding date had been moved."

My head spun with the new information being shared, and I had trouble keeping it all straight.

"I need to know everything that happened, Felix, from the beginning," I told him. He nodded at my request before turning to face me fully.

"After seeing what happened between you and Dash on that dance floor and watching him flee, I knew something was wrong. Once I told you to go, I ran after him and didn't stop until I located him in the War Room. He was..." Felix shook his head back and forth as he dragged his hands down his face. "When I found him, he had his hands on his head and was gasping for breath. I thought he was physically injured. Ainsley, he was a wreck, and I had never felt such torment and anger from someone before. When he saw me, he yelled at me to get out, but I couldn't. I ran for Dash as he slid to the ground, crying and pleading for me to leave. He was so distraught, and I had no idea what to do, so I threw my arms around my brother and just held him as he broke down. Eventually, he spoke and told me what he had learned.

"When he went to see his father after Annette's body had been found, he was told the truth about who you were. King Perceval explained that he and your father were close friends growing up and that he had learned of a plan to kill your parents because of their relationship and you. Your father was friends with a Magusier who betrayed them and informed the King of Tenebrae about your existence and that you possessed a Gift from each of your parent's kingdoms. When King Perceval learned of this news, he set out to find and rescue your mother and father but instead found their bodies with you nowhere in sight. After searching for hours, he said he managed to locate you in the arms of a soldier from Tenebrae who was to deliver you to their king. King Perceval killed them and stole you to keep you safe even though he knew your existence was illegal. He kept you hidden in Caelum with the help of a specific kind of magic to keep anyone from ever finding you. He decided that when you were old enough, you would move to the palace and marry Dash to keep you safe and protected forever."

Felix blew out a breath and tilted his head toward the ceiling. He looked exhausted but also like he was trying to ensure he didn't forget a single detail of the story. It was a pretty tale, but one I wasn't sure I believed. Sure, the things King Perceval had said made sense, but I had no way of knowing if he was lying about his relationship with my father, however... However, something deep inside me was whispering to tread carefully when it came to that king. I was surrounded by the people I had always thought were my enemy, yet I felt safer now that I was free from the king who swore to protect me. There was still so much I needed to know—needed to ask.

"And what was King Perceval's reason for wanting to drain me of my magic completely?" I asked.

"He knew that you would be forever hunted because of the Gifts you possessed and wanted to remove that threat entirely. He told Dash that he had searched for a way to rid you of the Gifts for years, but the only way it could be done was by Entwining you together."

"But then, wouldn't Dash be the one who would spend his life in danger from possessing magic from multiple kingdoms?"

I knew what Felix's answer would be before I even asked the question. There would be no scenario in this world where Dash didn't put *my* safety above his own. He would gladly choose to be hunted for the rest of his life if it meant keeping me out of harm's way.

"Yes, he would. When I brought that up, he said he didn't care about his own safety, only yours," Felix explained.

"If Dash was okay with all this being done, why was he so upset?"

I pulled on my fingers, looking anywhere but at Felix. Just because I understood Dash's desire to protect me didn't mean I forgave him. He may not have liked what he was going to do, but he didn't deserve to play the guilt-stricken victim because of a choice *he* made.

"He was never *okay* with it, Ainsley. I told you about the pain I felt from him when he ignored us. I mistakenly assumed it was because he killed those men in the orchard. He was torn up for days as he sat with the revelation of who you were and what he was commanded to do. I know you're furious at him for keeping it a secret, and I'm not defending his choice, but I'm telling you that I *felt* his anguish and don't wish it upon anyone. After he told me everything, he said he couldn't do it to you. He couldn't take away what he knew you wanted, and we would devise another way to keep you safe and hidden. I instructed him to tell you what was happening, and he promised he would the next day, not wanting to ruin your birthday more than he already had. Before discussing it further, King Perceval showed up and demanded to speak with his son alone. I waited outside Dash's room all night, but he never showed up.

"The next day I stayed away from you, knowing I couldn't look you in the eyes after what I learned. I finally understood why Dash had done the same. After you were attacked that night, his mind was made up, and he refused to listen when I tried to talk him out of it. He said it was the only way to keep you alive and safe. He talked about how you almost died in the orchard, and he couldn't let that happen again, and he—"

"But I survived," I interrupted. "That's not a good enough reason to take my magic."

"I'm not saying it is, but you didn't see him that night, Ainsley. He was terror-stricken. When he arrived at the palace with you in his arms, he was covered in your blood. I'd never seen his eyes that dark and wide with horror. He clutched you so tightly and threatened to kill anyone who tried to take you away from him, demanding that he carry you to the Medicus facility himself. When he had gotten you to the room and on the table, the three Medicus there told him to leave so they could work on you, but he refused to go. As much as I wanted to comfort my friend, I had to focus on keeping you calm and asleep as they cut off your dress and tried to heal you. Ainsley, I was terrified that we had lost you, but what I felt was *nothing* compared to what I could sense radiating from Dash.

"He stayed next to your head, cleaning the blood from your face and talking to you as the Medicus and I did what we could, but your immortal self-healing wasn't working fast enough. Eventually, the Medicus concluded that they had to physically tend to the injuries inside your body, or you would die. They gave you a tonic to keep you asleep but couldn't waste time waiting for it to take effect before trying to heal you. Dash lost it when you cried out in pain as they cut into you, and it took three guards and me to get him away from you. He screamed and fought us as he tried desperately to get back to you, and I had to use my Gift on him for the first time since we were children to calm him enough to drag him from the room. The Medicus sealed the door shut with magic but Dash didn't stop trying to break in. His knuckles were bloody, and I was sure his hands were broken, but he kept trying to get to you. I had never seen him so scared in my life."

I didn't know how to process what Felix was telling me. Did Dash's desperation of that night excuse his decision?

"After a while, I convinced him to sit with me outside your door," Felix added. "I held him for hours as he shook, cried, and begged the Gods not to take you from him. It was the longest night of our lives. Finally, the Medicus emerged and told us that you survived the procedure, but only time would tell if it was enough to keep you alive. I'm not saying he was right in deciding to take your magic, Ainsley; I'm saying I saw firsthand how scared he was to lose you."

I blew out a breath, desperate to fill the space with anything but words. But, Felix wasn't finished.

"When King Perceval returned and discovered that Dash had called a meeting of the Kings of Disparya, he laid into him. I could hear muffled shouts from the hall, even with their silencing shield up. When Dash returned to the room, he refused to tell me what was said between them. I didn't push the subject, figuring Dash needed time to sort through his feelings. When you started to heal, I tried reasoning with him again, but quickly realized that King Perceval had already gotten to him because Dash brought up his mother. She was never a subject he liked to discuss, but he kept saying he wouldn't lose you as he had lost her. His father knows Dash's mother is his weak spot aside from you. For years, King Perceval has guilted Dash into believing that the queen's death was somehow his fault and never wasted a chance to throw it in his face. I wouldn't put it past King Perceval to compare what happened to her and what happened to you so he could manipulate his son into doing what he wanted.

"One night, when you were asleep in the Sanctuary, Dash told me that his father had come to him the evening prior, bringing news regarding Tenebrae. King Perceval said that he received word that soldiers from Tenebrae were making their way towards Caelum, and he feared that this meant they somehow had learned who you truly were. We were running out of options and time, but Dash didn't want to tell you something that would devastate you without a solution, and I agreed. Neither of us was getting anywhere in our research, and you and he were mending your relationship. I didn't know what to do. I trusted that he would tell you before—"

"But he didn't tell me, did he?" I replied flatly. Even with Dash's reasoning, I was still enraged.

"No, he didn't," Felix said, releasing a deep breath. "And then King Perceval announced that your wedding would be moved up, and we ran out of time. That was the day I knew for sure you were an Empathi. After Dash and his father left the terrace, I was so scared and furious for you. You were talking, but I could barely process your words until you knelt before me, and I felt you. I could feel this warm light wrapping around me, trying to soothe and comfort my emotions, and I knew that you were the same as me. Looking back, it makes sense because of how close we have gotten and how much we understand one another. Your Gift as an Empathi isn't only the ability to feel and calm heightened emotions; you can also relate to and empathize with those around you. You can sense when someone is being genuine, and I believe that is part of the reason you were so quick to give Dash and me a chance in the first place after you learned of our past."

The more I thought about Felix's words, the more they made sense. It would explain why my feelings toward him and Dash changed drastically after Felix and I spent that day at the lake. Once I had learned about their tragic history and loss, I felt for them and wanted to know more. I had opened myself up and willingly let them in.

"Is that all?" I asked.

"No. That night, after I walked you to your room, I went back to Dash and asked him what he planned to do now that the wedding was approaching. He told me he was going to go through with it and that it was the only way to keep you safe. Dash said that his father was worried that your powers would start to show soon and that the drugs you were being given in your tea wouldn't hold them off for much longer. That's why he moved up the Entwining Ceremony. King Perceval didn't want anyone to know of your magic for fear that someone would betray us and share the knowledge with Tenebrae. Dash thought that the sooner the transfer of magic happened, the sooner you would be safe. He said he would never use your Gifts, so no one would ever know what truly occurred during the ceremony."

A perfect plan, all wrapped up and tied with ribbon.

"What are your thoughts on Dash?" I asked.

Did his belief that my life was in danger excuse his decision? Would I have chosen to do the same if I thought he would be hunted down, enslaved, and bred like an animal because of his Gift?

"I think Dash has accepted everything his father has said to him, and based on the information he's been told, he truly believed that the only way to keep you safe was by taking your magic," Felix answered.

"And King Perceval?"

The story he told Dash about what happened to my parents was similar to what he had once said to me. I had believed him then, but I wasn't sure if I should now. The king's explanation of everything sounded too careful and calculated, but that didn't mean I would be quick to believe whatever Evander would tell me next.

It was a long moment before Felix finally answered. "I think he's full of shit."

I kept my breathing calm and steady as I ran through everything Felix had shared with me, replaying his words repeatedly in my mind.

"How did I end up in Tenebrae?" I asked.

It was a question that I still couldn't figure out the answer to. I didn't think my captors had found us by coincidence, but if that were the case, then why did Felix seem so shocked when they appeared? He had even stood in front of me with his knife drawn across his chest as if he were ready to defend me. Nothing was making sense, and I needed to know what, if anything, Felix knew.

"When Dash mentioned his father's claims regarding Tenebrae making their way to, I was panicked," Felix explained. "I knew the type of magic their kingdom possessed, and all I kept picturing was you beaten and bloody in Dash's arms. The more I thought about it, the more fearful I became, but also the more it didn't make any sense. No king would be stupid enough to make their motives that obvious, especially one accused of attempting to kidnap a princess and a prince's bride. Nothing was adding up, so I decided to investigate further. Every year, King Perceval has me visit villages and speak with the people of Caelum to gauge how they feel about him and his decisions for the kingdom. I suggested to King Perceval that I conduct my visits as soon as possible due to the events that had transpired over the weeks. I told him it was to see if the Kings of Disparya had approached anyone in hopes of forming a coup against him and that we could end any unrest before it started. I knew he would agree because he had always been paranoid about losing his power over the people and would do anything to keep it.

"I set out immediately following my argument with Dash the morning after your Primum Celebration and traveled to the nearest village, an hour's ride away. I knew a few soldiers stationed there that hated King Perceval and who I could trust not to relay my whereabouts or questions back to him. No one had heard about or seen soldiers from Tenebrae traveling through Disparya. King Perceval ensures all his camps stay in contact with one another and are up to date on information. What one camp of soldiers know, they all know. The fact that my acquaintances hadn't heard of anything was a red flag. So I went to see your caregivers."

I narrowed my eyes, confused at whether the two hateful women who kept me alive for nearly twenty-one years had anything to do with the situation. They were happy to be rid of me, and I couldn't picture Looks or Mouth willingly answering any of Felix's questions if they pertained to me.

"Because King Perceval claimed to be close to your father, Dash firmly believed that one of your Gifts would be from Caelum. But the more I thought about it, the more that didn't seem likely," Felix explained, and my brows furrowed in confusion. "If you were from Caelum, then why drain you of your magic? Most of the other Gifts in Disparya aren't physical; therefore, they can't be seen when used. With even the most basic training, no one would ever know you had anything else. Which means—"

"My Gift had to be physical," I told myself, putting the pieces together.

"And only one kingdom besides Caelum possesses physical Gifts."

"Tenebrae," I finished, tilting my head toward the ceiling as I let everything soak in. "So when you learned I was an Empathi, you figured out my second Gift must have come from this kingdom. Why else would King Perceval want to hide it."

"Exactly," Felix answered. "So I visited your caregivers to see if they could offer any insight. I knew they probably wouldn't openly tell me anything, but I had to try. However, when I arrived, the house was empty, and they were nowhere to be found. I checked your village, asking around, and that's when I learned..." He halted and looked at me, his face falling as his eyes softened with sympathy.

"You learned what, Felix?" I asked, fearing I already knew the answer.

"They died a few days after you arrived at the palace," he replied, and I let out the breath I had been holding. I hated those women for how they treated me my entire life, but it didn't mean I wanted them dead.

"King Perceval was covering his tracks," I deduced. It wasn't a question, but Felix confirmed the theory anyway. "So what happened next?"

"At the kings' meeting, I could sense that King Tallis didn't harbor the same hatred for King Evander as the others did. I realized that getting word to Agnitio would be my only hope of discovering what was truly going on. If the two kings were on friendly terms, I had a chance of getting King Tallis to arrange a meeting between myself and the King of Tenebrae. There was one person I knew I could reach out to that could get my message into the hands of King Evander, and that was Elenora—King Tallis' niece. I wanted to meet her in person, but she was stationed at the border of Agnitio and Ministro, which was at least a five day ride away. I couldn't bear leaving you for that long, so I grabbed some transfer parchment and wrote an encoded message requesting her to arrange a private meeting with King Evander for me immediately. I told her it was regarding the attacks he had been accused of, and that the information I had suggested otherwise. Eleanora's response appeared within the hour, detailing a meeting time and place."

"And that's when you went to see Evander?" I asked.

My head spun at all the information I had been given. The more I learned, I realized the less I knew. While Felix was plotting to meet with the King of Tenebrae, I was tangled in bedsheets with Dash, blissfully happy and unaware of everything going on around me. Felix stood and began pacing the small cell as he recounted what had happened.

"Well, not exactly," he answered. "When I was about to leave the village, I felt unease and anger swirling around me, and as I tried to detect where the feelings were coming from, I noticed one of King Evander's advisors leaning against the door of a small house. When our eyes met, he disappeared inside, leaving the door open. I knew it was a command to follow, so I did. I entered to find the house unoccupied, save for Olivier sitting alone at an empty table, waiting for me. He tried to get me to tell him what information I had, but I refused to speak to anyone except for King Evander. Eventually, he told me to return in two days for the meeting. As soon as I agreed, I made my way home. The following day, we learned that the Entwining Ceremony was being moved up. Once I realized that Dash wouldn't be convinced otherwise due to his fear for your safety, I knew I couldn't wait any longer and had to get you out.

"I immediately found Imogen and told her everything I knew and my plan. She was shocked, of course, but wasted no time telling me to get my ass out of the palace to find King Evander while she did what she could there. Though it was the middle of the night, I found Olivier awake and sitting at that same table.

I quickly explained that things had changed, and I couldn't wait any longer to speak to his king. To my surprise, King Evander was already there and sat down to hear me out."

I forced my mind to go back to that night. The three of us had spent it drinking and laughing in the Sanctuary like a typical day. I had no idea that would be my last night of peace, the last night I would spend with Dash. I didn't know that my whole world would be turned upside down the very next day.

"It was a huge risk, but I didn't know what else to do," Felix said. "You weren't safe in Caelum, and I knew King Harbin would have you killed if he learned about your Tenebrean Gifts so Ministro wasn't an option either. I don't know what it was, but I had this feeling that telling King Evander about you was the right choice. I can't explain why I knew that—I just did."

Felix's expression was soft and thoughtful, like he was recounting everything about that night in great detail. I couldn't imagine the fear he must have felt over contemplating what to do about me. We had all been under the assumption that King Evander was trying to capture and hurt me, so Felix must have really been at the end of his rope if he chose to take a chance and trust him.

"What happened when you told them?" I asked.

"Their faces were impassive and blank the entire time, like the information I shared meant nothing to them. At one point, King Evander said that if King Perceval wanted to conduct an illegal ceremony and put his son and his kingdom at risk for war, then that was his decision to make. He didn't care about the repercussions it would have. He didn't care about anything... Until I mentioned your name.

"The change was slight, but I felt it, and now I realize it was because he had met you during the kings' meeting. I didn't understand what caused his sudden interest at the time, but I didn't care as long as he offered his aid to get you out of Caelum. I would figure the rest out later. We spent the next hour devising a plan for your rescue. I gave them a general idea of where I would be taking you and how they could pick up the trail to find us. Olivier and Evander would meet us in my secret spot, and together we would explain what was happening."

He walked back over to the bed and sat closer than before. A part of me wanted to scoot away and create distance between us, and the other wanted to lean into him for support. In the end, I stayed where I was.

"I returned just before dawn and found Imogen. She had created two tonics for you and explained that one would help rid your body of the poison from the tea, but the side effects wouldn't be pleasant. If it were too much for you to handle, I was to give you the other tonic to help lessen your pain. I struggled during the journey, going back and forth on whether I had made the correct choice. It wasn't until I heard you speak about how much you loved Dash and the friendship you and I had built that I knew I had made the right decision. As much as I was doing this for you, I was doing it for Dash too. He's been my best friend and brother for years. I know him better than I know myself. Taking your magic would destroy who he truly is, and I love him too much to allow that to happen. I know he is better than his fears and weaknesses, and I couldn't stand by and watch him make a choice he would regret for the rest of his life.

"When we arrived at the location, you were sicker than before. I didn't realize the second tonic would weaken you as much as it did, and I began to worry that Imogen had made it wrong or your body wasn't accepting it like it was supposed to. Olivier and King Evander hadn't shown up yet, and I didn't want to leave our spot, but I had to get you somewhere you could rest with fresh water and shade."

I had been so sick that day, and positive it had to do with the amount of alcohol we had consumed the night before. Little did I know my best friend and mother figure had drugged me, and I was about to be stolen from the life I knew and the man I loved.

"When I saw that Olivier showed up with two other companions and King Evander was nowhere in sight, I thought they had set a trap for us," Felix continued. "I couldn't sense any ill will or malice from them, but it still made me uneasy that they changed the plan without my knowledge. After you fainted, Olivier said he would be taking you to King Evander, and I was free to return to the palace and lie about our arrangement. I, of course, refused to go and demanded to stay at your side. After some arguing and threats, he agreed but promptly knocked me out, and I awoke here in this cell with Calidore watching me. I didn't leave until Marceline retrieved me so I could speak to you. And that's everything," Felix finished, and I let out a long exhale. I had no idea what to make of his confession and needed time to sit with it.

"I don't know what to say," I answered honestly. My mind was a jumbled mess at the constant stream of revelations, and I couldn't form a single coherent thought. "But thank you for telling me." I rose from the bed and made my way over to the door. "I know that you and I have our shit to work through, and I'm not going to pretend that I'm not hurt by what you did, but right now, I need you, Felix. At this moment, you are the only person in my life who I know would never purposely hurt me. I want to repair the trust that you broke, but to do that, the lies have to stop now. I can't let you in again if I don't trust you."

"I swear to the Gods, Ainsley, I have told you everything I know. I don't plan on ever keeping anything from you again. Regardless of my intentions, it was wrong not to tell you the second I found out, and I'm so sorry. I love you, Ainsley," he said as a single tear spilled over. "Just tell me what I can do to make this better."

"I need time. I want to forgive you, but I don't think I can right now." He nodded as understanding, shame, and guilt flooded his pale features. "However, I would still like you by my side while I try to move forward," I added as I opened the cell door and gestured for him to follow.

"Always," he responded. I offered a small smile before we made our way out of the dungeons and onto the primary levels of the palace.

When Felix and I entered the dining room, Evander and Olivier were seated at a long table. The king casually looked up from his book as we approached.

"Happy family once more?" he quipped though it didn't seem like he cared about the answer.

"I'm ready to talk to King Tallis, but we need to get some things straight before I do," I said, and Evander straightened with excited anticipation. "My mother may have been from this kingdom, but I am not your subject nor your property."

"Noted," Evander said, boredom coating the word.

"And Felix stays with me. I want him out of the dungeons." Olivier snorted as if annoyed. Evander smiled at his advisor before turning his attention back to me.

"Felix has never been required to stay in his cell. He was granted freedom to move about the palace directly after you were shown to your room but chose to remain in the dungeons until you forgave him. His cell door has never been locked." I twisted to Felix and lifted a brow in question. He simply shrugged.

"Your friend is quite... Dramatic," Olivier added, rolling his eyes as he popped a piece of bread into his mouth and refused to look in Felix's direction.

"That's putting it mildly," I said quietly. I could hear Felix laugh softly under his breath, and the sound tugged at my heart. So much had happened over the past week, and I missed hearing his laughter.

"Tallis is in the study waiting for us," Evander said, rising to his feet and dropping the book onto the table with a thud. Usually, I would have been tempted to read the title, but I was too nervous to even care. "Follow me," he commanded and led Felix and me out of the dining room and through the halls.

3.

The study was large, about the same size as the Sanctuary back in Caelum. My chest ached as I remembered that room and the joy and laughter I had experienced in it. There were floor-to-ceiling windows on the back wall that showed off the mountainous landscape in the distance, and in the center of the study were two couches that faced each other with a low rectangular table in between.

"Hello again, Ainsley," King Tallis said as he rose from the black leather couch and bowed his head.

"King Tallis," I replied, returning the gesture.

"Have a seat," Evander instructed, waving his hand at the couch facing Tallis as he sat next to his fellow king.

I sat as Felix poured a glass of water from the pitcher on the table and handed it to me. I drained its contents, the cool drink calming my nerves, and placed the empty glass next to the liquor decanter in the center of the table.

"I know the news I shared with you this morning may have been a bit jarring, and I apologize if I didn't deliver it as sensitively as I could have," King Tallis remarked.

"You were gracious, Your Majesty. It was more about the information itself rather than the delivery. I appreciate your apology, but it isn't necessary," I said. King Tallis seemed genuine with his words, and I felt like I could believe what he was saying. I turned to Felix, and he nodded slightly, giving me the confirmation I needed. "I'm ready to hear what else you wanted to tell me."

King Tallis smiled warmly and sat forward, interlacing his hands and resting his forearms on his knees. "Evander, you may want to pour yourself a drink for what I have to say next," he said.

"I'm fine. Just get on with it," Evander responded, laying his arm over the back of the couch as if he were getting comfortable.

"Very well," King Tallis drawled, not taking his eyes off me. "Ainsley, you are the Heir to Tenebrae."

"*What*?!" Felix, Evander, and I all yelled in unison.

"Ainsley has two Gifts from this kingdom, making her next in line for the throne," King Tallis announced as plainly as if he was noting the weather and not relaying world-shattering news. Evander leaned forward, grabbed the decanter of amber liquor, and poured himself a generous serving before draining it all in one swallow and then refilling his glass. "I tried to tell you," the king said, gesturing to the drink in Evander's hand.

"Are you positive?" Evander asked as he looked at me like the idea thrilled him.

"Yes," he said, smiling.

"How can you possibly know that?" I demanded.

I felt the panic rise, and it was like I was suffocating under the weight of his declaration. Evander and King Tallis gave me a confused look and then stared at Felix as if he could explain my question.

"Ainsley, you remember what a Magusier is, right?" Felix asked kindly.

"They are the ones that have the power to see bonds and what Gift someone possesses," I answered, and Felix nodded in confirmation.

There was still so much I was learning about our world, but Magusiers were used as a cautionary tale of what could happen if someone became too greedy with their Gift. Magusiers were used during the Great Wars in Disparya to say if a pregnant female was carrying a child with abilities from two different kingdoms. If they weren't, and the child only possessed one Gift, the mothers and their unborn children were killed and discarded because they were of no use. If the unborn child *did* possess two Gifts, they didn't survive for long. After the war ended, they were hunted down and slaughtered for fear of the power they possessed. Magusiers were killed for their involvement, and the Gift was now extremely rare.

"Magusiers hail from Agnitio," Felix explained.

As the sovereign ruler, King Tallis possessed all three Gifts from his kingdom, so of course he would have the ability of a Magusier. I nodded in understanding and then turned back to face the kings.

"She didn't know of King Tallis' Gift?" Evander asked though it sounded more like an accusation than a question.

"She knew what a Magusier was, just not that they came from Agnitio," Felix corrected, and Evander rolled his eyes as he took a sip from his glass.

"It's alright, Evander," King Tallis added.

"No, it isn't," he replied under his breath as he stared at the drink in his hand. There was anger in how he said the words, but I didn't understand why.

"Evander..." the king warned, his tone holding more of an edge than his usual calm demeanor, but it was no use. Whatever seemed to be pissing off the King of Tenebrae had simmered over and he slammed his glass down on the table, the amber liquid splashing over the lip, as he glared at Felix.

"She has been in your care for months, and you never bothered to explain the basics of the world around her?" he demanded, rising from his seat on the couch, his stare fixed on the man next to me.

"We thought you and your kingdom were trying to hurt her, so we taught her about Tenebrae's magic. Everything else didn't seem as important at the time," Felix answered, not meeting Evander's harsh gaze.

"Yes, because clearly Tenebrae was the one she needed to worry about," he snapped, dragging a hand through his dark hair. I looked at Felix to find him staring at the table as guilt and shame washed over his face. Evander was treating him unfairly, and I wouldn't stand for it.

"That's enough!" I yelled, standing to face the king. "You don't get to treat him like that."

"You are Tenebrae's heir, set to take the throne should something happen to me, and you seem to know nothing about Disparya," he said furiously. I still didn't know what to make of king Tallis' proclamation, and to be honest, I wasn't sure I believed him, but given Evander's rage on the subject, *he* clearly did.

"I can't be the Heir to Tenebrae," I told no one in particular.

"And why is that?" Evander asked, crossing his arms over his chest as if he were settling in to debate this.

"I'm female," I explained. Evander raised his hands and clapped slowly, dramatically, as he stared at me, his grey eyes hard.

"Glad to know you know at least *one* thing," he gritted, glaring at Felix.

"Females can't be heirs or sovereigns," I added, refusing to play into Evander's insult.

"Says who?" he quipped, sounding annoyed at my defense.

"History," I explained. "Tell me one female that ruled or was destined to."

I may not have known much about the kingdoms or their powers, but as a woman, it was drilled into my head growing up that we were nothing more than property. We were nothing more than what we could offer to the men we were chosen to wed and Entwine with. Evander tongued his cheek as he glanced around the room, clearly trying to come up with an answer or a snarky retort. My eyes drifted to King Tallis to see his lips tug at the corner as he observed this exchange.

"I can't," Evander admitted reluctantly. "But that doesn't mean it isn't the case now."

"Whatever," I snorted. "Leave Felix alone. It's not his fault for my lack of education."

"You're right," he said coldly. "It's *yours*."

"Excuse me?"

"Did I stutter?" He stepped closer, still feet away yet towering over me. "It's your fault that you're this clueless. You should have asked questions. You should have demanded to know your history or at least the history of your world. You should have cared enough to educate yourself about how the world works and the Gifts within it. You should have been less concerned about fucking your prince and more involved in the decisions around you."

Rage surged forward like wildfire, setting every inch of my insides ablaze as I closed the distance between us.

"Go fuck yourself!" I spat.

"Right back at you," he growled.

I lunged for him, but strong arms wrapped around my middle, pulling me away as Evander flashed a wry smile and winked, only pissing me off further. White light, warm and soothing, shot through me, slowing my heart rate and relaxing my body. Though I tried to fight it, Felix's magic was too strong for me.

"You have to stay calm, Ainsley," my friend whispered.

"The fuck I do!" I yelled, feeling my pulse quicken once more. Felix's Gift sank further into me, building pressure in my chest and making it hard to focus as I struggled to fight my way to Evander.

"The drugs are out of your system now, so your magic will release freely. You haven't learned how to control it yet and could hurt yourself," Felix explained.

"Or I could hurt that asshole!" I snarled. Evander puckered his lips together and kissed the open air. Oh, *fuck* him. Shadows spooled from my fingers, and Evander's face lit up with delight as he watched.

"No, Ainsley!" Felix exclaimed, tightening his hold on me as he pushed more of his power through my body. My eyes drooped as my head swam with dizziness. My arms fell to my sides as I felt myself being carried and then set upon a soft cushion. "If you promise to calm down, I will release my hold."

"Yeah, love, just relax," Evander added snidely.

"I hate you," I mumbled before darkness enveloped me and swept me away.

"You are not helping, Your Majesty," Felix said, and my eyes fluttered open to find Evander seated next to King Tallis, his back against the couch as he swirled his glass of liquor. I sat up, glowering at Felix, who wore an apologetic look.

"How long was I out for?" I grumbled, rubbing my temples as a headache began to take form.

"Just a couple of minutes," Felix answered, reaching to grab my hand. I flinched beneath his touch, and he pulled back, hurt flashing in his eyes as he did. "I'm sorry," he whispered.

We had always been so close, but now our relationship was tainted by lies and deception. He was my best friend, and I wanted desperately to get back to where we once were. I took a deep breath as I placed my hand over his and looked deep into his amber eyes.

"Go ahead," I told him. Felix nodded softly, knowing what I wanted, and closed his eyes.

I felt a warm white thread weave around my heart, searching and exploring. His eyes squeezed tight as he reached my hurt and suffering, followed by hope and desperation. I couldn't describe exactly what I felt, but I knew his Gift would allow me to show him. It would let Felix see that though I was in agony and our relationship was fractured, I still loved him and wanted to mend it.

When his eyes opened again, they were cloudy with unshed tears. I squeezed his hand, wishing that I could explore the emotions he held. I now knew I had the capability and had accidentally done it before, but I didn't know how to access it. Did the magic come forth when called or simply on its own.

"I'll teach you," Felix whispered, seeming to read the look on my face.

Evander snorted, and I shot him a glare, finding him swallowing the remainder of his drink while shaking his head. His unearned anger continued to piss me off the longer it went on.

"Do you have something to say?" I asked flatly.

"Many things," he replied. "Starting with—"

"Can we not do this now?" King Tallis cut in, his voice even-tempered and calm. Surprisingly, Evander closed his mouth, following his friend's instruction. "As you now know, Ainsley," King Tallis began, leaning forward to address me. "Your mother was from Tenebrae, and your father was from Ministro. As such, you possess Gifts from both kingdoms. Whether you believe me or not, you *are* the Heir to Tenebrae."

I let out a long sigh as I looked toward Felix, trying to read his reactions. I knew that his Gift would not only keep me calm, but he had experience in discussions and negotiations with politics. He could read emotions and sense if something seemed out of place.

"If you would like, I can tell you exactly which Gifts from Tenebrae run through your veins," King Tallis continued. Felix glanced down, meeting my eyes as he subtly nodded.

"Tell me, King Tallis," I said, directing my attention to him. He smiled warmly as he bowed his head in answer.

"Just Tallis is fine unless you prefer me to address you as Your Highness." I shook my head. Hearing that I possessed more than two Gifts was enough information to process. I didn't want to think about what being an heir would mean for my title and status.

"Very well, Ainsley," he said, flashing his straight white teeth. "In addition to shadow magic, you possess the Gift of illusion." I felt more than I saw Felix stiffen beside me.

"Rosella," he said to himself.

"Care to share with the rest of us?" Evander quipped, and Felix's eyes drifted to mine, ignoring the Dark King entirely.

"That day, you threatened Rosella in Dash's room," Felix said to me. My mind traveled back to her naked in his bed and our conversation. "I overheard her in the hall telling Felicity that you turned into a snake. I had thought she meant metaphorically, but now..." he trailed off, giving me a look to suggest that he believed Tallis' words.

"Felix, I can't turn into a snake. Don't you think I would have noticed if I did?"

"No, but you can make someone *think* that you had. That's what illusions do, love," Evander added, sitting forward as he studied me. "What happened that day?"

"I told her to stay away from Dash and me and—"

"No," he interrupted. "That's not what I meant. Think back to that day and walk us through everything in your mind and what you felt beneath the surface."

"I don't know. I was angry," I admitted. "I let that emotion fill me and imagined I was as deadly as the vipers that Dash always compared me to."

"Your prince compares you to a snake? Charming," Evander snarked, and I rolled my eyes. "But that's exactly what happened, love. You imagined yourself as a snake, so you became one in Rosella's mind. You need training, and as my heir, I will ensure you get it."

I rested my head in my hands as I attempted to digest the plethora of information shared with me today. Last week, I was in love and on my way to becoming the Princess of Caelum, and now I was brokenhearted and set to take over an entire kingdom. This all felt like a nightmare I couldn't wake up from. It was far too much.

"Are you okay?" Felix asked.

"No," I told him. "My entire life and everything I have come to know and love has been a lie. I don't know what to believe or who to trust."

I pulled my head back and glanced around at the three men in the room. Their eyes were all on me, their faces full of concern, wonder, and maybe even pity. I still had so many unanswered questions, so I waded through the murkiness of my mind to seek the truth.

"Was I born here or in Ministro?" I asked, keeping my gaze on Tallis' kind eyes.

"Here in Tenebrae," he answered. "Your father fled Ministro long ago and found refuge in this kingdom."

"Why did he—" I started but was immediately interrupted by Evander.

"We need to be focused on what is going on now and not what happened in the past," he argued, and I felt the little restraint I had on myself slip. He did not just give me shit for being clueless and not asking questions, only to interrupt me the second I did. The audacity of that man was something else.

"Why don't you want me to know?" I demanded, my cheeks heating with anger. "Did he find refuge here just for you to betray him and my mother years later because of their illegal relationship?" Evander turned, narrowing his eyes as they held me.

"Love, I was three years old when you were born and your parents slaughtered. I'm not sure I could betray them at that time."

"So it was your parents that did then?" I retorted. Fury flashed in his eyes as he straightened, ready to attack.

"Van," a deep voice warned, and we both turned to see Olivier standing in the doorway, quietly listening to the conversation.

Evander clenched his jaw and reluctantly tore his gaze from Olivier to peer back out the window. For whatever reason, he decided to heed the advice. Olivier walked through the room, stopped at my side, and knelt to meet me at eye level.

"I was there the night your parents were murdered, and I swear to you that I will tell you everything you want to know," Olivier said quietly. His turquoise eyes were piercing but soft, and I couldn't place the odd sensation I had as I stared at him. I knew nothing about this man other than that he was close with Evander, he aided in my rescue, and he claimed to know my parents, yet something inside told me that I could trust everything he said. "But right now, you should focus on the other questions you'd like to ask." I nodded, unable to speak. "You look like him," he added. Olivier stood and walked over to Evander to rest his hand on his king's shoulder.

I accepted that I would get to learn the truth of my parent's demise later on, and for now, I could focus on other pressing topics. Like why the hell I had been allowed to be born in the first place.

"Conjoining is illegal in Disparya," I stated, and Tallis nodded in acknowledgment. "So why are you both allowing me to live right now?" My stare wandered to Evander, needing to see the truth in his eyes as I asked the question.

"Because we don't punish those for loving who they want," Evander answered, and I wanted to snort at the irony of that statement. He had done nothing but punish me with harsh quips for my loving the Prince of Caelum since the moment I arrived in Tenebrae. He must have picked up on where my mind had gone because he quickly added, "We don't murder people for having a relationship with someone who hails from a different kingdom. Not here, nor in Agnitio. However, I cannot speak for the other three kingdoms. We provide refuge to those who need it."

"Is that why King Perceval wanted me? Because I was the Heir to Tenebrae?" I asked, looking up at Felix as I prayed to the Gods he didn't know this truth and chose to keep it from me. The only thing that made me think otherwise was that he seemed just as shocked to hear the news as I was.

"Does King Perceval have a Magusier on his Council?" Tallis asked before my friend could respond.

"No," Felix answered immediately. "He's been searching for someone with the Gift for years, but he hasn't been able to secure one." Tallis studied Felix skeptically as if he wasn't sure he believed his answer.

"The King of Caelum has tried many times to add one of the few remaining Magusiers in my kingdom to his Council, but I have denied his request throughout the years. I wasn't sure if he had managed to find one by other means, so I had to ask," Tallis replied.

"Last year, rumors surfaced that someone with the Gift resided in Arcanus with the Incantis. He dispatched a group to investigate, but they returned empty-handed, so as far as I know, nothing came of it," Felix explained.

I forced my mind back to when I learned of the Incantis. I had been told they were unique immortals said to be chosen by the Gods themselves to worship them and spread their word. They resided on private land within the continent of Disparya, known as Arcanus, that did not belong to any of the five kingdoms. The Incantis were considered sacred and protected by our laws. They performed rituals and ceremonies throughout Disparya, like the Entwining Ceremony Dash and I would have participated in on our wedding day. The kings in the room exchanged worried glances, and the unease was palpable.

"If your friend is being truthful, then no, Ainsley; King Perceval has no idea that you are the Heir to Tenebrae. The Gods would not have chosen you for that title until Evander's father passed, and he was crowned as the new King of Tenebrae. At that time, you were two years old and already in Caleum. Only a Magusier can detect your magic by using their Gift on you. If he has none on his Council, there would be no way for him to know of that development." Tallis explained, leaning forward and interlacing his fingers as he observed me with his light brown eyes. "I know this is a lot to take in right now."

"You think?" I asked incredulously. "Days ago, I was nothing." An almost unnoticeable growl came from Evander, but I caught it. "And today, I'm told that I'm the Heir to Tenebrae, have three Gifts, and none of those powers come from the kingdom I thought I belonged to my entire life."

I rubbed my temples and looked toward Evander. His face was unreadable, but some feeling I couldn't place told me sadness and excitement were swirling within him. Perhaps my Gift as an Empathi allowed me to detect his hidden emotions.

"I don't understand why the Gods chose me to be the heir," I whispered more to myself than to anyone else.

"They work in mysterious ways," Tallis said gently. It was meant to be a statement of comfort, but it provided anything but. What did the Gods see in me that was worthy of holding such a title—such responsibility?

"And you didn't know I was the Heir to Tenebrae until today?" I asked Evander.

"I only just found out the moment you did," he replied, glowering at Tallis as he said the words.

"You made your choice, so I respected your decision," Tallis said unapologetically.

"Had I been aware of all the facts, my choice may have been different," he countered bitterly.

"What *choice*?" I asked before Tallis had a chance to respond.

"It doesn't matter now," Evander said, keeping his gaze locked on Tallis'.

"What choice," I demanded again, but neither answered. Neither of them looked in my direction and instead stared each other down.

"Van, let it go," Olivier said, squeezing his king's shoulder.

The gesture was brotherly, like something I would have witnessed Dash and Felix do, and I began to question the dynamic of their relationship. I had assumed Olivier was Evander's right hand, an advisor of sorts, but maybe he was more than that. Evander reluctantly peeled his eyes from his fellow king and brought them back to me, the grey within them dark like billowing storm clouds. I clawed through the scrambled thoughts in my mind, now full of new information that I was barely starting to digest.

"I can't... This is all just..." I couldn't form a sentence as I looked at the three sets of foreign, questioning eyes that stared back at me.

"She needs a break," Felix said as he stood and helped me to my feet. "She's been through enough today."

I was thankful for his objection to continuing the conversation. Today alone, I had been told that King Perceval stole me because he knew I was the product of Conjoining and wanted to keep me safe; Dash had lied to protect me based on what his father told him; Felix and Imogen both aided in my kidnapping which turned out to actually be a rescue; And I not only had two Gifts, but three. Two from Tenebrae, making me heir, and one from Ministro. Felix knew me well enough to know that adding to the growing list of revelations would only bring more stress. He walked around me, taking my hand as he led me across the room to the exit.

"We're not done here," Evander said, making Felix halt immediately. It took me longer than it should have to understand why.

Though the conversation was conducted in a casual setting with titles forgone, it didn't change the fact that Evander *was* a king, and Felix knew that. He had been trained his entire life in the game of politics and how to act around royalty. Even if he didn't care for Evander, he still respected and recognized that we were standing before a king in the very kingdom he ruled.

I squeezed Felix's hand as he twisted toward me, his face now full of frustration and defeat. Thanks to his Gift and the close friendship we had built, he knew precisely how scared and overwhelmed I was. I could tell that he wanted nothing more than to get me out of that room and somewhere safe where he could help talk me through everything I had learned. It was killing him that he couldn't do just that.

"Yes, we are," I announced as I turned to face the other men in the room. "At least for now." My tone was cold and unyielding, daring them to challenge me. I stalked for the door as I pulled Felix behind me, not bothering to say another word to those present as we left.

4.

"Tell me what you're thinking," Felix said as he closed the door once we reached the safety of the bedroom I had been staying in. I walked over to the window bench and peered out at the snowcapped mountains in the distance as I ran through Tallis' words repeatedly, trying to make sense of it all.

"Somehow, I'm thinking nothing and everything all at once. It's like my mind is filled with multiple voices screaming thoughts at me simultaneously, and if I try to focus on only one, they all disappear, and I'm left feeling heavy and disoriented." I dragged a hand through my unbound hair as I closed my eyes, willing silence into my head. "I don't want to think about everything I was told today. I just... I can't, Felix. I can't handle attempting to understand my powers or why I am the heir to a kingdom."

"Then how about we not think about it, at least for now," Felix suggested.

I wanted to agree, but I knew if I chose to shove out the knowledge I had just learned, my thoughts would travel to only one other place. I would be forced to face the truth and emotions I had refused to let surface for days. I would have to acknowledge and relive the betrayal and heartbreak caused by the person I had given myself to. I ran my fingers over the gemstone flame that hung from my wrist as I contemplated if I was strong enough to go there.

After a moment, I unclasped the delicate bracelet Dash had given me as a birthday present and let it fall to the window bench with a soft clink. I wasn't ready for the wave of agony crawling its way free, but it was inevitable, and I needed to get it over with. I took a deep and shuddering breath. Finally, I allowed my mind to flash through images of Dash and me, and gave my body permission to feel the mix of love and hurt.

"Ainsley?" Felix asked cautiously, no doubt sensing my creeping devastation.

I turned to face my friend, my eyes lined with tears and my hand clutching my heart as I doubled over from the pain. He rushed for me, catching me in his arms as I slid to the ground, letting the tears flow and the screams finally break free. It was time to cry. It was time to feel.

The night was long and torturous to get through, but Felix never left my side. He gripped me tightly as I came undone and questioned everything that happened between Dash and me. He listened to me cry, vent, and beg the Gods to take the pain away. He held my hair back as my body worked to vomit, but because my stomach was empty, I heaved painfully on nothing but air. When that was finished, and I still wasn't ready to move, he rubbed my back as I wept and laid my face on the cold marble tile of the bathing room floor.

Felix scooped me up at some point in the night and carried me over to the bed. He rested his back against the velvet headboard and pulled me into his lap, cradling me against him as the tears continued to flow. I stole a glance at my friend to see his face sullen and wan, his eyes hollow and blank.

"I loved him, Felix," I sobbed, choking on the words as he wiped my tears and pressed a cool, wet towel to my reddened cheeks and swollen lids. "I loved him," I repeatedly chanted, as if saying the phrase could somehow erase its truth.

"I know," he kept whispering as he brushed my sweat-slicked hair from my face and pressed me harder against his chest, holding me firm as he rocked me gently. "I know."

Dash had lied to protect me. He had thought my life was in danger and that I would be killed if it had been discovered that I was a product of Conjoining. It had broken him to make that decision, but I was still furious because it wasn't his to make, it was *mine*. I had always been honest with Dash about my feelings regarding my lack of freedom over my own life. Before we were even friends, I had told him that he represented the choice that had been stolen from me. In the end, after everything we had been through, that's all he would ever be.

Felix was quiet yet reassuring as he listened until the sky turned a gentle shade of lavender, followed by the bright gold of a new day. He had never offered advice since he knew that wasn't what I needed. Only once did he speak up and object to my rants, and that was when I took full blame for what had happened. I cursed myself for being naive and trusting, for falling in love in the first place.

"If I didn't, Felix, I wouldn't be hurting like this. It's my fault, and I was stupid to think—"

"No, Ainsley," he interrupted, pulling me from his chest to set his amber eyes upon me. "This is not your fault whatsoever. Dash should have told you the truth the second he found out, and I should have too. You let us in and we failed you. None of this is on you, and you didn't do—"

A throat cleared from across the room, and Felix stiffened against me as he looked toward the door. I didn't bother to take my eyes off my friend as I kept my voice low and sharp, knowing precisely who had intruded.

"What do you want, Evander?" I croaked, my voice raw and hoarse from the hysterics.

When silence passed for entirely too long, I turned to find him leaning against the door frame with his arms crossed over his chest and a serious look on his face. His charcoal eyes were piercing as they stayed fixed on me, and his jaw was clenched so tight that it made his face look furious. His chest rose and fell heavily, and there was purple under his eyes as if he hadn't slept. Evander's gaze shot to the man holding me. Suddenly, Felix winced as if in pain, his grasp on me tightening with the movement.

"Felix, are you okay?" I asked, pushing back from him as he pressed his hand to his heart.

"You do not get to know what I'm feeling unless I allow you to, Empathi," Evander said.

"It wasn't intentional," Felix explained, rubbing his chest. "It's a habit."

"Then break it," the king responded coldly.

"Why the hell are you here right now, Evander?" I snapped, setting my gaze on him as Felix straightened.

"We have things we need to discuss."

"Not now," I said, returning my attention to Felix. I was about to ask how he was feeling and what exactly Evander had done to him, when the king spoke again.

"Yes, now. I gave you the night to work through your shit; I'm not giving you another day." His declaration had me sliding out of bed and striding for him as anger boiled within. I could feel the darkness creeping through my veins, begging me to release it, but I refused. It had been a struggle through the night to keep my magic locked away when it craved to be let loose, but I couldn't let it out. I didn't want to; I didn't want *it*, which was the greatest irony. The magic I had once wanted so badly had become the thing I wished I could get rid of. The Gift was supposed to bring me happiness and a sense of fulfillment but instead had brought me nothing but pain, loss, and suffering.

"I don't want to speak to you," I said as I stopped before him.

"I don't care. You can throw your little temper tantrum, but I'm not leaving until we finish what we started yesterday." I wanted to call him on his bluff, but I could tell that he meant every word.

"Fine. Then discuss."

"Alone," he said as he looked past me toward Felix. I heard blankets shuffling as he climbed out of my bed, following Evander's order.

"You can say what you want in front of Felix," I replied, and my friend stopped his advance, positioning himself at my side.

I wasn't thrilled with the idea of being alone with this king. I didn't think Evander would hurt me, especially after his face lit up at hearing that I was the heir to his throne, but something felt odd whenever I was in his presence. It was unease and danger mixed with intrigue and curiosity, and I constantly felt as though there was a build-up of pressure in my chest when he would look at me.

"He goes."

"He stays," I snapped back, crossing my arms over my chest as I readied for this fight. "Say what you came here to say, and then leave, Evander." He observed me for a moment as if he were debating how to continue.

"She's had a hard night, Your Majesty," Felix said, trying to reason with the king. "She needs time to adjust to everything she's gone through and has been told." I was so grateful to Felix for understanding that I wasn't in the headspace for the conversation Evander wanted to have. Wrath flashed over Evander's features, and he straightened, unfolding his arms and lowering them to his side as he made his way for Felix.

"I've heard enough from you," he said bitterly. "I let you coddle her last night, but that's over now. You have done absolutely nothing to help her and everything to destroy who she is. Who she should be. The only reason you're still breathing is that you got her out of there and brought her to me, but my gratitude only goes so far, Empathi." Felix walked forward, closing the distance between them, and I was taken aback by his brazenness. He had always shown respect to royalty, but it seemed that even Felix had his limits regarding how he was treated.

"I have done *everything* I can to help Ainsley. Since she showed up at the palace, I have been there for her in every way. I've spent months building a genuine friendship, so I think it's safe to say that I know what she needs better than you do, *Your Majesty.*" Felix spat the title like it was venom in his mouth, and Evander let out a breathy laugh, the sound cruel and menacing.

"You've done *everything* to help her? You haven't done shit," Evander sneered as he stepped even closer to Felix, their chests almost touching. "You never saw her as anything more than your fucking little toy to play with."

"That's not true!" Felix argued.

"Bullshit," Evander said, teeth bared in fury. "From what you've told me, her life has been threatened at that palace nearly since her arrival. Would you like me to list all of the incidents you told me about? You know what, don't answer that; I'm just going to go ahead and say them: the illusion that sent her jumping from the roof." Evander turned his focus on me as he spoke again. "Which, by the way, you cast upon yourself, but we'll deal with that shit later." I swallowed hard at his suggestion, and he brought his cold stare back to Felix. "The bodies being found around the palace, including one outside her room. And finally, when she was fucking beaten to an inch of her life. All of this happened while she was in *your* care."

"You don't think I fucking feel guilty for all that?!" Felix yelled. His amber eyes looked like molten steel as rage flooded his features.

"No, I don't," Evander said. "What the fuck did you bother to do about it for her?"

"Dash and I tried to figure out who was behind—"

"No. I said *for her*." Evander tilted his head in my direction. Felix's eyes grew wide, and his mouth opened and closed as if trying desperately to figure out what to say but was coming up short. "She was scared and hurt, and you assholes couldn't be bothered to teach her the tools she would need to defend herself. The tools she would need to survive! You and your prince seemed to care more about being her friend and fucking her than giving her what she actually needed," Evander snarled. His outrage and frustration were palpable. "If you think that you honestly *helped* her… If you think you made her a better person, you are a pathetic excuse for a friend." I glanced at Felix to find him staring at the floor with his head hung slightly. "I won't tell you again, Empathi; I need to speak to my heir, so get the *fuck* out of this room before I send you back to Caelum in pieces."

Before I could object, Felix stalked passed Evander and out of the room, slamming the door shut loudly in his wake. My gaze found the king watching me. His eyes were dark like a relentless storm, and my heart thundered under the pressure of his stare. My anger began to build, and I felt the darkness creep through me once more as I replayed Evander's threat to Felix's life. I took a deep breath, closing my eyes as I clawed and scraped at the shadows, pulling them back down and refusing to allow them to surface.

"Let it out," Evander commanded, and my eyes flew open to find his face severe and unyielding.

"No." I suffocated the shadows within until they dissipated. Evander's jaw was tense, and he shook his head in disappointment before storming across the room and throwing the double doors to the balcony open wide. Crisp air drifted through the space. Autumn seemed to have already made herself present in Tenebrae. I watched as Evander walked out, resting his hands on the balcony railing and gripping so tightly that the whites of his knuckles showed through his tan skin. With my temper already white-hot, I knew that I shouldn't follow, but I couldn't let him get away with what he said to Felix.

"You don't get to treat him like shit," I snapped, my arms wrapping around myself at the chilled breeze as I made my way onto the balcony. Evander turned to face me as a look of shock flashed over him. "You don't get to be angry with Felix."

"Yes, I do." He strode past me then and called over his shoulder, "But I'm more furious with *you*." My mouth hung open as I stood there, still trying to comprehend what he had just said. What reason did he possibly have to be upset with me? I twisted to go after him and demand he explain, but before I could, he reappeared on the balcony and shoved a fur blanket into my arms. "Put it on," he said as he took up his spot against the railing again. I wanted to argue and throw it to the ground to make a point, but I was freezing, and I had a feeling that Evander would wrap me in shadow if I refused. I covered myself, and my body relaxed instantly under the heat of the fur. "You're welcome," Evander said flatly.

"What gives you the right to be angry with me?" I said bitterly, and a muscle in his jaw ticked as if he were trying to suppress his amusement.

"You're the heir and—"

"I'm more than that, and just because I may be the heir, it doesn't give you the right to—"

"*Exactly*, Ainsley," he interrupted. "You're more than that; more than simply a title. It's a fact that you seemed to have forgotten."

"That isn't true."

"Isn't it?" Evander questioned, raising a brow. "When I met you that day in Caelum, you were fierce and took none of my shit. You were a fighter and wouldn't let me push you around. You even threatened me at one point." I thought back to that day and how, even though I was scared, I stood up to Evander, refusing to back down. "I'm angry because I thought you were strong and intelligent. I thought you were determined and capable, but everything I've learned so far tells me otherwise. Everything was—" He stopped, crossed his arms over his chest, and shook his head. "Never mind."

"No, please continue insulting me. I insist." Evander stared at me for a moment before nodding to himself.

"Fine. Everything was right fucking there in front of you, Ainsley, and you missed it. Every sign that something was wrong was laid out plain as day, but you were too concerned about fucking your prince to see it."

I flinched slightly at his words but didn't dare retort. Instead, I swallowed the lump in my throat and lifted my chin higher. "Anything else?"

Evander's eyes darted across my face as if searching for something. He must have come up empty because he continued again.

"Yes. I'm angry because you stopped fighting. You stopped caring and asking questions. For fucks sake, you lived in a palace with a massive library and never once bothered to pick up a damn book and educate yourself on the world around you, or at least demand that your *friend* or your *fiancé* teach you." He spat the endearments like they were poison on his tongue. "If you had, you might have noticed something wasn't right. Maybe then..." Evander cut himself off and dragged a hand through his dark hair as he watched me.

"Continue." It was all I could say.

"You were so blinded by your love for your prince that you lost yourself, which almost cost you everything. You were willing to offer him a piece of your magic, a piece of who you are. I understand that you love him, Ainsley, but that isn't a good enough reason to give up part of who you are. And he shouldn't have been okay with taking it."

"He wasn't *okay* with it. He was trying to keep me alive," I argued though I had no idea why I was defending Dash when I disagreed with his decision.

"Then he should have shown you how to protect yourself," Evander finished. The silence stretched between us for minutes.

"Are we done here?" I asked as I quickly wiped away the tear that trickled down my cheek.

"Yes."

"Great," I said, turning on my heel and heading for the hall. I needed to get out of this room and out of this Gods forsaken palace before I killed him.

5.

My knees were pulled to my chest as I picked at the grass beneath my feet. The air had a chill, and goosebumps spread over my flesh as I pulled the blanket tighter around me. Near silent footsteps approached, and a strong arm draped across my shoulders as Felix tucked me into his side.

"I hate how he treats you," I said, dabbing a fallen tear from my frozen cheek. Felix sighed beside me and kissed the top of my hair.

"He isn't wrong," he said. "I should have done more to keep you safe. I should have taught you more. I failed as your friend, Ainsley."

I clenched my jaw as I pulled back to look at him. Etched into his features was a sense of sadness and guilt that seemed to run deeper than any physical scar. I reached my hand up to cup his cheek. Without trying, my Empathi Gift spilled out and pushed itself into him, wrapping around his heart and trying to calm and heal any emotional damage. It moved on instinct like it knew what it was always meant to do without my control or direction. His eyes fluttered closed as he felt me. I could finally offer the peace I had longed to give him.

"You've made mistakes, but the only person I have to blame is myself, Felix," I explained. "As much as I hate him, Evander is right. I could have and should have asked questions and demanded answers. I shouldn't have let myself be blinded by my love for Dash and my fear of losing him. If I hadn't, things would be vastly different right now." Felix shook his head as he opened his mouth to argue. "And don't bother trying to argue, cupcake. It won't change my mind," I mocked, and he smiled as he wrapped me in his arms and squeezed me.

"What are you going to do now?" he asked, and I shrugged, not bothering to remove my face from where it was buried against his chest. "Whatever you decide, we'll do it together. I'm not going to leave you, Ainsley."

We had sat like that until the sun dipped below the trees and the temperature plummeted with the darkening sky. We desperately needed that silent moment for the two of us to be alone with no pending titles and unlearned magic, no betrayal or hurt. Just two friends who loved each other and were both equally as lost as the other in this new world. Finally, when the air grew too cold for me to endure any longer, Felix led me back to the room I had been staying in.

"Do you want me to get you something to eat?" Felix asked as he tucked me beneath the sheets of the bed.

"I don't think I can stomach anything." The look on Felix's face had my heart breaking even more. "But I'll try to eat some bread," I amended, and my friend nodded as he left the room. I knew it wouldn't stay down, but I could at least try for him.

I took deep, steadying breaths as I prepared myself for another sleepless night in a bed that wasn't my own, next to a man who wasn't Dash. Every time I closed my eyes, his deep blue ones were staring back at me, bold and bright—filled with a love so deep I was drowning in it even now.

I let Felix lead me around the palace grounds as he explained that I needed the sun on my face to feel normal again. What the hell was *normal* anyway? Was it feeling lost and hopeless? I felt that before I met Dash and Felix, and I felt it again now. I knew it didn't make any sense, but I didn't *want* to feel better. I wanted to wallow in my pity and thrive in my pain. I didn't want to pretend I was okay and fake a smile for the people I didn't even know and the one I hated beyond all reason.

I tried to keep Evander's words out of my mind, but they kept seeping into my bones like a bitter frost, refusing to let me thaw from the sting of them. He hadn't shown his face since our argument yesterday afternoon, and I hoped his absence would continue. The man was cruel and unforgiving when he had no right to be. I wasn't his property or his family. He had met me once, and even back then, I hated him. Just because I had two Gifts from Tenebrae running through my body, he thought he had a claim on me.

The more I thought about it, the more I wanted to leave this place behind too. I wanted to run far away where magic didn't exist, where I could be left alone while I broke into tiny pieces.

Felix seemed to be enjoying himself, and I didn't understand how that was possible. He would talk to Ophelia and Calidore whenever they stopped by to deliver my meals, and occasionally they joked and laughed like the world wasn't fucked up. Maybe their world wasn't, but mine was. Mine had fallen apart.

I was vaguely aware of Felix speaking to someone now, but the voices were muffled, and I didn't care enough to focus on making them clear. I didn't care about anything.

"Are you okay if I go and spar with Calidore?" Felix asked as he deposited me back into my room.

I nodded because what the hell did I care? Good for him for moving on so quickly and acting as if nothing had happened. Good for him for replacing Dash already with someone new.

"Are you sure?" he questioned, and I nodded again, not bothering to try to speak. I knew being angry at Felix for making new friends wasn't fair, but I didn't understand how he could do it. He was an Empathi, so shouldn't he be empathizing with *me*? Shouldn't he have been hurting to the extent that I was?

Whatever. It didn't matter.

"I'll be back as soon as we're done, okay?" he said—another nod.

The moment the door closed, my body took it as its sign to give myself entirely over to the hurt. I slid to the floor as I watched the sun slip behind trees; another day had come and gone. Another day of me feeling empty and hollow.

6.

Every fractured piece of myself hurt, the broken fissures cutting wounds deep enough to draw blood. My knees hit the ground as wave after wave of suffocating sadness washed over me, drowning me in a darkness blacker than the shadows that lived inside me. My body swayed as if I was being tugged back and forth by a phantom wind—a long blade of grass undulating in a meadow. I was weak and pathetic. I was useless and broken. I was heartbroken and lonely.

So fucking lonely.

I barely registered the press of the cold floor against my cheek and the small puddle of tears it rested in. When had I laid down? Every inch of me, inside and out, was a roaring fire that needed my pain to grow and burn ever brighter. My stomach was in knots, and my throat felt raw and exposed, as if I had swallowed sharp blades. Had I been screaming? My lungs ached with an intense burn and I quickly focused on my features to assess why. My mouth was open as salt water spilled from my eyes, and my hands fisted in my shirt, clutching my chest like it was the only thing preventing my heart from being torn free. My ears picked up the sounds of silent sobs until an agonizing scream tore through me.

My magic swarmed inside me, banging against my walls and desperately trying to free itself. I didn't know why it always wanted out, but it seemed it was just as quick to abandon me as everyone else. I wanted to forgive Felix—honestly, I did—but it was a struggle to forget that he had chosen to protect someone else when I needed him most. And Dash...

I recoiled in pain as talons dug through me at the mere thought of his name. Images flashed through my mind of his piercing blue eyes and dazzling smile as he stared at me with all the love in the world. I was dragged through memory after memory of us: laughing, playing, and tangling ourselves together in the warmth of the bedsheets. I could feel his searing touch on my skin as if he were here with me now, holding me in his arms and swearing to love me forever. For eternity. For as long as he existed.

I screamed my anger, my pain, my heartbreak as the tears flowed relentlessly. My eyes squeezed shut, and I let the despair rake through my body like a succubus, feeding off my pain and taking what it wanted. I wasn't strong enough to fight it off and didn't know if I would ever be.

I laid there on the floor, my body forming a tight ball as I held myself together for what felt like hours and also like no time had passed. Arms scooped around me, lifting me from my spot and pulling me against a hard chest. Felix had promised to come to my room after he finished sparring, and I cursed myself for letting him find me so distraught. With me suffering like this, his Empathi Gift was more like a curse.

I didn't open my eyes. I didn't want to see the look of guilt and hurt that I knew would be present within the brilliant amber color of his. Instead, I buried myself against his neck and apologized between the sobs.

Felix didn't respond.

He lowered me down onto my pillow before covering me with a fur blanket and tucking the sides in softly. Footsteps echoed as he retreated for a long moment before returning to my side.

The bed shifted with weight as I felt him lean close and run a hand across my face, smoothing back my matted hair that was stuck to it from sweat. A cool, wet cloth then swept over my cheeks, collecting the tracks left from the remnants of my tears. He brushed it over my swollen eyes and then around my nose as I sniffled. Though the screams had stopped, I still couldn't fully calm down. My chest rose and fell faster, and my breaths came in shuddering gasps as soft whimpers of pain occasionally slipped from between my lips.

Would this pain ever stop?

Lips pressed against my cheek, and I groaned at the intimacy as my whole body tightened. I didn't want to be touched like that, even if it was only meant to comfort. He pulled away quickly as if realizing his mistake, and I fought the urge to explain myself so he didn't feel like he had done something wrong. I needed to break that habit. My actions were mine, and I didn't need to apologize or explain them to anyone. Putting other people's feelings above my own was part of what led me to this point.

I took a deep breath and then released it as I forced my mind to take me to the dank cavern I had once been stuck in. There, I could scream and cry freely. I could rage in my anger and bask in my sadness. There, I could be alone.

Rather than climb into my bed as I expected him to, Felix's soft footfalls sounded as he departed my room. He must have recognized my desire to be alone. It wasn't that I didn't enjoy the small comfort he gave me daily, but when I was as broken and shattered as I was at that moment, I didn't want anyone to see. Least of all, the man who helped contribute to it.

A chill brushed over my skin, and I cracked an eye open as the blazing sun flooded my vision. My room was quiet and still, not giving anything away about the pain it witnessed me experience last night. I swallowed as my eyes drifted to a figure sitting across the room with his stare glued to the horizon beyond the window. I inhaled deeply, preparing for whatever onslaught of insults Evander would sling at me this morning. My mind was foggy, and my body still ached from the emotional trauma it had been put through. I was in no mood to deal with whatever he had planned for me.

"Do you want me to take you to him?" Evander asked quietly as he peered at the mountainous landscape in the distance.

"What?" I asked, the word coming out hoarse and raw.

I pushed myself into a sitting position, resting my back against the headboard as I studied him. At first, his posture seemed to be what it always was—filled with arrogance. He was leaning back into the armchair, one leg crossed over his knee as his elbow sat on the armrest, propping up his chin. He was dressed in his usual black attire as he stared out the window like he was bored.

But as I observed him more closely, the unaffected mask fell away. His hair was messier than usual, like he hadn't had time to style it to give off that perfect balance of unkempt and put together. His clothes were the same as yesterday's, and his toe tapped lightly on the wooden floor. I would have assumed it was his impatience with me dwindling, but the evidence led me to believe otherwise.

"To Prince Dashiell," Evander replied, finally peeling his gaze from the view to set it upon me. His eyes were darker than usual, with a small amount of purpling underneath, as if he had a rough night. "I can have you back with him before the sun sets. Just say the word."

My magic swirled and thrashed within me, alive at the mention of his name. My Gifts pushed and pulled me as a portion of them desperately wanted me to return to him while the other half was urging me to remain there in Tenebrae. My magic was a part of me, so why didn't it recognize the danger of going back? And why was Evander even giving me an option?

I tilted my head, trying to uncover what trap he was setting. He had been adamant about training me—the Heir to Tenebrae—so why would he willingly let me go? I knew I wasn't being held captive, but still... To offer to take me to Dash—it just felt off. Like it was the last thing, he'd ever want to do.

"No one will judge you if you choose to go," Evander said when I didn't respond, and I snorted.

Loudly.

"You've been doing nothing but judging and insulting me since I was brought here," I shot back. "Why would I believe that would stop now?"

Evander shifted, placing both feet on the ground as he leaned forward and rested his forearms on his thighs. He linked his fingers together and stared down at his hands. His head tilted up to look directly at me, and I was snared in the depths of his deep grey eyes, unable to form a single thought.

"I swear to you, Ainsley," Evander said slowly. "No one will say a word or possess an ill thought about you if you decide to return to him."

I was momentarily stunned as I examined each carefully laid promise, unable to detect a single falsity within. I swallowed hard as I dropped my stare from his, needing to break the intense contact, and instead focused on the hands in my lap.

"I can't go back to him," I whispered, more so to remind myself of the fact rather than to relay it to the man sitting across from me.

"If you want—"

"I can't," I interjected, my voice loud and forceful. It was hard enough to convince myself that Dash and I were no longer anything, let alone worry about trying to persuade others.

"Why not?" he asked, and I looked up at once. His tone was softer than usual as he tried to understand my reasoning, but what kind of question was that?

"I thought the answer would be obvious," I replied, crossing my arms over my chest.

Evander shrugged as he straightened and leaned back in his chair, getting more settled. "Sometimes the things that seem straightforward are actually the most complicated."

There was truth in that, and I didn't want to admit it. I wanted everything to be as easy as just me hating Dash, but it wasn't. I hated that I loved him still. Even after everything that happened, I loved him. I knew I couldn't be with him, but it didn't erase the mark he left on my heart.

"King Perceval would take my magic the second I crossed over the border of Caelum," I told him. That reason was, in fact, straightforward.

"He won't," Evander said. "Because he can't."

Okay, so apparently, it wasn't straightforward. What did that even mean? He could take it before, so what changed? I arched a brow in a request for an explanation.

"I spoke to one of my trusted advisors who is familiar with the way of the Incantis. I inquired about your situation, and she assured me it's not possible anymore."

"I don't understand. Why is it different now?" I asked.

"He can't take it forcefully. The power transfer during the Ceremony only works if you say the vows. He can't take what the Gods gave unless you give it freely. I was almost positive that was the case, but I wanted to be certain before I presented the option to you."

"So that's why King Perceval and Dash kept it from me. They needed to keep me in the dark to manipulate me into giving it away," I mused, putting the pieces together.

It was all starting to make sense. Was anything the king told me about my parents and his relationship with my father real, or had it just been a way to gain my trust?

"I can't speak on the motives of your prince," Evander began, stretching his long legs out in front of him as he tucked his hands behind his head. "But from what your friend has told me, I could gather he wasn't aware of the stipulation that you must give your magic to him of your own free will."

"He still kept me in the dark," I countered.

"Yes, but that doesn't necessarily mean he manipulated you."

"Why are you defending him?"

Did I enter an alternate universe where Evander and Dash were friends? This king sitting before me had nothing nice to say about him or myself days ago, and now it felt like he was trying to get me to leave. Maybe he decided that I wasn't worth the hassle anymore.

"Trust me; I'm not," Evander scoffed. "All I'm stating is that if King Perceval stealing your Gifts is what's holding you back from leaving, it needn't be. And as far as you and the prince go, that's for the two of you to figure out."

My heart picked up in rhythm as I thought about his offer. I didn't have reason to be scared of returning to Caelum because there would be no world where I would willingly give up my Gift now that I knew the truth. My magic would remain safely inside me, guarded and protected until my last breath.

Did King Perceval want to drain me of my magic for his gain, or was what he told Dash the truth? Had he been friends with my father and felt he owed it to him to protect me by removing the thing that could cause my death? Felix didn't trust the king's excuse, but Dash seemed to have. And Felix trusted Dash, so did that mean Dash was right in believing his father, and Felix just didn't like their choice for me? Or did Felix truly not buy the king's story about my past?

Did King Perceval even know my father at all? If I went, would I even be safe in that kingdom? They wouldn't be able to take my Gift, but was breeding me an option? King Perceval said that had been Tenebrae's aim all along, but perhaps it was actually he and Dash who planned to do that to me.

No.

I banished the thought the moment it drifted into my mind. Dash may have been a liar, but he would never force himself on me. He would sooner die than lay a hand on me in that way without my consent. My instincts tingled, and my magic brushed against me as if reaffirming that belief.

I rubbed my temples as a headache formed from all the impossible questions. Draining me of my magic wasn't an option, and Dash would never consent to breed me like an animal, so I had nothing to fear as far as my safety went if I chose to return to Caelum.

"If I went back to him, wouldn't that make me weak?" I asked, knowing that was the only thing I was truly afraid of. Evander studied me before lifting a single shoulder in a shrug.

"Some would say it makes you forgiving," he countered.

"I think you mean *naive*," I responded.

"Understanding."

"Stupid."

"In love," he said, and I flinched at the painful word. A single word that had meant so much was now the thing I loathed the most. Love had made me trusting, faithful, and so fucking blind.

"Like I said, stupid," I breathed. Evander shook his head, conceding the fight.

I released a heavy breath and gathered my thoughts, for this wasn't a conversation I wanted to have. There were too many unanswered questions and things I'd been told that didn't add up. I couldn't go back. At least not until I uncovered every shred of truth.

"I'm staying. At least for now," I told him with unwavering determination, so he knew this wasn't a topic I was willing to discuss again.

Evander observed me momentarily before nodding to himself and rising from the chair. He twisted around and grabbed two large bowls from the nearby dresser before striding for me and plopping down on the end of my bed. He extended his hand, placing the bowl in front of me on the blanket. I peered down at the contents as steam wafted up, smelling of delicious stew.

"Eat," Evander commanded gently, holding his own bowl in his lap.

I grabbed the spoon and stirred the food before bringing it to my lips for a bite. A thought pushed its way to the front of my mind, and I hesitated, bringing my eyes from my meal to Evander, who was staring at me intently.

"How do I know it isn't poison?" I questioned as I remembered that was how King Perceval kept my Gifts a secret from me.

Evidently, tainting what I consumed wasn't outside the realm of possibilities. I wondered if it was only my tea that had been affected or if what I had eaten had also contained traces of the suppressing drugs. I let the stew spill from my spoon and back into the bowl, then mixed everything around as if I could somehow see the answer hidden within.

"Because I'm not your fiancé," Evander answered, and my eyes sliced to him. His lips twitched in the corner, and I realized there was no malice in how he said the words. He was making a joke.

Though it was a pretty shitty one to make.

I snorted but scooped the food onto my spoon and took a bite. My stomach grumbled as I swallowed like it was saying, *'thank you for finally feeding me, you asshole.'* It wasn't until the stew traveled down my throat that I became aware of my hunger. It had been days since I had eaten, even though I tried. I couldn't swallow any food, and if I did, the second it hit my stomach, it would come back up in full force.

I breathed in and out through my mouth, readying myself for the sickness that plagued me constantly, but nothing came up. My stomach took my offer and left me in peace.

Baby steps.

"So, now you're making fun of my misfortune?" I jabbed, before taking several full bites.

"Sometimes humor is the only way to light the darkness," he answered, and I looked skeptically at him. Why was he being philosophical and wise? Where was the usual pigheadedness and overall assholery he loved to display? "Plus, it was too good of a line to pass up," Evander added.

Ah, there it was.

"You look like shit," I told him with a bright smile.

"Would you like me to grab you a mirror?" he said without hesitation and with a smile just as big.

My face fell as I glanced across the room and found the large wall mirror. Even from this distance, I could see how red and puffy my eyes were. My lips were chapped, and my cheeks were stained with tears that had escaped my lids overnight. I inhaled deeply before going back to my food as if the sight didn't faze me, though I knew I would never be able to forget the image of the girl looking back at me.

"I have reason to look the way I do. You have no excuse," I shot back, shoving the last spoonful of food into my mouth.

"Maybe I could get some rest if I wasn't constantly feeling your pain," he replied. The words came out soft, though with more of a bite than I sensed he intended.

My face heated, and my stomach knotted from embarrassment. I really needed Felix to teach me how to control this Empathi Gift so I wasn't unintentionally filling everyone with my dread and anguish. However, the idea of Evander suffering along with me felt like a reasonable punishment for all of the hell he'd given me so far. He wanted me to use my Gifts, after all. Well, beggars can't be choosers.

"I'll work on that," I said, as sweet as sugar.

"I bet you will," he responded in the same exact tone.

It was clear neither of us could stand the other and somehow we found ourselves thrown into this situation. Evander was stuck with an heir who refused to make anything easy or give him an ounce of respect. And I... Well, I was stuck with an asshole king whose favorite pastimes seemed to be dealing insults and flirting with me until I struggled to refrain from stabbing him. This was clearly going to work out exceptionally well.

"As for your other Gifts, I'll train you when—"

"No, you won't," I interjected, and Evander cocked a brow. "What makes you think I trust you? I may technically be from this kingdom, but I don't know that you won't hurt me or use me for your gain, just like King Perceval supposedly tried to do."

"Yes, you do," he said confidently. "I know for a fact your magic is telling you that your safety is not a concern when it comes to me."

I reached internally and found my magic resting there, not giving a care in the world to the conversation taking place. It was further confirmation that Evander was right. My magic knew not to be fearful of him, but it didn't mean I trusted his motivations. I was still unsure what they were, but my instincts told me it was more than he was leading on. I had to trust that, at least.

"So stop being a brat so I can train you."

"I'm not being a *brat*; I'm being cautious," I countered, annoyed once again at his persistent insults. "Not to mention, my magic is also pulling for me to return to Caelum, so I'm not sure that I really trust its judgment."

Evander narrowed his eyes as if he could see straight inside me and witness the back and forth I was experiencing. His stare was intense, and his eyes darted around like they were keeping pace with the rampant thoughts brewing in his mind. The darkness in his gaze made me long to know what he was thinking and how it pertained to me. After a second, he shook his head just barely, denying whatever his mind had conjured.

"If you're staying, then you will train," he said. I opened my mouth to argue, but Evander held up a hand, halting all excuses from falling from my lips. "I will not allow you to sit on your ass and do nothing. If you don't want to train, fine; that is your right. But know that if that's your choice, I will bring you to Caelum and leave you there to fend for yourself. Deciding not to live up to your potential is your choice, love, but I will not aid in your self-destruction."

Anger surged through me at his unfair ultimatum and the false pretense of *choice*. Shadows began to slip from my fingers, and I reached down to grip the blanket to anchor me. Evander's grey eyes tracked the movement, and joy sparked within them at the sight of my struggle.

"Let it out," he growled, and I gritted my teeth in pain as I struck at the darkness.

"No," I ground out as I sank my claws in deeper and dragged it back to the bottomless pit it belonged in. The shadows twisting around my fingers dissipated like smoke on the wind, and I breathed a sigh of relief as sweat beaded on my brow from the effort. Evander curled his lip in disgust and his face filled with disappointment. He turned away, no longer able to look at me, and I took several deep breaths as I willed my body to calm from the exertion.

Dash and Felix had always used their magic so effortlessly, and I had no reason to suspect it would be physically painful for me to keep mine in. Even when Dash had said it became challenging to retrain himself, he never mentioned that it hurt to do so. I closed my eyes as I was taken back to that moment at the lake and the look on his face as he held himself back before finally letting go. The world around me had come to life with his magic as he gave himself to me completely. I cringed as I remembered how it felt to hold and kiss him—to know he and his magic belonged to me.

When I opened my eyes, Evander stood at my side, looking down at me. Without saying a word, he removed the empty bowl before me and placed his full portion in its spot. I eyed the untouched food skeptically, realizing he hadn't taken a single bite. It was like he purposely held off just to make another demand.

"Eat," he commanded, and I clenched my jaw. I hated his domineering presence and how he ordered me around as if I would fall in line like a loyal subject.

"So let me get this straight," I began, drifting my eyes back to his as I lifted my chin in defiance. "I have to eat when you say eat and train when you say train... I have to either do whatever you want when you want it, or I have to leave? That really is *some* choice."

Evander rolled his eyes like I was being overdramatic, and maybe I was, but it certainly didn't feel like that. It felt like he was being unreasonable and didn't like the idea of someone calling him out on it. He leaned in so close that I could make out details on his face that I couldn't see earlier. There was a slight stubble along his jawline, and his eyes held more than his words were saying. Pain and fury—sadness and longing—were hidden beneath the cold slate exterior. There was a sort of desperation in the way his gaze held mine. Like he needed me to stay more than he needed to breathe.

It made me even more suspicious of him.

"No, love," Evander said as he raked his stare across my face appraisingly. "You either better yourself, or you leave."

I didn't know what to do. Being as far away from him as possible sounded perfect, but where could I go? And why did part of me want to stay? I took a deep breath and blew it out slowly.

"The people who kept trying to take me had shadow magic—a Tenebraen Gift," I said quietly, and Evander nodded.

"They did," he responded. "I had nothing to do with your attacks and will continue to search for who did." I read the truth of those words in his grey eyes. After a moment, he straightened and backed away toward the exit of the room. "I don't need an answer right now, but if you decide to stay, we'll be leaving in thirty minutes."

"Where are we going?" I blurted before he could disappear into the hallway. He smirked, and I knew it was because I had given him my answer before I fully decided it was what I wanted.

"Home."

7.

Idle conversation accompanied boots slamming to the ground as our traveling party dismounted. I stayed saddled upon Nox, my eyes pinned to the massive house before us. From the outside, the building seemed warm and inviting, beckoning me to step inside and enjoy the comfort it promised to provide. The wood and stone exterior gave it an aged character, letting me know this wasn't just a random house but a home that had been lived in and loved over countless years.

"Are you coming or just going to sit there and gape?" Evander drawled in his usual arrogant tone as he headed inside, not bothering to wait for my reply. I rolled my eyes but jumped down from Nox and strode for the door.

Light flooded the ample entry space, and I glanced up to find the source coming from a window in the ceiling that let the sun shine down and illuminate the area. Directly to the right was what looked to be a living room filled with furniture in bold, rich colors that mimicked the design I had seen at the palace.

"You'll want to take your boots off first," Ophelia whispered before I could step into the adjoining room. "Van is a bit overbearing when it comes to keeping the house clean."

"It's not overbearing to not want dirt dragged across the floor every day," Evander called from somewhere in the house, having heard her hushed explanation.

"Onyx and Nova track far more dirt in this house than I do," she countered. Great, two more names I didn't know. How many people lived in this house?

"We both know that's not true," he yelled back.

She rolled her eyes and helped me shrug out of my coat before hanging it along the wall next to everyone else's.

"Thank you, Ophelia," I told her.

"Just Lia. I hate my full name."

I kicked off my boots and placed them in line with the others as Lia grabbed my arm to lead me through the house. She pointed out room after room, giving me a quick tour while she pulled me along until we managed to stop in what I assumed was the library.

Bookcases were stacked from the floor to the vaulted ceiling along one wall and housed thousands of novels. My fingers twitched, and I drifted across the room with intrigue as I plucked one of the titles from the shelves. It was a story I had read countless times, and I browsed the other options, seeing if there were more I could find. I pulled another—my favorite. A book I could recite word for word without looking at the pages. It was a comfort read; a story I always went back to whenever I felt alone or lost, which happened to have been most of the time. A story about unwavering friendship and love—two things I seemed to be lacking these days.

"May I?" I asked tentatively as I turned around, noticing for the first time that Evander and Calidore had been in the room too. They sat on a leather couch that looked comfortable enough to fall asleep on. Evander swirled a glass of amber liquid as he observed me curiously.

"Of course. It's your house," he said, and I scoffed as I pocketed the book.

"Just because I'm the heir and agreed to stay here does not make this my house," I responded pointedly as I scanned through the other novels hoping to find more to read. A large, worn spine caught my eye, and I removed the title from its spot on the shelf.

"I don't mean it in a chivalrous way, love. I mean you actually own this house."

I dropped the aged book, causing a loud thud to reverberate through the otherwise quiet room. Did I hear him right? This place *belonged* to me?

"How about we not damage the ancient and priceless literature," Evander said sarcastically as he stared at the large book at my feet. I reached down quickly, scooping it up and inspecting it for any damage. Thank the Gods there wasn't any. I slid it back onto the shelf and opted for one that looked less breakable should I receive any other mind-blowing news. It was becoming an unwelcome occurrence this week.

"If it's mine, does that mean I can kick you out?" I said to him with just as much sass. Evander's lips spread into a creeping grin as he crossed a leg over his knee. He slowly shook his head back and forth, letting me know that wasn't an option.

"I'm afraid we share this happy little abode together," he replied, and I hated the pleasure his voice was filled with. "This house belonged to both of our mothers long before they met our fathers and created us."

I chewed on that little bit of information. Why would our mothers have shared a house? I knew Evander and I weren't siblings but perhaps cousins. Maybe our mothers were sisters, and that's why they chose to live together. The thought of sharing blood with Evander made me sick to my stomach.

"So we're related?" I said flatly.

"Gods, no," he replied like that was the worst possible notion I could have had. "Our mothers were just close friends who grew up together. They had this house built and lived here until they moved to the palace after my parents wed. It was then left to both of us once they died."

"Why not just you?" I asked. Evander looked at me with pinched brows and a question in his grey eyes. "I wasn't here."

Evander nodded his understanding and leaned forward to place his glass on the coffee table. He rose from the couch and slid his hands into his pockets as he crossed the room in my direction. His intense gaze trapped me, refusing to relinquish hold of my focus though I wanted to pull away. If his cold and calculated steps along with his searching stare were a tactic to intimidate me, it was working.

And I hated it.

I swallowed hard and straightened my posture as he approached, raising my chin in a defiant way that always seemed to either piss him off or turn him on. I wasn't sure which one it did more, but I hoped it was the former. His commanding presence snuffed the air from my lungs and demanded my full attention. I was vaguely aware of Lia climbing the bookcase ladder as she spoke to Calidore. The magic I forced to stay below the surface stretched and flexed its metaphorical claws. Was it warning me of some impending danger? No, it was something else entirely. Something I couldn't put my finger on as I stared at the king standing before me, the distance too close for my liking.

"No, you weren't," he said, his voice as smooth as satin and as sharp as a blade. "But I knew one day you would be."

Evander's words felt weighted and layered, as if a deeper meaning was woven within. I was quickly learning that he was secretive and cryptic, his statements never quite as simple as I was supposed to believe. There was a deep and dangerous way about him that I wasn't sure I wanted to dive into. Was uncovering the truth worth the risk of being around this man, a king who wanted far more from me than he was letting on?

"You didn't just assume I was dead too?" I asked, keeping my voice strong and fluid despite the lump in my throat and pounding of my heart. He shook his head as his gaze dragged up and down my body. The way his eyes raked over me was night and day to what King Perceval would do. Evander wasn't appraising my body or what I had to offer; it felt closer to something that resembled wonder at the fact that I was in his presence at all. Like he was doing it to verify I was really standing there in that room with him.

I took a step back from Evander and instantly felt like I could breathe again, thanks to the added distance. He broke our eye contact and diverted his attention to the thousands of books lining the walls.

"You can take anything you'd like, but just try and put it back where you found it when you're finished," he said, reaching up high to remove a book from the shelf. He glanced over the title before deciding against it and selecting another.

"Van has them all organized by genre and gets a little overbearing when they get misplaced," Lia called from the top rungs. She didn't seem to be deciding what to read but just enjoying herself as she slid the ladder back and forth along the wide bookcase.

"Is there anything you don't find I'm overbearing about?" Evander drawled as he backed away and returned to his spot next to Calidore.

"Not really," Lia chirped sarcastically, and Evander threw up his middle finger without ever looking her way.

I was still getting used to the playful informality of the relationship between these people and their king. Back in Caelum, King Perceval never seemed lax with his company. It was always formal titles and stiff postures. It was the constant fear that one wrong word would mean the end for you. After my introduction to that man, I lived in continual fear whenever in his presence, though that was primarily due to my sharp tongue at the worst possible time. With Evander, it seemed like he considered the people surrounding him to be more like family than advisors. Were they even advisors to begin with? I still had many questions, so I made a mental note to ask Lia for the answers—the only one I felt wouldn't give me a difficult time for being curious.

"Holy shit," Felix declared as he and Olivier entered the room. My shoulders fell, and I loosed a long breath as my friend strode for me. Evander refused to let him accompany us on our journey, stating that Felix needed to be thoroughly questioned first to ensure he wasn't a spy come to betray Tenebrae. I knew he wasn't, and I truly believed that there was no way they would kick him out of Tenebrae, resulting in my leaving too, but until he walked through that door, I didn't realize just how nervous I was.

I hugged my best friend tightly as he glanced around the extensive library in astonishment. The warmth and hominess of it reminded me so much of the Sanctuary, and my chest ached knowing I wasn't going back anytime soon—possibly ever. That decision was the best thing for me, but it didn't change how much it hurt. My heart continued to break a little more each day as the truth of never seeing the man I loved again set in. His dark teal blue eyes haunted me whenever I closed mine, never able to escape him or the memories of us together. Being in a room similar to the one we had spent countless days in wasn't helping either.

"How was the journey?" I asked as I released him and wandered to a leather armchair stationed along an enormous wall made of glass, giving us an unobstructed view of the snowcapped mountains and a dark blue lake behind the house. Having a window of this magnitude should have felt intrusive and too open, but instead, it made me feel safer. It was like physical proof that there was nothing to fear or hide from anymore. I could just be.

"Quiet," Felix answered as he sat in the chair next to mine. "He refused to say one word to me the entire trip. No one has ever been able to resist my charm to *that* extent." I looked at the man in question as he sat next to Evander and poured himself a healthy serving of alcohol. Olivier picked his head up and glared at Felix will all the disdain in the world before downing his drink in one swallow.

"What did you do to make him hate you so much?"

"I wouldn't exactly say he *hates* me. More like he's struggling against his desire for me," Felix whispered low, and I smirked at his ever-present confidence.

"No, I hate you," Olivier clarified, clearly having heard our private conversation. He drank another serving of his liquor before getting up and leaving the room.

Felix was always popular in Caelum. Everyone loved him, and he made friends and lovers at every turn, so it was an odd sight for someone to despise him so openly. Evander also didn't make it a secret that he couldn't stand my best friend, and I began to worry about his potential happiness in this place. If he wanted to leave, then we would, no questions asked. At this point, the only ones we had in our corners were each other, and I wasn't about to give that up for people I had just met—people I could tell were still keeping things from me.

"Let's go, you two," Evander announced as he set his drink down and rose from the couch. "I need to show you to your rooms."

"You're down there, Empathi," Evander said, pointing to a door at the end of the hallway on the right. We weren't staying together? I wasn't sure I liked that idea at all, and by Felix's hesitation, he didn't either.

"We can share a room," I said, placing a hand on my friend's chest to halt him from heading down the hall. Evander tracked the movement, and his eyes lingered longer than they should have. His jaw clenched just barely as he dragged his stare from my hand to my face and shook his head.

"No. You can't," he declared, and the defiance in my blood boiled at his domineering attitude. There was no reason Felix and I couldn't stay together. He was who I trusted—the only comfort I had in this strange new place, and I wasn't about to give that up simply because Evander wanted to be a prick.

"It's okay, cupcake," Felix said, stepping out of my hold and making his way around us. "Come and find me when you're done with whatever this is," he added, gesturing between Evander and me.

When Felix's door closed behind him, I crossed my arms over my chest and glowered at Evander, shifting on my feet to get into a more comfortable position. I wasn't going anywhere.

"Your room is through there," he said smugly.

"Great," I replied in the sweetest voice possible. Evander rolled his eyes at my sass and twisted to open the door. As soon as his back was to me, I turned on my heel and stormed down the hall toward Felix's room. My friend said to find him when we were done, and I was most definitely done.

Evander appeared in a puff of shadow before me, and I gasped in shock as I jumped back, startled. Before I could say a word, he leaned in and threw me over his shoulder like an inconvenient sack of potatoes.

"What the hell do you think you're doing?!" I demanded, slamming a fist against his lower back. Shadows crept along my fingers the more I hit Evander, and I was forced to stop my assault to prevent any more from escaping. I needed to figure out how to be angry without losing control of my magic. I had to keep it locked away.

"You want to act like a child, so I'll treat you like one," he said shamelessly as we stepped into the room he claimed was mine. Rather than set me down on my feet like any decent person, Evander dropped me on my ass before fixing his ruffled hair and sliding his hands into his pockets.

I glared at him from the floor, my rage making magma seem like a glacier. My chest heaved, and my fingers dug into the carpet beneath me in an attempt to stop my shaking. I was a fuse poised to explode, and he held the match between his fingers, primed and ready. My Gift of shadow leaked through my skin, but I couldn't stop it. I was too far gone in my anger. The back of my throat rumbled in something that sounded strangely like a growl. I was a feral beast he had uncaged and was now baiting me to strike.

Evander leaned forward and pressed his lips together, kissing the open air in the most asshole way imaginable. My barely-there leash snapped, and I lunged for him with fingers outstretched like claws, prepared to shred him apart. Shadows swirled around me, untamed and untrained, moving chaotically and without direction. I had no control over anything—not my magic and certainly not my fury.

The second my hands reached Evander, he spun me, slamming my back hard into the wall and pushing my legs apart with his knee as his body held mine in place. He grabbed ahold of my wrists, pinning them above my head with only one hand while the other...

The other held a dagger to my throat.

8.

I sipped on shaky intakes of air, careful not to move too much or else I'd feel the sting of Evander's blade. I was stuck, unable to fight my way out physically or with my sharp tongue. The king's gaze was cold yet possessed intrigue as he looked down at me, his face only inches from mine. I held my breath, too afraid to move, though my entire body trembled. Evander tilted the dagger, so the smooth flat metal was pressed against my skin as he delicately traced it across my exposed neck.

"Now love," he said gently—a lover's purr. "You really need to get that anger under control." He smiled, and his eyes sparkled as if an idea had just occurred to him. Evander tightened his grip on my wrists and leaned in, whispering softly into my ear. "Or if you'd like to channel it into something else, I have a few ideas for you." My anger grew at his suggestion, and I did everything I could to keep myself from making a stupid decision that would end with me hurt or looking more like an idiot than I was at that moment.

"You're an asshole," I spat, trying to shift from beneath him, but Evander tightened his hold, not allowing me an inch of freedom. He flipped the dagger over in the same movement, so the sharp edge was pressed to my skin, and I instantly halted my attempt.

He clicked his tongue disapproving and tilted his head, his face full of exaggerated disappointment. The whole situation was just another Gods damn game to him.

"It isn't wise to insult someone who holds a dagger to your throat," he drawled, pressing the blade harder to my flesh, just enough to sting but not cut.

"You're not going to hurt me," I said confidently, and Evander cocked a brow.

"No?"

"No. You need me," I responded, calling his bluff.

The king grinned a crooked, wicked smile before dipping his face closer, so his lips hovered just above mine. The heat from his breath caressed my skin as his charcoal eyes bore into me, loving every second of his twisted game.

"Desperately," he whispered before pulling back and letting the dagger dissolve into shadows. I took a deep gulp of air, my hand flying to my throat as Evander strode for the door. "Dinner is downstairs in an hour, and training starts at dawn," he called over his shoulder, not bothering to turn around before leaving me alone in my room.

I breathed a heavy sigh, my hand still clutching my throat. I wasn't going to make it here. I chose to stay in Tenebrae because I wanted answers about my past and who I truly was, but there was no way I could live under the same roof as that man and survive. One of us was bound to destroy the other, and I knew I needed to be smarter with my choices. Trying to attack him had worked out for me a grand total of zero times, and if we were keeping score, I was definitely in the negative when we squared off. If I wanted to beat Evander at his own games, I needed to study him and discover his weaknesses. He already knew anger was mine, and he was using that every chance he could. I would stop at nothing until I figured out how to break him.

After a while, I managed to pick myself up from the floor and explore my new room. Though it was half the size of the one I was given in Caelum, it felt just as spacious. Wide, floor-to-ceiling windows lined the far wall on either side of a large fireplace already roaring to life as if someone had prepared it for my arrival. There was also a set of doors that led to a small balcony overlooking the lake. I could see myself spending most of my time there once I got used to the chilly weather of Tenebrae. Even though autumn was only beginning, it was already colder than our winter months back in Caelum, and I assumed that was because of the elevation and the surrounding mountains. I pulled open dresser drawers to find them fully stocked with clothes that looked to be my size. Who had done that?

The bathing room was one straight out of my dreams. It was bright and open and housed an enormous copper tub that was already filled with bubbles and had steam snaking through the air. An actual squeal of delight slipped from my lips as I quickly undressed and climbed into the bath. The hot water greeted my skin like a lover's kiss, and I sighed euphorically as I submerged myself deeper into the bath, finally feeling a sense of relaxation for the first time in nearly a week.

"Am I interrupting some *alone* time?" Felix asked as he strode into my room without knocking. I gave him a flat look that relayed nothing of the sort was happening or would be happening any time soon. "It sounded like you were enjoying yourself," he explained as he shrugged.

"Definitely not in that way," I said before dipping my head below the surface. My Gods, I wished I could live in that tub. The water was the perfect temperature—scalding hot to match my temper.

"Can I join?" Felix asked once I came back up for air.

"Only if you keep your undergarments on," I demanded, giving him a pointed look that dared him to object. "And go get me a fresh pair of mine to put on. I don't need you grazing certain parts of my body on *accident*," I said, playfully emphasizing the last word. Felix laughed and gave me a wink before doing as requested.

"How are you holding up?" he asked from behind as he piled a handful of bubbles onto my head to mold some sort of hat. We had been in the bath for close to an hour, and the water hadn't dropped in temperature one bit. I would have loved to have this magic tub in Caelum, but I was positive Imogen would have never let me fully enjoy it. Rarely did she ever allow me to bathe longer than necessary to get myself clean. *Fuck*, I missed her.

"As best I can," I answered honestly, running my fingers over the water's surface absentmindedly.

I had never felt more lost and confused than in the past week. Everything I thought I knew was revealed to be a lie, and there was still so much I needed to uncover. Countless questions about my parents and the magic I possessed pounded in my mind like the beating of a persistent drum. But the unanswered questions that drew me in the most, capturing my focus like a moth to a flame, all pertained to Dash. He had broken my heart, but it didn't change my love for him, no matter how much I wished it had, though I knew I couldn't return.

"You're late for dinner," a cold voice claimed from the bathing room doorway. My head snapped up to find Evander standing there with a scowl on his face. His eyes slid back and forth between Felix and me, and his jaw clenched as he took a deep breath like he was preparing to scold me.

"I'm not hungry," I declared, and Evander's gaze hardened.

"I don't care. Sit at the table in silence then," he demanded, and his condescending tone was enough for me to snap.

This time, I remembered to keep a leash on the full might of my anger as that always seemed to be my demise when it came to our altercations. I stood at once, bubbles dripping down my body in soapy streams. Evander's eyes dipped briefly before eyeing the bubble hat on my head and settling back onto my pissed-off face. I could have sworn amusement flickered in his stern gaze, but it was gone so quickly that I couldn't be sure.

"When you agreed to stay, you—"

"Never agreed to happy family dinners," I said, cutting Evander off. "If I want to soak in the bath for hours with my friend after having a week from hell, then I will do that. As I said before, I'm not hungry. If I change my mind, I know where the kitchen is."

I placed my hands on my hips as I stared him down, welcoming the challenge of his rebuttal because whatever he said wouldn't change my mind. Evander broke eye contact, turning his head away from me as he tongued his cheek. His lips twitched in the corners, and I couldn't tell if he was amused or angry I had outsmarted him. Never in our quick terms did Evander specify that to stay, I had to play nice and go along with what he wanted. Perhaps the key to defeating him was being clever.

"And another thing," I said, forcing his attention back to me as his lips tilted in a grin. Oh, he absolutely hated that I now had control of the situation. I turned the tables on him and would be the one making the demands now. "Since I own half this house, I get to make some rules too. The first being: don't barge into my bathing room unless I fucking invite you to," I said firmly.

"Noted," he stated.

"Great," I replied. "So you can take your arrogant attitude and get out."

Evander smiled wide though it looked anything but pleasant as his eyes assessed me. He slid his hands into his pockets as usual and slightly dipped his head.

"Apologies, love. Next time I'll try not to be so cocky," he said, and Felix choked behind me. Apparently, he was just as surprised that Evander was capable of apologizing as I was. "Have a ball, you two," he added before departing the bathing room and closing the door behind him.

I let out a sigh of victory, happy that I finally bested him for once. I put that asshole in his place and reminded him that I wasn't someone who was going to be bossed around. I was going to make decisions for myself and—

A reflection in the mirror caught my eye, and I gasped.

"Felix…" I breathed.

"I'm so sorry," he whispered, and my hand clasped over my mouth as I stared at myself.

A pile of bubbles was on the top of my head, but not in the shape of a hat as I had previously thought.

No.

On my head was a giant bubble cock and balls. A mortified scream left my mouth, and I was almost positive I heard Evander's laughter from down the hall. I had stood my ground and told him off, all while sporting genitalia atop my head. Evander wasn't pissed—he was holding in his laughter.

Oh, Gods, fucking kill me now.

"I'm not going to tell you again. Get up," Evander demanded, and I threw my middle finger at him. After the unfortunate bubble incident last night, I didn't dare leave the room. Felix had gathered me a dinner tray from the kitchen after apologizing profusely for not at least smacking his creation off my head the moment Evander appeared in the doorway. Still, I didn't plan on letting him off of the hook for that anytime soon.

Felix had offered to stay with me through the night, but I chose to be alone. I still had trouble sleeping, often waking from nightmares of reliving the moment I learned of Dash's betrayal or what might have been had he taken my Gifts. I didn't want to worry Felix or keep him from sleep. He was going through a lot too, and I was sure the weight of betraying Dash was getting to him, even if he never spoke of it.

Evander had let himself into my room just before dawn and demanded I get up and ready to train. I, of course, refused after politely reminding him of my demand last night that he not barge in without being invited, to which he so happily pointed out that my request was only specific to the bathing room and not where I slept.

The back and forth between us had been going on for close to half an hour, and the light of dawn now streamed through the wide windows. Neither of us was any closer to giving in to the other, and I was curious just how long this argument would last before Evander finally gave up.

"You said you'd train," he said between clenched teeth, pulling the blanket off my body when I refused to leave the bed.

"I. Didn't. Say. *When*," I yelled, throwing pillows at him between each word. "The sun is barely up, and I'm tired." I shoved the last pillow over my head and turned to the side to go back to sleep. I wasn't happy I no longer had my blanket, but I wasn't about to fight him for it.

"That's not how this works," he snarled, and a warm pair of hands wrapped around each of my ankles. What the hell?!

Evander tugged, and I barely managed to grab the iron headboard to prevent myself from being ripped away. I held on for dear life as he pulled and pulled until my body was wholly taut and my stomach lifted from the mattress.

"Let go!" I exclaimed, using all my might to keep my grip firmly on the metal frame. I thrashed my lower body around until Evander's hold on my ankles slipped, and I quickly brought my knees to my chest.

The bed shifted as Evander crawled towards me and grabbed one of my ankles again. I kicked back my foot with all my might and landed a hard blow to his face, causing him to swear loudly as he clutched the side of his cheek. I internally applauded myself for finally being able to strike him.

"Stop being so difficult," Evander growled, moving towards me again.

I flipped to my back, determined to land another kick to his face, but he moved out of position. Instead, I wrapped my legs around his middle and slammed his body to mine, hoping to use the momentum to flip us over. That way, I could punch his stupid face as he was pinned beneath me. The only problem with that was Evander was strong as hell. His body was pressed firmly against mine, but I couldn't get him to roll, no matter how hard I tried.

"If you wanted me in your bed, all you had to do was say that, love," he announced seductively as he glanced down at me with a victorious smirk. I growled my frustration and changed my tactics, fighting to shove him off of me to no avail. "But maybe later. We're already late," he said before leaning down and flicking the tip of my nose up with his. I jerked my face away as shadows engulfed us.

One second I was in my bed with Evander on top of me, and the next... I was outside in the training area, with Evander *still* on top of me. I glanced around the space, panicked and confused about how we'd gotten there, though no one else seemed concerned. Four sets of eyes watched me curiously, including Felix, who gave me a cautious little wave from the other side of the ring.

"How did you do that?" I demanded breathlessly as Evander stood and dusted the dirt from his pants.

"A perk of being king," he said. I thought magic was limited to one of the three Gifts of a kingdom, along with basic powers like creating silencing shields or turning on and off lights with a flick of the wrist. I had never heard of anyone being able to do what Evander could. "And before you ask, I'm the only king who can do it."

Why? What made him so unique to possess such an ability? I opened my mouth to demand answers, but Olivier's voice cut me off.

"What is she wearing, Van?" he asked, his tone filled with annoyance.

"She refused to get ready, so I brought her how she was," he answered as he shrugged, seeing nothing wrong with the fact that I was wearing thin silk night clothes.

"You could have at least given her boots," Olivier replied, and Evander grinned like he was well aware of what he *could have* done but chose not to.

Olivier scrubbed his hands over his face just as Lia ran inside after announcing she would collect me something more appropriate to train in. She returned minutes later, and I quickly slid the pants and shirt over my nightclothes. I thought about going inside to change, but I feared Evander would have followed me and brought me back completely naked just to humiliate me some more.

Once I was fully dressed, everyone made their way to the center of the training ring. Olivier instructed each person on what task they would be working on today, and I patiently waited for him to get to me. I bounced on the balls of my feet, trying to warm myself as I glanced around at Lia working on archery and Calidore and Felix throwing daggers at a target. I hoped I would be paired with Felix. Not only was he the only one I knew, but it would have been quite cathartic to throw sharp objects at a target I could pretend was Evander's face.

"You and Evander—" Olivier began, but I interjected immediately.

"Absolutely not," I said. "I will not be working with him."

Evander could teach me the ways of politics and the inner workings of our kingdom and court, but he was not training me in physical combat. With my hatred for him and his disdain for me, there was no way any good could come from that session.

"I'm the only one who has the Gift of illusions here, so it makes the most sense that I instruct you on how to use your Gifts," Evander said. I turned to face him so there was no mistaking where I stood on the matter.

"I'm not using my Gifts," I told him firmly. "I'm willing to be trained to defend myself physically, but I want nothing to do with this magic."

The Gifts I was given terrified me. I had nearly killed my best friend because I let it out, and I didn't think any amount of training would tame that terrifying darkness I felt lurking in its presence. The shadows seemed to be fueled by my anger, and that wasn't going away anytime soon, so there was no way in hell I would let that Gift out to play. I could always have Felix teach me the basics of using my Empathi Gift, but the illusions and shadows would be staying locked away.

"That's unacceptable. You need to take control of your life and hone your Gifts, Ainsley. And I'm going to teach you how to do that whether you like it or not," Evander replied furiously.

"No," I said again. "It's my choice whether or not I want to explore them, and right now, I don't. But even if I did, you wouldn't be the one instructing me. I don't trust you, Evander. There's more going on than you're telling me, and until I know what it is, I'm not listening to a word you have to say."

"If you want to be a stubborn brat and have nothing to do with me, fine. But at least have Olivier teach you how to use your shadows."

"I'm not being a brat," I snapped and Evander huffed a sarcastic laugh that set my teeth on edge. "You want me to take control of my life? Well, that's what I'm fucking doing. I'm choosing myself and will not be bullied into doing something before I'm ready. Everyone has made decisions for me all my life, and I'm to blame for a lot of that, but I won't allow it anymore." I took a deep breath as I stared into Evander's grey eyes. His face was unreadable, and I couldn't help but wonder what was running through his mind. "As I said before, I don't trust you. I won't look stupid by giving the benefit of the doubt to people who care more about themselves than me. I won't make that mistake again."

"You don't have the option of not using your Gifts, Ainsley," he snarled as he stepped closer, closing the distance between us completely. "You possess magic and are untrained, therefore a danger to yourself and others. Do you not recall nearly leaping from the palace roof in Caelum? That was your magic trying to break free, and because you couldn't control it, you cast an illusion upon yourself and almost died because of it. If you keep burying your magic down, it *will* happen again."

We were so worried that night that someone from Tenebrae had cast an illusion on me, and technically, that was true, though we had no idea that *I* was the culprit. I didn't want anything like that to happen again, but I couldn't just give in to his demands, especially when I didn't understand the way of my magic. I would talk to Felix later, and if he agreed that I needed to be trained in my dark magic, I'd do it. But if learning to control my Empathi Gift was enough to sate the need to expel my magic, then there was no need to access my shadows.

"My answer is no," I replied, looking directly into his eyes. I wasn't going to let him intimidate me. "And if you have a problem with my terms, then I'll leave."

Evander's chest rose and fell heavily as he took in my words. I had given him an ultimatum that benefitted him in no way, and he was pissed. He shook his head before storming into the house, deciding there was no point in arguing anymore. I glanced up at Olivier, waiting for him to comment or demand that I learn my Gifts, but he only instructed me on how to stand properly in a fight.

9.

Two weeks had come and gone, and I was getting used to my life in Tenebrae. Training for hours each day was exhausting, and I still wasn't ready to access my magic, though it constantly scraped against me in a demand to be set free. Evander and I hadn't spoken since that first day in the training ring, and I got the impression he was avoiding me, but I didn't mind. I had no desire to be near him.

Felix had come to my room after dinner every night to instruct me on using basic magic and my Empathi Gift. I wanted to ensure I was doing everything I could not to push my emotions on others accidentally, and that started with creating a shield and learning to master an internal defense. Thankfully, Felix was confident that using my Empathi Gift would be enough to sate the need to expel my magic, so for now, my darkness could stay locked away.

My nightmares were getting worse day by day. It was like my mind could sense that I was getting stronger—more capable—and it wanted to remind me that I could lose it all in an instant. I wasn't ready to face what my dark Gifts were capable of, but that didn't mean I wanted them to be stripped away. It was a comfort to know they couldn't be stolen from me, but in the midst of my dreams, it felt real enough to warrant fear.

"Save some for Ainsley! You've already had three," Lia said from her spot at the end of the bed.

Lia had wormed her way into our little friendship through her persistence and Felix's obsession with her. She was a breath of fresh air at all times, and despite my desire not to form any new relationships, she was quickly becoming a fast friend. She respected my choice to hold off on learning all my Gifts and never pried when

I was lost in my head about things. She and Felix had gotten along during our stay at the palace, as they bonded over both being from Ministro, though Lia was a Medicus rather than an Empathi.

When I asked about how she ended up in Tenebrae, she said she wanted a change of scenery. I could tell there was more to her story, but she never made me divulge information before I was ready, so I wouldn't do the same to her. She had met Calidore shortly after arriving more than a century ago, and the two have been inseparable ever since.

"Well, then she should eat them faster," Felix quipped, shoving a cookie into his mouth. Lia tossed a pillow at him, and I smiled at the exchange as a soft knock sounded on my open bedroom door.

"Can I join?" Calidore asked tentatively, and I nodded. I hadn't gotten to know him much, only learning small details that Lia shared, but I knew he meant everything to her, so I didn't want to be rude. Calidore jogged to the bed and plopped down happily as if my allowing him to stay made his entire month. He leaned in and kissed Lia on her cheek before grabbing one of the cookies from the plate and shoving it into his mouth.

"Your shield is shit, by the way," he said around a full bite. Okay, so maybe I wouldn't let him hang out with us after all. "You lose it the moment you fall asleep. Whatever your nightmares are of, they must be pretty bad because you're so loud until you wake up." Lia shoved him hard in the ribs to silence him.

I looked at Lia and Felix, who were both averting their eyes like they couldn't bear for me to see the truth inside them. If I didn't already experience yelling at Evander with a dick made of bubbles on my head, this conversation would have topped the list of the most embarrassing things to have happened to me.

"Well, that's just great," I mused.

"I only meant that I can help you with it," Calidore explained, and I glanced skeptically at him. "As soldiers, we're trained always to keep a penetrating shield up when we sleep. It'll take some practice, but a silencing shield is far easier, so I'm sure you can pick it up quickly. Unless you don't want—"

"No, I do," I said at once. "I want to learn how to do that. Thank you, Calidore."

He bowed his head slightly, and Lia beamed at him. I desperately wanted my emotions and fears to stay only mine—to be private once again. It seemed that would be the case soon.

"Whenever you decide you're ready, I can help you with your shadows too," he said as a dark tendril escaped from his palm and curved around his wrist. I felt gratitude at his offer and that he wasn't pushing me to access that Gift until I deemed myself ready. I could see why Lia loved him.

"Someday, but for now, just the shield," I told him, and he nodded like he expected that response.

"Maybe we'll all actually get some sleep tonight for a change," Calidore said before reaching for the last cookie.

Felix and Lia's eyes widened at his comment. I was sure one of them was about to punch him when the corner of his lip lifted in a grin, and I realized he was joking. His eyes sought mine, hopeful that I wouldn't take it the wrong way. It may not have been the best timing, but I appreciated him helping me and trying to make light of a dark situation.

"Just for that, I'm going to be even louder tonight," I told him, leaning forward, snatching the cookie from his hands and shoving it into my mouth before he could stop me. Calidore threw his head back with laughter at my playful response.

"I guess I'll just have to make Lia scream louder," he joked, wrapping his arms around her and kissing her face as she squealed in his hold. I smiled as I watched their exchange, though a piece of me broke as it reminded me of what I had lost with Dash.

I knew tonight's nightmare was going to be brutal.

I sat at the breakfast table, sipping my coffee and enjoying the early morning silence, when an envelope slid next to me. I looked up to find Evander standing there, his eyes darting from the paper to me. It was the first time he had approached me in two weeks, and now he was doing it with some cryptic message.

"What is this?" I asked, looking down at the envelope like it was poison.

"Something to help you," he said simply as he pushed the paper closer. I eyed it for a long moment before finally looking back at him and shaking my head.

"I thought I made it clear that I don't trust you," I said, and Evander sighed dramatically before taking the envelope and striding into the next room. Rather than throw it away, he created a clip from shadows and hung it above the fireplace in the living room. I couldn't lie and say I wasn't curious about what the envelope contained, but it certainly wasn't enough to give in and read it.

"By the way, you look good enough to eat today, love," Evander called from the other room, and my grip tightened around my mug as I forced myself not to respond. He just wanted a reaction out of me after not getting one for two weeks, and I wouldn't let him have it. A moment later, he returned and placed himself in the seat across from me, watching intently as I sipped my coffee.

Evander rested his elbows on the table, interlacing his fingers and resting his chin atop them. He arched a brow but didn't bother to say a word as we sat quietly. I opened my mouth to ask what he was doing when his eyes sparkled and widened a fraction at the act. I quickly closed it, realizing this was another way to bait me. Instead, I leaned back and took a long drink of my beverage as we stared daggers at each other. If he wanted to play this game, he would soon find out he was no match for me. I wasn't going to be the one to look away or speak first.

Soon, commotion filled the room as the rest of the house residents came to grab their breakfast, but Evander and I paid them no mind—our eyes locked firmly on one other, and both too stubborn to retreat first.

"What's happening?" I heard Felix ask from somewhere behind me.

"Her and Van are having some sort of pissing contest, though I can't quite figure out why," Lia answered.

I assumed the answer was obvious: Van was an asshole who needed to learn that things wouldn't go how he wanted. If winning this stupid game showed him that I wouldn't easily back down, he would hopefully take the hint and leave me alone.

"I bet it's because he threw some insult at her again," Felix suggested, and I opened my mouth and closed it quickly as I fought against the urge to correct him. Evander caught my almost slip and straightened as if that little opening was all he needed.

"Nah. If that were the case, she would have just tried to attack him again. This seems more of a battle of stubbornness. I think he told her to do something, and she didn't like his tone," Lia said, and I internally applauded that guess. Even if it was wrong, it was definitely something I'd do.

"Personally, I think he made a pass at her again, and she's fighting the urge to take him up on it," Calidore supplied, and I rolled my eyes at his ridiculous assumption, realizing one second too late that the move had cost me the game.

Dammit.

Evander grinned even wider before rising from his chair and casually strolling out of the room. I squeezed my hands tighter around my mug, furious that I had lost and would no doubt have to deal with Evander's arrogance about it tenfold today. I wasn't sure why he suddenly approached me again, and I hated that I found myself curious about it.

"What just happened?" Calidore asked as he looked after Evander.

Everyone began to move about the room as if they couldn't depart it fast enough. A gentle prickling sensation began forming in my fingers, and I glanced down to find my shadows creeping around them like growing ivy. I swallowed hard, focusing on recalling the Gift rather than on my frustration at letting my control slip with both Evander and my magic.

"Ainsley's met her match," Felix whispered low, and I bristled at that thought.

When I first moved to the palace in Caelum, I made Felix and Dash's life with me as difficult as I could. They wanted nothing more than to get to know me and establish a friendship, but I made it clear at every turn that I hated them. I spent my days in silence, refusing to give in to their attempts at conversation, and I was damn good at it. So why was I struggling so much with Evander? He had bested me at every attempt, drawing out my anger whenever he wanted. Even when I kept my fury on a leash, he still managed to beat me at a damn staring contest. He wasn't my *match*; he was a challenge.

One that I was going to win.

I took a deep breath as I paced back and forth in the hallway, hesitating outside Olivier's door. I could knock and get it over with, but some part of my brain wanted to stay in the dark.

Fuck it.

"Come in," Olivier announced after I gently rapped on his bedroom door.

I twisted the knob and pushed it open, though I remained in the hall. Olivier looked up from where he was seated at a desk and dropped the papers he had been holding when he saw me standing there. We only spent time together during my training sessions and never spoke outside of them. It wasn't because I hated him like I did Evander, but I could tell he was waiting for me to ask about my parents, and I wasn't ready to.

Until now.

"Do you have a minute?" I asked, half debating just turning around and returning to my room.

He nodded fervently and gestured to the sitting area on the other side of the room. I closed the door behind me and crossed the space before sliding into an empty chair as Olivier did the same. Nervously, I blew out a breath and began pulling at my fingers as I tried to figure out how to start.

"It's not that I didn't want to know about what happened to my parents," I said, feeling the need to explain why I hadn't sought him out sooner. "It's just that I don't know who I can trust and what stories to believe. King Perceval hasn't been entirely truthful, but that doesn't mean you will be either."

Olivier didn't seem offended by my explanation, nor did he seem frustrated or angry by it. Instead, he smiled warmly, like he understood my reluctance, and his bright turquoise eyes softened. I may have been unsure of things when it came to this conversation, but I also felt at ease in his presence.

"Regardless of my skepticism, I need to hear what happened the night they died," I admitted as I averted my gaze. He offered to tell me anything I wanted, but it still felt like I was putting him on trial and forcing him to prove his innocence.

"Of course," Olivier replied gently.

I leaned back in my chair as I gave him my full attention. I wanted to look him in the eyes as he spoke and prayed my Gift would allow me to pick up on any hint of dishonesty. Olivier leaned forward, resting his forearms on his knees as his stare locked on mine. I wanted to buckle beneath the intensity.

"Your parents—Julian and Viviette—were two of the best people I have ever known," Olivier began, and my breathing quickened at hearing their names for the first time in my life.

I didn't think something so little would affect me as much as it had. I didn't know my parents. I never had a chance to get attached and have them ripped away. I shouldn't have been reacting like I was, but it was like they were never truly real until learning their names. It represented who I was and what I'd never have.

"And I miss them every Gods damn day," he continued. "Julian was a mentor to me for most of my life—the only father figure I've ever known. And Viv was the kindest, sweetest soul. I went through a lot of shit growing up, most of my own doing, but she never once judged me for my mistakes and was always quick to welcome me into their home. Your parents became family to me over the years, and losing them was one of the worst days I've ever experienced."

I blew out a breath as I watched him and read the clear emotion on his face. How he spoke of my mother and father differed significantly from how King Perceval had. When the King of Caelum mentioned my parents, it was like he was recounting a memory from long ago, but when Olivier spoke of them, his voice held such an air of grief it was like he could remember every encounter with them as clearly as if it occurred yesterday. It was obvious which of the two men who claimed to know my parents truly had.

"What happened?" I asked, needing to hear the rest of the tale.

"Every week, we'd have a family dinner at the palace, but that day in particular, Viv wanted to do it at one of the village restaurants. Since you were expected to arrive any day, your mother got whatever she wanted," he said with a soft laugh, seeming unbothered by that fact. "When I arrived at the restaurant, your parents were already there, but we were still waiting on Uriel and Dahlia."

"Who?" I asked, unsure of the names.

"Evander's parents."

I should have known that was who he was referring to, but he called them solely by their names, leaving out their royal title of king and queen. Olivier claimed my parents were family to him, but given his informality with the rulers of Tenebrae, I was sure the same could be said for them.

"Of course, the moment we sat down, your mother went into labor," he continued, smiling to himself. "Your father brought her to the inn across the street, and I retrieved a Medicus for them. Everything happened so fast, and you were born within the hour. I remember you were so tiny in my arms, and I was terrified of breaking you, but Julian kept telling me you were stronger than you looked. After a while, I headed back across the street to pick up food and give the three of you time together. That's when everything changed."

Olivier looked away, and his turquoise eyes gleamed in the room's dim light. He was lost in the memory of that day, and judging by the way he tensed and swallowed hard, I knew the next part of his story wasn't going to be a pleasant one. His stare stayed fixed on a random point across the room as he spoke again.

"All at once, people were screaming and running away as the streets were filled with men brutally cutting down anyone in their way. I sprinted for the inn, pushing my way through the crowds of people fleeing from the building. Somehow the enemy had gotten inside already. People were yelling and fighting for their lives, but over all of that noise, the only thing I was focused on was the sound of you crying."

Olivier blew out a shuddering breath as he closed his eyes, and tears gently streamed down his cheeks. My heart ached, and my eyes filled with moisture as I listened to his story, knowing it ended in tragedy.

"By the time I got to the room, it was too late. Julian was on the ground, and his lifeless eyes stared up at the ceiling while Viv screamed as she fought. Your mother was a skilled warrior, giving everything she had to protect you. I joined the fight the moment I stepped through the door, trying to take as many of them down as possible, but we were outnumbered—two to seven and…"

Olivier trailed off, and the pain etched on his face had me reaching for his hand. I clasped it in mine, sending my Empathi Gift out to try and lessen the hurt he was experiencing. I was briefly met with an internal shield, but he lowered his defenses at once and let me in. That act alone said how much he trusted me. I wasn't skilled at calming emotions like Felix was, but I could at least let him know I was there for him at that moment. Hopefully, that would be enough.

"After they killed her, they went after you, and before I could stop them, a blade was shoved through my chest. The last thing I heard was you screaming, and then my world went black," he said as his eyes fluttered open to meet mine. There was nothing but agony and truth swimming in those bright blue depths. "The next thing I remembered was Uriel's voice yelling commands and the smell of fire all around. Somehow I survived the massacre, the sword just missing my heart, but I didn't care. Julian and Viv were dead, and you were missing. My family was *gone*.

"Dahlia said they looked everywhere for you as the inn went up in flames, but there wasn't any clue as to where you'd gone. We didn't even know if you were alive or dead or where to look. It was like you and every assailant vanished without a trace. We didn't have a single idea as to who was behind the attacks, and it killed me. For years Uriel and Dahlia searched for you but kept running into dead ends until their own lives were taken on their hunt."

"They believed I was alive all this time?" I asked though it was more of a statement than a question.

"Yes," he said. "Uriel swore a death vow to your father that he'd stop at nothing until you were brought home."

I didn't know what to do with that but feel shame and guilt. I knew it wasn't directly my fault that they died, but I couldn't help feeling like I played a part in their demise. Evander's parents were dead because of me. If they hadn't been out searching, then they'd probably still be alive, and he would have never experienced the pain of losing them.

Olivier's story was so different than King Perceval's but there were elements that were the same. Both men claimed I was stolen and my parents were slain just after my birth, though King Perceval said he knew who was behind the attack. Even though I had shadow magic, it was still possible that King Uriel wanted to breed me since I also possessed another Gift from a different kingdom. But if Evander was telling the truth, about our mothers being best friends, then I couldn't see the former King of Tenebrae wishing me harm. Especially if Uriel and my father were close like Olivier had said. Even though King Perceval's story provided the most answers, it made the least sense.

"So King Perceval and my father were never friends," I told myself, deciding that the King of Caelum's story was one I would no longer believe.

"They were," Olivier replied, and my eyes widened in shock. That definitely was not the response I was expecting to hear. "King Harbin of Ministro, King Perceval, and your father were all close friends growing up. In fact, Harbin and your father were cousins. I don't know exactly what happened, but once Harbin was crowned king after his father's passing, Julian developed a second Gift, making him the new Heir to Ministro. He wanted to keep it a secret."

"Why?"

"Because that meant the Gods had chosen a different bloodline to rule. They didn't deem Harbin's children worthy enough of the title. Even though they were friends, Julian was afraid his cousin would kill him in an attempt to force the Gods to choose his direct line. Somehow Harbin found out about Julian's second Gift and ordered his murder. Your father barely managed to escape and fled north. He ended up in Tenebrae, and Uriel granted him refuge. That's when he met your mother; the rest became history."

"And he didn't maintain a relationship with King Perceval?" I asked, and Olivier shook his head. I nodded to myself, knowing exactly why that was. "Because Perceval was behind Harbin learning the truth. My father knew it, so he cut him off."

"Yes."

"And then he had him killed and stole me," I breathed, the emotion thick in my throat.

I had been in the company of that man for months. I sat there and listened to him spew lies about my father and what had happened to me. And I had believed every damn word out of his vicious mouth. My magic scraped its claws against my skin, begging me to let it out and claim retribution.

"He will pay for this," I vowed, and Olivier squeezed my hand tight.

"Yes. He will."

10.

Another envelope slid next to me the following morning and I promptly set two fingers on it before sliding it back and sipping my morning coffee. Evander sighed dramatically before snatching it up and hanging it next to the one from yesterday. He sat down in the chair across from me again, resting his chin in his hands like before.

"Are you still fighting the urge to resist my passes at you?" Evander asked with a seductive grin and a hint of amusement in his eyes. Apparently, we weren't playing the quiet game today, but that was fine. I was determined to win whatever game he chose.

"Do I look like I am?" I asked sweetly, giving him a *fuck you* smile. He shrugged noncommittally.

"I think you enjoy our little back and forth more than you want to admit."

"And I think you're delusional," I responded just as the sounds of people filling the kitchen reached my ears, followed by several low groans as they took in Evander and me.

"Last I checked, *you* were the one who pulled me on top of you."

"You know the reason why, but it's cute you think that means I want you."

"It's cute you think it doesn't," he said. I snorted, which only caused him to chuckle in self-satisfaction. I couldn't figure out if he was just trying to get under my skin or if he actually believed in what he was saying. None of the interactions we'd ever had were pleasant, and I'd given into his flirtations a grand total of zero times, so I was leaning toward the former.

I stood, resting my palms flat on the table, and leaned closer; Evander followed suit, mimicking my every move. I gritted my jaw, forcing my anger and annoyance to stay in line as I focused on my opponent.

"You're full of yourself," I responded, shaking my head slowly.

"And you're in denial, Your Highness," Evander said smugly, and I cringed at the title. He only said it because he knew it would force me to recognize this twisted game of fate the Gods forced upon me.

"I don't think so, Evander... or would you prefer I use *Your Majesty*?" I asked sarcastically, showing him that his use of my title wouldn't cause me to buckle, even though I hated that it connected me to him.

"Whichever one you'd rather use while you beg for me later," he said with a single-shoulder shrug. "However, my name *does* have such a nice ring to it while it's being screamed."

Our onlookers sucked in their breaths, preparing for my wrath, and I pressed my fingers into the wood to stop my shadows from slipping out with my rage. Evander's eyes twinkled as he caught the movement, and I took a deep breath to remind myself that he was only saying it to get a rise out of me. He knew how short my fuse was and that getting me pissed off was the most effortless way to victory. Well, not today.

I cocked my head and pursed my lips as if I were seriously considering the choice.

"Let's go with your name then," I finally said after a moment. "But given that your obnoxious ego is clearly just you overcompensating for your tiny dick, I doubt any screaming will be involved. And the only thing I'll be begging for is for you to put it away so I don't die from laughter at the sight of it."

Evander's lips twitched in a ghost of a smile, doing the opposite of what I intended. What guy gets his manhood insulted and then grins about it?

"Oh, my Gods... There's two of them," I heard Felix say softly, and I stole a glance to find everyone nodding as they watched us intently, nibbling on their toast and sipping from their coffee. They seemed to be thoroughly enjoying the show, and this time I didn't mind, as I was the one who would be walking away the victor.

"Don't worry, love," Evander started as my eyes drifted back to him, noticing he stood straighter like my insult had only heightened his desire to win. "If you find my size lacking, I'm sure I can more than make up for it with my tongue."

"The only thing your tongue seems to know how to do is talk shit."

"How about we go upstairs, and we can put that to the test?" he quipped and winked.

"You're so egotistical."

"And you're stubborn."

"You're an asshole," I shot back, leaning closer.

"You're a brat," he bit out just as forcefully before closing the distance between us by another inch.

"Narcissistic."

"Self-centered."

"Obnoxious," I said back, mentally keeping note of all the insults I had in my back pocket.

"Annoying," he responded as his Gift of shadows began to slip out and snake slowly around his arms.

"Arrogant," I breathed as I watched them move, knowing he only released his Gift to intimidate me and assert his dominance.

Evander broke our stare and followed my gaze to the darkness swirling around his body. He held his palm up, and I watched as the shadows gathered, spinning around themselves faster and faster until a small vortex appeared. After a moment, he twisted the fingers of his hand, and the shadows halted their twirling and flattened themselves before reshaping into the form of a jasmine blossom, dripping in darkness. The shadows kept their texture, making the flower's petals seem fluid and moving. The leaves weren't fully formed but instead were twisted trails of wispy darkness.

The magic he held up was beautiful, but I knew how dangerous it could truly be. It wasn't long ago that I held that same Gift between my hands but rather than create something delicate, it chose to be deadly.

"Afraid," Evander said, and my gaze broke from the creation he held. His face fell flat, and his eyes knowing as he stared back at me. Gone was any trace of his playful and arrogant presence. Instead, I was met with the cold, hard king that had always been lurking just below the surface.

My throat bobbed, and my mouth went dry as I tried to come up with something to say back to him, but there were no thoughts in my mind other than the word he uttered.

Afraid.

I was, and I couldn't even lie about it because everyone in that room knew it too. Evander's shadows slithered away, leaving him standing there just as he was a moment before. He leaned forward, grabbed my mug, and finished the rest of my coffee.

"Same time tomorrow, love," he said before he backed away and headed out to the training ring.

Rather than slide the envelope back over to him this morning, I opted to pick it up, giving him hope that I would open it before tossing it over my shoulder. I was still pissed about my loss yesterday and wouldn't likely be over it soon. Once he took up his usual seat after hanging the envelope next to the others, I made sure to be the one who chose the game. I couldn't let Evander resort to opening his mouth, as I knew that was the quickest way for me to lose now that we learned he could bring up my refusal to use my magic.

I crossed my arms firmly over my chest and settled back in my chair as I glowered at him. Evander realized very quickly what I wanted and mimicked my movements. I wasn't sure how long we sat in silence. The steam from my coffee had disappeared a while ago, and the other house residents had come and gone a few times already. We had the day off from training as Olivier announced that he had some meetings planned with a few of our generals stationed in a nearby camp.

I had nowhere to be and today was going to be the day I won.

Lia and Felix were conversing as the scent of roasted chicken filled the space. Holy Gods, was it already time for lunch? That meant Evander and I had been playing this game for more than six hours, and there was no end in sight.

"What's going on here?" a voice I hadn't heard in weeks said.

"Welcome back, Marce!" Lia said enthusiastically, and I stomached a groan.

That woman seemed to hate me. The day we left the palace, I caught her asking Evander why he was even bothering with me—saying that I was nothing more than a wasted use of space. She wasn't wrong, but that still didn't make it any easier to hear. I thanked the Gods when I found out she wouldn't be coming with us as we mounted our horses to depart the palace. And yet, here she was anyway.

"Ainsley and Evander have a pissing contest every day, but this is the longest it's gone on," Lia continued.

"Because she's determined to win finally," Felix added.

"So she hasn't beat him yet," Marceline mused, and ice shot down my veins at her sinister tone. Footsteps approached, and soon I could feel her presence next to me. "Just add it to the list of your failures," she said, and my gaze drifted to hers. "I can't say I'm surprised, though." Her turquoise stare dragged up and down my body, a look of disgust on her beautiful face.

Evander pushed back from the table at the same time Marceline did, and my eyes snapped back to him. He wore a triumphant smile as he stretched his stiff arms above his head.

"That wasn't fair!" I shouted, rising from my seat. Marceline had interfered, and because of that, I lost a game I knew I could have won.

"Better luck tomorrow, love," he called over his shoulder as he turned and strode out of the room with Marceline following close behind him.

With Marceline's words ringing in my mind, I slammed my fists against the table, cursing loudly as I pounded them repeatedly.

Failure.

The following two days didn't start any better. Evander had gotten up earlier than me to ensure he'd make it to the table first, which completely threw me off. He also made sure that he was the one to choose the game and refused to select one that didn't involve speaking. He knew how close he had come to losing before.

The first day, he brought up my fear of magic, and though I was prepared for him to go in that direction, it still unsettled me. I didn't have a response and lost the game within the first few minutes.

On the second day, I was more prepared and devised a way to steer the conversation far away from magic. But it was like Evander knew precisely what I had planned and directed us to a point where he could bring up Dash. My blood went cold as he commented on my love for the prince and where it had gotten me. I opened and closed my mouth several times before giving up.

Evander said his usual goodbye before striding away to the training ring. I sat there longer than I should have, listening to metal clanging and laughter echoing from outside as everyone sparred. I was half surprised that Olivier hadn't come to find me, but I was sure the arrogant look Evander would be wearing would explain why I was running late.

I took another minute to try and push the sickening reminder of Dash from my thoughts, not wanting Evander to see how much his words had affected me. I couldn't allow him to ever win by bringing up the prince again.

I trained hard that morning, covering my body in sweat and dirt. I allowed Olivier to push me to my limits, wanting to feel the pain in my muscles rather than the ache in my heart.

"Take a break," he said as I rested my hands on my knees and gasped for breath.

"I'm fine," I told him, wiping the sweat from my brow. I certainly wasn't fine, but I didn't want to stop. I didn't want the chance for Evander's words to creep into my mind and fester. I lunged for Olivier again, but he quickly deflected, spinning me around and pinning my wrist behind my back.

"You're tired and therefore sloppy. Take a break, Ainsley. It's not a request."

I grunted as he twisted my wrist harder before shoving me away. I stumbled a few steps before righting myself and glaring at the man with turquoise eyes. He only smiled back before striding over to the table where water was set out. Looking around the space, everyone was sitting down, stretching their limbs and rehydrating before the next session, but I had no desire to do the same. I was still pissed off after my loss this morning and opted to go for a walk instead. If I broke down over Evander's words, I'd rather be alone when it happened.

I headed down the dirt path that led away from the house and into the woods. Felix and I had ventured down here before, so I knew there was a small meadow just beyond a thicket of trees—a perfect place to lose myself without anyone seeing or hearing. As I walked, I had the strange sensation of being followed, but when I turned around, there was nothing there. Maybe it was just my paranoia of others seeing my weakness.

Calidore had trained me each night as promised, and though I couldn't keep a shield up while I was asleep, the magic was becoming easier and easier each day. Cal had said if I kept the progress up, I would have it down within the month.

I entered the clearing and sat beneath a large oak tree as I stretched out my legs from the strenuous workout. The wind blew softly, causing the autumn leaves to fall all around. There was a quiet sense of peace and tranquility in this place, and though I was afraid my mind would drift to Dash now that I was alone, that wasn't the case. I was still broken, and it hurt to even think of him, but I found that he frequented my mind less and less lately thanks to staying busy. If I kept myself preoccupied, there wouldn't be time for my mind to drift to the man I loved and the betrayal he inflicted.

The breeze whistled through the trees, and a snapping branch had me glancing around. Nothing moved, but I had a sinking feeling that I wasn't alone. I stood slowly, taking up a stance that had become second nature to me, thanks to Olivier's training. I wanted to call out for Felix in hopes it was just him coming to join me in a spot we dubbed ours, but before I could, a massive figure to the left caught my eye.

My body stiffened with fear as a large grey wolf shifted from behind the cover of the trees and slowly made its way to me. Its body was enormous, close to half the size of my horse, and deadlier in every way. I wanted to flee but wasn't stupid enough to believe I could outrun a wolf. I could scream for help, but I was too far out for anyone at the house to hear me, so that wouldn't work either. Taking a deep breath, I did the only thing I could.

I called for my magic.

11.

Shadows leaked out, curling around my fingers as I outstretched my hands toward the animal. I bent my knees, keeping my stance limber in case the wolf attacked and I needed to run for it.

"Stay back!" I yelled, letting more darkness spill around me, but the animal didn't listen. It kept on its journey, watching my magic with interest as it closed the distance between us. I gulped down air laced with fear as the wolf paced no more than twenty feet away.

"Don't come any closer!" I tried again, my voice coming out broken and shaky. My whole body was trembling as I stared into the deep brown eyes of the vicious animal that would surely tear me to pieces within seconds.

The grey wolf continued to creep closer, and my anxiety increased. I pushed my magic out harder, but it did nothing but continue to swirl around me instead of slamming into my target as it had with Felix that first day. I was untrained, and it was about to cost me my life. I closed my eyes and waited for the sharp feel of the animal's teeth shredding into my skin, but instead felt fingers trail down my arms.

"She won't hurt you," Evander whispered in my ear. My eyes flew open to find him standing behind me, his hands wrapped tightly around my wrists as he held my hands out firm. My breathing came in rapid gulps as the wolf inched closer and closer, but Evander wouldn't let me retreat. He kept my hands extended as the animal's face stopped inches away.

"Breath slowly," he whispered again. I followed his order without a fight, sipping on the air around me. "Good," he praised, and if the wolf didn't kill me, then surely his compliment would. "Now call your magic back."

"No," I said at once. He had to be kidding.

"So you refuse to use it for weeks, and now you won't put it away?"

"Not when there's a feral animal inches from my fucking hand," I said incredulously, breaking the wolf's stare to look up at the king pressed against me. Evander smirked as he met my eyes like this conversation was taking place casually and not in front of a killer.

"As I said before, she won't hurt you."

"I don't trust you," I breathed. Evander thought on that for a moment.

"Okay, then she won't hurt *me*." At that, I recalled my magic. I didn't believe Evander had my well-being high on his priority list, but I knew he valued his.

A soft, wet nose pressed to my hand, and my focus slid back to the wolf who was now sniffing me curiously. I held my breath as she tilted her head while staring at me. An odd sensation ran through my veins, much like when I first met Nox.

I was surprised when I woke up one morning to find my horse grazing outside the palace. Felix had told me our captors had brought her with us rather than leave her behind because she was from Tenebrae. Perhaps the connection I felt with her and now with this wolf was simply because we were all from the same kingdom. Maybe it had something to do with me being the heir to it.

Evander let go of my wrists, but I didn't lower them, too afraid to make any sudden movements and change the civility of the animal. He crouched down and released a soft whistle as if calling a dog. The grey wolf moved from me and immediately leaped into him, pressing her large paws against his chest as he scratched behind her ears.

What the hell?

"This is Nova," he said as he stood, pulling out some food from his pocket and handing it to the wolf. She scarfed it down in one bite and then began pouncing around the meadow after the butterflies that filled the space. "And that..." he said, pointing to a dark figure in the distance that was now entering the meadow. "Is Onyx." The enormous black wolf prowled toward us, and I could tell even from this distance, he was far bigger than Nova.

Onyx didn't approach slowly the way Nova had. Instead, he strode right up to us and smelled the hand I hadn't offered before sitting in front of Evander like a trained beast. Evander reached into his pocket and tossed Onyx something flat and round. The wolf devoured it and strode away to hunt down butterflies with Nova.

"They're your pets?" I asked, confused. They seemed docile, but their sharp claws and fangs told me they were vicious and wild.

"They're family," Evander said as if that answered my question. "They come and go as they please, but yes, they do belong to me. To *us*." I turned toward him at that last word and pinched my brows together. Did he mean it in the literal sense or that they serve the two of us as the kingdom's rulers? "They were given to us shortly before your birth. Onyx was meant for me, and Nova for you."

"Why?" Was it normal to give wild animals as gifts to babies?

"Their species of wolf is rare and sacred to Tenebrae. They were meant as a present to honor our kingdom and the children our parents had created," he answered, and I guess that made some sense. Why wouldn't someone want to give something so treasured to the children of two powerful men?

"I felt something with her," I whispered, unsure why I bothered to divulge that information to him. Evander nodded as he kept his eyes firmly on the two deadly animals that were catching insects in the flowers. "It was similar to what I felt with Nox once."

"The wolves are bonded to us," he answered.

"Like the Entwining Ceremony?" He shook his head.

"It's not magic that binds us together." I waited for him to continue, but he didn't, instead focusing his attention and a crooked smile at the wolves before us.

"Are you really going to make me keep asking you questions? We both are aware that I know absolutely nothing, so instead of giving me answers that will only lead to more questions, how about you just tell me everything at once?" I demanded. Evander chuckled under his breath.

"Sorry, love, but no. I enjoy your company far too much to tell you everything you want to know in one fell swoop. I'd much rather drag this out for as long as possible."

"Fine," I gritted, crossing my arms over my chest as I watched Onyx's teeth clamp around an unsuspecting butterfly, ending its short life too soon. "Tell me about what binds us with the wolves."

"Onyx and Nova may have been given to you and me, but it didn't have to go any farther than that. They would have lived their days on the grounds or in the wild, never making contact with anyone. But, for whatever reason, they *chose* to serve us."

"And that's why they're here now," I deduced, and he nodded.

"What you felt was her bond and commitment to you."

"How does she know who I am?" I asked.

"As I said, their species is rare and sacred. There's a lot I still don't understand about them, but it's clear she knew you and wanted to relay her decision to be yours. With Nox, she was your father's horse. Her immortal breed chooses a family to bond with and serve for life. That's what you felt."

I nodded, still not fully grasping what precisely that meant, but I guess I would figure it out along the way. Evander sucked in a sharp whistle, and the wolves perked their heads up at the sound. He jerked his chin, indicating that our time in the meadow was over, and I watched as Onyx opened his jaw and dropped a slobber-coated butterfly to the grass before he and Nova ran over.

The four of us walked along the path that led back to the house in silence as I pondered the information I had been given.

"Where do they stay?" I asked, realizing that though I had been living there for weeks, I hadn't once seen them.

"They have their own room in the house, but they've been staying in the woods since you arrived. I didn't need you freaking out and crying when you woke up to find a wolf at the foot of your bed," Evander replied, and though I rolled my eyes at his dramatics, I wasn't sure how far off from the truth it actually was. "Now that you're acquainted, they'll stay in the house again."

Once we reached the training ring, everyone was already warming up, including Marceline, who seemed to be joining us for the afternoon session. Great. Her eyes caught on our approach and slid to Evander as she arched a brow. He shook his head without saying a word, and her gaze moved to me before she offered a glower and then turned away. What was her problem with me?

Onyx followed Evander to the weapons table, and Nova sat stoically at the edge of the ring as she observed me sparring with Olivier. With her watching me like that, I suddenly felt nervous and like I had something to prove. Maybe it was the motivation I needed because I had never fought harder than I did then.

12.

Dinner was quieter than usual. I found myself glancing between Evander, Olivier, and Marceline, who all had a look of concern etched into their features. Calidore's smooth voice and my friends' gentle laughter were drowned out as I focused on Evander and the way his jaw ticked. The three of them were clearly on edge, and I couldn't concentrate on anything but that.

"What's going on?" I demanded, interrupting Cal in the middle of his story. Everyone's eyes moved to me, but my attention was locked on the king across the table. Evander set his fork down and shifted in his seat, but before he could answer me, Marceline did.

"What do you care?" she snapped, and I flinched at her harsh tone. "You've already stated you want nothing to do with your magic or role here, so this is none of your business."

"Marce," Olivier warned his sister, and they exchanged a long look before she pushed away from the table and headed out of the room.

I wasn't sure what I did to warrant her hatred of me and what my refusing to use my magic had to do with it, but tonight I would find out. If she lived here too, I wasn't going to feel uncomfortable around her constantly.

"It's nothing you need to worry about," Evander announced.

"Liar," I said back. The way he constantly dragged his hand through his dark hair or across his jaw since dinner had started told me that this was serious.

"I'm not lying," he replied, and I tilted my head to study him. Nothing but honesty shone in his eyes, and I immediately realized why. Because Marceline was right—I had made my feelings clear. This was none of my business and, therefore, nothing for *me* to worry about.

"But you're concerned," I said, and Evander looked to the others around the table before nodding. "Tell me anyway."

He held my stare for another moment as if trying to determine whether he would give in to my request. If he tried to deny me, I wasn't going to back down. I may not have wanted to take on my role as heir yet, but I couldn't deny the tug of protectiveness I felt over this kingdom. The look on Evander's face the moment he sat down tonight stirred something in me that I didn't know was there.

"Soldiers from Pravus have been spotted entering Ministro," Evander said while looking at Cal rather than me. Calidore swore under his breath as he looked to Olivier, who nodded in confirmation. Cal began asking questions about when it happened and how many were seen, but I turned my attention to Felix, hoping he could shed some light on what Pravus was.

"It's the continent to the west of Disparya and is made up of those who lost the First Great War," Felix answered.

"And over the past few centuries, they've been slowly trying to reclaim their homeland," Evander added. Felix narrowed his brows as if this was the first he'd heard of it. "With the help from a couple of our kings, I might add."

I glanced between Felix and Evander as they stared at one another in some sort of showdown. Was this king accusing Felix of helping people from Pravus take back Disparya? Evander crafted a dagger in his hand and flipped it, repeatedly balancing the hilt and then blade on his finger. Felix shook his head slowly as if denying some unspoken claim, and I felt the hair rise along my arms as I watched the display between the two men.

"Someone fill me in on what's happening," I demanded. Felix tensed beside me.

"He believes King Perceval has been conspiring with the leader of Pravus and that I've known about it," Felix answered. "But it isn't true."

Felix didn't have to say that last statement for me to know the answer already. He may have betrayed me, but that was because he was stuck between myself and Dash. I couldn't see him aiding in treason and not telling me about it once we left Caelum.

"Then you won't mind if we have Tallis interrogate you," Evander said casually.

"Not at all. If you want to waste everyone's time, then have at it. I've been here for weeks and have answered every question you and Olivier have asked me. Accusing me of knowing about all of this and keeping it from you is bullshit, and you fucking know it," Felix replied with an unusual bite in his tone.

Evander flipped the dagger one final time and caught it at the hilt before pointing it across the table at my friend. His grey eyes were dark and hungry after Felix's outburst, and I was terrified his thirst wouldn't be sated until he drew blood.

"Let's get something straight," Evander said, his voice icy and commanding. "I allow you to live because you brought her to me, and I allow you to stay here because you are important to her. Do not mistake my generosity for respect or admiration. We are not friends, and I do not trust you, Empathi."

Felix swallowed hard, and his hands balled into fists in his lap. I covered them with my own, and squeezed tightly as I stared Evander down.

"If Felix says he didn't know, then he didn't," I announced, and the king's gaze flickered to me. "If King Perceval was conspiring with someone from Pravus, then Felix had nothing to do with it. There isn't a reason for Tallis to—"

"There is *every* reason, love. Tenebrae is my kingdom, and I will not let her fall because you want to take your friend at his word. A friend who is an advisor for King Perceval and has proven to be a liar," Evander interrupted. My palms pressed to the table and my fingers dug into the wood. I couldn't argue with him on that fact. I couldn't expect him to know and trust Felix as I did.

"*Was*," Felix said quietly. "I *was* his advisor. I promise I knew nothing of King Perceval's involvement with Pravus, but I will talk to Tallis and tell you anything I can." Felix closed his eyes briefly as he composed himself before looking back at Evander with a renewed sense of purpose. "But I'll also need you to share everything you've learned about it with me."

"That isn't an option," Olivier interjected. "You are not on our council, and this information isn't to be shared outside it."

"Then let me on it," Felix replied.

"It's only for those we trust," Olivier countered bitterly.

This conversation was getting nowhere, and I wasn't sure it ever would. Evander and Olivier obviously would never trust Felix enough to include him in what had been going on, and Felix wasn't likely to divulge information without getting some in return.

My friend blew a heavy breath before unclenching his fists and scrubbing a hand down his face, clearly frustrated with the conversation.

"You don't trust me," Felix said, directing the statement to Evander, and the king shook his head. "Do you trust that I love her?" Evander looked at me momentarily as he considered the question. Then he nodded. "Then trust that I would never let anything happen to her. If Pravus is planning on declaring war on Disparya, that means she would be a target because of what she is. I would never help a cause that would harm her."

Evander stared at Felix as if trying to detect a lie, but I knew he wouldn't find one. Everyone besides Lia and Cal may have hated Felix, but no one could deny my friend's love for me. He betrayed his childhood friend, his king, and fled his home to save me.

Evander rose from his seat, giving Olivier one final look as he debated his decision. Olivier shook his head, begging his friend to reconsider, but Evander turned towards us again with his mind made up.

"You'll accompany us after our morning training session to the camps along the border. We have a meeting with some of the generals, and perhaps what you hear there will help jog your memory of any information you may have overheard while working for Perceval," Evander said. Felix nodded at once, and a moment later, the king and his right-hand man departed the room.

Felix's eyes dropped to his plate like he was replaying every conversation he had with King Perceval in his thirteen years of living in Caelum. His nose scrunched and his eyes narrowed as he continued staring like the answers would unfold if he just concentrated hard enough.

"Is it really bad?" I asked Calidore. He nodded, making my gut knot with worry.

"The leader of Pravus has been a threat for years. Oli and Van have kept a close eye on the situation, but it's been worsening over the decades," Cal said.

"How does Evander know other kings are involved?" I asked.

"He and Oli have had the theory for a while now but started looking into it when those attacks on you and Princess Cordelia occurred. The events seemed too calculated for the culprits to be random rebel groups. Not to mention, Van does a good job at ensuring groups like that don't exist," he responded. I wanted to ask what he meant by that last fact, but something told me I already knew. Evander didn't seem like the type to ignore traitors or keep bad fruit amongst his people.

If King Perceval was working with the leader of Pravus, wouldn't Felix or even Dash have known? It didn't seem possible for either of them not to know about an alliance of that magnitude. Maybe Dash was aware, and it was just another thing he kept to himself.

I stood outside my bedroom door, unsure how I'd gotten there. My thoughts had been so plagued since dinner that I didn't remember making the journey back to my room, yet there I was, standing there like an idiot. I looked down the corridor, wondering if I should just go to Felix's room instead. He seemed to be in such turmoil after being accused of aiding in King Perceval's possible treason, and I wanted to be there to help him in any way I could. Before I could step in that direction, the door across from mine opened, revealing a very pissed-off-looking Marceline.

"What?" she demanded harshly, and I averted my eyes as if I had been caught doing something wrong. I put my head down, determined to ignore her and go to my friend, but her self-satisfied snort echoed in my ears, and I whirled around.

"What the hell is your problem with me?" I demanded, marching right to her. She was at least a foot shorter than me, but fuck if that didn't make her even more terrifying. Her turquoise eyes widened, and a slow smirk formed on her face.

"I have to pick just one?" Marceline mused, and I clenched my jaw as I felt the familiar prick of magic against my skin. "Fine. You're a coward and a brat."

"I am not—"

"You're useless and pathetic. You have a responsibility to your people and refuse to acknowledge it," she continued as if I hadn't spoken. "You were given three Gifts and choose to disregard them because of fear."

"You don't understand—"

"You complain about your life being stolen from you, but you've been given it back just to throw it away yourself," Marceline added, pushing forward and forcing me to walk back into my room. The second we were inside, she slammed the door shut and continued her insults. "You're stubborn, arrogant, and unreasonable, and thousands of my people—*your* people—will die because of it."

Her blue eyes were bright with rage, and her lip curled back in disgust as she dragged her stare up and down my body, making me feel so much smaller than her. Her blond curls were tied back into a knot on top of her head, and for a split second, I was reminded of being reprimanded by Imogen so long ago. I wasn't sure if it was my longing to have her with me again that had me opening my mouth, but whatever it was, I found myself spilling my truth to Marceline.

"If I use my magic, then they'll die because of me anyway," I said, and the emotion in my voice seemed to throw her off. She uncoiled her tense body for a moment, and I could have sworn her eyes flickered with something like pity. "I almost killed Felix because I couldn't control it. I can't risk it again. I can't—" My words were cut off as a sob escaped my throat. I knelt down with tears in my eyes. She was right to call me a failure because that's exactly what I was.

I couldn't get a grip on my emotions or magic, making me weak and pathetic. I hated myself and everything I was. My feelings got pushed onto the residents constantly, and I knew I was waking them up each evening with my screams from the nightmares that raged through me. I was a fucking failure.

"You're stronger than this, so act like it," she said before walking away and leaving me to my misery.

13.

I stared at the ceiling for hours, contemplating Marceline's words. Was I stronger than I was acting? It sure didn't feel like it, and given my breakdown as soon as she confronted me, I'm not sure why she thought I was.

A soft melody drifted through the room like a wisp of wind, and I sat up, looking around for the source. There was a light creeping into the room from under my door. Usually, the hallway stayed dark at this hour, given that everyone was sound asleep.

I slid from my bed and padded across the room before peeking my head out. The corridor was dimly lit and silent, except for the quiet music coming from downstairs. I followed the sound, enjoying how the soft notes swelled before falling, only to rise again. The gentle melody brushed over my skin in a caress that soothed my aching heart and filled my soul with a sense of belonging.

I kept walking as the music beckoned me closer until I stood in the library doorway and stared at Evander across the space. He was seated at the grand piano, his fingers moving over the keys in delicate strokes as we were enveloped in a piece that embodied desire and longing. I should have walked away and given him privacy, but I was ensnared in his song; captivated by the beauty of it and found my feet pressing forward to go to him.

He quietly whispered the lyrics with each note he played like he was singing only to himself. The melody coming from the instrument couldn't compare to the elegance of his voice, and I desperately wished he were singing louder so I could be fully wrapped in it.

I sat down next to him on the bench, watching in amazement at how his fingers moved with such precision across the ivory keys. He didn't stop playing or comment on my arrival though I knew he was aware of my presence; instead, he continued his song until it reached its end. Only then did he withdraw his hands from the keys to flip a page from the book atop the piano as he selected another piece to perform.

"Did I wake you?" he asked, stretching his fingers as he hovered them over the keys again, readying himself to play.

"What's a death vow?" I asked, changing the subject. It was a question I had since Olivier first mentioned the words days ago, but I wasn't sure why I decided to wait until tonight to bring it up.

Evander's fingers pressed lightly on the keys as he played another haunting song, though no lyrics were involved this time.

"So you spoke to Oli about your parents," he observed, giving me a sidelong glance while continuing to play the piano with such expertise. "A death vow is a promise made to someone dying or in honor of a life already lost," he answered, focusing on the notes. "It's made to fulfill their last wish."

"Does anything happen if the vow is broken?" I asked, wondering if the oath was enforced by magic and if there were consequences for it not being carried out.

"It's said that when the death vow is made, that person's soul cannot find peace until the promise is fulfilled," Evander answered, and there was a sadness in the way the words drifted from between his lips. I couldn't blame him for that, especially knowing I was why his mother and father were killed.

"Do you think he found peace?" I whispered.

I reached forward and pressed down on one of the keys, causing a low note to cascade out of the piano. It would have interrupted Evander's song, except he stopped playing when the question left my mouth. We hadn't gotten along since the moment we met, and I was starting to understand his resentment toward me and the hostility he always showed. I only hoped that Uriel's vow was fulfilled when I arrived in Tenebrae.

"I do," he replied quietly, and I sighed deeply at the knowledge. I obviously had never met either of our parents, but I hated the idea that someone's soul was left aching and wandering the next life, unable to rest because of me. "I have something for you," he added, and I turned to look and him just as he slid from the bench and strode for a desk across the room.

I watched as he pulled out a small key from his pocket, unlocked one of the drawers, and removed a small black box. He walked back slowly and set the package between us as he sat. I raised a brow, unsure if I wanted to open it. I had denied every envelope he tried to give me, so why should this be any different?

Evander rolled his eyes, picked up the box, and removed the lid before reaching inside and pulling out a long thin silver chain. He held it up, and I took it from him as I inspected the dainty jewelry. At the end of the delicate chain was a small silver pendant, no bigger than the pad of my thumb. Small black stones encrusted around the circle, and in the middle, the outline of a bird was etched into the metal.

"What is it?" I breathed, running my fingers over the symbol.

Evander shifted beside me as he leaned closer to inspect the jewelry in my hands.

"I'm not sure," he admitted, eyeing it skeptically. "People have been trying to figure it out for years, but no one seems to know what it is. But if I had to guess..." he reached for the pendant, and I let him place it in his palm as he looked it over.

I held my breath as my curiosity grew by the second. Evander's eyes squinted as he drew his face closer, seeming to pick up on something he hadn't before. I swallowed hard as he tilted his head, and his eyes widened in wonder before meeting my bewildered stare.

"I'd say it's a necklace," he breathed, and my face fell as he smiled, the anticipation in my lungs deflating just as quickly as it had filled. Evander chuckled under his breath as I ripped the jewelry from his fingers, and he returned to playing the piano. "It's a present from your parents—something meant to represent home. The etched bird is a symbol for Tenebrae" he added. "It's said that species can always lead you home—no matter how lost you are." Any annoyance I felt towards him dissipated at his words.

He held up his wrist and showed me the bracelet adorning it before lowering it back to the keys. It was similar to my necklace though rather than a small pendant, he had a solid silver band encrusted with the same black stones around its perimeter and a bird etched in the center.

"Yours was meant to be given at your naming ceremony, but clearly, that didn't happen," Evander said.

"Obviously," I replied flatly, and his lips twitched in the corners. Why did he always find so much joy in being a prick? "We both know I have no idea what a naming ceremony is, so are you really going to make me ask, or can you just be nice for once and explain without prompting?"

"Maybe I just like that you're forced to speak to me."

"I don't know why. Nothing I ever say to you is nice," I pointed out. Evander chuckled again, finishing his song and turning the page to find another. This new piece was softer and slower than the last—something meant to be danced to with a lover while the world around faded away.

"True, but maybe I like that," he said seductively, and I rolled my eyes before slipping the chain around my neck and tucking it beneath my nightgown. "It's a tradition in our kingdom to hold a ceremony shortly after a child's birth where their name is revealed to friends and family."

"It isn't known beforehand?" I hoped there was a possibility he was aware of what my name would have been. Evander glanced over to me and shook his head. His eyes softened a fraction, and I was sure it was because he knew the reason I inquired.

"It's considered bad luck to speak the name to anyone before the ceremony," he said, removing his hands from the piano and placing them onto his lap. He ran his fingers over his bracelet absentmindedly as he watched me with sympathy in his gaze. I didn't want pity, especially not from him.

I had accepted the death of my parents long ago, and though it hurt that I would never know them, I didn't want to dwell on what I had lost. I would seek revenge for their murder but wouldn't shed a tear for a life I had never known. Movement caught my attention, and I looked past Evander to find Felix standing in the library doorway.

"Hey," I said as Felix looked back and forth between Evander and me. It must have been strange to see us sitting so close and not at each other's throats for a change.

"Hey," he answered cautiously as his eyes lingered on the man at my side. Evander's back was straight, and his attention was now firmly on the instrument in front of him though his fingers didn't touch the keys. "I came to check on you, but you weren't in your room. Is everything okay?"

"Yes," I told him, offering a weak smile. "I just couldn't sleep."

"I'll stay with you tonight," Felix responded, stepping to the side in a gesture for me to follow.

Evander rolled his neck as his jaw clenched. He was annoyed for some reason but didn't say a word.

"I'll be up in a minute," I said, keeping my gaze locked on the king.

After a moment, retreating footsteps filled the otherwise silent space, and I arched a brow as Evander turned his attention to me once more. Gone was any trace of kindness, and instead, I was looking at the man who spewed his insults to me days after I arrived in Tenebrae.

"What is your issue with him?" I demanded harshly.

"I have many, but right now, my main concerns are with you," he answered in the same tone. Great. What the hell could I have done now? "You refuse to let him go. You continue to use Felix as a crutch when you should be figuring out who you are without him."

"He is my best friend—"

"He lied and betrayed you, yet you rely on him as if he hadn't. You refuse to use your dark Gifts or to separate yourself from him. You're holding on to every scrap of your old life when you've chosen to live this one."

"That's not fair," I tried to argue, but Evander cut me off again.

"Everyone in this house has been trying with you—*I* have been trying with you."

"Are you fucking kidding me?" I demanded, rising to my feet.

There was some remnant of truth in his declaration: Lia and Cal both had become people I enjoyed being around. They offered their help and friendship and never tried to push me before I was ready, but Evander? He's been domineering and demanding, cruel and compassionless. He hasn't once tried to get to know me and instead has tried to transform me into the person he thinks I should be.

"Felix and I may have shit to work through, but never once has he made me feel worthless and deserving of what happened to me," I spat, and Evander's eyes widened at my accusation. "You have made it perfectly clear exactly what you think of me. I'm not strong or intelligent, determined or capable. Being betrayed by the man I love was entirely my fault because the only thing I cared about was fucking him."

Evander flinched as I threw the words he had once said to me right back at him. He could hate Felix all he wanted, but there was no way in hell I would allow him to act like he was better than my friend. I wasn't sure if Felix and I would ever get to the level of trust we once had, but he was trying every day to ensure we would.

"Felix has his faults, but at least he's there for me and wants the best. *He* saved me from Caelum—not you. You may have brought us to this kingdom, but he's the one who risked his life and everything he had to get me out. You claimed to believe I had been alive all this time, so where the fuck were you?" I yelled. Evander didn't answer. His grey eyes stayed cold and blank as he listened to my rage. "I don't care if you don't like Felix. I'm not giving up the only person I know I can count on."

With that, I walked around the bench and headed for the hallway. Evander called after me, but I didn't stop until I reached my bedroom and locked the door behind me.

"What happened?" Felix asked from his spot in my bed, but all I kept hearing was Marceline's words echoing once again.

Useless. Pathetic. Failure.

14.

The next morning, after refusing to take the envelope from Evander, I didn't try to win his game, let alone play it. I just sat there in the kitchen, staring at the mug of coffee between my hands, too tired from my night of crying to give a shit about anything. I thought I was getting stronger, but it seemed I was breaking a little more in a different way. Before, my pain consisted of Dash's betrayal, but now it was something else. Marceline's words had planted themselves in my mind and were growing like weeds in a garden, destroying the beautiful things I thought I had created.

"Love?" Evander asked cautiously. I looked up to find him watching me with a soft expression on his face, void of the usual arrogance that always danced around his features. He knew that even our argument last night wasn't enough to warrant the behavior I was displaying today. "What's wrong?"

His voice was small and caring like he was approaching a hurt animal, not the woman he loved to irritate. I shook my head as I stared through him and not at him—not seeing anything except my own misery. My Gods, I really *was* pathetic.

"Good morning," Marceline announced as she fluttered into the room and captured Evander's attention. My fingers wrapped around my mug a little tighter as I braced myself for the possibility of another verbal assault.

"Marce," Evander said stiffly as his gaze fell to my hands which were holding onto the cup for dear life. "We discussed this."

"And I disagreed," she said simply as she wandered to fix herself a breakfast plate and left the room.

Evander continued to watch me, and I didn't enjoy seeing the pity in his eyes. He had done nothing but purposefully piss me off since I arrived, and now he was concerned about my mental state? Perhaps he just didn't enjoy that someone else broke me before he could have his fun.

"What did she say?" he asked after a moment.

"Nothing that wasn't true," I replied, pushing away from the table and disposing of my mug in the sink before heading outside to train.

The session was brutal, and I spent most of it in the dirt, flat on my back after being knocked down for the hundredth time. My mind wasn't focused, and it was causing my downfall. I should have taken the day to myself, but I didn't want to give Marceline another reason to hate me. I wasn't sure why I cared so damn much what she or anyone else thought of me, but I couldn't get her words out of my thoughts. Failure, stubborn, pathetic, and coward repeatedly echoed each time I hit the ground.

"We're done for today," Olivier said when he finally had enough. He had spent the morning yelling at me for being sloppy and unfocused, but no matter how hard I tried, I couldn't get into the mindset I should have been in. "You're wasting my time with this bullshit."

"I'm trying—"

"No, you're not," he said derisively. "I've seen you try, and this isn't that. We're done, and it's not up for debate."

Olivier turned and walked out of the ring without another word, leaving me even more pissed off. I grunted my frustration before stripping off my training gloves, throwing them into the dirt, and storming off across the yard. My eyes met Evander's from the other side of the ring where he was working on throwing daggers at a target with Cal. His face held a question that I refused to acknowledge. I continued on my journey, ignoring everyone and everything as I replayed Marceline's words in my mind again.

Failure, stubborn, pathetic, coward.

I paced around the living room while waiting for Felix to return. The sun had gone down hours ago, and I assumed they would have returned from their meeting with the generals by now. Lia was the only one who didn't join them, saying she'd rather stay at the house than attend some boring meeting, though I knew she did it to keep me company. My mind had been searching through countless conversations I had with Felix and Dash, trying to come up with something that could help, but nothing did. We spent our days pretending horrors didn't exist rather than diving head-first into them.

"You're going to ruin that rug if you don't calm down and have a seat," Lia called from the couch as she flipped through a book.

"They should have been back by now."

"I thought you didn't care about politics," she commented, giving me a knowing glance.

I thought I hadn't either. Being named the Heir to Tenebrae was at the very bottom of things I concerned myself with, but lately, I found myself more intrigued about what it would mean to hold that title. I would also lay awake at night, letting my shadows slip through just enough to curl around my fingers, though I wouldn't admit that to anyone. Baby steps.

"I just want to know what's going on. I don't like being left in the dark," I replied. Lia arched a brow, letting me know she knew there was more to it than that, but thankfully she didn't push me on it.

Another hour came and went when the front door finally opened. I ran for the entrance, pushing past everyone as I made my way to Felix, and threw my arms around his neck. Before they left, Evander gave his word that nothing bad would happen to my friend, but I didn't trust him completely. I couldn't be sure he wasn't lying until I laid my eyes on Felix for myself.

"How did it go?" I asked, pulling back as I examined his face to ensure there wasn't a scratch on him.

"We'll discuss it in the study," Evander interrupted before Felix could get a word out. "There's a lot you need to know." The worry in his voice had me shifting my attention to him, and I didn't like what I saw.

Evander was often so confident and composed, but there was a look of terror deep in his grey eyes that I could see him fighting as he looked at me. The sleeves of his shirt were rolled over his forearms, and I noticed a tattoo that looked like wispy shadows stretched over his skin. For a split second, his tattoo appeared to move before stopping abruptly, like he didn't mean for it to happen. Everything about him, from how his face had fallen to how his shoulders slumped forward just barely, seemed off. I swallowed the lump in my throat as I nodded, and Evander escorted us all to the large study.

The room was almost identical to the one back in the palace but on a smaller scale. I sat down on one of the leather sofas, pulling Felix to sit next to me as everyone else filed into the room. Olivier and Marceline stood at a far window, carrying on a hushed conversation as Cal and Lia joined them, no doubt wanting to be filled in on this afternoon's events.

Evander sat across from me, his forearms resting on his knees and his hands linked together tight. The air around us was thick and heavy, pregnant with worry and fear. My magic prickled along my skin, and I fought the urge to let it out like I had been doing in private. I couldn't control it when my emotions got the best of me, and something told me this conversation wouldn't be easy.

"Our parents," Evander began, looking at me. "Believed that the leader of Pravus—Oberon—had been planning an attack on Disparya for centuries. They tried to convince other kings to join their cause, but no one believed them. The kings all thought it was a ploy to cause unrest within Disparya so that Tenebrae could capture their kingdoms. Because they had no proof of their claims, they were sent away at every turn. Our fathers then traveled to the continent of Vorsutos to try their luck there, and fortunately, their leader believed them. For decades they worked closely with the leader to our east, combining our forces and working on strategies that could potentially get the other kings on our side." I sat a bit straighter as I listened.

"Tallis' father was the first to be persuaded," Evander continued. "He could see the honesty in my father and didn't require physical proof as the other kings did. Unfortunately, having him on our side did nothing to change the minds of the other stubborn leaders, so our fathers decided to focus their efforts on something most considered ridiculous. They hunted for Inmuto," he continued.

Felix stiffened beside me, and I glanced up to find the blood had drained from his already pale face. Apparently, this story wasn't something he had learned this afternoon.

"It doesn't exist," Felix breathed, though the way he said the words made it seem like he wasn't quite sure he believed them.

"It does," Evander said slowly. There was nothing in his face that would lead me to believe he was lying. "The sixth kingdom isn't a myth. It's real, and I've been continuing my parents' search for years."

"How do you know?" Felix asked, and it wasn't a harsh accusation. He was genuinely curious.

Evander stood from his spot on the couch and beckoned us over to a desk that contained several old maps sprawled across it. He pointed to a spot that showed the border where Venator met Tenebrae and the Northern Sea, tracing his finger along the ridges.

"I've stared at this map for my entire life, and every time, I always come back to this area," Evander breathed, and Felix leaned in to get a closer look. "When we go through our coronation, our land gives us some of its magic, binding us to it."

Felix nodded as he followed along, but I just stood there confused. All of this was news to me. My eyes flickered over the worn parchment as I trailed my fingers over it, trying to understand what Evander was saying. As if he could sense my frustration, he placed his hand over mine, causing me to glance up.

"The Gods choose who the rulers of this continent are, but the land has to accept them. If it doesn't, then during the ceremony where the magic as king—or queen, in your case—is solidified by an Incantis, then the land will reject the bond, and the ruler dies," Evander said.

My heart sank into the pit of my stomach. I thought this world was as simple as the heir inheriting the third Gift once the sovereign died and taking their place. I had no idea the land itself had to accept that transaction. If Evander fell and I took his place, then the land of Tenebrae could decide I wasn't worthy and kill me rather than let me become queen. I was going to be sick.

"It's only happened twice in the history of Disparya, love. And our history goes back eons, so your chances are very slim," Evander comforted, though it didn't help. A chance of death was still a chance.

"So because of your bond with the land, something feels off," Felix clarified. Evander nodded in confirmation.

Felix walked around to the other side of the desk, looking at the map from different angles as if that would present him with the answer to the question written on his furrowed brows. His amber eyes were serious, and he tied his silver hair back as he concentrated on the land before him.

"Everything I've read about Inmuto is riddled with theories. Almost every piece of information contradicts something written elsewhere, and not one scrap of proof of its existence has ever been found," Felix said as he surveyed the map.

"And that's why it's been discarded as a myth for so long. But those stories had to start somewhere. Just because we haven't found proof doesn't mean it's not out there," Evander added as he pointed to Tenebrae's northern border. "Here is where I feel the strange sensation the strongest. I have several camps set up near the area that I occasionally visit to see if I can locate anything," he explained, and Felix's eyes lit up.

"Can we go?" he asked.

"I plan on taking a trip in the spring. The mountains we have to cross to get there are too harsh in the colder months, and I don't know the area well enough to use my traverse magic to get us there safely," Evander replied.

Both Felix and I looked to the king. What the hell was *traverse magic*? Evander smirked and then disappeared in a puff of smoke before reappearing across the room just as quickly. He slid his hands in his pockets as he strode for us, and I glanced at my friend to see his eyes wide with amazement.

"When the land accepts someone as sovereign, it gives a special power—known as an obscure—to the person it binds to. I call what I was given *traversing*," Evander explained.

"Why wasn't I aware of that?" Felix asked, more to himself than to any of us. "King Perceval doesn't seem to have anything out of the ordinary like that."

"He does. All of us kings do, but most of us choose to keep it a secret from everyone, including each other. You know the rulers of Disparya will do anything to have an edge over anyone else. You've witnessed it time and time again," Evander said.

"So everyone's obscure is different," I mused.

"Yes," Evander answered. "No one knows for sure how the Gods choose what obscure is given to each sovereign, but there does seem to be a correlation to their Gifts or personality. For example, my father was known for his desire to help people. He would have done anything to ensure the safety of all people in Disparya. His obscure was his ability to summon. He could literally pull a person through space and time and make them appear in front of him. With that power, he could save someone from impending death by removing them from harm's way." My mouth dropped at the magnitude of King Uriel's obscure. "My own obscure is a variation of his. I can't bring someone to me, but my manipulation of shadows can bring me to them," he continued.

My mind spun with this knowledge. Not only did kings have more magic than anyone else, but they also had a secret power that no one knew about. I dragged a hand through my hair as revelation after revelation poured out. Fucking Gods, how much of this world had I been oblivious to? Did Dash know about his father's extra power, or was he just as in the dark about this as Felix and I were? No, if Dash knew, then there was no doubt in my mind he would have told his best friend about it.

"So the sixth kingdom isn't a myth, and the kings all have an extra power," I began. "But what does all of that have to do with the meeting today?" I was sure by Felix's surprised expression that none of this was the topic of conversation this afternoon. Both my friend and Evander grew still, their eyes drifting to each other rather than the map they leaned over.

"Nothing and everything," Evander said, meeting my gaze. "We didn't discuss those topics at the meeting, but it could be the key to winning this upcoming war."

"Then what did you talk about?" I asked.

"You," the king answered, and how he said the word sent a chill down my spine. "If Perceval is involved—which I firmly believe he is—then what he was planning with you would have just been the start."

"What does that mean?" Felix asked before I had the chance to do so.

Evander gestured to the couches, and the three of us headed that way again, just as Lia, Cal, Marceline, and Olivier joined us. The seven of us sat around the coffee table, settling in for what I assumed would be another world-shattering piece of information. I didn't know how much more I could deal with, but I had to be close to reaching my limit.

"How many females have gone missing from Caelum in the past decade?" Evander asked, and Felix cocked his head to the side.

"A handful, but that's not unusual," my friend answered. "Every kingdom has rebels and traitors who go against the law. It's not uncommon."

"That's true," Evander agreed as he adjusted in his seat, leaning forward to pour himself a serving of amber liquid before getting comfortable again.

I watched intently as he swirled the alcohol around, sipping lightly on it rather than throwing it back in one swallow like usual. My mouth salivated as I stared at the glass, thirsty for the relief it promised. My mind was a cluster of jumbled up thoughts and feelings, and dulling the constant noise was something I desperately craved. As if he could read my thoughts, Evander leaned forward, handing me his glass, and I took it on instinct, not even realizing what I had done until the sweet burn of liquor was searing its way down my throat. I clutched the frosted glass tightly as the ice clinked against the sides, dinging in a beautiful melody that had me relaxing in my seat.

"But those females were never found, correct? No clues were left to be discovered, and no suspects were caught. It was like they vanished into thin air, never to be heard from again," Evander added as he fixed himself another drink. Felix didn't respond.

The room grew silent once more, with nothing but the sound of rattling ice as we sat around the small table, waiting for Evander to finish whatever he was getting at. I looked toward Lia, who was watching me with green eyes full of worry.

"I believe Perceval sold those females to Oberon for him to use in his Conjoining experiments," Evander finally said. I stopped breathing as the air was stolen from my lungs. "And I think if it weren't for Perceval's greed, you would have been one of them, Ainsley."

I drained the rest of the liquor, welcoming the sting as it traveled down my throat and into my empty stomach. Evander reached out to hand me his fresh glass, but I shook my head. I didn't want to get drunk; I just wanted to take the edge off and numb myself a little. Evander reached into his pocket and pulled out a piece of rolled-up parchment. He carefully opened it to reveal hundreds of names neatly scribbled across the paper, front and back. There were so many that nearly all the parchment was covered in black ink.

"Everyone who's gone missing in the past ten years," Evander announced, and my stomach knotted as bile crept to the back of my throat.

"That isn't a lot when you consider there are five kingdoms," Felix argued. He still didn't believe Evander's claims.

"This is just Caelum," Evander countered, and Felix went still as he stared at the paper tossed onto the table. "And this is Ministro." Evander pulled out another piece of parchment with just as many names scrawled across it. "And this is Venator, Tenebrae, and Agnitio." Evander opened the final list with a grand total of fifty names.

Fifty names between three kingdoms, while both Ministro and Caelum had well over ten times that amount from each of them. There was no way anyone could argue with the facts Evander presented. Felix reached forward and grabbed the slips of paper as he carefully looked over the names, shaking his head in disbelief. He turned to me, his mouth open and his eyes glassy.

"You didn't know," I soothed, but I knew my words would offer no comfort to him.

"I should have," he replied, pointing at the paper he held between his hands. "Seeing their names all listed like this makes it all so fucking obvious that something bigger was going on."

The look on Felix's face reminded me of just how lost I had been after learning truths that had been kept hidden from me. I was alone and questioned everything I had ever been told. I'm sure Felix felt the same since this had been happening under his nose.

"I take it you didn't discuss this at the meeting either?" I asked, and Felix shook his head as his eyes locked on the victims between his fingers. I moved my attention toward Evander, wondering if he was about to drop yet another bomb of information rather than relay the conversation that was held today.

"I was given the list of names after we finished," he said, answering my unspoken question. "During the meeting, we discussed how Caelumian soldiers had been spotted gathering near the western coast, and your friend denied that meant anything substantial."

"That was before this," Felix sneered, holding up the paper. "Had you informed me about everything, perhaps I could have been more useful."

Evander smirked as he leaned back on the couch, shooting Olivier a look that he returned. It brought me back to the days I had watched Dash and Felix do the same thing, the two of them able to know what the other was thinking thanks to their years together. I studied Evander for a moment longer as I tried to put all the pieces together. Why would he invite Felix along just to keep vital information from him—information that could have allowed Felix to remember critical details that could help save Disparya from an attack?

"He was testing you," I breathed, and Evander's eyes sparkled with pride. "He wanted to see how you would react in the meeting. Whether you would be relieved that it seemed Tenebrae was missing key facts, therefore showing your hand that you knew all along what King Perceval was up to."

"But I wasn't relieved, was I?" Felix said, glaring at Evander.

"And that's why he waited to tell us the rest here," I explained. "He wanted to watch my face when you denied it to see if I could detect a lie. You've been untruthful with me before."

My focus stayed on Evander as his grin grew, and he tipped his glass in my direction in a friendly gesture. I hated his games, but I understood why he orchestrated this one. He didn't trust Felix, but for some reason, he trusted me and my opinion of my friend. If I believed him, then it was good enough for Evander. I raised my chin and nodded, indicating that Felix wasn't lying about any of this. The king dipped his head in acknowledgment and placed his glass on the table before clearing his throat.

"King Perceval has been hunting you ever since you left Caelum, love," Evander said, and I sucked in a sharp breath. "He's doing it discreetly, of course, so as not to get caught, but my sources tell me he is dead set on bringing you home."

"Caelum isn't my home," I interrupted, and Evander cocked a brow. "At least not anymore. Not after what he's been doing and what he tried to do to me."

"Noted," Evander responded, and I didn't miss the way his eyes softened with hope. I knew without certainty that Caelum wasn't my home, but I still wasn't sure if I wanted Tenebrae to be. "Regardless, he still wants you back there. As I said before, the choice for you to return is yours, but no one in this room will let him take you without your permission."

I looked around, meeting the eyes of everyone surrounding us and seeing nothing but sheer determination shining through. Even Marceline looked like she'd prepare to battle to the death if she needed to. It was an odd sight to behold, especially because she seemed to hate me.

"So what happens now?" I asked.

"Now," Evander began, glancing at Cal and Olivier, who nodded as if excepting some unsaid order from their king. "I'll be heading to Vorsutos in the morning. I'll be meeting their leader to discuss our latest report and your Gifts."

"What do my Gifts have anything to do with this?" I demanded.

I didn't like the idea of him discussing their rarity with anyone. I didn't trust that I was completely safe here, and the fewer people who knew I had three Gifts, the better. How was I supposed to know I wouldn't be hunted as thoroughly as I had been in Caelum when others found out? Someone clearly wanted me, and spreading information about just how valuable I was seemed like an idiotic idea.

"Everything, love," Evander replied. "Just because you don't want to accept them right now doesn't mean they won't be vital to our cause once you finally do."

So I was just another pawn in a long game. Someone to use and wield the way another king wanted. How was what Evander was doing any different than what King Perceval wanted to do? Each man wanted me to further their idea of what the future should look like, and I was to have no say in it.

"Take me with you," I demanded. I wouldn't sit back and let him decide yet another thing for me.

"Absolutely not," he replied. I felt my rage surge to the surface as my magic jostled awake, ready for me should I call. "You aren't experienced in these sort of things, love." His patronizing tone had me rising to my feet, but before I could argue, Evander disappeared into shadow, leaving his spot empty as everyone's eyes fell on me again.

"He's such a fucking dick," I ground out, stomping out of the room as everyone grunted their agreement. I heavily enjoyed that they felt the same way too, but I was pretty sure it was in a more playful way and not the burning hatred I aimed at the king.

15.

I barely slept that night, my mind too focused on everything I had learned and what that could mean for the kingdom I was growing unexpectedly attached to. I tried to slip into Felix's room last night, but he locked me out for the first time since I'd known him. I couldn't help but feel hurt, but I also understood wanting space while going through an internal struggle. Still, I hated knowing he was suffering alone.

I journeyed downstairs an hour earlier than usual, before the light of dawn managed to seep through the windows. I had given up on sleep long ago. I was doing myself no good staring at the ceiling and letting my thoughts run rampant, so I figured I might as well make myself useful.

After the floor was swept and all dishes from the previous night were cleaned and put away, I worked on the living room, fluffing pillows and picking up large bones that I assumed were meant for Onyx and Nova to chew on. As I folded blankets and put them into the basket on the side of the couch, a bag at the front door caught my eye. I quickly padded over to it and inspected its contents, finding food, water, weapons, and clothes all neatly rolled to fit. They were no doubt there for Evander to take with him on his journey today. Smiling, I lifted the heavy pack and carried it out the front door, looking left and right to ensure no one had been watching. The house was dark and quiet, with everyone still sound asleep upstairs, so I was in the clear.

I shut the door behind me, carefully releasing the handle so the latch wouldn't click loudly and indicate someone was leaving. The second I was free and clear, I raced through the grounds with the pack slung across my back. I skidded to a halt once I reached the training ring and looked around as I tried to figure out what the hell I was going to do next. As much as I wanted to say to hell with Evander and just go alone, I had absolutely no idea where Vorsutos was or how to get there, so that wasn't a viable option. But I couldn't just let Evander get away with his arrogant, better-than-everyone remark, so I had to think of something.

My head twisted toward the glistening light of the lake, and I sprinted in that direction, my mind entirely made up. Once I reached the water's edge, I opened the pack, shoving heavy rocks in for extra effort. I couldn't afford for the damn thing to float, though I was pretty sure it wouldn't. When I was finished, I closed the bag back. As I tried to lift it again, I fell onto my ass, hitting the rocky shore hard.

Shit.

I wrapped the straps around my hands and tugged as hard as I could, dragging the pack along the wooden dock step by painful step. My shoulders were burning, and sweat dripped down my face as I pulled the bag with all my might, giving myself a workout that made Olivier's training look like a child's game. There was no way this thing would float, and I smirked as I finally reached the edge of the pier. I stepped to the other side of the bag, unwrapping it from my hands and dropping to my knees. With a final grunt, I pushed it over the wooden edge and into the black depths of the lake.

Fuck. *Yes.*

I allowed myself ten seconds to appreciate the feat before I stood and sprinted back to the house before anyone woke up and noticed my absence. The sun was beginning to paint the sky a dreamy hue of pink and lavender, so I knew I didn't have much time left to get inside and wipe away the sandy evidence of what I'd done.

There was no way I could go back to my room and risk being seen by someone in the hallway, so I ran to the kitchen sink and used a towel to rinse off every grain I could find. Next, I wiped the sweat from my face, and though there was nothing I could do to hide my pinking cheeks from exhaustion, I hoped I would cool down enough before the others arrived. I quickly made my usual cup of coffee and plate of food before sitting firmly in my seat at the table.

Evander appeared shortly after I drained half the mug, holding a white envelope per usual. He slid it towards me like he did every morning, and I slid it right back… like I did every morning.

"Are you sure you don't want it, love?" he asked, and I perked up at the question.

He always had just accepted my refusal without so much as a word, so this was out of character. Perhaps it was an angle for a new game he wanted to play. I shook my head, though my instincts were on high alert on what his next move would be. Evander shrugged and promptly hung it next to the others before sitting across from me. His eyes flickered to where he had pinned each envelope, and I couldn't help my gaze from following as well. He sighed dramatically before turning back to me with a single brow raised.

"How'd you sleep last night?" he inquired, tapping his fingers along the table like he was bored and just trying to make conversation to fill the silence.

"Fine?" I was suspicious of his tone.

"That's good," he replied, tilting his head back and pursing his lips like he was trying to come up with more things to ask me. "Are you excited you get the day off since Oli has meetings to attend to?"

Okay, what the hell was this game he was playing? He was being civil, and that was sending me into a spiral as I desperately tried to figure out what was going on.

"Is this a new game?" I asked, and Evander chuckled under his breath.

"Nope," he said. "I already won the game this morning. This is just me trying to have a nice conversation with you."

"We haven't played a game yet," I said, confused. Had I missed the staring or the insults? When the hell did it even start, and why did I care so much?

"Haven't we?" he said, giving me a wolfish grin. Before I could demand he tell me more, Olivier strode in, fully dressed with his travel pack in hand, and Felix following close behind.

"I don't know why you just can't admit it," Felix said flirtatiously, grabbing a cup of coffee and claiming the seat next to me. "It can't be a coincidence that I see you in the hall every morning."

Olivier's jaw clenched, and I could hear his teeth grind together as he glowered at my best friend, obviously not buying whatever Felix was trying to sell. His hand clasped around the handle of his mug so hard I thought he would break it.

"We live in the same house," Olivier snarled like he hated the fact, which I was sure he did. Felix only shrugged as if that response meant nothing and only furthered his point. I watched as Olivier's rage turned his face various shades of purple before he slammed his mug down and stormed out of the room, muttering how Evander should have let him kill Felix from the start.

"I'm not sure that's the impression you were aiming for," I whispered, and Felix smiled.

"As long as he's thinking of me, I don't care in what way. I'm playing the long game, cupcake," he replied.

I laughed at my friend's response just as Olivier appeared in the kitchen again, this time bag free as he piled a plate full of breakfast foods and sat across from Felix. I didn't miss that he stabbed his food with more force than necessary while he glared at my friend, but Felix didn't seem to mind. He was just happy Olivier was paying him any attention at all.

Evander pushed himself from the table and headed out of the room toward the front door. I grabbed my coffee and held my breath while waiting for the show to begin.

Here we go.

"Olivier?" Evander called as he returned to the kitchen empty-handed. "Have you seen my pack?"

"You put it by the front door last night," Olivier replied, not taking his eyes from Felix as he jabbed his fork into an unsuspecting sausage.

"I know where I put it last night, but it's not there now."

I leaned back in my chair, the wood groaning beneath the weight, and took a long sip of my coffee as I tried to hide the smirk that begged to be displayed. At the sound, Evander turned to me, angling his head slightly as a slow smile crept up his face.

"Love, you wouldn't happen to know what happened to it, would you?" he asked with a twinkle of intrigue in his eyes. Sitting next to me, Felix cursed softly under his breath, and I didn't need to look at him to know he was shaking his head at me.

"How should I know? I'm just so… inexperienced when it comes to those sorts of things." Let him eat his words from last night. Evander gasped in mock excitement and rested his hands on the dining table before leaning across it to close the distance between us, his face mere inches from mine.

"Oh, Ainsley, I think I'm going to love this little game we're playing." His eyes flickered to my mouth. *Ass.* His smile widened as if he could read my thoughts. "Until next time, love," he said as he straightened himself, popping a grape that he stole from my untouched plate into his mouth and headed out of the room. I pushed my chair back, the legs scraping loudly against the floor, and hurried after him, ignoring Felix's protests.

"I'm coming with you to Vorsutos," I said once I caught up to him in the hall.

"The hell you are," he declared with a low laugh.

"This is about me, so I deserve to be there. I deserve to know what's going on."

"You're right, you do. But you refuse to train, to even *try* to access your magic. You're more of a liability than anything else, Ainsley. I don't mind kicking your ass; in fact, I'd be more than willing to. But know that I'd let this realm freeze over before I let anyone else so much as try." I felt my blood begin to boil.

"I can defend myself."

"Oh yeah? And how did that turn out for you back in Caelum?" he said, his cold grey eyes simmering with rage. I flinched at his words, at the memory of those attackers' hands all over my body in the orchard—at the feel of the dagger against my throat. My hands began to tremble slightly with anger, and Evander watched as I clenched them into fists at my side, willing my body to calm. He studied me for a moment longer, gears seeming to turn in his mind.

"If you want to head out in the practice ring, I wouldn't mind laying you out a few times before I leave. Although…" he said, stepping closer, his lips spreading in a seductive smile. "I could think of a few other things that I'd prefer to do with you on your back." That smug, arrogant prick. Before I knew what was happening, shadows shot from my hands, aimed at Evander's face. He deflected my attack with a slight flick of his wrist, no more than the movement one would make to swat away a fly. He was quick. Too quick. The evidence of years of training and practice.

Evander's smile grew more wicked. "There you are," he said. My eyes widened as I met his stare, my breathing heavy. Evander's face became serious and determined as he put his fingers around mine to steady them.

I held up my shaking hands in front of me, not knowing what to do or what to make of this power. It was also so much stronger the angrier I was, and that's what scared me. I was terrified of the magic itself. Of its force. Of its strength. Of how *good* it felt to wield it.

"Train Ainsley. Learn how to wield these Gifts you were given. Because they *are* a gift, not a curse. It is a part of you and it will not steer you wrong." He backed away toward the front entrance. "Train Ainsley. You're a key player in this war, but the level of your involvement is entirely up to you. You choose how big of a role you want to play." I gaped at him, unable to come up with any response. I turned on my heel to head back into the dining room when Evander called out again. "Oh, and love?" I turned slightly, throwing him a glance over my shoulder. "Decide quickly." And then he was gone, nothing but swirling shadows in his wake.

I stood there for another moment until I turned and saw the envelopes hanging above the fireplace. They beckoned me like a siren, and I found myself striding for them. I unclipped the first one and looked around, ensuring no one was watching as I broke the black seal on the back. I removed a folded piece of paper from inside and flipped it open to read. "

Ways I plan to piss off Ainsley today
1. Hand her this envelope
2. Explain that it's to help her even after she claimed she didn't want my help
3. Tell her she looks good enough to eat
4. Stare at her until she notices

What the hell was this?!

5. Compliment her ass

6. Make some comment about how much she wants me

7. Steal a piece of her dessert

Oh. My Gods. He did every single thing written on that list. I quickly tossed the parchment to the ground and ripped open the next envelope.

Ways I plan to piss off Ainsley today

1. Attempt to hand her this envelope

2. Establish a new morning game and beat her

3. Insult her

4. Insinuate how much she wants me

I quickly read through the rest of the items and tore open another envelope... And then another, and another, until I had gone through nearly all of them. Each piece of paper detailed precisely how he planned to annoy me that day, and every action was carried out as promised. There wasn't one line he missed. I reached for the envelope he had tried to hand me today and quickly withdrew the final folded parchment.

Ways I plan to piss off Ainsley today

1. Tell her I already won the game when she tries to figure out what we're playing

2. Refuse to let her come to Vorsutos with me

3. Annoy her enough over the past week that she caves and decides to read these letters the moment I leave the house, ensuring I win the final game.

- Why hello there, love.

I know you're standing in the living room, reading this letter with your mouth open and eyes wide.

I closed my mouth at once and narrowed my eyes as anger filled me at his arrogant assholeness. The fact that he knew exactly what would happen and planned it down to the second only pissed me off more. I took a deep breath, clutching the letter as I continued reading.

And you're calling me every name you can come up with in that pretty little head of yours as you realize how right I am and just how well I know you. You may hate me right now, but consider my letters a training exercise—the lesson being: never let your stubbornness or pride get in the way of accepting help. Especially when you need it. Had you taken my letters when I offered them, you would have known what I planned to do to rile you up and get under your skin each day. You could have prevented it all but instead you let your ego get in the way and suffered for it. You're a strong woman, love. Don't let fear and anger cloud your judgment. I hope you learn from this, and I look forward to our next match.

- Van

His Royal Majesty - King of Tenebrae - Master of Orgasms

I audibly laughed at that last title—a good, honest to Gods laugh. A sound I hadn't heard myself make in weeks. I was shocked that Evander had mastered this whole thing, and I played right into his trap because I was too stubborn to see it.

I ran through everything Evander had said before he left and how I felt about it. I didn't want to be left out of the decisions, but I was still terrified of what my magic could do. I knew I would have better control over it once I started to train, but what about when I slipped? What would happen if I got so angry that I couldn't stop and hurt someone I loved?

Evander had seen what I was capable of, but it didn't seem to worry him. In fact, it was like he was excited by my potential. I couldn't figure out if it was because I was another pawn he could wield or because he had a powerful heir in his pocket. It most definitely wasn't because he was happy for me and the magic I held. Did part of me not want to access my Gift because I didn't trust his motivations? Was that even a good enough reason to hide away?

Failure, stubborn, pathetic, coward. Though I felt Marceline's words through every aspect of my life, if I continued to deny myself of the magic I had been given, then her words would continue to ring true. If I continued to run from my role as heir, then I was doing exactly what King Perceval did to me my entire life—staying hidden.

I didn't want that to be my life going forward. I knew I had a lot to overcome, and I would still struggle every day with it, but I wanted the chance to take control of my destiny. I wanted to have a seat at the table and be involved in the decisions, especially when they pertained to me. I couldn't keep cowering away, too afraid to move forward. My darkness terrified me, but I also had this strange calm whenever it brushed against me. And even though I couldn't trust him, something deep in my soul told me Evander would never let me lose control in the way I feared.

I was safe with him.

"Train me," I said, stopping before Marceline as she took a bite of her eggs. Felix, Lia, and Cal all exchanged fearful looks as I made demands of the tiny yet terrifying woman. If I was going to do this right now, then she was the one that needed to oversee it. I didn't even know what her Gift was, but I didn't care. I'd demand she'd help me in whatever way she could.

"I'm busy," she said, bringing the fork to her mouth again.

Of course she was. She already made it crystal clear what she thought of me, so why would I have expected her to be willing to train me? I took a step back, accepting that she wanted nothing to do with me when my magic tingled beneath the surface. No. No, I wouldn't accept that answer. I wanted to learn and wouldn't leave until she agreed to teach me. I leaned down, grabbed her plate, and slid it across the table until it landed in front of Lia.

"Not anymore," I told her with all the confidence in the world when in actuality, I was trying extremely hard not to piss myself. Everyone in the room stiffened, and I held my breath as I prepared for the consequence of that action. I would either get what I wanted or die a very slow and painful death.

16.

Marceline dropped the fork onto the table and tilted her head to stare up at me. I kept my face serious and determined, not wanting to give an inch to the fear coursing through my body as I awaited her next action. After what felt like a lifetime, her lip curled in the corner.

"It seems like it," she replied, letting her smile take more form. "You have thirty seconds to get your ass in that ring before I change my mind."

I turned and sprinted for the door, releasing a sigh of relief. Holy Gods, I couldn't believe that actually worked. I was half expecting her to end my life right there for that stunt. I was grateful she decided to spare me, though something told me she would get me back for it with this session.

I quickly learned that Marceline was a Tremo—a magic wielder with the Gift of inducing fear into her enemies. It suddenly began to make sense why she always terrified me, and I wondered if her Gift had any connection to her personality. I didn't possess the same Gift as her, but she explained how important it was to learn to defend myself against mental powers like hers. She gave me a little taste of what she was capable of, but never let it get to the point of my body shutting down and turning into a lifeless husk like Josephine and Pecus had when they were killed in Caelum after being exposed to fear magic.

She would use her Gift on me for only a few seconds at a time, but it never failed to leave me hysterically crying in the dirt. She dug her way into my mind, extracting my darkest fears. My thoughts would go through the nightmares I experienced every night, but this time it felt real—like I could reach out my hand

and touch Dash, who stood just a foot away. I could feel the magic draining from my veins and screamed at the burning pain it caused.

Even though she would only expose me for a short amount of time, the images I was trapped in seemed like they lasted for hours. I would come to, gasping for breath as I clutched my stomach, screaming from the pain my mind had sworn I felt, only to realize it wasn't real. Felix and Lia would rub my back and try to calm me down as Marceline demanded we go again.

Eventually, she determined we were done with her type of magic and instructed Cal to teach me how to wield my shadows. That Gift came easily, though I was still cautious about the amount I wanted to release. Cal seemed to misunderstand my hesitation for lack of ability. He encouraged me to keep at it and that the more I practiced, the better I would get at controlling the limited amount of shadows I had. Little did he know, I didn't think I had a limit. Darkness filled every ounce of my body, and it didn't feel like there was an end to it. The only way I could know that for sure was to let it all out, but I didn't feel comfortable doing that. What if I wasn't able to call them all back?

After the sun had begun to set, Marceline decided to call it a day, and I collapsed onto the ground in relief. I was drenched in sweat, panting for breath, and every muscle in my body ached. Using my magic seemed to exert far more energy than sparring had. I didn't see how I could master both skills at once.

"You did well today," Marceline said, extending her hand for me to take. I eyed it cautiously before letting her pull me to my feet.

"Not a complete failure?" I joked, and she grinned.

"I wouldn't go *that* far," she replied. "But interrupt my breakfast again, and I'll skin you alive."

"Noted."

I stretched and shook out my aching limbs as we strolled toward the edge of the ring. I may have been terrible at defending against her attack, but at least I had tried. I finally found it in myself to access my powers and felt confident in my decision.

"Does this mean you don't hate me anymore?" I asked, and Marceline laughed.

"I've never hated you," she responded, and I cocked a brow in disbelief as she rolled her eyes. "When you got here, you were in a dark place, and Evander and I differed greatly on how to pull you out of it. He wanted to take it day by day, and I just wanted to push you and see if you'd land on your face or fly. Anger seemed to be the only emotion you held on to, so I decided to use that to corral you closer and closer to the edge. If that meant letting you overhear me talk about how pathetic you were, then so be it."

"So you were baiting me," I said, thinking over every unpleasant encounter I had with her.

"Yup," she said shamelessly. "Clearly, it was the correct route to take with you. Like usual, I was right, and Evander was wrong."

I may not have liked her tactics, but I couldn't deny they played a part in what got me to start using my magic. Her cruel words had festered like a virus until they became too much, and I needed to cut them out.

Marceline dipped her head in a slight bow—a sign of respect—and strode into the house. Lia, Cal, and Felix headed inside to prepare dinner, but I opted to stay out a little longer. I didn't want to stop practicing. I let my shadows out, enjoying how the tendrils caressed my skin as they slithered over it. My senses seemed to heighten, and I could taste the air around me as my magic drifted into the world, claiming it for my own. I couldn't create an object or do much of anything with my darkness yet; Cal had chosen to start me on the basics of calling and recalling my Gift until it was like second nature.

Eventually, my hunger gnawed at my focus too much, and I gave in to my rumbling stomach, putting my shadows away for the night. Olivier came home from another meeting with the generals while we were having dinner, and Marceline told him about our training today.

"Starting tomorrow, your morning sessions will be physical, and your afternoon will solely consist of accessing your magic," Olivier instructed as we cleaned the dining table. "I take it Felix will assist you with your Empathi Gift?"

"Yes," I told him. "He's been helping me for a few weeks with it already. I didn't want to keep shoving my heartbreak on everyone."

Olivier nodded his approval, and we silently finished the rest of the dishes. All I kept thinking about was how good it felt to finally be putting myself to use and how annoyed I was that it was Evander's stupid note that pushed me over the edge. If it weren't for him, I would have still been too afraid to access that integral part of me, and I hated that I would eventually have to thank him for it.

A cool breeze skated over my bare skin, and I yanked the blankets higher, desperate for the warmth they provided. Sleep should have come easy with how exhausted my body was from a full day of magic use, but my mind wouldn't quiet. I kept waking with thoughts of Evander and what could be happening in Vorsutos. Was I truly safe once he told the truth about my three Gifts to his contact there?

My skin tingled, and my magic swirled with the feeling of being watched. I sat upright the second I felt a presence in the room. My hands flew up, and shadows curled around my fingers, ready to fight my intruder. I scanned the room to find Evander at the window, closing it tight to prevent any more cold air from blowing through.

"Fucking Gods," I breathed, clutching my hand to my chest like the pressure could stop my pounding heart. "What are you doing?"

He walked to the other window and locked it before kneeling at the fireplace and tossing another log on. The fire roared to life once more, and the room instantly began to heat as he made his way to my bed and sat on the edge. His eyes raked over my body as he assessed me and then twirled his fingers to create a fur blanket that he then draped across me.

"You should dress warmer," he said, gesturing for me to lay my head against the pillow as he tucked me in again.

"This is all I have," I responded.

Lia had ensured my dresser was fully stocked, but the nightclothes she purchased were all of thin materials like silk and satin. Normally I would have been fine with that, but I still wasn't used to Tenebrae's climate, so I spent most of the night freezing. Evander nodded to himself like he was mentally noting that fact.

A soft snore came from the end of the room, and we both turned to find Nova sleeping on the floor. Since that first day I met her, she'd been sneaking into my room each night. She always kept her distance though, and I wasn't sure if it was for *my* benefit or the fact that she just didn't like me. Regardless, I enjoyed that she was here.

"You didn't answer my question," I said, directing us back to the conversation and away from the adorable sleeping wolf. "What are you doing here?"

Evander created another much smaller blanket this time and placed it along the end of the bed, covering my feet. I wasn't sure how he knew my toes felt like icicles, but he'd guessed right.

"Olivier said you accessed your magic today," he said, ignoring my question. A slight smile curved his lips, and I couldn't help but return one. "Tomorrow, we'll work on your illusions. That is if you'll allow me to teach you." I nodded. I still didn't trust him, but I wanted to learn.

"I don't think I can, though. When I call for my magic only my shadows ever come out."

Evander twisted to face me more fully. "Close your eyes and reach out to your magic. Concentrate on what you feel."

I did as he instructed, diving into myself and focusing on the power running through my veins. The familiar feel of my magic brushed along me, warm and comforting, a bright flame that would protect and soothe but never burn.

"First, you need to understand how magic works in order to grasp how to properly utilize it," Evander explained. "The power you feel inside you is the raw magic that lives in your soul. Your Gift is the physical manifestation of that outside of your body."

I dove deeper, circling around the raw energy Evander was talking about. The magic felt both familiar and new. Like it was land I had grown up on my entire life, yet never explored. It was vast and all-encompassing... and powerful. So Gods damn powerful. How was it possible that so much magic resided inside me? How strong did the suppressants I was given have to be in order to keep my magic dormant?

"Everyone has at least a small amount of that raw power, even if they don't possess a Gift. That energy is what gives us our accelerated aging and then our self-healing abilities once we become immortal," Evander continued.

I had known that when we turned seventeen, our growth sped up so we aged two years rather than one. And once we turned twenty-one and became immortal, we stopped aging altogether. But I hadn't been aware that everyone had this raw power inside them.

"That raw magic is what is given during the Entwining Ceremony," he added. "But what would have happened to you if you had stayed in Caelum wasn't that. It was a vastly different spell designed to strip you of the Gifts of the land that the Gods had bestowed upon you. Had you gone through with those vows, you would have become a powerless immortal. That ceremony wouldn't have only given Dashiell your raw magic, but access to your Gifts as well."

I swallowed hard and tried to anchor my mind to stay in the present and not drift back to all I had almost lost, unbeknownst to me. "If everyone has at least *some* magic in their soul, why aren't they given a Gift? Why is the magic limited to just their aging and immortality?" I asked as my eyes fluttered open once more.

"I don't think we'll ever know why the Gods make the decisions they do. For whatever reason, they chose not to grant everyone the magic of our lands."

I chewed on the inside of my cheek. That didn't seem fair. The base of magic was already inside them, so why couldn't the Gods allow them to access it beyond what immortality offered? What was so wrong with allowing those without a Gift the ability to flick their wrist and create a shield or turn the page of a book without ever touching the paper? The Gods seemed like selfish assholes who held too much power over our lives.

"Do you want to continue to be pissed about something you can't change, or would you like to learn about the magic you were given?" Evander asked, disrupting my thoughts.

"Both," I snarked, closing my eyes again. I could feel his smirk on me as I focused back on the raw magic living in my soul. A shimmer in the depths of the power caught my eye, and I instinctually moved toward it, my hand reaching out as if to cradle the strange magic in my palms.

"Picture your soul having three separate doors—one for each of your Gifts," Evander announced. I flinched at the interruption and pulled away from my task to carry out his instructions instead.

I squeezed my eyes shut tighter and visualized three large doors within me. One of them had a white light surrounding it, and I knew it was the door that would release my Empathi Gift. The second door was black with tendrils of darkness swirling beneath the crack at the bottom—my shadows. The third door was different than the others. At first it seemed plain and ordinary, but the longer I stared, the more it changed. It grew in size and shifted its shape to be arched. It was constantly evolving and developing into what my mind desired it to be. It was my Gift of illusions.

"Go to that door," Evander said. He must have read the confusion or wonder on my face and had known exactly what I had discovered. "Visualize yourself holding a key and unlock it. Let the magic out." I gripped the imaginary key in my hand and unlocked the door before swinging it wide. "Now look."

My eyes fluttered open, and a small golden key flickered in my open palm briefly before disappearing altogether. I gasped, opening and closing my hand several times as if that would make the key reappear.

"Did you see that?" I asked excitedly. Evander smiled wide but shook his head.

"You were able to cast that illusion on yourself. We'll work on keeping it around longer next time, but for now, try and get some sleep. Using magic will take a lot out of you so you need to keep your body well-rested."

Evander slid from the bed, creating one more blanket to throw over my body before retreating from the room. My mind was wild with the illusion I conjured, but I still needed to ask him the question that had been gnawing at me all day.

"Vorsutos," I called out, abruptly stopping his retreat. "How did it go over there?"

"As well as I could have hoped."

I nodded, happy things seemed to go okay, though my thoughts were still plagued by what Evander might have told the leader there. He observed me curiously, like he could tell there was still more I wanted to say.

"Did you tell them about me?" I asked quietly, needing to know the answer one way or the other.

"Yes," he said, and I released a heavy sigh. "But not that you have three Gifts."

Well, I wasn't expecting that. I sat up again, cocking my head as I watched the king who stood across the room. His hands had found their way into his pockets per usual, and he looked relaxed and unbothered by the stress we were under.

"Why not?" I questioned, and Evander shrugged.

"Because you didn't seem to feel comfortable with me doing that. The leader of Vorsutos—Declan—is a close friend, someone I consider family. I may trust him but you don't, and it's not my secret to tell."

I opened and closed my mouth several times as I tried to come up with a response to that. I didn't think he'd care about my feelings and would do what he felt was best. This side of him wasn't one I had seen, and I couldn't help but fear it was an act. A part of me hated that I was cynical and suspicious of everyone, but after how naive I was back in Caelum, I couldn't blame myself for it.

"Thank you," I said, and he nodded once. "Why are you back so soon anyway?" I assumed he would have stayed on the continent to our east for at least a few days, especially now knowing he was close friends with its leader.

"Because it was clear by you stealing my pack that you didn't want me to stay away for long. You just couldn't bear being apart," he quipped, and I rolled my eyes. Evander lingered in the doorway for another moment before crossing over the threshold. I don't know what came over me or why I couldn't just let him disappear, but for whatever reason, I spoke again.

"Master of Orgasms. Really?" I said sarcastically. Evander chuckled and shrugged.

"It's a demanding title, but someone has to do it," he said smoothly and his lips pulled into that crooked grin he loved to wear.

"I'd imagine it would be for someone who's never given one," I replied, laying my head back on the pillow as I brought the blankets higher once more. "Good night, Evander." I didn't let him respond with a quip since I wanted the last word.

"Sleep tight, love," he said, and I didn't miss the humor in his voice.

That night, I didn't have a single nightmare, and I refused to believe it happened for any reason other than that I was too exhausted to dream.

I hurried to the kitchen, excited to start my training today and not at all wondering what game Evander would want to play now that I had opened all of the envelopes. As usual, I was the first one to arrive, the quiet house feeling comfortable and more like a home each day that passed. I walked over to the coffee and began to fill my cup when I glanced out the window to see a figure standing in the training ring, gilded by the dawn's light. I placed my mug down and rushed outside, where Evander was dressed and waiting. Why was he out here and not meeting me at the table like we had every morning?

Without being instructed, I mirrored his stance. Evander held up his palm, and I watched as shadows snaked around his fingers. I mimicked the magic, letting mine out and forcing the darkness to move in the same way his had. He nodded to himself, satisfied with my work, and had his magic curve up his arm and around his body. I studied him for a minute before trying to get my shadows to bend in the same way. Sweat began to bead on my brow, and I stuck out my tongue as I concentrated hard on the motion and feel of the magic. Eventually, the shadows moved up my body, though not as fluid as Evander's had for him.

Evander recalled his Gift, and I did the same, resting my hands on my knees as I gasped for breath from the effort of that small use of magic. He had done everything so effortlessly, and there I was, struggling to do something so basic. How the hell was I ever supposed to create something like a blanket or dagger when I could barely command the shadows to move the way I wanted?

When he determined I had enough of a break, he held his palm up again, and I followed suit. Instead of curling the shadows around his fingers as before, he created a little vortex of darkness in his hand. I cursed under my breath at the sight and reluctantly called my magic back to the surface. I had no idea what I was doing as tendrils of darkness weaved around each other, doing nothing but resembling two fish flopping back and forth.

"Fuck," I said, closing my fist, and Evander smiled at the display.

"Better luck tomorrow, love," he said before striding back inside toward the kitchen. So this would be the new game—who could outdo the other in magic. I had never felt so determined to win and vowed to practice every day until I could defeat him. I wasn't sure how high those chances were, but I was damn sure going to try.

17.

Another week had come and gone, and each day I had gotten stronger in my fighting and magic. I was still nowhere near where I needed to be, but each morning I lasted a little longer against Evander. Every afternoon, I would spend an hour with each trainer to hone my Gifts. Marce had me working on strengthening my mind against her attacks, though I was still complete shit at it. Olivier and Cal instructed me on bending my shadows at will, twisting them into shapes, and curling them around my body. I wanted to learn how to craft and solidify objects, but they said it was beyond my current skill level. For now, I was to master the basics of how the shadows moved while studying the objects I would eventually craft.

Every day I would examine the daggers on our weapons table, committing every detail to memory. In order to solidify my shadows, I needed to know every little thing about the object I was trying to transform them into. When Cal and Oliver deemed me ready, a dagger would be the first thing I would craft.

Evander and I spent the most time together, training for up to two hours each day, as illusions were the hardest of my Gifts to master. He first taught me how to detect if an Illusio was using their magic on me, explaining that if I knew right away, I could get control of the illusion just as quickly.

"Most Illusio are shit with their Gift," Evander said as he directed me to stand in front of an empty table at the edge of the training ring. I rolled my eyes at his arrogance. All he meant was that they weren't as good as him. And though that may have been the case, it didn't change that he was an ass for saying it. "So they'll be sloppy with their cast," he finished.

Evander gestured to the empty table just as a dinner setting appeared. A plate, bowl, wine glass, fork, and spoon were positioned neatly as if we were about to eat.

"What do you see?" he asked, crossing his arms over his chest as he observed me studying the objects.

"Exactly what it looks to be—a place setting," I said, and he shook his head.

"How can you tell it's an illusion?" he asked. I opened my mouth to answer, but he cut me off. "And don't be a smartass and say because you watched me cast one, or I'll have you running up and down Mammoth Hill until you puke." I groaned loudly at that idea.

I was so lovingly introduced to the steepest hill I'd ever seen the other day when I decided to mouth off to Olivier after he yelled at Felix and me for taking too long during our water break. He had me going up and down the hill at full speed until I collapsed after twenty minutes, swearing to the Gods above that I'd rather die than ever do that again.

I rolled my eyes at Evander but leaned in closer as I looked over each object, not knowing what I was supposed to be looking for. After a minute, I gave up, stepping back and informing Evander that I wasn't sure. He pointed to the fork, and I stared down at the utensil.

"It has one too many prongs, and the color is a different shade than the other items," he said. The moment the words left his mouth, the answer was obvious. "You're unlikely to encounter someone with the same skill level as me when it comes to illusions, but you need to inspect every aspect of your surroundings when you're in the presence of an Illusio. Even the slightest mistake will allow you to regain control of your mind. Now, how else can you tell this display isn't real?"

I shook my head to tell him I wasn't sure, but he leveled me a flat look that commanded me to take my time and figure it out. I knew what to look for now, but Evander already gave me the answer, so it couldn't have anything to do with that. I glanced around the space, catching Lia's eye and wrapping my hands around my mouth to make my voice travel.

"Can you see this?" I yelled before pointing to the table. She shook her head, and I looked to Evander, smiling wide as I figured it out.

"Asking someone wasn't what I meant, but points for creativity," he said, and I didn't miss the slight twitch of his lips. "Try again."

I huffed in irritation as I inspected the illusion again. Asking if someone else could see it wasn't the answer, and I already knew the visualization was off, so what else was there? A thought sparked in my mind, and I reached my finger out, pushing through the wine glass as it if wasn't there—though I suppose it wasn't.

"Very good," Evander praised, and I bit my lip as I swallowed the pride I felt for solving the riddle. "Other people can't solidify illusions. You'll always be able to push right through the objects, immediately indicating that what you're seeing isn't real."

"Other people?" I asked, getting caught on that phrase as I looked at him questioningly.

Evander grinned and strode forward, casting an ornate wine glass in his hand. He picked it up by the stem and handed it to me. I expected the object to go straight through my fingers, but instead, I felt the cool glass press against my skin. My eyes widened in wonder.

"How?" I asked breathlessly, holding his illusion in my hand.

"It's extremely difficult to master, and I'm the only one I know who can do so. Another secret only my closest council members know."

I stood there, marveling at his mastery over the skill before it flickered out of view, and I was left with my hand outstretched and wrapped around nothing but air. Shit, I wanted to learn how to do that.

"Will you teach me?" I asked immediately, and Evander smiled wide as he nodded.

"In time, yes. But you must master the basics before starting on the more advanced aspects."

He had a point, but the more I learned about what I could do with each of my Gifts, the more I wanted to practice. I was addicted to the feel of my magic on my skin and how it filled my senses and coated the air around me. I loved breathing it in and experiencing the strength and power it granted me.

"Once I grasp the basics of everything, will I learn how to use my Gifts all at once?" I asked, rolling my neck and shaking out my limbs to get myself ready to cast an illusion of my own.

"No," Evander answered. I opened my mouth to argue, but he held up a hand. "Because it's not something that's possible."

I narrowed my eyes at him, not entirely believing his response. I hadn't seen him use multiple Gifts at once, but that was because he always wanted to focus on only one Gift at a time with me. I reluctantly let my mind drift back to the times Dashiell had accessed his magic in my presence and was quickly realizing he never used two at once either.

"Why not?" I asked, trying to call forth my shadows and illusions at the same time, but found I couldn't. They were both stuck below the surface.

Evander held his palms up, and I watched in interest as shadows swirled in his hands. He crafted a long cylinder in one hand and two balls the same diameter as the cylinder in the other. He positioned both balls side by side at the entrance of the tube, but they were too large to fit through together.

"No matter how hard you call for your Gifts, you won't be able to pull both at once," he explained, demonstrating how both balls couldn't pass through the cylinder at the same time. "You can only call them one at a time." He shoved one ball through and then the other directly behind it. "With training, you'll master them enough to seamlessly switch between your shadows and illusions in the blink of an eye."

My heart raced with the idea of being *that* skilled with my Gifts. The more I thought about it, the more excited I was to learn and hone my magic. Evander's face split into a grin as he watched me practically bouncing in place at the mere thought of what I could do.

"Your Empathi Gift works a little differently," he added as I listened intently. "You can't reach your Empathi Gift out to someone or manipulate emotions while you're using another Gift; however..." My stomach knotted, and my excitement built at that one little word—*however*. "You can still feel emotions if someone is projecting them onto you while you're accessing a different Gift." I smiled wide.

"So I can use my shadows and still detect if someone is angry or fearful?" I asked, wanting to make sure I was understanding.

"Yes, but only if *they* project those emotions onto *you*. You can't shove your Gift into them and extract those feelings if you're already accessing your shadows or illusions," he explained.

I released my shadows, letting them wrap around my skin before watching them drift away in the wind. Then I called for my illusions, casting a small black rock before letting it flicker away. Then the shadows again, followed by another illusion. I switched back and forth, wanting to practice as much as possible so I could use my magic as seamlessly as Evander. I loved my Gifts, and I had never felt more alive than I did while wielding them. The more I used my magic, the more comfortable and trusting of it I became.

"I'm not training today," I announced as I reached Olivier and Evander, who were deep in conversation. They looked up questioningly as they found me striding toward them with Nox's lead in one hand and another mare's in the other.

"What do you mean you're not training?" Evander asked, sounding not too pleased by my decision to take the day off.

I had kept up with him the past few mornings for our little game, and he had to pull out illusions to beat me, knowing I couldn't cast them well yet. However, I did manage to cast a cookie that Felix almost lunged for last night before it flickered out of sight, thanks to my lack of control. I was lucky if I could hold a mind for longer than thirty seconds, and it only pushed me to try harder each day. I was thankful that Lia, Felix, Cal, and even Marce volunteered for me to train on them each night after dinner when the five of us gathered in my room for nightly shield and Empathi sessions.

"I have other plans today," I declared as Felix strode outside, dressed and ready for his usual sparring match with Cal. He gave me one look over and furrowed his brows as he took in my casual clothes and the horses on each side of me.

"And what plans could be more important than honing your Gifts?" Evander asked, crossing his arms over his chest.

"Felix and I have a date," I replied and shrugged.

"We do?" my best friend asked, looking confused as he stepped closer. I nodded vehemently and gave him my brightest smile.

"Did you honestly think I'd forget your birthday?" I asked, and Felix's eyes instantly misted over as he grinned. Pure joy flooded his face. How could he ever think I'd forget him? "You've been there for every one of mine, so I figured the least I could do was be there for one of yours."

Felix lunged for me, wrapping me in his arms and forcing me to drop the leads as he spun me around. I giggled as he kissed my face, satisfied to give him a day of carefree happiness. Lia and I planned a little celebration later tonight, but I wanted to have some Delicious Duo time during the day. I felt like I had barely spent time with my best friend the past few weeks, and we had some serious catching up to do.

"I thought you two first met when Ainsley moved to the palace this summer," Evander commented.

"We did," I answered, thrown off by the statement.

"Then how did he celebrate every birthday with you?"

My face fell, and I felt the blood drain as I replayed the words I had said to Felix. I hadn't realized I mentioned those birthdays he and Dash had made so special for me, and now I was drowning in the memories as I struggled to tread water. Felix's question-filled eyes met mine, but I shook my head, determined to make this day about him and not my own issues. It was hard enough that he didn't have Dash with him and knowing their friendship, I was sure there was some stupid tradition they always did each year.

"I'm going to go grab the lunch I packed, and then we can be on our way," I told Felix, ignoring Evander's question as I backed toward the house. As I turned around, the three men's reflections in the window snagged my attention, and I watched as Evander and Olivier drew closer to my friend with curious looks on their faces.

"Speak, Empathi," I heard Evander command as I reached the house. Evander was definitely not someone I wanted to know about the twenty birthday celebrations Dash had planned and how my pathetic heart still broke whenever I thought about what he had done for me. I only hoped Felix was strong enough to resist Evander's order or at least smart enough to lie about it for me.

I returned five minutes later, swinging the basket of food I had packed just as Evander and Olivier stepped away from Felix. The apologetic look on Felix's face let me know he spilled his guts at Evander's feet. I groaned loudly and headed for Nox, attaching the basket to her saddle as Evander appeared at my side.

"Ainsley," he said, but I held my hand to stop him.

"I don't want to hear it," I responded, continuing my work to prepare for our journey.

Evander tensed, and I could feel his discomfort radiating as he placed his hands over mine to halt me from my task.

"I didn't know," he said, and my stare drifted from where his fingers grazed mine to his charcoal eyes. They were hard and furious as they bore into me. I wasn't sure what to do. One moment Evander was insulting me as he burrowed beneath my skin like an infection, and the next, he was understanding and trying to relate to me on some level. The constant back and forth was giving me whiplash.

"Well, now you do," I replied harshly. "Not everyone grew up with people who loved and cared about them, people who celebrated birthdays and were genuinely happy to see them." I made a pointed look at Evander's friends, who were clearly family to him. "I didn't have what you had. I had no one until I met Dash and Felix. And yes, I may have been stupid and naive, as you have loved to point out in the past, but for a little while, I felt loved and wanted for once."

"Ainsley," Evander started, but I cut him off again.

"I understand that you hate Dash for planning to steal the Gifts of the woman who is your successor, and even I hate him for that. But it doesn't change the things he did for me or why I fell in love with him. So please, Evander, keep your comments to yourself because no one can make me feel more pathetic than I already do."

I mounted Nox, not caring to listen to him as he tried to speak again. Once Felix was saddled and ready, I took the lead and galloped down the dirt path. Today wasn't a day to be sad about what I lost; it was a day to celebrate my best friend and give him the quality time he deserved. I wasn't going to let Evander's pity ruin that.

"I know it isn't a lot," I said, biting my lip as I handed over a large box wrapped in black tissue paper. Felix rolled his eyes dismissively as he forcefully snatched the present from my hands and began tearing the paper from the box like an animal shredding apart its prey. This man was like a child when it came to presents.

I watched nervously as he ripped the lid from the box and peered inside. I had spent the past two weeks trying to figure out what to give him, and when the idea came to mind, I sent Lia to town immediately to pick up the supplies. She was more than happy to do so and decided to grab a few presents of her own for Felix, which I couldn't wait for him to see tonight. Especially the shiny gold underwear that was going to expose his ass completely.

"Do you like it?" I asked as he stared at his present without saying anything for far too long. He dropped the box onto his lap and crushed his body to mine, squeezing me so hard I could barely breathe. "I take it that's a yes?"

"It's perfect," he answered, the emotion thick in his voice.

"I just know how much your story meant to you, and I hate that we left it back in Caelum," I said as he released me and removed the large journal and new set of pens from the box. "I figured you could rewrite it or work on a whole new story if you wanted to."

"Thank you," he breathed, dabbing tears from his eyes. "It means the world to me."

We sat in silence for a few minutes as Felix held the journal in his hands, nothing filling the space but the sounds of the wind whistling through the trees and the songbirds flying through the air. I could feel his pain, though; each shard was like glass to the heart, and it killed me that I knew I couldn't fix it for him.

"I'm so sorry, Felix," I choked out. "I know how much you miss him."

"I do," he breathed, his voice breaking on the words. "I miss him so fucking much, Ainsley. But I also miss *us*. I miss the way the three of us were a family. I miss our lazy days and jokes. I miss the way we all were. I know my situation wasn't the best, but I had the two of you and now…"

Felix released the journal, and his head fell into his hands as sobs climbed free from his throat. I wrapped my arms around his neck as I broke alongside him. There was nothing I could do to make the day better for Felix. The only thing that would do that was for Dash to be here. And that wasn't possible. So instead, I just held my friend as we both mourned our loss.

The days without Dash were beginning to come easier for me, but it seemed to be getting harder for Felix, and I was now watching him unravel because of it. I wanted to find a way to make this right for him. He didn't deserve to feel this hell. If it weren't for me, he and Dash would still be together now, most likely drinking the day away and celebrating by daring each other to do stupid shit that could get them killed. He missed Dash and his life, and I wanted him to have that again.

"You can go back," I whispered, and Felix shook his head as he pulled away from his hands to meet my gaze. The amber of his eyes was brilliant in the sunlight, and the tears that welled made the color seem bolder than usual.

"I can't leave you," he replied, and I reached up to hold his face in my hands.

"Felix—"

"I won't leave you, Ainsley, so don't ask me to," he said, and I breathed a heavy sigh at his stubbornness. "Even if I wanted to return to Caelum, I couldn't. King Perceval would brand me a traitor and kill me. Even if I managed to lie my way out of it, Dash would know the truth. He'd see right through my deception and know I betrayed him when it came to you."

I didn't doubt that Dash already knew Felix was why I was taken from Caelum, or at least had his suspicions about it. I didn't have proof, but it was a strong feeling. Dash was insanely clever, and the way his mind was constantly working was one thing I loved about him. Because of that, I had little faith that Dash wasn't fully aware that something was happening behind the scenes with Felix. I knew the two had been friends nearly their whole lives, but would that friendship survive a betrayal of that magnitude? I couldn't be sure.

"I'm so sorry, Felix," I said again, releasing his face. "I wish I could make this better."

"Me too," he whispered before curling me in his arms again as we both cried for the life we had lost and the friendship I wasn't sure he'd ever get back.

18.

When we returned to the house in the late afternoon, Lia had everyone gather in the library for a night of drinking games to celebrate Felix's birthday. Olivier had protested, of course, but for some reason, Evander gave him a look that shut him up. I internally groaned at the gesture, not wanting the king's pity now that he knew just how shitty my life had been growing up. A story, I might add, that he never once bothered to ask me himself. Instead, he just assumed that I was a spoiled brat who was only concerned about fucking a prince. I tipped back my glass, swallowing the rest of my drink as I reached for the wine bottle to refill it. Damn, I missed those magic goblets in Caelum. It was so much easier when the glass just refilled itself.

"How about truth or dare?" Cal suggested, and Lia waved him off.

"Top and bottom?" Lia asked, and Felix snapped his finger and pointed excitedly.

"Yes!" he said, and we all filled up our glasses for the game.

The rules were simple, once a category was picked, each player said their favorite and least favorite thing having to do with that topic. If an answer matched someone else's, both players drank. Back in Caelum, I learned that Felix enthusiastically chose whatever game he knew would get him drunk the quickest.

"Are you sure you want to play?" I asked as Evander filled a glass with his favorite amber liquor. He arched a brow in question, and I shrugged. "You just don't seem to enjoy fun, so I figured you were too boring to play games." Besides the games Evander and I played every morning, he was always so serious, often side-eyeing Felix and me whenever we cracked jokes or just goofed off. I constantly felt like he was judging me when I'd catch him staring, and it always made me self-conscious though I knew it shouldn't have.

"I'll never turn down a game, love. You should know this by now," he said, settling back in his chair. I turned my attention back to Cal and Lia as I pointedly ignored Evander's comment.

"Felix, since it's your birthday, you get to pick the first category," Lia announced, raising her voice so the idle chatter around the room quieted. Felix bobbed his head back and forth momentarily before finally settling on one.

"Turn-ons," he said, and we all thought about our answers.

"Bondage is a top," Marce announced, breaking the silence. We all looked at her with shocked expressions. That definitely wasn't the answer I'd expected to hear from her, but I was here for it.

"Gross," Olivier said, and she shrugged.

"Cover your ears next time, brother," she said, and we all laughed, though none of us drank.

"Role-playing is a top," Lia announced. Cal clinked his glass against hers, and they both took a sip of their drink, indicating their favorites matched.

"When my partner takes control is mine," I said, and the others hummed their approval, but it was Evander that grabbed my attention. He raised his drink to me and took a slow and deliberate sip as I stared at him. There was no way his top matched mine, and he was only drinking to piss me off after my comment about how boring he was. Evander cocked a brow and gestured to the glass in my hand as Felix and Olivier rattled off their tops. I reluctantly gave in and followed the game's rules, even though Evander was obviously cheating.

We each listed our bottoms, and surprisingly no one's least favorite was the same. Lia selected the next category, and in sticking with the theme, she chose sexual positions.

"From behind is my top," Felix and Olivier both said in unison. I covered my mouth as I snickered over the shocked look on Olivier's face. He was horrified that he and Felix had something as simple as a favorite sexual position in common. The man prided himself on being as opposite to Felix as someone could possibly get. I think he actually got off on it. Felix, on the other hand, was beaming ear to ear as he toasted his glass high and swallowed the contents whole.

"We could always go back to my room where you can show me exactly how you enjoy it," Felix offered.

Olivier refilled his drink and downed it again. "I'd rather fuck my sister."

"Dude, that's fucking gross," Marce exclaimed, looking utterly disgusted that Olivier would even say such a thing.

"Exactly. That's how much my dick wants to stay away from him," Olivier replied, glaring at Felix, who only smiled wider.

"I don't know. The more you deny it, the more I think you want me," he said with a wink. A low growl left Olivier's throat, and I couldn't help but snort at their antics, the alcohol seeming to be doing its job and getting me lax.

"I'd have to say me on top… is my top," Lia said, getting the game back on track.

"Oh, me too, me too!" I exclaimed, clinking my glass to hers as we laughed and drained the contents.

I reached for another bottle and noticed Evander watching me intently, a question seeming to play in his mind. Thanks to the copious amounts of liquor we had been consuming this evening, two Evanders were swaying gently on the couch, and each one was looking at me. Why was he always staring at me like he either wanted to fuck me or kill me?

"I noticed you didn't drink with Lia and me," I told him, slurring my words slightly. His eyes narrowed, and a crooked grin formed on his face. I was vaguely aware of Cal and Marce talking about their choices for top, but I was too preoccupied with calling out the liar staring at me. "If your partner taking control truly *was* your favorite, then why wouldn't them being on top be your favorite too? It's a position that gives them full control," I said, taking another sip of my drink.

"Because—" Evander started.

"Because you're a liar and just wanted to copy me because you knew it would get under my skin. Just admit it!" I demanded. Evander bit his lip to hide his laughter, though it didn't do any good. I still heard it.

That dick.

"I didn't drink because I've never had sex in that position," he countered.

"You've never had sex with someone on top?!" I yelled entirely too loud, and everyone glanced in our direction. My face flushed with embarrassment as I realized I probably shouldn't have screamed. "You've never had sex with someone on top?" I whispered, though it definitely still came out more of a quiet yell, and Evander laughed at my ridiculous attempt.

"Nope," he said with zero shame. I looked around the room, but no one else besides Felix seemed surprised.

"Why not? It's good. Like *really* good," I said, completely aware of how drunk I was but unable to stop myself from talking. Evander's smile grew, and *fuck* if it wasn't a beautiful thing to see. He was handsome, gorgeous even... but a total ass, and that's all that mattered.

Obviously.

"I'm sure it is," he said with amusement.

"Van is saving that for the Claiming," Olivier added as he rolled his eyes.

"The Claiming? Is that some virgin thing? Oh my Gods, are you a *virgin*?" I asked, clasping my hands over my mouth. I had been talking sex positions with an inexperienced virgin—his poor little ears.

The room roared with laughter, and I looked around, confused as hell. Was this some kind of joke they were all playing on me? I took another sip from my glass while waiting for everyone to calm down and include me in on the fun.

"I'm definitely not a virgin, love, and I'd be happy to prove it to you if you want," Evander said, and heat rushed to my cheeks. Nope, I would absolutely not like that. It had been over a month since I had sex last, and the alcohol and topics were clearly just getting me in the mood. It had nothing to do with this weird back-and-forth banter Evander and I had or the fact that he was seriously attractive. It was just hormones and the game we were currently playing. That was it.

"That tradition is still upheld here?" Felix asked incredulously as he took a long drink from his glass, his gaze locked on Olivier as if he were undressing him with his eyes. Go, Felix.

"It is, but not everyone follows it," Evander answered, tearing his stare away from me. I made a mental note not to drink around him again. At least not until I released some of this apparent pent-up sexual frustration I harbored.

"Interesting," Felix mused. Before I could ask anything more about the Claiming and what exactly that was, we all moved on to list our bottoms.

I hadn't heard a single word anyone else said as I tried to figure out my answer. I wasn't inexperienced when it came to sex—I had plenty of it—but I hadn't been adventurous enough to know what I didn't like.

"Am I allowed to just say any position that has rocks digging into my back, and I don't get to come?" I asked when it got around to my turn. Ugh, I wasn't sure I would ever be able to erase the memories of Logan from my mind.

"Or when your partner doesn't use his tongue the way he should," Felix added knowingly, and I clicked my glass with his.

"Wait, Dash never..." Lia began, but I shook my head to correct her.

"No, he did. A lot... Like a lot, a lot. It was his favorite thing to do," I rambled, recalling how it felt to have Dash's head between my thighs, working me until I was screaming his name with my release. Gods, I missed how good that felt. I threw my head back as I closed my eyes, replaying each delicious moment in my mind.

"We're talking about a douche noodle named Logan," Felix said and I nodded without opening my eyes.

"I miss sex," I pouted, and everyone besides Lia and Cal mumbled their agreement. Well, at least I knew I wasn't alone in that.

"Come on, cupcake, let's get you to bed," Felix said, rising to his feet. He tried to lift me from the ground but dropped me before falling over my body. We both laughed at the realization he was just as wasted as I was. "Maybe we should just stay here tonight," he said, but before I could agree, Evander cut in.

"I'll take her," he announced, appearing beside me and picking me up as if I weighed nothing. I wanted to protest, but I was entirely too drunk and tired from the day. I wrapped my arms around his neck and rested my head against his shoulder as I closed my eyes and let my body sway with each gentle step he took. There was something comforting and familiar about being in his arms, but

I couldn't place what it was. I inhaled his cedar and fresh fallen snow scent as he carried me to my room and tucked me into bed.

"What's the Claiming?" I asked, my voice muffled with sleep. Evander pulled the blankets over my shoulders and brushed the hair away from my face.

"It's a tradition held in Tenebrae. When you find the person you want to spend your life with, you can Claim each other. It binds you together, but not with magic that is *made* as the Entwining Ceremony uses. It's your own magic that Claims one another. It's then solidified by an act that can be as simple as a kiss or more complex like sex," he answered, and I hummed my acknowledgment.

"Why did you choose that position?"

Evander was quiet for so long that I thought he either wouldn't answer or I had fallen asleep and missed it completely.

"Because, as you said earlier, it gives the person on top full control. There's only one person I want to have that kind of power over me—the one I choose to Claim and who Claims me in return. They're the only person I would relinquish all control to."

"Mmmmm," I said, unable to come up with any words as sleep began to steal me away. I liked that Evander kept something for the person he was meant for. I liked that they would have something no one else had. There was a poetic beauty in that, and I was envious of whoever it would be. Not because I wanted Evander for myself but because they would share something sacred, something that couldn't be touched. I knew I could never go that deep with anyone again, but it didn't change the fact that I missed feeling loved.

19.

"**Y**ou're going to love it there!" Lia said, pinning my hair back away from my face. "The food is amazing and the music and dancing are so much fun."

I smiled back enthusiastically at her reflection as she finished her work on my hair. Apparently, we were all going to some tavern for a night out and everyone was excited about it. The only tavern I'd ever been to was back in the village I grew up in, and that was because it was the only thing to do there besides screwing Logan. Neither activity was worth remembering, so I hoped this tavern experience would top it.

Felix dug through my dresser, pulling out random dresses as he tried to find something for me to wear once Lia nixed my outfit. I was going for comfort and warmth with a sweater and pants, but she explained I would regret that choice when we got on the dance floor, and I began to sweat from all the layers.

"This one," Felix said, tossing a thin, deep blue satin dress onto my lap. I looked at the piece of fabric with wide eyes, knowing I would freeze my ass off the moment I stepped outside. Before I could object to his ridiculous choice, he held up a thick white furred coat that looked long enough to hit my ankles.

"The tavern is only a twenty-minute walk, but Van's just going to traverse us, so we don't have to deal with the cold," Lia added, dropping down in front of me as she painted my lips a deep mauve color.

My chest ached slightly as I thought about how Imogen would also do this for me. She'd paint my lips, pin my hair, and always select gorgeous gowns for me to wear. I missed her more than anything. I missed her cinnamon and honey scent and her warm hazel eyes. I even missed how she'd purse her lips and scold me for my attitude. Hopefully, she was doing okay, and I'd see her again one day.

"We're leaving in two minutes!" Oli called from down the hall, and the three of us hurried to finish getting me ready.

Five minutes and several groans from everyone downstairs waiting on us later, we were set to go. Everyone was dressed immaculately. The men in the room wore fitted pants and tight dress shirts that showed off their hard muscles beneath. Marce and Lia were donned in a dress similar to mine, though in a different color. We huddled around Evander, and though he couldn't take us all at once, it only took him about ten seconds to traverse us in two trips.

The village streets were filled with people enjoying their night out, laughing in conversations as they passed. Everyone seemed so careful and happy, and I felt a little pang of guilt to know it potentially wouldn't last. War was on the horizon, and unless we figured out a way to stop the leader of Pravus from invading Disparya, nights like this would cease to exist.

Evander's hand brushed my back as he steered me to the massive building across the street with the word *Tavern* written into a large wooden sign above the door. The windows were illuminated, and silhouettes of people drinking and laughing inside made the establishment seem welcoming from the exterior. I tugged my coat tight around me as the chilled autumn wind blew, and Evander moved to my side, blocking the breeze as we crossed; I wasn't sure if it was done intentionally or by accident, but either way, I was no longer getting slammed with cold air.

Olivier reached the door first, holding it open for everyone, and we all rushed inside the warm space. The room was spacious, with people sitting around tables, enjoying food and drink with their company. Evander nodded to a barkeep and pointed to a private table in the back that I assumed was meant for us. As we passed through, I glanced over the scene, enjoying how every group of patrons seemed to participate in a different activity. Some were eating a nice meal, while others were drinking and laughing; some were in the midst of what looked to be a serious card game, and others were reading in dimly lit corners, even though this didn't seem like the place for that.

"I thought you said there was music and dancing," I whispered to Lia as we settled into our chairs.

"That's downstairs. This level is the restaurant," she replied. I nodded as I continued to observe my surroundings. The restaurant looked cozy and welcoming enough, but there was something about it that I couldn't quite put my finger on—something *different*.

The barkeep from earlier arrived with our drinks, and shortly after that, our table was covered with platters of different types of foods—all of which were new to me. The smell of unique spices permeated through the air as I piled my plate full. I sampled everything, not finding even one item I didn't like, and by the end, my stomach felt like it was going to explode. I wasn't sure how I was supposed to dance in this condition, but as the music from below reached my ears, I found myself willing to try. It was so nice to take a break from the training and talks of war—to just be carefree for a little while.

A tall blonde woman who reminded me a lot of Rosella approached the table and came to stand directly behind Evander. I watched intently as she leaned forward, sliding her hands over his shoulders and down his chest before whispering into his ear. He hadn't mentioned having a lover. Evander smiled at whatever she told him and clutched her hand in his before rising from his chair.

"I'll meet you all downstairs," he announced, draping his arm around the woman's shoulders. Everyone mumbled their acknowledgment, too lost in their own conversations to care about what he was doing or where he was going. I got the feeling that this happened quite often.

Evander and his new companion strode across the room to a large staircase that spiraled up to another floor where a wall was lined with doors. I watched shamelessly as she pulled a key from her pocket and unlocked the door before wrapping her arms around the king and pulling him inside. My focus darted across the restaurant as men and women sat on laps and whispered into the ears of other patrons. A few even pulled them from their seats to lead them to the staircase, just as the woman had done with Evander. My mouth dropped open as the pieces of where we were began to click into place.

"Is this a brothel?!" I whispered to Lia.

"Yup," Marceline answered before Lia could as she smiled wide. "It took you long enough to figure it. I thought you would have when the waiter came by with his ass practically hanging out of his pants."

"I thought it was the uniform!" I argued. I didn't know what to expect, but it certainly wasn't going to a brothel.

Everyone laughed at my naivety, including Felix, who had enjoyed the look of shock on my face far too much to defend me. It wasn't that there was anything wrong with brothels, but I just didn't understand why we were here. Besides for Evander to get laid, I guess, because I had no doubt that was what was happening upstairs right now.

"Van owns this place," Lia explained as she shrugged and dabbed the corner of her mouth with a cloth.

Of course he did.

Why wouldn't the *Master of Orgasms* own a place that's sole purpose was to offer pleasure?

"Can we go dance now?" Cal whined as he pushed back from the table. "Van said he'd meet us, so there's no point in waiting for him up here. He could be in there for hours, and I don't want to miss out on the fun downstairs."

Hours?! What the hell were they going to be doing in that room? Sure, Dashiell and I used to spend all night tangled up with each other, but we had breaks in between. If it was lasting hours straight, then maybe Evander wasn't the *Master of Orgasms* after all. Perhaps it took that long because he sucked at pleasuring someone. I don't know why that image brought me such happiness, but it did.

Actually no. I knew exactly why: he was always a dick, and it was satisfying to think he had no clue how to use his.

We moved our little party to a large couch in a dimly lit corner of the bottom floor. Dozens of people were dancing, moving their bodies to the slow and sensual melody of the music. It was haunting and sexual, giving the same energy as what I'm sure was happening on the top floor with the workers and their clients.

Marce was the first one in our group to go dance, pulling some unsuspecting bystander by the shirt and making him join her. He looked like he wanted to object for all of two seconds before falling prey to her stunning beauty and intense turquoise eyes. She placed his hands where she wanted them, and together they moved as one to the beat, enjoying each other's company.

"Dance with me. I want to make him jealous," Felix whispered desperately, angling his chin to point to Olivier, who was sipping on his drink and talking to Cal.

"He's not going to get jealous if it's *me* you dance with," I countered. Everyone knew we were just friends, so they'd never believe our ruse. Felix bit his lip as he contemplated my reasoning before nodding to himself.

"Good point," he said before standing and pulling me up with him. Felix ripped off my fur coat and clutched my hand as he dragged me to the edge of the dance floor despite my protests.

"Felix, I don't know how to dance like that."

"Yes, you do," he said flatly, looking around the room until he found his two victims and gave a crook of his finger to call them over. "Just move your body like you're having sex. You'll be fine." I opened my mouth to argue with him, but something sad in his pleading eyes made me decide to do this one thing for him.

"Okay," I said, nodding, and my best friend grinned from ear to ear.

"You're with her, and you're with me," he said to the two men who appeared before us. Neither tried to argue or even question.

"What's your name?" I asked as my partner led me through the undulating crowd to the center where Marce had also stationed herself.

"Taren, Your Highness," he said, and I cringed as he made it known he knew exactly who I was. I wanted to tell him to call me by my name, but a voice in my head demanded I have him address me by my title only. For some reason, I decided to listen to it.

"It's nice to meet you, Taren," I said, wrapping my arms around his neck as I pushed myself closer. His green eyes were bright and his blonde hair fell forward over his brow as he smiled down at me.

Just move your body like you're having sex—I could do that.

Taren's hands slid down my spine to my lower back and I instinctively arched against him. It had been a while since I had been touched that way, and my body seemed to crave it. I closed my eyes and gave myself over to the music, letting my desires free as we danced. He spun me, so my back was pressed to his chest. I reached my arms up and dragged my hands through his hair as his fingers moved down my sides. I focused on his touch, willing it to erase every trace of Dashiell from my skin—every memory of his hands on me. It wasn't enough. He was still there, and I needed to rid myself of him completely.

I twisted in Taren's hold to face him again and leaned on my toes to bring my lips to his. He didn't try to resist, instead pushing me back to my normal height as his tongue forced its way into my mouth. I let him take what he wanted, and it reminded me so much of the kisses I had shared with Logan. They were hollow and void of passion or feelings, just something to do to pass the time. This kiss was so much like that, but I didn't care—I needed it. I needed to claim myself back, my autonomy back, and this would help me do it.

I wasn't sure how long we had been wrapped up in our embrace as we danced, but I was vaguely aware of the music changing for a third time when an arm yanked me away from Taren.

"She's done," Felix said politely, though I didn't miss the edge of protectiveness in his voice. Taren dipped his head in a respectful bow to me before heading back into the crowd of dancers as my friend dragged me away.

"What the hell?" I demanded once we got back to our empty private couch.

Everyone was on the dance floor, including Evander, who must have made his way down at some point. I looked out at my friends, who were all having a great time with each other, as Felix stared at me with concern and judgment.

"What was all that about?" Felix demanded, gesturing to where we had just been. I shrugged because I thought it was pretty obvious. Not to mention, I didn't owe him or anyone else an explanation for my actions.

Felix's jaw ticked as he looked away from me, disappointment edging his features. I suddenly started to feel self-conscious about what I'd chosen to do, even though there wasn't a reason for me to. I was a grown woman, and if I wanted to kiss someone I was allowed to do so without being made to feel guilty about it.

"Everything okay over here?" Evander asked as he approached the two of us. Sweat glistened on his brow and his hair was messier than before. I couldn't help but wonder if it had to do with him dancing or what had transpired upstairs earlier. Evander slid his hands into his pockets as he looked between Felix and me, no doubt picking up on the obvious tension.

"Felix is pissed because I kissed someone who isn't Dashiell," I said bitterly as I crossed my arms and settled into the couch. It wasn't fair for him to act that way towards me just because I decided to enjoy my night after *he* forced me to dance in the first place.

"That's not true," Felix argued, shaking his head. "It doesn't have anything to do with it not being Dash, but what happened out there... I understand that you're hurting still, but that's not how—"

"Leave, Empathi," Evander commanded, interrupting Felix before he could finish his sentence. Felix closed his eyes as if trying to reign in his frustration toward the king. "And I highly suggest you don't say another word."

Felix opened his eyes and looked in my direction, but I couldn't meet his stare. I was too pissed at him for trying to tell me how I should and shouldn't behave. I promised myself that I wouldn't lose who I was again and let someone dictate my actions. Felix wasn't excluded from that just because he was my best friend.

My eyes stayed firmly locked on Evander as he turned and motioned for someone to come over. Olivier appeared a moment later and was given the order to take Felix home, which he reluctantly accepted. A part of me enjoyed that Felix would have to deal with Olivier's hatred toward him for the next twenty minutes, so he could feel just as miserable as he made me. Without saying another word, Felix rose from his seat on the couch and followed Olivier out of the tavern.

I took in a deep breath and let it out slowly. Though I was angry at Felix, I hated fighting with him. And even though tonight hadn't turned into an argument, it was heading that way if Evander hadn't stepped in. For once I found myself grateful for his nosiness.

"Have you been enjoying yourself tonight?" Evander asked as soon as it seemed the two men had left.

"I think so. At least I was before all of this happened," I admitted and glanced back at the dance floor to find Taren watching me from across the crowd. He waved tentatively, and I gave him a small smile that didn't reach my eyes.

"Then come on," Evander said, jerking his chin toward the dance floor. I didn't let myself overthink it and instead followed him into the sea of people until I had Lia's arms wrapped around me as we laughed and danced to the music.

20.

Felix and I hadn't spoken for the rest of the week, and it seemed he was actively keeping his distance from me. The longer he stayed away, the more pissed I got at him, but there was no way I would be the first to give in and confront him about our issues. I wouldn't apologize for what I did that first night at the tavern or every night since.

The music swelled around us as my back pressed harder into the wall, and my fingers fisted through dark brown curls. My mind fogged just how I liked it as hands trailed down my body in idle strokes.

"We could go somewhere more private," she said, but I shook my head as I kissed her again, completely content to stay there. I was on a desperate journey to find a part of me Dashiell hadn't touched—hadn't tainted—and though I was having shit luck at it, I wasn't ready to see if the answer lay in the bedroom. I wasn't ready to cross that line.

I held her face, loving the feel of her soft skin between my fingers as she kissed me hard. I couldn't help but sense that she was trying to erase a lingering pain of her own. It seemed like most of the people here were. Occasionally, I'd reach out my Empathi Gift and feel the overwhelming emotions of longing and desire. Everyone here wanted to be wanted—to feel something—yet here I was, trying to accomplish the opposite. I didn't want to hurt anymore or have to feel Dashiell's fingers on my skin like a brand. I wanted to numb the pain and feel nothing at all.

"Ainsley?" a familiar voice called, and I automatically turned in the direction it came. Felix stood a foot away, looking sad and alone. "Can we talk?"

I found myself nodding before I decided to do so, and after a quick goodbye to the woman I had just been spending my time with, I followed Felix outside to the front of the tavern. We stood awkwardly in the cold night air, neither of us speaking though I had already decided that Felix would have to be the one to start. He had gotten mad at me for no reason, so he would have to explain himself before I bothered to do the same.

"I handled everything between us poorly last week," he finally said, and I pressed my back into the cold stone building as I listened. "I need you to know I wasn't upset because you weren't kissing Dash. I was upset with how you were trying to get over him."

"It's my right to do that as I see fit, Felix."

"I know," he said before taking a deep breath and coming to stand before me.

His amber eyes looked like flickering flames in the dim light from the windows, and I noticed how they were slightly misted over. His throat bobbed as he swallowed his emotions before clutching my hands tight.

"I know how deeply you let yourself feel and how much love means to you," he said. "And I hate that what I did has steered you from that. I hate that it's making you into someone like me. Someone who wants to be numb, so they never have to hurt."

My eyes burned with unshed tears, and my heart splintered at his words. Love had meant everything to me. It had been what I craved most in my life, and when I thought I finally had it, it was ripped away and replaced by lies. And now... Now I understood why Felix went through so many lovers. Being with people you didn't care about was better than being alone. I could give in to my body's desires without giving away my heart, and it felt good to finally hold that power again.

"You deserve so much more than that, Ainsley," Felix added, and I closed my eyes as a tear ran down my cheek. "You deserve to be loved and treated right. Dash didn't do that, and neither did I as a friend. I know you're still hurting, and I'm not sure those scars will ever fully fade for you, but please don't do what I do. If you want to move on in whatever way, I'll support you. But I am begging you, don't do it just to stop the hurt. Because it'll only make it worse, and I need it never to get worse for you. I don't want you to lose yourself."

My breathing was shaky as I replayed every broken plea from Felix's lips. I understood what he was asking, and I knew he was right. It wasn't about me moving on. With that first kiss, I had managed to claim a tiny piece of myself back. And with that, I had felt power and strength for the first time, possibly ever. But I also knew that each time I allowed myself to do it again, it was only to numb the sting of a still-open wound. It became less about claiming and more about concealing. I wanted to forget Dashiell, and I was using whoever I could to help me do it. I wasn't ashamed, but I knew it wasn't working and couldn't go on.

I met Felix's gaze as I nodded slowly. He sighed in relief as he wrapped me in his arms and held me tight. I inhaled his leather and spice scent, letting it fill the cracks of my broken self and keep me grounded.

"There you are!" Lia announced, pushing through the doors and striding straight for us. "I saw you both downstairs, and then you were gone by the time I made it to that side of the room. Is everything good now? Are we friends again?!"

I couldn't help but laugh at her enthusiasm.

"Ainsley couldn't get rid of me if she tried," Felix joked.

"Well, in that case, come on," she said, grabbing our hands to pull us back inside the tavern.

I missed spending time with them but after my conversation with Felix, the only thing I wanted to do was leave. I was exhausted, and the hurt of Dashiell's betrayal was fresh in my mind again.

"I actually think I'm going to head home," I said, and Lia stuck out her bottom lip in a pout. Felix placed a kiss on her cheek before offering his arm for me to take. "Stay," I told him, knowing how much he wanted to take his mind off this past week. "I know the way back, and it's not a long walk."

"I don't like the idea of you walking alone," Felix said.

"She won't be," a satin voice said from the shadows, and we twisted to find Evander approaching. "I'll take her home."

I had no plans to go back with him, but if it got Felix to ease up and have fun with Lia and our friends, I'd agree to anything. I kissed his and Lia's cheeks before wishing them a fun night as they disappeared inside the tavern.

"Shall we?" Evander asked, but I shook my head.

"You can go back inside too. I just agreed so they'd let me leave."

"I'm going home, love. The offer wasn't just me being chivalrous, though I always am."

I rolled my eyes at his usual arrogance and crossed the street before he could say another word. Having him traverse me would have been much faster, but I wanted to walk and clear my head. However, with Evander's footsteps padding after me, I wasn't sure how successful I'd be at that.

"You know you could have invited Karly back home," he offered, and I looked up at him questioningly as we stepped onto the dirt path. "It's your house too, so you can bring whomever you want home. I just wanted to make sure you knew that."

"Thanks, but I'm not ready for that anyway," I replied, not knowing why I'd decided to share. We weren't friends, so why did I feel the need to tell him? "How did you know her name, anyway?" I asked, hoping it would be enough for him not to comment on me being too afraid to have sex again.

Evander was quiet for so long that I didn't know if he had heard me. I looked up to find his eyes narrowed on the path straight ahead, like he was trying hard to focus on it so he didn't have to answer. I shoved him in his side and he dropped his gaze to me as his face filled with a medley of emotions. He opened and closed his mouth several times before giving me an apologetic smile.

Oh, Gods, no.

"How long ago?" I demanded, bringing my attention to our surroundings, so I didn't have to look at him while he told me about his past relationship with the woman whose throat I had my tongue down tonight.

"A couple of years. It only happened a few times."

"Well, now I'm *really* happy Felix interrupted when he did," I said. I half expected a snarky response, but Evander grew quiet—too quiet. I stole another glance to find him smiling at me in that same pitiful way. I groaned loudly, knowing what it meant. "Who else?"

"Do you really want to know?" he asked. Nope, but also, very much, yes.

"Just tell me."

"Karly, Elizabeth, Gavin, Haden, and Isla," he answered, and my breathing stopped. Nearly every single person I had kissed, Evander had already done the same. "Oh, and Taren was *definitely* waving to me that first night, not you. Did you kiss him? Because if so, then add him to the list too." Scratch that. *Every* single person I had kissed, Evander had done the same, if not more with.

"You have got to be kidding me," I said, dragging a hand through my hair.

"Look at it this way: we both have exquisite taste."

"How does that help the situation at all?" I demanded, and Evander shrugged.

"It doesn't, but I still think it's a fun little fact."

The lights to our house loomed in the distance, and I could make out Onyx and Nova's silhouettes as they lay next to the lake under the moonlight. I wanted to get inside and scrub the memory of this night from my body.

"I'm going to need a list of everyone you've ever been with so I know who hasn't been tainted by you."

"Or... and hear me out," he said, holding a finger in the air as if to make a point. "You can just take out the middle man and kiss me instead."

"Why would I ever want to do that?" I snorted at his ridiculous offer.

"Because it's clear that you want me and don't want to admit it. That's why you've been going after those I've already had. That way, you can have a little taste without admitting you want the real thing."

I stared at him unblinking. He was always so full of himself, especially regarding me, but this was a whole new level. Was he honestly suggesting that I had only kissed those people because it brought me closer to him? He was insane—absolutely delusional. And as his lips broke into a playful grin, I realized he was also joking. I shoved him hard as he laughed, and I couldn't help my own laughter from creeping up, but I quickly smothered it with my hands.

"Please tell me you were also joking about everyone we've both kissed," I begged, and Evander's grin spread even more.

"Sorry, love. That was all true."

21.

I lunged my sword, and Olivier swatted it away like it was nothing but an insect buzzing around his ear. I stumbled from his deflection and worked to regain my balance before I fell on my ass. Again.

"No more going to the tavern. You're fighting like shit, and I'd be willing to bet it's from your late-night drinking and dancing," Olivier seethed as he spun his sword and landed a blow hard to my back, making me fall forward and eat dirt.

I had been at the tavern every evening lately—we all had—but the past few nights, I left at a decent hour and had barely drank anything more than a glass of wine. Olivier wasn't wrong; I was horrible today, but I had no idea why. I had gotten a good amount of sleep, knowing Oli said today would be a challenging workout with me trying to incorporate magic and fighting simultaneously. I had been looking forward to this session all week, which was why I left the tavern so early yesterday. So what was going on with me?

I gasped for breath as my cheek pressed into the dirt. My arms shook hard as I pushed myself back to my feet, and I swayed side to side as I stood there, trying to get my bearings. Sweat dripped down my face, and my chapped lips stung as a bead of moisture touched them. My chest rose and fell heavily as my vision doubled, and two Oliviers were standing in the middle of the ring, ready to punish me for my carelessness.

I gripped the hilt of my sword hard, took a deep breath, and ran for him again. Our weapons clashed as sharp pain radiated through my body at the impact. I jumped back, grunting as we circled each other again. I felt so weak and didn't even have the energy to call my magic forward to aid me.

"This is pathetic," Oli snarled. I gritted my teeth in determination as I ran for him once more. He spun and kicked me in the side, knocking me into the dirt again, and I cried out in frustration and pain. "Focus! Pick up your sword and push through the pain. It's your own fault you're this exhausted."

I lifted my head to see everyone still going through their exercises but glancing our way to watch my failure. I sucked in a sharp breath as I got back to my feet and faced my opponent again. My hand held my sword while the other clutched the excruciating pain in my stomach. The agony was so great that I was less than two minutes away from getting sick all over the ring. At least we were outside.

With nothing but sheer will, I ran for Oli again. This time, I only made it halfway before a searing scream ripped through my throat, and I fell to the ground. My eyes closed, but the world still spun in the darkness, making me feel dizzy and even weaker. My stomach churned from the effects of my mind, and I twisted my head as I vomited onto the ground.

My friends yelled my name, and soon, hands were all over me as they shouted panicked questions at each other and me, but I couldn't answer. My body trembled, and tears streamed down my face as my stomach felt like it was being stabbed with daggers and shredded apart slowly. Sweat poured down my face and body, leaving me feeling sticky and wet. Too wet.

Someone's hand pressed onto my thigh, and there were gasps of shock followed immediately by sighs of relief though I had no idea why.

"Her cycle," I heard Lia announce. "Is she not on a tonic?"

No one answered, but that wasn't surprising. How would they have known? My caregivers had placed me on a contraceptive tonic when I was seventeen years old, after learning of my exploits with Logan. That meant I hadn't had my cycle since then either. As soon as I got to the palace, Imogen made sure I still took the tonic, but I hadn't been in Caelum for over a month now, and hadn't had a reason to keep up with it here.

"Fuck," Felix breathed, shame and panic coating his voice. "Imogen gave me a ton of different tonics to bring for her as a precaution. I'm sure the contraceptive was there, but once we got here, I completely forgot."

"You forgot?!" Evander yelled, and heavy footfalls descended as he was no doubt approaching my friend. "She's lying in a puddle of blood, too weak to fucking move and screaming in pain because you *forgot*. I swear to the Gods, Empathi—"

"Van, this isn't helping," Marce cut in. I said a silent prayer for her unintentionally saving my friend's life because I was positive Evander was just about to kill him.

"Why is she still in pain?" Evander growled. "Why aren't you healing her? You're a Medicus. That's what you do."

"Because her cycle isn't an injury. There's nothing for me to *heal*." Lia shot back. "She needs Sirona."

"Olivier—" Evander started, but Marce cut him off.

"No, Van, it needs to be you. You're the quickest."

The space around me grew quiet, making my nausea worse. Instead of keeping my attention on their quarrel, I had nothing else to focus on besides the pain. My stomach turned over and I twisted, vomiting onto the dirt as the pain of my cycle slammed into me repeatedly.

"We have her, Van. I swear," Marce said quietly, and I wasn't sure why he was fighting so hard to stay.

"Fine," he ground out. "But get her to her room right now, and the Empathi stays far from her."

The sound of him traversing echoed in the otherwise silent space, and only now was I becoming aware of what Evander had said before. I was lying in a puddle of blood—my blood. My cycle blood. In front of everyone. Fucking great.

"I'm not staying away from her," Felix warned in a tone that said he wasn't going to be backing down.

"I wasn't going to make you. Marce, go turn on the water in her tub," Lia said, giving orders to everyone around. "Felix, go gather a bunch of clean towels and sheets for her bed; she'll need them. Oli and Cal, I need you to help me carry her to the bath."

I groaned and cried as I was lifted from the ground, the pain worse with each step they took. The roaring in my ears drowned out their apologies as they tried to carry me as gently as possible to my bathing room. Olivier mumbled a lot in my ear as he held me, and I had the strong sense he felt guilty for pushing me so hard and not seeing how sick I was.

"Perfect. Now set her down carefully," Marce instructed. I was submerged in hot water that instantly lessened the pain of my cramps. I sighed and took the first deep breath I could as I sank into the water. "It feels amazing, doesn't it?" Marce asked, brushing the hair from my face with a cloth.

"Okay, thanks so much, you two; we have it from here," Lia said, dismissing Cal and Oli.

Together, Lia and Marce worked to strip me out of my clothes until I was completely naked in the bath. I gripped the tub's edge as another painful cramp came through, and Marce dug her fingers into my lower back, somehow lessening the pending aches.

"This reminds me, I need to take my tonic next week," Marce announced, and Lia swore under her breath.

"I was supposed to take mine last week. Shit. I better do that as soon as we're done here," she said, and Marce laughed.

"I have ten towels and three different sheets for her," Felix declared as he strode into the bathing room and dropped to my side. His hand brushed over my face, and I hummed at the comforting feel of his cool fingers on my clammy skin. "I'm so sorry, Ainsley. I completely fucked up."

"S'okay," I whispered, pressing my cheek into his hand, needing to feel that colder temperature.

"Get. Out," Evander demanded angrily as he arrived and saw my best friend going against his orders. Felix didn't move, keeping his hand against my face. "I won't tell you again."

"She wants me here," Felix tried, but Evander wasn't having it. He marched forward with a look of vengeance in his eyes. "You can threaten me all you want but I'm not leaving her alone with *you*."

The way Felix spat the word had Evander halting halfway to us. There was more Felix wasn't saying, and by the way Evander cocked his head in interest, told me he knew it too. My friend looked down at me with concern etched into his features.

I wasn't sure if it was worry for my health or for the wrath he was undoubtedly about to incur.

"Ainsley told me what happened to her father and why King Harbin wanted him dead," Felix stated, directing his attention back to the king in the room. Evander's face hardened and a muscle in his jaw ticked.

"Your point..." Evander replied angrily, the words squeezing between his clenched teeth. We all knew what Felix was getting at.

Like my father, I was chosen as the heir to a kingdom even though I wasn't the sovereign ruler's direct bloodline. My father was nearly killed because of it, and Felix was rightfully worried that I would suffer the same fate at the hands of a different king. I knew I wouldn't, though. Evander was far too happy at the news of me being the Heir to Tenebrae.

"My point is: your bloodline wasn't chosen to continue the line of rulers," Felix argued. "How do I know you won't kill her so you can open that possibility up for your future children? How do I know—"

I moaned in agony as another wave of pain broke through the surface. I could barely make out Felix's soft whispers of comfort as I gripped the side of the tub and screwed my eyes shut. Evander mumbled something about *not having time for this shit*, and then a swooshing sound filled the space three times in a row. Suddenly, it was Evander's fingers on my skin, brushing back my hair from my face. Did he just traverse Felix out of the room and leave him somewhere?

"Felix...?" I croaked.

"Is in a timeout for continuously ignoring an order from the ruler of this kingdom," Evander answered calmly as he backed away, only to return a moment later to press a cold cloth to my face. I sighed in relief at how good it felt. The cold kept my nausea at bay while the heat from the tub soothed my cramps. "I've got you, love," he said.

My eyes fluttered open, and I was met with a soft smile and relieved eyes from Evander. Lia and Marce were now standing at the far end of the bathing room, talking to a woman I hadn't yet met. She was stunning with long dark hair that reached her waist and a deep tawny complexion. She wore a bright smile that complemented the warmth in her honey eyes, and I couldn't help but feel safe in her presence.

"Love, this is Sirona. She's going to help with the pain and ensure it doesn't happen again," Evander explained as she walked forward.

"Ainsley, it is so nice to finally meet you," Sirona said, kneeling next to Evander to meet me at eye level. I nodded, unable to speak as another round of pain surged through my body, and this time a scream came forth with it. "I'm going to need you to take this," she said as I worked on coming down from that last wave. "It will dull the cramps for now."

I eyed the vial skeptically, not keen on taking a tonic from someone I didn't know. My eyes automatically drifted to Evander and he nodded as if knowing I needed the reassurance that it was okay to trust this woman.

"You're a Medicus?" I asked as I tipped the open bottle into my mouth and swallowed the contents.

"Yes, but I am also an Incantis... well, I used to be one but that was long ago," Sirona answered. I glanced back to Evander who gave me a look that said *I'll tell you about her later*. "How long has it been since you've taken a contraceptive tonic?"

"About two months," I answered weakly, remembering the last dose I took was shortly after the night at the lake with Dashiell.

"And when was the last time you've missed a dose before now?"

"Never," I told her, breathing through my mouth as more nausea crept up. Evander seemed to know that was his cue because he instantly placed the cold cloth back on my face.

"I see," she mused, popping the lid off a vial and pouring the contents down my throat. "That's why this is so bad for you now. You haven't had a cycle in over four years, so your body is in overdrive. But don't worry; with a few of these vials and another contraceptive tonic, you should be as good as new tomorrow. However, I'd prefer you stay off your feet for at least two days to ensure the medicine works as it should."

"Done," Evander said, even though she hadn't been talking to him. Normally I would have told him off and spoken for myself, but I was so damn tired and just wanted the day to end. "Is there anything else she needs?"

"No," Sirona answered. "But we should get her out of the bath and to the bed because the medicine will make her sleepy. Lia, Marce, will you help her? I need to have a word with Evander before I go."

Lia and Marce had me dried and changed into fresh clothes in record time, even leaving several sets of new clothes out in case I bled again. According to them, one of the medications Sirona gave me would instantly stop the bleeding, but it seemed they'd rather be safe than sorry. I climbed into bed and beneath the warm blankets while Lia lay in the spot next to me. At my request, Marce headed downstairs to try and figure out where Evander had taken Felix.

"Marce and I will take turns staying with you until you're feeling back to normal," Lia said, and I nodded sleepily.

"Thank you for everything," I whispered before the tonic took hold and dragged me under.

When I woke, it wasn't Lia sitting next to me, but Evander, flipping through the very filthy book I had been reading with a smirk on his face. I groaned as I scrubbed a hand down my face and looked to the window to see the setting sun. I had slept the entire day thanks to whatever Sirona gave me.

"What are *you* doing here?" I demanded, rolling to my side to face him better.

"I'm stuck on babysitting duty until Lia is finished making your dinner."

"And Marce?"

"Probably heading back from the camp I stashed your friend at," he answered, arching a brow as he seemed to read a particularly interesting line. I was still pissed at him for what he did to Felix, but dammit if I didn't want to know what part he had just read.

"He's okay, at least?" I asked because scolding would do nothing; it never did.

"Your friend is fine, but if he continues to disobey me, I won't be able to say that again."

"You can't just—"

"I can, love," Evander interrupted, shutting the book and placing it back on the side table. "I understand he's your friend, but he's also a guest in *my* kingdom. If I give an order, I expect it to be followed whether he agrees with it or not. He has to abide by my rules; if he can't, he doesn't get to stay here. I've given him far more chances than anyone else, and that's only because of what he means to you."

I wanted to stick up for my friend, but I wasn't sure what to say because Evander was right. He and Felix hadn't gotten along, yet he still allowed him to be here. I had watched the two of them argue, and if it had been King Perceval in place of Evander, Felix would have been put to death long ago. I may have hated how he treated my friend, but he had a point. He was a king, and he needed to be respected as such.

I sighed, knowing I didn't have an argument. Sitting up, I leaned over Evander to retrieve my book and bring it to the nightstand on my side of the bed. I didn't need him to know exactly what I was reading, not to mention I still wanted to finish it.

"So Sirona is an Incantis?" I asked, changing the subject.

"She used to be but was exiled from Arcanus once her powers as a Medicus manifested. Incantis aren't supposed to possess magic—only the ability to speak to the Gods."

"And then she came here to Tenebrae?"

"Yes. A very, very long time ago. She serves our kingdom as a Medicus, but her knowledge in the way of the Incantis and their skills with spells and tonics has helped Tenebrae immensely," Evander answered. I wanted to ask about what exactly she's helped with, but he cut in before I could. "Enjoying your book?" He angled his chin toward my nightstand.

"Yup," I answered with zero shame.

"I bet you are." A devilish grin spread over his face. I rolled my eyes at his insinuation and shrugged.

"At least I don't have to pay for *my* entertainment," I said sweetly, and Evander's eyes lit up as his mouth dropped into an open smile. It had been a while since we played this little banter game, and I'd be lying if I said I didn't miss it. "But if you own the establishment, do you still have to pay?" I asked sarcastically.

"Being one of the owners has its perks, so I make sure to give them a massive tip."

"I'm sure you'd have to, given how small your cock is."

"Sorry, love, I think I must have misspoken. I meant that I make sure to give them *my* massive tip."

"I already claimed a small cock insult. You can't try to turn it around simply because you messed up the wording. Get your shit together, Van," I teased.

Evander's answering smile was bright and dazzling as a laugh broke through, and I couldn't help but return one of my own. Our insult games had always left me frustrated and angry, but today, this one felt lighthearted—fun, even.

"It seems you're right," he conceited.

"Does that mean I actually won?" I asked, and Evander shrugged.

"If you want to claim the win when I clearly gave it to you, then be my guest."

"You did not give me the win; I earned it."

"Do you think I'd really perform my best in a game where my opponent has been weakened? Where she's drugged up on medication, in pain, and not at her full potential? Come on, love, get your shit together," he replied. I couldn't tell if he was being honest or trying to maneuver me out of my win.

Shit.

He could have been lying, and this was a last-ditch effort to claim victory since he'd never lost against me. But also, why would I think I could beat him now when I was so clearly at a disadvantage? But maybe that was the point, and I *was* supposed to question myself. But if he *was* taking it easy on me, then I didn't truly win. My head spun at the questions rapid-firing off in my mind.

"Try not to hurt yourself thinking about it too much. I don't want another reason to have to hand you a victory again," he said, and I shot him a frustrated glare.

"Did you let me win? Just tell me!"

"I don't think I will," he said as he leaned close to me. "And that right there makes *me* the winner."

I grabbed my pillow and smacked him with it. I had let him get into my head again, which cost me just like it always did. Ugh, I hated the man. Evander ripped the pillow from my grasp and smacked me with it just as hard before shoving it back behind me.

I reached for it again.

"Try it, and I'll toss it out that open window, and you'll be left with no pillows," he promised, and I contemplated if the crime was worth the punishment.

Ultimately, I decided it wasn't and laid my head back down as I stared at the ceiling. I wasn't sure how long Evander had been sitting with me before I woke up, but I figured Lia would have returned by now and relieved him of his babysitting duty. Hopefully Felix would get back soon too, so I could find out precisely what happened when Evander traversed him away.

"You're the other owner, by the way," Evander said, slicing through my thoughts. "You and I share the tavern. I figured you should know that."

"Why?" I asked.

"Because you are the Heir to Tenebrae. Everything I own also belongs to you."

I was just getting used to sharing this house with him because of our mothers and now I was sharing a business with him. I didn't know the first thing about running an establishment, let alone a place like the tavern.

"I think you're better suited for that type of business," I said while giving him a pointed look, and he chuckled softly under his breath. I knew nothing about brothels, and given that Evander seemed to be a frequent customer, the business was in better hands with him. "Why do you do it, anyway?"

"Do what?" he asked, furrowing his brows.

"Pay for sex. You're a king. I'm sure people throw themselves at you all the time, so why not just pick one of them? Why pay for what you can obviously get for free?"

"Who says I'm paying for sex?" he said. I rolled my eyes at the bullshit coming out of his mouth.

"I saw you go into that room the first night at the tavern," I pointed out, and Evander grinned like he had been caught redheaded and was proud of it.

"Maybe I just enjoyed talking to her."

"The way her hands moved down your body makes me believe she had no desire to only *speak* with you."

Evander laughed and nodded like he knew exactly what I was referring to and how right I was. It was plain to see that she desired him, and I didn't miss how his grey eyes lit up when she approached. I'd wager a guess that she was his favorite to frequent when he stopped in. There was nothing wrong with that, but I just wanted him to admit it, and I didn't understand why he wouldn't. Was he trying to be as difficult as usual?

"There's nothing wrong with paying for good company or conversation, love," he argued, and I snorted.

"Yes, because a conversation was all she wanted to have with you." He couldn't have been serious.

Before I could comment further, Lia pushed into the room carrying a tray full of food for me. Evander hopped from the bed and strode for her, taking the tray from her hands so she could climb onto the mattress next to me. Once she was situated, he set the food before us, said goodnight, and headed for the exit.

"Oh, love," he called, and I glanced up from my food. "The second book is better." He jerked his chin toward the novel on my nightstand, winked, and left the room.

Lia cocked a brow for me to explain, but I shook my head, too tired to get into any conversation centered around Evander.

Over our shared meal, she explained that Felix and Marce were on their way home and should arrive within the hour. She said she gave Evander an earful about traversing people without their permission, and he promised not to do it again. I narrowed my eyes at her, to which she promptly amended her statement and said he promised not to do it *as often*. Well, that was better than nothing, I guess.

A gentle knock sounded at the door just as we finished eating, and Lia answered it to find a large platter of chocolate desserts and a note with the word *love* written across the front. She handed me the paper before switching out our dinner tray for the desserts Evander had left as I flipped it open.

Payment for your company earlier.
- Van
His Royal Majesty - King of Tenebrae - Master of Orgasms - Winner of All Games

I rolled my eyes as Lia grabbed the note from me, and she laughed as she read his self-appointed titles. Evander wasted no time adding that last one, and it only fueled my fire to get back at him for tricking me out of my win earlier.

"I don't understand the payment part," she admitted, and I took a large bite of a chocolate pie.

"We were discussing the workers at the tavern earlier and this is his idea of a joke. He's paying me in food for my *company*."

"Ooh, I get it," she said, laughing to herself. "I guess you're officially a tavern worker now."

"Except there's no way in hell I'd ever sleep with Evander, so I don't think I have the proper qualifications."

I thought about if I were in their position and had to sleep with the king. Evander was always so arrogant, so I doubt he'd be any different in the bedroom. He was probably controlling and rough, dominating, but in the most delicious ways. He'd be the type of person that wanted to have you bend to his will and every desire, but something told me he'd make sure you were screaming in pleasure before he ever thought about claiming his own.

"And that makes you the perfect tavern worker," Lia said, interrupting my intrusive fantasies.

"What?" I asked, not understanding what she meant.

"Van doesn't have sex with them," she said simply, picking at a chocolate-covered strawberry.

"Yes, he does," I argued. She looked up from her fruit with a confused expression. "Were you not paying attention when he took that blonde woman upstairs that first day you took me to the tavern?"

"Who, Giselle? They were probably conducting a report," she answered. Okay, what was going on, and what was I missing? She must have read the desperation in my eyes for an explanation because she tossed her dessert onto the plate so she could focus on our conversation. "The tavern is a brothel, yes, but Van also employs them all as spies for him. They report any happenings they overhear, and oftentimes, Van conducts meetings upstairs so no one bothers them. The brothel is a perfect cover as long as all its patrons believe he's there for its simple pleasures just like them," Lia explained.

My mouth dropped open in shock. It was a genius operation and one I hadn't expected, though I'm sure that was the point. I felt tension release from my shoulders, knowing that Evander wasn't sleeping with anyone from the tavern. Why the hell did I care?

I *didn't*.

22.

"Again!" Evander bellowed as I crafted a dagger from shadows and flung it at the target across the woods. "Faster!" he demanded, and I did it again and again until I was panting for breath and continuously throwing the weapons short of the target.

Evander lunged for me, and I barely had enough time to block his attack as I jumped back and took up position. We circled the small clearing in the woods, and he didn't give me time to catch my breath before striking again with his fist. I ducked out of the way, narrowly missing the blow.

"Verus," he demanded as he dropped to the ground and swept out his leg. I quickly jumped over his attack.

"Truth tellers," I answered. "They have the ability to detect lies." I threw my fist out the moment Evander stood. I missed as he spun gracefully, avoiding my attack and instead landing one against my back.

"And they hail from?" he prompted as I quickly righted myself and got out of the way before he could strike me again. He crafted a long sword in his hands, and I did the same, ready for the battle.

"Agnitio."

"And the other two Gifts of that kingdom?" he asked, slamming his sword against mine and making my hold shake from the force of his strength.

"Seers who can see the future and Magusiers who can detect bonds and Gifts within a person," I answered, pushing away from him and going on the offensive.

I struck repeatedly as the sounds of metal clinking filled the otherwise quiet location, but I couldn't land a single hit. Evander was too fast and skilled; no matter what I did, I couldn't defeat him. He let his sword disappear into shadows and pointed to the target across the clearing as I worked to catch my breath.

"Craft and throw," he commanded. I wiped the sweat from my brow and internally groaned at the task, but still did as instructed. "Venator."

"They possess stealth magic," I said, working my shadows as quickly as possible to craft a dagger. The darkness solidified in my hands, leaving me with a deadly blade. "The Oculi with preternatural vision, Sonor with preternatural hearing, and Venari with preternatural tracking abilities."

"Their role in Disparya?"

Evander was incredibly demanding regarding my studies, claiming he had years of incompetence to try and correct. He may not have been wrong, but he was still a prick for saying it. He never missed the opportunity to shove that fact in my face, but I couldn't deny how happy I was to learn. The more I studied and trained, the more ready I felt for my role as Heir to Tenebrae.

I learned that each kingdom essentially had a role in Disparya to keep her safe and prosperous. Caelum held elemental magic, which provided water and fire. Ministro's anatomical magic provided our land with healers and people who understood how the body worked. Agnitio's magic wielders were crucial in our justice system and could also predict any pending threats to our continent. However, those visions were subject to change as frequently as the direction of the wind. Our Shadow Shifters in Tenebrae were casters able to create any inanimate object Disparya would need.

"Venator are our fighters. With their Gifts, they're spies and assassins who take out anyone wishing to harm our people or land," I answered confidently as I crafted and threw five daggers in a row at my target... and missed every single one.

"Good. Now take a break because you should have been able to craft ten daggers in the time it took to make three."

I grunted in frustration, pissed off that my stamina was shit and I couldn't craft the objects as quickly as I wanted to. One morning during our game, Evander determined I was ready to start working on using my magic to mold items. So, for the past few weeks now, I had been doing just that. I was crafting objects perfectly from my shadows, and my illusions had been getting stronger, but I still didn't feel good enough. I wasn't where I wanted to be, though everyone swore I was miles ahead of schedule.

"You need to rest," Evander commented, and I rolled my eyes.

"I need to get better and faster," I said, striding across the deep line of trees to readjust the target.

"You will, but for now, we need to get home. I just got word from Marce that she and Felix may have found something about Inmuto," he said, holding up a piece of transfer paper. I watched as he scribbled on the parchment before the ink disappeared and delivered our message to our friends back at the house.

Evander and I were about half a day's hike from where he could safely traverse us back home. He had suggested we come out here so I could meet some of our soldiers and explore the camps. The task would be part of my role as heir once I was fully trained and ready to take on the responsibility. I wasn't thrilled at the idea of it being just him and I alone, but everyone else claimed to have things to do, though I had a feeling they just didn't want to get stuck with the two of us.

The entire trip had been spent bickering about the most pointless things. Evander had such a way of getting under my skin that it set my teeth on edge and made me want to rip out my hair. Yesterday, he had refused to let me bathe in peace, stating that he needed to watch the treeline for any potential threats. When I pointed out that the trees were opposite to my naked body as I hid it under the water, he refused to turn around and claimed the potential for *that* view was far better than bark and leaves. I had to use my shadows to keep myself covered, which I'm sure was the point. Everything was a Gods damn training exercise to him.

It was going to be a long hike back.

"We'll be heading to the palace in a few days," Evander announced as we packed up our small camp and began the trek home. "It's the monthly check-in meeting with our advisors and—"

"I get to sit in on it?" I asked hopefully. I wasn't allowed at the generals' meeting all those weeks ago, and I wanted a seat at the table.

"Nope," Evander answered, and I groaned. I hated that he kept me out after constantly pushing me to accept my role. "We've apprehended a few people this week, and they've been taken to the dungeons. While I'm with the advisors, your job is to interview them and assign a sentence based on the crime."

I looked at Evander with wide eyes. That wasn't a small task, and I wasn't sure why he was trusting me with it. I had no experience when it came to doling out punishments. I wouldn't even know how to go about doing it.

"Are you sure?" I asked. He had to know I was in over my head and was waiting for me to fall on my face.

"Yup."

Yup? That was all I was going to get? No elaboration, no pep talk, no sage advice? He could have at least explained what I should expect while down in the dungeons or how the process would go.

Evander kept his eyes straight ahead, and I bit my lip as I contemplated what he was about to throw me into. Our people were important to him, so I couldn't picture him letting me take the lead with something so significant without properly preparing me, though maybe he had a different outlook on criminals. I was stressing out about my upcoming task, and that was the last thing I wanted to be doing. I sighed and twisted to look at him as we walked through the woods. His eyes were still straight ahead as he paid me no mind.

"How should I go about everything?" I asked. Evander smiled as if he had been waiting for me to say those words. Of course, he had. He always pushed me to be more assertive and confident in my training, and this task was no different. I should have known.

"Well," he began, jumping in front of me and walking backward as he spoke. "The new arrivals have all committed petty crimes, so they were placed in the first-floor palace dungeons. You'll be given a report on each inmate that details what they did and a list of potential sentences."

"And I just pick one?" I asked, trying to follow along. Evander bobbed his head back and forth, letting me know it wasn't as easy as just that.

"Essentially, yes, but there is a bit more to it," he said. I nodded, giving him my full attention in hopes he'd elaborate and not make me ask more questions. "If someone is arrested for stealing bread from a market, we will give out a sentence we feel fits the crime. As rulers, it's also our job to ensure no one in our kingdom is going without basic needs like food, shelter, or clothing. During the interview, you will inquire as to what the inmate's motivation was so we can help. After you learn that information, you'll choose their sentence. The list will contain various jobs for you to choose from, such as working in the palace kitchens and cleaning up around the local villages. You'll also select the length of their sentence."

"If they stole something like food because they had none, why are we punishing them for trying to survive?"

"Because theft is a crime, love. The palace is open for anyone to come should they need a place to stay or a hot meal. Our citizens know this, but sometimes pride gets in the way of asking for help when you need it. We do our best to help our people with what they need, but a crime is still a crime, and they must be held accountable."

I could understand his point, and it annoyed me that this conversation was making me see him in a different light. Honestly, my opinions of him had been steadily changing over the weeks, but I still wasn't ready to admit that out loud, which was why it was frustrating when he forced me to acknowledge how kind and just he was. He was a good king who cared about his people, unlike what I had experienced in Caelum. I couldn't ever imagine Evander having people put to death simply because they disagreed with him, as Felix told me King Perceval would do. I hated to admit it, but I was in great hands with Evander.

It was evident that he had my best interest in mind regarding my role as heir, thanks to the constant studying and training he'd have me do. He wanted me to be as educated and prepared as possible to lead our people. But what had been developing between us was more than that. We had formed some sort of odd truce and understanding with one another. I would even go so far as to say it was a *friendship*. Even though he still was an ass seventy percent of the time, I found myself laughing with him more than visualizing his death at my hands. I looked forward to our games each day, happy to be on common ground for once.

Evander tapped my nose before turning back around and walking in a different direction.

Well, that pleasant thought about him lasted all of two seconds.

"You're going the wrong way," I sneered as I rubbed the tip of my sore nose.

"I promise you, I'm not," he said sarcastically, and I mocked him behind his back though I knew he heard. "Brat."

"Asshole," I replied, pushing past him and marching down the hill.

"That's not the right way," he called, but I threw my middle finger over my shoulder and kept on. It most certainly was the correct way. "You're going to get us lost."

"I am not. I distinctly remember all the fuzzy trees!" I said, pointing to the moss that grew along the bark. "That's how I know we're on the right path."

"Look around, love! They all are fuzzy trees!" he replied, blowing out a frustrated breath as he stretched his arms wide to survey the land surrounding us. I looked around, and sure enough, most of the trees had moss growing along the sides. Shit. "Now, will you stop being so stubborn and just listen for once?"

"Can you stop being an ass and—"

"Shhh."

"I will not—" I started, but Evander threw a hand over my mouth to silence me. His eyes went wide as he looked around, and a second later, my magic prickled against me, and my instincts raged. Something was wrong. I met Evander's stare as mine went wide, and he nodded, pulling me by the hand as we ran through the woods just as footsteps and shouts grew louder.

We sprinted as fast and silently as we could, not daring to steal a glance behind us as we raced through the trees.

"They went this way!" someone yelled, and I swallowed a lump of fear as I forced my legs to continue and not give up. I was suddenly reminded of being hunted back in Caelum. Men had chased me from the orchard through the woods before beating me so badly, I had almost died. I couldn't let that happen again. I wouldn't.

Evander led us through the trees as if he knew exactly where he was going. I didn't question him or try to argue. Instead, I clung to his hand like it offered the only safety I needed as I followed him through the thickets. The sun was beginning to set, and the deeper we moved into the woods, the darker it was.

"This way, love," he whispered as our pursuers continued to close the distance, though they didn't know it. Somehow, they still hadn't seen us. I knew it was sheer luck and not Evander shielding us with an illusion. We couldn't see our hunters to slip into their minds and seize control of what they saw.

"Can't you just traverse us out?" I asked, already breathless as we sprinted.

"No," he replied. "I don't know this area well enough, and if I try to traverse I risk us appearing right in front of them. It's safer to hide."

Dammit.

I could hear them gaining on us, and I knew we didn't have long before they caught up. If we were going to hide, we needed to do it soon. Evander threw a look over his shoulder, and I could see the worry carved into his features. He knew we were running out of time.

"Over there," he said, pointing.

We stopped before a large boulder with a small hole beneath, barely big enough for Evander to slip through. He shoved me down first, forcing me into the cramped space, and then tossed our packs in. Next, he shimmied his way down just as the voices grew louder; the men hot on our trail. He held up his hands, crafting small rocks to cover the opening so nothing but a sliver of light leaked into the underground space.

My heart pounded against his, the area so small we had no choice but to be pressed against one another. My fingers splayed against Evander's chest, and his hands held my waist firmly as we listened to the approaching men.

"I saw them come over here," a man said, and several footsteps gathered near where we were hidden. I squinted through the cracks in the rocks and saw nearly ten men, all dressed with weapons and brutal scars adorning their flesh. Warm hands cupped my face as Evander forced me to look at him. He shook his head slowly as he held my gaze, and I nodded, understanding he wanted me to keep my eyes on him and only him.

"Their footprints stop here," another man called, and Evander closed his eyes in frustration as his jaw ticked. Shit.

"Van," I whispered, barely loud enough for him to hear.

I began to panic, feeling the sting of the blade on my throat as if I were standing in that orchard again. I could feel my ribs breaking and skin splitting apart as I clawed and fought for my life. This couldn't be happening again. Evander's grip on me tightened, and he leaned close to whisper in my ear, sensing the suffocating fear paralyzing me.

"Breathe, love. I've got you," he said. My heart instantly slowed at his words, like my body knew it was the truth.

The sound of the men searching the area filled our small space. We were going to be found. I had no idea who these men were, but the fact that Evander chose not to stand and fight didn't give me any hope that they were friendly. The rocks he had crafted began to shift—someone was digging their way into our little hiding spot. My lips wobbled as my mind flashed through memories of being kicked and slapped, bound and gagged. Evander rubbed his thumbs over my cheeks as his gaze stayed firmly on mine.

The last of the rocks disappeared and though I wanted to turn and look, Evander refused to allow me to move an inch. I held my breath and waited for the man to announce he had found the people they were hunting, but instead, he threw the rock back down in a fury and stormed away. I scrunched my brows, and Evander tapped his temple, indicating he cast an illusion over us now that we were stationary and he could concentrate.

"Nothing," one of the men declared before cursing loudly.

"They had to have gone somewhere. We just aren't looking hard enough," another said.

"Perhaps they have a stone," a third man suggested, and murmurs broke out over that.

Evander's eyes darted across my face as he listened intently to the conversations happening above. I fisted my hands in his shirt, involuntarily pulling him even closer to me. I needed the comfort of knowing I wasn't alone. Evander allowed me to take what I required and pressed his forehead to mine, giving me even more of the contact I craved.

"Maybe," the first man said. "For now, let's go and report what we know. We'll keep hunting once night falls."

Grumbled conversations broke out as the men moved, and eventually, the only sounds in the woods were insects chirping and small animals shifting through the trees. Another twenty minutes passed but I didn't dare make a sound until Evander was sure it was safe. He released my cheeks as he peered out of the hole before nodding to himself.

"They're gone," he announced quietly, and I buried my face in his chest, unable to stop myself from letting the fear and panic take over. "It's okay, love," he said, pulling my face back to look at him again.

My hands trembled and my entire body shook as I looked up at him with terror-stricken eyes, unable to separate the past and present in my mind. It was like I was back in Caelum all over again. I didn't know how to calm my body and force myself to remember that I was in a small hole with Evander, even though I could clearly see that.

"What's your favorite thing about Felix?" Evander asked, and I blinked several times at the odd question.

"What?" I asked, and he repeated the question. I looked around as I thought about the answer and what that had to do with what was happening. "His sense of humor," I breathed.

"His jokes?" Evander asked, but I shook my head.

"No, those are terrible," I admitted. Evander chuckled softly under his breath, causing my lip to lift in the corner at the sound. "He can turn any situation into something humorous and make me laugh even when I don't want to."

"And what's your favorite thing about me?

"I don't have one," I answered flatly.

"Because there are so many options that you just can't choose?"

"No," I said, as my breathing continued to slow. "You're a pain in my ass, and there isn't anything I like about you."

"You really are shit at lying, love," he said, pressing his forehead to mine again.

I was no longer suffocating or drowning in the memories of being attacked in Caelum. I was finally back in the present, in a small, cramped space with Evander at my side.

"Better?" he asked as my grip on his shirt loosened, and I nodded. "Good." He flicked my nose up with the tip of his, and I groaned as I pushed him away.

"I hate that," I complained. He flashed his perfectly white teeth.

"I know."

Evander tossed our bags through the opening and climbed out of the space before helping me up. He interlaced our fingers together as he led me through the woods again, neither of us feeling safe enough to discuss what had happened yet.

We reached our destination in a third of the time it would have usually taken us. After our close call with those men, we decided we'd run the entire way. Evander and I were both dripping in sweat and beyond exhausted as we collapsed on the grass outside our house, the effort it took to traverse us draining most of the energy from him.

"Are you close to your baseline?" I asked. It was the first time I had seen him that weak, and I didn't like it.

"No, love. Just tired as fuck," he answered, and I felt the tension in my body release at his response.

I would have been furious if he dipped below his baseline and risked his magic not refilling just because he wanted to get us home quicker. Ever since I started using my Gift, I stayed as far above mine as possible. Truth be told, I wasn't sure how much magic I'd need to expel to reach it. Finding out how much I could use before hitting my baseline wasn't a risk I wanted to take any time soon.

"What the fuck happened to you two?" Cal demanded as he ran for us with Felix close behind. He draped Van's arm across his shoulder as he helped him into the house, and Felix scooped me up with a look of worry lining his features. They sat us on the couches in the study, and I closed my eyes to rest as Evander relayed the story of what had happened and who those men could have possibly been.

"Do you think Venator was behind it?" Olivier asked, and Evander shrugged.

"I'm not sure if they were or not. Tenebrae and Venator have always had a good relationship, but it doesn't change that those men were tracking us, and they knew what they were doing. I couldn't fucking shake them, Oli."

After an hour-long conversation, we still didn't know who had been hunting us or why, so we focused on what Felix and Marce had located... which turned out to be another dead end. They had discovered an ancient text that mentioned Inmuto, but when scholars in Agnitio translated it, it was said that the kingdom was nestled between what was now Caelum and Ministro. That seemed to be false as Evander was certain Inmuto resided north of Tenebrae.

"So, what's our next move?" Olivier asked, and Evander sighed as he hung his head, seeming lost for words.

I looked around the room, but no one else was coming up with any suggestions. If Venator was behind our attack in the woods, then that meant three out of the five Kings of Disparya were working with the ruler of Pravus. Our odds of winning the war as it stood weren't good on an average day, and I didn't like the idea of adding another powerful kingdom to the side of our enemy.

"Why don't we find out if Venator was truly involved? We'll hold a meeting," I suggested, and Evander shook his head.

"If they are responsible, then going to their kingdom to accuse them of that would be extremely dangerous. There's no way they would accept an invitation to come here, despite trying to keep up appearances," he explained. I bit my lip as I tried to come up with another solution.

"Then we'll hold the meeting on neutral ground, like Agnitio, and we'll disguise it so it doesn't seem like a meeting at all," I said, and Van leaned forward as he listened to my plan with intrigue. "We'll do what you did to Felix with the generals. We'll casually mention incidents without giving too much away and gauge the king's reactions. If he's being truthful and Venator had nothing to do with what happened to us, then it's the perfect opportunity to try and get him to join our side."

Van grinned, and his grey eyes shone with pride as I finished my pitch. I glanced around at everyone else as they watched me just as intently, and I couldn't help but feel solid and secure in myself and the role I was taking on. Months ago, I was scared and cowering in a room, doing what I was told to stay hidden, and now I was concocting plans to win a war. I had come a long way since then, but I knew I still had further to go.

"And what do you suppose we disguise the meeting as?" Evander asked. I knew he could have come up with an idea, but he wanted me to finish this plan on my own.

"We say it's a celebration for me. We say that the Gods have finally chosen an heir for Tenebrae, and for the first time, it's a woman. It would be suspicious to turn down an invitation to meet someone of my unique stature," I said before rising from the couch and pacing back and forth as I finished molding my idea. "We don't mention where I've been for the past twenty-one years. My name was never given during the kings' meeting in Caelum, so he should have no reason to know who I am. If the King of Venator gives any indication that he knows my identity, then there's our clear sign that he's been working with Perceval and Oberon," I finished, exhaling deeply as I faced the room.

"I don't know," Cal said skeptically.

"We need their aid. I honestly don't know if we can win this war without Venator's assistance. If they aren't working with Oberon to take over Disparya, we must do whatever we can to ensure they are on our side during this fight," Evander replied. However, it seemed like he was saying the words to himself rather than commenting on what Cal had voiced.

Everyone was silent as they looked to Van, waiting for his word on whether or not this was a plan we were going to carry out. After a moment, he stood and walked around the couch to his desk before rifling through the contents and pulling out a single piece of transfer paper.

"What are you doing? I asked curiously, wondering why he hadn't said anything about my damn good idea. Evander finished writing his note, and I stood on tiptoes as I watched the ink disappear to wherever its destination was.

"Telling Tallis he has a ball to plan."

of Conjoining wasn't being forced on anyone, but I had no doubt that we could come up with them.

I had made it clear to Van and Tallis that though they were free to advertise the ball and myself as they saw fit for our plans, I would not be entertaining any proposals seriously. I would do what I needed to uphold our ruse, but that was the extent of it.

In the weeks leading up to the ball, I trained tirelessly, honing my Gifts until they were damn near perfect. I could craft my daggers with a twirl of my fingers and faster than the blink of an eye. My illusions were coming easier though I still couldn't solidify them the way Van could, and it always pissed me off as that's how he won our stupid game every morning. Thanks to Felix, my Empathi Gift was the one I learned the quickest but didn't use often.

The more time that went on, the more confident I felt in my role in this kingdom, and the less Dashiell crossed my mind. He was still in my heart, and I wasn't sure he'd ever fully leave, but he didn't plague my nightmares anymore.

"Ready?" Evander asked as we stood in Agnitio, just outside the gates that led to the palace.

"As ready as I can be," I said.

They opened for us as we strode through.

The Kingdom of Agnitio was beautiful, covered in bright white stone buildings and sprawling hills of the deepest reds and oranges in the distance. Children played in the streets and everyone waved as we passed down the long road to the palace entrance, where Tallis was waiting with open arms.

"Welcome, friends," he said, hugging the six of us. Calidore drew the short straw and had to stay back to watch over Tenebrae in our absence. At first, he threw a fit about it, but then Evander promised he could sit on the throne while we were gone, and Cal's tune quickly changed.

"Have they arrived?" Evander whispered as he wrapped his arms around Tallis, and the king nodded. It looked like it was time to put on the show earlier than we had planned. We had hoped arriving a day before everyone else would give us an edge, but we should have accounted for King Arden having the same idea.

"Ainsley, this is Naideen," Tallis said, gesturing to a tall woman with jet-black hair. "She will be your maiden during your stay and will show you to your room so you may get ready. Prince Jahier and the other lords have been anxiously awaiting your arrival."

I dipped my head before my eyes slid to Evander. He gave a subtle nod of encouragement, and I headed off with Naideen as she led me through the palace. There were some similarities to the one in Caelum but mostly vast differences. There were more open windows that offered the sun to shine in a way that illuminated the entire space. It was grander, but felt more like a home than a display of wealth.

I entered the room Naideen had brought me to and found that it resembled my room at my house in Tenebrae. The bed and fireplace were in the same position, and the bathing room was along the same wall though it didn't have as big of a tub as mine contained.

"Ainsley?" Lia called, and I turned to find her holding several gowns as she entered the space. "I wasn't sure what we should go with for this trip, so I brought as many options as possible. I think you should wear this one today."

I studied the soft lavender gown she held, letting my fingers trail along the delicate fabric. It had been so long since I had dressed up. The cold weather of Tenebrae meant most of my days were spent in oversized sweaters or my black training suit. I began to miss the way the dark fabric hugged my body. It felt like a second skin, but one as strong as armor and as light as a feather. Unfortunately, there was no way I could wear it on this trip. Here in Agnito, the climate was like the dead of summer rather than nearly winter.

"The purple it is," I told her, and she smiled as she grabbed my hand and led me to the bathing room to get ready.

An hour later, I was changed into the dress she had picked, and my hair traveled down my back in gentle waves. Lia added light rouge to my cheeks and lips and a thin line of kohl to my lids, making me look put together but still like myself. The lavender material of the dress scraped across the floor just barely as I walked, and I was thankful Lia had suggested something so thin and lightweight as the heat was already getting to me after having acclimated to Tenebrae's colder climate.

"Lost?" a familiar satin voice called. I rolled my eyes as I turned to find Evander standing directly behind me. He had also changed into something more weather appropriate, and I couldn't help but notice how the thin material of his shirt showed off the muscles hidden beneath.

"Aren't you supposed to be seducing some poor unsuspecting victim?" I snarked back.

We agreed that it would make sense for him to advertise himself as someone looking for a partner as well. The more people we could get to attend this event, the more chance we had at figuring out who might be working with Oberon and getting people to join our side.

"I'm far more interested in seducing you."

"You're only saying that because I look pretty right now," I pointed out, swaying my dress side to side playfully.

"No, you don't." My face fell.

"Ouch. Your seduction skills need polishing. You may want to work on that before the big party," I bit out, pushing through the doors to the gardens before he could stop me.

Dozens of eyes fell upon me as I walked, and I suddenly felt self-conscious. Did I really look that bad? Evander appeared beside me, but I paid him no mind.

"That's not what I meant," he said, barely moving his mouth to ensure no one would overhear.

"Well, that's what you said," I replied coldly, just as a man with pale green eyes approached.

He was tall *and* handsome, his light eyes complimenting his darker skin in a way that captivated me whole. He looked muscular and strong, but there was also a gentleness about him that made me feel secure. His features weren't harsh or angry; they were soft and held an air of excitement and wonder within.

"Am I interrupting?" the man asked. There was something familiar about his voice, but I couldn't place it.

"Of course not, Prince Jahier," Evander said, and my eyes widened in recognition. He had been the kind voice I had overheard that day the kings had their meeting in Caelum. "May I introduce the Heir to Tenebrae, Princess Ainsley."

Prince Jahier smiled wide as he bowed, and I returned the gesture, unable to hide the grin from my face either. I had never met this man before, but everything I had gathered from that small meeting told me he was a kind soul... and his father was a dickhead.

"It's so nice to meet you, Your—"

"Just Ainsley," I said, cutting him off.

"Ainsley," he corrected. "And please, just call me Jahier. We can forgo the boring titles."

"Deal," I said, holding out my hand. He took it and we shook, solidifying our agreement.

We stared at each other for a few moments, neither of us able to come up with what to say. Jahier looked to Evander with an unspoken question, and I followed suit. The moment I turned toward the king, his eyes were on me, and there was an emotion on his face I didn't understand. I wanted to ask what was happening in his mind, but we didn't have time for that. We came on a mission and needed to stick to the plan. I widened my eyes exaggeratedly as I jerked my head in Jahier's direction, hoping Evander could tell what I wanted. He cleared his throat and then excused himself, finally grasping that he needed to leave the two of us alone.

Jahier held out his arm for me and I took it as we strolled through the gardens while everyone stared. I was instantly reminded of my first day in Caelum and how everyone had watched Dashiell and me as we walked through the grounds, though this was night and day to that situation. Still, I didn't like having an audience then, and I definitely didn't now.

"They're all jealous that I snagged you first," Jahier said as I made eye contact with our onlookers.

"How can you tell?"

"Because we were discussing who would get to be the first to talk to you, and while they bickered about it I took my chance," he explained, and I enjoyed how much he didn't seem bothered by it.

"I do love someone who takes control," I declared. Jahier flashed me a dazzling smile that would have swept anyone off their feet. So why didn't it do that for me? Why was I still thinking about the look on Evander's face and how I was desperate to make sure he was okay?

Thirty minutes later, we were still laughing and enjoying each other's company as we continued to stroll the perimeter of the gardens. He was easy to talk to, and I genuinely enjoyed his presence though I knew I should be mingling with the other lords to gather intel.

"Can I tell you a secret?" he asked, and I nodded.

Jahier tightened his hold on my arm as he led us away from prying eyes and around a large hedge trimmed to resemble an owl. He looked left and right, checking to make sure no one had followed or was still watching us. I began to worry about whatever he was about to tell me. He seemed nice enough, but we had only just met, and he was already acting odd.

"I like you, Ainsley. I find you intriguing and exciting," he said nervously, and there was shining hope in his green eyes. Oh shit. Was he about to propose? I tried to come up with the best way to turn this man down after knowing him for less than an hour. "I think you're truly great, but I'm not going to propose to you."

"Oh, thank the Gods," I said, breathing a sigh of relief.

"Ouch?" Jahier replied, seeming a bit thrown off and offended by my response. "I didn't think I was *that* bad. I mean, maybe a little awkward initially, but I thought I recovered quite nicely."

I couldn't help but laugh at him, and he joined in, though I was pretty sure he was doing it just to be polite and cover up the awkwardness of the situation.

"No," I said through my quiet chuckles. "I think you're amazing too, but I don't want you to propose. Hell, I don't want anyone to," I admitted. I knew it went against the plan Evander and I concocted, but I had a deep feeling that I could trust Jahier. He was the Heir to Venator, so perhaps if I was in his good graces, he could convince his father to work with us.

"Really?" he asked, and I nodded vehemently.

"It's just what's expected of me," I told him. It wasn't a lie. Sooner or later, I would have to marry, but I hoped Evander would at least let me choose the person rather than try to convince me to be with someone he thought would be a good fit for Tenebrae. It wouldn't be a battle he'd win by any means, but it was still one I didn't want to have.

"I can understand that," Jahier said. "Once my father heard about the ball and what you are capable of with having three Gifts, he said I didn't have a choice. I was supposed to lay my charm on thick to get you to choose me."

"Your father seems like a jerk," I said, forgetting that I couldn't actually say those things aloud even if I thought them. Jahier laughed, and I felt a small amount of relief that maybe I wasn't screwing everything up.

"He is, but how did I do? Were you thoroughly seduced?"

"I think you've ruined all other men for me."

"That's what I like to hear," he said, continuing our banter.

"How about we stick together this weekend? Your father will be pleased to think you've won over a princess, and I don't have to fake laugh at people I find intolerable," I suggested, holding out a hand to make another deal.

"Count me in," Jahier responded, shaking hard and solidifying our plan.

We spent the rest of the day together, refusing to give anyone else a chance to speak to me. I caught Evander's eye a few times and gave him a look that beckoned him over so we could talk, but he wouldn't come. Instead, he focused on flirting incessantly with anything that walked on two legs. I was thoroughly annoyed, but that was only because he was ignoring me. It had absolutely nothing to do with him flirting. I glared at Lia and then gave a pointed look toward Evander. She shook her head and shrugged, not understanding what his issue was either. What the hell?

When I was tucked in bed and ready for sleep, my mind was starting up again, replaying how Evander looked as I met Jahier. I wouldn't be able to focus tomorrow unless I got some answers, and since he was keeping his distance from me, I would have to go to him.

I knocked on his door once, twice, three times. No answer. Footsteps sounded beyond the room, so unless Evander had lost his hearing, he was well aware someone had been knocking. I went for my fists, banging hard against the door until Evander yanked it open, his features full of rage and then morphing to confusion as he witnessed me standing in my night clothes and wearing a pissed-off expression.

"What are you doing here?" he asked. My eyes drifted to his body, and I found him wearing nothing but a pair of soft pants to sleep in, with the drawstring dangling loosely in the front. His muscled chest was perfectly carved, and his shadow tattoos were displayed, though they weren't moving like I knew they could. His hair was in its usual messy but perfect state and slightly damp, as if he'd just bathed. He was perfection embodied, and I struggled to regain control of my anger as I returned my stare to his face.

"Well, you've ignored me every chance you could, so I figured I'd come to you so you couldn't run away," I announced, shoving past him and pushing the door wider to reveal a beautiful petite woman on the other side.

She wore a deep blue gown showing her full curves and warm brown eyes. Her hair was short and styled so that one side hung longer than the other. She was gorgeous... And she was in his room.

"Oh Gods, I'm sorry," I said, backing away as I realized I had interrupted whatever was about to transpire between them. "I didn't mean... I'm just going to go," I said, stumbling over my words as I hurried out of the room, but before

I could make it more than two steps, Evander caught me by the wrist and pulled me back inside.

I did not sign up to watch him have sex with someone, so that better not have been what he was going to try and convince me to do. I looked back and forth between them as my face heated with embarrassment. I couldn't believe I just barged in and cockblocked him. That was a total Felix move.

However, I wasn't exactly upset by it either. What the hell was wrong with me?!

"Ainsley," Evander said slowly like I was a child that needed handholding. "This is Elenora, Tallis' niece." He gestured to the woman who waved awkwardly from her spot across the room. "She's been trying to track down information about the men we encountered in the woods."

"I was just telling Evander that there have been whispers of an elite tracking unit from Venator making its way through Disparya, so that may be who you encountered," she explained.

I offered a tight smile of thanks as I tried to gauge the situation. Elenora was gathering information, but that still didn't mean she and Van weren't about to hop into bed together. Maybe they exchange information for sexual favors. I didn't know how any of this secret mission stuff worked. If he was willing to flirt with everyone to get answers, maybe he was willing to sleep with them too.

"The library is also a great place to do any research you may want to conduct. We have several works regarding Inmuto, so maybe you could find something to aid you on your journey of discovering it," she offered. I gave a thumbs up like an idiot because I still couldn't form the words to ask her if she was planning on fucking the king standing next to me. Okay, it was definitely time for me to leave them to it. I waved a hand awkwardly as I backed toward the door, still not saying a damn word.

"Stay," Evander whispered, his hand clasping around mine as he turned to thank Elenora for her help. She dismissed herself and promised to follow up if she learned anything else.

I pulled my hand from Evander's as I roamed aimlessly around his room, noting how much bigger it was than mine. Everything was the same, except on a larger scale and the exact opposite layout of mine. I ran my fingers along the soft fur of his bed, biting my lip as I sipped on the tension the air was filled with.

"You didn't interrupt anything," Van finally said, and I nodded as if it wasn't a big deal.

"It's fine if I did," I said before realizing my mistake. "I mean, it's not fine that I interrupted, but it's fine that you had something for me to interrupt." The words stumbled out of my mouth, not making any sense, and I blew out a frustrated breath. "You know what I'm trying to say. It's fine if you have someone."

"Noted," he replied, and I didn't like how that sounded. "And you know it's fine if you like Jahier. It's okay to move on from Dashiell."

"I know," I said quietly, and for the first time, the mention of me moving on from the prince didn't hurt quite as much. "Were you okay earlier?" I asked, remembering why I had come to his room in the first place. Evander regarded me for a minute before nodding and offering a smile that didn't reach his eyes.

"Are you excited about tomorrow?"

"I'm just ready to go home," I said honestly, suddenly wishing we were arguing like usual in the library rather than stuck here playing a part neither of us wanted to for the good of our kingdom.

"So am I."

"Can we play a game tomorrow?" I asked, wanting to bring some sense of normalcy to our situation. Evander smiled wickedly, and I bit my lip in response. His eyes immediately dropped to the action.

"What do you have in mind, love?"

24.

A knock sounded at my door, and I glanced from my vanity to find Felix striding in, all dressed up and handsome as hell. His clothes were tailored to fit his toned body, which had gotten even more muscular since we arrived in Tenebrae, thanks to Olivier's impossibly difficult training sessions. His silver hair was tied into a bun atop his head, a style Calidore always wore. Something told me Lia was behind it.

"Are you escorting me tonight?" I asked playfully, and he stuck out his bottom lip in a pout.

"I promised Lia I'd be her date since I thought you were going with Jahier. The two of you seemed to be inseparable these past two days."

It was true, of course. The deal Jahier and I had made to stick by each other's side all weekend had worked out perfectly. No one dared to get close to me for fear of infuriating the prince and King of Venator, and I much enjoyed Jahier's company, so it wasn't terrible. The only annoying part of the situation was the vicious looks I received from King Arden's closest advisor, Mishal. Whenever I made eye contact with him, his lip would peel in disgust. I had to fight my magic on more than one occasion not to lash out at him.

"He was going to, but his father requested his presence earlier, so I'll be walking downstairs by myself," I said, fixing my hair as Felix met my gaze in the mirror.

"I'll take you both. I don't think Lia would mind, and I don't have any objections to having two beautiful women on my arm."

I smiled at my friend's reflection before putting the final touches on my bold look. I needed to make a statement about exactly who I was, so no one ever forgot my name and the power I held.

"I appreciate the offer, but I'm actually looking forward to entering on my own. It may sound stupid, but it feels like I'm taking back my independence and showing the world that I'm okay on my own. Or at least, just showing *me* that," I told him. Felix smiled proudly before squeezing my shoulders. "But, if you want to assist me, you can help decide which gown I should wear. I'm torn between those two." I gestured over my shoulder to the stunning dresses that hung on the wall.

"The one on the right," Felix said without hesitation. I twisted in my chair as I cocked my head and studied the dress he selected. If I wanted to have all of my potential allies wrapped around my finger, that was the gown that would do it. "Oh, and here," Felix added, reaching into his jacket pocket. "Evander asked me to give this to you."

I smiled wide as my fingers enclosed around the metal, and I couldn't help the rush of adrenaline I felt as I held it in my hands. The look was coming together, and this last item completed it. I glanced at my gown as my friend began to retreat from the room.

"Felix?" I asked, and he stopped his advance, twisting around to face me again. "Do you think it'll bring them to their knees?" I jerked my chin toward the gown and waved the object in my hand.

A slow, sly grin crept up his face.

"Yes," he said, and I nodded, satisfied. "And I know exactly which man will be the first to fall."

I gripped the railing as I reached the top of the stairs. As I began my descent, the crowded ballroom grew deathly silent, all eyes focused solely on me. I held my posture straight and my chin high as I glided down the stairs as effortlessly as floating, while simultaneously praying to the Gods I didn't trip. The midnight black dress I wore hugged my chest and hips as it flowed to the floor. The sides were strategically cut out to show off the most amount of skin, and the dress was completely backless. There was a long slit up the front that revealed my bare leg all the way to my upper thigh every time I took a step.

I kept my hair down and in long curls with one side pinned back with a matching comb in honor of Imogen, as it was always the style she loved to do for me. My lids were lined with thick kohl and winged out to the side, and I painted my lips blood red. Though I adored my outfit, my favorite part was the black diamond diadem atop my head—the present Evander had asked Felix to deliver to me.

I let my shadows seep out behind me as I walked, making it look like I had a train of billowing darkness in my wake. I wanted everyone in the room to see what the Heir to Tenebrae looked like. I wasn't a weak and pathetic pawn for them to use, nor was I a power piece for them to try and gain to their side with marriage. I made my own decisions and the reason we gathered tonight proved that. It was my idea—my plan, that set this all in motion, and I wasn't going to sit back as a traitorous king plotted to take away what belonged to me.

I reached the halfway point when my gaze immediately locked on Evander's. His chest stopped moving as he saw me, and his fingers tightened around the glass he was holding. Was he angry, or was he trying to hold himself back? Last night, I told him I wanted to choose the game and keep it as a surprise until this evening. We were going to see who would break who first. By the hunger now in his darkened stare, I could tell he was up for the challenge.

The room was still silent as I reached the bottom of the stairs where Jahier was waiting for me with a smile. The music struck up again, thanks to someone clapping in demand for it across the room. Jahier reached for my hand and spun me around to get a better look at me.

"You look lovely," he said, flashing a bright smile. "I'm kind of tempted to take back what I said about the whole marriage proposal situation."

"Awww, you're too late. I've already accepted five offers," I teased, and he clicked his tongue in disappointment.

"Point them out, and I'll take care of them. I'll make it quick and painless."

"What if I want it to hurt?"

Jahier tilted his head as he observed me and the seductive smile on my face. He narrowed his eyes as they sparkled with intrigue and questions. I bit my lip, and his gaze fell on my mouth. It didn't entice me the way it had when Evander had done it.

"Something tells me you mean that," he responded. I shrugged before removing a glass of wine from a serving tray and lifting it high in cheers before draining it. "Okay, now I'm *really* reconsidering what I said about a proposal." I laughed as he wound his arm around my waist to drive home the point.

"You forget that I don't want a proposal either."

"I think I can change your mind," Jahier said confidently.

"I don't know about that. I've heard that I'm pretty stubborn."

"I like a challenge," he whispered as he pulled me into him, his eyes dropping to my red lips again.

My heart skipped a beat as I prepared myself for what Jahier was about to do. His pale green eyes searched my face for any sign of hesitation, but rather than stop him, I just stood there as he leaned in close and pressed his lips to mine.

The kiss was soft and gentle, a hesitant first time, and though my lips moved against his like we had done this before, it didn't feel right. It was perfectly fine, but it wasn't what I wanted to be doing. He wasn't who I wanted to kiss. Jahier pulled back, and my fingers instantly pressed to my lips as I felt them tingle from the embrace.

"And now I'm definitely going to propose to you," he breathed. I smiled as I shook my head.

"I'll say no," I warned.

"Then I won't stop trying to charm my way into your heart until I get a yes," he vowed. I rolled my eyes as I pushed him playfully.

What was wrong with me? Jahier was handsome and thoughtful, and kind. He made me laugh and was fun to be around. He wasn't intimated by my title or my

Gifts, and he listened—really listened—whenever I spoke. He was interested in being my friend first, so why was I turning him down? An alliance with him could help keep Tenebrae and the rest of Disparya from harm's way, not to mention my instincts were letting me know that he was a good man, and I trusted that.

It had been months since I showed up in Tenebrae, and though it may not have seemed like a long time, so much had happened that it made it feel far longer. It wasn't my fear of marriage or the Entwining Ceremony that got in the way. I would sooner die than willingly give my magic to anyone ever again. I'm pretty sure Van would lock me in Tenebrae's dungeons if I so much as considered it, so that wasn't an issue. Though I still loved Dashiell, there were no feelings that prevented me from moving forward.

A month ago, I wouldn't have been able to grasp the concept of marrying anyone after what I'd gone through, but as more time passed, the idea became easier to digest. The more I grew comfortable in my role as an heir, the more I accepted what would be expected of me. Even though I wasn't a queen, and Van was the leader of our kingdom, I was still one of its rulers and would sacrifice what I needed to ensure the safety and stability of our people. If that included marrying for an alliance, then so be it, but I would have the final say on who that person would be.

"Ainsley," Evander said, suddenly appearing beside us. I jumped back, startled like I had been caught doing something wrong. My fingers automatically reached for my lips again, as if he could see what happened between Jahier and me just by looking at them. The hard press of his jaw and his steel gaze as he stared at me let me know he was already well aware. "This is King Arden," he continued, and my eyes flickered to the man standing beside him.

He looked so much like his son that I had to do a double-take. They shared the same build, height, dark skin, and pale green eyes; the only difference was where Jahier wore a permanent smile, his father's lips were set in a hard line. There was no light and laughter in King Arden's eyes that which was so present in his son's.

"Your Majesty," I said, dipping my head, and I could sense Evander's unease at the gesture. Why didn't he want me bowing? I hated that this trip kept us from one another to the point that I couldn't just ask him what was going on in his mind.

King Arden didn't return the bow as his gaze dragged over my body appraisingly, and I internally cringed at the blatant disrespect he was giving me. He looked at me like I was some potential possession he was less than pleased with.

"Can I help you with something?" I asked harshly, as his stare lingered on my body rather than my face.

"Excuse me?" he sneered, clearly picking up on the hostility I was gladly serving. Jahier stiffened beside me, and I watched as King Arden's gaze finally reached my eyes. I straightened my posture and raised my chin to show I would not be backing down from him.

"For someone with excellent eyesight, you seem to be having difficulty locating my face. We have a talented Medicus on staff, and I'd be happy to send her your way if you wanted someone to take a look at that for you. We can't be too careful with our Gifts, now can we?" I said, keeping my voice smooth and polite.

King Arden's green eyes grew colder, and his jaw ticked with rage as he glowered at me. I half expected Evander to cut in and say something to recover the situation, but he just stood there quiet and stoic. The only thing that gave away what he was feeling was the slight twitch at the corner of his lips as he fought to keep the smile from his face.

"How dare you?" the king's advisor—Mishal—began, but King Arden held his hand to his advisor's chest, signaling him to silence his thoughts. I hadn't seen Mishal approach, so his voice startled me, knocking my gaze from the king to him. His lip was pulled back in a snarl as he bared his teeth at me, ready to verbally rip me to shreds should his king allow it.

"Isn't she fun?" Evander asked, breaking the silence as he placed a hand against my lower back. The move wasn't meant to comfort but to show me I had his support. That we were a team, and he had my back through this.

"Quite," Jahier added with a light chuckle as if trying desperately to diffuse the awkward situation. "I'm rather very fond of everything she is." I smiled gratefully at the prince.

"Prince Jahier," someone shouted, and we all turned to find a group of eager men striding toward us.

They looked at me hungrily, and I groaned, knowing precisely why. I had a part to play, but I was enjoying my time with Jahier far too much for it to be over so soon and have to spend my evening faking flirtations and batting my lashes.

"We've all determined that you've had enough time with her Highness and should make room for others," another man said playfully, though completely serious.

Jahier placed a hand over his chest and bowed at the men. When he straightened, his eyes were bright as he reached for my hand, pulling me away from Evander and closer to him. The prince wrapped an arm around my waist as he stared at me while speaking to the men.

"My apologies. I didn't mean to monopolize all of Ainsley's time," he said, not sounding the least bit sorry. "But I find myself unable to share her." Jahier gave me a flirtatious wink, and I was happy he was willing to help me delay the inevitable a bit longer.

"Nonsense," King Arden cut in. "Lords, have your time with the princess. My son is needed elsewhere for a while."

I swallowed, knowing that my little stunt caused the king's sudden desire to keep Jahier away from me. It was my own fault for snapping the way I did, and now I would have to deal with the consequences. I offered the prince a warm smile, but before I could step out of his hold, he pulled me into him and dipped his head to kiss me again, not caring one bit who was watching.

"I had to steal one more," he said against my mouth before withdrawing.

I touched my lips again as I flushed, stepping away and glancing around at our audience. A few of the men shifted uncomfortably as they cleared their throats, unsure how to carry on now that it seemed the prince had made his intentions with me clear. But something told me it wouldn't be enough to stop the others from trying to make their claims, too.

Evander's hand found mine, and he guided me to his side once more. Jahier's gaze dropped to the point of contact, and his brows scrunched together momentarily as if some thought fluttered through his mind. His eyes slid back and forth between us before he finally settled them firmly on Evander.

"I'd like to speak with you later, Your Majesty," Jahier said, a question in his eyes and hopefulness coating his voice. My breathing hitched as I thought about what the conversation might entail and hoped that Jahier had taken my lack of desire for a proposal seriously. I wasn't playing a game of hard-to-get—not with him, at least.

Evander's body shifted just barely, his hand splaying wider on my back like he was using me for support. I looked up at him to find his eyes locked on Jahier, his face falling into an unreadable mask that only I knew meant he was trying to contain whatever emotion he was struggling against. What we had been working toward was potentially in our grasp, and I wondered if that's what he was sensing too.

"Of course," Evander replied cooly, dipping his head to the prince. "Come and find me when you've finished."

Jahier nodded before disappearing into the crowd with his father. Mishal lingered longer than necessary, looking furious. I arched a brow in a challenge, but rather than spit any insults, he gave one last look of disgust before hurrying after his king. I got the impression he was going to do whatever he could to ensure Jahier stayed busy for the rest of the night.

"I need to steal the princess away for a quick word, and then she's all yours," Evander announced, and the waiting crowd of eager men mumbled their acknowledgments to the king.

Van's hold slid from my back to my hand as he pulled me through the packed room. Several people waved or greeted us as we passed, but Van paid them no mind, leading me to the far end of the ballroom and through a small door designed to look like one of the many murals painted across the walls.

He shut us in the small dark space, the only light coming in from the lattice-work along the hidden door, giving me a clear view of the party on the other side. I felt Evander's presence grow closer and I spun to find him a foot away, observing me intently.

"Arden hasn't given any indication that he's been working with Oberon," he announced after a minute or two of silence. It felt like the words were rushed and unplanned, as if it wasn't what he originally wanted to say.

"I don't think Jahier knows anything. We've had conversations about Venator, and nothing he's said has given me any reason to believe he's aware that his father may be committing treason."

Evander crossed his arms as he inhaled deeply, nodding to himself. I rested my back against the wall, looking over my shoulder as I watched everyone drink and converse while soothing music played in the background. I rolled my neck as I prepared myself for the sweet-talking I would have to do the moment we went back out there.

"I think I can convince Jahier to hear us out," I said, watching a few of the men who had approached earlier peer over the crowds of heads as if searching for me within the sea of people. Evander huffed an amused breath, and I twisted to face him, his eyes on his feet as he stood there. "Is something funny?" I asked. He shook his head.

"I'm just impressed by how quickly you've gotten him to fall for you," he answered, picking his head up. "You know he wants to make you his, right? He'll convey his intentions to marry you when we speak later."

I had hoped Jahier's comments earlier were just banter, but I knew Evander's assumption had merit. Though I enjoyed my past two days with the prince, I didn't want to establish a future that was more than friendship.

"Wasn't that the whole point of parading me around like a prize mare? We wanted people to come based on my potential as their bride, and that's exactly what happened. And the man who wants it most is the one who could offer the assistance in this war that we need," I replied.

"So, will you say yes?"

I chewed on my cheek as I pondered Evander's question. Jahier could offer everything we needed, so wouldn't I be a fool if I didn't entertain the idea of marrying him?

"If we decide that's what is best for Tenebrae, then yes. I'll do whatever I have to," I told him, taking a deep and steadying breath. "He seems like a good man. And he's nice."

"And what about what's best for *you*?" Evander asked, and my brows pinched at the question. Would marrying Jahier be what was best for me? I knew I would never let myself love again, so perhaps being with someone I could see as a friend wouldn't be so bad.

I turned away, looking back at the crowd as the music began to change into something that reminded me of what was always played at the tavern. The melody was fierce and passionate, like a hunter that captivated its prey, making them bend to their will before it devoured them. Couples pressed together, swaying their hips and rolling their bodies, feeling the energy the music was feeding them. Desire and longing laced every moment as they danced, lost to the sounds around them.

"He laughs at your jokes," Evander said, his body so close I could feel his breath on my skin.

"He finds me funny," I offered, focusing on the dancers and not on the heat radiating from the man behind me.

"You're not," he said. "Your jokes are shit, and you're the only one who laughs at them."

"You're an asshole."

"Yes, but that doesn't change the fact that you're not funny," Evander breathed as he grabbed my wrist and spun me around to face him. His cedar and snow scent enveloped me in the small space, and my head swam with dizziness at his proximity. "He also said you looked lovely."

"So it's a problem that he finds me attractive?" I argued, though there was none of the usual bite in my tone I was trying for.

"You're not *lovely* or even *pretty*," Evander claimed, and I opened my mouth at his insult, ready to spew venom right back.

But before I could, he rested his hands on either side of my head, forcing my back to press against the latticework as he leaned close. My mouth went dry as his dark frame caged me in and his chest pressed to mine. His striking grey eyes captured me, refusing to relinquish their hold as he spoke with unwavering certainty.

"You are devastatingly breathtaking, Ainsley," he whispered, and I blinked several times at his words. "Anything less is an insult. Don't settle for anyone who doesn't value your worth."

I swallowed the thick lump in my throat as his gaze held mine, unsure how to respond. I clenched my fingers and was met with soft fabric rather than the feel of my own skin. Apparently, I had fisted my hands in his shirt as he spoke, my body desperate to bring him closer.

"You shouldn't be with someone *nice*. You deserve someone who feeds your passion and stokes the sparks of your flame. Someone who challenges you and won't ever let your fire burn out. *Nice* is boring," Evander said, and the caress of his breath on my skin had my legs trembling beneath me. My chest swelled at each word as I struggled to keep my composure and not give in to how my body felt around him.

"He may not think that I'm *devastatingly breathtaking* or look at me like I steal the oxygen from the room. The kiss we shared may have lacked burning heat, but I've had that kind of passion before, and look where it got me. Maybe *nice* is exactly what I deserve."

He gave me a look that told me he didn't buy that for a second, but I knew what falling in love was like and the destruction it could cause in its wake. I knew how dangerous undiluted passion and desire could be, and I couldn't ever teeter on its edge again, no matter how good it felt. Evander pulled my hands from his shirt before guiding my arms around his neck as he kept his eyes on mine.

"You promised me a game tonight," he said as his eyes flickered to my mouth. I bit my lip, my mind drifting to how much I enjoyed these games between us. I lifted my hand, trailing my fingers up his neck and through his dark black hair. Evander groaned in desire at the touch, and I basked in the feel of his soft strands against my skin. "Interesting game you chose," he said breathlessly, and I smiled, loving that I had just an ounce of control over him.

"I had to pick something I knew I could win," I said innocently, and Evander's hands traveled to my waist, pushing me back to gain some space between our bodies. I mentally noted how much I had him breaking already, and we had barely begun.

"Is that right?" he asked with a slight tilt of his lips. I nodded, digging my fingers into his scalp as I tugged playfully on the back of his head. Evander sucked in a sharp breath laced with desire as his fingers tightened on my waist. It wouldn't take me long to win, and soon, he'd be begging for me. He dipped his head close, bringing his lips to my ear, and a shiver danced down my spine. "Then let's play, love."

Conversation flowed all around me, though I barely partook in any of it, only needing to bat my lashes and bite my lip as potential suitors promised to give me anything I could think to desire. I didn't see Jahier again. His father kept him busy enough to stay away from me, but occasionally my eyes would find Evander across the room, whispering secrets into some random woman's ear and making her blush. His gaze always seemed to find mine as we both worked, fulfilling our mission to find allies and uncover information.

The only problem with that was I was so preoccupied with winning the game between us that I could barely focus on anything these men were saying. Evander's fingers stroked along a different woman's arm as he sipped from his wine glass. My stare lingered on the way he licked his lips, getting every last drop of the sweet drink, and I wondered if I would taste the wine if I pressed my mouth to his.

"So, would you like to?" someone in the group of men asked, and my mind snapped to, realizing he was directing his question at me. I scrunched my brows as I met his brown eyes, and he pointed to the floor of people grinding against each other to the beat of the music. I was about to object, but then an idea sparked in my mind. We were here for a reason, after all, and I couldn't let this game with Evander cause me to mess up my mission. It also didn't hurt that this dance could aid me in the game I was starting to lose.

But that was just a minor detail.

"I'd love to," I said, finishing my wine before placing the empty glass on a passing tray.

"I get her next, Ian," another man said. Ian? I had been calling him Ronald in my head. Whoops. It's a good thing I didn't call him that aloud, though I'm sure I could have just blamed the slip on my wine.

Ian—not Ronald—led me to the center of the dance floor before spinning me once and bringing me in so I pressed against him as we moved to the music. His clammy hand slid down my back, leaving a sweat trail that had me suppressing a gag. He dipped me once and then again, twisting my body to his will as he forced me to move how he wanted. No. I wasn't here to give these men power over me. I was here to take theirs. To show them that *I* was in control, and they would bend to *me.* I stepped out of his hold, grabbing his hands and placing them where I wanted as we danced, but he fought against me, desperate to hang on to control. Well, that wouldn't do.

I pushed away from Ian, done with our time together. If he couldn't play how I wanted, then he lost the chance to play with me at all. I strode across the floor like I owned it, my eyes capturing another of the men from the group that followed me around. I raised a brow as I made my way toward him, and he nodded vehemently. As I reached him, I grabbed his hand to pull him onto the floor and he trailed behind, understanding that it was my lead he'd be following.

My eyes caught Evander watching me with curious interest, his hand resting on the back of yet another new person. I clenched my teeth to hold back my anger. He was getting to me without putting on a show the way I was. Evander tipped his drink to me in smug acknowledgment, and my blood boiled with a renewed purpose. I would win this game if it was the last thing I did. I was going to put on the best damn show of my life.

25.

I stopped us in the center, where Ian was still standing there, gaping at me like he was confused about why I had left him. Well, maybe he should have given me what I wanted. I pressed myself against my new partner, snaking my arms around his neck and running my fingers through his hair just like I did to Evander. Our bodies moved in time to the music, and unlike Ian, this man allowed me to control the dance.

"Are you enjoying yourself?" I asked, and his throat bobbed as he nodded excitely.

"Yes, very much so, Ainsley," he replied. I immediately halted my movements.

I never permitted him to use my name. I was a Gods damned princess, Heir to the Throne of Tenebrae, and he was beneath me in every sense. Tonight wasn't just about putting on a show to win mine and Evander's game, it was about making sure these men knew who I was. I was the power they longed to have, and if they weren't going to acknowledge or respect that, then they weren't worth my time.

"Your Highness," he corrected quickly, but it was too late; I had already pushed away and was on the hunt for my next victim.

A hand wrapped around my wrist, yanking me back and whirling me around, so I collided with a hard chest. The man's muscles bulged beneath his shirt, making the fabric look like it would rip apart with the barest of movements.

"Care to spend your time with someone worthy of it?" he crooned in my ear. The words were meant to be seductive, but instead, they sent bile creeping up my throat. I quickly crafted a dagger from shadow and pressed it to the man's neck before he could make another ridiculous remark. His eyes went wide with shock as they dipped to the weapon I held at his throat.

"Absolutely," I said sweetly. "I'll be sure to let you know if I find one. Now release me right this second, or I'll gladly stain your pretty clothes with blood."

The man's hands slid away a moment later as he turned and sprinted from the dance floor. I waved at his back before scanning the group of men practically salivating at the display. I pointed to one, and he rushed over, dipping his head in a bow before placing his hands across my upper back like he was terrified to move them any lower.

"What's your name?" I asked, stroking the man's cheek as shadows swirled around my fingers, caressing us both.

"Devon, Your Highness," he said, watching my Gift with piqued interest. They were all hungry for it. Not just for me but for the power I had running through my veins. They wanted to taste what it would be like to align themselves with it—to have it running through their blood—though they had no idea that wasn't an option.

"Devon," I mused, trailing my shadow-covered fingers down his neck in a slow, taunting movement. "Is that really where you want to touch me?" I whispered. He swallowed hard before shaking his head and sliding his hands to my lower back. I arched a brow, and his eyes widened with need as he moved one hand to my ass and pressed me tight against him. I wrapped one arm around his neck while the other fisted in his shirt as we danced.

I moved to the music, getting lost in the melody as Devon's hands roamed across my body. I gave myself over to it, drunk off the power of being in control and loving the feeling of being touched in this way again—of being wanted. Even though it was only a desire for my body and my power, I didn't care. I could feel good without worrying about my heart breaking, and I craved that physical release. It was an animalistic need of desire that had gone too long unsated.

One second I was rolling my body against Devon's as his fingers dug into my back, holding me firm against him, and the next I was spinning away and colliding into someone else. My eyes fluttered open to find Felix standing there with a smirk.

"You're putting on quite the show, cupcake," he said as we danced, though not as sexually as with my previous partner.

"And you just halted my fun," I told him with a pout. Felix grinned and shrugged like that had been his plan all along. "How has your night been?"

"Frustrating," he admitted with a sigh. "I've been trying to make Olivier jealous all night, but he's barely noticed." Felix spun me out and back in, and I couldn't help but smile at his continuing struggle to pursue Oli. I wasn't sure if it was because he genuinely liked him or was just thriving off the challenge of winning him over. But there definitely was *something* between them.

"Perhaps it's time to aim for easier prey," I suggested, gesturing around the room. "You know you could have anyone."

"It's not as fun," he breathed, and I understood what he meant. I was getting off on the high of being in control, but Evander's words kept ringing in my mind. I wanted a challenge—*needed* one—and it wasn't here with these men. "It seems like your plan to dangle yourself in front of Evander has been working. He hasn't been able to look away from you all night," he added. His words cut through my mind. My gaze met his as he tilted his chin in Evander's direction, but when I looked, I saw nothing of the sort. Van's eyes were firmly locked on two women as he smiled dazzlingly at them, no doubt trying to charm himself between their legs. "Okay, *almost* all night," Felix amended as I gave him a flat look.

Perhaps I had picked the wrong game and should have stuck with our usual choices. I blamed the decision on seeing him with Elenora last night, even though it was an innocent encounter. I was bold and daring, wanting to see how far we could push each other this way, but it looked like Evander wasn't interested. Either that, or he was bored and I wasn't captivating enough. The words *devastatingly breathtaking* echoed in my mind. Was it part of his strategy to throw me off and make me ache to hear those words from him again?

The song bled into another, and this time the music was haunting and more sensual. The bodies around us slowed, adjusting to the pace flawlessly as they held their partners close. As I scanned the party, my eyes accidentally lingered too long on a man at the edge of the dance floor, and he took that as a sign that I wanted him next. I groaned and pulled back to look at Felix with an apologetic smile.

"Time to get back at it," I whined, not looking forward to dancing with another stranger.

"Don't be too mad at me, okay?" he said, and I furrowed my brows, not understanding his meaning. Felix spun me around several times before he released me, and my back slammed into a warm, toned chest.

I inhaled the intoxicating scent of cedar and snow as I lifted my arm and wrapped it around my new partner's neck while my other hand interlocked over the one he had resting on my waist. Our bodies danced to the music like they weren't our own, matching each other's movements in perfect synchronicity. Evander dragged his knuckles down the length of my extended arm, leaving a trail of goosebumps on my skin. I shivered though my whole body was filled with burning flames as I savored the feel of him against me.

He spun me around to face him, the movement fluid and slow. I didn't miss a beat, snaking both arms around his neck and pressing my fingers roughly through his hair. Evander's throat rumbled in pleasure as he leaned forward, putting his forehead to mine as we ground against each other to the longing melody. My heart hammered wildly as I drank him in, needing so much more of this passionate embrace. Though I felt in control with the others, I felt *alive* with him.

Evander's stare flickered to my mouth, and I bit my red lip as I enjoyed how he seemed ready to devour me whole. His hands roamed over my body in a possessive need, and I fisted my hands in his dark strands as I kept him against me, wanting to feel so much more.

"Careful, love," he said breathlessly. "If you keep it up, you'll have every person here begging at your feet. It's dangerous for one to wield that much power."

I smirked and cocked my head in a display of confusion.

"But what if it's my goal to have at least one person on their knees before me tonight?" I asked seductively, as I gave a show of looking around at the people watching us. I could have sworn there hadn't been that many eyes on me until this second, each person watching with bated breath as if waiting to see something happen between Evander and me. In the crowd, my attention snagged on Jahier, who was just as engrossed in the show as everyone else, while he chatted absentmindedly to the company he was keeping.

"If you want someone to worship you tonight, I'd happily assist with that,"

My lips parted at his proposition, and I worked to push away the deliciously intrusive thoughts roaring through my mind. I could practically feel his fingers digging into my hips as he held me still while on his knees. There was power in knowing I could make him bow for me, but I wasn't stupid enough to think that it wouldn't be *me* who was at his mercy if he did.

My hands slid down over his chest as I stood on my toes to place my lips next to his ear.

"I'd normally accept such an invitation," I said, pressing my mouth to his neck to place a soft kiss. Evander shivered, and I smiled against him, loving the effect I had on his body. "But," I added, moving my mouth back to the shell of his ear to whisper. "I'd rather have someone who can actually satisfy me."

I took the bottom of his ear between my teeth and tugged gently. Evander's grip on my hips tightened, but before he could so much as try to respond, I pulled back and turned to walk across the dance floor without so much as another glance in his direction.

The rest of the evening was spent with me fulfilling my side of the mission—talking with the men who wanted me to be their bride and subtly trying to find out if anyone had caught wind of any treasonous activities. Whenever they tried asking me questions about what I was looking for in a partner, I always expressed my desire for strength and capability. Someone that would be faithful to me and my kingdom. Someone who could prove their loyalty to me. My hope was that one of the men would try to barter information in exchange for marriage, but so far, that hadn't been the case. Either no one knew anything, or they were too loyal to their cause to betray it so soon.

I made sure to avoid eye contact with Evander again, though I caught him staring at me more often than not. He seemed to follow wherever I wandered, and I immensely enjoyed that fact. Eventually, I realized I wasn't getting anywhere with my goals, and I didn't want to fake my enjoyment any longer. Jahier was still conversing at his father's side while Mishal stared daggers at me anytime I glanced his way, letting me know that approaching my new friend wasn't an option.

I scanned the room one last time, trying to decide my next move when I accidentally got snared in Evander's grey eyes. He was standing with the two women from earlier, but his gaze was pinned on me as he spoke. There was a hunger in his stare, and I realized we hadn't finished our game yet, so I couldn't call it a night even though I was ready to.

After draining the rest of my drink, I set my wine goblet down on the nearest table and strode out of the room, my gown hissing against the floor as I walked. I made it only halfway down the corridor before I heard soft footsteps echoing behind me. I knew he would follow. That had been the point of me leaving so early, after all. We had been playing our little game all night, and I was determined to end it and win. Smiling, I halted my steps and half-turned, pressing my back against the cool, rough stones of the palace's walls.

"Is there something I can help you with, Evander?" I asked, picking at my nails and paying no mind to him as he stopped before me.

"Well, if you're offering, I can think of a few things." His eyes drifted up and down my body—a predator assessing its prey.

I had him right where I wanted him. I rolled my eyes and lifted a brow as if to say *tell me why you're really here.*

"I was just wondering why you decided to leave early. You aren't feeling ill, are you? If you need someone to nurse you back to health, I wouldn't mind," he claimed with a flirtatious wink.

I snorted at his blatant lie. "Nope. I just got tired of seeing you stare at me all night," I said sweetly.

"Now love, how would you know that were the case if you weren't watching me as well?" He was always so cocky, so sure of himself. It didn't help that I was giving him a reason to be. I hated how often I caught myself staring at him, watching him talk to other women. Watching him give them attention—the same attention I kept telling myself I didn't want. But my Gods, did he have to look so good tonight? His close-fitting black jacket was tailored just enough to show the signs of his hard muscles underneath. Even his cedar and fresh fallen snow scent was more intoxicating than usual, and as he stepped closer, my head spun as it filled my senses.

"And could you blame me with the way you look tonight?" His gaze raked up and down my body for a second time. "Nice dress, by the way," he said, his eyes finally finding their way to mine. "I don't think I've told you that."

"Thank you," I responded, smoothing the fabric of my gown. My hand rested just below my hip where the long slit of the dress started, my bare leg coming into view. "But you did call me breathtaking, so I assumed you were referring to my outfit."

Evander's gaze flickered to my exposed thigh for just a moment before setting his stare back to me.

"*Devastatingly* breathtaking," he corrected. "The shadows were a nice touch, by the way. The diadem pulls the whole look together."

"Thanks. It was quite lucky that it matched the dress I selected specifically for Jahier," I commented, running my fingers over the black diamonds of my crown.

"So you chose this with him in mind?"

"I wanted to make a *very* good impression," I said, shrugging—a lie. I had chosen it for him—for that dark, hungry look that he had in his eyes the moment he saw me descend the stairs. The same look he was giving me now.

"I'd say you accomplished your goal, love. I know he ended up being rather preoccupied tonight, so we never got to have our little chat. If you'd like, I can go find him now so you can accept his proposal," he offered cooly. We both had the same air of indifference in which we spoke, as if we wanted to show the other just how unfazed we were.

"And how do you know I didn't already pull him aside myself and accept it? I mean, you're the one always telling me to take what I want. Maybe that's exactly what I did."

"What *do* you want?" he asked seductively, raising a brow in question.

I smiled wide and shrugged in response, not giving him the satisfaction of a verbal answer. Evander leaned forward, resting his forearm against the stone on the side of my head, and my heart began to pound harder at the proximity. I almost had him. I was so close to winning this stupid little game of desire we had been playing together all night.

"I suppose you *do* have needs that must be met." He glanced down at my mouth, and I bit my lip. Partly for show and partly because of the heat building within me at every glance he gave. I took a long, deep breath before replying.

"And what exactly do you know of my needs," I asked. He shook his head ever so slightly, his lips curling in that devious smile of his.

"Nothing yet, but I know of mine." Of course he was more concerned with his own desires. Before I could open my mouth to reply, he closed the slight gap between us. His broad muscled chest, so prevalent even covered, now pressed against me. "Like my need to have your body against mine." My hands reached behind and grasped the stone blocks for support. I prayed my legs wouldn't give out as he came closer, our breath mixing. This was a very dangerous game we were playing. "My need to feel the warmth of your skin."

His free hand wrapped around my exposed leg at the knee, slowly gliding it higher and higher, his fingers pressing into my skin and stopping at my upper thigh. He squeezed tightly, a territorial claim, and my blood boiled under my skin. In a swift motion, Evander lifted me. My back pressed harder into the wall and my legs wrapped around his middle on instinct. I was playing with fire, and I sure as hell was about to get burned.

I stopped breathing as his lips grazed my neck, working their way up to my ear. My fingers dug into the stones as I felt him harden against me, and the sheer, massive size of him made my mouth go dry and my body ache with want.

"My need to taste every inch of you," he said as his teeth brushed over the shell of my ear.

My arms flew around his neck, and my fingers found their way into the hair at his nape. I tugged his strands slightly as I felt his arousal hard like granite against me. I ground myself over it, and Evander let loose a deep growl, the sound low and guttural, primal. His hands gripped my hips tighter as he whispered breathlessly into my ear.

"My need to have my tongue between your thighs." *Fuck*. I arched into him further, and an almost inaudible moan escaped me, but I knew he heard it. "The way your skin prickles under my touch, your heart pounds against my chest, your breathing turns shallow... And the way you let out that delicious little moan," Evander continued, and I swallowed hard at his words. "Your body is telling me that your needs are the same as mine, and it's begging me to fulfill them."

My breathing came so heavily I was practically panting with want for this man. The thought of winning was drifting away and being replaced with images of me weaving my hands through his black hair as he dragged his tongue up my center, giving me exactly what I was craving.

"You're misreading it," I whispered.

"Is that so?" Evander asked as he pulled back to look at me with hooded eyes. His desire-soaked words were having just as much effect on him as they were on me. He reached up and wrapped his hand around my wrist, removing it from his hair and bringing it between us. "There's only one way to find out," he said as he guided my hand up my leg until it dipped below my dress.

Our eyes stayed locked on one another as he directed my hand higher and higher until I was just an inch away from where he wanted it. He cocked a brow as if giving me a final chance to back out, but I raised my chin higher. I was determined to not only stick to this little game he was playing but also not give him any indication of the answer he was looking for.

Evander smirked as he guided my hand the final distance.

My eyes widened, and I immediately sucked in a breath as my fingers grazed over myself, feeling just how fucking drenched I was for him. I forgot all about not giving that fact away. Evander's throat bobbed, and his jaw clenched as he read the answer on my face. His eyes grew darker—feral and wanton, and his grip on my wrist tightened ever so slightly as he saw the clear desire in my stare.

He released his hold on my wrist, and I slid my hand out from beneath my dress, bringing it back to the wall for support. Evander swallowed hard and then dipped his head to press his lips to my neck, sending fire scorching through my veins.

"I guess we have our answer, love."

He was right, and though I hated it, it didn't change the fact that at that moment, I wanted him. Gods, did I want him. His breath tickled my skin as I arched my neck in a silent request. I needed so much more from him, and I didn't fucking care that I would lose the game for admitting it. I felt him smile against me before he withdrew his mouth, bringing it mere inches from mine, his breath hot and laced with yearning. I brought my lips closer, wanting to finally taste him.

"But you know... I think I want to hear you *say* the words first."

Evander pulled his face back and set me on the ground as my legs threatened to give out completely. He casually pushed himself off the wall and met my widened eyes as I dropped my mouth open like a gaping fish, gasping for air. A half-smirk spread across his face.

Van knew he had won, but that wasn't enough. He wanted me to say the words. He wanted to hear me tell him that I wanted him. Even if I wasn't entirely too stubborn, I couldn't form coherent sentences with my mind completely foggy with lust. The absence of his body left me feeling weak, with my head spinning from his lips on me.

"Just something to think about tonight." He backed away slowly, sliding his hands into his pockets. "You know... when you're alone," he said with a wink, before disappearing into those Gods forsaken shadows he loved so much.

That. Fucker.

 26.

I walked through the corridor to my room, on shaky legs. My breathing was uneven as my mind flashed back to Evander's hold on my body and being pressed against him as his hands gripped me with need. I remembered his lips hovering over my ear and his tongue gliding against my skin as he kissed me. I shook my head to clear the intrusive yet unbelievably desirable thoughts.

Breathe, Ainsley. It's not going to happen, and you don't even want it to because you don't want him, I told myself, though my inner monologue laughed at the obvious lie.

"Ainsley?" a soft voice called, startling me. I turned to find Prince Jahier striding towards me with a grin on his beautiful face. "I'm sorry it took so long for me to slip away. I don't think my father likes the idea of me trailing after you so much."

"I didn't get that impression," I deadpanned. Jahier laughed and shrugged apologetically.

"You're leaving so soon?" he asked, tilting his head to the side.

It wasn't late by any means, and the party had only been going on for a few hours. From what I've learned of Agnitio's celebrations, it wouldn't be ending anytime soon, so I *should* go back to the ballroom and socialize. I should drink and dance and try my damnedest to figure out if any of these people knew of Pravus' leader and his war plans. The problem was that there was no way I could go back and focus on my task without thinking of Evander. Maybe that made me a shitty heir but whatever. My mind wasn't working properly, and I would be useless to our cause. I would have to let my faith lie with our friends who were trying just as hard to uncover truths.

"I'm a little tired," I lied, giving him a weak smile. Jahier frowned but extended his arm for me to take.

"Then let me at least escort you back to your room," he offered. Always the gentleman.

A pang of guilt spread through me. He was kind-hearted and good-tempered. Given that Jahier had seemed to change his mind about marriage tonight, I shouldn't have allowed him to walk me to my room. I was giving him false hope and was an asshole for it. But I'd made a promise to myself and my people that I would do what I must, so I could do this.

"I'd love that," I said, looping my arm through his. He smiled widely and led the way down the hall to the guest rooms we had been placed in. "Did you enjoy yourself tonight?" I asked as we walked slowly, savoring the warmth and kindness I felt radiating from him.

"I did, yes. But I'm sure I would have enjoyed my time more if it was spent with you."

"I think I would have too," I admitted, and it wasn't a lie. Being around Jahier was easy. He was sweet, thoughtful, and funny. He was polite to servants and those beneath his status. There wasn't anything not to like about this man, and whoever he ended up with would be incredibly lucky. "How long will you be staying in Agnitio?"

"Only for another day or two. My father wants to get back and discuss King Evander's proposal privately," he explained and rolled his eyes. I focused on the movement rather than the fact that I hadn't been aware Evander had made any sort of offer to King Arden.

"You don't agree?" I asked curiously, pretending that I knew what he was talking about. Jahier took a deep breath at my question.

"I don't think there's anything to discuss," he said flatly. My stomach plummeted. Was his mind already made up? Did he not want to aid us? "Any threat against Disparya, whether great or small, should be dealt with. We should defend and stand by one another. If a king of this land requests aid, I think it should be granted." Jahier shrugged as if that was the simplest thought in the world.

"You want to help us?" I said, surprised. I knew he was our best bet in who to convince, but I didn't think that only one conversation would have captured his allegiance. What exactly had Evander said?

"Yes, I do," he replied as we reached my bedroom door. I pressed my back to it, showing him I wasn't ready to head inside yet. "And it wasn't your plan to feign interest in me that convinced me." My face paled, and I tensed.

"I…" I started, but I had no words.

There was nothing I could say to defend my plan, but it wasn't like that with Jahier. I genuinely enjoyed his company, and when he said he didn't want to offer me a proposal that first day, I was so relieved that I could just be myself around him.

"I'm sorry," I offered weakly. "That *was* my plan, and I've executed it with everyone except for you, Jahier. You mentioned changing your mind about marrying me, but I can't. It's not that I don't think you're wonderful because you truly are. It's just that…" I began, not knowing how I was planning to finish that sentence.

"I'm not him," he finished. My eyes snapped to his. Not *who*? I raised a brow and he laughed under his breath. "It wouldn't take someone with my Gift as an Oculi to see the way you and King Evander look at each other. You both command the attention of everyone who looks your way, but the only person who captures yours is one another." I shook my head to argue, but he raised his hand to stop me. "You may not realize it yet, and that's okay, but it's obvious to everyone else."

"The man infuriates me," I replied.

"They say there is a fine line between love and hate, Ainsley. I'd say you're straddling it now."

"It's not like that with us," I pointed out—because it wasn't. Sure, we teased each other and he just had me pressed against a wall a moment ago where I forgot my own name, but that was just a *game* we were playing. That's all we were to one another—a game. "His sole purpose is to get ahead—to beat me in everything we do. He would rather me admit that I want him than actually have me."

Jahier laughed as he shook his head and brought my hand to his lips for a gentle kiss.

"Goodnight, Ainsley. I'll see you in the morning."

"Goodnight, Jahier."

I walked to the bathing room, stripping out of my gown and tossing it to the floor as I went. I needed to clean up and go to bed. The sooner I was asleep, the sooner I could have Evander and his arrogant self creep out of my mind.

Ten minutes later, I was bathed, changed into my silk nightgown, and tucked beneath the soft sheets.

Two hours later, I was still staring at the ceiling, picturing Evander's fingers trailing up my thigh and his mouth pressed below my ear. I thought about how he directed my hand where he wanted, making me feel myself and how wet I was. Without thinking, my hand began to move.

My fingers idly trailed down my body, over my breast, and dipped below the hem of my nightgown. My breathing quickened as I brought my fingers higher up, the skin on my thighs burning as they made the ascent. I imagined Evander pressed against me, feeling how hard he was—how much he wanted me. I sucked in a sharp breath as I felt how soaked I was again, and my hips bucked in demand.

Obeying my body's request, I slipped a finger inside myself, moaning softly as I imagined it was Evander doing the deed. Another finger filled me, and I covered my mouth with my other hand to stifle the euphoric sounds that escaped me as I pumped in and out, pleasuring myself to thoughts of him.

It was *his* fingers that moved inside me, *his* tongue that devoured me relentlessly as I gripped his dark hair. It was the groans of his desire for me that echoed in my mind as he demanded my body to give him everything he wanted.

My thumb swirled around my clit and I screamed out, biting the back of my hand hard as I finally came with the image of his relentless tongue between my legs ripping through my mind. I withdrew my hand, breathing heavily as I realized what I'd just done. I had pleasured myself to him just as he insinuated I would.

I pulled a pillow over my face and screamed my frustration into it.

I was late for breakfast, but I didn't care. I had barely slept through the night thanks to Evander's mind fuck. When I arrived at our usual table, everyone was chatting together, their plates now empty. Evander looked up from his book and half-eaten piece of toast the second I approached. I scowled at him, and a wry grin crept up his gorgeous, stupid face.

"Sleep well, love? You look well rested," he teased with a wink. I hated him. If he wanted to play this game, then fine—I'd play.

"I sure did after running into Jahier on the way back to my room," I announced, pouring myself a cup of coffee from the kettle on the table.

"Oh, is that so?" he baited.

"Yup," I replied, adding cream and sugar to my coffee before sipping my hot drink. "We had a very long and satisfying conversation." Evander scoffed and rolled his eyes, not believing my insinuation. Dammit.

"How was *your* night?" I asked, hoping that putting the pressure on him would give me a break. "You looked awfully cozy with those two brunettes at the celebration."

Evander smiled wickedly and tongued his cheek as he glanced around the room before waving his fingers at someone. I turned to find those two women in question waving back with wide smiles.

"You could say my night was also eventful," he replied, placing his book on the table. Unwanted jealousy coursed through me as I thought about him performing everything he promised to me—on them.

"Good. I'm glad," I said, forcing a fake smile.

"Are you, now?" he teased, baiting me to admit the truth.

My fingers pressed into the side of my cup as I stared at him and tried to get myself under control. If my shadows slipped through, he would know how bothered I was by the idea of him with them. I told myself it had nothing to do with the women themselves, and he was free to do whatever with whoever. I was only frustrated because he got into my head and riled me up. That was the reason—the *only* reason.

"Good morning, everyone," Jahier's voice rang out over my thundering heart, and I twisted my head to see him standing at my side with an empty plate and cup.

"Good morning, Jahier," Evander said, his voice confident and all-knowing. "Ainsley here was just telling us that she ran into you last night on her way back to her room."

Shit.

My eyes pleaded with the man not to give away that nothing happened between us in front of Evander. The fact that I got off to thoughts of Evander was mortifying enough, and I didn't need to be proven a liar in front of him too. A sly smile appeared, as Jahier narrowed his eyes.

"That is quite correct, King Evander," Jahier offered. Thank the Gods for this merciful, chivalrous man. "We bumped into each other, and I offered to walk her back to her room. I hope I didn't overstep," he said.

"Oh, not at all," Evander replied smugly, satisfied that seemed to be all Jahier did.

"Good. Neither of us was ready to go back to the party, so we spent a good amount of time talking. It was a very... *fulfilling* conversation," he said as he grinned. "I do hope you felt the same, Ainsley." I smiled widely at him and his willingness to play along. I was forever in his debt.

"It was quite a... *stimulating* conversation, and I'm glad to hear it left you satisfied as well," I answered, biting my lip to play up the rouse.

"Very satisfied," Jahier said, letting his gaze drag up and down my body slowly. "Until next time."

He lifted my hand and kissed it before bringing his attention to everyone else. Jahier nodded politely before striding back through the dining room. After a long display of watching him walk away, I turned my focus back to Evander, who was gritting his jaw so tightly I thought he would break a tooth. I picked up my mug, keeping my eyes locked on him as I slurped my coffee loudly.

"Oh, come on!" Felix drawled as he stood from his chair. "You both are absolutely ridiculous. We all know that the only thing either of you fucked last night was your own hand, so stop being so stubborn and just do something about all of this pent-up sexual tension because you're making the rest of us miserable!" I shot him a glare that had him raising his hands in innocence and sitting back down.

Evander cocked a brow at me, his previous torment disappearing after my friend's little outburst.

I was going to kill Felix.

"What do you say, love? Why don't you and I go do something about all of this pent-up tension?" Evander said as he took a slow, seductive bite of a peach.

I fucking *snapped*.

I leaped across the table, my hands aimed at his throat as I tackled him to the ground. I was faintly aware of the sounds of dozens of scraping chairs as his taunting laugh boomed around us. He wasn't even trying to fight back, which pissed me off more. I rose, planting my foot against his throat as I bared my teeth at him.

"You and me, outside, NOW," I seethed. Evander's leg swept out, catching me off guard and sending me falling to my back. Before I could even think about flipping over, his boot was against my throat.

"Meet you there, love," he said, tossing his peach into the air before taking another bite and striding away. I rolled onto my stomach, coughing as the pressure on my windpipe disappeared.

I was going to kill *two* people this morning.

I was aware of our friends' muffled whispers behind me as I followed Evander outside. Behind the palace there was a large training ring, much like the one we had at our home in Tenebrae. Evander eyed me with a cocky grin as he unbuttoned his shirt before ripping it off. Toned muscles flexed beneath his tanned skin as he shook out his limbs to stretch. His shadow tattoos spilled over his flesh like ink, rippling around his body rather than staying stagnant like they usually did.

"Seriously? Is that necessary?" I asked, stepping into the ring.

"I don't want to get it filthy. If my being shirtless is distracting, that's your problem. I have a few ideas of how to help you deal with it, though," he said, and I lunged with my shadows. Evander batted them away like nothing as we circled the ring, glaring at one another. "So, what part of me do you want the most? Is it my mouth or my huge—" My darkness surged forth, enveloping us both, but when it dissipated, Evander was gone. "Playing dirty, are we, love?" he asked from behind. I twisted quickly just in time to be kicked hard in the chest and fall to my ass.

"Slow down, Ainsley!" Felix yelled from outside the ring. "Take your time."

"I'd love for her to take her time with me," Evander called, and I rose to my feet and sprinted for him.

He blocked every punch I threw, but I was quick, too, deflecting his attacks in return. I crafted two shadow daggers to join the fight when my physical blows weren't landing. Evander followed suit, stopping everything I threw at him. I was getting nowhere, and my energy was quickly depleting. As our weapons halted in a clash, he whispered close to my ear.

"Was it my hand or tongue you imagined last night as you pleasured yourself?" I roared my fury as I pushed him away and repeatedly struck with my blades. Evander parried, spinning around and kicking me in the back until I fell to the ground, my weapons disappearing as I lost concentration.

"He isn't helping her. He's making it worse," I heard Felix say.

"He *is* helping her. He's trying to teach her to stop and think. To tune everything out and force her rage into her attack," Olivier replied loud enough for me to overhear. "Slow down and breathe, Ainsley. He isn't just baiting you for fun," he yelled.

"Now, don't tell her all my secrets, Oli," Evander whined playfully.

I whipped my head in his direction to find him spinning a dagger between his fingers, paying no mind to me. I stood, brushing off the dirt from my pants as I inhaled deeply and formed another two daggers with my magic. Evander transformed his into a long sword and pointed it directly at me.

"I'd be more than happy to take you back to my room so you don't have to only rely on your imagination anymore," he teased. I didn't rush him this time.

Instead, I crouched into my stance and circled the ring, ready to defend rather than attack.

"Good, Ainsley! Don't let him trick you into anything," Olivier called.

"Don't forget to use your magic in conjunction with your weapons. The two together will do more damage than one on its own," Lia offered.

Tendrils of shadow swirled beneath Evander's feet, but before they could wrap around his ankles, he leaped out of the way.

"Nice try, love, but you'll have to be less obvious," Evander said, striking with his sword. I deflected, spinning out of the way, and landed a blow to his ribs with my elbow.

"YES!" Lia boomed, clapping loudly.

I smirked as I spun around, ready to face him again. It was the first time I had ever landed a hit on Evander, and a sense of pride filled me at the accomplishment—along with a renewed purpose. I could fucking do this.

"Good job, girl," Marceline praised under her breath.

Evander lunged and I deflected, moving to land the same hit again, but he anticipated my movements, and instead I took a knee to the gut.

"As I said, you'll have to be less obvious," Evander commented as he let go of his sword, which drifted apart into nothing before hitting the ground.

He rolled his neck and placed his hands in his pocket, letting me know he wanted to fight me without using weapons. He didn't think he needed them and that I was easy to defeat. Out of all the insults he spat, this one stung the worst, and the gleam in his eye told me he knew it.

I lengthened my daggers into short swords and ran hard, but he traversed out of the way before I could reach him. I skidded to a halt and turned, swords held up and ready for an attack from behind, but he was just standing there with a stupid smirk on his face as he watched me.

"Gotta be quicker than that, love." I swung my sword, and he ducked out of the way, the motion easy and fluid like he had practiced it a million times. I threw my leg up to land a hit to his side, but he caught it, spinning my leg hard until I was thrown off balance and landed in the dirt. I swept my leg around quickly, hoping to catch him off guard and take him out from below, but he jumped back and away from my assault. No matter what I tried, he was always ready.

"Anticipate his moves as he does yours. Slow down and *think*," Olivier suggested.

"You can do this, Ainsley!" Lia called supportively.

"You do know that I'm your *king*, correct? This is a clear act of treason," Evander teased as he circled me, his hands now tight behind his back. *Anticipate his moves*. I could do that. We'd spent months training, and I was familiar with his tactics. I knew the attacks and defenses he preferred. I knew the way his magic felt as he called it forth. I could do this.

I swiped my sword at him, cutting the open air as he disappeared. The second he was out of view, I jumped to the side, missing the swipe of legs from below as he appeared behind me.

"Good, Ainsley. Very good!" Felix bellowed and joined in with Lia, clapping loudly and encouraging me. I let go of my swords, allowing them to turn into shadows once more as I threw a punch. Evander blocked it, and I quickly brought up my knee to hit him between the legs, but he deflected that too.

"Now, now, love. Surely you don't want to damage me there. Not until I give you what you've been dreaming about." I saw red—crimson red.

I swung again and missed as Evander kicked me in the back. I stumbled but caught my footing before crashing to the ground again.

Deep breaths. Don't let him get to you. That's his game. That's what he wants. Anticipate his moves and beat him.

I crafted my daggers again and struck at him relentlessly, pushing him back farther and farther toward the edge of the ring. I didn't give him a chance to attack, keeping him on the defensive and forcing him to retreat. The moment he traversed, I spun, tucking in my leg and letting it loose in a hard, straight kick. At first, there was nothing but open air, and then a hard chest in the spot I guessed Evander would appear. He went flying back a foot and over the white line that marked the boundaries of our ring. He was barely more than a step out of bounds, but a step was still a step.

Holy shit, I had won.

Evander's eyes narrowed at my stunned expression as he followed my stare to his feet. Slowly, he picked his head up and a bright and brilliant smile was plastered on his face. He crossed his arms over his chest and tilted his head to the side in that cocky and gorgeous way he always did.

"Well done, love. It's about time."

A body collided with my back, and several arms wrapped around me as cheering broke out. I did it. I really fucking did it. Lia and Felix took turns kissing my cheeks as Olivier gave me a hard pat on the back, and Marceline nodded approvingly from the edge of the ring. My face lit up with the deepest sense of accomplishment I had ever felt. I had overcome Evander and my own mind when I needed to.

My eyes found Van's watching me intently, with pride shining within.

"Again," I told him, crafting daggers in my hands.

"As you wish, love," he said, forming a sword of his own.

He didn't bother pretending like he didn't need it anymore.

27.

Three hours later, I was exhausted and gasping for breath. Evander didn't go easy on me, and I never beat him again, but I didn't care. I had defeated him once and gained so much knowledge after this morning's training.

"That's it for today. Both of you take a break and get washed up for lunch," Olivier instructed, walking into the ring. I shook my head to say I was fine, but he gave me a look that dared me to argue. Olivier wasn't against pushing me, but he was also a knowledgeable trainer, knowing just where my limits were. I wiped the sweat from my brow, smearing the dirt I felt caked to my skin, and let my daggers disappear on the wind.

"Fine, but I want to go again tomorrow morning," I demanded. Evander nodded with a wry twitch of his lips. I retreated back inside, looking forward to a hot bath and a full plate of food. I had forgotten that I hadn't eaten this morning, too caught up in Evander's inappropriate proposals and letting my anger get the best of me.

"Look who it is," a snide male voice called. I hadn't been aware that my head had dropped in exhaustion until I picked it up to see Mishal walking towards me in the empty corridor of our guest rooms. "The little slut."

Shock flashed over my features at his insult. I could tell he hated me, but to call me that? He certainly was brave to insult a member of the royal family of Tenebrae. I wasn't just some random woman he didn't care for—I was a princess. More than that, I was the Heir to the Throne. I looked around, certain that he must have meant the words for someone else, but we were alone.

"Excuse me?" I questioned.

"You heard me," he sneered as he entered my personal space. I backed up to gain distance, but he kept coming forward until I was pressed against the stone wall. "Don't you think for one second that I don't know what you're doing." His breath was foul as his face came inches from mine. I was thrown off by the audacity of this man—what made him think he could speak to me like this?

"I don't know what you're talking about," I replied, making my way to shove around him, but he reached out, halting me with a tight grab of my wrist.

"You can seduce this court's unknowing lords and ladies, but you will stay away from Prince Jahier."

My eyes dropped to his hold on my arm, and my lips pulled back in a snarl as my magic slammed against my barriers. No matter how much I wanted to, I couldn't let it out. Anger had never gotten me anywhere, and I needed to think this situation through. We were here on a mission, and if I slipped up, I could ruin that for us all.

"You're mistaken, Mishal," I said, pushing forward to escape his hold.

He slammed me back against the wall so hard my teeth rattled in my skull. I wanted to scream and fight, but Evander's words echoed through my mind. *We need their aid. We must do whatever we can to ensure they are on our side during this fight.* If I caused a scene now, I would fail my people. I'd fail *him*. I couldn't be the reason Disparya fell. I couldn't be the reason the Kingdom of Venator refused to help us. I bit my tongue and tensed as his hand curled around my throat so tightly I knew he was leaving a bruise.

"You don't fool me, nor is King Arden falling for your tricks. So go fuck your way to the top somewhere else, whore," he snarled.

I turned my head as I struggled to breathe against his grip on my windpipe, but he didn't like that. He grabbed my chin with his free hand, making me stare at his hateful face. His eyes were a piercing black, like a bottomless pit of darkness and his features were too sharp and angular, making him look hard and unfriendly. His greasy brown hair spilled over his forehead, partially covering several small scars.

"If I see you sniffing around my prince again, you will regret it. Not even King Evander will be able to save you." He released me, and I fell to the ground, gasping for air as Mishal dipped his head in a condescending bow. "Your Highness," he spat before walking away as if nothing had transpired.

There was no doubt in my mind that he was going to convince King Arden not to consider whatever Evander's proposal was. I stood on shaking knees and hurried into my room, locking the door behind me before letting the silent tears stream down my face.

"Olivier will be pissed if you don't get your ass down to lunch. You know he's ruthless when it comes to fueling your body after a workout like we had this morning," Evander called from the other end of the room. I hadn't noticed the sound of him traversing in here, too lost in the memory of being strangled.

After I pulled myself together, I washed the dirt and feel of Mishal's hands from my body. I wore a long-sleeved collared shirt to hide the marks on my wrist and neck that were taking far too long to fade. Granted, thanks to my self-healing properties the evidence of what happened would disappear within a few hours rather than the days it would have taken if I was still mortal. But it still wasn't fast enough. There was no way I could head downstairs into a dining room full of people until the marks were gone completely.

"I'm not very hungry," I said, refusing to turn and face him.

My eyes were focused entirely on the sandy hills in the distance, knowing that if I met his stare, I would surely crumble. I couldn't let him know I failed our mission—not yet, at least. Not until I figured out a way to fix it.

"That's not a good enough excuse. Let's go," Evander demanded, but I didn't move. The sound of him approaching rang in my ears, and I instinctively shifted closer to the window to keep as much distance between us as possible. "Ainsley, look at me. What's going on?" I reluctantly turned to face him, keeping my eyes down and praying he couldn't see the bruises on my throat.

"Nothing. I'm just exhausted," I told him, casually crossing my arms over my chest.

Evander's glare hardened, and I followed his stare to the sleeve that had shifted slightly with the movement, showing a fading bruise. Before I could adjust, he reached for my shirt. I stopped breathing as he pulled the fabric back to reveal the purple marks that adorned my wrist.

"What the fuck happened."

It wasn't a question, and each word was said slowly, the fury in his tone chilling my blood instantly. I yanked my sleeve back down and shrugged off his concern.

"It was probably just from our session today," I offered, but Evander shook his head.

"I never touched you there," he said, furiously.

"Evander, it's nothing. Really, I'm fine, so please just let it go," I begged, turning from him once more.

He caught my chin to stop me before I could fully retreat, and I sucked in a painful breath between my teeth. Evander released me at once and stepped closer. Ever so slowly, he raised his hand, tilting my face gently until the bruised fingermarks on my throat and chin were on full display.

A deep growl emanated from the back of his throat, and his jaw clenched tight. His eyes were wild with the kind of fury only a God could have as his gaze met mine. Tears pricked the back of my eyes as the full force of my failure came forth. I was ashamed and embarrassed I had let this happen, and now Evander was pissed at me for it too.

"Who did this to you?" he demanded in the voice of a king and not the man I'd come to know over the past few months. I shook my head, terrified to give him the name because if I did, he would absolutely lose his shit. He would cause a scene, and everything we were fighting for would be ruined worse than it already was. "Ainsley, don't you fucking keep this from me."

"It's fine, Evander—"

"THE FUCK IT IS!" he yelled, stepping away and running a hand through his black hair. "Nothing about this is *fine*, Ainsley."

His chest heaved as he paced back in forth in front of me, unbridled rage present in every thunderous step. Shadows swirled around his hands and blended in with the tattoo viciously slithering across his skin. I had never seen him that angry, and the potential of what he could do with that rage frightened me to my core.

"If I tell you who it was, will you hurt them?" I asked, and Evander laughed bitterly.

"*Hurt* doesn't begin to describe what I will do to them, love," he seethed, and I shook my head again.

"And that is exactly why I can't tell you," I replied, and he stared at me, completely dumbfounded. "If I give you a name, you'll make everything worse."

Evander stepped closer, his gaze wild as he spoke slowly, each word calculated and precise. His eyes were storm clouds billowing violently, holding no ounce of the calm and confident man I'd dealt with daily. This man before me was the embodiment of rage—of our shared darkness. When he replied, his words were careful and concise. He didn't raise his voice, only speaking in a flat and even tone, which made me all the more terrified of his deadly vow.

"I *will* find out who touched you, Ainsley. I will question every single person in this Gods damn kingdom until I am given a name." I swallowed hard as he approached, the look of destruction and the need for blood on his face. "And if I have to torture it out of them, then so be it. I don't care if they are innocent; someone *will* confess. So I will ask you one more time, love." He leaned forward, his breath caressing my face as he spoke. "Who the *fuck* did this to you?"

I swallowed, fighting the bile that was stuck in my throat. I glanced around the room as if it held the answer to my problems and an escape from my failure. But it didn't. If I kept this from him, then the blood of innocent people was on my hands. I would have called his bluff, but I had never seen that crazed look in his gaze, and I wouldn't have put anything past him. So, I closed my eyes and blew out a defeated breath.

"It was Mishal," I said quickly, "But—"

He vanished instantly.

Fuck.

28.

I hurried out of the room and sprinted through the halls. Lunch was still going on, and there was no doubt that Evander was headed to the dining room, where he'd likely find Mishal still eating or just finishing up. As I turned the corner to my destination, loud crashes and screams broke out in the distance.

Oh, Gods.

I picked up my pace, gasping for breath as I pushed through the doors to find everyone cowering to one side of the large room and Evander on the other. He had Mishal against the far wall, holding him in place by his throat as he whispered into his ear. Though I couldn't hear his words, I had no doubt they were vengeful promises.

"What is the meaning of this!" King Arden demanded as he entered the room to see the encounter between his advisor and Evander. The watching crowd stayed silent, no one daring to answer his question for fear of retaliation from the other powerful king in that room—the king whose shadow magic curled around Mishal like deadly vines.

"Just having a conversation, Arden," Evander remarked in that arrogant tone I knew would piss off the King of Venator.

And it did.

King Arden's face twisted in rage at the lack of respect Evander was giving him. They were both rulers of powerful kingdoms, yet King Arden held himself in such a manner that made me believe he felt he was above Evander and anyone else in every way. I was beginning to get the feeling Evander was about to prove him wrong.

They all feared Evander in some aspect, and that was evident in what I overheard during the kings' meeting in Caelum. They were terrified he would come after their kingdoms while they were away and take them for his own. He was strong, powerful, and skilled enough to wipe them from the map with the right motivation. And they all knew it.

"Drop him right this second! He is under my protection!" King Arden demanded as his hand gripped the sword's hilt at his side.

I frantically searched the room for help and found Olivier and Marceline moving around the crowd slowly. Their hands were on their weapons, ready to defend their king against any attack. For a split second, I thought about getting their attention to help me convince Evander to back down, but the serious look on their faces told me it would be useless. They were there to aid their king, not me.

"Your protection is no longer in play when he touches something of mine," Evander countered back, not bothering to take his eyes from the man in his grasp.

"What are you referring to, Evander?" King Arden demanded, moving closer to the two men though still keeping enough distance to stay out of harm's way.

"He's accusing me of touching his *whore*," Mishal spat, and Evander punched him so hard that bone cracked and blood splattered everywhere, leaving Mishal's nose crooked.

"Call her that again. Please, I beg you to utter the words," Evander seethed, tightening his hold on his prisoner's neck.

Mishal coughed, spitting blood and gasping for air. My Gods, Evander was going to kill this man. I rushed forward, pushing through the crowd of gawkers, determined to stop him from falling over that edge of destruction.

"Evander, don't," I pleaded, and his head twisted slightly at the sound of my voice, but he didn't break his focus on the task at hand.

"Here is the little liar now, My King," Mishal choked out, and King Arden turned his attention to me. I couldn't even deny his claim because I *was* a liar. The whole mission revolved around me leading people on and giving them the false hope of a marriage alliance. I wasn't innocent by any definition.

Evander growled, pulling Mishal forward and slamming his back against the stone wall. I flinched as the sound of crunching bone washed over us, and the audience audibly gasped at the brutality of it.

"I never touched her," Mishal lied, and my lip pulled back in anger. "Her Highness must have slipped and fallen and is now blaming me to try and cause discourse. It's clear they don't want peace with us, Your Majesty."

Yes, because the marks on me were clearly made due to my clumsiness and not from the hands of someone vile. What Mishal was suggesting didn't even make sense. Why would we seek Venator's aid just to spew untruths and end any allegiance before it ever started?

"See, King Evander. Tenebrae's heir slipped and inflicted her injury upon herself. Now let my advisor go this instant!" King Arden demanded, and my jaw dropped at his demand. Mishal was obviously lying, but it seemed the King of Venator didn't care. Perhaps he never truly wanted to consider Evander's request, and this was just an excuse to back out.

"Are you fucking kidding me?" Evander quipped, and a sardonic laugh broke through as he turned to look at Mishal. "The last I checked, falling doesn't leave bruises in the shape of fingermarks on one's *throat*."

"I don't give a shit about what you think is possible or not. You will release Mishal right now or have the Kingdom of Venator to answer to. Choose wisely, Evander, as we know you can't afford any more enemies."

Evander gritted his teeth before reluctantly dropping Mishal to the ground. He stood over the advisor's bloody body with a look of disgust on his face and a dark promise in his eyes. My throat bobbed as I swallowed a hard lump, watching the men nervously. No one in the room seemed to be breathing as we all waited to see Evander's next move. Would he walk away or finish what he started? I loosed a sigh of relief as he turned from Mishal and stalked towards me before pressing a hand to my back to steer me out of the room.

"Perhaps one of her lovers got a little too rough in bed. She looks like she'd like that sort of thing," Mishal added, and the air from my lungs was stolen as I felt Evander's fingers press into my back just a tad firmer than before.

Evander abruptly halted as his face filled with a rage like no other. A tendril of darkness shot out from his hand, aimed right at Mishal, and in the blink of an eye, a crisp snapping noise echoed in the nearly silent room. Mishal's lifeless body slumped to the floor, his neck at an odd angle as a strip of black rope dissipated into the air.

"What did you just do!" King Arden yelled, rushing to his advisor's body.

"Sorry," Evander said under his breath as he guided me to the exit. "My magic must have *slipped*."

Evander opened the door to my room, holding it wide for me to enter first. I passed him without meeting his eyes, too nervous about the pending conversation. I didn't like the intense feelings coming off of him, and I had no idea how to calm them down. When I got halfway into the room I turned, finding him shutting the door and latching the lock before resting his hands on the frame as he tried to hold himself together.

"Thank you for—" I started weakly, wanting to dissolve the tension, but Evander interjected immediately.

"What the *fuck* were you thinking?" he seethed, whirling on me with his features full of anger and disappointment. I knew this would happen when he found out I had failed. I knew I would let him down, and now things had gone entirely to shit.

"We can fix this," I offered, taking a slow step toward him. "Let me talk to Jahier. Maybe I can convince him to ally with us. It's my mess, Evander; let me try to clean it up," I pleaded, and Evander's face twisted in a confused rage.

"You think I'm mad because we don't have a shot in hell at an alliance?" Evander asked incredulously. He stalked for me with a sense of purpose, and I shuffled back several steps. "I'm fucking furious because you let him touch you like this," he said, gently grabbing my forearm and holding it up for me to see the bruises still adorning my flesh. "You didn't fight, Ainsley, and you could have. You *should* have. We've all taught you better than this. We've taught you to defend yourself, and this is what you do with that knowledge?" he growled, dropping my arm and rubbing his hands through his unkempt hair. His posture was rigid yet feral, but it was nothing compared to the look in his eyes.

"I'm sorry, I—"

"You should be. This is fucking unacceptable." He paced back and forth in front of me like a madman.

"What would you have had me do, Evander?" I demanded angrily. He halted his relentless pacing and stared at me confused. He opened his mouth to answer, but I spoke first. "And don't say *fight him off*. You had drilled in me over and over how important this meeting was. How important it was to our mission and our people. You said this may be our only shot. What kind of person would I be if I did something to ruin that and doom Tenebrae and the rest of Disparya? What kind of ruler, Evander?"

His brows creased, and he shook his head as his gaze darted across my face, not wanting to accept what I was telling him. Saving our people was more important than my pride.

"You taught me to pick my battles, so I did. I took the pain and the embarrassment and the shame so I could potentially save thousands of lives. Don't stand there and act as if I fucking enjoyed it," I added, crossing my arms over my chest as if the position could shield me from his disappointment.

Evander moved, closing the gap before us and reaching down to gently tilt my chin up. I wanted to look away and not see the pity on his face, but his soft eyes ensnared me. He ran his cool fingers over my discolored flesh, and my skin burned at his touch.

"This," he whispered, cupping my jaw with his other hand "Is never okay. It will never be a price you have to pay." My eyes watered, and as a tear escaped, he wiped it away with his thumb. "Fuck the alliance, Ainsley. You are worth far more than a few promised words from strangers. When are you going to start realizing that?" I squeezed my eyes shut as the tears flowed, and Evander leaned down and pressed his forehead to mine. "Promise me you'll never let someone touch you without your permission again."

"I promise," I croaked, choking on the lump in my throat. Evander released me then, walking back to the door before calling over his shoulder.

"Go get something to eat."

"I'm not hungry," I replied. The thought of food after this afternoon had my stomach churning. I just wanted to curl up in bed and forget the past hour.

"It's not a request, love," Evander said in his no-nonsense way. "Taking care of yourself includes fueling your body whether you want to or not. Not to mention, Olivier will have your ass doing sprints if you skip a meal," he added teasingly.

"Where are you going?" I asked, as he began to leave. Evander halted on the threshold, not turning to face me.

"I have some things to work out."

And then he was gone, closing the door quietly behind him. I headed to the bathing room to wash my face and scrub away the cowardly tears from my cheeks when a gentle knock sounded at the door. I answered it, finding a servant with a tray of food.

"His Majesty, King Evander asked me to deliver this to you, Your Highness." I took the tray and expressed my gratitude. "He also wanted me to inform you that if you are still unwell, he will have dinner sent up for you this evening." She curtsied before shutting the door and leaving me to myself.

Half an hour later, my entire plate of fruits, bread, cheeses, and assorted meats was clean. Apparently, Evander knew best, as usual. I stood from my bed and paced my room, still unsure if I was ready to face the countless people who would be gossiping about the encounter in the dining room earlier. I half expected to see Felix barging in here but knowing Evander, he probably ordered him to stay away until I was ready.

I drifted to the window, peering out at the view. Agnitio truly was a magnificent kingdom with winding sapphire rivers and bright white houses that were striking against the red sands beyond. It made me miss my home. I'd become accustomed to seeing her giant grey snowcapped mountains and sprawling green fields.

Movement below caught my eye, and I twisted to see Evander in the training ring with Olivier. I would have thought it was any ordinary session, but I could feel his tension from here. His shirt was off, and his muscles flexed as he struck Olivier again and again relentlessly. I had never seen him move like that before.

He was nothing less than a trained warrior, dodging every attack and striking just as fast. Oli blocked, but Evander didn't let up in his pursuit, managing hit after hit.

Olivier raised his hands in surrender before his king could come at him again. Evander halted, scrubbing his sweat-slicked hair and creating a towel from his shadow magic. I studied his movements as he wiped his face. His brow was pinched, and his expression tight and distraught. As if sensing me, he looked up and I froze in place. I wished there was something I could say or some gesture I could do to show him that I saw what he was going through. Today had shaken him, and I didn't know if it was more because of the life he took, the allegiance he lost, or the disappointment he felt at my lack of action. Maybe it was a bit of all three. I turned then and walked back to my bed to leave him be.

"You're too slow. Focus, Ainsley," Olivier said disapprovingly as he deflected my hit and knocked away my dagger.

I freaking sucked this morning. My head was clouded, and my thoughts were on the fallout of yesterday's dining room display. My bruises had entirely disappeared by the time dinner rolled around, and I felt up to joining my friends.

Evander skipped dinner, and Lia explained that he was with Tallis and King Arden, discussing the repercussions of his actions. The members of Venator departed back home immediately following the meeting. Jahier had given me a slight wave from across the hall as they left, not daring to speak to me in person. It hurt because of the friendship we had established, but I understood his decision.

"It's a little hard to focus when my mind is clouded by the meeting I'm currently being kept out of," I bit back, striking and missing miserably yet again.

Fuck this stupid fucking morning. Tallis and Evander were in the council room discussing potential allies to recruit now that we had lost a significant prospect.

And I was being cut out. I was willing to bet it was because Evander was still pissed at me for yesterday.

"As I told you earlier when you asked for the twentieth time, you are not needed there. If you were, you'd be participating," Olivier argued, sheathing his daggers, and I rolled my eyes at the excuse he had given me all morning. "Fine," he said, crossing his muscled arms over his chest. "Name five lords that could help, and I'll take you there right now." I opened my mouth and quickly shut it. I had nothing, and the smirk on his face said he knew it too.

"Whatever," I said, stomping off to the edge of the ring to take a swig from my canteen. Was this what dealing with a sibling was like? Olivier had once said that the only father figure he'd ever known was mine, and I briefly wondered if the role of older brother was one he was trying to fill.

"We're done for the day," Oli called out. "There's no point continuing when you've been shit all morning." I threw my middle figure over my shoulder, not bothering to look at him, and felt Felix's presence a heartbeat later.

"Your boyfriend is an ass," I told him, taking another mouthful.

"He's not my boyfriend," Felix whined. "Not for lack of trying, though. He's so stubborn—worse than you are sometimes." I snickered, wiping the sweat from my brow as I faced him. "I know he totally wants me too," Felix added. "I'll make him admit it one day. If it's the last thing I do, I'll make him admit it."

I laughed and shook my head at his tenacity. The two of them were so different, and Olivier seemed to want nothing to do with Felix, but that wasn't going to stop him. Felix had been laying the groundwork for Olivier to be his since we had gotten to Tenebrae. If it worked, Felix could truly be considered a mastermind.

"Library today?" I asked, changing the subject to try and detract Felix's attention from the man currently walking away shirtless through the courtyard. I waved a hand in front of his face when he didn't respond.

"Sorry, cupcake. He's just so fucking gorgeous," he explained. "But yes, the library sounds good."

"Ok, perfect. I have some things I want to research that may help us find aid after all."

"Oh?" Felix questioned, now intrigued.

"Yes, but keep it between us, please. I don't want to get anyone's hopes up if it turns out to be nothing,"

We agreed to meet outside the library in an hour, giving me plenty of time to eat and bathe. I hurried to my room when a familiar voice caught my ear, and I turned the corner to find Evander nodding politely to two lords before walking away.

"Evander!" I called, jogging up to him. He turned at the sound of his name, and his eyes widened briefly as he saw me. "How did the meeting go? Any prospects?"

"A few," he said, continuing his walk down the hall, and I followed.

"And?" I asked when he didn't elaborate.

"And we'll have to see how it pans out."

So this is how the conversation would go then—quick responses to my questions without any real additions. I understood that he was mad, but this was ridiculous. We were running out of time to secure alliances, and his silent treatment only hurt us.

"Why weren't you at breakfast this morning?" I asked, not wanting to be dismissed so easily.

"I had the meeting," he said as if it was apparent.

"Cut the shit, Van." I grabbed his arm to stop him. He turned and smiled at a few passing servants before returning his attention to me. He arched a brow, silently commanding me to explain my antics. "You're avoiding me."

"I am not," he countered, making to move again, but I tightened my grip, refusing to let him run until we had it out.

"Is it because you're still mad at me for yesterday?"

He stiffened slightly but didn't answer. I hated the way he was acting toward me. It was so unlike the man I had come to know and enjoyed being around despite my attempts to hate him. This wasn't us. We played games and pushed each other's buttons; we teased and bantered—we didn't fight like this.

"Or is it because you're afraid I'll beat you in the ring again?" I tried, hoping to bring some playfulness back into our dynamic. His eyes lit up, and my heart lightened at seeing the challenge within. It was just a glimpse of my normal

Evander, and now that I had him, I couldn't let him go yet. Not until I knew we would be okay. "You are, aren't you? You're worried I'll have you flat on your back," I said, closing the small gap between us as I stared up into his beautiful face. He crossed his arms, tilting his head as he studied me, and a cocky grin formed. Thank the fucking Gods for that smile.

"Are you flirting with me, love?" he asked seductively, and I snorted, rolling my eyes and shaking my head to deny his claim.

"Not a chance," I replied, loving that I had this side of him back, even if it was only for this moment.

"Oh, but I think you are. You could have said I was afraid you'd defeat me, show me up, or even knock me on my ass, but you didn't." He leaned down, whispering the last words, "You wanted me to have that visual of me on my back with you above me."

"In your dreams," I said weakly, as my mind flooded with that very description, making breathing hard as his body pressed closer to mine.

"Always, love. Always."

I stepped back, creating some much-needed distance between us as I struggled to fill my lungs with air once more. Evander smiled, seeming to know exactly what I was doing, and I didn't even care. I was just happy to play with him.

"Then come spar with me," I managed to get out.

"I can't. I have a—"

"Meeting," I finished for him, and he nodded. I tried to ignore the deflated feeling that took over. I had grown accustomed to the friendship we had built, and it hurt when he forced himself to keep busy, not letting me in on his feelings. "Okay," I said, backing away and accepting his answer once and for all.

"But I'm free tomorrow at dawn," he called. "Unless you're rethinking your invitation."

A smile spread wide across my face.

"Never."

"See you then, love," he said as he winked. And then he disappeared, leaving shadows in his wake.

29.

"So what is it we're looking for in there?" Felix asked as we waited outside of the library. The massive two-story stone doors stood tall and blended into the walls seamlessly, so no one could find it unless they knew where the entrance was. Elenora had shared its location and password with me when I expressed my desire to see inside. She also offered to give me a tour, but Felix was the only one I wanted with me for this side mission of mine.

"Books on Inmuto," I told him, running my hands along the coarse white stone. "Excero," I breathed, and a loud cracking sound filled the space. Fissures slipped up the rock in a jagged pattern as if lightning had been etched into the wall. Had I said the wrong word?

When the cracks reached the top of the door, the stone groaned as it scraped against itself and separated, leaving an opening big enough for two people to walk through at a time. Beyond the doors, the small tunnel was dark, and even though my instincts weren't picking up on any danger, I still didn't like the mystery this place offered.

I glanced up at Felix, who looked far too excited for this adventure as he bounced in place. The library of Agnitio was renowned in our country, and the rulers of this kingdom were particular about who they selected to enter, so not many people had ever been inside. I'm sure I had to thank Evander's friendship with Tallis for the invitation.

"Come on," I told Felix, swallowing my nerves and heading into the opening. We were enveloped in darkness, and the groaning of the door behind us told me it shut the moment we passed through. I took another hesitant step forward, hating that we couldn't see, when my face smacked hard into the stone wall. Felix swore under his breath as if he had just done the same thing. I pushed out my hands, feeling around and being met with nothing but the hard wall. What the hell was going on?

"Try to the left, and I'll check the right," Felix suggested, and I did as instructed. I turned to our left and held my hands out as I stepped hesitantly again, running into a wall once more. "Fuck, it's a dead end," he said.

"Same over here," I added, feeling my way around until I found my best friend again. We were enclosed on all three sides, with only the exit behind us. There was no library anywhere to be found unless it was above or below us, though we had no way to figure that out. "Maybe Elenora gave us the wrong password, or maybe I messed up the directions," I said, trying to figure out what went wrong.

"Perhaps," Felix mused as he slipped his hand in mine, making me feel more grounded in the dark. "Why don't we just head back out where we can see and try to work through this?" Felix tugged on my hand, and we took a few steps before we were met with the hard stone of the doors. I leaned forward and whispered the same password hoping it would let us back out.

The splintering sound of cracks slicing through stone echoed off the dark walls, and I sighed in relief to know it had worked. The doors groaned as they opened again, and this time, light from the hallway flooded through, blinding us immediately. I squeezed my eyes shut from the intense brightness as hushed voices flooded around us, which was odd because the corridor had been empty when we arrived not more than three minutes ago. Now, it sounded like dozens of people were crowding around, watching us come through the hidden door that led to nowhere. Perhaps few people saw it, not because they weren't invited but because no one could ever locate it.

"Holy Gods," Felix whispered in amazement, and my eyes fluttered open.

All around us were white stone pillars as tall as I'd ever seen and holding up a roof that wasn't there. The only thing above us was a bright blue afternoon sky and fluffy white clouds. A gentle warm breeze rolled through, carrying the scent of fresh grass and honeysuckle, and I sighed at how relaxed it made me feel. I turned to Felix to ask if he could smell it too, but his stare was firmly fixed on the stone walls that stretched hundreds of feet into the air and housed thousands, if not millions, of books.

I spun, taking in the fact that there wasn't a single inch of wall in this room that wasn't covered in literature. In the center of the enormous space were tables, couches, and cozy little spots to curl up and read under the sky above. I was worried for a second that the books weren't safe from the elements, but then a shimmer caught my eye, and I realized the whole space was protected by a shield. I wasn't sure how a breeze could escape through unless there was a window open somewhere I couldn't see. This place was a literal dream, and I never wanted to leave. Forget a marriage alliance for aid in a war; I'd make one solely to stay in that library.

Felix clutched my hand tight and smiled wide as he ran for the bookcases, pulling me along with him. I laughed under my breath, trying to keep the volume down so as not to disturb anyone around who was reading.

"What are you two doing!" a stern voice called out, and Felix and I halted at once as we located the source of the interruption.

Four tables, all covered with parchment and books, had been set up in the shape of a rectangle, and in the center sat a man with a pissed-off expression. Felix and I slowly approached, wondering what the hell his problem was. I opened my mouth to inquire, but he slammed a pen down on the table, making me flinch at the sound.

"Everyone who enters has to sign in," he barked, pointing at a piece of paper covered in names. We both nodded, and Felix picked up the pen to do as instructed. "In this library, there is no running, no conversing loudly, no laughing, no food or beverage, no sudden movements, no Gift usage, no removing books from the premises, no sleeping, no playing, no—"

"Fun?" Felix offered, and I clamped my lips together to stifle my laughter as it apparently wasn't allowed. The man gave my friend a flat look that said he was in no mood for his antics, and I wasn't sure he'd ever be.

"No sexual activity, no singing, no humming, no arguments, no explicit language, and no questioning the rules," he finished.

"Is smiling okay, or...?" Felix asked, and I snorted before quickly disguising it as a cough and mouthing an *I'm sorry* to the very unhappy librarian. The man didn't respond, and Felix took his loss, jotting down two names before offering a polite, tight smile to the man and leading me back to the stone bookcases.

"Marjorie and Abigail?" I asked, noting the names used were ones from his manuscript. Felix winked.

"It wasn't in the listed rules that I couldn't write down fake names," he said conspiratorially. "And for some reason, I have the feeling you don't want them to have our real ones anyway."

I bit my lip because he was absolutely correct.

The sky overhead was a beautiful orange hue as the sun began to set. Felix and I had claimed an oversized couch and table for our own as we flipped through countless books they had detailing limited information about the lost sixth kingdom. We learned absolutely nothing new, and I huffed in irritation. Only three books claimed Inmuto was located in the north, but even those said it bordered Venator to the west and not Tenebrae.

As far as their magic was concerned, we were no closer to uncovering that either. Some books claimed they could manipulate the earth, wind, or stars, while others claimed they were shifters. One document even said that Inmuto held a piece of each of our kingdom's Gifts, making them all-powerful, and that's why they were wiped out. But if any of that were the case, why hadn't we ever encountered someone with those abilities? It seemed unlikely that there hadn't been at least *one* person alive today that descended from that kingdom. Unless, of course, it really was a myth.

Though everything seemed to point in that direction, I trusted Evander's intuition because I felt it too. I hadn't been in Tenebrae very long, but when Evander pointed to the map and relayed his theory, I couldn't help but feel the truth in it. I was drawn to the same point, and it just didn't feel right—like it was missing something. As soon as the weather transformed into spring, we'd head to the border and see what we could figure out. Van had explored it before, but hopefully, with a new set of eyes with him, we'd have better luck.

"We have to be missing something within all this damn bullshit," I hissed angrily, and the librarian shushed me loudly.

"No explicit language!" he whisper-yelled, and I gave him the middle finger. He looked as if he were about to argue, but I aggressively whispered back before he could.

"It's not against the rules," I said, giving him my other middle finger for good measure. He glowered at me as he scribbled on a piece of paper, no doubt adding inappropriate finger gestures to his insane list.

"I think we should take a break," Felix suggested, and I threw myself onto the couch and looked up at the dimming sky. Though the light faded from above, all around us, lanterns lit with a gentle glow, just enough to be able to read in a calming ambiance.

"Time is running out, and we're getting nowhere."

"I know," he replied, climbing on top of me to block my view and force me to look at him. "But we're going to figure it out. It may take some more time, but I know we can do it. If we have to spend every day in this dreadful library, we will."

I smiled, knowing he would love nothing more than to spend our days in here from the moment the sun rose. Unfortunately, I had the distinct feeling it wouldn't be enough.

"No sexual activity!" the librarian said in outrage, and Felix and I looked up at him from the couch. We were certainly in a precarious position, but our clothes were still on, and nothing inappropriate was happening. This man just wanted a reason to scold us like children again.

Felix climbed off of me, glaring at the librarian the entire time as he muttered curses under his breath. It took a lot to piss off Felix, and it seemed like this man managed to hit every button possible.

"How do you feel about breaking one of the rules?" I asked just loud enough for only my friend to hear. Felix's answering wicked smile was all I needed to see.

30.

"Why are we training at night?" I asked Marce as we trekked through the sparse, thin trees of the forest on the outskirts of the palace. As soon as Felix and I finished in the library, Marceline cornered me, demanding we go train. My protests of being tired and hungry did absolutely nothing, and she forced me to change and head out with her.

"Because I'm hoping the dark and quiet will sharpen your senses enough for you to conquer this Gift. You should have mastered how to defend against it by now," she said.

"Thanks," I told her flatly. Every other Gift I had been taught, I'd managed to pick up quickly, but fighting against her powers as a Tremo always left me reeling, completely defeated, and under her spell by the end of the session. Even when I knew the wielder wished me no harm, it didn't take away the pure terror that filled my body. I wasn't getting any better, and it was a problem.

"It isn't something you should be ashamed of," Marceline said absentmindedly as she held up a branch for me to duck under. "The rate of your progress in all aspects of your training has been incredible. We just need to figure out how we can get you to overcome this as well."

"And you think using your Gift on me in total darkness will allow this?" I questioned. I didn't see how it would do anything but make me worse at defending it than I already was.

Most of the fears brought forth were seeing those I held dear to me, like Felix, lifeless in my arms, screaming as the pain of loss ripped through me. Other times, I was in the woods of Caelum, being held in place and cut open by the men that had attempted to kidnap me. But the worst scenario was being tied down, screaming as King Perceval stole every drop of my magic while his son stood by and watched with a smile plastered on his face.

Most times, Tremos used images of deadly creatures and impending death to terrify their victims to the point that their bodies and hearts gave out from the fear. But Marceline wanted me to learn to defend against the ideas that truly scared me. She explained that if I could do that, I would be able to defend against any possible attack. I would be able to differentiate between real and fiction. So I prepared once again for my greatest fears to be pulled to the forefront of my mind as I tried to use everything I had learned to fight them off.

"I think the darkness will aid your mind in deciphering what is truly there and what is not. I think the quiet will help you focus. And if it doesn't," she said, cresting the top of a red sandy hill. "I'll have a fantastic time watching you flail around in the dark."

"Asshole," I told her as a smile tugged at my lips.

Marce took us down a path that led to a small clearing on the edge of a moonlit lake. Sounds of insects chirped, and a warm breeze blew around us. Though I loved the climate of this kingdom, I couldn't help but feel a little homesick for the cold weather of Tenebrae.

I took up my stance and she faced me, readying her Gift for our session. I reminded myself that nothing I experienced was real, just as I had every time before we started, though it never did me any good. Marce raised her arms and attacked my mind until I was standing in a black room as Felix screamed in pain at my feet.

I dropped to my knees as my hands moved to the wound on his chest, trying desperately to help him as I was drenched in his blood. Felix coughed, red liquid spilling from his mouth as he grasped my arms with pleading eyes for me to save him.

"Hang on, Felix," I begged, pressing my hands to the wound. I tried to call my magic to the surface to craft something to plug the gaping hole in his chest, but nothing happened. I was an empty shell void of any magic. Felix began to weaken in my arms. "Stay with me, Felix. Please!" I cried, digging through myself for any scrap of power.

Tears sprang from my eyes as I watched his life slowly drain away, unsure how to save him. I couldn't lose my best friend. He was a bright light in this dark world and didn't deserve to be taken from it so soon.

"What a shame," a cruel voice murmured. I clutched Felix protectively as I twisted to find King Perceval striding for us with Dashiell at his side, wearing a wicked smile. "If only you had magic, you could have spared him from this fate."

"Please save him," I begged, sobbing as I held him, his body growing colder by the second and his breathing becoming much too shallow. King Perceval and Dashiell watched with interest but didn't move to help. "He's your best friend," I claimed, staring directly at the prince in hopes of getting through to him.

"It's too late," he replied harshly, and I shook my head as I turned back to the man in my arms, but he was gone. All that was left in his place was a puddle of crimson blood. I reached forward, pressing my hands to the thick liquid as if I could still find him there.

"Ainsley," King Perceval bellowed. I turned quickly at the sound to find him now standing only a foot away.

I scrambled to my feet, startled at his sudden proximity. He moved closer, and I stepped backward as I looked down to ensure I didn't slip, but the blood had disappeared completely. There wasn't a trace to be found on the floor or my hands. It was like it hadn't been there at all. "You have something I want," the king said.

I brought my palms up, calling my magic, and this time I could feel a tiny ember within me, fighting to ignite a spark. My shadows pressed against my skin, but I couldn't get them to break through no matter how hard I tried. They were trapped, caged below the surface, and I couldn't find the key to free them.

"Having issues?" Dashiell asked cruelly as he held up a small teacup and poured its contents onto the ground. The liquid splattered, hissing and sizzling as it hit the floor, resembling the poison it truly was. I shuddered to think that's what it looked like as it infected my body and sunk its claws into my magic to keep it from manifesting.

King Perceval gripped my shoulders to stop me from retreating as Dashiell stalked for me with a serpentine smile, looking so much like his father. I thrashed against the king's hold, trying to fight him off, but he was too strong. With my magic sated, I felt weaker than I ever had before. Dashiell drew closer, and as I attempted to bring my leg up to kick him, I found that I wasn't able to. My eyes dropped to see my feet rooted to the spot. The poison had spread across the floor to reach me, crawling over my feet and around my ankles as it claimed me like it was furious I had escaped it in the first place. I was stuck, and I could do nothing to get free.

"I won't let you take it," I snarled as I looked into the deep blue eyes of the man I had once loved. The color was different than I remembered, being more of a plain dark blue rather than the medley of deep teal and navy that I was always so captivated by.

A flicker of memory fluttered into my mind of the two of us smiling while I selected a vase that matched the color of his eyes and inhaled the scent of the crisp white rose inside. I looked around, realizing something about this room wasn't right, but before I could question it further, Dashiell's hands wrapped around my arm and I screamed as a burning heat spread through me.

My shadows leaked from my skin, no longer belonging to me as Dashiell drained each tendril slowly from my body. Hot tears coursed down my cheeks as the poison at my feet seeped into my skin, paralyzing me and making me bend to the prince's will. My body shook and my knees trembled from the excruciating agony of having my Gifts torn from me.

The physical pain was near impossible to endure, but the emotional trauma was far worse as it left me begging for a quick death. I was nothing without my magic. I couldn't help save my kingdom or the other people of Disparya. Thousands were going to die because I was too weak to fight and too stupid to avoid being captured. Evander was going to hate me.

King Perceval's boisterous laugh echoed in my ears as every ounce of my power was stolen for the benefit of his son. And as I looked at the man who had shown me what it was like to feel alive, I found I didn't recognize him at all. Had he always been this cruel? I tried to recall why I claimed to love him, but every time I pushed my thoughts toward memories I could have sworn had taken place, a wall was put up, blocking me from seeing the view. As soon as chocolate tartlets, raspberries, and a soft meadow by a lake at night flashed into my mind, the memory was just as quickly replaced by sinister eyes and wicked smiles.

I screamed out as Dashiell grabbed a fistful of my hair, yanking hard as he forced me to look up at him while the final bit of my magic drifted away, leaving me empty and hollow. Tears pricked the backs of my eyes, and my body ached as if I was being handled roughly, though the only hands touching me were Dashiell's. King Perceval had let go of my shoulders the moment his son approached, no longer deeming me a threat now that I was immobilized. The prince's fingers curled in my hair as he sneered at me, and the pain throughout my body intensified. Why was I feeling this pain in my limbs rather than just the point of contact between Dashiell's hand and my head? Was it because my magic was gone, and this was the result?

A scream pierced the dark space, but it didn't come from me. I squeezed my eyes shut as the sound reverberated through my bones and placed my hands over my ears to try and muffle the screeching noise. The louder the scream got, the more pain I felt filling every inch of my body. My head was stinging from Dashiell's violent hold on my hair, and my skin felt raw and tender like I had been brutally beaten.

The scream ended abruptly, and the claws that had sunk into my mind retracted, giving me back complete control. A crushing weight had been removed from my chest, and I sucked in a gasping breath as Marceline's Gift released me from its hold. But rather than drink in the warm night air, my lungs filled with water.

"We've been looking for you," an evil voice called out, and though it was muffled from me being underwater, I'd recognize the owner anywhere. A moment later, I was pulled from beneath the surface and a vicious, rotten-toothed smile peered down at me. The men from the orchard had found me again, and it wasn't another trick of a Gift; it was real.

And I was going to die.

31.

I wheezed and coughed, desperate to suck down fresh air, but the moment I took a single deep breath, he shoved me back into the lake. I gripped the hands clasped around my neck, my nails digging into his skin as I tried to claw myself free from his hold. He pulled me up again, and I inhaled another breath at once.

"I can't kill you just yet," he breathed as he hovered over me, his face only inches from mine. I was enveloped in the smell of sweat, dirt, and rotting flesh as he kept me close, giving me an eyeful of his yellow teeth. "Not until I have a bit of fun first."

I glanced around, finding Marceline on her back several yards away with her eyes closed and blood dripping down the side of her head. My heart sank as I stared at her, praying to the Gods that she was alive. As if they heard my call, her chest rose and fell steadily, indicating she was still with me and hadn't fallen to these assholes. I looked past my attacker to see several men observing us, and their faces were once more hidden in shadows to hide their identities. The man with the scarred hands was there again, and I watched as he strode forward and whispered something into the leader's ear that caused his face to spread into a twisted smile.

"My companion here just shared some interesting news with me," he said before dunking me below the water again. I hadn't had a chance to gulp down any air before his assault, and I thrashed below the surface as my lungs burned and panic took over. I tried to recall every bit of training I'd had, but my mind was only filled with terror. I couldn't remember how to fight or even how to call my magic. My focus was solely on trying to breathe, and it was going to cost me my life.

He pulled me up, and I coughed heavily as my captor laughed in my face. All thoughts emptied from my head as I was struck across the face with a blow so hard, I saw stars. My teeth rattled as the metallic taste of blood coated my tongue, and my hands fell to my sides as my vision blurred.

"That was for getting my men killed," he snarled before hauling me upright to knee me in my side. The hit was so hard a snapping sound echoed in my head, and I screamed as burning agony ripped through my body.

He lifted me so my feet no longer touched the ground before slamming my back onto the rocks at the lake's edge with all his might. The air from my lungs was knocked out of me, and my vision spotted with darkness. He wasn't going to make it a quick death. No, he would take his time and make it last as long as possible while he relished in my misery.

Months of learning and training, all for nothing—I was failing when it mattered most. My attacker wrapped his hands around my throat again as he dragged me closer to the water, not entirely done with his torture. I sucked in a painful breath a second before he dunked my head below the surface. This time, he only held me down briefly before bringing me back up.

"You see," he began with a hint of amusement in his voice. "I had only planned to locate *you*, but my friend here tells me you're in the company of some pretty important people."

He dipped me again, and the cold water stung my busted lip as my blood tainted the lake. His brow arched when he lifted me back up like he wanted me to comment on his statement, but I wouldn't.

"It seems King Evander has been staying close to you, and I bet he's going to come looking the moment you don't return to him," the man replied cheerfully.

I swallowed the bile that crept up at the mention of Evander and what these people could do to him. He was a king and could take down any opponent, but would he have a chance when he never saw the attack coming? Marceline was ruthless and terrifying. She led our armies and was renowned as a great warrior, and they still managed to catch her off guard. Evander had no reason to believe I wasn't safe here in Agnitio. If he came looking, it would be because he thought we were still out training and would have come to offer his help like he had done so many times. He wouldn't think that we were in danger.

"Now, I *was* just going to beat you senseless before dragging you off with us, but I'd much rather make you suffer in other ways first. Not to mention, taking out a king is a feat I'd love to claim for my own," he said, and my blood went cold. "So, what I'm going to do instead is make you watch while I kill everyone you love—starting with her." He pointed to an unconscious Marce before plunging me into the lake again.

His booming laughter was muffled and drowned out by my underwater screams as I frantically clawed at the arms around my neck. I couldn't let him hurt her or any of the people who had started to become my family. Marce didn't deserve the cruel fate she'd been dealt.

He pulled me up, and my screams roared around us as I broke the surface, making him laugh harder. This couldn't be happening. My life—*our* lives—couldn't end this way. I had worked too hard and given too much. I tried to call my magic again, this time feeling a slight prickle as I did. My attacker leaned into my face, his lips curling in disgust as he finished his vow.

"And ending with King Evander."

He slammed me below the water again, and the world grew dark as my magic tore from my body at the mention of his name.

A tall figure slowly led me through the castle, yelling orders I could barely comprehend. The roaring in my ears was so loud, I couldn't make out the words around me. I held up my hands as they shook uncontrollably and dragged the pads of my thumbs over each of my fingers, feeling the odd sticky substance that coated them. Blood. My hands were covered in blood.

"And take Felix with you!" a familiar voice commanded.

The once warm blood had now gone cold. So cold. So *thick*. Not an inch of skin was visible. I had killed him, and now his very life's blood stained my hands—a stain I wasn't sure I could ever erase.

"You're not coming with us?" someone replied, the sound distant yet close as if echoing off stone walls in a vacant room.

A faint tapping sound caught my attention, and I looked passed my fingers to the marble floor to see a small puddle forming inches from where I stood. I realized the source of the mess wasn't coming from my soiled hands but rather my hair as dark red blood dripped from its ends. Was there any part of me that wasn't covered?

"I am not *fucking* leaving her," the first voice spat out, enraged.

Evander.

I turned my head, trying to follow the sound—trying to find him, but my body shook so hard I couldn't see straight. At once, soft hands were on my face holding me still. Evander was now in my line of sight, his gaze darting across my face and settling on my shocked stare. Whatever horrors he saw there had his eyes going cold and his jaw clenching. He called out, never taking his gaze off mine.

"And Olivier... bring them back alive." The tone of his voice told me they wouldn't be staying that way for long.

Evander draped my arms around his neck and picked me up in one smooth movement. I laid my head against him as I savored the warmth and safety he provided. Servants murmured as we passed, and Evander gave them orders that I didn't care to hear. All I wanted was sleep. All I wanted was to wake up from what was clearly just a nightmare. I couldn't have killed someone in that way. I couldn't have.

"And make sure Tallis knows exactly what happened," Evander commanded, his voice serious and detached—the voice of a furious king. He slammed the door shut and carried me into the bathing room. Tallis and Evander may have been friends, but two of Evander's own were attacked tonight, and he wasn't likely to forget that anytime soon. He was going to want answers.

He set me down gently on a bench near the tub and drew the warm water. I watched quietly as he grabbed bottles, dumping their oily contents into the already steaming bath. The smell of lavender and sage quickly filled the room; they were scents meant to calm, I realized.

Evander walked back over and knelt as he looked me up and down, his eyes soft and sorrowful. There was pain and anger on his face, along with emotions I couldn't comprehend through the haze of my mind. After a moment, he stood back up, nodding to himself.

"I'm going to go get Naideen so she can help you bathe, Ainsley." He spoke each word slowly, deliberately, like he was afraid I wouldn't understand. "I'll be right outside the—"

"NO! No, no, no, please. Please don't leave me, Evander. Please don't go. Please." I begged, grabbing the sleeve of his jacket with all the strength I could muster. The back of my eyes burned as the tears began to flow down my cheeks, smearing tracks through the blood already there. Evander was back in front of me in less than a heartbeat, with my face between his hands.

"Okay. It's okay," he said softly, his eyes pleading for me to believe him as he wiped his thumb back and forth over my bloodied cheeks. "I'll stay, Ainsley. I won't leave you."

I closed my eyes and breathed deeply in relief. I didn't know why but at that moment, his presence was the only one I wanted. Not Felix. Not Lia. *Him*. Over the course of our time together, we had developed a deep bond between us. I wasn't sure if it was simply because we were ruler and heir, but whatever the reason, his company made me feel protected. The feeling wasn't only regarding my physical safety; I knew this connection had also kept my emotional and mental welfare intact. It was an odd sensation and one I had never experienced before, not even with Dashiell or Felix.

"Come on, let's get you cleaned up," Evander whispered, and held my hands as I lifted myself on wobbly legs, praying to the Gods above that they could hold my weight long enough to undress. Pain shot through my body as I reached for the hem of my shirt, and I winced. Evander's hands were immediately on me and the blood-soaked fabric.

"Are you hurt?" he demanded, panic coating his voice.

"Yes," I answered honestly, remembering each blow I had taken.

"May I?" he asked as he held the bottom of my shirt in his hands. I nodded my permission, and he lifted the fabric before sucking in a sharp intake of air at whatever it was he saw. His breathing increased, and a mix of pain and fury flashed across his face. "This will hurt slightly," he said as he brought his fingers to my side, brushing against the skin. I looked away as I let out a cry, the pain sharp like lightning shooting through my body. "It looks like a broken rib. I'll call for a Medicus shortly to have it looked at." I nodded over my shoulder, still in too much pain to speak.

Evander quickly removed the rest of my clothing, never letting his eyes stray from mine. I wasn't sure whether it was his way of letting me know he wasn't stealing glances or if he was too afraid to look away. Like if he did, then I'd be left alone to deal with the horrors he saw there. When he finished his task, he gripped my hand steadily as I slowly climbed over the lip of the copper tub. Heat caressed my body, soothing the muscles I didn't even know had ached, and I melted into the warm water.

As I submerged myself up to my chest, panic began to rise, and I squeezed my eyes shut as tight as I could while images of tonight flowed into the forefront of my mind in flashes. A vision of a man holding me down in the water, trying to drown me for the purpose of his torturous game. Images of Marceline lying there unconscious and bloody. I began to shake again, gripping the sides of the tub so hard I was sure my knuckles were about to break skin as my breathing came in short, fast spurts. This wasn't the lake. This wasn't the lake. This wasn't the lake. Sobs burst from my throat, followed by the sound of boots hitting the floor and water splashing.

Evander's arms came from behind me, his hands gently prying mine from the sides of the tub. Once free, he interlaced our fingers and wrapped our arms tightly across my chest as his sodden clothes made loud dripping noises into the water while he held me still. He leaned forward and whispered into my ear.

"You're okay, Ainsley. You're safe. You're okay. You're safe."

Over and over and over again. Like a chant. Like a prayer. And with how his voice broke on the words, I wasn't sure if he was saying it more so for himself or for me. I tried to clear my mind, focusing on his voice and steady heart beating loudly. Concentrating on the feel of his chest rising and falling against my back. I slowed my breathing, trying to match the pattern of his own until we were moving as one.

"Good," he said. "Keep breathing. Slowly. You're okay now. You're safe. I have you."

Nothing had ever felt more true than those words.

32.

When my sobs reduced to shuddering breaths and the heavy flow of tears dissipated to nothing more than a gentle trickling down my cheeks, Evander's weight shifted slightly as he released his hold on me. Before the panic could rise at the thought of him letting me go before I was ready, he whispered. "Lean forward for me." I obliged, and after a moment, a warm cloth swept gently over my shoulders, and I watched as the blood that coated my skin began to drop into the bath and disappear beneath the surface. Evander's touch was careful as he washed away the physical traces of the night, though I knew the evidence ran far deeper than what was showing on my skin. He didn't know what I did—the extent of how far I'd gone.

Bottles opened and closed, and soon, his hands were in my hair. His touch was methodic and soothing. It was comforting and cautious. It was exactly what I needed. Without thinking, I leaned back against him as I focused on the movement of his fingers working and the way they seemed to quiet my raging thoughts and broken soul.

"I was fourteen the first time I ever took a life," Evander whispered. My posture straightened slightly but he ignored the change in me and continued," It was when I was visiting Vorsutos one summer. Our trip had to be cut short because Declan received word of an attack by rebels. He and Olivier ordered Cal to take me back to Tenebrae while they went to fight." He wrung a cloth over my hair, and the suds slowly rolled down my back. He reached for another bottle and began his work through my hair once again, the scent of lavender filling my nose.

"I was pissed that they refused to let me go," he continued. "They said I was too important to risk and too inexperienced for a battle of that magnitude. Of course, they were right, but I didn't care. We didn't make it to our ship before sundown, and back then, I couldn't traverse the distance I can now, so we stopped for the night. I waited until Cal was asleep and snuck out, determined to join Declan and Olivier. I had only made it a few miles when I ran into this man with one eye. I'll never forget the hunger within it as he stared at me like I was the answer to his prayers. I wasn't sure if he knew who I was or why he was looking at me like I was a treasure to be kept until I glanced down and saw my shadows had curled around my hands on protective instinct. I called my magic back, but it was too late. He knew I was from Tenebrae.

"Tilt your head back," Evander instructed. I did as asked and rested my head against his shoulder as he gently poured water across my scalp. When he was finished, he helped me sit up straight and guided me until I was twisted around to face him. He reached for the cloth again and brought it up to my forehead as he carefully cleaned the caked-on blood from my face.

"It's not a secret that Disparya is a far wealthier country than Vorsutos. The man wanted to ransom me. He didn't possess magic, and by the look of him, he wasn't strong or a trained fighter. I didn't want to hurt him, let alone kill him." Evander took a deep breath as he continued his work. "But he wouldn't stop. When he lunged for me, my Tremo Gift surfaced before I knew it was happening, and he was snared in my magic instantly. I was paralyzed by fear as I watched the life drain from him in the most gruesome and grotesque way imaginable."

Evander submerged the cloth in the water, letting the evidence of my guilt drift away until the fabric was clean once more. The crimson liquid dripped into the bath but instantly disappeared as the magic of the tub kept the water clear. He wrung out the excess water and hung it over the side of the tub as he turned his attention back to me. His fingers gently tilted my chin from side to side as he inspected the bruises I could feel on my throat.

"Once my Gift released him and returned to me, I emptied my stomach on the grass next to the body. I was so shaken and guilt stricken that I wasn't sure how I would be able to make it back to the camp. But somehow, I found the strength to stand and was back inside my tent within a few hours. Cal had never even noticed that I had been gone, and the next day, we returned home. As soon as we arrived, I locked myself in my room for about a week. Cal assumed I was throwing a tantrum over being kept out of the battle, so he left me alone, never disturbing me except to leave meals outside my door. It was the worst time of my life," Evander said, moving his fingers up to the side of my face, where my skin instantly stung at his touch. Another bruise, no doubt.

"I couldn't keep any food down, and I sure as hell couldn't sleep. Night after night, I was plagued with visions of that man—reliving his death over and over again. And I was powerless to stop it. My grief consumed me whole until I was nothing but a raging fire of anguish. My heartache and anger were so great that I nearly lost myself to it. I wanted to give up right then because what kind of king was I after taking a life that could have so easily been spared? If I had listened to the words of the men more experienced around me—if I hadn't been so damn stubborn and arrogant in thinking I could handle myself—then that man wouldn't have died at my hands."

I averted my eyes as I was filled with shame. Not at what Evander had done, but because I felt no remorse for my own actions.

"You're the only one who knows," he said.

His hands fell away from my face, and my eyes eagerly sought his; the truth of the words held so tightly within them that I was shocked he had managed to speak it. A secret kept like a sacred oath that would never reveal itself, but for some reason, he chose to share it with me.

"Did it ever get easier—living with that guilt?" I asked him on a shaky breath. Evander's face filled with sorrow and pity as he stared at me.

"I wish so much that I could tell you what you want to hear, love. But there hasn't been a day that I don't remember that moment and regret my loss of control."

"I didn't just kill him, Evander," I said, my gaze deathly serious. "I eviscerated him." I took a deep breath as I looked into his grey eyes and spoke the words I knew I needed to say.

"When they found us, we were caught completely off guard. They attacked Marceline before she even had a chance to defend herself. I thought they killed her, and the only saving grace was that I saw her chest slowly rise and fall. They came for me next," I recounted hollowly, as my mind traveled back to that moment, and I sensed Evander's body tense. "The sound of the leader's voice was a shock to my system, and it was like I was suddenly back in Caelum, too weak and paralyzed with fear to do anything." I blinked away the tears and steadied my breathing as I tried to calm myself enough to continue my story.

"He grabbed me by the hair and dragged me to the lake, dunking me underwater until I started to lose consciousness, then brought me up for air before I could. Over and over again, he played his game while spewing his insults." I sat up straighter, and my stare became serious. I wanted to relay my following words to Evander with importance. "I tried to remember how to fight, Van. I promise I tried," I sobbed, and his hands found my cheeks as he wiped away the tears that had formed. I needed him to know I didn't decide to be weak and let them hurt me. I didn't want him to think I had allowed it to happen again after what occurred with Mishal.

"I know, love. I know you did," he said, trying to soothe my guilt.

"I couldn't fight the panic and clear my mind. It was like everything I had been taught had just vanished from my head. And then…" I swallowed as I remembered the moment the fog cleared and clarity came through. "And then he said he would come after everyone I loved and make me watch as he hurt them. He said he'd start with Marceline, and then when he threatened to come after you, I just fucking snapped." There was a rush of adrenaline and power unlike anything I'd ever experienced. Magic surged from me like a wave of destruction, ready to protect me—ready to kill him. I still wasn't sure what exactly I had experienced, but I knew I couldn't hold it in any longer.

"Van, something happened. I don't know what it was, but…" I said, trying desperately to come up with the words. Evander sat there patiently as he continued to stroke his thumbs over my cheeks in an effort to comfort me. I took a deep breath and swallowed hard. "Magic ripped from me, but it wasn't my shadows or my other Gifts. This power felt different but also familiar, and I wielded it with little effort."

Evander watched me without ever giving away what he was thinking. His face was thoughtful but passive, his eyes warm but distant. I could tell he wanted to know more but was afraid of pushing me too far. His mind was at work, carefully curating a response.

"Can you tell me what it felt like?" he finally said. I thought about it, forcing myself to go back to the moments I ended my attacker's life.

"It was like my magic was trying to claim his body as my own. I could feel the pulsing of blood flowing through his veins, the way his heart beat and his lungs expanded. It was as if I was there inside him, experiencing the way everything worked," I explained. Evander's stare was blank and patient as he waited for me to continue. "I wrapped the magic around his organs until I reached his heart. And then I looked him in the eyes and squeezed."

I shut my eyes as if I could picture everything perfectly behind closed lids. I could see the shock and pain on his face, knowing he was about to die at my hands. A shiver of pleasure ran down my body at the memory of how good it felt to see him terrified.

"I squeezed and squeezed until he was begging me to stop. And then I squeezed some more. I didn't stop until his blood poured from his mouth, his ears, his eyes. Only then did I let go—and only because I wasn't done with him yet." I opened my eyes again to find Evander as still as a statue as he listened. "Once his body slumped to the ground, I climbed over him and used my shadows to craft claws on the back of my cestus. And then I stared into his eyes as I tore him apart until nothing was left but shredded flesh and crushed bone."

I flexed my fingers as if I could still feel the weapon strapped to my hands and the blood that poured over them. And maybe I could. Perhaps this phantom feeling of taking a life would always stay with me like it had Evander. But the man sitting before me didn't want to take the life he had. I enjoyed taking my first tonight. He deserved it. He deserved every brutal thing I had done to him, but what did that make me? Was I just as evil as that man? Did killing him in such a horrific and grotesque way make me a murderer?

Evander dipped his head, so his nose nearly touched mine. His stare never wavered—never indicated he was bothered by what I had done. It was as if the details of my abuser's death didn't matter to him. But it did to me. I had never felt stronger than I had when I was tearing him apart, and that scared me.

"Tell me, love," he whispered. I knew what he meant: tell him the things I wasn't saying aloud. The secrets of my mind he knew I was holding onto tightly.

"I'm a monster, Van," I breathed, my eyes instantly welling with tears at the admission. "It's no wonder the world fears what we're capable of. No one should ever wield so much power."

"I don't agree," he said.

"Evander, I killed him in the most horrific way. I could have ended it quickly, but I didn't. I chose to draw it out and reveled in his suffering," I argued.

"I snapped a man's neck the other day. Do you think *I'm* a monster?"

"No, but that was different. You were—"

"Protecting someone I care about. It's no different than what you did tonight. And the only thing I regret is how quick of a death he received." I took a deep breath and let his claim wash over me as thoroughly as the soap, wanting his words to scrub me clean of every sullied thought I had about myself. "Make no mistake, love, I enjoyed what I did to Mishal and would have liked it even more if I got to dish out half of what you did tonight." He pressed his forehead to mine as the final tears fell from my eyes. "You are not a monster, Ainsley. You are strength and love and vengeance. You took the payment you were owed. Lines to cross do not exist when it comes to avenging those we love or ourselves."

I wanted to believe him. I wanted to accept his words as truth, but I didn't know if I could.

"I feel so weak and broken, Van," I admitted as I pulled back just enough to meet his gaze again. He nodded as if he knew exactly how I felt. Like he too, had experienced the same lows.

"You're not," he said, dragging my nose up with the tip of his. I let out a soft groan of annoyance before reaching my hand up to bat him away. "See," he said, smiling. "There's that fight I adore." I couldn't help but let out a breathy laugh as I rolled my eyes at him.

"What happened to me?" I asked. The look in his eyes when I shared my story, told me he knew exactly what was going on. Evander swallowed hard, his throat bobbing with the movement. I held my breath as terror began to sweep over me. The moment Evander sensed my panic, his hold on me tightened.

"Breathe, love. It's okay," he soothed. I did as instructed, sipping on small intakes of air as I waited for him to clue me in on why my magic had acted the way it had. "That magic you felt tonight was your Gift." I narrowed my eyes at him. It didn't feel like my shadows, illusions, or Empathi magic at all. It was something wholly different. "I'm not sure how it's possible, but what you described is the Gift of an Imperium, love."

My brain clawed through the knowledge I had learned about the five kingdoms and their unique Gifts. Imperiums hailed from Ministro and had the magic of anatomical manipulation. They could control how blood flowed in the body and how the organs worked. They could wrap their magic around someone's heart and end their life instantly. Evander had said it was arguably one of the strongest Gifts in existence and just as rare as the Magusiers.

"How?" I asked shakily.

"I don't know, but we're going to figure it out, love. It's going to be okay. I have you," Evander said.

I loosed a breath and let his words wrap around my mind and caress me until I started to relax. If I had a second Gift from Ministro, then that would mean I was also the heir to that kingdom. I didn't see how that was possible, but I knew I could believe Evander when he said we'd figure it out. We would.

"Can I ask you something?" Evander said.

"Yes."

"Why did you ask for me? When Oli found me, he said you refused to talk to anyone but me. You just kept demanding for me repeatedly," he said, and I let out a deep breath before nodding. There wasn't anyone I wanted more at that moment or this one than him.

"The first reason was that I knew you wouldn't judge me. You wouldn't look at me differently once you discovered what I had done. I know the others love me, but you... you understand me, and that's what I needed."

I gripped the hands that held my face as I breathed him in. I was safe with him, and he didn't run after learning the depths I had gone to as I enacted my revenge.

"And the second reason?" he asked, and I parted my mouth to speak, but no words came out. I tried again, and still nothing. "It's okay, love," Evander said. "Let's get you out so we can take care of that wound."

He stood, stepped out of the tub, and walked to the towel rack. He was fully clothed and dripping all over the floor but didn't seem to notice or care as he strolled for me. Evander held the towel open as he turned his head to the side to give me privacy so I could step out of the tub. Once free, he wrapped me in the warm fabric, bundling me up tight before leading me out of the bathing room and over to the bed. He set me down on the edge and then strode for the dresser across the room.

A moment later, he returned with a shirt and underwear. I dropped the towel from around me as he slid his shirt over my head and carefully pulled my arms through each hole. I sucked in a sharp breath as I tried to get dressed, my possible broken rib sending a striking pain through me. Evander clenched his jaw like the noise hurt him just as much as it did me, and I wondered what was going through his mind. After sliding his underwear up my legs so I could wear them as shorts, he stood, still drenched in his clothes, and made his way toward the bathing room.

My whole body tensed with his absence, and Evander stopped on the threshold as if he could feel the change in me. I stilled, trying to coax the shadows that wrapped around my fingers to retreat back inside my body. I was being ridiculous. It wasn't like he was leaving me alone; he was just going into the next room. So why was I starting to panic? Why was fear suddenly consuming my thoughts?

Van turned to face me and, without hesitation, walked back to the bed. He stripped off his shirt, and I turned my head to let him change in peace. Once he was donned in a dry loose shirt and soft sweatpants, he tossed his soaked clothes across the room so they landed on the bathing room floor with a loud, wet thud.

"I'm sorry," I told him, sounding just as pathetic as I felt. He knelt before me, gripping my chin softly between his fingers and forcing me to meet his piercing grey eyes.

"Apologize one more time, and when we get home, I'll be having you running up and down Mammoth Hill until you're drenched in sweat and your own vomit." Evander raised a single brow as if daring me to argue, but I knew better than to.

At least right now. "You're not a burden, love. You are allowed to feel—especially after what occurred tonight." I nodded just as a soft rapping sounded at the door. "Come in," Evander said, his gaze still firmly on me.

"Your Majesty, I was told you required my assistance," a smooth female voice said from across the room.

Van stood and faced the Medicus, who was now making her way toward us. He told her about my injuries but left how they occurred out of his explanation. Whether he decided they weren't relevant for her to be aware of or if he was taking precautions and didn't trust her, I didn't know.

She lifted my shirt, slowly moving her hands over my bruised skin as I struggled to remain still.

"It's a cracked rib, but it won't take too long to heal," she explained, though her eyes were fixed on Evander when she spoke. Which, by the way, happened to be incredibly rude, seeing as *I* was the patient.

She pressed her healing powers into me, and I felt the familiar prickling and pull of magic as she worked on healing a cut on my thigh that I hadn't notice until now.

"How is my companion, Marceline, doing?" Evander asked, and my head whipped to him. How could I not have asked about her? I was suddenly overwhelmed with guilt for being so lost in my own weakness and trauma that I hadn't thought to check on my friend. I knew she was alive when I handed her over to Lia the moment we entered the palace, but that didn't make not inferring about her progress any better. I swallowed down the shame as I fixed my stare on Van. He was leaning his back against a dresser, and his arms were crossed over his chest as he stared pointedly at the ground.

"She's well, Your Majesty. We gave her a tonic so she could sleep through the night, and her injuries were minimal and healed quickly," the Medicus replied.

Van nodded as he exhaled a sigh of relief, but his body seemed to tense even more instead of relaxing. Without thinking, my Empathi Gift drifted out, wanting to reach him and offer some comfort. But instead of being met with the agony of guilt I knew he was experiencing, I was enveloped in feelings of lust and greed.

I angled my head toward the Medicus, who was now tending to my broken rib. I watched her cheeks flush pink as she dragged her stare up and down Evander with hunger. In her distraction, she pressed too firmly on my side, and I hissed at the pain.

"Apologies, Your Highness," the woman quickly said. Maybe it wouldn't have happened if she had stopped eyeing the man in the room with us. I glanced back to Van to find him closer than before, his eyes wide with concern. I opened my mouth to tell him I was okay when the Medicus beside me gasped.

"Your Majesty, what happened?" she asked urgently, stopping her work on me and getting to her feet.

I followed her line of sight to see red marks adorning Van's forearms and even the sides of his neck. Marks made from fingernails—from me. I hadn't been aware I had been clutching him that tightly. Evander leveled me with a flat look that promptly reminded me of his vow should I apologize for anything to him again. I bit my tongue, swallowing my condolence, and turned away.

"I'm fine," Evander told the woman.

"Nonsense, Your Majesty. I'll take her Highness down to the ward and return to heal your wounds," she insisted.

My heart dropped into the pit of my stomach at her suggestion. I couldn't be alone long enough for Evander to step into the damn bathing room to undress, and now I was to be taken away? I gripped the blanket beneath me, hoping it would somehow ease the fear right out of my system.

"I would prefer Ainsley stay here," Evander explained, and I relaxed immediately. Soft footsteps sounded within the space as she reached him. I closed my eyes and gritted my jaw as her desire swept through me as if it were my own.

Minutes ticked by as she healed him, asking questions about Tenebrae and giggling softly at his responses, though they weren't freaking funny. His tone was polite and cordial, and I didn't get the sense he was interested in her, but I could have been wrong.

"She should really get some rest," the Medicus whispered to him. "Though I've healed her injuries, I would prefer her to stay in the ward so we can monitor her as a precaution. I'd be more than happy to come update you through the night on her progress." Oh, I bet she would. I felt the energy within her spike at the offer. Her heart picked up in rhythm, and there was a sense of hopefulness in her proposition.

I glanced over my shoulder at them to find her hands wrapped tightly around Evander's arm, even though his flesh had no more visible injuries. His posture was rigid, and his face forlorn. He looked exhausted. A man haunted by the events of tonight and the terror brewing in his mind. It was apparent that he was going through something, yet she didn't care. She wanted him.

My blood heated, and fury flowed through me as I realized she was trying to get me out of the room so she could be alone with him. No—absolutely not. I wouldn't sit there and let her take advantage of him like that.

"Get out," I spat, twisting around to face them. Evander and the Medicus looked up from their conversation with confused expressions as if they weren't sure to whom I was directing my demand.

"Love?" Evander asked, taking a few tentative steps towards me, but my glare stayed locked on the woman.

"You need to leave," I told her again. "Now."

The Medicus looked to Van, waiting for his response, but I could feel his eyes firmly on me.

"Your Highness," she said, raising her palms placatingly at me. "You've been through an ordeal tonight. If you just follow me—"

"No," I interrupted, and I could feel the ebb of my shadows flow over me.

"We'll be fine, Lilith," Evander said calmly. "Thank you for your assistance tonight." She offered him a weak smile before hurrying to the door.

"Lilith," I called before she managed to cross the threshold. "If a Medicus needs to check on me, be sure it's Lia. I doubt I'll have to worry about her being too focused on trying to fuck the king next to me rather than doing what she came for." The color drained from her face at my insinuation, and she dipped her head in a slight bow before quickly shutting the door.

I took a deep breath and let it out slowly as Evander came to stand in front of me. The anger wouldn't dissipate as I finally looked up to find him watching me with intrigue.

"Care to fill me in on what just happened?" he asked with a cocked brow. *Not really, no.* But I knew Evander, and there was no way he would just let this go.

"I could feel her lust for you," I admitted, dropping my gaze to the hands in my lap as I pulled on my fingers. He crouched down and took my chin gently in his hand, forcing me to meet his eyes for this conversation. He wasn't going to let me hide or be timid with my actions. He was going to make me own them.

"And it's fine that she felt that way. Why wouldn't she?" I rambled, wanting to clarify that I didn't have an issue with people wanting him. Because I absolutely did not. Obviously. "But," I began, searching for the right words. "But you're not okay right now, Van. And she knew that. I couldn't allow her to manipulate and use you while you were grieving and guilt-stricken. You don't deserve that."

Evander's fingers dropped from my face, and his eyes softened just before he turned to the door as if he still saw the Medicus standing there. Did I read the situation wrong? Did he want her? My stomach churned, and I felt as if I were going to be sick. I groaned and scrubbed a hand over my face as a thought washed over me.

"And now I realize that the distraction she was offering may have been exactly what you would have wanted," I told him, and his eyes sliced to mine to see an expression of horror. "You can make me run up and down Mammoth Hill for a week straight if you want—I don't care. I need to apologize for this. I stepped over a line—" Evander took my face between his hands and leaned in, pressing his forehead to mine.

"You didn't," he said. "You did nothing that Lia or Olivier wouldn't have done themselves if they were here. Thank you for looking out for me." I nodded against him before pulling back. "For the record, it wouldn't have been a distraction I wanted," he added. "I didn't even realize what she was doing."

"Because people throw themselves at you so often that you don't notice it anymore?" I teased, hoping it would do the one thing I wanted more than anything at that moment.

And it did.

Evander's grin was bright and beautiful, and I couldn't help but return a smile of my own at the sight.

"Obviously," he replied. I rolled my eyes but didn't let my face fall. "Come on, smartass. It's time for bed," he said, gesturing for me to crawl into my spot.

"Hey, Van?" I asked tentatively as he tucked me in.

"Yes, love?" he said absentmindedly, shifting my damp hair to bring the blanket higher.

"The second reason," I began, suddenly feeling nervous. But I had to continue. He deserved to know the truth. "Was because I trust you."

Evander's hands stilled, and his gaze zeroed in on mine. His brow was furrowed, and there was a light in his eyes that I had never seen before. It was as if I had just presented him the world, and he wasn't sure why or what to do with it.

Maybe I had.

I knew how important trust was to Evander and how much he sought mine, but it was something that I made clear over all of these months that I wasn't ever going to give it to him. After everything that happened in Caelum, I wasn't sure I could even offer that vulnerable piece of myself to anyone. Sure, I didn't believe that any of my new family would purposely hurt me or put me in harm's way, but this trust between Evander and I wasn't that. It was something deeper and more profound. It held a significance that even I didn't fully understand.

He infuriated me most days, but it didn't alter the fact that when I was hurting—when I was terrified and lost—he was the one I sought. He was the only one I wanted to see. The only one I dared speak to. I knew in my soul that I could trust him more than I could myself. I hadn't felt that deep of a connection since Dashiell, and it was terrifying. Things weren't romantic between Van and me like they were with Dashiell, but I still opened myself up to him. To trust anyone that deeply was terrifying, but I also couldn't keep denying it. If anything, tonight proved just that.

A smirk crept up Evander's lips, though it didn't hold its usual cockiness. Instead, it bared something more like hopefulness and joy. And maybe just a smidge of victory.

"It's about time," he replied mirthfully.

"Well, maybe if you weren't such a prick most days, it would have happened sooner," I said sweetly, and Evander's smile grew.

"Noted." His face fell slightly, becoming serious, as he stared into my eyes. "I trust you, too," he admitted, and the words were like a crushing weight.

Not in a bad way, but in this all-encompassing, heavy way. A way that made that truth more precious than anything in this world. Until he had spoken the words, I didn't know how much I craved to hear them, but every nerve ending in me sparked at the knowledge.

There was something between Evander and me from the beginning. Some sort of connection that grew more prominent with each passing day. I wasn't sure if it was because of our relationship as sovereign and heir—like the Gods had made it so that there would be some untouchable bond between us. Whatever it was, the more I gave it a chance and let it in, the more I wanted it.

"I'm afraid to go to sleep," I admitted weakly. "I'm on edge, and I can't cage my magic. It's loosely leashed, at best. What if I lose control while I'm unconscious and it comes out again?"

Evander nodded like he knew the feeling all too well.

"It won't hurt you," he reassured me, though I already knew that.

"I'm not worried about me," I told him.

My Gift prickled beneath my skin, begging me to let it out and hunt down the others I had let get away. There was still a debt to be paid, and my magic urged me to go collect. I wasn't sure it would settle until it was paid in full, and those men suffered as horrifically as their leader did tonight.

"If your darkness slips out, I'll be here to coax it back," Evander said as he stood and walked around the bed to climb in next to me. I watched as he propped his back against the headboard and plucked a book from the nightstand. He flipped through the pages until landing on the spot he had left off and giving me a sidelong glance.

"Do you swear you won't leave?" I asked, sounding like a child afraid of the dark. I needed to get a grip on myself and soon.

"I promise."

With his vow, I closed my eyes and hoped the Gods would be kind enough to grant me a dreamless sleep. But the fact that they'd been a bunch of assholes lately didn't give me much hope.

33.

When my eyes fluttered open again, the room was lit with sunlight pouring in from every window. Evander was in the same spot he was last night, still reading a book, though it seemed to be a different title. Had he not slept? The purpling under his eyes and the look on his face as his stare met mine gave away that answer. He looked exhausted and his complexion was wan.

"You didn't sleep, did you?" I asked though it came out more as an observation than a question.

"I couldn't," he admitted as he closed the book and twisted to grab a glass of water on his nightstand. He handed me the cup, and I sat up, drinking from it deeply, the cold water waking me even more. Evander watched me intently before leaning over and lifting the side of my shirt.

The fact that I didn't flinch surprised me. If anyone else had tried to pull up my clothes, I would have fought them off, especially after last night. But with Evander, my body knew I had nothing to worry about.

His fingers skated over my ribs as he nodded to himself, seemingly pleased with whatever he saw. I looked down to find the redness and bruising around my side almost nonexistent. That Medicus may have been a manipulative asshole, but at least she was good at her job.

Evander let the soft fabric fall from his hand and I stifled a yawn. How was I still tired?

"Go back to sleep," he demanded.

"Any word on Marce?" I asked, changing the subject. Evander gave me a stern look but answered my question nonetheless.

"She's fine," he answered. "And currently out with Oli and Felix trying to track down your attackers."

"They still haven't been found?"

That wasn't a good sign, making me lose hope that they would be. Van shook his head, and his stare drifted to the open windows like he could see them out there now. His arms tensed just barely in his lap like he was fighting the urge to get up and join them.

"You should go and help them look," I offered.

"I'm not leaving you," he said calmly as his attention focused back on me, his grey eyes warm in the morning light. I wanted to argue and tell him I would be okay by myself, but I knew he wouldn't believe me. Hell, even I didn't believe me. I wanted to be brave and shove down the scared part of me that needed someone here, but I couldn't. It was a lie, and like Van had said—I needed to be more honest with myself. And the truth was that I wanted him with me.

"Then, at least try to get some sleep," I told him.

"You're the one who needs to rest," he declared, waving a hand over my body to point out the small but still visible marks. "I'm fine."

"Actually, you look like complete shit. Keep this up for much longer, and you won't have anyone throwing themselves at you," I teased. Evander rolled his eyes like that was the most ridiculous thing to have come out of my mouth. I smiled wide as I scooted back down and placed my head on the pillow before arching a brow to demand he do the same.

Reluctantly, he did.

Van rested his hands overtop his chest as he stared up at the ceiling, thoughts seeming to brew in his mind like a tumultuous storm. I hated seeing him like this. Right now, he wasn't the arrogant, cocky man I had grown used to. He was tense and reserved. I could sense this wall he had put up around himself stronger than any I had seen with him before. But I would scale it to get through to him if needed.

I reached for him, taking one of his hands in mine and interlacing our fingers. I needed him to know I was here for him.

"Thank you for last night," I said, realizing I hadn't yet expressed my gratitude. "For taking care of me in more ways than one."

Evander's throat bobbed as if readying to speak, but he stayed silent. Instead, he simply nodded, his gaze still rooted above. I tightened my hold on his hand and decided to try and give him the same comfort he had given me. I rolled to my side, pulling his hand with me, but he didn't budge. He didn't even look my way. He just stayed there, staring up at the ceiling. I tried again, pulling a little harder in an attempt to get him to roll to his side with me.

Nothing.

He tilted his head in my direction, and my pleading eyes were met with his sorrowful ones. The look of pain, guilt, and fear was all too familiar, and I hated seeing him go through it. I locked my eyes on his as I tugged his arm playfully in an obvious demand of what I desired. When he held me in that tub last night, it was the only time I had felt safe and secure. I longed to give him that, but he was keeping me out. He wouldn't allow himself to unravel like I had.

Evander swallowed hard before returning his stare to the ceiling above. I sighed as I accepted that he didn't want what I was trying to offer. He wanted to get through this on his own, and I had to respect that.

"I'm here if you need me, Van," I said quietly, though loud enough that I knew he heard. I unlocked our fingers, placed his hand back on his chest, and gave one last reassuring squeeze before I let him go. Evander's attention dropped to his hands—the loss of touch—before his stare found mine. "Try and get some sleep, okay?"

I offered a weak smile and rolled onto my side so my back faced him. I may not have wanted him to leave me, but I could at least give him space to go through his emotions without having an audience.

Only a moment had passed when the mattress shifted with weight. His strong arm wrapped around my waist and pulled me against him. My fingers automatically found his, and I interlaced them as our legs tangled together. My body molded perfectly against his as if it were made to do so. He buried his face in my hair, and his lips grazed the back of my neck.

"Thank you," he whispered against me, and I clutched his hand tighter—happy to offer this one thing to him. Happy to be his safe space.

"Do you want to talk about it?" I asked, even though I could sense the answer.

"No," he admitted, and I nodded.

Evander gripped me tighter, and I automatically scooted backward in his arms until there wasn't even an inch between our bodies. He didn't want to discuss what he was going through. He didn't want to think about it or feel it. He wanted an escape. And I would give it to him.

"It's fine if you want to cuddle me like a child with a stuffed toy, but if you snore in my ear, I'm kicking you out," I said lightly, hoping he would take the bait. His smile spread against my skin, and my heart fluttered in response.

"Noted," he mumbled. "I don't snore, but even if I did, I doubt it would compare to those noises you made all night."

"Liar," I scoffed, and I felt him shrug.

"It was like a bear got into a fight with a dog."

"Shut up."

"At first, it was like this low rattling sound," he explained. "But then it grew louder and became this horrifying gargling noise. Like you were drowning underwater. I was worried for a second until you started snorting."

I smacked him hard on the arm with my free hand, and he chuckled close to my ear, quite pleased with his nonsense.

"You should have a Medicus check that out," he added smugly.

"If it's really so bad, then maybe I should go back to my own room and leave you to sleep in peace."

Evander's feet weaved in between mine, and he burrowed his face between my head and the pillow like he was trying to fuse himself to the spot.

"Shhhhh," he said into the pillow. "I'm trying to sleep."

My lips twitched in the corner as I held him tight against me, content and safe. This was what we both needed. There was no pressure for this to be more than it was—two people being there for one another in every way they could.

Evander breathed deeply and let out a sigh of contentment.

"Did you just smell me?" I asked as I twisted to try and catch a glimpse of him.

"Yup," he said shamelessly, shrugging like it was no big deal. "The shampoo I selected compliments your scent, and I was admiring my good taste."

"I have a scent?" I asked, horrified at the thought.

"Yup." He sounded way too happy about it.

Oh, Gods, was it something horrible? I wasn't sure he was entirely joking about the snoring, but right now, I would gladly take that fun fact over the idea of having some unappealing scent. A part of me didn't want to ask, but a much larger part needed to know.

"What do I smell like?" I asked tentatively, hoping it wasn't something disgusting.

"Undying lust and desperation for me," he answered without hesitation.

I lightly elbowed him in the stomach, and he laughed as he shifted behind me. My skin prickled with goosebumps as I felt his nose drag along the back of my neck as he spoke.

"Like eucalyptus and jasmine," he announced before inhaling deeply again. "And cold, crisp air. Like on a winter's night."

Okay, that definitely was better than the odd combinations my mind was coming up with. Evander nuzzled into me, his head resting against mine, his mouth pressed next to my ear. His breaths came in gentle waves of relaxation, and I felt an edge of relief at the tension slowly starting to ease out of him.

I dipped my head just barely as I pulled his hand gently towards my face, trying to inhale his scent.

"Did you just smell me?" he mocked sleepily.

"No," I lied, and his cheek lifted against me in the cocky grin he was undoubtedly giving me.

"And?" he asked.

I inhaled again, letting his familiar scent envelop me. Feelings of comfort and peace, annoyance and frustration, all mingled together.

"Like misplaced arrogance and desperation for me," I teased.

"That sounds about right," Evander responded, and I leaned forward, bringing his hand to my nose and breathing in.

"Like cedar and freshly fallen snow," I answered, closing my eyes and basking myself in it. "And a subtle hint of mint."

"Well, it's no wonder you're always falling over yourself for me. I smell delicious," he said, stifling an exhausted yawn. I rolled my eyes as I put our hands back across my body.

His arm tightened infinitesimally, and I noted the change. It wasn't the way he gripped me before, which was coded in comfort. This was dipped in desperation and fear. His heart drummed in his chest, heavy against my back. Our lax conversation and attempts to shove our feelings away was quickly fading, and back were the emotions he was struggling with.

I instinctively reached out to my Empathi Gift, trying to find a way in. I now understood why Felix always used his Gift on me when we first met all those months ago. It was nearly impossible to control when in contact with someone hurting.

I was met with an internal wall of ice.

"Just ask," he said, sensing my intrusion. Though it was unintentional, it didn't mean it was okay.

"I'm sorry," I told him, but he shrugged off the apology. Did he really mean I could inquire, or was he simply telling me not to try to use my magic on him again? "You said you hadn't told anyone about that night when you were fourteen. Why did you choose to tell me?"

"Because you needed to hear it," he answered. "Because you needed to know that even though what happened will haunt you, you will grow and learn from it. You needed to know that you would be okay." I twisted and found him watching me intently. "And because I knew you wouldn't judge me. You wouldn't look at me differently once you discovered what I had done," Evander added, giving me a comforting smile.

I nodded as I stared into his grey eyes. Fear flickered there momentarily before it was driven away behind his cold gaze. He straightened, still clutching me to him as he watched me like if he turned away, I would be taken again.

"I'm okay," I whispered. "All of us are okay."

He swallowed hard, letting the words roll down his throat. I gripped his arm hard like I could force him to believe the words by touch alone. Evander stifled a groan as he dropped his head to look at the point of contact.

"Your magic is reaching out," he said quietly as he lifted our interlaced fingers before us.

"What do you mean?" I asked, staring at our hands. I mentally checked over myself and all my Gifts seemed to be put away. "Am I hurting you?" I ripped my hand away from his as the fear of injuring him in some way surged forward. I inspected myself, but there were no shadows. Evander grabbed my hand back and traced my palm with his fingers. Beneath his touch, my skin prickled, and I felt the tiniest pull of magic, though I couldn't be sure if it was mine or his.

"You're not hurting me," he said, and I was flooded with relief. "Your magic is pushing against me." He interlaced our fingers once more but still held up our hands to view. "It's like your magic is knocking gently at my door and asking if mine can come out and play with it."

It was an odd sight to picture. The dark magic that had viciously shredded a man to pieces last night was now asking if it could be friends with Van's darkness. What the hell was this strangeness that I was born into?

"Does magic usually do this? Reach out in this way?" I asked.

Evander was quiet for a minute before finally answering.

"No," he admitted. "At least not that I've ever experienced."

"Is it because of our bond?" I asked, and Evander's intense stare moved to me. There was a question in his eyes, and I felt the need to explain. "Our bond between sovereign and heir," I clarified. His gaze softened as he turned the words over in his mind before shaking his head slightly.

"I'm not sure," he said. "My father died before my Gifts emerged, and I don't know if other people in our position share what we do."

I thought back over my time with Dashiell and King Perceval. Their relationship was strained and broken—something more like a dysfunctional father and son rather than what Van and I shared. I hadn't been around Jahier and King Arden long enough to decipher if they were different, though given what I had witnessed between them, I doubt they were.

"How do I make it stop?" I asked, turning back towards our hands and watching Van twist them this way and the other as if he were looking for a way to do just that.

"I don't know," he breathed before slowly releasing his magic and letting his shadows spool around our locked fingers.

My own Gift surged forward without permission, and this time I felt it as strong as if I had made the choice. My shadows swirled around his, and we both sighed in satisfaction. Feeling our magic mix was pleasure and relief, like I could finally suck down air after being underwater for so long, suffocating without it.

Evander lowered our hands as he pulled me tighter against him, and I melted into his touch. I let his shadows and his scent calm and soothe me. And even without searching his emotions, I could tell that mine were doing the same for him.

The events of last night forced their way to the forefront of my mind, and I released a shuddering breath. I was safe, and so was he. We were together and alive. That was all that mattered at the moment. We would find the others and make them pay for what they did to Marceline and me, but for now, this night with him was enough.

A silent tear ran down my cheek, and Evander wiped it away before adjusting us, wrapping his free hand around me in a tight hug. I let my breaths mimic his like I had last night, making sure my chest rose and fell when his did.

"I hate feeling this weak," I whispered.

"I know, but you need to," he said. "Tomorrow, you can go back to being stubborn and strong, and I'll go back to being ruthless and an asshole. But tonight..." His hold on me was firm and unyielding, and I found myself never wanting it to stop. "Tonight we break, and we feel." I nodded and let the tears flow as he held me.

We both needed this. We needed to be able to go through our emotions and be scared and feel our guilt. We needed a safe space, and we were that for each other. The foundation of friendship and trust had been built between Evander and me. And as we held each other like our lives depended on it, I didn't see any way for it to crumble.

34.

When I awoke again, the room was dark, and Evander and I were still tangled in each other's arms. I twisted around to face him, careful not to wake him up. He looked so peaceful and calm, the exhaustion finally drifting away like a bad dream. I reached up, pushing back a loose strand of his dark hair from his face. His brow furrowed beneath my touch, and I pulled my hand away before I could disturb him anymore.

I glanced around the room, trying to gauge the time. The moon was large and bright in the night sky, though it didn't offer me much. We had slept away the day and into the night, and my stomach grumbled at the realization that I hadn't eaten since before Felix and I sought out the library.

I carefully untangled my limbs from Evander's and slowly slid free. He had taken care of me so thoroughly, the least I could do was ensure he had something to eat when he woke up. I slid out of bed and into a pair of slippers that had been left out for me. I glanced over my shoulder to ensure he was still sound asleep and then disappeared into the dark hall.

Tallis' residents always were up late, but the empty corridors told me they had long gone to sleep. It had to be the middle of the night then, if not verging on a new day. I walked through the halls, heading toward the dining room. Every night, the room was full of food throughout the hours, and the servants would set up for breakfast as they took away dinner, so there was bound to be at least something I could bring back to the room for Van and me.

I rounded a corner and spotted two men having a hushed conversation at the far end. They seemed to be the only other people awake at this hour. I paid them no mind, and they didn't seem to notice me either as I made my way closer.

All at once, the air was taken from my lungs, and I froze in paralyzed fear as my gaze zeroed in on one of the men. He was tall, slender, and dressed like a guard, though his uniform wasn't that of those they wore here in Agnitio. But it wasn't his attire that incapacitated me so thoroughly. It was his hand—donned in intricate scars. The hands that hurt me in Caelum. The hands that were present at the Lake.

I needed to get out of the hallway before he spotted me, but I couldn't move. I was back to being that scared girl from last night as my fear consumed me.

All at once, a hand wrapped over my mouth and around my waist. I thought about screaming half a second before a cedar scent curled around me, and a low voice whispered in my ear.

"It's me," Evander said as he pulled us away from the middle of the hallway and pressed me against his chest. He wrapped us in shadows as the two men looked up from their conversation. "They can't see us," he explained into my ear before I could ask. I nodded, his hand still firmly pressed over my mouth while the other splayed over the bare skin on my stomach from my shirt shifting.

I worked to level my breathing and calm my nerves as we watched the conversation before us unfold, though we couldn't make out the words. Evander released his hand from my mouth, and I twisted in his arms to face him, my fingers fisting in his shirt as I held him close. He took in my shaking hold before his eyes went wide with worry.

"Ainsley, what happened? What's wrong?"

I swallowed hard as his eyes wrapped around my trembling fingers.

"The guard," I began, and Evander's gaze drifted towards him." Is one of the men who attacked me."

Evander's eyes hardened, and his body stiffened to stone against me. Gone was the haunted and broken man from earlier, and in his place was a vicious king who thirsted for bloodshed. His jaw clenched hard, and his fingers dug into my back as he held me against him.

"Are you positive?" he ground out.

I nodded, and Evander let out a low growl, just loud enough for only us to hear. I held him tighter as my fear began to take hold once more. My shadows released from me, wrapping tight around my hands, and panic was like a strike of lightning through my veins.

"Van," I whispered, staring at the magic I couldn't stop from surging forth. But his eyes were locked on my attacker and his companion. "Van," I tried again. It was no use. His mind was turning, and there was death in his eyes.

I cupped his cheek as my shadows slithered over his skin.

"Evander, please," I whispered, the desperation in my voice spilling over and breaking his focus. His eyes sliced to mine as he took me in. "Please get me out of here," I begged, burying my face in his chest as I fought to rein in my power.

A swooshing sound echoed in my ears, and I was wrapped in the familiar scent of his room. Before I could open my eyes and verify that we had been traversed to safety, Van's hands were on my face, shoving my hair back as he pressed his forehead to mine.

"I'm sorry, love," he said, holding my face between his hands. "I shouldn't have let my control slip like that.

"It's okay," I told him as I opened my eyes. I watched him drop his mouth like he was about to object. "Try to argue, and I'll have you running up and down Mammoth Hill until you're drenched in sweat and your own vomit," I warned.

But Van didn't crack a smile. He dragged a hand through his hair and glanced around the room as if searching for the answer to what to do next.

"I wanted to kill him," he admitted, still not meeting my eyes.

"To be honest, I'm surprised you didn't. After what happened with Mishal, I thought you would have ended his life when you found out."

Evander took a deep breath as he nodded to himself.

"Do you recognize the man he was with?" Evander asked cautiously. I got the sense there was more to his question than just trying to see if I could identify the man's companion. I thought back to the stranger's appearance though nothing was familiar to me.

"No," I admitted, shaking my head. "I don't think he was part of that group."

Evander scrubbed a hand down his face, and I wasn't sure if that was the answer he wanted to hear or not. He stepped closer and rested his hands on my shoulders as he looked deep into my eyes.

"The man that was with your attacker is King Harbin, Ainsley." My blood went as cold as ice.

"Are you saying he orchestrated the attacks?" I asked.

"I'm not sure. Princess Cordelia was supposedly attacked not long before you, so either it was faked, or Harbin has no idea that one of his men is behind it. There are still too many questions in the air to know for sure."

The possibility of this being some masterminded ordeal created by King Harbin sent my head spinning. Every time we thought we were getting one step closer to uncovering truths, we were set back again.

"So what now?" I questioned. Evander stepped away and crossed his arms over his chest as he thought about that.

"First, I need to speak with Tallis and find out why Harbin is here and why the fuck he didn't think to give me a heads up. After that, we're going home. Oli, Marce, and Felix still haven't returned, so I'll get the word out to them about our plan. You, me, and Lia will leave as soon as we can. We need to get home and figure things out."

Evander scrunched his face, and I braced myself for another wave of information I knew I wouldn't like.

"I hate to do this to you, but given what we just found out, I don't know what else to do," he said cautiously.

"What is it?"

"Until we figure out if Harbin is behind these attacks, I don't want you to be alone. We can have Felix or Lia move into your room. At least for a little while. I need to know you're safe."

"You think they'll attack us in our home?" I asked incredulously. I, in no way, liked the idea of giving up the small amount of freedom I had.

"Our home and Tenebrae in general, is the safest place for you, but I still don't want to take any risks until we learn more about what's going on," Evander explained. The pained look in his told me he would fight to find out who was behind this so he could grant me my freedom again. I decided at that moment not to fight him on it.

"Felix or Lia?" I clarified, and he nodded.

"We can have them move in as soon as we get home."

I glanced around, trying to decide which of them I would ask to be my new roommate. Neither would decline, and both would be happy to take on the task. But Lia had Calidore, and I knew Felix was still trying to find his way. He valued his alone time just as much as I did.

"But not you," I said, still not looking at him. Fingers slid below my chin as he directed my stare to his.

"I'd prefer that, but I want you to feel comfortable, love. I want you to feel safe."

I turned over his words as I pondered them, knowing how I already felt and what I wanted to do.

"I feel safest with you," I admitted. It was the truth. I loved Lia and especially Felix, but with Evander, it was different. I knew in my soul that I could trust him without restraint. I knew he would sooner die than allow anything to happen to me.

I made a mental note to speak to Sirona and learn more about the possibility of some unwavering bond between sovereign and heir, causing me to feel like this. Or maybe I just wanted there to be some magical reason rather than admitting the truth. I trusted Evander because I allowed him in after swearing I would never do something like that again.

He smiled as he looked down at me, that cocky grin curving his lips in its usual way.

"Then it's settled: you'll move into my room when we get home," he declared.

"Don't you mean that *you'll* move into *my* room?"

"Nope."

"What? Why? You would have Felix or Lia move, so why can't you?" I asked, already annoyed with this agreement. Was it too late to say that I had changed my mind?

"Because my room is better," he said, shrugging.

"So?" I pushed. That wasn't a good enough reason. If I had to give up my freedom and privacy, then I should be allowed to do it in the comfort of my own room.

"And my bed is more comfortable."

"Doubtful," I shot back. "Do you even have a bathing tub as big as mine?" I did not want to part with that thing. It was my favorite part of the day.

"As big as yours, no," he said, and I grinned triumphantly. "It's slightly smaller, but I have a pool in my bathing room that easily makes up for it." The smile on my face immediately fell, and Van's only grew. An entire freaking pool? How the hell was I supposed to argue with that?

Dammit.

"Fine." I ground out, conceding the luxury of my room for his. I quickly turned around so he wouldn't see the excitement and curiosity in my eyes, but I knew he could sense it by his chuckle of victory.

"I have to go and speak to Tallis," he reminded, and I twisted to face him. "I know you just went through a lot, so if you want to remain here, I'll have Lia come up to stay with you. But I would rather not leave your side, so if you're up for it, I'd like to bring you along." I practically bounced over to him, happy he felt the same desire to stick together.

Okay, I definitely needed to talk to Sirona as soon as possible because this was getting out of hand.

Evander guided my arms around his neck and pulled me flush against him as he traversed us out of the room. A second later, he slid his hands from my back down to my waist as he held me steady while I looked around the new room we were now in.

"You know you could have just held my hand, right?" I said, stepping out of his embrace and walking around a room that appeared to be a large study.

"I know. But that was so much better," he said shamelessly. I scoffed as I peered over a map of Disparya that lay on a table in the center of the room.

The doorknob twisted, and a very tired-looking Tallis strolled in, wearing robes of deepest blue and gold, his white hair thrown back messily rather than styled in its usual pristine braids. Evander stalked for him, looking pissed off. I released an annoyed sigh at the exchange that was about to unfold. Rather than ask questions calmly, Van was going to lose his shit. I knew the reason had nothing to do with not knowing that King Harbin was here and everything to do with the fact that he seemed to be consorting with the man who tried to kill me last night. Honestly, I couldn't even blame him for his reaction because if our roles had been reversed—if he had been nearly killed—I would have handled it the same way.

"Explain," Van demanded, crossing his arms as he stopped before his friend. Tallis raised his hands in defense, trying to calm Van down from his temper tantrum.

"He requested to discuss trade matters in person, but I had no idea he was going to come early," Tallis defended.

"I had no idea he was coming at all," Van spat back, his temper rising. I rolled my eyes and strolled over to Tallis, who glanced around Evander to me.

"How are you feeling, Ainsley?" Tallis asked as he stepped around Van to approach me. "I'm so sorry this happened. I have members of my army assisting your friends in their search," he said, reaching out to take my hands in his. Evander huffed at the gesture, and I shook my head and mouthed a quick *'sorry'* before addressing him aloud.

"I'm doing better, but..." I looked to Evander, a question on my face that only he could answer. He nodded subtly and stepped forward, taking the lead for the pending conversation.

"One of her attackers is at Harbin's side and dressed as a guard from Ministro."

Tallis walked forward, closing the distance between him and Evander as his eyes grew wide with alarm.

"Is Harbin—" he began, but Van interrupted.

"We don't know if he's behind it or not. That's what I need you to help us figure out." Tallis nodded vehemently, striding for his desk and rifling through it as he gathered a handful of papers. "There's more, Tallis," Evander said cautiously, and the king looked up from his task with furrowed brows. "Ainsley received a second Gift from Ministro."

Tallis dropped the stack of documents as he shook his head, refusing to accept Evander's claim, though his eyes held an air of uncertainty. There was no reason for us to lie about it, and he knew that. He stepped forward to meet us again, his gaze never moving from me.

"I'm certain she's an Imperium, but I want you to verify," Evander instructed, and Tallis nodded absentmindedly.

I stared into his warm eyes, watching his pupils dilate slightly as his Gift as a Magusier came forth. Tallis released a low breath, his mouth parting like he wanted to speak but was unable to. He broke his stare from me and sought Evander instead, wonder flooding his features.

"This shouldn't be possible," Tallis whispered, confirming Evander's suspicions of my new Gift.

What that meant for me that was setting us all on edge. I was not only the Heir to Tenebrae but the Heir to Ministro as well.

"If King Harbin finds out—" Tallis warned, but Van interjected.

"He won't. I'm not going to let him kill her like the others." The others? Evander's eyes collided with mine as if he could sense my question before I was able to ask it. "Ministro hasn't had an heir since your father. At least not one anyone has known about," Van elaborated.

"You think he's having them killed the moment someone manifests a second Gift," I breathed, and he nodded, confirming my suspicion. Fuck.

"She'll have to be taught how to wield it," Tallis said, directing the statement to Van. "The Imperium Gift is rare and powerful. It isn't safe for her to possess it without training."

"I know," Evander answered. "Her and Lia's Gift as a Medicus are in the same family, so she can help Ainsley with certain aspects of control until we find an Imperium—"

"We already know one," Tallis cut in. I perked up at the conversation and the way Van went still, his body rigid at the suggestion.

"I don't trust him," Evander said coldly, and I couldn't help but wonder who he was referring to.

"It's imperative that she learn, and he's her best option," Tallis reasoned as he took a deep breath and pinched the bridge of his nose, letting me know this person had been a frustrating topic of discussion between him and Evander before.

"He's a prick, and we don't know where he stands," Van added. "His father—"

"He doesn't consider that man his father, and you know that."

"It still doesn't make him trustworthy, and you want me to leave her training to him. The training of a Gift that very few people possess," Evander argued. "That Gift is powerful, and you want me to allow him to potentially hurt her."

Tallis sighed, displeased with his friend. I understood where both of them were coming from. Tallis was right in pushing for me to learn how to wield my Gift as an Imperium properly, but Evander's priority had always been my safety. He wasn't quick to trust anyone with it, especially now that we knew my attackers from Caelum were working for King Harbin of Ministro.

"You know I understand better than anyone else just how important Ainsley's safety is," Tallis said, putting a hand on his friend's shoulder. "So trust that I wouldn't make this suggestion if I thought it would put her in danger."

Evander closed his eyes and blew a long breath as he debated what to do. I knew he trusted Tallis, but this decision wasn't easy for him, no matter the reassurance his friend offered.

"I just can't take the chance with how close he is to his father. I know you trust him, but he's done nothing to prove his worth to me," Evander pointed out.

"The information he's provided in the past has been pivotal."

"To our cause, yes, but not to *her*. You're asking me to trust him with *her*, and I don't," he explained. We were getting nowhere, and it wasn't looking like Evander was going to back down on his stance. "But I do trust *you*," he added reluctantly. "So have him send someone else who can train her. If they can pass your honesty test, I'll allow them access to her."

Tallis smiled as he nodded, no doubt aware that was the best offer he was going to get from Van. I grinned as well, excited that I would have another Imperium to show me how to use my Gift. It was terrifying what I was capable of, and I wouldn't truly feel safe until I mastered all of the magic I was given. I had no doubt that Lia would be a fantastic teacher, but she was a Medicus, and her aid would only be able to extend so far. I wanted to reach my full potential, which wouldn't happen unless I trained with someone who possessed my Gift.

The two of them poured over the documents through the night, trying to connect the dots on how and why Harbin might be involved and if they were missing any other connection. After the third hour, I had fallen asleep on Tallis' couch when the book I was flipping through led us to another dead end with Inmuto.

"Come on, love. It's time to go," Evander whispered into my ear, and I opened my eyes to find us back in his room with him now fully dressed and the sky beginning to light with the oncoming dawn.

I sat up, stretched, and spotted a set of clothes left out for me at the end of the bed. I hated to admit that I rather liked wearing his clothes. They were soft and comfortable. It also had nothing to do with the fact that they smelled like him and that his scent was quickly becoming synonymous with safety and trust.

I quickly changed, and within minutes, Evander and I were quietly sneaking out of the palace before the residents woke up. Thanks to my illusion Gift, we didn't have to worry too much about being seen. I hadn't planned on using it, but Evander gave me the task the second we slipped into the hall. He said to call it a 'training exercise,' and when I tried to protest because I didn't want to be responsible for our deaths if King Harbin caught us... Evander's response? *'Well, then I suggest you do a good job.'*

Asshole.

I tried to hide my satisfaction when we made it to the stables unseen, but it was no use. When he saw me attempt to stifle my smile, his smug ass boasted about his superior teaching techniques the entire time we got Nox saddled. We opted to ride back rather than traverse to see if we could come up with a clue to where my attackers had fled.

Lia appeared moments after we entered and threw herself at me, wrapping me in her arms as she squeezed.

"Evander refused to let me see you," she whined, and I threw Van an angry look.

"No, I refused to let you kick me out of *my* room so you could stay with her," he corrected.

"That's the same thing," she declared, unwrapping herself and holding me out at arm's length so she could inspect me. "How are you feeling?"

"Good. But I'll be better when we're finally home," I told her truthfully.

"Then let's get the hell out of here," she responded.

She mounted her mare and strode out of the stables. We waited until she was in the tree line and signaled that we were in the clear before Van helped me atop Nox. I took the reins just as he hooked his bag onto her saddle.

"What do you think you're doing?" I asked, and Evander gave me a devilish grin. "No," I told him. "Get your own horse. Nox is mine, and she doesn't even like you."

"Lia has the only other horse," he said triumphantly. "And Nox likes me *very* much."

"She won't let you up here," I told him confidently. Nox and I had an unbreakable bond. We understood one another, and she was always firmly on Team Ainsley. She even bit Felix once when he stole the last pastry from my hand during a casual ride one morning.

Evander stepped to the front of my horse as he watched her curiously. She huffed in irritation the second she noticed him, and a smile formed on my face.

And then very quickly faded as I watched Evander reach into his pocket and pull out not one—not two—but three plump, red apples. He outstretched them to Nox, and she gladly took his payment. When she was finished eating, Van held up a hand, and she nuzzled into him, granting her thanks and permission.

Traitor.

Evander looked at me with all the arrogance of a victorious king and winked as he patted my horse.

Prick.

He hoisted himself onto Nox, settling behind me as he took the reins from my hands.

"It seems she has a new favorite," he whispered into my ear before steering us out of the stables and after Lia.

I crossed my arms and refused to say another word for the rest of the morning. Nox earned herself no extra after-dinner treats for a solid week for that stunt. At least Nova still liked me more than Evander. Maybe I could train her to bite him whenever he pissed me off, though I wasn't sure Onyx would ever let us get close enough to him. I guess we'd have to find out.

We rode until the sun had nearly set, only stopping to give our horses a much-needed rest and some water. There was a camp of Tenebraen soldiers nearby, and Evander had decided that's where we would stop for the night. If we left first thing in the morning, we'd be safely home by tomorrow night.

"Are you excited to move into my room?" Van asked into my ear. I had been steadily ignoring him most of the day, but that didn't stop his efforts to try and get under my skin, a feat he didn't need to put much effort into in order to accomplish. I rolled my eyes, though he couldn't see from behind me on Nox.

"Not even a little bit. And it's my turn to steer," I said, ripping the reigns from his hands. Van chuckled softly.

"That's fine. It only means I get to hold on," he announced, moving his hands to grip my waist. My stomach knotted, and my body tightened at the touch. I swallowed, steeling myself as I focused on keeping Nox following Lia on the path ahead. "I am curious, though," he said, pressing his chest firmly to my back." If Felix was right."

I had no clue what he was referring to and wasn't sure I wanted to know. So why the hell did I find myself opening my mouth to inquire?

"About what?" I asked, allowing a tinge of annoyance to seep through my tone. His games were either fun or dangerous, but lately, I was discovering that the two seemed to blend the more and more we played.

"When he claimed that you didn't take Jahier to bed," he said simply. "And that the only company you had was your own hand." I swallowed—hard. Evander's fingers tightened around me like he could tell he'd love the answer. He absolutely would, given that Felix was completely correct.

"So, was he right?" Van asked, pulling my attention from his hands to his words.

"Not at all," I told him, but the denial spilled from my lips weak and sounding of untruths. Coarse stubble grazed the side of my neck, and Van's breath caressed my skin.

"You're shit at lying, love. You'll want to work on that."

I tightened my hold on the reins and kept my eyes straight ahead, trying desperately not to focus on how his lips felt so close to me. His hands flexed and dug into my side, causing the hem of my shirt to shift slightly and his fingers to graze the soft skin there. I sucked in a breath and shook my head to clear it, determined not to give into this game of his, though the stakes were tempting.

"So, did you think about all the ways I said I wanted to have you?" he asked in a dangerously low whisper.

"Who said I thought of you at all?" I shot back on a shaky breath. Evander dipped his head to settle his lips in the crook of my neck. I shivered at the intimacy of his touch and felt him smile against me.

"Your body gives you away."

He released one of his hands and swept my hair to the side before running his nose along the back of my neck like he had last night but now, the gesture was fueled with desire and longing. I unintentionally arched, tilting my head up slightly as I melted into him.

"Do you want to know what I thought about?" he asked seductively.

"No," I whispered. My eyes fluttered shut as I enjoyed the feel of him so close.

"I thought about your face when you realized how wet you were for me," he said, not caring about my answer. Probably because he read it for the lie that it was. My mouth dried as I remembered how I pictured that very same thing as I touched myself. However, it was his darkened eyes and hungered expression that was painted in my mind.

"I thought about what it would be like to touch you," he said, running his hands down my arms slowly, causing goosebumps laced with desire to form. "What it would be like to taste you." His fingers slid over mine, and I held onto the leather reins like they would stop me from succumbing to him. "I thought about your grip on my hair as you held me there and took what you wanted from me," Evander continued. An involuntary moan slipped from between my lips as I imagined doing just that. I hated him most days, yes—but Gods damn, did I want him just as fiercely. It seemed like lust and hate were a fine line for us.

Evander's lips grazed the corner of my mouth, and I automatically tilted back, giving him better access. My lips parted for him on instinct as I felt him draw closer. My chest beat uncontrollably, and the scent of cedar was intoxicating as I struggled to retain my grip on reality. Everything about him sharpened my senses and threw me into a frazzled mess of hormones.

I waited for him to close the distance and take what he had been demanding from the moment we met. But instead, his mouth moved to my ear.

"I think I'm really going to love our new living arrangement," he said before pulling back completely. In the same breath, I lost hold of the leather reigns as he took them from me, lurching me forward and straight out of my lust-filled fantasy.

What the *fuck*.

"Tell me, love," he said. "Was it my hand or tongue that got you off?" I clenched my jaw and crossed my arms at his ridiculous game. "Or perhaps it's some other part of me you've been fantasizing about."

"Go fuck yourself," I bit.

"Gladly," he laughed, and it set my blood boiling and my teeth on edge. I hated that he had this power over my body, and more than that, I hated that he realized it too.

"It's good that you and your hand are already well acquainted because you won't be getting anything from me."

"Or you could just stop denying yourself and go after what you want," Evander replied with swaggering arrogance.

"I would, but he isn't here," I said just to shut him up. Van stilled, and I had the feeling the words did more than what they were intended to. I wasn't sure why, but I needed to try and save whatever was happening. "When did Arden leave anyway?" I asked because I knew it was the only way Evander would relax. We both knew that wasn't who I wanted.

"So Arden is who you've had your eye on, huh?" he questioned sarcastically.

"Definitely. Didn't you pick up on the fact that I'm really into asshole misogynistic pricks now? They're such a turn-on," I teased and twisted to look up at Van, who was wearing his usual cocky grin. Gone was the tension from his body, and I felt my own ease at the knowledge.

Before he had a chance to respond, Lia's screams for him broke through

35.

"Van!" Lia yelled again, her voice broken and urgent as she called for her king. Van urged Nox forward, and we took off at full speed down the path and into the outskirts of the Tenebraen soldiers' camp. As soon as Nox slowed, Evander jumped down and rushed for Lia as she yelled for him again.

I dismounted and pushed through the crowd of gathering soldiers to find out what was happening. The camp was filled with the scent of burning fire and the sounds of chaos. Between the mumbled conversations and hushed whispers, I couldn't determine what was happening.

Growls and snapping teeth echoed up ahead, and I rushed forward, pushing through the last of the crowd as I set my eyes on Evander with his hands outstretched and a snarling Onyx in front of him. Van tried to sidestep him slowly, but Onyx cut him off, refusing to let his master pass. What the hell was going on? Onyx was loyal and obedient only to Evander and occasionally to me when I snuck him treats while Van wasn't watching. So what warranted a behavior like this? It looked as though Onyx would attack Evander without hesitation. But why? I peered around him the best I could and saw a bloody heap of fur lying completely still on a wood palette.

Nova.

I ran forward on nothing but instinct to get to my wolf, but the sudden movement caught Onyx's eye, and he left Evander. The black wolf leapt in front of me, landing just inches away, the sound of his growls deafening and the look of death in his dark eyes terrifying. He wasn't going to let anyone get to Nova. He was protecting her.

"Ainsley, back away!" Evander demanded, rushing to my side and trying to shove me half behind him. Onyx lunged and snapped his teeth around the open air. Not to attack, but in warning. A warning that clearly meant *stay the fuck back*. I reached a hand out toward him to try and let him smell me, but Van quickly thwarted the movement.

"Maybe he doesn't recognize us," I suggested. Perhaps he was too lost in fear and anger to see we were their masters.

"He knows exactly who we are, love," Evander said, taking a tentative step toward his wolf. "He's just hell-bent on protecting her." I looked again at Nova. Her body's gentle rise and fall was so shallow I didn't know how long it would continue. Her light grey and white fur was matted in dark red, so much so that I wasn't sure how she was still alive.

"Everyone needs to stay back. No one goes near them, is that understood?" Van demanded and was met with immediate agreement from the crowd of his soldiers.

"Van, we can't help if he won't let us get to her," I said anxiously. "Can you trap him in an illusion or hold him down with your shadows?"

"No. Our wolves can detect the use of magic before it ever leaves our bodies. If I so much as try it, he'll attack and we'll be fucked more than we are right now." I cursed low as I dragged a hand through my hair.

"We can't let her die, Van."

Evander took a deep breath before stepping forward, ignoring Onyx's warning growls as he did. Everyone surrounding the scene froze as they watched their king approach his feral pet. He knelt inches away from Onyx's sharp teeth as he held up a hand, trying to reach his wolf and show he meant him no harm. Onyx's dark stare flickered into something like recognition for a split second before a man's soft voice filled the silence, followed by a low whimper of pain.

Onyx whirled around and leaped across the space, his teeth bared and ready to attack. One of the soldiers had decided to take advantage of the distraction and stepped out of line to try and wrap one of Nova's bloody paws. It was with the best of intentions but it was the wrong choice. And he paid for it.

"No!" Evander bellowed, but it was too late.

Onyx shredded into the aiding man, ripping apart his limbs as easily as a knife cutting through warm butter. The man screamed, but the sound was cut off the moment Onyx's teeth locked around his throat and tore it out. The wolf turned away the second he was done, letting the man's bloody and lifeless body fall to the ground in a heap of flayed flesh and bone. Onyx backed up and rushed to Nova, stepping over her body and shielding her from anyone else who dared to get too close.

I turned to Evander to find his eyes wide with horror and his mind seeming to be at a loss for what to do. The soldier was only trying to help, but ignoring Van's orders brutally cost him his life. Onyx dipped his head as he eyed the onlookers, his muzzle drenched and dripping in the blood of the life he had so easily taken.

The crowd was silent, save for the sounds of rushed footsteps and vomiting from those who couldn't stand the sight before them. A gentle hand on my shoulder brought my attention to the red-haired beauty whose jade-green eyes, usually so bright and hopeful, were now filled with sorrow and pain.

"What happened?" she whispered to me, but before I could answer, Evander spoke.

"He got too close," he admitted under his breath. Van stood and backed away slowly, never taking his eyes off his wolf until he reached our sides.

"I got the message to Sirona. She's gathering her supplies and will be ready the moment you get there," Lia told him.

"I can't leave," he replied, throwing an arm out to gesture to the bloody corpse across the space.

"You're the quickest way to her, and Nova is running out of time, Van. She won't make it if you don't go," Lia explained.

My eyes shot to Nova, her breathing getting shallower with each minute that passed. I swallowed down air, the panic of losing her setting in more and more. I rushed forward, determined to make Onyx get out of the way. We couldn't just let her bleed out and die.

Firm hands gripped mine, and Van spun me around to face him.

"No!" he said as I tried to fight out of his hold.

"Please," I begged as tears welled in my eyes. "I have to do something!"

"There isn't anything you can do. He won't let you near her, love."

"Then go! Get Sirona. Nova won't last much longer. You have to go now!" I begged, choking on my plea. Evander glanced between the wolves and me, seeming torn on what to do. "Please, Van."

"Promise me you won't go near them," he said, the words rushed and desperate. I looked past him, eyeing the territorial wolf that was shielding mine. Onyx was practically begging someone to come closer so he could take out his rage again. It was crazy to try, but I couldn't help but wonder if I could get through to him. If I could just make him recognize me and understand that I wasn't there to hurt her, then maybe...

"Promise me!" Evander demanded, shattering my thoughts and directing my stare back to his. His grey eyes were frenzied and full of fear and guilt. The hands gripping me were trembling so slightly that I barely noticed. His throat bobbed, and his chest rose harder and faster as he watched me with bated breath. "Please, love. I can't leave if I don't know you're safe. I don't want Nova to die, but I won't sacrifice you to save her. I can't." I swallowed and closed my eyes, letting the tears spill down my cheeks.

"Okay. I promise," I told him.

Evander let out the breath he had been holding, nodded, and then disappeared. All that was left were swirling tendrils of shadow in his place. Lia wrapped her arms over my shoulders and whispered reassuring words, though I could barely comprehend what she was saying. My ears were too busy ringing with the fear that filled every crevice of my being as I waited for Evander to return with help.

I paced back and forth, unable to stay still. The more minutes that ticked by, the more anxious I became. A group of men standing in a circle caught my attention; their hushed whispers and quick glances at Onyx caused the hair on my arms to stand and my instincts to tingle with awareness. I marched for them, sure to leave a wide enough birth not to spook Nova's protector.

"What are you discussing?" I asked though it sounded more like a demand than a question. Which it was. The men went quiet, throwing glances at each other like they were silently pulling straws to see who would have to answer.

"Something needs to be done," one of the soldiers finally said, stepping forward. He was stocky and built, though smaller than his companions.

"Something *is* being done," I told him. "Evander went to get Sirona to heal—"

"No," he interrupted. "About *him*." The man jerked his chin toward Onyx, and I twisted to find the wolf snarling in response. It was like he could read every dangerous thought this man had in his head. My blood was pumping hard, as I prayed to the Gods that I was misinterpreting what this man was suggesting.

"What is your name?" I questioned, stepping closer to him.

"Jonothan," he answered, standing straighter as if that would grant him a few extra inches.

"Jonothan," I said with a deadly calm. "You wouldn't be suggesting putting down your king's wolf, would you?"

The man looked at his companions, hoping they would offer him some backup on the matter. But rather than help their friend, they looked in every other direction, refusing to speak up. Jonothan swallowed deeply, realizing he was on his own. I expected him to back down, but instead, he stepped forward, closing the distance between us.

"That thing killed one of our men," he said. "Henry was a good soldier. He was trying to help, and that wild beast shredded him apart for it!" He raised his voice louder, and I glanced around to find a few people nodding in agreement. "That wolf has no business being in this camp. He murdered one of ours. The payment for that is a life for a life."

Several cheers broke out, and my heart raced at what was unfolding. I didn't want to hurt these men, but there was no way in hell I would be letting them form a mutiny. In charge for ten minutes, and I was already shit at it.

"Your king gave you an order," Lia said, her voice as cold as ice as she moved toward me. I didn't miss the daggers she casually slid into her palms from the sleeve of her shirt. The soldiers began to close in around us slowly, and my blood sang with the oncoming fight. Onyx growled low from behind me, ready to protect Nova with his last breath, and I planted my feet to do the same. I extended my hands, letting the shadows spool and twist around my fingers.

"But he's not here to enforce it," Jonothan said confidently, and my lip peeled back in disgust.

"No, but your princess is," I declared, using my title willingly for the first time. As I finally said those words aloud, I found that I loved how they sounded. I *was* a princess. I was the Gods damn Heir to Tenebrae and I didn't want to run from it anymore. I wanted to embrace every ounce of my power.

Starting right here and right now.

"This is your last chance to fall in line," I announced to the crowd as I let the darkness spill from my hands like a cascading waterfall and pool all around me in delicate, dark ripples. "Stand down and back away."

Murmurs broke through as people watched my magic take form, debating what to do. Soon, the crowd dissipated, with more and more soldiers deciding this wasn't a fight they wanted to be a part of. I smirked as Jonothan's numbers dwindled, but I took a mental note of who was on his side to begin with. We didn't need an uprising within our ranks. Not at a time like this. We needed people we could trust.

A flash of movement caught in my periphery as someone darted out from the crowd with a sword aimed at Onyx's back.

Fuck that.

I threw my arms out and let my shadows rip from my body. They slammed into the crowd, sending everyone except for Lia and my wolves flying backward through the air. Bodies slammed into trees and tents before falling to the ground with grunts of pain. I stalked for the man who attempted to end Onyx's life. He scrambled to his feet and crafted a sword in his hand to defend himself, but it wouldn't do him any good. I twisted my fingers, and my shadows snaked around his feet and slithered up his body before he had a chance to even swing at me.

I enclosed my magic around his throat, letting my Gift solidify into rope.

"You made the wrong choice," I told him simply. I tightened my hold on him, cutting off his oxygen completely.

A presence appeared next to me, and I whirled around with my fist raised high, ready to attack. An arm curled around my wrist before I could deal my blow, and my eyes met Evander's as he stared down at me. His gaze was piercing as he assessed the situation that had unfolded in his absence, and his eyes sliced past me to the man I still had rooted in place by my magic.

"Sirona is here," he said as his attention drifted back to me. "Go to her."

"But—" I began as I glanced around at the scene. Dozens of soldiers were on the ground, bellowing in pain and hurrying to their feet to flee my reckoning. I needed to finish what I started with those who disobeyed us.

"I'll handle them, love," Evander said, his tone dripping in deadly promise. "You know I don't like to be kept out of the fun." I raised my chin as I nodded, content to let him take care of the mess while I tended to Nova the best I could.

"Fine," I told him. "The two men by that tree." I tilted my chin in the general direction. "The man cowering behind that tent, and the one over there on the ground clutching his balls and crying." I pointed to the targets, and Van smiled devilishly as his gaze sought each of them out. "Oh, and this piece of shit here."

"Noted," Van said, striding forward as his hands slid into his pockets.

I marched for Sirona, not bothering to turn around as screaming pleas filled the space. I didn't try to hide the smile that formed either. They deserved what they were getting. No one would mess with me and mine and get away with it.

By the time I reached Sirona, she had gotten Onyx to settle down enough to allow her within a few feet of Nova so she could assess her wounds from a closer distance. Thank the Gods. Lia and I stayed a few feet back, not wanting to crowd her as she viewed the injuries from different angles. I decided now would be the best time to take my chance with calming Onyx further.

I took a deep breath and slowly walked over to the wolf staring intently at mine while she lay there unmoving. A low grumble reverberated in his throat as I got within a few inches of him, but I didn't back down. The only way we could fully help her was by helping him.

I had seen the look in Evander's eyes last night when he saw the man who had attacked me, and it wasn't much different than the one displayed in Onyx's dark glare now. It was a tornado of fear, anger, and guilt. Him being an animal didn't make those emotions any less real. He couldn't lose her like I couldn't lose any of the people I'd come to call family.

I held up my hand and slowly brought it to his face. Onyx bared his teeth but didn't lunge or snap at me. He didn't snarl or attack.

"I know you're hurting, and I can see that you're scared," I whispered, and something flashed in his eyes as if he could genuinely understand me. "We just want to help her," I continued, reaching further until my hand was met with soft fur. I held my breath, and neither of us moved as we stared at one another. Van would lose his shit if he saw me right now, but I didn't care. Another scream in the distance told me that he was preoccupied at the moment.

I flexed my hand, allowing my fingers to rub along his muzzle until I petted him as thoroughly as if this was any other day.

"Good boy," I breathed, moving my other hand to scratch behind his ear. He sat there, still as a statue but no longer growling, so I guessed I could call that a win.

"Go ahead, Sirona," I told her, not taking my eyes from the wolf at my side. I continued to pet him while he stared at Nova, trying to comfort him the best I could. I knew it wouldn't mean much if she didn't make it.

We watched Sirona work with the aid of Lia, but no matter what they tried, it didn't seem to be working. A lump rose in my throat and my chest ached as they hastily moved over Nova's body, trying their hardest to fix her wounds. Onyx tensed at my side, and a whine escaped him like he could sense her succumbing to her injuries. This couldn't be happening.

"Go and help them, love. I've got him," Evander said, appearing at my side to sit next to his wolf. I shot my gaze back and forth between him and Sirona, wondering what I could do.

"I'm not a healer," I pointed out. I would just get in the way. My efforts were better spent keeping Onyx calm and sated.

"She belongs to you. Give her the support of just being there with her," he explained, but I just shook my head. It didn't feel like enough—it didn't feel like anything. "She needs you."

With that, I stood and hurried to Nova's side as Sirona and Lia gave everything they had to heal my wolf. The scene was gruesome, and I stifled my urge to cry at seeing Nova that broken and in pain, but I could do what Evander instructed.

I could sit there with her, stroking her head and offering words of hope and encouragement. I could let her know she wasn't alone, even if this was her end.

We worked like that for hours, and the sun had long set by the time Sirona had healed the last of the significant injuries. My body shook, and my hands trembled from the fear I was so rattled with, but Nova was alive, and that's all that mattered.

Onyx leaped from Evander's side and bounded to Nova the moment we stepped away, nuzzling into her. She huffed and whimpered, but they weren't filled with the sounds of pain and death as they had been earlier.

I smiled as I watched the relief fill his dark eyes and wiped a bloody hand across my forehead that was dripping in sweat. Van caught my eye with a grin just as big as mine.

"We did it," I said, sighing, and he nodded before taking my hand and leading me to a large tent on the other side of the camp. Inside was a tub of hot water with steam snaking through the open air. My legs were so wobbly I practically fell over myself as I rushed to it and dipped my hands below the surface. I melted into the heat and quickly bent down to untie my boots.

"When you're finished, we'll be at dinner. The tables are set around the corner from where we just were," Van explained, and I gave an unintelligible response that sounded like something between an *okay* and *thank you*.

After my entirely too-long bath, I changed into the clothes left on the bedroll, wondering where Evander had gotten them or how he knew I'd need them.

I slipped through the tent flap and strode for the location Van had told me, noting the stares accompanied by whispers I was getting from the soldiers as I passed. It had to be unsettling to know their heir was nearly as strong as their king, though they had no idea I had the potential to be even more powerful since I had four Gifts in total. We decided last night to keep that secret to ourselves.

I dipped my head at the onlookers who watched me. Most turned away in fear, but a few stood tall, dropping their heads out of respect, and I made a mental image of their faces. After what happened this afternoon, it was necessary to note who was against us and who gave us their loyalty.

"How was the bath?" Van asked as I plopped beside him on the wooden bench in what I assumed was my spot. The plate before me was already filled with all of my favorites: chicken, potatoes, carrots, and so many rolls. My stomach grumbled as I bit into the bread, enjoying the salty, buttery flavor as it hit my stomach.

"Perfect," I told him, digging into my potatoes next.

I glanced over my shoulder to find Onyx and Nova still on the pallet. Nova was sleeping soundly as Onyx stood watch over her, peeling back his teeth at anyone who looked at them longer than he deemed okay.

"How is she?" I asked, my gaze locked on our wolves.

"She's okay," Van said, placing his hand over mine and squeezing gently. "Sirona said she'll need to rest for a few weeks to ensure she heals properly, but she'll be just fine."

I breathed a sigh of relief as I turned away and focused back on my plate.

"What happened, Evander? Her injuries were... "I couldn't finish as I let my mind drift to how she looked and how much blood she had lost.

"The unit she was assigned to was attacked," he said, whispering low so only I could hear.

I scooted closer as I understood this was a conversation he wanted to be private. A shield appeared around the two of us as I directed my eyes to him.

"Oberon?" I asked, and Evander nodded.

"We received no intel that they were in Disparya, let alone close to Tenebrae. Our soldiers were blindsided. Only a handful managed to get away and dragged her on that pallet with them," he explained.

My mouth dropped open in shock, partly because of the attack and partly because those survivors risked their lives to bring her here. She was barely alive, but they didn't leave her. My gratitude for those men knew no bounds, and I looked around like I could somehow recognize them.

"They're being tended to by Sirona and the other healers right now," Van said, reading my silent thoughts as usual. "I told them to expect you after dinner. I figured you'd want to speak to them."

I nodded quickly, grateful he knew me so well.

"Onyx wasn't with them?" I asked.

"No," Van answered. "He was assigned to protect a different group of generals as they travelled and was here by chance. Nova and the soldiers showed up only an hour before we arrived. If we had gotten here any later, I'm not sure she would have made it."

I blinked and shook my head, desperate to clear that possibility from my mind. We *had* made it. We saved her, and now I made it my mission to destroy every last person who hurt her. I was sure Onyx and Van were feeling the same.

"What happened to the men from earlier?" I inquired, taking another bite from my plate.

"They've been dealt with," he answered, turning toward his food and dropping the shield around us.

"And by *dealt with*, you mean…" I arched a brow as I gave him a sidelong glance.

"There is no room in our army for soldiers we can't trust," he said matter-of-factly. I nodded, reached for my water, and took a long sip as I realized what he was saying. "Does what I did bother you?"

I thought about that for a moment before shaking my head. It didn't. Not even a little bit.

"I would have done it if you hadn't," I admitted, looking up at him and finding an edge of intrigue in his features. "You said there were no lines," I reminded. "And after hearing those soldiers threaten them, I found that to be the case. Onyx and Nova are as much my family as you and the others are. There isn't anything I wouldn't give to keep you safe or do to those who threaten to harm you." My voice was flat and even, with nothing but sheer honesty shining through. I didn't waver in this declaration because it was the truth, which somehow made me stronger.

Evander smiled and reached for his drink.

"Then may the Gods help the assholes who try," he said, clicking his cup against mine.

36.

I spent the meal conversing with soldiers and getting to know them the best I could. They were my responsibility as much as they were Van's, and I wanted them to hold me in the same regard as him. Given our current situation, earning their trust and respect felt like a priority.

When I finished eating, I stopped at the healer's tent as planned and thanked the soldiers responsible for saving Nova. I wanted to offer them something more than my gratitude, so I decided to allow them to head back to their homes for a few weeks once they were medically cleared to move. Though I wasn't in charge just yet, I knew Evander wouldn't object to me repaying their kindness how I saw fit.

"What did you give them?" Van asked as I sat down next to him, grabbed his cup of ale, and finished it.

"A few weeks with their families before heading back out," I said, reaching for the pitcher and refilling it. "And they drink for free if they ever visit the tavern."

Van nodded, satisfied with my arrangement. I turned around on the bench, and leaned against the table as I watched Nova. She was now awake, and her eyes roamed over the sea of soldiers while Onyx lay quietly beside her. Her fur was mostly clean, though a few reddish patches remained, and her breathing seemed steady. Her back flexed as she pushed herself to stand, and a deep growl ripped through Onyx. He immediately stepped over her, forcing her body back down and then licked a bloody area of fur on her face.

Nova seemed to comply for all of five seconds before she moved again, lifting herself as she tried to get out from under Onyx. But he was stronger than she was right now and he pushed her back down a moment later as if he anticipated her moves. Nova fought back, refusing to give in as she sneered at him, her sharp teeth bared. Onyx growled right back, and when she attempted to move again, he lunged, locking his jaw around the back of her neck as he snarled into her fur.

I stood up, but Evander caught my arm and tugged me back down.

"He's hurting her!" I exclaimed, trying to rip my arm away, but his hold was firm.

"No, he isn't," Evander said, yanking on my body until I sat beside him again. How the fuck could he say that?

Onyx's growls grew louder, and his hackles raised as he moved over Nova until she was entirely beneath him. Nova snarled in fury as she pressed her body back onto the wood, forced to submit. Once her belly hit the surface, Onyx pressed his weight onto her, pinning her in place so she couldn't move, and then finally released his jaws from around her neck. She let out an irritated huff as he returned to tending to her wounds like nothing had happened.

"See?" Evander said. "Your wolf was just being stubborn and trying to get up before she was ready." He swung his legs over the bench so he was now seated like I was and crossed his arms over his chest.

"Or maybe she's fine, and your wolf is just an overbearing asshole," I shot back. I didn't like him taking jabs at Nova.

Evander scoffed and rolled his eyes.

"They've been together for a long time, love, and I'd wager that Onyx knows Nova better than she knows herself. She clearly is still injured and has no business walking around."

"Whatever," I snapped, peeling my eyes from him and back to the wolves. Onyx nuzzled into her, resting his head on top of hers. I stifled the smile that was beginning to form at the scene. Nova looked annoyed, but I could tell by how she shifted her body to make more room for him that she was happy he was with her.

"Nova is Onyx's to love and protect," Evander said thoughtfully. "In the same way that he is hers. They belong to each other. Trust me, Nova is just as overbearing whenever Onyx gets injured."

He was right. They did belong to one another, and this display was evidence enough. I found myself envious of their bond. Of meaning more than the world itself to someone. I had thought I had it once, but it had all been a lie. A love tinged with betrayal.

A soldier stepped forward, interrupting my thoughts and presenting Evander with two plates full of raw meat. Van looked them over before nodding, and the man turned around and carefully walked over to the wood pallet with plates in hand.

Onyx's head snapped up at the intrusion, but Nova's tail wagged in a fury as the food came closer.

She was definitely mine.

The soldier placed the plates in front of each wolf before practically sprinting away. Nova dug right in, but Onyx sat stoic and tall as he kept watch while she enjoyed her meal. It was like he thought someone would come out and attack her while they were distracted.

Once Nova cleared her food, Onyx lowered his face to his. I expected him to dive right in, but instead, he scooted the full plate with his nose until it was firmly in front of Nova before sitting straight again. My eyes widened in shock and adoration as I watched. Nova didn't move until a low growl emanated from Onyx's chest—a dare for her to protest. She expelled air through her nose like a sigh of irritation and worked on his plate until it was spotless.

Once she had finished she laid back down. Onyx resumed his spot next to her, resting his chin on the top of her head and taking up watch once more as she shut her eyes. My heart swelled until it was about to burst from my chest, and I felt Evander's eyes burning a hole into me.

"They display emotions just like we do," I said, amazed, and turned to face him.

"They are intelligent creatures," he said simply. "It's part of why they are protected here and coveted everywhere else."

Most of the camp had gone to sleep, but I was too restless to try. Van sat at the table, drinking and laughing with a group of soldiers as they shared stories throughout the evening. I had left them to it hours ago, instead deciding to help another group clean up for the evening.

"Is it okay if I take this?" I asked, gesturing to a platter of meat left on the table.

"Of course, Your Highness," one of the soldiers said. "If you're still hungry, I can bring the rest of the meal back out."

"That won't be necessary, but thank you," I told him, grabbing the platter and two empty plates before striding away from the table and toward my destination.

Onyx perked up as he heard my approach, but once he saw it was only me, he quickly lowered his chin back atop Nova's head, flattening her ears in the most adorable way. I placed one of the overflowing plates on the pallet next to him, but he simply side-eyed it and went back to watching the last of the soldiers turn in for the night.

"Eat," I told him. He didn't move, so I walked in front of his line of sight, forcing him to look at me. "Eat Onyx," I said again, and this time he climbed off Nova and moved to his plate. My lips curved into a victorious smile... until he dipped his head and scooted the plate in front of Nova just like he had before. I rolled my eyes, though my insides squeezed at the gesture.

"She's already eaten. Twice, in fact," I told him, crossing my arms over my chest. "Plus, she's asleep."

Onyx sat straight, looking me dead in the eyes with a look that said, *'she'll wake eventually.'*

"I had a feeling you would do that," I said, twisting and grabbing the second full plate and setting it before Van's stubborn wolf. It wasn't hard to tell who he learned his behavior from. Onyx glanced down at his plate but stayed sitting, and I huffed in irritation as I leaned closer to the wolf.

"Eat," I said, and his stare softened for a moment like he was genuinely struggling to restrain himself from obeying my command. If I couldn't make one damn stubborn wolf eat, how the hell was I going to make thousands of soldiers fall in line when I commanded my own unit? I would not let Onyx defeat me today.

I straightened, lifting my chin high and letting any warmth in my expression disappear.

"I said, *eat*." My tone was dipped in command. The voice not of his friend or even master, but of a ruler.

Onyx lowered his head to the food, albeit reluctantly, but still. I watched triumphantly as he devoured his entire meal in minutes. When he finished, he shot me a glare that was a medley of annoyance and gratitude. I shrugged, not caring how he felt, and just happy he had a full belly.

He stretched his back and yawned but didn't take up his spot next to Nova, and I realized that he was fighting the pull of sleep. Was he planning on watching over her all night? He had to know that she was safe with us here, right?

"You got him to eat," a smooth satin voice called from behind, and I twisted to find Van walking up to us. "How much of a fight did he put up?" I leveled him a flat stare.

"He takes after you," I told him, and his face broke into a dazzling smile as he stopped at my side.

"For future reference," he said, dipping a hand into his pocket and pulling out a stack of treats wrapped in a napkin, "He's a sucker for oatmeal cookies. You can get him to do anything for them." He whistled through his teeth and Onyx perked up as he watched his master hold up four oatmeal cookies.

The wolf made to move but then stopped and glanced down at Nova. He whimpered as he shifted from side to side, torn on what to do.

"Apparently, anything but leave her," I pointed out, snatching the cookies from Van's hand and bringing them to the wolf. I laid the treats at his feet and scratched behind his ears as he gobbled them up in a single bite. "He's refusing to sleep."

Van appeared at my side again and knelt down to face his wolf. Onyx stared at his master with sad eyes for a long moment before Evander released a breath of understanding.

"You need to sleep," Van whispered, and Onyx gave a soft whimper of refusal.

My eyes watered watching the exchange and the fact that even now, he still didn't feel like Nova was safe. Or maybe he was nervous that she wouldn't survive the night and would succumb to her injuries even though she had been healed. It was like he was afraid that if sleep came for him, the one thing that meant everything to him would be taken while he was under.

"I'll watch her," Van said, pressing his forehead to his wolf in a gesture I had seen him do so many times to me. A gesture that had come to showcase trust and understanding—love and compassion. "I promise," he whispered before looking at Onyx. The wolf wavered briefly before finally lowering his body to the pallet. He snuggled into Nova, nuzzling his face to hers before shutting his eyes and letting sleep claim him.

Van stood and moved to Nova's side as promised. He ran his hands along her grey fur and kissed her softly between the ears. Though she technically belonged to me, Van had as much claim on her as I did. The three of them had been together since he was a toddler, and they were just pups. Nova had history and trust with Van that I wasn't sure I would ever truly gain.

Evander flicked his wrist, calling his Gift forward, and I watched in awe as he twisted and twirled his magic, bending the shadows to his will. His control was immaculate, and the care in which he worked was something to desire. Tendrils of darkness curved and expanded to create a large nest of blankets and pillows right next to my wolf. Once he manipulated his magic to the desired size and specifications, he solidified his creation before plopping down.

"Our tent is just around the corner." He pointed, and I followed his finger. "I figured you wouldn't want to be too far away from her, so I moved us over here. There's a tub and a change of clothes ready for you." I opened my mouth to express my gratitude but instead found myself walking for his nest and sitting beside him.

"I'd rather stay here and watch her," I said, and Van nodded before throwing a blanket over me. I rested my back against the large wall of fluffy pillows, still amazed at his ability to mold his magic with such expertise. If I attempted to create a pillow, it would look more like a disproportionate potato. And it would probably be just as hard. It made sense that he was so good at this all, though. Not only did he possess more power than others since he was a king, but he had also inherited that title at the mere age of five. He had been training endlessly for nearly twenty years to master his craft.

"I didn't think he'd actually sleep," I told Van as I looked at the black wolf whose tongue was now lolling out of his mouth.

"If it were anyone else besides me offering to watch her, he wouldn't have."

"He trusts you that much?" I asked, remembering the feral look on Onyx's face when he wouldn't so much as let Van take a step in Nova's direction earlier. Van seemed to understand that's where my mind was at.

"Nova is his Solum," he said, and I couldn't help but feel I should have known what that meant; like that word held a meaning more substantial than the air itself. "It means one and only."

I looked up at Van with pleading eyes for him to elaborate.

"It's said that the Gods created two souls to mold and match each other in every way—a perfect pair written in the stars. When they find their other half, an undeniable bond forms. A love deep and pure," he explained, and his eyes drifted to mine.

"Is it magic?" I asked curiously, but Van shook his head. "So then, how do you know it occurs? Can you see it?" I turned, looking over our wolves as if I could find some indication that this bond existed between them—some physical marking or glowing light to tell me that they were Solum, but there was nothing that I could detect. I reached out my Empathi Gift but was met with a solid wall, unable to get through.

"You can't use that Gift on them," Evander declared as if he knew exactly what I was trying to do. "No internal magic works on them. It's a defense their species has developed over time. Their venom also neutralizes our magic."

"Forever?" I asked as I slumped onto the pillows and called my Gift back.

"Just until it leaves our system. It can take anywhere from several minutes to a few hours, depending on the amount of venom in the bloodstream."

Onyx and Nova's sharp fangs became a whole lot scarier. It was a good thing they were on our side.

"You said their bond occurs in their species, but can it occur in others too? Can it happen between people?" I asked. Evander shrugged, and I was annoyed by his lack of knowledge or interest in the matter.

"Some people claim they are Solum," Van said after a moment, as he stared at the wolves. Onyx had shifted onto his side and put his paw over Nova as they cuddled. I was instantly reminded of last night and how Van and I must have looked similar to this as we comforted each other. "But who knows for sure."

"So it's not something that can be seen then," I deduced, and Evander shrugged again. "Is there anything you *do* know?" I asked, annoyed.

Evander grinned at my impatience and shrugged again. I swung my fist, determined to punch him in the arm for messing with me, but was met with a soft pillow he had crafted a split second before he could take my blow. He chuckled as he tossed the fabric shield onto our nest and leaned against the pillows to get comfortable.

"Some say it's a physical occurrence—like a shock to your system, a searing touch, or the air being taken from your lungs. Others have said it was more of something to be felt internally—as if they were two magnets being drawn to one another despite reason. A few have said it was intuition—that they saw the other and just knew. Some say it was their magic that called to the other," Evander explained. "Thanks to the Magusiers of the past, the Solum Bond has only ever been identified in the wolves throughout our history, so it's hard to tell if the people who claim to experience it are being truthful."

"Why don't you just have Tallis use his Gift on them?" I asked curiously. It seemed like the easiest way to find out the answer.

"Because what would be the point?" Evander countered. "If they truly believe they found the person the Gods had created for them, why would I take that away? We honor the Solum Bond between the wolves in Tenebrae. We even have a holiday to celebrate it. It's something rare and beautiful, so who wouldn't want to experience it?"

Evander fell quiet as he glanced down at me, and I nodded, understanding exactly why he didn't want to know the truth. Those people didn't deserve to have their happiness taken away with just one glance from Tallis. They might have been accurate in their assumptions, but given that this bond seemed to only exist in the species of wolves sleeping before us, it was most likely not the case.

"I hope they have it," I whispered, and Evander smiled.

"I do too."

37.

Felix, Olivier, and Marceline were gathered in the library when we arrived that afternoon. Because of Nova's injuries, Sirona thought it best that Van traverse her back rather than have her try to heal on a day-long journey.

The moment his amber eyes met mine, Felix sprinted for me. His arms wrapped around me as his eyes roamed over every inch of my face, searching for injuries or markings from that night at the lake.

"I'm okay," I told him. "You didn't find them, did you?"

"No," he said solemnly. "We followed a trail we found, but just like back in Caelum, it disappeared into thin air. It was like they were there one second and then just vanished."

I glanced over my shoulder to see Olivier filling Van in on the details of their journey.

"You're the only one with the traverse ability, right?" I asked the king. He and Olivier both looked up from their conversation and headed over to us.

"I've never encountered someone with my ability, nor have I discovered anything about it during my research. I have no idea how they are pulling it off," Van answered.

"I think we should revisit the possibility of Venator being involved," Felix said. "With their tracking Gifts, it's more than possible for them to make it so that they are untraceable."

Evander and Olivier nodded, both seeming to agree with Felix for once.

Progress.

But we were still running out of options and time and getting nowhere.

"I'll go over the texts Ainsley and I stole—" Felix began, and Evander's eyes snapped to him. "I mean, *borrowed with expressed permission*," he corrected, and Olivier pinched the bridge of his nose.

I had my mind made up that if we couldn't find what we needed before leaving Agnitio, I'd smuggle the books out and take them with us. After the hell the librarian had given us during our time there, I didn't feel bad about it, and Felix was all too willing to help.

As we were leaving, he created a diversion by stripping out of his clothes and plopping down on the couch to read completely naked. After the librarian had rushed him, demanding he get dressed, the two argued about how reading in the nude wasn't against any of the rules. I used the distraction to grab as many books as possible before casting an illusion to make it look like I was holding a potted plant as I fled. I'll never understand why no one stopped to question me on why I was caring around fauna in the library, but I also wasn't complaining.

"And I'll go help him read over the books that we definitely did not steal from the library under a false name," I said as Felix and I both backed slowly out of the room, not taking our eyes off the furious men before us.

"Love," Evander growled in warning, but the second my foot stepped over the threshold, I turned, grabbed Felix's hand, and sprinted for his room. Evander could have followed, but I was pretty sure he was more impressed than angry, judging the lack of pursuit. I just hoped we could return the stolen texts before Tallis could find out what we had done.

When we arrived at Felix's door, Lia was sprawled on his bed, flipping through the pages of a worn book. I smiled at my friend as I made my way for her and sank down onto the mattress.

"Any luck?" I asked, peering over the stack of open books lying about.

"Nope," she whined. "We've been at it all night and haven't found anything yet."

After Nova had been healed, Evander decided to traverse Lia back home so she could fill the others in on what had happened to the camp. Hopefully, the five of them could figure out how soldiers from Pravus had gotten through our defenses.

"Maybe if you and Cal hadn't spent most of the night fondling each other, we'd be farther along," Felix teased as he took the book from her hands and turned the pages.

"Well, maybe if you and Oli weren't filling the room with aggressive sexual tension, then we wouldn't have had to distract ourselves," Lia shot back.

I raised a brow at Felix, demanding an explanation, but he rolled his eyes and returned to the text in his hands. I turned to Lia instead, knowing she'd tell me exactly what I wanted to know, but a deep voice interrupted before she could open her mouth.

"The two of them spent most of the night arguing about where to start and why they were right while the other was an idiot," Calidore said as he strode into the room with a platter of food for everyone. "Then they would stare at each other in this longing way like they were about to rip each other's clothes off and just hate fuck right in front of us. It was really hot."

My focus shifted to Felix, who was now shaking his head at the explanation.

"That's not how it was," Felix argued, but a little smirk began to curve his lips. I might not have been here last night, but I had witnessed several instances where it was clear there was something present. The growing tension between them didn't magically vanish just because Oli refused to acknowledge what was happening. Felix had made his intentions clear, so it would be up to Oli to change their path. But it seemed like he was too stubborn to do it.

The three of us stared at my best friend incredulously as he tried to deny what obviously happened.

"Fine," he said, slamming his book shut as he stomped for the bed. He climbed between Lia and me and threw himself backward until his head hit the pillow. "That's exactly how it was. But what the fuck am I supposed to do? I can literally *feel* the sexual tension, and there isn't anything I can do about it."

I felt bad for my best friend. I had never seen him so obsessed over one person. In Caelum, Felix would bounce around, taking a new lover nearly every night, and it wasn't like he didn't have that option here. Cal and Lia both tried to convince him to join them, and every night we went to the tavern, Felix would spend most of the time dancing and flirting with someone new. But it was like he just didn't *want* to do it anymore. Even when his body was elsewhere, his attention was always fixed on Oli. Felix had never had the chance to fall for anyone, and now that he found someone he was interested in and free to pursue, it was unrequited. If anyone in this world deserved love and happiness, it was Felix.

I leaned back and set my head next to his as I stared into his amber eyes. He pouted out his bottom lip to be dramatic and make light of the hurt I knew he was feeling. My hand found his, and I interlaced our fingers together. I didn't have to say anything for him to know I was there for him. It seemed like Felix and I had developed that same secret way of communicating that I had been so jealous he had with Dashiell.

My heart ached as I thought about that prince and his friendship with Felix. What would he have said and done if he were here? How would he have comforted the man that had been his best friend since they were eight years old?

I knew Felix had chosen to spend his time with those he couldn't see himself caring about, but Dashiell had witnessed it for far longer. He and Felix had shared nearly every aspect of their lives with one another. They were brothers in every way besides blood, and Dashiell knew him better than anyone. And now that was just... over.

I opened my mouth and closed it as I struggled to come up with what to say, and felt overwhelming guilt at Felix being here. I was the reason he was no longer with Dashiell. I was the reason he was here—feeling this pain over wanting someone who didn't want him back.

"It's okay, Ainsley," Felix whispered. "I'll be okay." I closed my eyes and swallowed hard. I wanted to believe him, but I just didn't. There was nothing I could do about the situation with Dashiell. Felix had made it abundantly clear that he couldn't return to Caelum and wouldn't leave me even if he could, but perhaps I could get through to Olivier. I had to at least try.

"Didn't you say you and Evander overheard something about a stone?" Cal asked, bringing us back to the present by referring to the day Van and I had hidden from our pursuers in the woods. I nodded, recalling that one of the men had suggested we possessed a stone, though we didn't know what that meant.

He held up the book, revealing a drawing of a man wearing a large pendant with an emerald stone in the center. I slid off the bed and took the book from his hands, checking the title as I did. But there was no description of the man or stone on the page he had held up. That particular text mainly consisted of stories about important people throughout our history and only held a small part about Imnuto and the magic it was said to have.

"What do the stones they discussed have to do with Inmuto?" I asked, trying to understand why he thought to show us the drawing.

"It doesn't," Cal responded, flipping the page to show another drawing of a man with dark rubies embedded in the hilt of the sword sheathed at his side. "But we keep hitting dead ends with it, so maybe we should focus our energy more on how our enemy keeps evading us."

"It's not a hard feat for Venator to accomplish," Felix suggested, but Cal shook his head.

"Only if it actually *is* Venator behind the attacks, but Van tried to get King Arden on our side, and he wouldn't have done that if he believed he was working with Oberon. I trust Van's gut instincts, and if he felt Venator wasn't involved, we should focus on other avenues until it's proven otherwise."

Calidore had a point. Venator could have been behind the pursuit of Van and me, and if so, it would have explained why we didn't hear them coming until it was almost too late. But that didn't explain why Oli and Felix weren't able to track the men who attacked Marce and me in Agnitio. They said the trail seemed to vanish without a trace, and given that the men possessed shadow magic from Tenebrae, that shouldn't have been the case. Perhaps the stones that were mentioned held the answer.

"Cal's right. Our best bet is to wait until spring to keep hunting for Inmuto. Right now, our biggest concern should be figuring out how our attackers keep managing to disappear without a trace. Let's approach this as if Venator isn't involved and assume they are using some kind of aid to help them escape," I said, closing the book and tossing it onto the bed.

We couldn't afford to waste any more time chasing possibilities. I trusted Van's belief that the lost kingdom still existed and I would help him find it, but for now, we needed to focus on something tangible, and these stones were that.

"Sirona will have books regarding magical objects or practices," Lia announced, rising from the bed as well. "Felix and I will go get them, and then we can reconvene in the library later."

We all agreed to the plan and headed our separate ways. I wasn't sure if these stones held the answer to anything, but it was worth the research. Nothing else had been going our way, and after my mishap in Agnitio with Mishal, I felt the need to prove my worth more than ever.

I sat in my new bed, looking around the massive space Evander called his. It was a similar setup to my room, but with a bigger bed and an even larger bathing room to account for the pool it held. As soon as I finished adding the last of my things to the dresser Van had provided, I stripped out of my clothes and dove in. He still had a copper tub sitting next to it for some reason, though it made no sense. The pool was superior in every way.

The water grew hotter as I dipped below the surface like it magically sensed the warm temperature it had been set to wasn't enough for me. I sighed in contentment as I reluctantly gave in to the fact that staying in this room was a million times better than mine.

Lia, Felix, Cal, and I had sprawled out in the library earlier this evening with our noses in the books Sirona had lent us while Marce, Oli, and Van strategized different tactics to take when it came to the pending war. Van was supportive when I expressed my desire to research more along the path with the stones and said he'd inquire if his friend from Vorsutos, Declan, had any information that could be useful. I wasn't sure if giving up on Inmuto was the right path, but I had made my decision and needed to stop questioning it.

Once finished with my swim and scrubbed clean, I changed into my silk night-clothes, cursing the cold weather as I padded back into the room. The windows were shut tight, but his room felt so much chillier than mine ever had. Perhaps some kind of magic regulated the temperature, just like with the pool.

I twirled my fingers, letting my shadows craft a blanket around me as I headed for the fireplace. My creation was thin and terribly made, but at least it warmed me slightly as I blew on the fading embers.

"It's easier if you add the kindling that's atop the mantle," Evander called as he entered the room and strode over.

He reached for a small box and tossed the kindling into the fire as he tended it. Within moments, the logs caught, and the heat from the flames licked over my skin, bathing me in its warmth. Evander placed the contents back down before walking to the bathing room and closing the door behind him. I heard the water from the shower turn on and decided it was time to climb into bed and get some sleep.

I let my poorly crafted blanket disappear before crawling beneath the covers, still too thin for my liking. The fire had warmed the room slightly, but it was still entirely too cold, and I shivered as I struggled to get comfortable.

Before I decided to let sleep claim me, I used my shadows to craft as many pillows as I could and lined them down the center of the mattress to create a barrier between us. The bed was big enough that neither of us would get close throughout the night, but I didn't want to take any chances. We had slept in each other's arms in Agnitio, but that was because we had both experienced something traumatic and needed one another. This was something entirely different, and I wasn't about to give him any ideas.

"You're in my spot," Evander said, and I opened my eyes to find him standing in the doorframe with damp hair and his tattoo creeping across his skin slowly. He was dressed in a thin shirt and sweatpants that looked so much warmer than what I was wearing.

"I was here first."

"It's *my* bed," he argued, and I shrugged because I gave zero shits.

"You should have thought about that before you took a shower and left me to choose what side I wanted."

"Honestly, I thought you'd still be sitting by the fire and crying about how cold it is in here," he shot back, going over to his dresser and rifling through it.

"Because it *is* cold in here! You keep it at an unreasonable temperature."

"Then you're really not going to like it when I open the windows in a minute."

"Don't you fucking dare," I growled. I didn't care if I agreed to stay in his room; if he let it get any colder in here, I was leaving. There was no way I would willingly stay and freeze my ass off all night.

Evander flashed a bright and wicked smile before shutting his dresser drawer and strolling over to my side of the bed with what looked to be a ball of thick yarn. He pulled the blankets off me, and I yelped from the instant cold that washed over my body, causing goosebumps to appear over my flesh. Evander grabbed my ankle before I could cover myself back up and unrolled the ball to show a pair of chunky knit socks. He put them on me, and my feet thawed at once as he tucked them back beneath the blanket. I blinked several times in confusion as he walked around to his new side of the bed.

"How did you—" I began.

"You always sleep with an extra blanket over your feet, so I assumed you'd want those," he answered as he unlatched the window and pushed it open just as he said he would.

Cold air blew into the room, and I lifted the blanket to hide my face from the breeze. My body shook beneath the sheets, the silk fabric doing absolutely nothing to keep me warm on such a chilly night. The socks were a nice gesture, but they wouldn't keep the rest of me warm.

Evander chuckled under his breath as he watched me tremble from the cold, and I glowered at him. Of course he'd find my misery entertaining. With a slight flick of his wrist, his shadows emerged and formed a thick fur blanket that was the perfect size for just one person. He climbed onto the bed and draped it over my body before looking pointedly at my crafted pillow barrier and then at me.

"Really?" he said flatly.

"Yup."

Evander rolled his eyes and waved a hand over my pillows. One by one, each of them disappeared into swirling tendrils of shadows, leaving the bed exactly how it was before.

"What the hell?!" I demanded as Evander lay down to get comfortable.

"If you need to craft a barricade to stop yourself from wanting me, that sounds like something you should really work through."

"*I don't want you*," I said between my teeth. "If anything, you're the one who wants me, and you know it."

"I'm not too sure about that, love," Evander tsked. "I'm not the one who created a divide down the bed because they can't control themselves."

"I can control—"

"And a line of pillows? Really?" he interrupted. "Do you honestly think a stack of fluff would keep me from fucking you if you asked? Come on now, love. Be more creative next time," he said, rolling onto his side to face the window.

My mouth dropped open as I stared at his back, unable to come up with a retort as my mind filled with images of him breaching the pillows to get to me the second I requested it. I shook my head to clear the thoughts and rolled onto my side to face the opposite wall.

I built the barrier to prevent ending up wrapped in each other's arms as we had days ago, but now all I could think about was doing so much more than just cuddling.

Shit.

38.

I reluctantly found that moving into Evander's room wasn't the worst thing imaginable. The large pool in the bathing room more than made up for the two weeks I'd spent freezing until I slipped beneath the warm fur blanket. Despite my protests, Evander refused to shut the windows every night, and whenever I complained, he'd let his shadows drift out and craft a binding to tie around my mouth before I could stop him. After I was free, and he had a good laugh about it, he'd form an additional blanket to throw at me. But every morning when I woke up, that blanket was gone. It was as if he enjoyed tormenting me every night rather than just putting an end to my suffering.

One day, I found my drawers stuffed with thicker sleepwear and a note that said: *So you stop shaking the bed all night.* But as I browsed the warmer options, there was only one thing I wanted to wear. I padded over to his dresser and dug through it until I found a shirt to steal. Sure, I could have just put on one of the new options I had and been perfectly fine, but once I had worn his clothes in Agnitio, I found myself desperate to be wrapped in his scent again. It made me feel calm and grounded—safe and secure. But there wasn't a chance in hell I'd be telling him that, so I'd make up a lie if he inquired. Thank the Gods, each night he never did.

Our research regarding the stones had proved to be the right course to take, and for the first time, it felt like we were finally making progress. Sirona's books depicted hundreds of different stones and gems throughout history, most of which were said to be either myths or no longer existed. That fact would have deterred anyone else, but because the same had been said about Inmuto—which we firmly believed still existed—it gave us hope that it also applied to the stones.

Three stones in particular, were said to have been around since before the events of the First Great War and quickly disappeared after. Two of those three seemed to be exactly what we were looking for. The Lapsus stone was said to allow objects to vanish and appear elsewhere, much like what Van could do on his own. The Tectus stone was said to be able to conceal things from sight, making them completely invisible. It also made the objects undetectable unless you possessed the third and final stone. The Indico stone was said to be kept with the other two, for its magic unfolded differently. Where the Lapsus and Tectus worked to remove and conceal, the Indico had the opposite effect by revealing their hidden secrets.

Whenever the two stones were used, they would leave a magical signature on the land that only those who held the Indico could uncover. There was no description of how it all worked or even what the stones looked like, but I knew we had to find them. My instincts were screaming at me that the three of them held the answers to our questions. However, I had no idea whether there were several of each of the stones or only three in existence.

Regardless, we needed to find them all.

"He has the information," Evander said, subtly nodding toward a table in the back of the tavern. I followed his gesture to see one of the tavern workers kissing someone's neck sensually before he looked up and locked his eyes on mine for the briefest of moments. "Your test is to retrieve it."

Ever since I learned about Van's operation at the tavern, he had given me tasks to retrieve planted information from our spies without being obvious about it. And thanks to the fact that he was paying them double to watch me like a hawk for any mistakes, I failed every time. I was too quick when I walked, too overly flirtatious, too suspicious because I glanced around... the list went on and on.

But not tonight.

I rose from my seat at the small table Evander and I were at. Because I failed so often, he determined that the rest of our group was a distraction and that they had to stay away until I successfully completed my mission at least once.

I shrugged out of my thick coat, revealing the thin black satin dress Lia had lent me. I didn't miss the way Van's eyes roamed over me hungrily as I backed away from the table and walked to the bar at the other end of the room. I climbed onto the seat and ordered myself a drink as I casually glanced at my mark. I looked at him and only him, as that was where I seemed to have gone wrong nearly every time. According to Evander, looking around the room made it seem like I was either looking for someone in particular or checking to make sure I wasn't being watched. It was best to focus only on who I was there to see.

My eyes locked with the worker a few times, and I bit my lip and looked away quickly as if I were shy about having been caught. I crossed my legs, revealing my bare skin from the high slit of my dress as I sipped on my drink. *Interested but not overly flirtatious,* I reminded myself as my gaze traveled to the worker leaving the man he had been tending to. I forced color to my cheeks as I held his stare across the room while he strode for me. Once he was a few feet away, I straightened my posture and turned, glancing at my drink before casually taking a sip. *Interested but not overly flirtatious.*

His fingers roamed down my arms and I let my head fall back to his chest as my eyes fluttered closed. I focused on only the feel of his touch, which took away the pressure of my task. I had to treat this like just another night downstairs, dancing with strangers and enjoying myself.

"What brings you in tonight?" the worker—Flynn—asked. "Are you lonely or just looking to have a good time?" A code phrase: did I have information, or was I looking for some.

"Both," I said breathlessly, tilting my head back, so his mouth met my neck. He kissed along my throat, and I moaned softly; not too loud to be over the top, but just enough so that anyone watching knew I was enjoying my time like any other patron. His lips worked their way up until they were primed at my ear.

"Then how about we go upstairs and take care of that for you?" he whispered before pulling back to look at me. He swiped his thumb along my bottom lip and I nodded, keeping my gaze pinned to his as I stood from the bar and let him lead me upstairs. My role tonight was just to be a lonely customer who wanted attention and the hope of a good time.

Flynn grabbed a key from his pocket and unlocked one of the rooms on the top floor before opening it wide for me to enter first. The second he shut the door behind us, the sound of Van traversing filled the space.

"Well?" he asked, and I spun around to face Flynn as I bit my lip nervously. I had no idea how I did tonight. Van always let the scenarios play out before informing me that I failed rather than stopping them as soon as I messed up. My leg bounced impatiently as I stood there, waiting for the verdict.

"She was perfect," Flynn declared, and I leaped at him, wrapping my arms tightly around his neck. "Fantastic job, Your Highness."

I squealed with delight knowing I had finally freaking done it! Who knew there were so many rules when it came to gathering information from a spy. I thought it would have been as easy as just following them upstairs, but Van quickly pointed out that wasn't the case. Our operation had to be as covert as possible, and therefore we had to make the task believable.

Van thanked Flynn and then dismissed him so we could review the notes from his observation of my performance. Surprisingly enough, he said it was nearly flawless, but I could have allowed Flynn to touch and flirt with me more so that it seem like a genuine transaction. Other than me rushing through the encounter too quickly, I received top marks from him.

"Next time you'll be the one to pursue him, but for now, you'll practice on me," Evander said. I arched a brow skeptically.

"You're joking," I accused, but Evander's face was serious.

He strode to an armchair nearby and dragged it to the center of the room before sitting down. I stared at him, unblinking, as I processed his demand. "You can go ahead downstairs, try to seduce one of the other workers, fail miserably and embarrass yourself, or..." I hadn't moved from where I stood near the door. "You can practice on me in the privacy of this room without our spies picking apart your every move."

I swallowed hard as I chewed on his proposal. There was no way I wanted to try and seduce him, but I also didn't want to look like an idiot in a room full of people observing me. And I was positive that if I refused him, Evander would ensure I failed.

"Unless, of course, you're too afraid, love," he teased, and I rolled my eyes.

"What do I possibly have to be afraid of?" I countered, narrowing him a flat look.

"Perhaps you'll find that you enjoy the act. It's clear you want me, and now you get to play off of that."

I gritted my jaw and rolled my knuckles into fists. He was obviously baiting me, but I couldn't stop myself from playing into his hand as usual. I let out a frustrated groan as I shook my arms like I was preparing for a training session with Oli. Evander's lips lifted in the corners as he watched me, no doubt thoroughly enjoying how much I didn't want to do this.

"I'll have you run through it once without instruction, and then I'll give you notes on how to improve. Your goal is to do just as Flynn did tonight," he explained, and I nodded. I understood what was expected of me; I just didn't want to do it. Not with him.

I took a deep breath and glanced around the room as my eyes narrowed on my target. If he wanted a damn show, I'd give him one. I wouldn't leave any room for improvement or notes. I would do this once and *only* once. I walked right past where Evander lounged in his chair, ready for me.

"Giving up already?" he drawled, and I ignored his commentary, instead focusing on my task at the liquor cart.

Once I was finished, the sounds of my heels clicking on the wooden floor echoed between us as I returned to him. I kept my pace slow to give my mind more time to decide how I wanted the scenario to play out. I thought about how Giselle approached him that first night, making her performance so believable that I genuinely thought he was a customer of hers. Everything about her was confident and bold as she made a show of claiming him, and I would have to do the same to pass his little test.

I walked around the chair to stand before him again, swirling a glass of amber liquor in my hands. I brought the drink to my lips and took a deliberate sip as I pinned him in my gaze. The alcohol burned on its way down, warming the pit of my stomach the moment it hit, and I ran my tongue over my lips, collecting the last remnants of the smokey drink. Evander's eyes darkened as he tracked the movement, and I mentally noted the change. I reached out, placing the drink in his hands, and began to circle him, running my fingers up his arm as I passed.

"Just setting the scene," I said, stopping behind him and placing my hands on his shoulders before slowly dragging them down his chest as I had seen Giselle do. I leaned forward so my lips hovered above his ear. "What brings you in tonight?" I whispered as I moved my fingers back up his chest before undoing the top button of his shirt and sliding my hand beneath.

His heart thudded heavily, and his flesh burned beneath my touch. I was supposed to be turning *him* on, but the feel of his bare skin had me swallowing hard and my body aching with need. I closed my eyes as I thought back to the way he had me pinned against the wall while telling me everything he desired from me. Rather than get lost in my lust for him, I would use it to my advantage. I would do to him what he did to me that night.

I pressed my lips to Evander's neck, letting my tongue brush over the point of contact. His body tensed under my kiss, and he shifted in his chair as his control began to slip away. I smiled against him before pulling back. I withdrew my hands from his chest, letting my nails graze across his flesh as I did. Standing once more, I walked around to his front to continue this game face-to-face. Before I could ask the code phrase, Evander spoke another.

"It looked inviting," he said, which meant the pending conversation was dire and needed to be had immediately. It also meant he was bowing out of our game before we had truly begun. I tilted my head as I smirked at him. There was no way I was ending it early.

"Are you lonely or just looking to have a good time?" I asked, lifting my foot and setting it on his lap.

"Did you not hear my response?" he said, curling his hand around my ankle.

"Oh, I did. I just don't care," I replied, giving a pointed look at my shoe in a clear demand for him to remove it. His fingers grazed over the strap, hesitating at the buckle like he was battling himself. "Unless, of course, you're too afraid, love," I mocked.

With that, Evander placed his drink on the arm of the chair and unhooked the clasp. The straps wrapped around my calf unraveled, leaving my leg bare. He guided my foot out of the shoe, and I brought it back to the ground before placing my other one in his lap so he could do the same.

"So, are you lonely or just looking to have a good time?" I tried again.

Evander tossed my shoe to the floor, and before he could guide my foot back down, I pressed it against his chest and pushed until his back slammed into the armchair. He groaned at the force I used and gripped my ankle as his other hand held onto my leg. Carefully, he ran his fingers from my calf to my thigh before tracing back down in a long stroke. Every nerve in my body was firing off at once, and I zoned in on his tender touch.

"Both," he whispered breathlessly. I bit my lip as I met his darkened eyes. They were wild and frenzied—the look of a beast needing to be set free.

I pulled my leg from his hold before slowly climbing onto his lap to straddle him. I kept myself lifted so my face hovered above his because I liked the dynamic of being the one to gaze down on him for a change. Reaching for the drink he had set down, I took a small sip and then held it out for him to take.

"Finish it," I demanded. Evander's chest rose and fell rapidly at the sound of command in my voice. He did as instructed before placing the glass back down and moving his hands to my waist. I swiped my thumb across his bottom lip, gathering a small bead of liquor, and then pressed it to my tongue. I'm sure it would have tasted far better coming from his lips.

His fingers dug into my sides as he watched me savor that stolen bit of alcohol, and I couldn't help but smile at the restraint he was losing. He had me entirely undone for him back in Agnitio, and it was my turn to do the same to him. It was my turn to leave him breathless and panting. It was my turn to leave him wanting more.

I slid a hand behind his neck and up his hair until I had a fistful of his soft black strands between my fingers. I pulled hard, yanking his head back and making him suck in a sharp breath as I crafted a dagger with my free hand and pressed it to his throat. Evander's eyes sliced to the hand that held the weapon and then back up to my gaze as a sly smile took form on his gorgeous face.

"Now, love," he drawled. His voice was sensual and filled with excited anticipation. "The task was to seduce me. I don't believe our marks will want to have a weapon primed to end their life while we conduct our business."

"Oh, but I am," I said innocently. "You told me to seduce *you,* not a mark. *You* want a challenge. *You* enjoy me like this."

I could feel the tension in the room and his struggle to resist me. It only fueled my fire more. I let my mind travel to that night in the corridor and the way he took control of my body, making my resolve shatter as I urged him to take what he wanted.

"And by the way your fingers are digging into my flesh, and your eyes keep dropping to my mouth like you want to claim *that* instead of the weapon aimed at your throat, I think it's pretty safe to say I'm doing just that," I said confidently. "So much so that I'd be willing to bet you want nothing more than to take me here and now, exactly as we are—dagger and all."

Evander didn't answer. He only stared at me with wild eyes and a throat bobbing hard as he swallowed my words. I leaned forward and pressed my lips to each corner of his mouth before letting my dagger turn into shadows as I climbed off his lap. Then, I gathered my shoes from the floor and strolled for the door.

"Oh, and Van," I called without turning around. "I don't think I need any notes, but here's one for you: close your mouth; you're drooling."

And then I left him there. I couldn't turn into shadows and traverse the way he could, but I thought it was a pretty damn good exit.

39.

A permanent smirk was etched on my face as I replayed the scene between Evander and me in the tavern from three nights ago. We hadn't discussed what had happened, nor did Van offer me any notes on improvement. We both knew they weren't required. Occasionally, I'd catch his stare, and within the shadowy depths of his dark eyes, I could almost see the flashing images of me straddling him while his fingers dug into my waist. I swallowed hard, refusing to let my body react to the memories.

I stretched my arms above my head, enjoying the warm rays of the sun while being bundled in a thick blanket. Felix demanded we have a Delicious Duo day, and though I agreed because it had been too long since our last one, I wasn't keen on spending the day in the cold. Winter was far more frigid in Tenebrae than it ever was in Caelum. I grew up with the colder months being more mild than freezing, and I wasn't sure if it was because of the Aerians controlling the weather or that Caelum was the southern part of Disparya, where Tenebrae was the far north. I suggested that our day would have been better spent indoors next to a fire, but Felix was adamant we go on a picnic. It was something we used to always do together back in Caelum, and even though I didn't want to freeze my ass off, I wanted to be able to offer him that little reminder of our past.

"You *do* know picnics are supposed to entail food, right?" I asked, pulling the blanket tighter around me as I looked over at Felix. He rolled his amber eyes before shifting beside me to dig into the pack he brought. He withdrew a loaf of bread, a plate of meat and cheese, and a bowl of raspberries. My stomach rumbled as I sat up and ripped the food from his hands. Van had only agreed to let us have the afternoon off if we trained for an extra hour this morning, which meant we had to skip lunch.

Within ten minutes, nearly every scrap of food had been consumed by the two of us. The only thing left was the full bowl of raspberries. Felix grabbed a handful and tossed them into his mouth before offering me the bowl. I shook my head.

"Sorry, I thought you liked them," Felix commented, placing the fruit bowl in his lap before popping another berry into his mouth.

"I do, but...But they held a hidden meaning between Dashiell and me," I stated, swallowing the phantom pain of the memory. The raspberries had been our own inside joke and a way to tell the other that we were proud of them. I had unconsciously chosen to stay away from the fruit and the unwelcome reminder it brought.

Felix flicked the bowl of raspberries with his wrist, tossing them all behind him on the grass. "I never cared for them that much anyway," he said with a ghost of a smile on his lips. It was small moments like this that made me love Felix even more. "How about chocolate instead?"

My head perked up as Felix took out a small clump of fabric and began untying it. I waited impatiently as the cloth unraveled, revealing several round pieces of chocolate. He handed it to me before digging into the pack and pulling out his own portion.

"How are things going with Olivier?" I asked as I shoved pieces of the dessert into my mouth. Felix shrugged, but I could tell there was more he wanted to say. I nudged him with my hip. "Talk to me."

"I don't know," he answered. "Olivier can be so hot and cold. Sometimes there are these moments when I think he's going to let me in, but then he immediately slams his walls down and shuts me out. Whenever I think I'm making progress with him, he pulls away again."

I felt frustrated for Felix, knowing how much he liked Olivier. There had been several times when I thought things would turn around for the two of them, only for it never to happen. And I knew that was due to Olivier's stubbornness and not for lack of feelings. I'd often catch Oli staring at Felix from across the room or grinning to himself after overhearing a joke my friend had made.

Just last week, Oli had cooked a side dish of some sort of potato casserole that was overly sweet. He had served it to us once before, and everyone hated it except for Felix. My best friend ate the entire pan as the rest of us chastised Olivier for cooking something so disgusting. When we complained about him making it for us again, he claimed he had forgotten that we didn't like it, but I didn't believe that for a second. Especially when I saw how happy it made Felix as he slid the entire pan next to himself. Oli had stolen glances at him that whole meal, and I could see the longing in his gaze as he watched Felix's joy radiate through the room.

Last night after dinner, Felix offered to help Oli clean up, as he did every night. I had expected Olivier to tell him no, per usual, but instead, he simply shrugged and said if Felix wanted to waste his time, that was fine by him. It wasn't much, but it was *something*.

"I'm sorry," I told him.

"It's okay," Felix replied absentmindedly as he took a small bite of his chocolate. He had barely touched his share, while I had finished mine within the first minute of him handing it to me. I reached forward to steal some of his portion when he shifted his body to block me from doing so. "This isn't for you," he said as I tried to climb over him to get to it.

"You're barely eating it," I argued. Felix held it higher out of reach.

"It's my sad chocolate."

"Well I'm sad too." I wasn't. I just wanted the damn chocolate.

I crawled onto his lap as he twisted around, trying to keep the food from me. It only fueled my desire to have it more. I pressed all my weight into him, knocking him over as we wrestled for control. Felix extended his arm as far as possible, but it was useless. I was too hungry and too determined to stop. I lunged forward, wrapping my hands around his wrist to pry his bag of chocolate free.

"Ainsley, no!" Felix yelled as I managed to pull out a single decedent piece and shove it into my mouth.

The flavor of berry and chocolate burst on my tongue, and I was thrown off by how different Felix's share tasted from mine. While my portion was sweet and had a nutty flavor, Felix's was tart with a subtle hint of spice. It was far better than mine, and I was slightly pissed off that he had saved the better-tasting chocolate for himself.

Felix's hand enclosed around the bag to stop me from stealing anymore. I released my shadows and crafted a dagger. In the blink of an eye, I sliced the bag within Felix's grip, and the chocolate spilled out, falling into the grass around us. I dove for them, shoving each morsel into my mouth as Felix tried pulling me away by my feet.

"Ainsley, stop!" Felix yelled.

"No!" I exclaimed, my mouth completely full and cheeks bulging. My best friend huffed and dove to the ground, stuffing his face full of chocolate, knowing it would be the only way to stop me from eating them all. We fought for each loose piece until nothing was left.

"You're going to regret that," Felix mused.

"Doubtful."

Felix rolled his eyes and handed me a canteen of water. "Drink all of this," he instructed.

"Drink all of this," I mocked with a giggle. Felix smiled brightly as a knowing look twinkled in his eyes. I chugged the entire container. "I need more," I demanded, my lips going dry around the words.

"There's a stream over there," Felix replied, pointing through the tree line. I followed his gesture, marveling at how the pink leaves blew in the wind.

Wait. The trees had pink leaves? How the hell had I never noticed that before?

I jumped up from the ground and ran over to them. Within three seconds, I was standing across the field from where I originally was. Holy shit, I was fast as fuck. The instant we returned to the house, I was going to challenge Van to a race.

"It took you long enough," Felix drawled. I looked down to find him lying under one of the trees, spinning a pink leaf between his fingers. How the fuck did he get here before me?

"What are you talking about? I got here in just a few seconds," I argued.

"Try ten minutes." Felix sat up and did a somersault before jumping to his feet. "You tiptoed the entire way because you feared any sudden movement would scare the trees."

I shrugged. It sounded like a valid fear to me.

"Well, I'm here now," I replied. Felix stepped toward me with a concerned look on his face. "What is it?"

"Your eyes," he said, leaning in so close that there was only an inch of space between us. "There's fire in your eyes!"

I jumped back and repeatedly smacked my hands over my eyes to extinguish the flames.

"Put it out! Put it out!" I yelled.

"I'll save you, cupcake!" Felix announced, and I could hear him rustling through his pack frantically. "Got it!" A moment later, I inhaled sharply as cold water splashed against my face. "Open your eyes," Felix demanded, and I did. He breathed a sigh of relief before pulling me into his chest to squeeze me tightly. "The fire is gone."

"Thank the Gods," I said, wiping my face back and forth over his shirt to dry myself.

My eyes fluttered closed as I stepped back and breathed deeply to compose myself from my near-death experience. But when I opened my eyes again, Felix was no longer in front of me. I whirled around, noticing the leaves had shifted from bright pink to light blue.

"Felix?" I called as I began to search the surrounding area.

"Yes, my gummy gum drop?" he answered, and I looked up to find him sitting on a high tree branch, swinging his legs back and forth like a small child. I wanted to be up there too.

I circled the trunk, trying to find the best way to climb up there, when a flash of white caught in the corner of my eye. I turned around quickly, trying to find the source, when I noticed a giant bear picking berries off a bush. My heart pattered excitedly as I tiptoed in its direction, loving how the soft grass felt beneath my toes. When did I take my boots off?

It was winter, so I should have been cold, but I wasn't. I was filled with warmth and happiness, and I didn't want it to ever go away. I outstretched my arms and waved them up and down slowly. That way, if the bear noticed me approaching, it would mistake me for a large bird and not a person. I was so damn smart.

"Hey, bear," I whispered aggressively. The white bear picked his head up to look at me. "Do I look like a bird to you?"

"Not really," the bear said, and I swore under my breath. Maybe if I jumped from a branch and tried to fly...

"Wait," I said as a thought occurred to me. "Did you just speak?" The bear cocked its head to the side, and I was given a clear view of a long scar over one of its eyes. I swiveled my head over my shoulder and called for Felix. A heartbeat later, he was at my side, looking up at my new large friend. "It's a talking bear," I told Felix.

"I didn't talk," the bear replied.

"Oh," I said. "Nevermind. I could have sworn it spoke before."

"Are you sure you didn't speak?" Felix asked the bear.

"I'm positive. Bears can't talk," the bear replied.

"Dammit," Felix answered. "It would have been really awesome if you could."

"I agree," I chimed in. "Oh well. Thanks for your time," I told the animal as I turned to walk away. My magic stirred inside me, giving me that usual indication that something wasn't right. I spun back around. "Wait! You're speaking now!" I accused the bear. It shook his head. "Yes you—"

"Hey, buttercup, look!" Felix interrupted. "I'm riding a talking bear!"

My eyes widened as I beheld Felix on the bear's back, his hands clutched around thick white fur to stay on. He must have snuck around the animal while the bear and I argued about his speaking ability.

"I want to ride it too!" I demanded through a fit of giggles.

"No one should be riding me!" the bear yelled, standing on its hind legs while trying to grab Felix to throw him off its back. Felix chuckled as he dodged out of the way and continued to climb up the bear until he was sitting on its shoulders. I clapped enthusiastically, even though I was really fucking jealous of him. Why did he get to ride the bear, but I couldn't? I bent down to pick up several rocks and tossed them at Felix.

"What the fuck?" Felix yelled as one hit him in the face.

"I want a turn!" I barked, like we were children and he was hogging my favorite toy.

"No one is getting a turn!" the bear argued, and I threw another rock, hitting the animal on the nose. "Fuck," it said and then held out its paws to stop my assault. "How about we play a game instead?"

Ooh, I liked games.

"Yes!" Felix said excitedly as he leapt from the bear's back and ran back to my side, ready to hear what we would be playing.

"I'll hide," the bear said, backing away slowly. "And you two count to one hundred, and then come find me."

Felix and I both covered our faces immediately and began to count. By the time I reached twenty-five, I had forgotten what we were supposed to be doing. So, I just stood there with my eyes shut and enjoyed the cool breeze on my skin and how it made every nerve in my body tingle. It was like a million little feathers were brushing over me simultaneously, and I couldn't help but giggle as they tickled my flesh.

"Love?" Evander's voice rang through my ears, and my eyes flew open to find myself now standing in the study of my house. I twisted my head in time to see Felix plop onto the couch. How did we get here? "Love," Evander said again, and this time I ran for him, leaping into his arms and wrapping my legs around his middle.

"Van, Van, my grumpy man," I whispered, pressing my forehead to his. He pulled back slightly to look into my eyes, and I couldn't help but melt at the sight of him. My Gods, he was so gorgeous. "Boop," I said, tapping my finger to his nose. Felix laughed from behind me, which caused my own set of giggles to break through.

"You didn't," Lia scolded, though I had no idea who she was speaking to, nor did I care. Van was too pretty to look away from.

"She took it from me!" Felix replied. "I didn't do it on purpose."

Evander broke my stare and looked past me, his brow raising in question.

"Cal and Felix made chocolate with inepta berries, and well…" Lia answered. A ghost of a smile graced Van's lips as he nodded. "I'll go grab the tonic."

I could barely comprehend any of the words being exchanged, entirely too focused on how Van's black strands felt between my fingers and the way a single dimple formed with his crooked grin.

"Did you eat chocolate today, love?" Evander asked.

"Yes. Lots of it. Lots and lots and lots of it. Felix wouldn't share his, so I had to steal it. You would have been so proud of me. I tackled him, crafted a dagger, and cut the bag open and everything. I took what I wanted," I explained, the words rushing from my mouth chaotically. "I should have saved you some. It was delicious."

"Maybe another time," Van said.

"Can I tell you a secret?" I whispered loudly, and Evander's smile grew.

"Of course, love," he whispered just as loudly back.

"I met a talking bear."

"Did you, now?"

I nodded enthusiastically, though I was disappointed Van missed it. It was really fucking cool. "And Felix rode it!"

"That was fun," Felix declared from the couch. "But I still liked the fish better." The fish? I twisted to look at my friend questioningly.

"What fish?" I asked.

"Oh, I met a fish earlier, and he had the cutest little hat."

Are you fucking me? My heart shattered, and I could feel tears in my eyes. How could he have done this to me? How could he have met a fish with a hat and not share that with me? Did he not think I was worthy of meeting it? Did he want the fish to be his best friend instead of me? My lip wobbled, and I could feel the trickle of tears on my cheeks.

"You didn't tell me that," I croaked, and the look in Felix's eyes said enough. He knew he messed up. "You betrayed me again!"

"I wouldn't!" Felix replied through a sob.

"How could you?" My body shook with the hurt of his betrayal, and I turned away, burying my face in the crook of Evander's neck as I cried.

"The hat wasn't even that cute," Felix said.

"You're lying!"

"I am," he cried. "It was really fucking adorable. Please forgive me, Ainsley."

Evander rubbed his hand up and down my back in gentle strokes, and I basked in the feel of him. His body trembled slightly as if he were laughing gently, but that couldn't have been the case. There was nothing funny about my best friend keeping a talking fish with a hat from me.

"Kill him, Van," I said through my tears.

"Of course, love," he replied, moving us closer to my ex-best friend.

"Wait, no!" Felix yelled, and I loved the fear in his voice. He shouldn't have kept yet another secret from me.

"Van..." Olivier warned, and Evander's posture sagged in defeat.

"She said it was okay," Van argued innocently.

"You know she's going to regret it in an hour," Oli replied. Evander sighed in irritation before forcing my head up to look him in his brilliant charcoal eyes.

"I'm not allowed to kill him," he answered, and my lip wobbled from the sadness. "But I can torture him a little for you." A second later, Felix jumped up and began screaming about bees attacking him before sprinting from the room.

"Van," Olivier drawled, and the sound of him running after Felix echoed around the space.

"The illusion of the bees will go away once he gets to his room," Van said, and I laughed, happy that he had made Felix suffer for his betrayal. "Now, can I tell *you* a secret?" I nodded excitedly as I leaned in close. "You are very, *very* high, love," he whispered. I burst out in laughter. That was the most ridiculous thing I had ever heard. "Lia is grabbing you a tonic, so you'll be good as new in an hour... Perhaps a bit longer, given how much you ate. In the meantime, I'm going to carry you to bed. Sleeping will help the effects wear off quicker." He brushed the hair from my face and pressed a light kiss to my cheek.

I closed my eyes, not caring if I was high or sober or riding a white bear with a scar over its eye. All I wanted was to be in Evander's arms a little while longer.

40.

I stared up at the ceiling, still feeling a bit off from my trip to the woods with Felix yesterday. Upon waking from my nap, Van explained that the chocolate I had stolen from Felix was made with inepta berries, which have a hallucinogenic effect. Seeing as I consumed an amount meant to last for weeks, even the steady diet of a tonic every few hours wasn't enough to rid me of the effects completely. Evander demanded Sirona come by and check me out this morning since I still wasn't feeling great. After a full inspection, she let us know that a few more doses of the healing tonic would be enough to restore me to perfect health. And that I should stay clear from anything containing inepta berries for at least a few weeks. Given how sick they made me feel, that wasn't going to be a problem.

I sighed and ran my fingers over the soft pages of a worn book as I waited for Evander to return from dropping King Tallis off at our palace. Two days ago we received word from Tallis instructing Evander to hold an emergency meeting with the three of us and the most trusted generals belonging to Tenebrae and Agnitio. When Evander probed his friend for more information about what was happening, Tallis simply said that his Gift showed him something. He also said it was information he wanted to verify and discuss in person. As the sovereign of the Kingdom of Agnitio, Tallis possessed all three Gifts which included that of a Seer. Evander explained to me once that his visions of the future can change as frequently as they occur and can't always be trusted. But if he wanted to call an emergency meeting regarding the possibility of one path for the future, then it had to be important.

Not long after we left Agnitio, Evander had decided to inform Tallis that Felix and I stole from his library. I was pissed he ratted me out but happy he at least did it after we realized the books we had taken were no longer of use to us since we were going in a different direction. Tallis was less than pleased about it but agreed not to rescind his invitation to use the library in the future. He was also kind enough to send books that could be helpful in our search for the stones, which made me feel all the more horrible for stealing from him.

The whooshing sound of Evander traversing into the library of our home filled the space and I looked up from my spot on the couch. Van walked over and sat beside me, throwing his head back and staring at the ceiling as he released a frustrated breath. He looked beyond exhausted and worried about whatever news Tallis was bringing. I placed a hand on his arm to offer him a small amount of comfort. We sat there in silence for another minute, neither of us seeming to want to do anything but enjoy the quiet together.

"I don't want to attend the meeting," he whispered. "Every time we have one, it's always more bad news."

He wasn't wrong. Lately, our reports always said one of two things: more attacks had occurred against our camps, or everything had been entirely too quiet. It was like Oberon had ordered his armies to test us, only attacking sporadically and at random locations so we could never predict his movements. I didn't want to imagine what news Tallis was planning to share and why.

"Is everyone waiting for us at the palace?" I asked.

"Nope. Two of the generals from the northern camps are still on their way and should arrive within the next hour. Everyone else decided to head to the dining room for lunch while they waited."

I nodded before sliding off the couch and heading to the far end of the room as Evander watched me curiously. His eyes lit up as I returned to him, now with a cashmere blanket in hand. I climbed back into my spot, covering us both and using his shoulder as a pillow again.

"Then we have some time before we have to be there," I said, shutting my eyes. I could tell Evander didn't want to leave this room yet, and neither did I. There was peace and comfort when it was just the two of us, and I was desperate to hold onto it for a little while longer.

"That we do," he replied, pressing his cheek to my hair once more as he let out a sigh of contentment.

"Someone better explain how the *fuck* this happened," Evander demanded, slamming his fist down on the council room table. Everyone kept quiet and avoided making eye contact with their king, which I knew would only piss him off more.

"Answer, Elenora," Tallis commanded, just as furious as Van.

The meeting had gone to complete shit the moment Tallis confirmed his vision came to fruition. Elenora stepped forward, and I didn't miss the slight tremor in the fists at her side.

"Our armies have been focused inland and on trying to stop the new attacks on our camps that we—"

"Forgot that a threat also rules in our homeland?" Tallis said, interrupting his niece. The king had always been kind and soft-spoken, but now... Now he had the voice of a ruler ready to wage war. "As one of my generals, I expect far more from you." Elenora hung her head, clearly disappointed in herself.

"Who is planning on accepting responsibility for this massive slip?" Evander demanded, looking over the line of generals standing around the table before his eyes settled on me, softening just the slightest bit. Whatever he read on my face had him moving in my direction just as one of our generals spoke up.

"Your Majesties, we still managed to report our findings," the man—General Roshard—said, his voice shaking with every word.

"Once their mission had been completed, and they were returning home!" Tallis exclaimed, and the general flinched as if he had been struck.

This wasn't a small problem or a minor inconvenience. This was a huge fucking deal, and everyone in that room knew it. It didn't look like the meeting would end until someone paid the price for this disastrous mishap.

"They haven't made it yet," General Roshard added hopefully. "We can take them out before they ever reach—"

"No!" Felix yelled, stepping forward, and I grabbed his arm to pull him back. Evander had already demanded his silence the moment the news had broken, and I knew he only obeyed the order so he could interject if the time called for it.

My eyes stayed pinned on Van's as he closed the distance and stopped before me. I was vaguely aware of his hand wrapped around mine as he squeezed my fingers tight, but my mind was too focused on the information we had been given.

According to reports, a dozen ships full of soldiers from Caelum were heading back from Pravus after what looked to be a friendly visit. And on one of those ships, Dashiell had been spotted.

"You can't," Felix begged, and Van broke eye contact with me to look at my friend. "I know Dash, and he wouldn't—"

"Oberon's forces have been attacking our people! Anyone who conspires with the land of Pravus is our enemy and should be dealt with accordingly," the general snarled, and a rumble of anger slipped from Felix's throat. "I motion we end the threat before it becomes a bigger one. We don't know what happened during the visit and shouldn't risk it."

Felix stared at Evander, his eyes wide and pleading as he shook his head. He wasn't going to back down regarding Dashiell's life. He wasn't going to stand idly by and watch the order to end it be given.

"I know you hate him," Felix tried, his voice breaking from the emotion in his throat. "But please, Evander. Please, don't."

I closed my eyes, fighting the tears that welled for my best friend as he desperately tried to keep Dashiell safe from harm. I didn't know what to do or what comforting words to offer because sparing the prince's life wasn't up to me. The two kings in this room would decide his fate and what actions needed to be carried out.

When my eyes fluttered open again, Van was watching me intently as an emotion I didn't recognize twisted his features. I stared at his face, though not really seeing him, as my mind shifted through everything we'd been told. I wanted this meeting to be over and to go home where I could think more clearly. This room was too crowded and suffocating, filled with people I had no desire to see because they only ever brought devastating news—like today.

"No," Evander announced, and I blinked several times as he came into view. Had I heard him right?

"But, Your Majesty—" General Roshard tried, but Van quickly cut him off.

"As you stated: we don't know what went on during their visit, and I'm not about to start a war with Caelum by killing a prince simply because I dislike his travel plans."

Felix sighed in relief, and I could feel the tension ease from his body as his shoulder slumped forward. I held his arm tight as he stumbled a step, losing his footing as the knowledge of his friend's life being spared rocked through him.

"We wait," Tallis added, agreeing with Evander, and mumbles of acknowledgment broke free. "For now, we're going to figure out how we missed this and ensure it never happens again. I should never receive a Gods damn vision of that magnitude once it is already too late."

Another two hours later, we still didn't have answers about how no one noticed the dozens of ships that left Disparya until they were returning weeks later. Or how no one seemed to know that the Prince of Caelum wasn't in Caelum. Neither ours nor Tallis' spies managed to catch any word of it, and that was the most unsettling of all.

After Tallis and his generals departed Tenebrae, Evander dismissed ours only after scaring them shitless first with promises of slow and torturous deaths if anything like that ever happened again. Felix left the moment the meeting was called to an end, and Olivier rushed after him. I would have been intrigued about that on any given day, but my head was still so heavy.

"Are you okay?" Van asked when we were finally alone in the council room. Throughout the entire back half of the meeting, he never left my side, often squeezing my hand or brushing his fingers along my lower back to let me know he was there for me. It was a small gesture, but it meant the world.

"No," I answered honestly, and Evander nodded like he wasn't surprised.

"Tell me what you're thinking," he said gently, and I lifted my gaze from where it had been pinned to the floor.

There was so much on my mind that I wasn't sure where to begin or what I even thought about it all. My best bet was to talk through the confusion and hope I would find how I truly felt along the way.

"I trust Felix with my life," I said, taking a deep breath and blowing it out. "But I don't know if I can trust him regarding Dashiell. It's in Felix's nature to want to see the best in people, and his childhood friend is no exception. I know he believes with his entire soul that Dashiell wouldn't betray Disparya, but it doesn't change the fact that he was spotted on one of those ships. It doesn't change what he tried to do to me."

I wanted to believe Felix, but the cards kept stacking against the prince. Felix helped smuggle me out of Caelum because he couldn't change Dashiell's mind. He didn't trust his friend wouldn't go through with stealing my magic. Dashiell also claimed I was the woman he loved more than anything, but that didn't stop him from betraying me. So how could he possibly be trusted not to betray Disparya?

"I'm still trying to fit the pieces together, but there is one thing that I'm certain of," I said, looking deep into his charcoal eyes. "Felix is blind when it comes to Dashiell, but I won't ever be again."

41.

The wood floor was cold beneath my feet as I stood at the edge of the bed. Wasn't I wearing socks a moment ago? And how did I get here? A gentle breeze rolled in from the window Evander had refused to close, and a chill brushed along my legs. I looked down to find them bare, with only my upper thighs covered by a satin nightgown. That definitely was not what I went to sleep in. Was this a dream?

Evander sat in the same position he had been in when I laid down, his back pressed against the headboard and a book in his hands. I ran my fingers along the mattress as I walked around to his side of the bed and stopped at the window. He didn't look up—didn't seem to notice me at all. And he noticed everything.

So this *was* a dream.

But I needed to make sure.

If I was asleep, I should be able to control what happened here. I held up my hand and watched a glass of water appear from thin air. I dropped the cup, and before it hit the ground, it disappeared. Evander still didn't stir, too engrossed in his book. Dream Evander didn't seem much different than real Evander in that respect.

I observed him for a moment as he casually flipped through the pages. His shirt was tight over his chest, the fabric so thin I could make out each curve of his muscles. His short sleeves showed off his tattooed arms, firm and toned. My Gods, he was gorgeous, and I couldn't help but imagine myself running my hands up and down his body. I almost banished the intrusive thought, but then an idea sparked in my mind like a tiny flame ready to roar to life in a blazing fury.

I could have him any way I wanted—because this was a dream. I was in control of what happened in this fantasy, and real-life Evander would never find out. He'd have no way of knowing that while I was lying beside him, sound asleep, my mind was doing unspeakable things to this version of him. As if dream Evander heard my thoughts, he perked up, and his eyes widened a fraction as he saw me standing there. I panicked for a split second before remembering this wasn't real. He twisted his head toward the closed door and then back in my direction, arching a brow as he studied me.

Dream Evander tilted his head to the side as he raised his eyes up and down my body appraisingly.

"See something you like?" I asked, pressing my back against the cold glass of the window. A shiver went down my spine, mostly from his intense stare rather than the temperature. He closed his book, setting it in his lap as he straightened and cleared his throat.

"Very much so," he said, his lips pulling in a crooked grin. My mind went wild with the game, wanting to see just how far I could take this, though I already knew the answer.

As far as I wanted to.

I bit my lip and slowly dragged my fingers up my thigh, hitching the nightgown's hem slightly. Dream Evander's eyes followed the movement like a bird tracking its prey.

"Want to come and show me how much?" I asked.

Knowing this wasn't actually happening made me feel more confident—braver. Dream Evander tilted his head toward the ceiling and closed his eyes as if debating his answer. That wouldn't do. This was *my* fantasy, and the answer wouldn't be anything other than a resounding 'yes.' He opened his eyes at once and smiled even wider.

"Very much so," he responded.

Perfect.

Dream Evander slid from the bed and stalked for me with a ravenous look on his face. He stopped before me, placing a hand on either side of my head as he leaned in close.

But not close enough.

I reached up, fisting my hand in his shirt and pulling him against me until his lips hovered just barely over mine.

"What are you doing, love?" Dream Evander asked seductively.

My heart thundered and my cheeks heated with anticipation. I had been flirting and teasing him for weeks—touching myself to thoughts of him—and now I was about to finally have him. Maybe not in the actual sense, but a sex dream was as close enough to the real thing as I was going to get.

"Taking what I want," I said before crashing my lips to his.

Our mouths molded together, moving as one in perfect synchronization. I slipped my tongue over his as soon as he gave me an opening and Dream Evander groaned in delight as he gripped my waist hard enough to bruise. I was disappointed that it wouldn't, though—that there would be no evidence to show for this moment.

I pushed myself off the window, walking us toward the bed without ever breaking our punishing kiss. Our lips moved brutally over each other's and I was drunk on the taste of him. Gods, I needed more.

Before we reached the bed, Dream Evander took control, and directed us to the dresser instead. My back hit the wood, stopping our advance, and his hands reached down, picking me up swiftly and setting me on the edge of the furniture.

Dream Evander tore his mouth from mine, moving it to my neck and flicking his tongue over my sensitive skin. Fucking hell, he felt amazing. My thighs clenched as my core pounded, wetness already pooling there. I wrapped my legs around his middle, and moaned loudly when I felt how hard he was. Dream Evander groaned as I rocked my hips, needing to feel that delicious friction.

"Tell me what you want, love. Name it, and it's yours," he said near breathless. *Desperate.*

He ground into me, and I moved on him again, gasping at how fucking good it felt. I was a corked bottle of wound-up tension and sexual frustration, and I was going to explode if I didn't get released soon.

"I'd rather show you," I said, grabbing his hand and directing it beneath the hem of my nightgown. Dream Evander's mouth captured mine, muffling the sounds of my cries of pleasure as he dragged a slick finger through me. Holy Gods.

I knew it wasn't real and just a fantasy I was having, but fucking hell did my imagination deliver tenfold. A tingle shot down my spine as I focused on how amazing it felt to have his hands on me, owning my body this way. He teased me relentlessly, sliding his finger back and forth but never entirely giving me what I needed. I bucked my hips, urging him to touch the spot I wanted, but Dream Evander simply smiled against my mouth as he pulled his hand back, denying me.

"You said you'd rather show me. So do it," he challenged. I gasped as he kissed me savagely, his hand staying stagnant as he waited for further direction. I arched my back and rocked forward, desperately trying to create that friction I needed so badly. "Show me," he demanded again, and I reached down, taking hold of his wrist and guiding him once again.

My fingers slid over the back of his as I moved two of them to my entrance. I kissed him hard as I tilted my hips forward, and he slid inside. I threw my head back and moaned as I gripped his wrist again, forcing him to pump in and out of me in a steady rhythm.

Evander buried his face in my neck as he kissed and bit the sensitive skin there, groaning as I clenched tight around his fingers. My hands traveled up his arms, and my nails dug into his flesh, leaving red marks in their wake until I was clutching his shoulders for support as I began to unravel.

"Van," I said breathlessly, and his mouth moved to mine so quickly it was like he was trying to taste his name before it drifted away. "I need more," I begged. "Please."

My plea was all he needed to hear to take complete control over my body. His free hand grabbed my waist and pulled me to the very edge of the dresser until I was primed to slip off it. I released his shoulders and moved my hands to grip the sides of the dresser to prevent myself from falling.

Evander's thumb swirled around me as his fingers went deeper, the new angle causing an intense pleasure to ripple through my body. I arched, moaning at the sensation as I ground myself against his hand, pushing myself closer and closer to the edge of ecstasy.

"Is this what you want, love?" he asked seductively, leaning down to graze his teeth over my nipple through the nightgown, and I gasped at the mix of pain and pleasure. The way he worked my body had me so high I didn't ever want to come down.

"Yes," I whimpered, tilting my head back towards the ceiling as I continued to move on him.

"So then take it. Take exactly what you want," he instructed.

His demand set loose a feral need in me that I couldn't describe. I thrust my hips forward harder, riding his hand as I gripped the dresser so forcefully I splintered the wood. I was so fucking close to that sweet oblivion I so eagerly needed. My breaths came in desperate gasps as I moved even faster, chasing my release with a relentless focus. Evander praised me through every movement of my hips, which only brought me closer. I opened my mouth, prepared to scream his name on that one final thrust of his fingers... And then jolted awake in bed.

Sunlight flooded my vision as I gasped hard like I had just sprinted up and down Mammoth Hill. Sweat beaded my brow, and my hair hung over my face as I gripped the blankets hard, struggling to come down from what I had just dreamed about. It was bad enough that I just had a sex dream about Evander, but couldn't I have at least woken up *after* my orgasm instead of before it?

I reached my fingers up, pressing them to my lips as if I could still feel his mouth on mine and his passionate kiss. My mind was an asshole for ending my fantasy early, but my Gods, was it good while it lasted. Real-life Evander could never compare to his dream counterpart that my brain had conjured.

"Are you alright there, love?" Evander asked, and I twisted to see him watching me intently with an open book in his lap.

Not even a little bit. I ran my hands through my tangled hair and took several deep breaths while nodding. There was absolutely no way in hell I was going to tell him what had just occurred while asleep. If he knew that he was the subject of my sex dream, it would give him an even bigger ego than he already had, and that wasn't something I wanted to deal with.

"Yup," I told him as I slid from the bed.

I needed to splash some water on my face and cool down, or else I'd think of Dream Evander every time I looked at Regular Annoying Evander, and that wouldn't do.

"Did you have a nice dream?" he asked curiously, and my eyes shot to him as my heart rate picked up. Oh Gods, did he know? I raised a brow in question rather than answer in case I was overreacting for nothing. "The sounds you were making lead me to believe you were enjoying yourself quite a lot," he explained as a cocky grin formed.

Fucking great.

He may have known I had a sex dream, but he didn't know who was involved, so at least I was safe there. I couldn't let him think I was embarrassed by my dream, or else he'd bring it up any chance he could, knowing it would get under my skin. I had to pretend it didn't faze me that he knew.

"Jahier made an appearance, so I most certainly did," I lied, shrugging like it was no big deal.

"Is that right?" he said suspiciously.

"Yup, and I had a great time." I turned away and headed toward the bathing room, not bothering to elaborate because I knew not playing with him would annoy him more than the thought of Jahier and me together.

"Tell me something, love," he said before I crossed into the next room. "Did you take what you wanted?"

I froze as the blood drained from my face and the air was knocked from my lungs. His question echoed in my mind, bouncing off walls and growing in volume each time it repeated. Oh my Gods, he knew—he *fucking* knew. Hesitantly, I turned around, finding Evander watching me with bright eyes and the widest smile I'd ever seen.

"What did you do?" I accused, and he raised his hands in innocence.

"I don't know what you're referring to," he claimed, though I could smell his bullshit from here. There was no way he would utter the same line he had in my dream unless he knew what had happened—unless he *made* it happen. My blood began to boil at the thought of him invading my mind that way.

"Did you send me a sex illusion while I was asleep?" I asked though it sounded more like an accusation.

"I enjoy getting consent, so no, love, I didn't force an illusion," he replied, and I believed him.

I wasn't sure why I had even bothered to ask the question in the first place. For months, Evander had every opportunity to take advantage of me in that way and hadn't, so there was no reason for me to believe he'd start now. Maybe I was reading into the situation too much. Perhaps I had uttered the words while asleep, and Evander was repeating them to get a rise out of me. I broke his stare, nodding to myself as I accepted his answer.

"But *you* did," he said, and I stopped breathing. My widened gaze met his, imploring him to explain. "I was sitting here, enjoying my book, when I looked up to find you across the room. I was confused for a second, but when I glanced at your sleeping body, I knew what it was. You had managed to slip into *my* mind and cast an illusion, all while asleep—not even trying to do it. I was so fucking proud of you at that moment."

I couldn't help but smile at him recounting what happened. It was no longer about what the illusion had entailed but instead that it occurred in the first place. And *I* was the one who cast it. Not Evander, *me*. I invaded his thoughts without actively trying, and it made me feel strong and excited about what I was capable of.

"I thought about waking you, but I wanted to see how long you could hold my mind for. And that's when your illusion took a turn..." he said, grinning knowingly, and I bit my lip. ..."

"So you and the illusion version of me..." I started, wondering how that was even possible.

I hadn't been able to make my visions into solid objects the way only Evander could, and I had a feeling if I had managed such a feat, he would have woken me immediately to share the news.

"When I finally have you, love, it won't be an illusion. I want the real thing," he answered, and I rolled my eyes at his use of *when* and not *if.* "You were quite persistent, and I didn't want to disappoint, so I slipped into your mind and cast an illusion of myself. I've never cast with someone before, so I didn't know what to expect or how to do it at first. But I watched us, letting you take the lead and making the illusion version of myself respond to you. I quickly figured out that doing it that way made the vision seamless."

I didn't know casting with someone was possible, and I became excited to try it out and see what Van and I could come up with together. Though, whatever it entailed definitely wouldn't be sexual like it was today.

"So that's why you had me make the decisions—so you could play off them," I deduced, and Evander tilted his head side to side in a noncommittal answer.

"Yes and no. It definitely made it easier just to have my illusion respond to the situation, but that's not the entire reason. I didn't want to lead because though you approached me, I didn't want you to feel like I was taking advantage of you. You were asleep and unaware of what you were truly doing, so it wouldn't have been right for me to choose what we did, even though it wasn't real," he explained, and I was grateful for his way of thinking.

I didn't believe I would have considered him to have crossed a line, as we were both illusions. I had also made my desires for him clear in that vision, but I appreciated that it didn't sit right with him.

"It was also *your* vision," he continued. "You casted it, so you deserved to control it how you sought fit. Not to mention, I loved seeing you demand what you wanted and going after it."

"You just like that it was *you* my illusion wanted."

"Of course I do, love."

I huffed a breathy laugh and shook my head at his confident arrogance. I couldn't be embarrassed or mad at myself for what had happened because I had slipped into Evander's freaking mind. That was the biggest accomplishment with my magic I had made thus far, and I wasn't going to feel anything less than proud of myself for it.

I backed away, turning around and heading for the bathing room. I was going to take a long hot bath to celebrate instead of the cold shower I was going to force myself under earlier.

"Do you need a hand?" Evander called, and I threw up my middle finger over my shoulder.

"Go fuck yourself," I singsonged, and he laughed.

"Oh, trust me, love. I plan on it now that I have plenty of new material to visualize."

I shut the door just as he managed to say the last word. Slowly, I shrugged off Evander's shirt and slipped beneath the pool's hot water. Though today started out shitty after learning about our forces completely missing a Caelumian fleet traveling to Pravus, it turned out to be a huge day for me. I reached a new level of my magic I didn't think I'd ever attain. So why was I focusing on the feel of Evander's hands and mouth on my body rather than that achievement?

42.

I had difficulty focusing on the book in front of me. For the past few days, my mind kept bouncing between the sex illusion I had cast on Evander and the meeting about Pravus. I wasn't concerned about my magic. In fact, that little stunt of mine had made me want to train even harder now that I knew just what I was capable of. But the situation with the continent to our west... That was something I was worried about. Oberon's forces had been moving into Disparya for months, and somehow, no one had noticed. Ships from Caelum had been spotted on the way back from Pravus, and again, somehow, no one had noticed. The new evidence that more was going on than we could figure out was unsettling, to say the least.

"No," Evander said, and I looked up to find him standing in the bathing room doorway with nothing but a towel wrapped around his waist.

His black hair was damp, and droplets of water rolled slowly down his bare tattooed chest, glistening in the dim light of the room. My gaze lingered for far too long as I studied their path down to his muscled V at the hem of the bunched towel.

"Absolutely not," he stated, and my eyes fluttered as I drifted my attention back to where it should be—his face. His eyes were hard, and he shook his head as he pointed to the spot next to me. "No wolves in our bed."

I followed his glare to the snoozing Onyx beside me and stretched my legs as I happily rested them on top of Nova.

"*Your* bed," I amended, going back to my book.

"Whatever. They're too big to be up there," he reasoned.

"Oh, they're fine," I told him, but as I looked over the mattress, I realized he was right. Nova took up the entire width at the bottom, and Onyx was nearly the same size as the length.

"Onyx," Van said while snapping his fingers. His wolf raised his head and cracked open an eye at his master. He stared at Van for a long moment before putting his head back down and shutting his eyes. "Onyx, get down!" Evander said, but this time with more force in his tone.

Onyx let out an annoyed huff, but rather than listen to the given order, he rolled to his back, letting his paws droop in the air as he got more comfortable.

A snort escaped me, and I clamped my lips down hard to keep from laughing as I turned back to find a red-faced Evander stomping away and mumbling something about flaying his wolf and eating him for dinner. I rolled to my side and scratched behind Onyx's ears as he began to snore contently.

"Good boy," I whispered. "We don't listen to the mean king when he's being unreasonable."

The mattress shifted as Evander climbed into bed and pressed himself against me, wrapping me tightly in his arms.

"What are you doing?!" I exclaimed as I tried to wiggle free.

"He's in my spot."

"So?" I demanded.

"So, you wanted the wolves in the bed, and this is the consequence of that. So either kick them out or deal with it."

I sighed in irritation as I realized there was no way I could get out of his embrace unless I made our pets leave. I glanced down at Nova to see she had wiggled in-between Van's legs as well, and Onyx now had his tongue hanging out the side of his mouth. They looked too damn happy, and I couldn't end that.

The second I conceited, Evander rearranged me how he wanted, reveling in his victory. He pulled me up, so I rested my head on his shoulder as his other arm curved around my middle. One leg hitched over me, while the other Nova had claimed as a pillow.

His body was wrapped around me like a human cage, and though I wanted to hate it, I didn't. I enjoyed feeling his heart thud against my back and how he buried his face in my hair. His tattooed shadow slithered across his arm and then stopped. The movement was so quick I was sure I might have imagined it. I freed one of my arms and traced the tattoo before gently tapping it. And then tapping it even harder and faster when it didn't do anything.

"What are you doing?" Evander asked, confused as he lifted his head to lean over me.

"I'm trying to make it move," I told him, not stopping my task. Why the hell wouldn't it move?

Evander threw himself back as he chuckled at my attempts.

"That's not how it works, love," he said, and I twisted in his arms until I was fully facing him.

"Okay, so tell me how it works," I replied, annoyed, and began to flick it instead. Maybe it thrived off of pain.

Nope. Nothing.

Maybe if I punched it...

Evander caught my wrist before I could land the blow and raised a brow.

"It only moves if I allow it to," he said before releasing me. "And sometimes without my permission, though that's rare. No need to assault me."

"But it's so fun," I teased, making Van roll his eyes. "How does it work, exactly?" I skimmed the outline of one of the markings, and he shivered beneath my touch, though the tattoo stayed in place.

"I can move them freely, should I choose," he answered. "But they are also connected to my emotions. When I'm experiencing one that's strong, like fear or anger, it'll shift on its own unless I have a hold on it. My emotions are quite literally on display for the world to see."

"But I've seen you without a shirt on and without tattoos before," I told him.

"The symbol on my back of the twisting shadows. When I want it away, that's where it retreats."

"Why would you put yourself on display like that?" I questioned. Evander didn't seem to be one to confide in someone about what he was feeling. He held a secret pain silently for a decade and only chose to share it because he thought it would help me. Why would he risk everyone being able to tell when he wasn't okay?

"As a reminder," he said, looking into my eyes with an edge of softness. "Never to lose control."

"For that man you killed," I breathed, as understanding washed over me. Van nodded, holding my gaze a while longer like he was waiting to see if I would judge him for it now that I had time to digest his story.

I wouldn't.

"I don't revel in the idea of people being able to read me, but I don't want to slip like I did that night ever again. Every move of the tattoo that occurs without my permission is a reminder of how easy it is for that to happen. I want to be better than that. I need to be," he explained.

The fear in his eyes when he mentioned that night was present and I felt like it might always be. But there was also a deep amount of determination and hope residing within, and I couldn't help but be proud of him. I glanced down at his arm and skimmed another line as it dipped below his wrist.

Onyx stretched his legs, shoving us hard and making us nearly fall out of bed. Evander grumbled at his pet before pulling me to my feet. "Come on," he said, as he led me to the balcony. The air was freezing and Van crafted a blanket to wrap me in.

"I want one," I breathed as I looked out over the moonlit lake. "Just like yours."

"It's not easy to control your emotions, especially when the world is watching you," he said. It didn't feel like he was trying to talk me out of the idea but instead wanted me to know exactly what I was doing.

"I'm not afraid of people knowing how I feel," I told him. "There is strength in that. But I want it because I never want to hide who I am again. I want my Gift tattooed on my flesh as a warning to those who tried to take it from me. This darkness is mine, and I'm never letting it go."

I twisted to find Van watching me with a smile on his face and pride in his eyes.

"Will you do it?" I asked, hoping he could understand how much this meant to me. He nodded slowly.

"Where do you want it?" he asked, and I looked over my body, trying to decide. I twisted my wrists, my arms, and my legs, unable to pick the perfect place.

"You choose," I told him.

Evander removed my blanket and spun me around so my back faced him. Slowly, he shifted my hair over my shoulder and ran his fingers down my spine in a delicate caress. I bit my lip as I fought off a shiver from his touch—something even the cold couldn't compete with.

"This will feel a little odd," he explained.

"Will it hurt?" I asked, suddenly worried.

"Not at all. It'll even feel good." Evander's hands moved to the base of my neck, and then I felt a slight pressure as he pressed his thumb to the spot he had chosen.

Warmth spread over me like flames licking my skin, but it didn't burn. I was wrapped in delicious pleasure as I felt my magic surge to the surface and mix with the fire, twisting and molding until they became one. I released a sigh of relaxation at the foreign feeling before it slowly retreated until there was nothing but embers remaining.

"All finished," Evander said as he removed his fingers and handed me a small mirror he must have crafted, still dripping in shadows. I held it up and peered inside to see him holding a matching one angled at my neck. There at the base sat a small black flower no bigger than a coin, with leaves in the shape of twisting shadows that matched his tattoo.

"It's a jasmine blossom," I said, taking in the delicate design. My eyes flickered to him in the mirror, and he nodded.

"The native ones bloom in darkness. I figured it was a fitting symbol," he explained as the two mirrors disappeared. "Now try to call the tattoo forth."

I closed my eyes as I focused on the magic, but it felt like it radiated through my entire body, and couldn't find an exit.

"I don't know how," I admitted, still focusing on where to lead the darkness. "It's everywhere all at once, and I can't feel where to direct it."

Evander's fingers skated over my skin. He leaned closer, and I felt his breath hot against me. Lips pressed to the base of my neck, and goosebumps spread over my flesh. Every nerve in my body fired off at once as I sucked in a shaky breath.

"Here," he whispered, kissing the spot again. "Direct it here."

I screwed my eyes shut even tighter as I forced myself to focus on my magic and not on what his mouth had just done. I zeroed in on that small spot at the back of my neck, now tingling thanks to Evander's kiss. I pushed the magic in that direction until it flowed out of me like magma, hot and destructive. It curved and caressed my body, and my eyes flew open to see it slithering down my arms. I held my hand up, watching thin tendrils of shadow spiral around my fingers, feeling like silk being dragged over my skin.

The tattoo ebbed and flowed, moving gracefully this way and that as I twisted around to face Evander. His smile was wide as he watched the delicate shadows ripple over me. He freed his own tattoo and held my hand up, interlocking our fingers as we watched our designs whirl around our limbs, twisting and mimicking the other's movements like they were dancing under the night sky.

"It'll only come when you call it," Evander breathed. "I didn't connect it to your emotions."

"Why not?" I asked, still too focused on the way our tattoos moved in perfect synchronization. A breeze blew in and Evander re-covered me with the blanket before I thought to do it myself.

"Because you deserve to keep that part of you to yourself. You've been hidden most of your life and had everything taken from you. You should be allowed to choose what to share with others and when. You shouldn't have to fight to keep that part hidden if you aren't ready for people to know."

I turned to face him, meeting his piercing grey eyes as they bore into me with shining honesty. He had known what I wanted and needed without me realizing it and had given me both.

"Thank you," I whispered, squeezing his hand in emphasis.

"Now you can scare everyone shitless on the battlefield with your tattoo—though it isn't as terrifying as mine."

"They are literally the exact same," I argued.

"Nah, mine is definitely scarier," he teased, and I rolled my eyes as I playfully slapped his arm.

I wanted to stay in this little bubble of peace, but Evander's words had cut through my thoughts like a knife. *Battlefield.* A place we were destined to be sooner rather than later. A place where everything would change.

"Are you nervous?" I asked tentatively. "For this war?"

Evander held my gaze as he nodded, unafraid to admit the truth.

"I worry for our people. This war will cost countless lives, and I hate that they will pay the price for it. I worry for our family. I know they can handle themselves and will gladly die for our cause, but I don't want them to," he breathed.

My heart tightened at the thought of something happening to any of the people we held dear. I swallowed the bile creeping up and forced the intruding images of lifeless green, gold, grey, turquoise, and amber eyes out of my mind. Instead, I called my magic back, letting it retreat into the beautiful flower he designed. I didn't need help this time. The spot was still prickling from Evander's lips—a kiss forever branded on my skin.

"But to be honest," he continued. "None of that compares to the fear I have over something happening to you." His hand tightened over mine, reminding me that he was still holding it, and I dropped my stare, needing to look anywhere but at the truth on his face. I didn't know why I wanted to shy away from his honesty—why his admittance infiltrated me so thoroughly.

"Are *you* worried?" Van asked, breaking the silence and easing the tension as I realized he was giving me an out to not have to comment on what he said.

"Yes," I whispered, nodding. "I've never seen battle, let alone been responsible for thousands of lives. What if a choice I make is the wrong one and people die because of me?"

Evander's face softened like he knew the feeling, and I supposed he did. He had been the King of Tenebrae since he was five years old, and though he wasn't marching with his armies at that age, he had to own the mistakes of his generals and others in charge until he could take up the mantle himself.

"I don't want to think about any harm coming to our family, and that possibility fills me with dread daily," I said.

I swallowed hard, and my mind raced with what more I wanted to say. My insides were pulling me left and right—one way being the truth and the desire to speak it, and the other being a hidden cove where I could bury my fear and feelings like I always had. But as I looked at the man before me and thought about how he had shared so much and been so open, I put my shovel down and walked out of that cave, determined to give him my secrets.

"But the thing that terrifies me the most," I began, still staring at our locked hands. I may have decided to share my truth, but I still wasn't ready to look him in the eyes as I spoke the words. "The thing that haunts me night after night…" I took a deep breath and let it out slowly. "Is the thought of losing you. I can't bear to entertain the possibility of you not here—of a life without you in it. You mean entirely too much to me, Evander." I closed my eyes, and a single tear landed on our hands.

The world was dark and quiet as I waited for him to respond. One minute had passed, and then another before he finally spoke.

"I know how hard that was for you to say," he whispered.

"Why? Because I'm stubborn and enjoy making your life difficult?" I teased, wanting to turn the conversation into something light and playful rather than deep.

"No. Because of how badly you've been hurt and broken," he answered seriously, and my eyes snapped up to him. Of all the things he could have said, I didn't expect it to be that. "You don't think I haven't seen how hard you try every day? You don't think I haven't noticed how you recoil whenever someone touches or hugs you or compliments you? Like you refuse to accept any form of love."

I swallowed the lump in my throat as my eyes watered and my hands trembled. Van gripped both of them in his as he stood straighter with an expression unlike one he'd ever given me before. I tried to piece together what it was, but it was as if he was giving me every emotion possible all at once. His stare held joy and fear, kindness and anger, but I couldn't figure out why.

"For months now, I have watched you struggle to put the broken slivers of yourself back together. I have watched you slowly allow others in—not all the way—but just enough to show that you were trying. And they may not have known what it meant, but I did," he said, moving his hands to cup my cheeks.

"So make jokes if you need to, or don't say anything at all. But know that I *see* you—I've always *seen* you. I have never once, nor will I ever, take your words lightly or your actions for granted. You mean entirely too much to me," Evander added, pressing his forehead to mine as his thumbs swept away the tears that had begun to fall.

I didn't realize he had observed me that closely or that he knew how much I had struggled. He never forced me to open up and fought daily to earn my trust. And now I was beginning to understand why it had been so important to him. He had witnessed my despair and anger. He watched me withdraw into myself and fight against everyone that tried to get close, never wanting to give them enough of myself to hurt me. Giving him my trust meant that I was healing, and that was what he wanted for me.

I wasn't sure if I could ever love or trust anyone the way I had before, and that was a painful reality. No matter how much I pushed and I gave, it wouldn't change what had been taken from me. I had loved Dashiell with every fiber of my being. I had trusted both him and Felix and was betrayed in the end. Though Felix and I had overcome the hurt, I knew that things would never be how they once were. Putting my blind faith in people had only destroyed me.

Now I had to be cautious. I had to give—but also keep. It was a balancing act, and I promised myself months ago that I wouldn't falter or stumble over to one side. I wouldn't trust completely, but I wouldn't give up either. It had gotten me this far, so why was everything inside trying to sway me one way? I had once fallen for pretty words—a breathtaking trap my heart had succumbed to. I couldn't do it again.

I wouldn't.

I straightened my posture, pulling back just enough so our foreheads were no longer touching, and took a deep breath as I closed my eyes. I needed to regain my composure—my control. So I let the memories of Dashiell's betrayal seep into my blood until it was all I could feel. And then I took that and bent it to my will, forging it in my own fire and wearing it like armor.

When my eyes fluttered open, Evander's stare was locked on me, and his face was filled with pain and regret. His grip on me tightened in desperation to hold on to the little scraps I had given tonight, but he knew it was useless. He could sense the wall I had put up the moment I opened my eyes.

"We should get some sleep," I announced as I pulled out of his hold completely. To his credit, he didn't try to inquire or argue.

"Okay."

I headed back inside and over to the bed, pulling back the blanket and settling in. Nova had left her spot where our feet had been and opted to curl into Onyx instead. The sun would be rising in a few hours, and we had an early morning planned. Van wanted to visit the nearby town to check on our supplies and see if there were any magic wielders we could recruit to help in some way during the upcoming war.

I closed my eyes and tried to focus on the pending task rather than Evander's words and how he made me feel or the look on his face when I shut him out again. But instead, all I kept thinking about was his lips on my skin and the feel of his body wrapped around mine when he came to bed earlier. I wanted to melt into his touch again and the safety of it, but I couldn't let myself go there.

A long moment passed before Evander spoke rather than lay back down.

"I'm going to go look over some of the texts for a little while—see if I can find anything we may have missed," he explained before I had the chance to ask.

I turned toward him with a question in my eyes, but his pained expression told me all I needed to know.

He was retreating too.

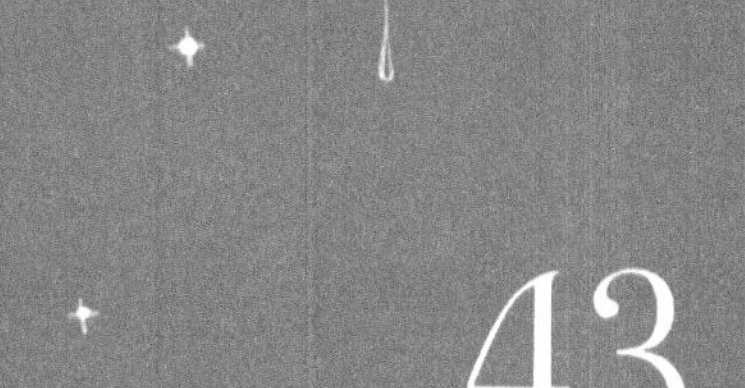

43.

The morning dragged on as the six of us walked through the villages, taking stock of the supplies and speaking with residents. Marce had decided to stay home and see if there was any merit to a potential lead Evander had discovered last night, though with everything we found directing us to dead ends, I wasn't hopeful.

Van had never returned to bed, and I only knew that because I found I couldn't sleep without him. I didn't know if it was not having the comfort I found in his presence or if the way we had left things last night was the cause. When I finally saw him this morning across the kitchen, he stared into his coffee mug, not bothering to say hello when he heard me enter the room. Instead, he announced to everyone we would be leaving shortly without looking at me at all. And now we were wandering the village, still not having said a single word to each other.

There weren't many magic wielders there, and those that were didn't possess enough experience for what we were asking of them. Anyone that had seen battle or had mastered their Gift was already serving in our armies. We came across a handful of Medicus willing to offer aid during the war. Though there weren't many, they were far more valuable than untrained Shadow Shifters who had a better chance of hurting themselves than the enemy.

While Van, Oli, and Cal spent their time discussing our next course of action, Lia, Felix, and I drifted over to a local orphanage. It was filled with children of all ages, and though several of them were there because they had lost their parents, most of them had never known theirs. They had been smuggled into Tenebrae from other kingdoms because they were a product of Conjoining. I wasn't sure if their parents did it to save themselves or their children, but at least they were here. Tenebrae had become a known safe haven for others, and I was proud that it was my home.

Lia tended to the kids' cuts and scrapes while Felix entertained them with jokes and elaborate stories. One of my contributions was creating tiny shadow wolves that ran around the room, playfully chasing the children before vanishing in a puff of smoke. The other, was toys.

"We have to figure this out, and soon," Felix said after I crafted a stuffed wolf for the kids. My ability to mold and create had become stronger each day, and the more I practiced, the easier it became. Soon, I'd be able to give Van a run for his money.

Okay, probably not *soon*, but I was at least getting better.

I handed the soft wolf to the last child in line and turned to look at my best friend. Felix was watching the crowd giggle and play with their new toys with such joy and sadness in his eyes. I realized that he was relating to them. Felix was an orphan himself, though I was willing to bet he didn't grow up with the same camaraderie and love that was evident between the maidens and children here. At least not until he found Dash.

"We will," I promised, knowing I couldn't allow anything to happen to these children. Most of them had escaped certain death from other kingdoms and didn't deserve to find it here. We had to do everything we could to maintain their safety.

We exited the orphanage and found our companions getting our horses ready to head to another village. Apparently, we weren't done for the day. I opened my mouth to ask where we were going next when a soldier galloped forward on his stallion, yelling for his king. He was covered in mud and muck, his eyes wide with terror and desperation.

"Your Majesty," he exclaimed again, jumping down from his horse as he ran straight to Evander. "It's the Borrus camp! They're under attack!" It was all he could say before Evander caught the man as he collapsed in his arms, a large wound on his stomach oozing blood.

Lia shot forward to her king's side, placing her hands on the man and doing what she could to heal his wounds.

"You three go back to the house and inform Marceline. See if she can find out what the fuck is going on and if any of the other camps have been hit," Evander demanded. "Oli and Cal: let's go." The two men ran to Van's side, and as soon as they each placed a hand on his shoulder, they were traversed away.

I dropped to the ground next to the soldier and glanced up at my friend to see the pain in her eyes as she looked at me. It was too late, and there was nothing we could do for this man as he coughed and choked on his own blood. His injuries were so extensive it was a miracle he had even made it here to begin with.

"Felix," I whispered as I moved to hold one of his hands. Felix came into view and knelt beside us, smiling at the man as he gripped his other hand. The most we could do for him was take away the pain as he passed into the next life.

"You seem to like to make an entrance," Felix teased, winking at the soldier. "What's your name?"

"Jacob," the soldier whispered through a rattling breath.

"I once knew a Jacob," Felix said as the man's breathing began to come easier, like it was no longer painful to sip the air that sustained his life. "But you're far more handsome."

Jacob laughed softly at Felix's compliment.

"How about, when you get better, we go get a drink?" Felix asked, and the man's eyes lit up at the thought as he smiled and nodded.

And then the light went out, and his body fell limp.

I sat back and tilted my head to the sky as tears for the lost soldier began to roll down my cheeks. This war was already claiming lives before it had even begun. Or perhaps it had, and we were too stupid to realize it.

"We can take him," a gentle voice called as I looked around to see a crowd had formed as villagers watched the scene before them. They weren't whispering or gossiping, their heads were hung, and their postures lax as some cried for the man.

Lia and Felix stood, giving the volunteers enough room to remove the body.

"We should go home," Lia said, sniffling. "We have to let Marce know what's going on." We didn't say another word as we walked to our mares to take the short journey back to our house.

A boom sounded in the distance.

At once we halted and looked around, trying to locate the source of the sound. Another boom. It was close enough to be near us but far enough that we weren't sure where it was coming from. The only thing we *did* know was that it wasn't coming from the direction Van had gone. Which only meant there was another attack somewhere.

"The Domus camp," Lia breathed as another sound came through, this time like cracking thunder, giving away the location. "It's a short ride just through there," Lia pointed. "It's the only thing in this area worth attacking."

I mounted Nox as Felix and Lia found their own horses.

"Get indoors and stay there," I commanded loud enough so every villager standing around could hear. I didn't wait for their acknowledgment as I sped toward the next attack with my friends close on my heels.

Insanity and chaos spread before us as we reached the camp. Screaming soldiers wielded their magic to fight off an attack that seemed to come from every direction. I dismounted and sprinted into the fray noticing the earth was sunken as if an explosion had occurred. I forced my magic forward to my fingertips.

"You!" I yelled and grabbed a random soldier. His eyes were frenzied and his face was smeared with blood as he stood frozen on the camp battlefield. Tents were ripped to shreds and supplies scattered. The earth was sunken in places like the explosion had taken place underground.

"What happened?" I demanded.

"I... I don't know," he sputtered, looking around as the shock of the events overtook him. The ground rumbled beneath out feet. "I can't be here! I need to go!" the soldier yelled, ripping himself from my hold.

He made it all of three steps before arrows shot into him; two to the heart and one between his eyes. I gasped, clutching my chest and wrapping myself in an impenetrable shield just as two arrows bounced off me.

"SHIELDS IN PLACE!" I yelled, my voice barely audible over the screams and shouts of the fight and slaughter. Lia and Felix both repeated my command, and soon, others followed suit, my order echoing through the ranks as soldiers protected themselves. Our men were trained and skilled, so why weren't they up in the first place? Had this attack taken them so off guard that they hadn't time to raise them? I looked around quickly, noticing that our casualty count was low and no one besides a select few had succumb to the attack.

The arrows came in fast and all at once, forcing our men to retreat into the camp and tighten their formation. My body tingled, and my intuition was firing off.

Something wasn't right.

"THE GROUND!" I screamed," DO NOT RETREAT!"

We were being herded to the middle of the camp where the explosions occurred. The arrows weren't meant to kill—though it was an added benefit for them if they did—they were meant to corral us into one area for the real attack.

My mind rolled over with panic at what to do as I was pushed further and further back toward the center of the camp by soldiers either not listening to me or too far gone in their own fear to realize this was a trap. I wracked my brain around everything I had been taught over these long months of training. My illusion Gift would take too much magic, and the fact that we couldn't see the enemy from their hidden spots surrounding us would make using that Gift impossible anyway. My Gift as an Empathi was useless right now, and I couldn't control the magic that came with being an Imperium enough to be helpful. It would have to be my shadows.

I closed my eyes and focused on reaching out to my magic as my body was pressed against the crushing weight of soldiers gathering closer and closer. It came forth in an instant along with my tattoo, and I let both crawl over my skin before directing my shadows high above us.

Shocked gasps broke out over the shouts as we were drenched in darkness. My shadows billowed out like storm clouds, violent and wild as they crept over our men. I took advantage of the hushed crowd as they watched with anticipation and horror.

"PUSH FORWARD!" I yelled. A few of the men repeated my command, but no one moved. Their eyes were locked on my darkness as it slithered down, forming a black dome around us to act as a shield. My magic took arrow after arrow but didn't falter, though I could feel a slight tingle in my body at each sharp attack.

"DO IT NOW!" I screamed again over the silence. This time, the demand was met with heavy obeying footsteps. My men pushed forward, still keeping a formation as we moved away from the center of the camp.

Just as the earth caved in with a crack that could rival any thunder.

Shouts broke out as we surged forward, trying to create as much distance between us and the sunken ground as possible. I whipped my head around as I watched some of our soldiers succumb to the crater, too close to the explosion not to be taken below or knocked out from the flying rocks and debris. I searched frantically over the sea of men as I tried to locate Felix and Lia. They had to have made it clear in time. I couldn't lose them. Red hair tied in a braid caught my eye from across the field as she shoved soldiers forward, trying to keep them moving. I breathed a sigh of relief as I continued my search for Felix, but I couldn't find him. He had to be okay.

The ground trembled beneath us as another blast from below shot dirt and rocks straight into the air like a geyser, but the earth didn't sink this time. I turned around, focusing my attention forward again as my body pricked and pulled while more and more arrows shot into my shadow shield.

"GATHER YOUR WEAPONS!" I yelled, and the order was parroted through the ranks. I pushed the shadows out further, expanding our line to the edge of the camp. The men stopped at the border, their arrows and daggers drawn, ready to attack on my word. A sense of calamity had now taken form as we killed the last of the dying chaos and gathered our wits. We were ready.

"NOW!" I yelled. Arrows were released and daggers were thrown out of our shield and through the darkness. We couldn't see if we had hit the enemy, but there were far too many of them to lower my shadows and leave us without protection.

"Where are our shielders?" I asked a soldier beside me, trying to figure out when to let them take over.

"They were taken out with the first wave of arrows, Your Highness," the soldier said.

Of course they were.

I took a deep and steady breath. I'd have to hold the shadow wall until we could take the risk of lowering it.

"AGAIN!" I yelled, and more weapons loosed. "Again!" I repeated.

If we berated them fast and hard enough, we had a better chance of hitting them before they were ready. I shoved more of my magic into the wall, spinning it like a tornado around us so that it would not only deflect the attack, but the wind might help send our arrows out further and in the directions we weren't aiming.

My tattoo slithered rapidly around my body, coating me in fire and fury as the strength of my Gift roared to life. I shoved myself to the front of the line as I held my hands up toward the wall, giving everything I could while being careful not to dip below my baseline. If I did, and this battle didn't take my life, then Van certainly would for acting so recklessly. My heart lurched as I thought of him. Was he okay? Was he winning his fight, or would it take him from me? I shook my head to erase the thoughts and instead focused on the here and now. These soldiers were my responsibility, and I couldn't fall into distractions.

I screamed command after command as an onslaught of weapons were released into the world. Slowly, the tingling from the attacks on my wall began to lessen. They were still present, but it seemed that our tactics were working. It was time.

"ON MY MARK, PUT UP YOUR SHIELDS!" I bellowed. I closed my eyes, diving deeper into myself as I gathered more of my magic. "NOW!" Murmurs broke out as the men did as they were told. I clenched my fist, ready to join the fight.

"DO NOT RETREAT. DO NOT FALTER. DO NOT STOP!" I screamed, and my words were met with grunts of approval and cheers—soldiers ready to take their payment in blood.

I took a deep breath and surged my magic forth, letting it spread beyond the tree line like a sickness plaguing the land. My ears picked up on two beautiful sounds: screams of terror as my darkness enveloped our enemies and the thunder of a stampede as my soldiers sprinted forward to collect their debt. I opened my eyes, crafted a sword in one hand, and followed them as my shadows disappeared the moment our soldiers reached the enemy.

Clanging metal broke out as our fight transformed into a physical one rather than magical. We had to keep them distracted enough not to be able to use whatever magic they possessed that allowed them to alter the earth so destructively. I had never seen such a thing nor read about it while studying our history. This was something foreign.

I lunged, slicing a man from belly to sternum and spinning in time to block a blow aimed at my back. I dug my feet into the ground, shoving with all my might and forcing my opponent to slide backward. We released our swords, jumping back from one another before attacking again. I pivoted and ducked, narrowly missing his blade as it swung over my head. I swiped my leg out, catching him off guard and knocking him flat on his back. Moving over him, I plunged my sword deep into his throat before he had a moment to recover.

Silver hair flashed in my vision as I saw Felix stabbing an unsuspecting enemy in the back before he could kill one of our soldiers. I was filled with relief and joy to see him alive, but I didn't have time to think about it any further before I was met with another fight.

The battle dragged on for what felt like hours as we cut through the enemy's line, taking their lives ruthlessly. I stepped over dead men, grey and deformed from our Tremos and slit the throats of others cowering in fear while their minds held them captive, too terrorized to move.

Before long, the grass had been stained red with the blood of our enemies mixed with our own, but it was over. And we won. Cheers had erupted over the crowd as they celebrated their victory after beheading the last enemy soldier, though we kept a handful alive as prisoners to interrogate as necessary.

My gaze roamed over the camp and the onslaught as I made my way for one of the craters within the earth. There was no residue painted over the area and no signs that any explosion had gone off. My suspicions were right, and these holes were created by nothing more than wielders who possessed the magic to do so. I swallowed my fear as I righted myself and headed for a group of huddled generals to find out what the fuck had happened here. Before I could make it to them, my body collided with Lia as she threw herself against me. I wrapped my arms around her before pulling her back to check over her body. She was a skilled warrior, but she didn't possess the physical or mental magic the soldiers had. Her Gift was meant to heal, not harm.

"I got thirty-two of those assholes," she said, sneering as she kicked the corpse of one of the enemy soldiers. "My previous record from the last battle I was in was thirty-six, so when we kill the prisoners, I get to do it."

And gone was my worry for her well-being.

"They're yours," I told her with a sly smile, and she beamed at me. "Where's Felix? I haven't seen him in a while." I scanned the sea of people, looking for my friend and spotting him on the ground with his back against a fallen tent. His leg was bloody, and he clutched his arm like he was in pain. Panic overtook me as I rushed for him with Lia right behind.

"Felix!" I yelled as I sank down next to my best friend.

"I'm fine," he said, wrapping his uninjured arm around me and pulling me close. "It's just a broken bone."

Lia knelt down, taking his arm into her hands and healing the wound as I crafted a sling for him to wear. She secured it around him before two soldiers appeared, holding a man whose own arm seemed to be barely hanging onto his body.

"Go. It's just a scratch," Felix said, gesturing to the deep cut on his leg. Lia nodded and directed the men to a tent set up for significant casualties.

"Did you get him for this?" I asked as I dabbed away the blood around his injury with a cloth I had crafted. Felix leveled me a flat look that said, '*really?*' and I smirked. Rushed movement caught my attention, and I glanced up to find Olivier sprinting for us. I shot to my feet at his approach, looking past him to see if Evander had followed but found nothing except our soldiers cleaning up rubble and bodies.

"What happened?!" Olivier yelled as he slowed to a stop before us, his gaze locked on Felix.

"Where is Evander?!" I asked, not caring to answer his question.

"He brought Cal and me here a few minutes ago. We all split up to assess the damage, and that's when I saw the two of you," he explained, not taking his stare from my friend. Tension eased out of my body as I learned that Van was alive and here. My eyes darted around, desperately trying to catch a glimpse of him somewhere in the crowd. "Now tell me what happened," Olivier demanded as I continued my search for the king.

"We were getting ready to go home when we heard—"

"No. With your arm," he ground out, and my attention flew back to Olivier to see his face filled with fury as he glared over Felix.

"It's fine," Felix started, but Oli cut him off as he knelt.

"It's not fucking fine. It's broken." Oli looked around as if searching for someone. He then snapped his fingers at a wandering soldier before directing him to tend to Felix.

"Lia already put the bone back in place," Felix argued, pulling away from the Medicus.

"But she was too fucking preoccupied to heal your leg?" Oli bit, his tone feral and pissed off. What the hell was his problem?

"Yes," I snapped, causing Olivier to direct his stare from my friend to me. "She was too fucking preoccupied reattaching limbs."

Oli huffed under his breath as he adjusted Felix's leg, and the Medicus got to work, cutting away fabric around the wound. His injury was bad, but thankfully not life-threatening. My focus drifted between the soldier removing fissures of sharp rocks from the wound and the intense stare-down that Oli and Felix were giving each other.

Olivier's jaw was set, his face tight with irritation.

"You can leave," Felix told him bitterly, and for just a moment, Oli's eyes flickered with something that looked an awful lot like pain.

"You need someone with you. You're injured," Oli replied.

"Well, it's a good thing that Ainsley is here."

"She'd rather go find Van."

My muscles coiled, ready to spring at the sound of his name, and my magic swirled and ached, wanting me to let it out as if somehow, it could find him.

"I'm still not alone. The Medicus—" Felix began but then stopped and directed his words to the man tending to him. "I'm sorry, what is your name?' Felix asked.

"Malcolm," the Medicus replied.

"That's a nice name," he mused as Oli glared at him.

"Thank you. Do you have any other injuries for me to tend to?" Malcolm's gaze dragged over Felix, noting every cut and scrape he could heal. His eyes narrowed on the small trail of blood that trickled from Felix's hairline. "How's your head?" Malcolm inquired as he worked on healing my friend's most prominent injury.

"No complaints yet," Felix replied flirtatiously, his eyes still glued to Olivier.

Malcolm blushed, and his fingers fumbled over the wound at the innuendo, making Felix suck in a sharp breath. Olivier leaned forward and fisted Malcolm's dirty uniform in his hands before shoving him away from Felix hard, causing him to fall. Malcolm hurried to his feet before sprinting away and not looking back. My eyes went wide and shot to Felix, but he looked just as confused as I was.

"You!" Olivier snapped, pointing to another unsuspecting soldier. "Job?"

"A healer," the man said, wiping his sweaty hands on his pants with a look of fear in his eyes.

"Good. Now heal him," Oli demanded. The man rushed forward, dropped to the ground, and immediately went to work.

"This is ridiculous. I'm fine. It's just a scratch," Felix reasoned as he shifted to get up. Oli's hand slammed into Felix's chest so hard I half expected the tent he was resting against to have collapsed. Oli leaned forward, leaving only an inch between his and Felix's face.

"Sit down and shut up," he snarled before pulling back. My friend's jaw clenched tight at the order, and his chest heaved in fury, but he didn't make to move again.

"Go find Evander, Ainsley," Felix offered, not taking his eyes off Oli. I hesitated, not sure if it was best to leave them together.

Another moment passed before I decided I couldn't take the suspense any longer. I had to find Van and see for myself that he was okay. I turned away and sprinted into the fray, scanning the sea of bloodied soldiers as I searched for the one I wanted.

Everywhere I looked, there was something new. Cal had found Lia and was helping to carry injured soldiers away when she was finished with them. Warriors dragged bodies across the field, bringing them to a large pyre already roaring to life. People worked to craft new tents and supplies, and even our wolves played a part by digging holes for support beams. When the hell had they arrived? I continued running, desperate to find Van, but coming up short each time.

I began to give up hope, thinking he may have gone back to the location of his own battle to assist there, when the sound of my name reached my ears. It was strong and commanding, frantic and fearful. It was *him*. I spun around, fervently searching. My heart hammered rapidly, and though I wanted to yell for him, I couldn't. My voice was caught in my throat with the panic and emotion that was bottled up there.

I looked and looked, chasing the sound of my name on his lips until a hoard of people cleared, and a dark-haired man appeared in the distance. Only a moment passed when his head snapped in my direction as if he had felt my presence. His grey eyes widened in relief, and I threw my arms out wide as I leaped forward, knowing that he'd catch me before I hit the ground.

Shadows appeared, and I collided with a firm body a heartbeat later as my arms closed tight around his neck.

"Love," he whispered as he held me, relief coating the word. I buried my face into him, inhaling his cedar and snow scent and letting it soothe me. I didn't want to ever pull back—to ever let go. He was *here*, and he was *alive*.

A soft whimper left me as my hands moved through his hair, trying to get as close to him as possible. His grip on me constricted, and a slight tremor went through my body. His heart thumped wildly against my chest, and I reached out my Empathi Gift.

"Don't," he warned, though it sounded like he was struggling to say the word.

I pulled back to look at him, and a swirl of movement on his neck caught my eye. It quickly disappeared, and I dropped my gaze to the arm clutching my waist.

A tattooed tendril dipped beneath the hem of his sleeve the moment I discovered it.

"Van," I breathed, stepping back and moving my hands to cup his face.

A muscle feathered in his jaw as he tried to keep it clenched. His eyes were focused and swirling with terror and frustration. His body subtly trembled, and his hands shook as they held me. He was losing control.

"It's okay," I told him.

He closed his eyes as he swallowed, trying hard to regain his composure, but it was useless. The more he seemed to try, the more it slipped away. His tattoo slithered back into view, crawling up his neck and around his fingers. I needed to get him out of here and fast.

"Van!" Olivier's shouts drew both of our focus.

He rushed for us as Felix hobbled along with an arm over Oli's shoulder. I wanted to go to them—meet them halfway— but Van seemed rooted to the spot, unable to move as he tried to calm down. He held onto me as if I was the only thing keeping him grounded and sane. I interlaced my fingers with his and clutched his hand just as tight. I could be this for him.

As he approached, Oli waved a piece of parchment in the air, lowering his voice to an urgent whisper.

"Marceline just sent this. She received word from Declan," Oli said, his face deathly serious. "We need to go home. Right now."

Evander swayed at my side, and I wrapped my arm around his waist to keep him steady. His chest began to heave as he looked around the space like he could spot the man he called family somewhere in the destruction. He opened his mouth and closed it again, unable to come up with the words as I watched the panic set in.

"Evander," I said gently, squeezing his hand. His eyes dropped to me, and I watched them mist over as he struggled. "Take us home." He blinked away the tears as he nodded, reaching a hand out for Olivier and Felix. They took it, and together we were pulled away from the camp.

44.

"What's going on?" I demanded the moment we appeared in the study. Marce stood over the desk, scribbling a note and letting the ink disappear. She turned and stormed for us with the letter she had received.

"Declan's been hit. Pravus's soldiers somehow got through our defenses and ambushed him. He's asking for aid," she explained as I took the paper from her. I read through it quickly before handing it to Olivier so he and Felix could go through it.

"We need to ready our forces," Oli said, reaching out to hand the letter to his king, but Evander didn't move to take it. His stare was pointedly set on the ground before him, and his hands were balled into fists at his side.

"Where are Cal and Lia?" I asked. Oli stared at Van's unusual behavior for a moment longer before lowering his arm and turning to me.

"They should be here any minute. I sent them ahead while I came to find you both."

I nodded and followed Marce back to the desk as words began to appear on another piece of parchment like spilled ink. We glanced at each other as we read the newest report.

Mass casualties.

I closed my eyes and swallowed hard. Marce swore under her breath and dragged a hand through her curls. We needed to help, but I wasn't sure what we could offer after the attack today without putting ourselves at more risk.

"What's going on?" Cal said as he and Lia stormed into the room. I held out the letter for him to take and watched his eyes widen with the news.

"How did this happen?" Lia asked as she read over his shoulder. "We should have had some warning of their passing through the straight." She was right. Our camps should have alerted us immediately of the movement, yet we hadn't received any notice. A fleet large enough to inflict the amount of damage being reported couldn't have been missed.

"They distracted us," Evander whispered. We all looked up to find him staring out the window, his knuckles gripping the pane so hard they were white. "The attacks today were to divert our attention from their true target."

My stomach knotted, and I felt as if I were about to be sick. Van's tattoo twisted violently around his hand, and the wood he gripped splintered and cracked under the pressure of his hold.

"We need to ready a fleet right now," Olivier announced, striding for the exit, but Calidore stepped in his way.

"We can't! We were just attacked. We can't leave Tenebrae vulnerable by sending our forces out. What if that's exactly what they want us to do?" Cal argued.

"We are not going to deny help, Calidore! You know Declan would never do that to us," Oli countered. Cal nodded as he listened, but his posture was tense and steady. He wasn't going to back down.

"I know," he whispered. "But we can't risk our people for theirs. Not after what happened today. You saw the magic they possessed. We don't know what else they are capable of." So they *had* also experienced the earth magic's effects as we had.

"I don't give a shit what else they can do!" Oli yelled, stepping closer to Cal.

"Sending our troops unprepared is the same as sending them to their death!" Calidore snapped back, straightening as he and Oli stood chest to chest to square off. "There isn't much we can do, and I don't think—"

"I don't give a fuck what you think," Olivier bit out, turning around to face Evander. "What do *you* want to do, Van? It's your call."

Calidore sighed and shook his head, seeming to accept his defeat. Evander considered Declan to be family, and because of that, we all knew he felt that Vorsutos was an extension of his own people. He wouldn't want to leave them to suffer this fate. But Van also cared deeply for Tenebrae and his soldiers. He was in an impossible situation.

Evander lowered his head but didn't answer, as his tattoo crept further up the back of his neck, slithering into his hairline and then retreating again.

"Think about Tenebrae, Van," Cal offered quietly as if hoping the mention of his own kingdom would sway his decision. Van clutched the pane even tighter as more cracks sounded through the room.

"We're running out of time," Oli said impatiently. He walked further to his king and placed a hand on his tense shoulder. Evander recoiled against the touch so subtly that I knew everyone except me missed it. He was about to break, and I refused to let them see it.

"How many ships do we have stocked and ready to send out with a full crew?" I demanded, letting my voice drop into the role of heir and not their friend.

"Only around twenty," Marceline said as she moved for me. "We'll need at least half a day to prepare the rest."

"Can you have it done by dawn?" I questioned, and she thought on that a moment before nodding. "Good. Go and gather the best soldiers we have and take the twenty ships now. I'll send word to Declan."

"Olivier," I stated, directing my stare to him now. "See that the rest of our fleet is ready before the sun rises."

"We don't have enough fresh soldiers. Most have just returned, and sending them back out to sea without proper time to rest will do more harm than good," Cal interjected.

I contemplated his warning for a moment before coming up with a decision on how best to act.

"Then we'll take from the nearby camps," I announced, turning back to Oli to give the order.

"Reach out to the camps closest to us. We don't have the time to waste going farther than a couple hours' ride. Take only half of each unit," I told him, and Calidore huffed in irritation, clearly pissed he wasn't getting his way, but I wasn't done yet.

I strode for Lia and she straightened, ready to take an order from her ruler.

"Gather as many Medicus as we can spare. They'll join Marce on her ships," I said, and her eyes widened a fraction at the odd request. Besides the trained soldiers, those who wielded that Gift weren't fighters.

"But—" Lia began, no doubt about to inform me that there wasn't much they could do in battle.

"Cal is right," I announced, twisting to look at my family. Their bodies were rigid, and their stares tense as they observed me. Evander had turned around now, though his head still hung, unable to look at any of us. I hated seeing him in that much pain. "There isn't much we can do. We won't win this fight, but we can offer our healers to aid as many of their injured and dying as we can. We at least owe Declan that. And if the Gods are merciful, we can hold them back long enough for our fleet to arrive."

My words were met with nods of approval and a smirk from Marce, clearly happy at the leadership role I had taken. Cal was the only person who looked ready to destroy the entire study. He shook his head as he crossed his arms over his chest.

"What about *our* people? We can't just leave them defenseless," he said, holding his hands as if pleading for me to change my mind. It stung a bit to know he didn't have faith in me. That he would assume I would leave our people exposed and ripe for another attack.

"No, we can't," I said, striding for him. "You will go to Tallis and inform him of what happened here. Have him send enough soldiers and Medicus to fill the camps until ours return."

"He won't want to do that," Cal argued.

"I don't give a shit what he wants to do," I bit back. "After what happened in Agnitio, he owes us, so go collect on that debt."

No one moved.

Instead, they all looked to Evander, waiting for his approval. They may have agreed with what I said, but he was their king. It was his word that they would follow. The problem was, he was in no state to acknowledge anyone, let alone give them an order. I walked to the center of the room and raised my chin as I looked each family member in the eye.

"Go now or step aside, and I'll find someone else who will." My tone was cold and final. I was done being challenged, and I had to protect Van. He wouldn't want them to see how far gone I knew he truly was.

At once, my family bowed and quickly rushed from the room to perform their tasks. I strode for Van, taking his hands in mind as he stared blankly at the carpet. A moment later, I felt Felix's presence appear beside me.

"His defenses are down," Felix whispered, and I nodded, knowing what he meant. Van's emotions were running wild, and he couldn't control them, let alone keep an Empathi out. "Do you want my help?" he asked, but I shook my head, knowing Van would never allow it.

"I'll be okay," I told Felix. "Go and rest your leg."

I waited until the sound of retreated footsteps faded, and we were completely engulfed in silence. I lifted a hand and slid it under his chin to force him to look at me. His grey eyes were dark and haunted—bottomless pits of despair that held such terror and anger within.

"And you," I breathed, moving closer to him. "Are coming with me."

I gripped his hand hard and led him through the house and into the safety of our room. Evander complied, following silently as his fingers tightened against my hold as if he was scared I would let him go. I took us into the bathing room and turned on the shower before leading him inside, fully clothed.

Evander didn't say a word as I positioned him under the water, letting the droplets drench his body and melt away the blood and grime covering his face. His eyes met mine, and I held his stare as I pushed the jacket away from his shoulders and unbuttoned his shirt, letting them fall to the tile. He swallowed hard before reaching for his pants with trembling fingers and undoing the belt. I removed my own clothes, leaving them in a pile next to his, and then crafted a cloth, hoping just a trace of my magic on his skin would help soothe him the way his always soothed me.

I grabbed a bottle of soap, letting the water create suds on the fabric before reaching up to wipe away the still-present dirt on his cheek. Van closed his eyes against my touch and moved his hands to my waist as I worked. The way his hold trembled against me let me know he was using me for support. I moved the cloth over his body, scrubbing away the traces of the battle from his flesh and swallowing down the growl in my throat as I washed over the scrapes and cuts along his chest. I would kill every last one of them for marking his skin.

Van didn't speak as I worked, dropping to my knees to clean each of his legs until every remnant of this afternoon was gone. I stood, gathering the shampoo and standing on my toes to massage it into his hair. Once satisfied with my work, I turned my back to him to retrieve a towel but was quickly halted by a hand grabbing my arm. The fingers of his free hand traced a line across my back, and I sucked in a breath at a sudden sting of pain. I twisted my head to look over my shoulder and discovered a long deep red cut stretching from my lower back to the top of my spine. Evander's grip on my wrist tightened as he explored the mark on my body, his hold shaking violently and his tattoo moving in a sudden whirl as he did.

His breaths came in heavy gasps, and a rumble sounded in his throat as his eyes darted over my wound. I spun quickly to face him, determined to calm him from the rage brewing and the look of destruction in his eyes.

"I'm okay," I told him urgently. "I'm okay."

Evander released my arm and closed his eyes as he shook his head. His throat bobbed, and his fist clenched as his body shook. His tattoos moved quickly and then slowed before stopping and then starting again. He was putting all of his focus into controlling them and not letting me see the storm inside him. I turned to face him fully and pressed my body against his as I raised my hands to hold his face.

"Look at me," I said, and his eyes flew open at my command. "I know you are a king, Evander, but you don't have to make these decisions alone anymore. I'm here now, and this is my family—these are my people. The weight of their fate no longer falls solely on your shoulders. Let me carry this burden with you. Please." A small noise escaped him, and his jaw tightened as he processed my words. His tattoo moved again before halting abruptly as his restraint continued to slip. He was teetering on the edge, and I needed him to know that if he fell, I would be there to catch him. Always.

"You don't have to hide from me, Evander. Not ever," I told him, gliding my finger along his tattoo. He shuddered a breath as his eyes bore into mine until they had misted over. I stood taller, pressing my forehead against his.

"You're okay now. You're safe. I have you," I whispered.

That was all he needed to hear.

Evander collapsed against me, and I held him tight as we slid to the ground. He buried his head into my chest as he broke, his body shuddering and his tattoos swirling violently across his skin faster and faster. My hold on him tightened as he came undone, refusing to allow even an inch of space between us.

"You're okay now. You're safe. I have you," I repeated again and again, just as he had for me. He wasn't alone, and now that I was here, he wouldn't ever be again.

A sob broke free from his throat, and tears spilled down my cheeks, mixing with the water from the shower to erase their evidence. His pain and sorrow were excruciating to experience, and my heart shattered alongside his. I threw up a silencing shield around us, wanting him to freely go through his emotions without others overhearing.

"I almost lost Oli today," Evander said, the words thick and rough in his throat. "If I was just one fucking second later, he would have been killed." He picked his head up from my chest and pulled back to look at me. The honesty and fear in his eyes were enough for me to vow on everything I would never let him hurt like this again.

I didn't respond, instead giving him the time to gather the thoughts I could see forming on his tongue.

"And now, Declan," he continued, swallowing another wave of emotion as his hands shook around me. "He was my father's childhood best friend. He's all I have left of my parents, Ainsley. He's family. I can't lose him; I can't."

I swiped away the tears that fell from his eyes at his declaration.

"You won't," I promised. "Marce will get to him in time. He'll be okay."

Evander held my stare as if he could force himself to believe my words that way. His hands moved from around my body to hold my face, and I snaked my arms around his neck. He dipped his head and ran his nose along mine before inhaling deeply. I held my breath as he gripped my cheeks tighter; not enough to hurt, but enough to let me know how much he needed to touch me.

"And you," he whispered, his voice strained and panicked. "I thought I was going to lose you. The second we heard that explosion in the distance, my first thought was not to stay and continue our fight, but to leave and get to you. I almost left so many fucking times."

I swallowed and ran my hands through his hair as I pressed myself closer to him, our bodies slick from the dripping water.

"I'm glad you didn't," I admitted. "They needed you there, fighting for them."

Evander nodded, knowing I was right. We were rulers and had to leave our emotions and feelings for one another off the battlefield in order to protect our people. No matter how much we hated it.

"You would have been proud of me," I told him. "I kicked ass today. I let my magic guide me, and I wasn't afraid of it or what it would do." Evander didn't respond, but I could feel the pride radiating from him. "And my tattoo was super scary," I added, and he huffed a breathy laugh.

Gods, I wanted to hear that sound again. *Needed* to hear it again.

"I actually heard one of the soldiers say how much more intimidating it was than yours," I teased, desperately trying to bring him back out of the dark cave he was in.

"You did not," he replied flatly, though I could hear his tone start to lighten. I gathered more moss and kindling, determined to nurture and grow this fire that was beginning.

"A few of them then started discussing how you should step down as king because there was no way you could ever compete with me. I tried telling them it wasn't necessary, but they seemed pretty adamant."

Through lowered lashes, I could see a muscle feather in his jaw.

"I think you're losing your touch, King of Shadows," I added. A slight smirk appeared across his face. Relief filled my body as I pulled back to look at him, seeing his eyes were brighter—calmer. His tattoos still twisted and turned rapidly across his body, but his breathing began to come steadier, his chest rising and falling at a slightly slower pace.

"Come on," I told him, taking his hand in mine as I got to my feet and brought him up with me. "Let's get you dried off."

I handed him a towel before wrapping myself in one and striding over to his dresser on the far wall of the bathing room. I rummaged through, gathering a change of clothes and offering them to him before picking my own. He lifted his brow as I slipped into his sweatpants and a large shirt.

"Am I ever going to get to keep my own clothes?" he asked skeptically. I smiled at the lighter tone in his voice, though it was still slightly edged in darkness.

"Nope," I said simply, taking his hand in mine and leading us to our bed. He grunted in irritation, but I knew it was a facade. He loved seeing me in his clothes just as much as I loved wearing them—perhaps even more.

We climbed into bed, and I arranged the pillows to prop myself up before pulling Evander to me. He wrapped his arms around my body and laid his head against my chest, letting himself continue to be vulnerable. My fingers raked through his damp hair and along the arm draped over me as I traced the slithering shadows of his tattoo, grateful he wasn't attempting to stop them anymore.

"You should try to sleep," I whispered. The sun was only now beginning to set, but I knew the events of today and the emotional turmoil he had gone through would have exhausted him as if he'd been up for days.

"I don't think I can," he admitted, adjusting himself so his leg hitched over mine and weaved in between. I thought about that for a moment before leaning down and placing a kiss on his head.

"I can help with that," I offered, and he stiffened against me.

Van never let Felix or even I use our Empathi Gift on him. He didn't like the idea of having his emotions manipulated or giving someone that much freedom to rummage through him at his most vulnerable. I expected that reaction from him, but I needed to show him that he would always be safe with me.

"I won't take away the pain or fear unless you ask me to," I told him. "I'll just calm you enough to sleep. I promise."

Evander lifted his head to meet my eyes, and I saw the worry dissolve away as he took me in. I had earned his trust over the several months we had spent together, and it was the one thing I treasured above all else. I wouldn't ever do anything to jeopardize that because I knew how much trust meant to him. How much it meant to me.

Slowly, Evander nodded and lowered his head back down. His grip on me tightened as if preparing himself for the surge of my magic he was about to feel. I dragged my fingers slowly down his arm until I reached his hand. I slid my fingers between his before lifting our locked hands and bringing them to my lips to kiss softly.

My magic drifted from me and into him, weaving its way through his body and wrapping itself around every ounce of pain it could find. I didn't let it alter the emotions, but instead let him feel that I was there with him, and he wasn't alone. Evander sighed contently as my Gift moved against his darkness, brushing against it like a cat offering affection. I moved towards his pounding heart and caressed it tenderly as my Gift eased into him, working to slow the frantic rhythm and calm him further. Soon, his breathing evened out, and the tension eased from his body as he fell asleep.

I held him for hours, continuing to rake my fingers through his hair as my magic kept his pain at bay, never taking it away but instead allowing it a safe place to exist. I wouldn't be sleeping tonight. I wanted to maintain my hold on him to keep his body calm. After today, there was a risk of nightmares creeping into his mind. The moment I felt his body respond to those thoughts, I would end them. The gentle rise and fall of his chest and his subtle, soft snores were all I needed to know he was okay.

The door to our room shifted open, though the sound was omitted due to the silencing shield I had placed around the bed to ensure nothing would wake him. My gaze drifted to the threshold where Olivier stood rigid. He gave a shallow shake of his head, and I inhaled deeply before reducing the shield to only encompass Van.

"There had to be a change of plans, but it can wait. I have it handled," Olivier said as he glanced at the man sleeping on me.

I gripped Van a little tighter—protectively—as his friend looked him over. Without thinking, my tattoo spilled over my skin and twisted around my limbs like ribbons, as if it could take the focus off Evander and camouflage him from peering eyes.

"I'm glad he has you," Oli added, redirecting his attention to me now. "That you have each other. That's how it was always supposed to be." He focused on the hold we had on one another and the support we gave. "You should have grown up together and been what you are for one another now. Neither of you should have had to experience the life you had alone."

I didn't want to focus any longer on the life stolen from me and the one I could have lived because what was the point? Evander and I hadn't been together since birth, learning and growing with one another—being the stable support the other needed. We were robbed of that chance, so it didn't make sense to dwell on it.

"I'm glad we have each other, too," I responded.

Oli began to retreat, and before I could extend the silencing shield back out, it disappeared like it hadn't ever been in place.

"Just say it, Oli," Evander announced as he shifted. He sat up and scooted his back against the headboard, though he didn't undo our locked fingers. His thumb gently swept over the back of my hand, and he offered me a small smile as he got comfortable.

Olivier stepped further into the room until he stopped at the foot of the bed and sighed.

"We can't send the rest of the ships out at dawn," he explained. "There's a storm about to roll in, and our fleet won't be ready in time to make it out before it does. We'll continue getting everything stocked as planned, but we can't depart until the worst of it passes."

"The Aerians?" Evander questioned.

"They said it's too strong for them to stop the pending weather completely. They could try to lessen its effects, but it's a blizzard."

"So even that won't do much," Van finished. He took a deep breath, and I watched his body, looking for any indication that his tattoo was about to run rampant again, but he seemed to have most of it under control.

"And Marce?" I asked.

"Is already gone and will miss the storm thanks to the headstart. Cal sent word from Agnitio that Tallis has agreed to aid in whatever way he can, and Lia is at the camps, helping to move the soldiers to safety before the storm hits," Oli stated.

Evander nodded, seemingly pleased with the direction Oli had chosen after the news of the storm. It wasn't surprising though. Oli and Cal had pretty much run Tenebrae as Van was growing up and into his role as king.

"We'll go to the nearby villages at dawn and help move them into the palace. Send word to the orphanage tonight and inform them to be ready by the time we arrive. I want the children settled in first, and then we'll work on the rest of the villagers."

Olivier bowed his head and left the room, closing the door just as Onyx and Nova slipped inside. Van's wolf moseyed over to my side of the bed and sat stoically as he whimpered. I reached over, petting him gently between the ears as I held his dark stare.

"Not tonight, boy," I told him.

Onyx huffed but didn't press it further and moved to curl up next to Nova, who had already claimed a stack of pillows on the floor. I twisted back to face Van, who was watching me intently with a curious glint in his eye. He raised a brow as if to say '*explain,*' and I shrugged.

"It's been a long day, and I figured you'd want a wolf-free night in our bed," I told him.

A beautiful smirk crept upon his face, and the force of it lightened my soul. For a moment, it was as if nothing terrible had happened today, and this was a night like any other we had shared.

"What?" I asked, not able to hide my smile from forming as I looked at him.

"You said *our* bed."

"No, I didn't," I argued, but Evander shook his head, his teeth flashing in a dazzling grin, and my heart melted at the sight. I turned away, refusing to look at him as he basked in his arrogance at catching a slip of the tongue. "How are you feeling?" I asked at once.

"Oh, so we're changing the subject when we've been called out?" he replied, scooting closer to me.

"Yup, so answer the question."

Evander narrowed his eyes playfully at me before releasing a breath of mock irritation and conceding.

"I'm okay," he said quietly.

"Your shadows have slowed." He held up his arms to inspect them. His tattoo was still moving quicker than it should be, but much slower than it had earlier—a clear sign he was starting to regain control.

"Listening to your heartbeat helped," he admitted.

I tugged on his arm, trying to get him to lay back down on my chest. If hearing it fiercely beat for him aided in his comfort, I would gladly lay here as long as it took for him to fully be okay. Evander resisted my pull as he shook his head.

"It's your turn to sleep," he declared.

"I can sleep like this," I told him, trying to yank him back down, but again he refused to budge. "What if the villagers don't want to go to the palace?" I asked, changing the subject. Evander gave me a flat look, letting me know he knew exactly what I was doing, but he didn't ignore the question.

"They don't have to go, though most choose to when we have a massive storm like this. However, if they decide to stay, we ensure they have provisions to get through at least two weeks." I nodded and opened my mouth to ask another question, but Van pressed a finger to my lips. "Now, head on the pillow," he commanded, not allowing me to deny him any longer.

I rolled my eyes but did as he said, knowing there was no way I would win the argument. Once I was situated, he twirled his pointer finger around, gesturing for me to turn on my side. I complied, rolling so my back faced him as he shifted on the mattress behind me. A second later, his hand gingerly rested on my waist, and his satin voice filled the space.

"Is this okay?" he asked tentatively, and for a moment, I wasn't sure why. But then the events of last night seeped through my mind, and I remembered how I had pulled away from him. I remembered the pain and desperation that had danced in his eyes as he watched me build my walls once again.

"No," I breathed. "You're too far away." I grabbed his hand, lacing my fingers through his as I scooted back into him. Evander pushed himself against me, wrapping his arms around me tight as our limbs tangled together, neither of us seeming to get as close as we wanted to the other. He sighed against my neck, and I shivered at his touch.

"I was scared today, too," I admitted into the darkness. "I can't lose you, Van."

His lips pressed against my skin as he softly kissed my jasmine tattoo, and I gripped him tighter. Everything in my body ached to tear down the fortress I had built and allow him in—to let myself feel again. But the voice in the back of my mind screamed and pleaded with me to remember the hurt and betrayal I had gone through the last time I had given my heart away, and I quickly shoved down the desire.

What we had now was enough. It had to be.

45.

I awoke to a massive weight crushing my body and wondered if Van had rolled us through the night and taken up his new spot on my chest. I cracked open an eye to find a giant black wolf snoring soundly on top of me and a grey one nuzzled between my legs. Leave it to these two to hop into bed while we were asleep and ignore my order from last night. I glanced to my left to find Van's spot empty and the midmorning sun pouring into the room.

Fuck.

I squirmed, trying to get my body out from under Onyx, but he was too heavy.

"Onyx, get up," I demanded, shoving the wolf hard until I could shift slightly. Onyx opened his eyes at the disturbance and lifted his head. After a moment he repositioned himself further onto my body as a deep growl rumbled from his throat in warning.

"You need to move right now. I'm late and have shit to do," I commanded, grabbing a fistful of fur from the scruff of his neck and pulling as I tried to fight my way free. He snarled at me, pushing even more weight onto my body before nuzzling into my neck.

You have got to be kidding me.

A low laugh came from the doorway, and I tilted my head to look beyond the massive wolf to find Van watching me with his arms crossed over his chest and a crooked smile on his face. He was dressed comfortably, his sleeves rolled up to his forearms, and his tattoo nowhere in sight.

"When you're finished being amused, can you tell your stubborn wolf to get the hell off of me?" I said, grunting under the weight of the giant fur ball.

"He's under strict orders not to let you leave," Evander explained as he crossed over to my side of the bed. He sat down on the edge, kissing Nova between her ears as she yawned and pulling on Onyx's fluffy tail as he growled in irritation.

"You seem better," I pointed out as I watched his playful exchange. His eyes were bright and alert—gone was the pain that had resided in them hours prior. His posture seemed straighter with more control, and his tattoo was put away between his shoulder blades. And his smile... My Gods, that smile.

"I am," he said. I loosed a sigh of relief.

"Why didn't you wake me up? We were supposed to leave at dawn."

"No, Oli and I were leaving at dawn. I was always going to let you sleep," he countered in that cocky, all-knowing voice of his. "Now hurry up and get dressed and eat. We have to finish moving the rest of the villagers into the palace, and your laziness has put us behind schedule."

I tried to smack him, but he quickly grabbed my wrist, halting the movement. He raised a single brow as if to say, *nice try*, and pressed my hand to his lips to kiss softly. There was something more intimate in the gesture than I anticipated. Like the exchange between us last night had altered some part of our relationship. The more trials we went through, the more we grew from them and leaned on one another. But it wasn't the same as it had been with Dashiell. I didn't depend on Evander in the same way. I didn't rely on him to keep me safe and protected. My dependence on him was more like expecting him to be there for me when I needed him, and he always was.

Evander released my hand and stood to leave. He was nearly out of the room before I called out.

"Van." He turned to face me, a question in his eyes. "A little help would be lovely," I said sarcastically as I jerked my chin toward the black wolf still on me. Van shrugged before sliding his hand into his pocket and walking away.

"You'll figure it out. Consider it a training exercise," he called over his shoulder. "We're leaving in ten minutes, and I suggest you be on time."

What a dick.

After entirely too long, I managed to get Onyx off of me. No matter what I did, I physically couldn't move him with my body or magic, and it took me an embarrassingly long time to figure out how to do it. Onyx had followed me to the kitchen after I changed to collect his seven promised oatmeal cookies and then bounded away back upstairs to no doubt sleep in my spot just to prove a point.

By the time Van had woken me, the first flurries had begun to fall, already coating the land in a thin layer of frost. It had taken nearly the entire day to get the villagers situated in the palace, with only a handful of them opting to stay behind in their homes. Though there were plenty of spare rooms for each family, all the children were set up on beds in the grand ballrooms. When I asked about this arrangement, Van said they look forward to the blizzards each year because it was like a big slumber party. The palace staff ensures the children have plenty of toys and games to keep them occupied, and they get to stay up late through the night hours eating sweets when their parents would rather them be asleep.

"It was something that my father implemented before I was born, and after he passed, Olivier kept the tradition going. Blizzard season became my favorite time of year because of it," Evander explained. I smiled at the thought of a dark-haired little boy running through the halls and slaying magical creatures with a group of other children, while outside the snow came down in heavy sheets. And for a moment, I imagined I was there too, sprinting after him as I struggled to keep up.

We had dinner in the dining hall with the new residents as darkness fell and the storm began in earnest. The wind blowing relentlessly outside the window hadn't fazed the villagers as they continued to laugh and share stories, enjoying their evening together. I spent most of the time making stuffed toys for all of the children after one of them had shown theirs off. They kept me busy, but I didn't mind, happy to use my Gift in a way that brought smiles to their faces.

I glanced around the room and watched intently as Van moved from group to group, meeting with families and receiving hugs and kisses on the cheek from the people who helped raise him. Though he had lost his parents, he had never been alone. The villagers of this kingdom and residents of the palace cared for him as if he weren't just the son of Tenebrae but as if he was their own flesh and blood.

My heart warmed as I watched him, knowing that even though so much had been taken from him at such a young age, he had these people and beautiful memories to cherish and hold on to. He was beloved.

Evander caught my eye, and with a crook of his finger, gestured for me to come to him. I finished the last stuffed toy—this time a small goose—and wandered over to the king. When I appeared at his side, he was in the middle of a story about some event I hadn't been around for. His smile grew as he took my hand in his, and I faced the group he had been talking to.

"Love, this is Peter, Judy, and little Tristan," Van explained as he introduced them. "They own one of the restaurants in the village, which happens to be my personal favorite," he added quietly.

"It's nice to meet you," I told them and was met with a slight bow.

"It's finally nice to formally meet you, Your Highness," Peter said.

"Just Ainsley, please," I interjected, and he dipped his head in acknowledgment.

"It seems that young Evander has kept you hidden from us," Judy added as Tristan clung to her leg, looking shy and nervous about being surrounded by so many people. He looked no more than six, and I was surprised he wasn't playing with the other children.

"Because I know the lies you will tell her," Van cut in, and Judy scoffed.

"Has he told you how insufferable he was as a child?" she asked me. "Always so arrogant and such a little shit." Her familiarity with the king surprised me, but it made me like her that much more.

"He hasn't, but seeing as that's exactly how he is now, it doesn't surprise me," I said, smiling at Van. Judy and Peter laughed, and even Tristan let out a small giggle though his blue eyes were firmly set on the children running past us.

"She's exactly like her mother," Judy commented, and my attention was immediately directed to her. Her expression went soft and sweet as she realized I wanted her to elaborate. "Both of your mothers," she said, gesturing between Van and me. "Were always in my restaurant growing up. From when they were toddlers until just before they passed, there wasn't a day they didn't stop by."

"It's nice to see her spirit still lives in you," Peter added, and I flushed at the compliment. Van let go of my hand and instead snaked his arm around my waist as if he knew I needed the small amount of support. Oli and Cal said I had taken after my father, but it was nice to hear that I resembled my mother in some way and that she was loved.

I glanced up to find Van staring down at me and smiling. He knew what her words had meant to me.

"So what I'm hearing is that our mothers were smart asses too?" Van said, flashing that perfect cocky grin their way.

I rolled my eyes as Judy huffed, apparently used to his arrogance. She then decided to scold him for his behavior, though I was only half listening as I watched Tristan stare after the children, still too shy to join in. I quickly crafted two stuffed wolves in my hands and bent down to meet the boy at eye level.

"Do you think you could help me with something?" I whispered, and he hesitated for a moment before nodding. I outstretched my hand showing him the two wolves—one black and one grey. "I accidentally made two of these. Would you mind giving one to that little girl for me?" I pointed to a small child around the same age as him. She had deep red hair and freckles and been sitting next to her parents all night, seeming just as shy as Tristan about joining the fun.

He eyed the little girl and then looked over the wolves in my hands as he contemplated my task. Eventually, he released his mother and took my offer. I watched as he strolled over to the girl, the wolves trembling in his tiny hands. When he made it to her, he outstretched his arms, allowing her to choose which one she wanted for herself. She looked at him curiously before her hands enclosed the small grey toy.

Fantastic choice.

My face broke into a wide smile as Tristan climbed onto the bench next to the girl. Rather than come back to his parents. I stood, happy to have helped them, and drifted my attention to the adults around me, still bickering about who was more annoying.

Apparently, Van had called Judy old and washed up, which prompted her to smack him upside the head. This led Evander to threaten her with execution and Judy to laugh in his face. I looked at Peter, and he shrugged like this was something that occurred daily.

"Ainsley," Judy began, "Did you hear of the time Evander pissed his pants?" I looked to the king to find him clenching his jaw tight, and a look of panic spread across his face.

"That was a long time ago," Evander cut in as I was about to inquire for more.

"He was seventeen," Judy added, and I burst out in laughter. Van grabbed my arm, pulling me away from the couple as I fought to stay.

"No! I want to hear!" I said, through giggles.

"Stop by the restaurant anytime, sweetheart!" Judy yelled after us, waving her hand. Van threw up his middle finger at the woman, and she laughed hard, knowing she had won their fight.

He led me through the palace as I begged him to tell me the story, though he refused at every turn. I would never let him live this down.

"You know I'm not going to stop asking," I warned as we entered a large room that I quickly realized was his bedroom. It was decorated similarly to our room back home though on a much larger scale. The bed was nearly double the size of our massive mattress, and the bathing room could fit our entire bedroom inside it.

"And you know I'm never going to tell you," he countered, shutting us in. I rolled my eyes at the truth of his words and sighed in defeat.

"Fine. I'll just have to visit Judy so I can find out."

"I think she'd like that," he said. "Not only to embarrass me but to get to know you. She was important to our mothers."

I thought about the two women spending their time in her restaurant, filling her days with laughter and snarky comments. What I wouldn't give to be able to see their exchange.

"I think I'd like that too," I said quietly, walking over to him.

Evander slipped his arms around my waist as I snaked mine around his neck, feeling his warmth against me. Though he seemed a world away from the darkness he was drowning in yesterday, I was still worried that it would come to the surface at any moment. He seemed to read the tension in my body and fear on my face as he tilted his head in question before bending at the knees to meet me at eye level.

"I'm okay, love. I swear."

I nodded, unable to speak. Emotion was thick in my throat, and I pushed my mind away from the memory of holding him on the shower floor as he broke. It wasn't that I didn't believe him; I was more scared that something would set him off and send him back spiraling down that path. What if I wasn't around next time?

He righted himself again, pulling me in as I buried my face in his chest, inhaling his cedar and snow scent as he held me.

"It's hard for me to see you with all of them sometimes," Evander said, and I tilted my head up to look at him questioningly. "With our people," he clarified.

"Am I doing something wrong?" I asked. I fought to free myself from his hold as I thought about every interaction I'd had with everyone since arriving.

"No," Van stated, refusing to loosen his grip around me. "You're perfect, and they love you."

My body instantly relaxed, and I breathed a sigh of relief while mentally cursing him for worrying me.

"It's just that..." he began, as he bobbed his head back and forth like he was trying to come up with how to explain his thoughts. "You should have been here with them. This should have been your life, and when I see you living it, it hurts to know how much had been taken from you."

I swallowed as I stepped away, and this time he let me. I wandered over to the bed before sitting down on the edge and looking around the space that could have been one I had grown up knowing. My fingers skated along the mattress that would have been the place I hid under while playing with Van as children.

"Oli mentioned a similar sentiment," I told him as I placed my hands in my lap and pulled at my fingers nervously.

Evander crossed the room and came to sit next to me, his features full of intrigue and hope. He took my hand and let his tattoo appear to move freely around his fingers. I called forth the ink hidden underneath my flesh and allowed it to mimic Van's. He grinned as he watched our magical tattoos bend and twist around in perfect synchronization.

"Do you think we would have gotten along?" I asked, still watching our fingers.

"When we were children? Not a fucking chance," Van scoffed, and I laughed under my breath. "We would have fought nonstop because young Evander was an absolute little shit, and you would have been too stubborn for your own good, though you still haven't grown out of that."

I nudged him with my shoulder playfully, but he was right. We would have caused nothing but destruction and a never-ending headache for our parents and those who would have had to deal with us daily. I thought about how he would have pissed me off and what I would have done to get back at him. Terrorizing each other would definitely have been our favorite pastime.

"But as we both got older, and you calmed down..." He flashed a cocky grin as I glowered at him. "There wouldn't be a force in this world that could stop us from creating what we have together now," he stated.

"And what exactly is that?"

We stared at one another for a long moment, and a look washed over his features that I couldn't place. There was a secret in his mind that I wanted to unlock and learn its truth. His eyes softened, and his lip curled in the corner, but it wasn't his usual smirk filled with arrogance. This was something wholly different—something innocent and pure.

"You're my best friend," he stated, like it was the only fact in the world that mattered.

His words sank into my chest, filling every inch of my body with that truth. I leaned into him, pressing my forehead against his as I fought the sting of tears welling in my eyes.

Evander reached up and held my face between his hands as we sat there in the silent dark, the only sound being the wind howling violently outside. I didn't know how I was supposed to feel, except I returned the feelings tenfold. There wasn't anything that could have made me doubt this bond that Van and I shared and the fact that he was truly my best friend.

With Felix, our relationship was genuine but straightforward. We had built our friendship on common ground and similarities. With Evander, we had something deeper and more profound than even I wanted to admit. It didn't feel like 'friendship' was a strong enough word for what we shared.

"I'm going to stay here tonight to make sure everyone has settled in and has what they need," he whispered. "I can bring you home to stay with Felix if you'd rather go back."

I shook my head, knowing that wasn't an option I would ever choose. If he were up against anything, I would always decide to stand beside him. I swallowed hard, shoving the possible implications of that truth back down.

"I'd rather stay here and do my job, too," I replied, knowing that wasn't the entire truth.

"Then let's get some sleep. The children will be screaming through the halls before the sun decides to rise." Evander stood and strode for a dresser. He tossed me a pair of his pants and shirt before heading into the bathing room to get ready so I could change in private.

By the time he returned, I was already tucked under the blankets and slowly drifting to sleep as I stared up at the ceiling, watching the shadows of trees bend with each thrust of the wind. I felt Van climb into bed and a hand curl around mine, clutching it tightly as we fell asleep.

46.

Evander wasn't kidding about the children. I threw a pillow over my head, whining into it as they screamed and played at an ungodly hour.

"Why?" I begged, the sound muffled beneath the fabric.

"I told you," Van said, grabbing the pillow from me and placing it over his own face.

"Get your own!" I whined, trying to rip it back from him.

The kids' voices grew louder as if standing directly outside our door. I pulled at the pillow harder, desperate to take it back as my ears filled with sounds too loud not to give me a headache.

"Craft your own!" he retorted, holding the pillow so firmly I couldn't get it to move even an inch. "Consider it a—"

"I swear to the Gods if you say 'training exercise,' the only thing I'll be crafting is a dagger to slit your throat with."

Evander dropped the pillow slightly so just his eyes were showing.

"Did you just threaten your king?" he asked, and I raised a brow in defiance. He lowered the pillow further, and I adjusted my grip, grasping more of the fabric between my fingers in anticipation of ripping it from him. "That's an offense punishable by death."

"Give. Me. My. *Pillow*," I seethed as more voices gathered in the hall, stopping outside our door. It was still dark in the room, though I was certain it wouldn't lighten much by the sound of the raging storm outside. Today would surely stay gloomy and cold as snow dumped heavily upon Tenebrae. I tugged again, but his hold held firm.

"Her Highness is in here, kids," Evander yelled, and my eyes widened as the door to our room burst open. Handfuls of children rushed into the space, jumping up and down and containing more energy than one person should ever be allowed to have. Especially this early.

"And she was just saying how much she wants to play with you all," he continued. My gaze snapped to him as my eyes widened in horror, and a wicked grin crept up his face. "Oh, and make sure to show her the music room. She hasn't seen it yet and would love nothing more than to hear you all play a song for her."

The children rushed for my side of the bed excitedly, their smiles bright and full of joy. I leaned down close to Evander's ear before they could pull me away.

"When we get home, I am going to torture you so thoroughly you will be begging me to make it stop," I whispered through a false smile. His eyes sparkled with life as they flickered to my mouth, making the long and deliberate drag back to my eyes.

"I don't doubt you'll have me begging, love," Evander whispered, giving me that annoyingly seductive voice he'd perfected, "But it won't be for you to stop."

Heat immediately rushed to my cheeks at the insinuation. Before I could comment further, the children grabbed my arm, yanking on it until I climbed out of bed and followed them to the door. I threw a pleading look at Van over my shoulder, but he simply waved and placed my pillow back over his face.

I would get him back for that.

"Do you need help, Your Highness?" a male voice called from behind as I carried a large stack of dirty dishes to the kitchens. The children kept me busy most of the morning and I only managed to slip away when the palace workers found us to announce lunch was being served.

"I think I've got it," I said at the exact moment I stumbled and nearly dropped the entirety of what was in my arms. With the number of people currently in the palace, I wanted to offer the staff as much assistance as possible when it came to cleaning up, but it turned out I was potentially doing more harm than good. Hands quickly reached out and grabbed the falling plates before they managed to shatter across the floor.

"Clearly," the man teased as I picked up my head to find him smiling at me. I blushed at my clumsiness as he took more dishes from my arms until we were carrying the same amount.

"I said '*I think,*' which left room for error," I pointed out, and he laughed, the sound filled with genuine happiness.

"My apologies for the incorrect accusation, Your Highness—"

"Ainsley," I interjected.

"Ainsley," he said. "I'm Marcas. It's nice to finally meet you."

Marcas followed along as we walked to the kitchens, quietly saying his greetings to people he passed as they addressed him. Everyone seemed to know who he was, and I felt a little embarrassed that I didn't.

"Do you live here?" I asked as we walked, but he shook his head.

"I live along the outskirts of the town of Vella," he explained. Evander and Olivier traveled to only the nearby villages, and Vella was about a day's ride away and clearly outside the radius, so I was surprised he was here. "We got a heads up about the pending storm, so we came early to stock the palace."

I glanced at him curiously, wondering what exactly he meant by that.

"My family supplies most of the wheat and grain for the kingdom. We wanted to ensure everyone would be taken care of during the storm."

"I'm sorry," I told him. "I'm still learning about how everything works."

"An apology isn't necessary, and for the record, I think you're doing a great job," Marcas said kindly. "It can't be easy to adjust to a life you hadn't grown up in and then be thrown into a role you weren't prepared for. Just know that you have the support of your people."

His words calmed my nerves and made me feel a bit better about the lack of knowledge I still possessed about Tenebrae. It was as though every time I learned more, I'd find something else I hadn't a clue about. I made a mental note to research the essential families within the kingdom and how they contributed to its success.

"Thank you," I told him, hoping the sincerity in my tone dripped through. He flashed a smile at me as he nodded and then held open the door to the kitchens. The servants rushed toward us, relieving us from the stacks of dirty dishes.

"I thought we told you to stop," one of the servants scolded as she dropped the plates into a sink filled with soapy water. "Go and relax. You've done enough."

"Oh, I was trying to, but this one over here was about to shatter all of your precious china, and I couldn't in good conscience allow that to happen, so I did the gentlemanly thing and helped," Marcas replied, giving me a wink as he spoke, and I rolled my eyes as a laugh broke through.

"My sincerest apologies, Marcas," I teased. "How can I repay you for your chivalry?"

"By helping me wash these," he replied, rolling up his sleeves as he strode for the sink.

The servant shoved in front of him in an attempt to stop him from completing the task. "Absolutely not. Go enjoy yourself. You deserve—" she tried.

"Melody, you and I both know I'm not going to walk away without doing them, so how about you save us both the time and let me help," he interrupted.

They stared each other down for a moment before she finally threw her hands up in the air and walked away, mumbling under her breath about his pigheadedness. Marcas closed the distance to the sink, grabbed a dish and cloth, and began scrubbing away.

"Are you planning on repaying the debt, or should I collect it some other way?" he called over his shoulder. I walked to the sink, stopping next to him as I rolled up my sleeves and crafted my own cloth from my shadows.

"Well, when you put it like that..." I said playfully, and Marcas laughed under his breath as we both got to work.

Though we finished our stack relatively quickly, more dishes and cooking utensils arrived, so we decided to wash them as well. Marcas spent the afternoon teaching me about what he and the other families do for the kingdom and who I should introduce myself to. He asked how my training was coming along and was quick to offer his assistance if I needed additional aid, especially when it came to navigating the political side of things.

By the time we had finished the last plate, the sun was already beginning to set, and my stomach growled in hunger after realizing we had skipped lunch and were late for dinner. As if my thoughts had summoned her, Melody appeared with two plates full of food.

"Will you at least eat now?" she implored, like the fact that we hadn't taken a break had physically pained her.

"If it will make you happy, then absolutely," Marcas replied, and Melody breathed a long sigh of relief as she set the food down on the large wooden island. I followed Marcas over, sitting beside him, and we both dove into our dinner.

I shoveled the food down my throat as I realized just how hungry I was and glanced up from a full mouth to find Marcas watching me with intrigue.

"What?" I struggled to say.

"Just wondering if I'm okay to eat too, or if you're going to try and take mine when you're finished," he said, placing a small bite of fish into his mouth. I shoved him as I swallowed, and he chuckled.

"Definitely the latter, so I suggest you hurry up," I replied, taking another full bite as I eyed his food.

Marcas scooted himself and his plate a little farther away as he winked, and I flashed him a devious smile. When we were halfway through our meal, Melody returned with a giant chocolate cake and placed it in front of us.

"For all your help today," she said before leaving us alone again.

Marcas and I picked over the dessert as we continued our conversation from earlier in the afternoon. This time, I did most of the talking, sharing with him my struggles in areas of my magic. My shadow and Empathi Gifts flowed effortlessly from me, but I found illusions to be a bit harder to navigate. I was determined to solidify them in the way I had seen Evander do, but the closest I had ever gotten was during that sex-dream-turned-illusion.

"What is the largest area you struggle with?" Marcas asked. "Is it invading the mind or keeping the vision molded?"

"Keeping it molded. I can only contain it for an hour at most before it begins to flicker and disappear." I told him. He straightened a bit as his hand rubbed the back of his neck like he was nervous. "Is that bad? It's bad, isn't it? Fuck. I thought I was progressing, but—"

"Ainsley, I'm Gifted with more magic than most, and I can only hold an illusion steady on my own for maybe ten minutes," he interrupted. "But you holding it for an hour... You should be proud."

I was filled with a sense of pride and astonishment at my own Gift. Here I had thought I was failing miserably, not living up to what I could be, and I was already surpassing those who had spent years perfecting their craft.

"It seems you may not need my help after all," he stated, and for some reason, I felt guilty about that. Marcas had been kind and willing to aid me all day, and now I was beginning to feel like I had given him the impression that he was useless.

"Can I see you do one?" I asked.

He grinned at my interest and held up an open palm. I watched as a beautiful carnation bloomed out of nothing. The petals were a vibrant and bright shade of red, full and bursting to life. I leaned forward and inhaled, smelling the sweet and airy scent of the flower as if it were really in front of me.

My fingers automatically reached out as if to pluck it from his hold but felt nothing but air as they passed through the illusion. Evander was the only one I knew of who was so strong and skilled in his magic that he could make any illusion become solid to its victim, so I wasn't surprised when Marcas wasn't able to do the same.

"It's incredibly detailed," I breathed as my fingers outlined the petals, though I knew I was only touching his hand. "Mine never look like this."

"It just takes practice. Pick an object and study it daily until you can see it flawlessly, even with your eyes closed," he instructed. "Do that every day until you perfect that item. Then pick something else and do it again."

His advice made sense. I had spent so much time focusing on expelling the magic instead of what I was trying to cast within a mind. No wonder I couldn't hold it as long as I wanted.

"He has a point," a voice called, and I looked up to find Evander watching us from the doorway. His eyes glanced over to where I was still tracing the red petals of the illusion in Marcas' hand before meeting my stare again. "You spend too much time focusing on the act itself rather than what you are trying to construct," he continued as he made his way for us, stopping across the table. I withdrew from Marcas, feeling the need to distance myself from him for some reason.

"Illusions take time to master, but with how long you can hold one, I'm sure you'll have no problem honing the skill now that you've learned how to improve on it," Marcas stated as he closed his palm, and the flower disappeared, freeing my mind.

"I hope that's the case," I murmured as I was snared in Evander's piercing grey gaze. He swallowed as he looked between Marcas and me, and I was sure he was noting the lack of distance between us.

"I have no doubt that it will be," Marcas responded, offering me a warm smile of encouragement that I returned. Evander shifted uncomfortably. He looked back toward the exit and then again at me before dropping his stare to the bench.

"I came to let you know it was time to head back to the house," Van began as his finger traced the wood grain pattern before him. "But, if you'd rather stay again, that would be alright too."

I watched Van's chest rise and fall slowly. To anyone else, it would look like he was simply just breathing, but I knew him. He was putting on a mask, and I wasn't sure exactly why. I wondered if something had happened while I had been in the kitchen all day, and he couldn't openly tell me with Marcas here. I twisted to face my new friend, who had such a look of hope flooding his features that it almost made me want to say yes.

Almost.

"We can head home," I said, standing from the bench. Marcas' expression faltered just a little, and I felt the need to explain myself since he was so thoughtful and kind today.

"Are you sure?" Evander asked, seeming not to believe it was what I truly wanted. I had thoroughly enjoyed my time with Marcas today, and it was nice to be with someone who treated me as a friend and not a princess, but I wasn't lying when I expressed my desire to go home.

"I want to check on Felix for myself, and I miss Nova," I explained as I reached for my plate to clean, but Marcas had beaten me to it, snatching it from the bench before I could.

"I've got this. Go and make sure your friend is alright," he said, and I opened my mouth to protest, but he cut me off. "Plus, I like knowing I have a debt over you." He winked, and I rolled my eyes as I shoved him away from me. He laughed as he bowed his head to Evander and walked over to the sink to take care of our mess.

"Thank you for today, Marcas," I called as I strode over to Van and grabbed his arm, ready to be traversed back to our house.

"Any time, Ainsley," he said thoughtfully before we left the room and I was pulled away into swirling shadows.

47.

We appeared in the study to find Olivier at the desk and Felix lounging on the couch as he chatted with Lia. I opened my mouth to ask Evander if anything had happened, but before I could, he pulled away and walked over to Oli without uttering a word. What was going on?

"I missed you, buttercup," Felix said as I climbed onto the couch and rested my head against his shoulder, unable to shake my weird feeling as I watched Van interact with his friend. "You missed quite the party last night. Cal had to go streaking in the blizzard because he lost at cards."

"I didn't lose; you cheated," Calidore growled as he strode into the room, holding four wine bottles in his arms.

"As someone who has played countless games with you, I'm going to have to side with Cal on this one," I said, reaching out my hand for the wine, knowing that if I chose to come to his defense, he'd give me a bottle. Cal smiled victoriously as he shoved the alcohol into my waiting palm.

"Do you want some, Van?" I asked loudly, but he didn't glance up. What the actual fuck. I uncorked the bottle with my teeth, then tilted it back and drank deeply before passing it to Felix.

"You too?" he noted, following my stare to the men at the desk.

"Oli ignoring your existence as well?" I asked, curious as to what I missed out on last night.

"The opposite, actually," Lia chimed. "They got into a huge argument because Oli has been going all over-bearing asshole when it comes to Felix's recovery."

"He won't even let me take a piss on my own," Felix added, "He literally stood outside the door, shouting at me to hurry up."

"So you went slower, right?" I asked.

"Obviously. And to punish me for it, he wrapped me in shadows so tight that I couldn't move and then carried me to bed," Felix explained. "I mean, it would have been pretty fucking hot if he wasn't so infuriating."

I stifled a laugh as I pictured the scene playing out and took another long chug from the bottle. It wasn't doing what I wanted fast enough.

"Cal," I said, rising to my feet. "Take me to the good liquor."

Calidore jumped up, ready and willing to comply, as he linked his arm through mine and guided us to the cellar. Last night, I felt so close to Evander. I thought our relationship had been on a steady path of profound trust and deep understanding and now here I was, confused and getting drunk.

I groaned in irritation as I plucked a random bottle from the shelf and blew off the dust. The dark amber liquid swirled inside as I pulled out the cork and took a swig before handing it to Cal. The alcohol burned like fire on its way down, searing my stomach as it settled, but I didn't care.

"Want to tell me what's going on?" Calidore asked, looking at me skeptically as he sipped the liquor.

"Van's being a dick. What else?"

"Well, yeah, I gathered that much," he commented, handing the bottle back to me as he grabbed my hand and led me the long way back to the study. I drank again, needing the alcohol to do its job and quickly. I didn't want to face the truth of how much Evander's rejection was hurting me.

"I just don't understand him sometimes," I explained as we walked the dark corridors. "Whenever I think we make progress and I don't want to kill him, he does something that pisses me off—like ignore me for no reason—and then I'm back to wanting to bash his skull in." Cal snorted as he listened. "Last night, there was this unspoken peace between us, and then today, when he came into the kitchen where Marcas and I were talking—"

"Wheat Man?" Cal inquired.

"What?"

"Marcas. The one who provides the wheat and grain," he explained, and I nodded. "I love that guy. He offered to help me make my own ale once—taught me how to do it and everything. I didn't realize he was there. I should stop by."

Okay, even Calidore liked him, so my talking to Marcas couldn't have been the issue.

"Yeah, he was great. He was trying to show me how to improve my illusions, and Evander came in and was all weird. Do they not like each other?"

"Nah, Marcas is a great guy and has contributed a lot to Tenebrae over the years. There isn't a reason not to like him, and even though Van can be a huge prick, he wouldn't overlook all the good Marcas and his family have done."

"So what the hell is his problem?"

"Did he say anything when he interrupted you?" Cal asked.

"Just that it was time to go home," I responded. "He even offered to stay another night at the palace if I wasn't ready to leave."

Calidore bobbed his head back and forth as he contemplated what could have caused Evander to become so withdrawn from me. We stopped outside the study door, and I took one last swig of the liquor as I prepared to go back inside.

"You know you could always just ask him," Cal offered, and I rolled my eyes.

"That would involve him speaking to me, which he doesn't seem to want to do right now."

I thought about how quickly he moved away from me and how he couldn't even look me in the eyes when I spoke. My heart tightened, and I worked harder to shove those intruding feelings down.

"You saw how he acted, right? I'm not just overreacting?" I asked him, hoping that I was blowing this whole thing out of proportion. Calidore offered me a sympathetic smile, letting me know I wasn't.

I groaned, pushing open the door to the study and stepping through a silencing shield I hadn't seen put up as I was enveloped in the screaming match between Felix and Olivier.

Fucking Gods.

"Because you're too fucking stubborn for your own good!" Olivier yelled, pointing a finger at Felix's chest. My friend stood with his arm around Lia for support, and I saw him still babying his injury. I had seen Felix over-exaggerate his wounds while sparring with Dash, but this wasn't that. I could tell he truly was still in pain.

"Well then, it's a good thing my Medicus said as long as I take it easy, I'm fine to do things on my own!" Felix shot back, gesturing to Lia at his side.

"Oli," Lia tried, but Olivier shot her a death glare that said to back off. She closed her lips and sighed as if this was just another night for them. I supposed it had been lately.

"But you're clearly not taking it easy! You still can't fucking walk, so you obviously need more rest. So sit the fuck back down, or I'll carry you up to your room. Your fucking choice, but you're not walking on your own." Oli said between clenched teeth, his chest heaving with fury.

"Why the hell do you even care, Olivier?! The last time I checked, you made it evident that you hated me and wanted me out of this kingdom."

Olivier balled his hands into fists at his side, and his face twisted with a medley of rage and pain. He had said time and again how much he wished Felix wasn't here, and though we all knew it was complete bullshit, I was willing to bet that Olivier had only recently realized it. Or at least come to accept it.

"Your injury makes you a liability. You'll put everyone else at risk if it doesn't heal properly. One of us will get hurt or killed trying to save you, and I can't have that," Oli said after a moment.

They stared at one another for a long minute and everyone in the room went silent at the exchange. Finally, Felix nodded to himself, seeming to accept Olivier's blatant lie.

"Fine, Olivier," Felix breathed. "You win; I'm done."

My friend turned to face me, his face full of sorrow, and I knew instantly what he was about to do. Before I could protest, he broke our stare and brought his gaze to Evander's.

"If Lia deems me well enough to travel, will you grant me passage to Agnitio?"

I closed my eyes as they pricked with tears. I wanted to beg him to reconsider, but I knew that would be selfish. Felix had struggled to find his place in this kingdom and had been hurting over Olivier's constant rejection of him. And now, to make matters worse, Oli told him that he only cares about his health because it makes him a liability.

Out of the corner of my eye, I could see Olivier stiffen and stumble back a step as if he had been struck with a physical blow. But he was still too proud to admit his lie and would allow my best friend's heart to continue breaking. Evander looked to Lia, and she nodded without him having to ask. I sucked in a shaky breath as I tried to cope with losing a member of my family.

"After the storm passes, I'll bring you there myself," Evander announced, and Felix bowed before turning around and letting Lia escort him away.

"This is bullshit," Olivier said, stepping in front of their path to prevent them from leaving. "He's obviously not well enough to travel, Van."

Felix leaned in until only a few inches separated the men. "Move," he growled. But Oli held firm.

"It's my responsibility to—"

"Then it's a good thing that I'm no longer your fucking responsibility, Olivier," Felix snarled. I had never heard him so furious and full of pain. I stormed over to them, determined not to let my friend deal with any more of this.

"You made your feelings on the matter crystal clear, Oli. You didn't want to put up with Felix from the start, and now you won't ever have to, so get out of the way and let them pass." I said, and Oli's eyes snapped to mine. They were dark and feral, and there was a challenge in them that I had never seen before. "That wasn't a request. It was a command."

Olivier held my gaze for a moment longer before turning on his heel and storming out of the room.

"I'm sorry, buttercup," Felix said. I grabbed his face between my hands.

"No," I told him. "Don't you ever apologize for protecting yourself and your heart. You don't deserve this."

His eyes misted over as he leaned in, wrapping his arms around me and squeezing tight.

"I'll miss you," he whispered.

"I just want you to be happy, and if you can't find that here, I want you to go somewhere where you have that chance. Maybe I'll even join you there one day,"

I teased, and out of the corner of my eye, I could see Evander shift and tense at the declaration.

"Maybe," he said, kissing my cheek before leaving the room with Lia.

Tonight was turning out to be one of the shittiest nights I had since arriving in Tenebrae. My best friend was leaving and the man who meant far more than he should have, was ignoring me for some Gods forsaken reason. I was slightly buzzed and pissed off. I needed to take my rage out and there was one person I was about to do that to.

I stormed through the house, heading for the back door and into the training ring. The snow was so thick I could barely see in front of me, but I knew he was there.

"Are you fucking kidding me?!" I yelled though the whistling wind drowned out my voice. It was freezing out here and I wasn't dressed appropriately, but the alcohol coursing through my veins gave me the illusion of warmth.

"What do you want me to say, Ainsley?" Olivier called back as he stepped closer, his silhouette now somewhat visible in the darkness. I slogged through the thick snow that was up to my knees as I closed the distance between us.

"I want you to stop being an asshole! Felix is leaving because of you."

"He's leaving because he's too stubborn and refuses to admit that I'm right. He pushes my buttons on purpose and can't deal with the outcome," Oli yelled, now inches from me.

I shook from the cold, and each snowflake that pelted my skin burned like fire, but I couldn't retreat to the warmth and safety of the house. Not yet, at least.

"No, he's leaving because you can't fucking admit how you truly feel about him. You're too afraid to acknowledge it, so you take it out on the man who has done nothing but try with you."

Olivier shook his head, refusing to accept what we all could see plain as day. I wasn't sure if it was because he hated himself for falling for someone he once considered an enemy or if he was just as broken as Felix and didn't believe he deserved love.

"Go ahead and deny it all you want, Olivier, but you're only hurting yourself. You've successfully pushed him away," I told him, not hiding the fierce bite in my tone.

He scrubbed his hands over his face, and shadows curled around his dark skin as he paced back and forth in a fury. He was struggling, which was evident, but I had difficulty feeling pity for him. That is until he stopped before me, and I saw the look in his eyes. The same look I had seen so many times as I peered into my reflection.

Undiluted fear and panic.

I had been in the same position as him—hell, I still was. No matter how much I wanted to, I was too afraid to offer my heart to anyone. Had Olivier been hurt similarly? Did he know from experience just how gut-wrenching love could truly be? I took a deep breath as I looked into his bright turquoise eyes. Part of me wanted to tell him to run and never look back—that love wasn't worth it. But then I thought of Felix and how much he craved finding the person he could call his. He would never do to Oli what Dashiell had done to me. He would cherish and respect this man until he took his last breath. Felix coveted love more than any treasure in the realm, and he would never do anything to jeopardize it now that he had been given a chance. For the first time, he was free to love who he wanted.

"Felix is going to leave, Oli, and I'm not going to try and change his mind; I love him too much to watch his heart break over and over again as he pines for you," I told him softly, not wanting to hurt him but knowing he needed to hear the truth. "If you want him—if you want the possibility of creating something with him—then only you can make him stay."

I backed away and headed into the house, leaving Olivier to contemplate his choice as the winter storm raged around him.

48.

I thought about returning to the study to retrieve the liquor bottle now that my aggression and the cold snow had sobered me up a bit, but I figured my best bet would be to call it a night and head to bed instead. Evander was leaving the bathing room right as I entered, with nothing but a towel around his waist. I made to keep my gaze focused straight ahead on my dresser and not at the godlike body that was on display for me.

"Did you talk any sense into him?" Evander asked, and I slammed the dresser drawer shut loudly.

"Oh, you're speaking to me now?" I demanded, stripping out of my pants and shirt—now wet from the melted snow—and into one of my satin nightgowns. I had no idea the last time I wore something of my own to bed, and the fabric felt foreign against my skin.

Evander's eyes raked over me, most likely realizing the same thing before he strode for his dresser and pulled out a black shirt.

"Change," he commanded, tossing the shirt to me. I caught it, balled it up, and threw it back at him as hard as I could.

"No." His eyes went wide, and his body tensed with irritation.

"Ainsley," he growled.

"Evander," I mocked in the same tone.

He took a slow and deliberate step closer like I was a prey he was hunting. I stepped back to create more space between us, and my gaze flickered to the exit he was now blocking. Shit.

"Put. It. On. Now," he demanded, each word clipped and forceful—a king's command.

"Go. Fuck. Yourself," I mimicked back.

Evander lunged, and I sprinted away, narrowly missing his grasp. I leaped onto the bed, trying desperately to make my way across, but strong hands grabbed my ankles. I fell forward, my chest and face hitting the mattress hard as Evander took control. He spun me onto my back and straddled me, pinning me beneath him as he struggled to slip the nightgown from my body.

"Fuck off!" I yelled, thrashing uncontrollably beneath him.

"I will when you stop being a stubborn ass!" he snapped back.

I reached up, slamming my fist into his cheek and causing him to swear. Taking advantage of his distraction, I attempted to squirm away, but Evander grabbed my wrists and pinned them to my side. He crafted a dagger from his shadows and then slit my nightgown down the middle until it fell completely open, revealing my bra and underwear.

"I liked this one!" I snarled.

"I'll buy you another," Evander bit back as he ripped the remaining scraps of fabric from my body and tried to shove the black shirt over my head.

I twisted and turned underneath him, but with his weight pressed into me, there was no way I could get free. He reached for one hand and guided it through the armhole as easily as if I weren't trying to punch him the moment he unpinned it. After both arms and my head were through, he leaned back, freeing the upper half of my body. My hands instantly flew to the hem of my shirt as I began to lift it.

"Take it off, and I'll just do it again," he promised, and his eyes were alive with the challenge. I huffed out a loud sigh of irritation as I crossed my arms over my chest and stared him down. "Care to tell me what the hell your problem is now?"

"I should be asking you the same. You just attacked me and forced me to wear this stupid shirt."

"No, I forced you to realize that you're being a brat," he countered, and my shadows slipped from my hands as rage coursed through me. The alcohol had entirely worn off now, and I was left feeling frustrated. Mostly because I knew he was right.

"You started acting weird the moment you came to retrieve me tonight, and then as soon as we got home, you did nothing but ignore me," I told him. Evander tilted his head to the side as he studied me.

"I wasn't ignoring you, Ainsley. Something was bothering me, and I needed a moment to get my head straight," he argued back, though his tone wasn't as harsh as earlier.

"Next time, tell me that!" I yelled, sitting up the best I could, though his position over the lower half of my body made it difficult.

"Next time, ask," he replied as he leaned forward, our faces now inches from each other. "Instead of getting drunk and throwing a fit."

I fucking hated when he was right.

"Fine," I ground out.

"Fine," he replied, pushing us forward until my head hit the pillow, and he was lying on top of me. "Are we good now?"

I thought about that for a moment. I had demanded honesty and openness from Van but was quick to deny him the same. What had changed to make me become so self-conscious with him?

"Yes, but I'm still mad at you," I whispered. "I really did like that nightgown."

Evander grinned as he looked down at me.

"You like my shirt better," he argued before flicking the tip of my nose up with his. I groaned and pushed him away. He chuckled under his breath before forcing himself to a sitting position with his back resting against the headboard. "Are you okay?"

I sat up as well, knowing exactly what he was asking, but I wasn't sure how to feel. "I want the best for Felix. If that isn't here, then I don't want to force him to stay for me," I answered. Evander nodded like he understood what I meant.

"Did you mean what you said to him? That maybe one day you'd join him?" he asked quietly, and I looked over to find him pulling at his fingers nervously.

"I don't know," I answered honestly. "Once upon a time, I never thought I would leave Caelum, and now look at me. I don't know what my future holds, but I do know that I don't *want* to leave Tenebrae."

I also didn't want to leave him, but I couldn't admit that right now. Evander loosed a sigh though it didn't contain any irritation or anger. It was more like contentment and acceptance of my response. He would never try and guilt me into staying if he knew that wasn't what I wanted.

"Do you want to play a game?" I asked, climbing off the mattress and going over to the liquor cart at the end of the room. I grabbed a full bottle of wine and a deck of cards before returning to bed. "Unless you're too afraid to lose, that is."

"Deal them," Evander responded without a thought as he let his competitive nature and need to win take over.

"Are you fucking kidding me?!" Van yelled as I laid down my winning hand—for the fifth time in a row. "You're cheating. There's no way anyone is that lucky."

"I don't need to cheat against someone who sucks. Now drink," I said, handing him the rest of the bottle. Evander groaned but drained the contents.

I had played countless times with Felix and developed a strategy I wouldn't be outmatched on. Like with everything else, Van was cocky and too sure of himself; his strategy at cards was no different. Felix had taught me that when it came to bluffing games you played your opponent, not the hand. Evander was finding that out the hard way.

"We're out of wine," he said, looking past me and over to the cart. We had already finished three bottles, and I had no desire to crack open the ones containing the hard liquor.

"How about we change the stakes then?" I suggested, and Van arched a brow in questionable intrigue. "We'll place bets instead. If I win, you tell me the story about the time you pissed yourself."

"Not happening," he replied. Even though I knew that would be his response, it was worth a try.

"Fine. If I win, you sleep on the floor, and I get the bed to myself tonight."

"And if I win?" he asked.

"Then *you* get the bed to yourself, and *I'll* sleep on the floor."

Evander shook his head, the terms not good enough for him. "Let's not pretend that I don't enjoy you in my bed, love," he said, gathering the cards from the floor and shuffling.

"What do you want, then?" I asked, and he shrugged.

"This was your idea, so you choose the stakes. But make sure it's worth it for me," Van said as he winked.

I rolled my eyes as I straightened, looking around the room like I could pluck suitable terms right out of the air. There never was a question that I refused to tell him—never a story he seemed interested in knowing. Anything he wanted me to share with him about myself, I did. But there was one thing I knew he wanted that I had refused to offer.

"If you win, I'll give you a kiss," I told him, and his eyes widened just a fraction. He bobbed his head back and forth, making a show of considering the offer though we both knew his stance.

"So if you win, you get the bed to yourself, and if I win, you get to kiss me. It sounds like you win either way, love," he replied cockily.

"If you dislike the terms, I'll pick something else for you."

"I didn't say that," he interrupted. "I accept."

He extended his hand for me to take, and I did, shaking once before letting go and attempting to snatch the cards from him. Evander withdrew quickly, keeping the cards out of reach as he shook his head. "I'm deciding this final game."

"That's fine," I told him. "You'll still lose."

"Do you need another pillow, or are you okay?" I asked from the large bed.

"I'm fine," Evander growled from the floor. I stifled my laugh as I got more comfortable, finally having a bed to myself for the first time in a month.

The last game wasn't even close, and I defeated him within five minutes of the first hand. Because I'm generous, I decided to make it best two out of three. And when I won those, I changed it to three out of five.

Evander didn't win a single hand.

After half an hour had passed, I stretched my legs out and rolled from side to side, unable to get comfortable. The room was quiet and dark, with nothing but the sound of snowflakes pelting the window softly. I closed my eyes and tried to relax my mind for the third time since crawling into bed over an hour ago. Evander had gone quiet, emitting no more sounds of him getting situated on the floor.

"I didn't like seeing you with him," Evander said into the dark, and my heart stopped at the sound of his voice. Not because he startled me but at what he said.

"With Marcas?" I asked, but he didn't respond. After a minute, I tried again. "It wasn't like that."

"I know it wasn't," he whispered. "But that doesn't mean it couldn't have been or won't be in the future."

"I can't," I said, hoping he would understand.

"I know, love. I know you can't right now, and it may be a long time before you decide you're ready, if ever. But someday you might be, and that was what I realized after seeing you together tonight," Evander explained. "Marcas is a good man. He cares about Tenebrae and our people and would treat you respectfully. He's the type of person you deserve to have when you're ready. If you ever are," he finished.

I went quiet, unsure of how to respond. I didn't want to picture myself with Marcas or anyone else, for that matter. I had sworn to guard my heart—not allowing anyone to get that close again. The last time I had done it, it nearly broke me, and I refused to do it again, no matter how much I may have wanted to lately.

"I can't sleep," I finally said, changing the subject entirely.

"Why not?"

"The bed feels too empty," I admitted. I couldn't find peace or comfort without him next to me, and I hated what that could have meant. "Will you come back up here?"

Before I could finish the last word, Evander appeared beside me as a puff of swirling shadows dissipated around him.

"Walking was too much?" I teased.

"No, but this was a much more impactful entrance." I shoved him, but he pulled me close, wrapping me in his arms as I buried my face against him.

"I'm sorry about earlier," I admitted. "I should have come to you instead of being childish. It triggered my insecurities and I acted without thinking."

"I didn't mean to make you feel that way, love," Evander said, constricting his arms around me.

"I know you didn't." I inhaled deeply, letting his comforting scent envelop me. His fingers skated along my spine, and I shivered at his familiar touch. "Was seeing Marcas and me together the reason you were upset tonight?" I asked, tilting my face up to look at him. His eyes found mine, and there was a slight edge of hesitation and embarrassment swirling within.

Evander nodded.

"You were different with him," he explained, and I narrowed my eyes in question.

The exchange hadn't felt much different. Maybe slightly less formal than how I was with the other villagers, but that was because they refused to treat me as something other than their heir.

"It seemed like maybe something could develop there," he added.

"I didn't think you cared all that much," I told him, pushing a strand of hair back from his forehead. "You've made it clear that I could bring someone home if I wanted to."

Evander broke my stare and looked past me as his eyes darted around, as if trying to find his reasoning. His throat bobbed, and his face scrunched as he worked through his thoughts. Finally, he brought his gaze back to me.

"I'm not going to say that I enjoyed watching you with other people each night, but I knew that you were doing what you felt you had to in order to heal and claim a piece of yourself back. I respected, understood, and supported that that was what you felt was the best choice for you. And I still do. If you decided to go to the tavern tonight and take someone to your bed, I wouldn't attempt to stop you, Ainsley. I wouldn't want to picture it, but I wouldn't deny you that choice.

"You and I flirt and tease and taunt one another, but I know that's all it is between us. Even in the times that felt more intimate, I could feel the wall you had put up with me. You focused solely on the physical release of it and refused to allow anything else to slip through, and I understand that's all it will ever be with us. If that's all you want and need, I will be that for you," Evander continued, and my mouth dried out.

I hadn't been aware that he could feel the guard I had within myself, especially at those moments. Did he just know me that well, or were my Empathi Gifts pushing themselves onto him when I'd been too distracted by my lust and desire? Why did his observation of our relationship make me feel sick?

"But with Marcas, it wasn't about the physicality," he added. "I came to find you earlier in the day while you both were washing dishes. You were laughing, and your smile was so fucking bright as you joked with him that my stomach knotted, and I left. I felt like I was intruding on you both and didn't know what to do."

My chest ached as I pictured Van's face as he watched us. It bothered me that even an innocent interaction with someone I had just met had upset him in such a way.

"I spent the rest of the day trying to talk sense into myself. I want to see you laugh and smile. I want to see you just as happy as you were today, even if the source of that happiness isn't me. I just had to remind myself of that," Evander explained.

I inched myself closer to him, pressing my chest firmly to his as I combed through the hair on the back of his head with my fingers. The idea of me doing this with anyone else sent bile down my throat. Evander had said that things were solely about the physical when it came to us, but it didn't always feel that way for me. I had tried to convince myself that was all it was—just two people attracted to one other and in close proximity, but it wasn't just that. I cared for him in a way I didn't think I would be able to again. And though I refused to let myself go over that edge, I couldn't deny how close I was.

"When I came to get you tonight, and you were touching him—"

"He was just showing me an illusion," I interrupted. I couldn't bear for him to think the interaction was more than that.

"I know he was, Ainsley. Trust me, I know what was happening, but it doesn't change how it felt. The fact of the matter is that I was jealous. I didn't like it, and I know I had no right to feel that way. I know our time together, this arrangement—all of it—won't last forever. There will be a time you'll be healed enough to move on, and you won't be in my bed any longer. You're not mine in that way."

"Van, what you and I have—"

"Is more than all that; I know," he interrupted. "I know the friendship and trust that we've built is strong, Ainsley. I know I can trust you with my life, and you can do the same with me, but I'm also aware that's all this is. I may flirt with you incessantly, and I don't hide my desire, but I'm not an idiot. I know what you want from this. You've made it clear, and I'm just struggling to reel myself back in from hoping that..." Evander stopped, not wanting to finish his thought, and glanced away. I removed my hand from his hair and gripped his chin, forcing him to look me in the eyes.

"That what, Evander?" I asked.

We were already knee-deep in this conversation and needed to lay everything on the table. I needed to know what he truly felt, and he needed to know where I stood.

Wherever the hell that was.

"That things may change," he admitted. "But every time I think that's a possibility, I'm reminded that it isn't. You have a wall up with me, and I get it. But you didn't with him tonight, and I just couldn't deal with that. At least not right away. I needed to distance myself—not from you—but from my thoughts. That's why I was so quiet. You can read me like a fucking book, and I didn't want you to see me fracture over something I've always known wasn't a possibility."

I released his jaw and slid my hand over his cheek. Van melted into the touch as he held my gaze, and for a moment, he wasn't the Dark King of Tenebrae. He wasn't the arrogant, confident man that was always so sure of himself. He was innocent and pure and desperate for the feelings I had tried so hard to push away.

I swallowed deeply as I let his words course through me, wrapping around my heart and filling my soul in a way I had sworn never to do. Brick by brick, my fortress was falling, and I clawed and rushed, trying to keep it together, but the effort was becoming useless. I was teetering over the edge, primed to fall into his waiting arms. And what was most terrifying was that I wasn't afraid of the descent, but rather how much I wanted to dive head first into it.

"I have a wall up with you because I've given you too much of myself," I whispered. "It isn't because I don't think you worthy or an option, Evander. It's because you're the only one with my friendship and trust. The only person I would allow to hold me and touch me the way you are right now. The only one I can tell my secrets to. I gave you what I swore never to give anyone else. You have the power to hurt me, Van. That is why I'm keeping you out."

Evander's brows furrowed, and I could feel his chest beat rapidly against mine.

"But I'm trying, Van," I admitted. "I don't want Marcas."

I should have pushed him away and enforced the distance I knew I needed, but I couldn't. With each press of his body against mine and stroke of his fingers along my back, I felt myself loosening. The walls that separated us from crossing a line were starting to crumble, and I couldn't keep up with my own demand to reinforce them. So instead of pulling away and clearing my head, I did the opposite.

I took a deep breath before tilting my head and pressing my lips to his right cheek and then his left. It was barely more than a whisper of a kiss, but he stilled as if he had stopped breathing completely, too afraid to move. His skin was hot against my lips, and his proximity had my heart thundering in my ears. Desire and panic mixed as I breathed in his scent before pulling away.

I worked to school my features into one of neutrality, not wanting him to see his effect on me from something as innocent as a kiss on the cheek. A kiss that *I* initiated. I wondered what it would be like to feel his mouth against mine. To feel his tongue sliding along my own. No. No, I couldn't let my thoughts go there. I counted to five, giving my mind time to clear, though I knew no amount would be enough.

"A consolation prize for losing earlier," I said, answering his unasked question. We both knew it was a lie—just an excuse to give myself for why I did it. But he would never pressure me to tell the truth. "Don't read into it." He nodded, and a sly smirk appeared across his face, causing my lips to twitch in response. "I was feeling generous... even though you threw a fit like a small child when you lost."

"That was not a temper tantrum. That was me questioning the validity of the games you chose," he defended himself, pointing his index finger at me. I leaned forward, clamping my teeth together inches away from his finger as if I would bite it clean off his hand if he moved any closer. He tapped my nose and quickly withdrew before I could make good on my nonverbal promise. "It's not my fault you pick terrible games."

"You only found them terrible because you lost every single time."

"I only 'lost' every time *because* they were terrible," he countered. "If we played a game of *my* choosing, the outcome would have vastly differed."

"You chose the last game!" I exclaimed. Evander rolled his eyes and waved a hand as if swatting the words from the open air between us would make them any less truthful.

"And you probably cheated at that one too," he said under his breath, almost too quiet for me to hear. Almost.

"I did not cheat!" I yelled, smacking him on his chest. He sat up and rested his back against the headboard as he rubbed the spot I had hit.

"There is no possible way that you won every time. Mathematically it doesn't make sense. Do you know what does make sense? *You* cheating," he claimed, crossing his arms over his chest. My mouth dropped open at the accusation.

"You are such a sore loser."

"I am not," he said stubbornly, refusing to meet my glare. Gods help me; even his temper tantrums were adorable. I bit my lip, but it did nothing to suppress the wide grin on my face.

"You are as stubborn as a child," I said through laughter, and Evander's eyes shot to mine, a small smile forming on his face. He shook his head, but I nodded vehemently, refusing to allow him an inch in this argument. "You may actually be *worse* than a child." He threw his head back and laughed.

"I just don't understand how you won every game. Even the one of chance," he explained. "I tried *so* hard. Like so fucking hard."

"I know," I told him, patting his hand placatingly. "I know you did."

"You're mocking me."

"I would never," I said mockingly, a sweet smile across my face. He ripped his hand from mine and groaned up at the ceiling. I watched Van pout for another moment before I slid out of bed and walked over to the fireplace.

"What are you doing?" Evander asked as I lit a match and tossed it in.

"I know it's the middle of the night, but I'm not tired," I said, sitting on the hearth as the flames grew larger and began sorting through the stack of books we had piled on the chair nearby.

The sound of a light puff caught my attention, and I looked up to find Evander had disappeared from the room. Apparently, moving without using his magic had become too much of a chore for him lately. A few minutes later, our door opened, and Van appeared, pushing a small cart stacked with food and drinks.

"I'm not tired either," he said, wheeling it over before plopping down on the hearth to face me. He handed me a cup of coffee as he grabbed my legs and placed them over his lap. He then slid wool socks over my feet—taking care of me as usual.

"I want to know more about you," I said as he sat back down. "And I don't mean the stuff you've already shared with me. I want to know the things I would have known if I was never taken."

Evander's face softened as he looked at me, and I could tell that he very much wanted to discuss this.

"I'll tell you everything, only if you do the same," he said.

We talked for hours, sharing stories and laughing as we drank and ate. We had discussed just about every aspect of his life and I even told him about the times

I had spent with Dashiell and Felix. The irony was that the more I talked about Dashiell, the less it hurt. The stories began to feel distant and old like memories of another life lived long ago. The sting was still present—a feeling I wasn't sure would ever entirely leave—but it wasn't heart-wrenching the way it had once been. Evander listened intently, asking questions but never pushing.

My stomach hurt from the laughter, and my eyes burned with tears. We had never spent this much time together simply enjoying ourselves. When the fire died, Van led us to the large window bench so we could continue under the light of the full moon. He propped himself up and pulled me between his legs so my back rested against his chest. Van draped a thick fur blanket over us as we watched the snow fall heavily, blanketing the world below.

Evander's nose grazed my ear, and he inhaled deeply as his arms tightened their hold. I sighed in contentment as the moonlight reflected on the chain around my neck and Van's matching bracelet. I interlaced our fingers beneath the blanket, hating how much I loved when he held me like this. It was dangerous to feel this wanted.

"Did you just smell me?" I teased, and Evander pressed a kiss just below my ear.

"Yup," he admitted shamelessly, and a grin spread across my face as I rested my head against his shoulder. I closed my eyes, content, happy, and wondering how Evander could have ever thought I had a fraction of this with Marcas.

49.

I awoke sprawled out on the window bench and under a plethora of blankets. So many, in fact, that sweat beaded above my brow. I kicked off the furs and stretched, catching the eye of Evander standing near my feet with two mugs of steaming coffee in his grasp.

I sat up at once and immediately reached my hands out like a child, begging for him to give me what I wanted. We had been up most of the night, so I wasn't sure how much sleep I had actually gotten. Van placed the cup in my hands and then jerked his chin toward the window in demand for me to look outside.

The world was so quiet that you could hear a pin drop. The blizzard had seemed to pass and nothing more than tiny snowflakes fell upon a blanketed earth. The trees were peppered with white, and the snow looked so thick it had to be at least a few feet high. I craned my neck as I surveyed the grounds and found Onyx sprinting in circles through the snow with Nova at his heels.

My lips twitched in the corner as I watched our wolves play in the remnants of the storm, their tales wagging furiously as they chased one another. Evander cleared his throat, and I twisted my attention to find him standing there with a food tray before I scooted over and made room for him. He set the platter down, and I surveyed the spread hungrily. There were berries, pastries, steaming meat, cheeses, and other assortments of things.

I reached for a blackberry, popping it into my mouth before hunting for another item. I could feel Evander's intense gaze on me as he watched, and I looked up to see him sipping his coffee but not saying a word. I glanced back down at the food, noticing a small white shell in the scrambled eggs, a piece of overcooked ham, and a slice of burnt toast. Realization dawned on me as I picked up the piece of bread.

"Did you make me breakfast?" I asked, meeting his eyes once again.

Evander's cheeks flushed slightly, and he bit his lip as he nodded slowly, watching me with bated breath. He brought his cup to his lips again like it could shield him from the shyness he was exuding.

I brought the toast to my lips, and Evander's eyes widened.

"Don't," he pleaded. "Let me get Lia to make you a new one."

I held Evander's stare as I took a large bite and chewed. The charcoal coated my tongue, and I tried my best to hide my struggle. Evander held his breath as he watched in horror at my attempt.

"It's delicious," I said around a mouthful of the abomination he had created. "The best I've ever had."

He closed his eyes as he threw his head back and groaned loudly.

"Please just spit it out," he begged, but I shook my head as I swallowed the seared toast and all the char that came with it. I reached for my coffee the second it cleared my throat and took a deep sip, not caring that it burned on the way down. "I'm sorry," Evander said, sounding defeated.

"It's the thought that counts," I told him, but he rolled his eyes at the explanation. I reached forward, grabbing his hand in mine. "I will eat every single burnt piece of toast you bring because you cared enough to make it for me," I said, and his eyes sliced to mine.

My chest felt heavy under his stare like I was trapped in a trance, and I found myself pushing aside the tray of food to get closer to him as my eyes stayed locked on his. He moved too, leaning forward to meet me halfway, and my gaze flickered to his full lips as I wet mine in anticipation.

My body was like a magnet being pulled to his by some force I couldn't stop. My breathing became heavy, and my mind fogged as my lips inched closer to his, desperately wanting to claim his mouth. Evander's hand reached up, sliding along the base of my neck and through my hair as he angled me how he wanted. My eyes fluttered shut, and I tilted my chin up, determined to finally take what I wanted.

The door banged open, and thunderous footsteps sounded around us. Van and I instinctively jumped back from one another as we directed our attention to Cal and Oli, now standing in the middle of our room. Evander got to his feet, his hands held out as he stepped toward our friends.

"Not yet," he said, but both men shook their heads. "Please, just let me have five more minutes with her, and then I'll let you do it twice," Van pleaded, but the men strode forward, grabbing him by the arms and stabbing him with a syringe. I leapt to my feet, alarmed.

"What the fuck is going on?!" I demanded, reaching for Evander, but Cal cut me off. Van only yelled a string of curses at them, too weak from whatever Oli had injected him with to physically fight back. He wasn't even using his magic.

Fuck. Wolf venom.

"Relax, it's just tradition," Cal said as he and Oli positioned Van so his arms were draped across each of their shoulders as they guided him to the exit.

"What kind of tradition calls for drugging and dragging him from our room?" I exclaimed, my irritation and worry for Van evident.

"The birthday kind," Cal replied, and my heart stopped. It was Evander's birthday? Why didn't he tell me? "Now, if you'll excuse us, we only have about seven minutes to do this before the venom wears off. Oh, and it's pretty cold outside, so you might want to wear something other than just his shirt."

I looked down at my bare legs and instantly pulled at the hem of the shirt that was barely covering my thighs, let alone my ass. The second they left the room, I sprinted for my dresser, putting on the first warm thing I could find. A muffled shout from outside rang out, and I ran to the window to see Oli and Cal leading Van onto the long pier with Lia and Felix laughing behind them.

What the actual fuck was happening?

I hurried down the stairs and out the door just as the men made it to the end of the dock. Oli grabbed Van's arms as Cal grabbed his ankles, and together, they began swinging him back and forth. Holy Gods, they were going to toss him into the lake.

I ran onto the pier, peeking over the side as I did, and relief flooded me. The lake had partially frozen over, extending a few feet beyond the dock. Cal and Oli were both in great shape, but they didn't possess the strength to throw Van far enough to reach the open water. He would simply hit the ice, and though it would probably feel less than great, at least he wouldn't be plunged into the freezing depths.

My relief melted away the second I reached them all and saw that someone had created a huge hole in the middle of the ice. Perfect for throwing a body into.

"Stop!" I yelled. Cal looked up at me, but they didn't halt their plans. "You can't throw him in. It's freezing! And he doesn't have his magic, so what if he doesn't heal quickly enough?" I argued, trying to come up with any reason to keep Van dry and warm.

"Why do you think Lia is here?" Oli asked. "She'll heal him. She always does."

"You do this every year?" I asked her, and she nodded excitedly.

"All of us do. It's a birthday tradition," she said. "Van has it the worst, though. He's the only one who has a birthday during winter."

I groaned, not liking this at all. I turned to Felix to beg for some assistance, but I knew he loved the idea of seeing the king he hadn't gotten along with take an ice bath in the dead of winter.

"We need to hurry," Oli announced as Van fought against the hold, his body seeming to gain some control. Cal nodded, and they swung their arms faster, gaining strength and momentum to throw him over.

"Wait!" I yelled again, pushing passed Lia and Felix to get to Evander. "I'll go too."

"It's not your birthday," Oli said, though he had slowed his pace as if he were considering this idea.

"I wasn't here for mine. Plus, it was my twenty-first, so I deserve to be thrown in," I told him, and the men shared a look before finally dropping Evander onto the pier. His fingers stretched, and he shook his arms out sluggishly as the venom began to leave his system.

"You're not going into that water, love," Van said as I helped him to his feet. "I appreciate the solidarity, but it's freezing, and you hate the cold."

"I do. But I'm not letting you do this alone," I told him as I interlocked our fingers together. "Though, I'm pretty sure I'll regret this decision the second we're under."

Evander looked down at me with a smile wider than I had ever seen and true happiness shining in those brilliant grey eyes of his. I squeezed his hand tighter as I peered back over the edge, groaning as I did.

"You don't have to do this, love," he said as his thumb swept over the back of my hand in a comforting stroke.

Yes, I did. I didn't know why I felt that way, but it was undeniable. I had to jump with him. I wasn't sure if it was because I wanted to initiate myself into this absurd tradition or because I couldn't bear the idea of him doing this alone.

"Whose ridiculous idea was this, anyway?" I asked, twisting to face our on-lookers. All of them smiled as they stared at Van, and a look of chagrin flooded his features. Of course, it was his idea.

"In my defense, I wasn't thinking about when my birthday was. I just wanted to throw Cal in the lake for being annoying on his," Evander explained, and I rolled my eyes as I turned back around, ready to get this over with.

My legs trembled like a shaky leaf, more from anticipation than the weather. I swallowed hard as I crept forward, letting my toes hang over the edge. I had run out of the house so fast I didn't bother to put on my boots, but at least I had socks on. Poor Evander was completely barefoot from the unexpected intrusion this morning. The hole in the ice was large enough to fit both of us, and the water was black as night, making me feel even more uneasy.

"Ready?" Evander asked, and my stare shot to his.

His eyes softened instantly as he took in the fear that undoubtedly filled my face. I hated the freaking cold, and now I was about to willingly jump into a frozen lake because of my stupid feelings.

Fuck my life.

Evander spun me to face him, clutching my hands tight in his.

"Keep your eyes on mine the entire time. The current is strong beneath the ice, so don't let go of my hand," Evander said gently, and I nodded. "It'll be over in a few seconds, I promise."

"Okay," I murmured, my hands trembling around his.

"On the count of three." I swallowed the lump in my throat before taking a deep breath. "One. Two. *Three.*"

We leapt into the air and, a moment later, plummeted into the dark black lake below. The water was so cold it felt like daggers were leaving cuts along every inch of bare skin. My body went numb, and my lungs screamed as I immediately exhaled in a rush. Panic surged through me as I struggled to swim back to the surface, unsure which way was up. The current was forceful, and my grip on Van's hand slipped as it tried to pull me away. His free hand grabbed my wrist as I kicked and kicked, trying desperately not to lose him. He yanked my arm hard until I collided with his chest. I wrapped my frozen arms around his neck as we swam for the surface. The second we breached it and I gulped down air, shadows wrapped around us. We were pulled away, appearing a heartbeat later on our bathing room floor.

I coughed up the frozen water as my throat burned and my lungs ached. Evander scooped me from the tile, cradling me against himself as he rushed us into the heated pool. I sank into the warmth as Van held me against him before stripping off my sweater and clothes until I was in nothing but my bra and underwear.

"Are you okay?" he asked, smoothing the frozen hair from my face and bringing me further into the pool.

"Yes," I said through chattering teeth.

The water around us grew warmer at once, thanks to the magic of our house. I sighed as heat wrapped over my body, and Van sucked in a painful breath. He always complained my baths were too hot, and I felt a little smug over making him suffer after jumping into that damn lake with him.

The fact that I volunteered for it wasn't the point.

"Why did you do that, love?" he asked through a huff of laughter as he set me down to stand next to him. I dipped my head below the surface, feeling the comforting sting of heat against my flesh, before coming back up for air. I scrubbed my hair away from my face and opened my eyes to look up at him.

"I'm going to have to do it next year, right? So I might as well have gotten used to it now," I said, and he raised a brow at me, waiting for more explanation. "And,

I guess I don't like the idea of you suffering alone. Even if it *is* because of your own stupidity."

Van laughed as he reached for me, pulling me against his chest. "If the roles were reversed, I would have jumped with you, too," he said, and my lips twitched in the corner. I liked the idea that I wasn't alone in feeling the way I had this morning and that my insanity was reciprocated.

Van's hand slid to my lower back while the other moved to the back of my head, and I arched into the touch, wanting even more from him. I internally groaned at how well he knew my body. It felt like uneven terrain, and I wanted to try and make him react to me the same way I always had for him. I pushed away at once and swam for the steps.

"I'm hungry," I called over my shoulder as I exited the pool. "My breakfast was rudely interrupted this morning."

He didn't try to follow as I wrapped myself in a towel and left the room. The sounds of his wet clothes hitting the floor told me that I had exactly two minutes to execute my plan. I ran for my dresser, pulling open the top drawer and riffling around until my hand closed around the thin black fabric.

I slipped into the lingerie Lia had purchased for me when I had first arrived in Tenebrae. She had said she wasn't sure what I preferred to wear, so she supplied me with every possible style of clothing in the realm. Though I never wore it, I was grateful to have it at that moment.

The lace underwear did absolutely nothing to cover my ass, and the nearly see-through corset top pushed my breasts up so they were on full display. I bit my lip as I appraised myself in the mirror before grabbing a pair of long, knit socks. They stretched up my legs, stopping just above my knee, and though they didn't go with my seductive ensemble, I was freezing, so it would just have to do.

"What are you wearing?" Evander questioned from behind me, his voice rough and deep. I spun around and tilted my head to the side as I narrowed my eyes at him.

"Oh, this?" I asked innocently, trailing a finger over the swell of my breast and down the front. Evander swallowed as his eyes raked over me with feral need—a feast he planned to devour. "You don't like it?" I stuck out my bottom lip in a soft pout as I watched him.

He strode for me slowly—deliberately—and I leaned back against the dresser as I waited for him to close the distance. My heart raced as I took in every carved muscle of his bare chest, letting my eyes drop down to the pronounced V that dipped below the waistband of his pants. My mouth went dry as I thought about what it would taste like to trace it with my tongue.

"I didn't say that," Evander replied as he reached me. He placed a hand on either side of the wooden dresser like it would keep him from shredding the lingerie right off my body. "But why are you wearing it?" His voice was pained, and his eyes were hungry as he took in every inch of me, giving me precisely the reaction I wanted. I had never seen him *that* desperate for me.

"It's your birthday, so I figured I would dress nicely. You disapprove?" I asked coyly, arching my back so my chest pressed against him. Evander groaned as he dipped his head so his lips pressed just below my ear. "I could always just change," I said breathlessly, and he kissed my neck, sending a shiver through me.

My hands reached for his shoulders, gripping hard as his tongue swept over my skin. I moaned softly at the feel of his mouth on me, and a low rumble left Van's throat at the sound. He pulled away, and his charcoal eyes were even darker with desire than before.

"Love, I very much approve of this choice. But looking and not being allowed to touch is absolute torture, and you know it," he explained. I smiled wide, loving what I was doing to him. His hands moved to my waist, lifting me and sitting me on the dresser's edge, just as he had in the illusion. He pushed my legs apart and stood between them, resting his hands on my thighs; a pounding began in my core at his proximity. Nothing but thin fabric separated us, and I was half tempted just to rip it off myself. "I think I may have to devise some sort of punishment for you doing this to me on my birthday."

A whimper left my lips as I raked my hands through his black hair, knowing that whatever punishment he came up with would be a delectable kind of torture. One that I was positive would have me screaming his name until my voice was hoarse. I felt slickness pool between my legs and shifted uncomfortably as I tried to regain control of this game. He knew what he was doing.

And my Gods, he was fucking masterful at it.

I shrugged at his words, pretending they had no effect on me though we both knew they did. I gripped his hair, yanking it back hard so he was forced to look up. Van hissed at the pain, but I could tell he loved it when I took control. I sat straighter, leaning forward so I could whisper in his ear.

"I think I'd like that game... But for the record," I said, dropping my voice even lower. "I never said you couldn't touch."

I pulled back to find Evander's eyes wide and frenzied. His chest moved rapidly as his stare darted between my face and body like he couldn't be sure whether this was actually happening.

"But if you'd rather play something else instead, we can do that," I offered, moving to hop down from the dresser. Evander's fingers pressed into my thighs as he slid them around to cup my ass.

"Don't you dare move a fucking inch," he demanded as he pushed himself against me, letting me feel just how hard he was for me.

Evander guided his hand up my ribs and over the fabric of the corset slowly, as if savoring the feel of me. He slid his fingers under the thin straps and pulled them down gently so they hung over my shoulders before leaning in and kissing my collarbone. I swallowed hard as I clung to him, wrapping my legs around his middle on instinct.

"I can't decide if I want to take you while you wear this or if I want to tear it to shreds," Van said, moving his mouth to my neck as he let his fingers swipe along the underside of my breast. I moaned, arching my back in demand for him to give me more.

"Why can't you do both?" I breathed as my fingers raked down his body before tugging at the waistband of his pants, needing them off right that second.

"I really don't want to be the one interrupting whatever is going on here—" Felix started but was quickly cut off.

"You have got to be fucking kidding me right now," Evander growled, twisting his head to stare daggers at my best friend.

I covered my mouth to muffle the snort that broke through. Felix had the worst timing in the world, and I wanted to wring his neck for stopping us, but the furious look on Evander's face was somehow both deadly and adorable, and I couldn't help but be amused by it.

"Leave, Empathi. Right now, before I rip your throat out," he continued.

"Do you honestly think I want to stand here and watch you try to fuck my best friend?" Felix asked, taking another step closer.

"So then get out!" Evander yelled, and Felix dragged a hand over his face.

"Just put your dick away and calm down. Oli received word from Marce and is waiting for you in the study," Felix finished.

Both Van and I straightened and looked at one another.

"Go," I commanded. "I'll be right behind you."

A puff of shadows swirled in front of me, and I jumped down from the dresser before digging through the drawers to find something more appropriate to change into.

"Care to share what all this is about?" Felix asked, waving a hand over my outfit. I shrugged as I threw a wink in his direction. "If I weren't falling for his best friend, I'd probably try to seduce you myself."

I huffed a laugh though I felt the sadness and frustration in his words. It hurt to see him fall for someone who was so set on pushing him away. The irony in that didn't escape me. I was well aware Oli and I share similarities in that department. I stripped out of the lingerie, not caring that Felix was still there because I knew my body was just flesh to him.

"You seem better today," I said, pulling a sweater over my head. He knew I didn't mean his leg, though he was walking a bit straighter than yesterday.

"Olivier came to my room last night," Felix admitted, and I spun around as I struggled to get my pants on. "I'm sure it had nothing to do with the screaming match between you two after Lia and I left."

I offered an apologetic look. Felix didn't seem bothered by it, but perhaps I had overstepped somehow. I probably should have minded my own business and let them figure it out themselves, but I just couldn't stand by and watch their potential go up in flames because Oli was too stubborn for his own good.

"Thank you," Felix said, and I breathed a sigh of relief as I made my way over to him, now fully dressed in something not intended to seduce the King of Tenebrae.

"What happened?"

"He asked me not to go," he admitted, and my jaw dropped in surprise.

"He didn't just *demand* that you stay?"

"Well, his exact words were '*don't go*,' and when I didn't answer, he threw in a *please*," Felix said. The corner of his mouth lifted in a grin.

"So you're staying?" I asked hopefully.

I would always support Felix's choice to be wherever he wanted, but it didn't mean I wanted him to leave. Yes, I was happy with the new people in my life, but Felix was family too, and I couldn't picture him not with me. He nodded, and I leaped at him, wrapping my arms around his neck.

"For now," he clarified. "If Olivier decides to be an ass again, then I can't stick around."

"He won't," I promised. "I'll order him to be nice. He's a rule follower and wouldn't dare defy his princess."

Felix laughed even though I was dead serious. Maybe I'd get Van to give the order as a royal decree or something. I could make being nice to Felix an official law, but after this latest interruption, I doubt Van would ever consider it. Maybe I could make it happen if I asked while wearing a little less lingerie. I made a mental note to find a more revealing set for later.

50.

Felix and I walked through the hall and towards the study, arms linked together as I savored the moments with him in case they would end too soon.

"The news Marce sent…" I began, mentally preparing myself for the worst. This was the last thing Evander needed—especially on his birthday.

"Is good," Felix said at once, and I stopped our walk, letting out a deep breath as I felt a crushing weight fall from my shoulders. I hadn't realized just how scared I was.

We entered the room, and my eyes instantly sought Evander, who was scribbling a note before letting the ink disappear. The moment the words vanished, he looked up, the worry and pain in his eyes replaced with joy and hope. He rushed for me, and I let him squeeze me tight as he whispered soft enough that no one else could hear.

"He's okay. They're all okay," he said. I returned the hug, moving my hands to his hair as he buried his face into the crook of my neck and inhaled my scent as if it brought him even more comfort. "Marceline made it just as Declan's other allies arrived. Between them and the rest of our fleet once it gets there, we should be able to do enough damage to force them to retreat. Marce is on her way back with their most injured so we can heal them out of the crossfire."

"Perfect," I said, yanking his hair back playfully so he was forced to pick his head up. "When will you learn that I'm always right?"

He laughed, and I was lost in the carefree sound of it. My heart melted to see him so lax for the first time in what felt like weeks. Even last night, when we had spent hours talking and laughing under the light of the moon, there was still an underlying edge of fear plaguing us both. We couldn't be truly happy or free until we knew those we loved were also.

"I will never doubt you again," he said, squeezing my waist and flashing a dazzling smile. Gods, what I wouldn't give to have his mouth on me right now.

His eyes roamed over me as a muscle feathered in his jaw as he leaned in close.

"You look adorable, but for the record, I prefer your earlier outfit choice," Van said.

My cheeks flushed, and my blood heated as I remembered how his gaze drifted over me like a predator. My thighs clenched as I thought about him pressed against me, hard and wanting.

"If you want to go back to the room, I can try it on again for you," I promised as I let my fingers trail over his neck in a seductive stroke. Van's eyes lightened, and he slowly nodded.

"We'll be back later," he announced to the room, not taking his eyes off me.

"No, you won't," Cal said from his spot on the couch. "It's time for the battle."

Evander groaned in frustration, and I arched a brow in question. A battle? Had we been attacked again, and if so, why the hell was this the first I was hearing of it?

"Unless you want to use your designated choice on this?" Oli offered, sounding bored. Van huffed as he released me, dragging a hand over his face before shaking his head.

"No, I'm saving it. We can do the battle now," Van announced, and Lia jumped to her feet, applauding excitedly. What was happening?

Evander turned to me, his face full of apology as he leaned in and kissed my cheek. My skin burned under his lips, and my pulse quickened at the intimacy. I needed more than this and *now*.

"We have a battle to attend," Van said, grabbing my hand and pulling me toward the front of the house.

"What happened? Where did they attack?" I demanded, picking up my pace as I shoved on my boots before crafting two daggers to slip into them for easy access.

"Not that kind of battle," he said as he chuckled under his breath and removed my weapons for me. I flicked my wrist, letting them disappear into tendrils of shadow as I waited for an explanation. "It's an ice battle."

"You say that like I'm supposed to know what it means," I countered as he ushered us outside.

Oli and Cal were speaking close as they pointed to different areas of the ground like they were strategizing. I would have assumed this battle would be taken seriously if it wasn't for Lia and Felix making snowmen rather than working out their plan.

"We split into two teams, and each team has a marker to guard," Van said, crafting two black flags from his shadows and holding one out for me to take. "We hide these within the designated playing area, and the first team to capture the other's flag wins."

It sounded easy enough.

"Where does the ice come in?" I asked.

"It's like a snowball fight but worse," he said, pointing to several buckets around the space. I walked over to one and peered in, finding it full of water. "You make a snowball and dip it in so the water hardens it. You aren't allowed to use any magic, which includes shields, so it hurts like a bitch when you get hit."

My eyes widened, and I looked at him in horror. Who in their right mind finds getting pelted with a ball of ice fun?

"Why are you all so sadistic?" I asked, shaking my head. Evander grinned devilishly as he shrugged.

"We get bored."

"So you throw each other in a frozen lake and then blast each other with ice?" I said in disbelief.

"We have a scary image to uphold," he added, wrapping his arms around my waist. Today, he was being much more hands-on with me than ever before, and I couldn't deny how much I liked it. We flirted and teased, yes, but this was entirely different.

The way Van had his hands on me this morning as I sat on that dresser was night and day to the intimacy of his hold now. And though I desperately wanted him in that physical sense, I craved this kind of touch the most. It had been so long since I allowed myself to be fully cared for in this way.

Piece by piece, I had been offering myself to him without my permission, and slowly my heart had begun to heal enough to accept it. I wasn't ready to completely hand it over, and I wasn't sure I ever would be, but I wanted to offer what I could and take what he was giving. And for every inch I handed him, he provided me miles of himself in return.

"Of course you do," I replied, reaching onto my toes as I curled my arms around his neck. Evander's cocky grin widened as he tightened his hold, pressing his body against mine.

"You two are on separate teams," Lia called, and I was immediately ripped away from Van by the back of my coat. "You both have *fuck me* eyes, and I'm not about to lose because of it."

I bit my lip to stifle my laughter as she released me and threw an arm over my shoulders. I wrapped mine around her middle while we made our way to Cal and Oli as they began to dip snowballs into the water.

"Seriously, though," she whispered. "What is it with you two today? There's always a crazy amount of sexual tension, but you're normally at each other's throats. This is... different."

"I walked in on them one second from ripping each other's clothes off," Felix added as he came to my other side. I wanted to argue and deny it, but it was the truth. I shrugged, dropping my voice.

"To be honest, I'm not sure. It feels like something has shifted between us," I admitted as I glanced over my shoulder at Van, following not too far behind. "We talked a lot last night, and after he explained how he felt about seeing me with Marcas—"

"The wheat guy? Fuck he's so hot. We spent the night together once, years ago, and let me tell you: that man explored the shit out of my map," Lia said, sighing as if remembering the perfect memory, and Felix laughed at her innuendo.

"You had sex with Marcas?" Calidore asked, overhearing our conversation. "Without me?" The disappointed look on his face was enough to make anyone feel sorry for him. Lia ran, leaping into his arms and peppering his face with kisses.

"It was such a long time ago, my darling, and you were out of town," she cooed. "I'm sure we can get him to join us."

Cal sighed, pouting like a child left out of a game, though I supposed, in this case, he was.

"It's fine," he whined, squeezing Lia's ass before setting her back to her feet. "I'm sure he'd rather spend his time with Felix or Ainsley... or both."

Felix and I looked at each other questioningly before turning back to Calidore as he shrugged.

"I say this with love, but the two of you are an absolute handful to deal with. Your tempers alone are enough to drive anyone insane," Cal explained as Oli and Evander both hummed in agreement. I rolled my eyes as I crossed my arms over my chest, displaying the exact behavior he was referring to. "And I'd be willing to bet that Marcas would be crazy into it. He seems like he'd be generous—"

"Oh, he is," Lia interjected. "*Extremely* generous. To the point where I thought I was going to combust from how many times he made me—"

"Why are we still talking about this?" Oli cut in, his tone deep and with an edge of irritation as his eyes stayed fixed on Felix.

"I'm just saying that Marcas would probably see them as a challenge. He'd try and figure out how he could break them in the best kind of ways," Cal added, shrugging. "They'd be too busy screaming his name to run their mouths—"

A ball of ice hit Cal square in the cheek, and he swore loudly as he doubled over from the pain.

"Just testing them," Evander said casually as he stared down at his friend. My body was coiled with tension as I observed Van until he brought those gorgeous eyes back to me. Sparkling within them was the promise of pain to anyone else who so much as mentioned Marcas and me together. I bit my lip at his territorial nature over the topic. He had always supported my choice to do whatever with whomever I wanted, but knowing how much it pissed him off right now was slightly flattering.

Okay, *really* flattering.

I liked seeing just how much I could rile him up over it. I'd already told him last night that I didn't want Marcas, so if he forgot that little detail, his suffering was on him. Lia cupped Cal's cheek as she healed the pronounced red mark adorning it, and Oli went back to making more ice balls. I held Van's gaze as I crooked my finger in demand for him to come closer.

Once he reached me, I snaked my arms around his neck, pulling his body flush against mine.

"Do you think Marcas would like my outfit from this morning?" I asked innocently, stoking the embers I needed to catch aflame.

"I think he'd hate it. He wouldn't appreciate it like I do, so you probably shouldn't waste your time," he responded seductively, and I bit my lip for show.

"So you're saying I shouldn't wear anything around him then," I decided, nodding like I agreed.

A low growl rumbled in Van's throat, and his grip on me tightened. I grinned in smug satisfaction as I watched him play through the images of me completely naked in front of Marcas. But before I could fully celebrate my win, his eyes narrowed, and his head tilted as he studied me.

"Are you trying to get into my head before the battle, love?"

"I would never," I replied innocently, giving him a wink. "But since we're on the subject, why don't we make this more interesting?"

"I'm listening," he purred.

I stepped out of his hold and began walking a slow circle around him, just as he had done to me the day we first met. Van watched me with a smile on his face as if he was reliving the same memory. Things were so different back then. He was a stranger intent on getting under my skin by flirting with me nonstop, and I was... Someone very different from who I was now.

"If I win, I get to ask you one question that you have to answer truthfully," I announced, stopping before him. Van arched a brow and offered me a flat look, assuming he knew exactly what I wanted to know. "Maybe it's the story, and maybe it's not. I haven't decided what I want to know yet."

Evander rolled his eyes and crossed his arms firmly over his chest as he watched me skeptically.

"And if I win?"

"If you win," I said, circling again. "I'll give you whatever you want."

Evander stiffened, and I suppressed the smile he couldn't see as I made my way around him, trailing my fingers along his back as I passed.

"Whatever I want?" he asked doubtfully as if trying to sense my bluff. I nodded, slow and deliberate, as a wide smile spread across my face.

"Anything you want. Name it and it's yours," I said, lifting my chin and letting him see just how serious I was. His gaze dragged up and down my body, and my blood heated as I imagined what he would ask for.

"You sure?" Evander asked, reaching out to brush his knuckles down the side of my face. I swallowed the thick lump in my throat as desire burned through my veins. I couldn't remember the last time I had been this sure of anything.

"Yes," I breathed before stepping back from him, creating some much-needed space. A breeze blew between us, chilling my bones and bringing clarity to my mind and body. I took a deep breath. "But it won't matter anyway because you're going to lose."

A crooked, cocky grin crept up his face, and his features flooded with excitement.

"Oh, love," he said arrogantly. "In the fifteen years we've been playing, I've never once lost."

Evander winked before turning and heading for the water buckets to help Oli with the supply of ice balls. My stomach knotted at his confidence, and I could feel it in my soul that there was no way I would come out victorious.

But I had to at least try.

"DUCK!" Oli yelled, and I instantly fell to my knees. My entire body was sore from being pelted with ice left and right for the past hour. No one had captured the other team's flag yet and I was half tempted just to hand ours over so I could go back inside and warm up.

We split into two teams, with Oli, Lia, and me on one and Evander, Cal, and Felix on the other. Felix still wasn't fully healed, and his injury made us evenly matched—the only reason Van allowed him on his team, to begin with.

To be honest, I was shocked he was allowed to play with how quickly Olivier objected to the idea. But once Felix gave him a flat look that seemed to hold more in the silence than in words, Oli took a deep breath and backed down. Clearly, he was on his best behavior around Felix, and I wasn't upset about it.

"Can we please be done?" I whined as an ice ball zoomed over my head, narrowly missing me.

"No! We are not done until a flag has been taken, so shut up, suck it up, and get up!" Lia sneered, and my jaw dropped in surprise at her ferocity. In all my time here, I had never so much as heard her raise her voice in anger.

"Lia doesn't like to lose," Olivier said as he launched an ice ball across the space, clipping Evander in the leg as he attempted to dive away from the attack.

"Yeah, I noticed," I replied sarcastically as I side eyed the red-haired beauty next to me. She could definitely give Van a run for his money in a race of who was more competitive.

"The sooner we get the flag, the sooner you can go sit by the fire. And I think I have an idea of where they've hidden theirs," Lia said as she gestured to a large willow tree on the far end of the yard. Olivier shook his head.

"Cal hid it there last year," he pointed out.

"Which is exactly why he'd hide it there again," I said, understanding what Lia was getting at. "He doesn't think we'd bother to look there because who would hide it in the same place twice."

Lia smiled triumphantly, and the three of us got to work, devising a plan. I was one step closer to not only thawing in the house's heat but getting to ask Van any question I wanted. I could practically taste the victory on my tongue.

The three of us split up, executing our carefully crafted plan. Olivier assured us that our flag was well hidden and that the other team hadn't so much as glanced in its direction. The battlefield that had once been the sparring ring was quiet and still, with no signs of the other team in sight. They were done with their constant assault and now waited for the perfect time to attack.

I crouched behind a bush, glancing left and right as snowflakes began to fall heavily, limiting our visibility. It wasn't ideal, but perhaps this development could work in our favor. The sudden weather change would help conceal us as we moved for our target. Unless Van, Cal, and Felix knew where we were, we could potentially stay undetected all the way to the tree.

I checked my surroundings before darting to the next nearby object and then ducked behind it. I did that repeatedly as I made my way closer. The snow was so heavy now that I couldn't hear anything but the flakes pelting surrounding objects and the sound of my heart beating. One of us had to be close by now. If I was allowed to use my magic, I could envelop everyone in darkness, make a break for the willow, grab the flag, and head back inside before anyone could realize what was happening. Whoever made the rule preventing us from using our Gifts was an asshole.

So my money was on Cal or Van.

I crept slowly to the heap of snow covering our weapons table and knelt beside it as I carefully watched the area. The willow was now in my sights and only about twenty yards away. I could sprint for it and hope to find the flag before someone noticed me, but the problem was I had no idea where Van's team was hiding. The deathly silence sent a wave of unease over me. If I'd learned anything in my training over the past few months, it was to trust my instincts and my magic, and both of them were screaming at me in warning. I inhaled a deep breath and then let it out, watching the puff of cold vapor twist and turn around itself like my shadows always did. My magic rubbed against me from the inside, cautiously asking me to let it out to play, and I hated that I had to deny it. My Gift was an inherent part of me, and keeping it locked away for any amount of time felt uncomfortable and just plain wrong.

A sudden flash of motion caught my eye to the left, followed by a thick crunching sound, like a heavy weight had been pressed into the snow. Olivier cursed loudly, and I watched his body descend into a hidden pitfall. On instinct, I darted out of my hiding place and instantly realized my mistake. But it was too late. Before I could move a step, a large ice ball slammed into the side of my face so hard I saw stars. I swore as my mouth filled with the metallic taste of blood, and time slowed as I glanced up to see another ball heading my way. I screamed as I turned, throwing my hands up to deflect the attack, but it wasn't enough. This time, thanks to spotting the ball quickly, I was able to twist my body so it hit right above my ear rather than a direct shot to my face again. It still hurt like hell, though.

"What the fuck!" Cal yelled, and I cautiously looked through my arm shield to find Evander on top of him as they fought in the snow. "I'm on your team, dammit!"

"You hit her in the face!" Van sneered back, punching Cal in the ribs before slamming his head into the ground. Calidore cursed and landed a sharp blow to Van's stomach before sliding out from under him.

"She'll be fine!" Cal exclaimed, dodging out of the way as Van lunged for him again. As hot as it was to watch Van go feral over me getting hurt—and as much as I wanted to watch—I had a game to win.

I hurried to my feet and sprinted for the tree, taking full advantage of their distraction. I could do this.

"Her lip looks pretty busted. It may take Lia a while to heal it," Olivier called from his trap, further instigating the situation. Evander growled, and I heard the crash of bodies once again.

The snow began to deepen, reaching my thighs, and my pace slowed significantly as I waded through the thick powder. Given the pitfall that captured Olivier and the snow being unreasonably thick only in this area, our guess on the flag location had to be correct. I gritted my teeth, using all my might to push forward. Just a little bit farther and I'd be there. Deep red caught my attention, and I spotted Lia on the other side of the tree, slowly approaching it as well.

"They had a shit ton of traps set up along my path, so I had to take the long way," she explained, shoving aside armfuls of snow as we plowed our way through.

"We're almost there," I told her, focusing on the task when the hair on my arms began to stand. Something wasn't right. My eyes darted across the tree, but I didn't notice anything off or out of place. I strained my ears to listen, but everything seemed fine—quiet and calm.

Shit.

I whirled at the same time Van's body collided with mine, tackling me to the ground as a scream left my lips. Flurries drifted through the air around us as we hit the snow hard, and I gasped as the cold flakes made their way into my clothes. Van's hands found my wrists, pinning them above my head as his crushing weight kept me from getting free.

"Where do you think you're going, love?" he crooned, offering me a victorious grin.

I scowled up at him, pissed off that I had come so close only to be taken down moments before I got to the damn flag. I turned my head to the side, and a renewed sense of hope filled me as I watched Lia reach the tree's base.

"Hurry, Lia!" I yelled, and Evander glanced up as she leapt for the lowest branch of the willow and hoisted herself up. He chuckled under his breath before diverting his attention back to me.

"Hmmm," he mused, his grey eyes shining bright was excitement. "What should I have you do for me?"

"You haven't won yet. She's going to get that flag and—"

"Why is Lia scaling that tree?" Felix asked, stepping into view.

My stomach dropped at the sound of his voice. I had completely forgotten about his existence and cursed myself for not noticing his absence as Van and Cal wrestled in the snow. My eyes dipped to the black satin fabric dangling from Felix's hands.

"How?" I demanded, squirming beneath Evander, but his hands constricted on my wrist, refusing to release me. Felix shrugged as he ran the flag between his fingers, and Lia swore a string of curses as she jumped down from the tree.

"I grabbed it about twenty minutes ago while you were all strategizing. Walked right past all of you while you argued about which way to split up and removed it from that shitty hiding place under the bush. Then I came back here, and we decided we'd rather watch your lousy attempt rather than end the game right then," Felix explained with a mischievous smile.

"How did you even know where it was?" I asked. Oli had sworn the place he chose was perfect and that the other team hadn't come close to finding it.

"I just decided to observe Olivier. I knew he wouldn't want to lose, so I spent the entire battle studying his movements and the way his glance would occasionally drift in that direction," Felix said, pointing to the row of bushes almost completely hidden under the cover of snow. "I wasn't sure if my assumption was correct, but when Olivier strengthened your defenses as I got within a close enough distance, I knew it was there."

"He then told Cal and me what he found out, and we devised a plan to keep your focus on our assaults so Felix could sneak around," Van added, grinning wickedly at me. I should be happy that he and Felix worked together for a change, but I was only pissed at the fact we had been tricked.

"So that little show between you and Cal was all an act?" I accused, yanking on my wrists.

Van pressed his body harder against mine, and I swallowed at the proximity. I should not have been enjoying this as much as I was. He released his hold on one of my arms before gripping my chin and tilting my head to the side as he surveyed the damage done by Cal's ice ball.

"Not even a little bit," Evander answered, dragging his thumb carefully over my busted lip. His eyes flashed in fury momentarily before he called Lia over and demanded she heal me. She did, of course, and I licked my lips, feeling that they were back to a normal size and without the taste of blood coating them.

Van shifted his weight slightly so I could breathe easier, though with his hands still pinning mine above my head and his body pressed against me, there was no way the movement was doing what it was intended to. His gaze roamed over my face and down my body as he leaned in to hover mere inches above me.

"I told you I would win, love. Now, to figure out what I want you to give me," Evander whispered, and my blood pounded with anticipation. I took a deep breath before lifting my chin to show him I wasn't afraid. I made these terms, and I was ready to fulfill them.

Shadows curled around our bodies, pulling us out of the training ring and onto our bedroom floor.

51.

"Change out of those wet clothes," Evander commanded as he untangled himself from me. I watched him walk to his dresser and search for dry clothes before stripping down. I rolled over, got up, and walked to my dresser at the opposite end of the room. Fisting the black lingerie from earlier, I spun around, holding it out for him to see.

"Into something more like this?" I asked innocently, and Van's throat bobbed as dark hunger filled his gaze. He took a deep breath before shaking his head.

"As much as I want to see you in that again, you're shivering right now, so dress warm," he instructed before tugging a shirt over his head. He wasn't wrong.

Goosebumps spread across my flesh, and my legs trembled as I stood there in my wet clothes. I quickly undressed, grabbing an oversized sweater and a pair of loose-knit pants to pull on. As I rifled through the drawers, a hand clasped around my ankle, lifting it from the floor, and I glanced down to find Van kneeling on the ground as he slid a thick sock over my foot.

"You're freezing," he said by way of explanation as he placed my foot down and reached for the other. "Now get in bed." He ran a hand over my calf and up the back of my leg. His command felt like it held a promise, and my cheeks flushed as I thought about what it could be.

"I figured you'd be trying to get me out of my clothes, not covering me in more," I teased, and he squeezed the backs of my thighs. I wobbled a bit and grasped his shoulders for support as he smiled wickedly up at me.

"The bed, love," Evander said again as he jerked his chin toward the mattress.

I did as instructed, watching as he climbed into his spot with slow determination. He rolled onto his side to face me and reached out, grabbing my body and pulling it into his chest. He intertwined our legs and positioned me so I was using his bicep as a pillow. One of Evander's hands cradled the back of my head while the other held my face, forcing me to lean my forehead against his. I closed my eyes as I felt his breath on my skin and his lips so close to mine that a simple lift of my chin would have them meet.

"What do you want?" I asked nervously as my hands trembled with anticipation.

"This," he whispered back. "Just to have ten minutes of uninterrupted time to hold you like this." My heart stopped at his request, and I was liquid in his hands, ready to bend and break for this man.

"I thought you would have demanded a kiss," I admitted breathlessly, and I couldn't hide the disappointment that coated my tone. His fingers constricted around my face like he was trying to restrain himself from taking just that.

"When we kiss, love," he began, his voice sultry and as smooth as silk. "It'll be because you want to. Not because you lost a bet."

"You had no problems with those terms last night," I corrected, remembering that I would have kissed him if he had won our card game. I glanced at his mouth through lowered lashes in time to see a crooked grin appear.

"Those were terms *you* chose, and you never specified where the kiss had to be. Your cheek would have done just fine," Evander responded, and there was nothing but honesty in his words.

To claim his prize, he would have simply demanded that my lips touch his cheek. If it had been anyone else, I probably would have felt self-conscious about it, with my mind jumping immediately to the conclusion that they weren't interested in me, but with Van, I knew better. Everything had always been *my* choice with him. From day one, he had been very clear about me being in control and going after what I wanted without anyone making those decisions for me.

"And this is all *you* want from me?" I asked him tentatively, breathing in his snow and cedar scent.

"Oh, I want many things from you, love, but this is all I'm asking for." Evander swept his thumb over my cheek as he spoke, and I sighed contentedly at his touch. I wanted more too, but this moment with him was perfect as it was.

"I didn't get you a present," I whispered, and Evander smiled as he narrowed his eyes at me.

"*This* is what I want," he answered, holding me a little tighter for emphasis. "I want just one day with you like this."

I raised my hand and cupped his face the same way he held mine, gently tracing my fingers over the slight stubble present. Evander pressed into my touch, and I felt his cheeks lift into a smile. There was no way that only ten minutes was going to be enough. I needed so much more of him like this—of *us* like this—and I found myself agreeing to his request. Just one day to remember what it was like to be touched. One day to let myself *feel*.

"Let's go, you two," Cal said from the doorway. "It's time for lunch."

Evander groaned in irritation as he turned to look at his friend. Even that slight movement made it feel like he was too far away. I buried my face into the side of his neck as I kept my hand firmly on his cheek.

"Are they always going to interrupt us?" I whined into him. Though the sound was muffled, Van heard it and chuckled.

"Yes," he said very matter-of-factly, and I huffed a breath of frustration.

"Unless you want to call it in now?" Calidore asked, giving his friend an ultimatum. Evander twisted to me again, his eyes searching my face as he debated what to do. After a moment, he leaned forward and kissed my cheek before pulling away.

"Not yet," Van answered as he got out of bed and extended a hand for me to take. He slid his fingers between mine as he helped me down and led us from the room. I looked up at him questioningly, but he shook his head in a carefree way, telling me not to worry about whatever it was that Cal was referring to. That was twice now that Van had been offered the chance to call in some kind of debt.

Lunch passed slowly and in much of the same fashion as it had every other day, with the only difference being the discussion centered around our next course of activity. I sat close to Evander, and my body came alive every time his hand would brush mine below the table as if this was some affair we were trying to keep secret. It wasn't, and it sure as hell wasn't an affair. I had no clue what I considered us to be doing, but all I knew was that I liked it.

And I wanted more.

"It's too cold to go to the tavern. I don't want to hike through all the snow," Lia whined, and I bit my lip as Evander traced his fingertips over mine delicately. I gave him a knowing look, and he returned it with a self-satisfying smirk.

"But it's so boring here," Cal reasoned. "Van will you traverse—"

"Nope," Evander said, cutting him off. "I'm not helping you drag me somewhere I don't want to go." Calidore groaned but didn't argue.

"Van won't help, and Lia's right; it's way too cold to be out this evening. We'll stay here, and you'll get to pick the first game," Oli offered, and I could sense Cal perk up at the compromise.

Evander's fingers moved from my hand to my arm, drawing long soft strokes along the inside. I swallowed hard as the sensitive skin tingled with each gentle passing touch. His smile grew as he watched me try to keep my composure and not melt into a puddle on the floor from his hold on my body. The confident asshole knew precisely what he was doing.

I reached for my water as I listened to the crowd discuss whatever game we would be playing and extended my free hand to rest on Evander's thigh. Right near the prominent bulge in his pants. I squeezed his leg tight, my fingers just a breath away from where he desperately wanted them. Evander stiffened and cleared his throat as he fought to regain composure from a move he obviously didn't think I would make. He was playing with fire and should have known it by now.

I glanced around the table, making sure no one had noticed this little game we were playing, when my eyes found Felix's. He wore a crooked grin and a smug look on his face that told me he knew exactly what was happening. I removed my hand from Evander at once and brought them high above my head as I stretched like nothing out of the ordinary was going on.

"Are you guys ready?" Calidore asked as he, Oli, and Lia pushed themselves away from the table.

"I am, but I think Ainsley is a little preoccupied," Felix said as he began to stand, and I shot him a death glare. Cal looked at me questioningly, but I shook my head, denying Felix's claim.

"I'm fine," I announced, getting up from my seat. "And I'm ready to kick your asses in whatever game you chose."

"Ainsley tends to get a little... *cocky* when we play games," Felix told Cal as he winked in my direction. I ran through every way I could murder my best friend as I stood there, trapped in his smug gaze.

"Well, don't get too confident. The first game is a challenge, and if you're not careful, you'll get knocked out early on," Cal said as we all made our way out of the dining room and to the library.

"Did you hear that, buttercup? It looks like you'll have some *stiff* competition," Felix purred, leaning close to my ear as we arrived. When we entered, Lia was already working on tending to the fire, and Oli rearranged the furniture so we could all sit in a circle.

"Say another innuendo, and I swear to the Gods, I will send you illusions of my wolves ripping your cock straight from your body and using it as their chew toy," I whispered through a sweet smile. Felix returned the gesture with a grin of his own before he drifted from my side.

"Yeah, it'll be really hard to stay in," Calidore said, replying to Felix's earlier statement, and my best friend's eyes lit up with renewed purpose.

"So you're saying Ainsley should pace herself so she doesn't finish prematurely?" Felix asked through a burst of laughter, and I lunged for him as he sprinted away in a complete fit of hysterics.

"Umm, I guess?" Cal answered, confused, as he dodged out of the way of my attempted attack on my friend.

Felix squealed as he narrowly missed my grasp, squeezing between two armchairs to escape me. Our friends mumbled around us, trying to figure out what had brought about Felix's excitement and *my* anger, though they didn't seem shocked at the display. I caught a glimpse of Evander out of the corner of my eye, tall, handsome, and carefree as he leaned against the doorframe, watching the hunt.

I ducked as Felix chucked a pillow to slow me down but instead hit Lia in the side of the head.

"Sorry!" he yelled as he rushed behind Oli and gripped his shoulder to use him as a human shield.

"Move," I commanded, and Olivier raised his hands in innocence, though he didn't get out of the way and turn over my prize. "Step aside, Oli. He's mine."

Felix gasped for breath through his laughter as he hid behind the man he was falling for, and I wondered why exactly Oli hadn't moved. Before, he would have never helped Felix, and now he was guarding him—albeit not by choice, but still. That had to mean progress, right?

Oli twisted and looked Felix up and down before addressing me. "He's still hurt," Oli said as if that was supposed to mean something to me.

"He's fine and clearly well enough to sprint away from me."

"I didn't authorize that choice," Olivier replied angrily while giving Felix a furious look, and I could have sworn color flushed in my best friend's cheeks. "And it won't be happening again." Felix nodded subtly like only Oli was meant to see it. What exactly happened between them last night? Was there more that Felix left out?

"Come on, love," Evander said, gently pulling on my arm. "Leave him be for now; you can get revenge once he's fully healed." A growl rumbled in my throat as Felix smiled victoriously from his safe place behind Olivier, and I let Van lead me away to the sitting area where Cal and Lia were already setting up the card game.

I lowered myself next to Van as Felix made his way to situate himself as far away as possible from me. I was about to call him a coward, but the words died in my throat as Olivier sat beside him. Mine and Felix's eyes met in a moment of truce as we both wondered what was happening. I arched a brow as my eyes widened, and Felix returned a subtle shake of his head to indicate that he had no clue what was going on. We would definitely be discussing that the moment we had a second alone.

"Are we playing or what?" Oli asked, breaking the silence, and I turned to see everyone else had been watching him as well.

"I'll deal first," Lia stuttered and gathered the cards as we all shifted in our seats like Oli didn't just catch us staring at him.

The only one who didn't seem to care was Evander. He was lying back against the sofa, his arm draped across the top, as he looked around the room with a bored expression. I leaned back, and his fingers instantly swept across my shoulder in a sweet caress. I bit my lip to keep from smiling, and my eyes flickered to Felix again, watching us—though his face held no trace of humor this time. His gaze was thoughtful and intense like he was reading a riddle hidden in the air between Evander and me.

Felix had witnessed me and Dash fall in love with one another. He had been there for the stolen glances and subtle brushes of our hands. He had felt our hearts beat wildly and watched us fumble for our footing as we navigated our feelings. Felix had been there for nearly every innocent and beautiful moment, and now he was here as it unfolded before him again. But this time, with someone else.

I leaned forward and moved out of Evander's touch as I broke eye contact with Felix. Van shifted next to me, and I could sense his confusion at my sudden need for distance, but I couldn't explain myself. How was I supposed to tell him I now felt shame and guilt, knowing my best friend had seen what had just transpired?

It wasn't the same as when Felix had walked in on me sitting atop that dresser this morning or even what he witnessed at the lunch table. That could be blamed strictly on the need to fulfill physical desires—something Felix was very familiar with. With how my cheeks flushed at the lightest touch of Evander's knuckles over my shoulder could never be mistaken for something lesser than it was.

And my best friend had seen it.

Felix knew where my feelings for Dashiell stood, but I didn't think he had ever given up hope that we would someday reconcile. That the three of us would be a trio again—a happy family, now stronger together after coming back from the pits of hell. But the look in his amber eyes as he read the emotions on my face told me he was starting to realize that wasn't going to happen. Dashiell and I couldn't fix what had been broken.

And I didn't want to try.

"Ainsley?" Lia said, waving a handful of cards in front of my face and cutting through my panicked thoughts. I blinked several times to clear my mind and forced a smile upon my face as I took the cards from her. "You okay?" she asked, and I nodded, playing off my mood as nothing more than getting caught in a silly daydream.

I didn't feel guilty for anything that was happening between Evander and me, but I also didn't want to flaunt it in front of Felix. He shouldn't have had to sit there and be reminded that Dashiell and I were over and his hopes for us would never come to fruition. It was a conversation that Felix and I needed to have soon.

The game was one I could have been decently good at if my mind weren't all over the place. I couldn't bear to make eye contact with Felix or Evander and instead kept my gaze on my cards or in my lap when I was eventually knocked out of the hand. Evander was a master at the game, always staying in until the final round with Cal and Oli. Even Felix had made it to the end a time or two, but never me.

As usual, I was first out, and rather than sit and watch the rest of the round, I decided to plop back into the couch and stare up at the ceiling as I contemplated how and when I was going to talk to Felix about where I firmly stood on the subject of Dashiell.

"Are you okay, love?" Evander asked, and I twisted to see him leaning back next to me, already out of the game. Cal was smiling to himself for being the one to take his king out of the hand, but I could tell that Van had thrown the match to steal this moment with me. He placed his hand over mine, and I moved out of his touch as I saw Felix watching us in his periphery.

"I'm okay," I whispered, directing my focus to Van, and the look in his eyes told me he didn't believe that for a second. He glanced around the space, his attention snagging on my friend for a moment before he took my hand and pulled me up from the couch.

Van guided me to the crackling fire and I basked in the heat from the flames, somehow still cold even with all the layers I was wearing. Felix's attention returned to the cards in his hands, and Lia swore loudly as she was taken out of the round.

"You don't want him to see us like this," Van deduced, and I nodded.

"I know he still has hope that things between Dashiell and I will work out one day. We were a family before I came here, so of course, he wants us to be together again."

"And what do *you* want?" Evander asked, and I didn't miss the hesitation in his tone at the question, like he wasn't sure he really wanted to know. Hell, I wasn't sure of the answer myself, but I knew what I *didn't* want.

"There isn't a future for Dashiell and me, and I should have ensured that Felix knew that long ago. I've loved every minute of today, but I don't want to subject him to it. At least until I have a chance to talk to him."

Evander offered a warm smile before leaning down and pressing his forehead to mine. I stiffened at the contact immediately. Had he not heard a word I just said? Before I could pull away, he wrapped his arms around my waist, keeping me firm against him.

"They think we're sitting on the couch, having a nice little chat," he said, and I twisted my head to find both Lia and Felix staring where we had just been sitting. Felix watched us curiously while Lia had the biggest smile on her face like she thought we were the most adorable sight in the world.

"An illusion?" I asked, and Evander grinned wide.

"I could tell something was bothering you and wanted to make sure you were okay," he explained, and I wrapped my arms around his middle before burying my face in his chest.

"Thank you," I told him, my words muffled in his shirt. His grip around me tightened as we stood there, enjoying one another's company for a little while longer.

52.

"That is not at all what happened!" Evander exclaimed through a fit of laughter.

The day was spent playing as many games as possible from the comfort of the library. Lia had brought up trays and trays of food throughout the afternoon and well into the evening as we snacked, laughed, and celebrated Van. We were now currently devouring cake as everyone shared their favorite embarrassing memory of the birthday boy, despite his persistent protests. Cal had announced that it was a tradition that would not be skipped, and I happily agreed.

I enjoyed hearing everyone's tales, but it also hurt to know I had missed out on so much. It was a game I would have been able to take part in had I never been taken, and though I didn't like to dwell on that fact, I was envious of the memories they had with him over the years.

"Are you alright?" Felix asked from beside me on the couch.

I had avoided him most of the afternoon, unsure what to say, seeing as it wasn't the time or place to have a heart-to-heart about Dashiell. I nodded and picked at my dessert before Felix snatched the plate away.

"Hey!" I protested as I tried to grab my food back, but he held it just out of reach and gave me a flat look that demanded an explanation. I sighed and slunk back into my seat, knowing he wouldn't drop it and let me be. "Sometimes I feel like I missed out on my whole life. I get angry because it was stolen from me, and then I feel guilty because if I had been here, I would never have met you. And being resentful about it makes me seem ungrateful for our friendship, and I struggle with how I'm supposed to feel." Felix's amber eyes softened, and he set my plate down in his lap to take my hand in his.

"You're allowed to be pissed about it, Ainsley. Wishing you had grown up here doesn't detract from how much you cherish our friendship. It doesn't lessen your love for me, I promise."

I chewed on my lip as I thought about that. Though his words were pretty and meant to comfort, it wasn't likely to suddenly make me not feel like an ass for wanting to have grown up in Tenebrae instead of Caelum. I offered Felix a warm smile that didn't reach my eyes.

"We should talk later," I told him, and he nodded thoughtfully as if he knew exactly what that conversation would entail.

"Deny it all you want, but I remember it like it was yesterday," Cal told Evander, draining the last of his drink and pouring himself another. "It's time for another game anyway, and I say we play Truth or Dare."

Felix sat up at the mention of his favorite game, and I took the opportunity to steal my cake back and finish the last bite before he could stop me. He glared as I attempted to give him my best smile though my cheeks were bulging. Felix got up and joined the circle of our friends, where Lia was promptly refilling everyone's drink in preparation for the new game. I had come to learn that this group managed to turn everything into a drinking game, even if it didn't start that way. I swallowed my food and downed the rest of my wine before rising from the chair and striding over to everyone.

"Although I love a good round of Truth or Dare, I think I'm going to head to bed," I said.

I was exhausted from the late night and early morning Van and I had, not to mention I wasn't quite feeling like myself ever since catching Felix watching me. My mind was more focused on how to open up the conversation about Dashiell, and I knew I wasn't the best company at the moment. I had been the first one out for every game we played, not even bothering to try my best, which was extremely weird, seeing as I was competitive as hell.

"Are you sure?" Lia asked with a pout, and I nodded before bending down to hug her.

I made my way around the group, saying my goodbyes as they threw out various names and insults surrounding my decision to bow out early—to which

I promptly gave each and every one of them the middle finger. Van's eyes were glued on me as I finally made it to him. We hugged and I instructed him that I'd skin him alive if he was too loud when he came to bed.

I looked at my reflection in the bathing room mirror, smiling to myself as I pictured Evander's face when he would return to the room only to find me wearing his favorite shirt—the one I had stolen so many times he had to keep finding hiding places for it. Tonight, I had located it rolled up tight and shoved into a pair of pants he had stashed away on the top shelf of the closet. I didn't know why he insisted on continuing the game when there was no chance he'd ever win.

"It's about time," Van said as I entered the bedroom, and I gasped as he scared the living shit out of me. He was sitting patiently on his side of the bed in a pair of black sweatpants and a thin shirt. His hair was damp and slightly mussed, like he had just washed it. "I took a shower in your bathing room," he said, reading the question on my face.

"Why aren't you playing Truth or Dare?" I asked, climbing into my spot. Evander's eyes narrowed as he took in my shirt, and I smiled victoriously. "It's mine now, so you might as well just give up," I told him, and he rolled his eyes and shook his head. He liked our games too much to ever forfeit.

"I played my veto," he said plainly as if I was supposed to know what the hell that meant. "Everyone gets to pick what we do on birthdays, except for the person whose birthday it actually is. It's a tradition we've always had. However, the birthday person gets to pick one thing they want to do."

"What do you normally choose?"

"The tavern, which is probably why Cal tried to get me to take us there tonight."

"But you didn't want to go this year?"

"No," he said, reaching forward to take my hand. His thumb swept over my flesh in comforting strokes, and my heart pattered frantically at his touch. "I wanted to use it to spend time with you."

"You knew I'd go to bed early?"

"You've been off most of the day, so I had a feeling you would. I wanted to save my veto so when that happened, I could leave with you," he answered, and I suddenly felt guilty. I didn't want to ruin his day or make him think I wasn't enjoying myself. "Knock it off," he said, cutting through my thoughts.

Evander slid a finger under my chin to force me to look into his grey eyes, and I melted into his stare, getting lost in the dark depths and never wanting to find my way out.

"You didn't ruin anything, so stop thinking you did," he said sternly. "I wanted to leave. I've wanted to leave all day and just be with you. I had hoped you would call it a night hours ago so we could be alone, but instead, you kept being stubborn and tried to ride it out."

"I don't mean to be a downer on your birthday—"

"So then don't be," he interjected, squeezing my fingers, and I rolled my eyes at the snark in his tone.

"I still wish you would have told me so I could have gotten you a real present," I told him.

I knew Evander didn't care about that, but I still hated that he didn't tell me. He had done so much for me since arriving, and I didn't think my just being around him today was enough to make up for it. He guided my arms around his neck and pressed his forehead to mine.

"The only thing I wanted was to have you like this," he said, gently brushing his fingers over my skin. It may not have felt like enough, but I could tell it was for him. "You smell like me," he whispered, dropping my arms and reaching for something behind his back.

Before I could comment, he wrapped his legs around mine, pinning me in place as he ripped the shirt from my body and threw it over his shoulder. I squealed as I struggled to get free, but Evander clenched his thighs so I couldn't move an inch as he fought to shove a new shirt over my head. Where the hell did that come from? Had he anticipated that I'd find his favorite shirt all along?

I arched, falling back onto the bed and bringing him with me as he forced one of my arms through the holes.

"I don't know why you're fighting me, love," he purred, getting my other arm to go where he wanted. He was so much stronger than me, and though I probably could have put up more of a fight, I was a bit distracted by how good his body felt on top of mine.

"I don't know why you're bothering with this when you know I'm just going to steal it back," I countered, and Evander smirked, his eyes bright with the challenge. Gods, he was gorgeous.

"We'll see," he said, removing his weight from my body and pulling me up to sit again now that I was donned in a different one of his shirts.

He climbed off the bed and strode across the room, picking up the shirt I planned to steal later and shoving it into his dresser. He then walked over to the fully restocked liquor cart and began to pour us each a glass of wine.

"If I had never been taken…" I started, watching his back muscles flex beneath his shirt as he prepared our drinks. "If we had spent every birthday together, what would you have given me for mine?"

Evander turned and walked back to the bed with a glass in each hand and a thoughtful look on his face. He cocked his head as he considered my question, handing me my drink and sitting back in his spot. I took a long sip as I waited for him to respond and found that I was nervous about his answer, though I wasn't sure why. Finally, he smiled to himself and faced me more fully.

"Well, I'd definitely give you a stupid present just to be a smartass," he admitted, and I laughed at how much I believed him. "But I'd also get you something I knew you really wanted."

He interlaced our fingers, and my skin burned at the point of contact. Just the barest touch from him had my head spinning and caused me to lose all focus on anything but how it felt to be so close to him. Today was so much more intense than usual because I hadn't pulled away. I welcomed each display of intimacy with open arms, and though that terrified me, it was a problem to be dealt with tomorrow.

"We would have had years of secret jokes and shared experiences, so my final present would have represented that. I would have taken you somewhere or given you something that held significance to our friendship and shown how much you meant to me," Evander finished, and my heart broke at how he said the words. There was such longing in his voice, like he mourned those missed moments and stolen possibilities as much as I did.

Unlike me, Van had been surrounded by friends and people who loved him like family his entire life, but somehow it still didn't seem like enough. It should have been him and I together—growing up and supporting one another through trials and heartache. We should have had the inside jokes and the fights, the long nights of talking and getting into trouble. We were meant to already have had years together and an established foundation of unwavering friendship, but instead, we were only just beginning.

"Close your eyes," I told him, an idea flickering to life.

"Absolutely not," Van responded without hesitation.

"You don't trust me?" He cocked a brow as he studied my face, the picture of curiosity. "Is someone afraid I'm going to take advantage of his vulnerability and kill him to claim the throne as my own?" I remarked playfully, coating the words with mischievous intent.

"The fact that you came up with that response as quickly as you did, yes," he countered as his lips lifted in the corner.

"Just shut up and close them," I demanded. He loosed a long dramatic sigh before following my command. "No peeking," I instructed, and he groaned in mock annoyance before mumbling his acknowledgment. "And hold out your hand."

"Why?"

"Because I know what I want your present to be, and I can't give it to you if you don't hold out your hand," I said as if it was the most obvious fact in existence. Evander groaned but did as instructed, angling his palm up so he was ready to receive my gift. "Perfect. Now, wait here," I told him, hopping from the bed and placing my and Evander's wine glasses on the side table. "Don't open your eyes until I return and tell you to."

"I know how surprises work, love," he said cockily, and it took everything in me not to punch him in the face while he was unsuspecting. But alas, it was his birthday, so I could play nice for the evening.

I hurried downstairs, tiptoeing past the library where the game of Truth or Dare was still in full effect. Our friends laughed boisterously as they played, and even though it sounded fun, I had zero desire to partake. The only thing I wanted to do was spend as much time with Evander alone as I could. I pushed aside the thoughts of why that might have been. Instead, I just kept telling myself it was because it was his birthday, and this was what he wanted.

When I returned to the room, Van sat patiently in the exact position I'd left him in. He perked up slightly as he heard me reenter, and I padded over to the bed, climbing into my spot next to him and smiling widely to myself.

"Are you ready?" I asked, and Evander nodded at once like he was actually excited about whatever I was going to give him.

I placed the present in his waiting hand and took a deep breath before instructing him to open his eyes. Evander stared at the burnt piece of toast for a split second and then broke into laughter, the sound beautiful and haunting. The kind of laugh you wish would never leave you.

"Do I have to eat it?" he asked, and I nodded. Evander scrunched his face in the most adorable, playful sort of pout, but I wasn't going to back down, and he knew it.

Without argument, he picked up the bread, inhaled a steadying breath to prepare for what he was about to eat, and took a large bite. I watched his eyes widen a fraction as he chewed, and a confused look flooded his features. He pulled the bread away from his face to reveal a regular piece of toast without a burn mark in sight.

Evander's gaze snapped to mine, and I grinned from ear to ear at my perfectly casted illusion. It may have been something as simple as char on top of toast, but it was still enough to fool him. And that, in itself, was the real present.

He dropped the toast and reached for me, placing his hands on either side of my face as he pressed his forehead to mine like he always did.

"That was amazing," Evander breathed, and I couldn't help but feel completely confident in my abilities for the first time. Sure, there were moments when I trusted my Gifts and had no problem wielding them in the required way, but this was different. I had never felt this sure of myself and what I was capable of before.

I pulled out of his touch, and his hands suspended in the air momentarily as if he were about to reach for me again.

"That was the *smartass,* and the *something that represented our friendship* present rolled into one," I explained, and Evander chuckled. "Now, eyes closed again so I can give you the last one."

With a dramatic sigh, he shut his eyes and held out his hand as he waited for his final present. I scooted closer, though kept just out of reach as I watched him nervously, my mind already trying to lay out all of the reasons why I shouldn't go through with the present. But I wanted to and had for a while now. Taking a deep breath, I swallowed the fear, letting it fade away like the last rays of the setting sun.

53.

I pushed forward on my knees and cupped his cheek in my palm as my mouth met his in a sure and deliberate kiss. Evander dropped his outstretched hand the second he realized what was happening and moved to hold the back of my head as our lips molded together. His tongue demanded entrance, and fire, hot and raging, burst to life inside me as it swept over mine.

The kiss wasn't slow or gentle—it was fierce and passionate. It was brutal in the way we were claiming one another, demanding and giving everything we had. My body's desires took over, and I crawled onto his lap, straddling him as my hands raked through his hair, tugging on it possessively. Evander's lips broke from mine, and I sucked in a breath of air as his mouth found my neck. His hands slid down the side of my body and dipped below the hem of my shirt so he could feel my hot skin as he gripped my waist tight.

Instinctively, I rocked my hips and was met with the feel of him hard against me. Evander groaned at the movement, so naturally, I did it again, loving that he was unraveling for me. I yanked on his hair, pulling his face from my neck and demanding that his lips meet mine again. He kissed me hard as his fingers traveled down to my ass, digging into my flesh as he guided my movements against him.

"Make that sound again, love," he said desperately, and it was all I could do to focus on his voice and not his touch.

"What sound?" I asked between gasps of breaths before I crushed my mouth to his again, taking more of what I wanted. The taste of him was driving me wild, and I couldn't get enough.

In a smooth movement, Evander spun us around so that my back hit the bed before he ground himself harder against me. I raked my nails down his back and moaned as the friction sent me closer to the edge.

"*That* sound," he said. "Never stop making it."

"Then don't give me a reason to," I countered breathlessly, angling my hips to meet his as he moved again. I closed my teeth around his bottom lip, tugging gently as I wrapped my legs around his middle, refusing to allow an inch of space. Evander groaned, and the noise alone almost sent me over the cliff and into a pit of ecstasy.

My breaths came in short pants as I moved on him, getting lost in how good it felt. I pressed my fingers into his back, his muscles flexing while he drove me to my release.

"Love," he warned, and I knew what it meant by how he said the word. He was barely holding on himself, and if we went any longer, there would only be one way this would end,

"Don't stop," I begged. "Please, don't stop."

I captured his mouth with mine, and he picked up the pace. I whimpered against his lips as I held on as long as I could, not wanting it to end but also needing the release it promised. Evander gripped my waist hard enough to bruise as he worked me until I was crying out his name. He covered my mouth with his, needing to taste the sound of my desire as he continued to grind against me, and my body shook as wave after wave of pleasure rocked through me. Soon Evander was grunting his own release.

We panted, desperate for air, as our chests moved rapidly against one another. Evander pressed his forehead to mine as we took slow, deliberate breaths to come down from our high. Before I could stop myself, a laugh bubbled up and escaped my lips. Evander drew back, looking at me curiously, though he had a broad smile on his face. Soon he joined me as we laughed at what we had just done. The two of us had ridden each other with our clothes on like two teenagers, afraid to have sex for the first time, and not the experienced adults we were. It was ridiculous, but there was also something so pure and innocent about it that I loved.

It made me feel more connected to him and what our past could have been like if I had never been taken. Would we have done something similar to this? Would it have just been an experiment conducted between two people who trusted each other, or would it have altered us from friends to something more?

"Just to be clear," I said, still trying to catch my breath. "The back half of what just transpired was *not* your intended present."

Evander laughed harder as he stared at me, and my heart shuddered at how dazzling his smile was. He was gorgeous on any given day, but seeing him so carefree and happy made it impossible not to be in awe of his beauty.

"And here I thought you were just being extra generous," he countered, and I shook my head before shoving him off me with a breathy laugh.

I slipped out of bed and into the bathing room to clean myself up, changing into fresh clothes before heading for the sink to splash water on my face and cool down. My eyes sought the mirror, and I was met with the reflection of a very satisfied woman. I dragged my thumb across my swollen lips as I remembered how his mouth tasted against mine. My cheeks were flush, and my hair was a tangled mess, and yet I wasn't sure I ever looked better—more alive.

I reentered the bedroom to find Van lying on his side of the bed in a completely different set of clothes as well. He eyed me curiously with a still-present grin on his lips as I crawled into bed and rolled on my side to face him. My smile matched his self-satisfying one as we stared at one another without saying a word.

"So," I began, but I had no idea what would follow. Evander was no help. He simply watched me struggle without offering any input of his own. He wanted me to have to start the conversation and had absolutely zero intentions of helping me navigate it. "Did you have a good birthday?" I asked, and his smile spread ear to ear.

"I did," he admitted but offered nothing else.

"And you enjoyed all of your presents from everyone?" I tried, and Van rolled onto his back and stared up at the ceiling as he nodded.

"I did," he mused as if going over what everyone had given him. "But I think the liquor decanter Cal gave me was my favorite." I lunged for him, smacking him hard as he laughed, gripped my wrist, and pulled me into his chest.

"You're the worst," I told him, though my face gave away that I didn't believe that at all.

"Don't I know it." Evander wrapped his arms around me in a tight cage as he hitched a leg over mine. I squirmed against him, trying to free myself from his hold, but it only constricted, refusing to give me up. "I won ten minutes of uninterrupted time, and since that ended early, I'm calling it in now," Evander explained as he cradled me like I was his favorite stuffed toy.

"That's fine and all, but you'll be holding a corpse if you don't let me get some air," I mumbled into his shirt. Van loosened his grip only enough to roll onto his back and rearrange me so I was lying with my head on his chest.

We stayed silent for a few minutes, neither of us needing to fill the space with words. I focused on the sound of his heart beating and the feel of his fingers trailing down my back and over my arm as he held me.

"I know my birthday is technically over, but can I ask for one last thing?" he whispered into the dark.

"Were my presents not good enough?" I joked, and he shrugged, the movement shifting me slightly.

"Your presents were more than enough, but I'm selfish when it comes to you."

"What is it that you want?" I questioned, my interest piqued.

"To kiss you," he replied hesitantly, and I lifted my head from his warm chest to meet his stare.

His charcoal eyes bore into me with a kind of longing and hope that I couldn't put into words. He wasn't requesting what had just transpired between us—that had been my choice to initiate. It had been my decision to take it as far as it had gone. And though this wasn't the first time Evander had mentioned or suggested kissing me, there was something about how he was looking at me that set this moment apart from the rest. It was the first time he *asked*.

"We've already kissed," I pointed out. "It sounds to me like someone is being a bit greedy." He nodded just barely, as if acknowledging his own thoughts rather than my playful jab. A vulnerability in his eyes had me lifting my head a bit higher to give him my full attention. I'd dealt with King Evander, with sinfully flirtatious Evander, with annoyingly skilled warrior Evander—fuck, I've even dealt with *snap someone's neck and walk away like it's nothing* Evander—but shy Evander? Shy Evander was someone new, and I eagerly wanted to meet him. He took a deep breath, and then I saw it; a switch in his face that told me he was about to retreat into himself the same way I had so many times.

"I know, and you're right, love. Just forget I said anything—"

"No," I replied, abruptly cutting him off. I desperately wanted to hold on to this side of him for a little while longer. "Tell me why you want one." He raised a brow suggestively.

"Besides the obvious?" he teased, and I knew he was trying to use humor and his cheeky ways to reach the shallows from the depths he was currently wading through. I wouldn't let him.

"Yes," I said, and his eyes softened as he realized I was not going to return my usual banter. He shifted uncomfortably beneath me, and even in a room full of advisors and discussing the subject of war, I had never seen him this on edge. My intrigue heightened.

He released my hand that was clutched to his chest and dragged his knuckles slowly over my cheek, the skin there instantly flushing under his touch. Goosebumps exploded over my body as he went down to my bottom lip and gently brushed his thumb over it, his eyes glued to his work. He swallowed thickly before he spoke.

"Because it wasn't enough. Because though I love when you take charge, I want my turn to initiate it. If I only get to have you like this for tonight, I want to make the most of it. And because I want you at my mercy just once. The way you have me completely at yours." I stopped breathing altogether at his confession, and before I could contemplate it any longer, I found myself nodding.

"Okay," I said weakly. His eyes narrowed as he tried to place my meaning. *Okay,* to his confession, or *okay* to his proposal? I'm not sure even I knew when I first said it, but the hopeful look on his face made my decision for me. "Just once?" I clarified.

"Just once."

"And then tomorrow, we go back to how things were," I stated.

"If that's what you want, love, yes. It doesn't have to mean anything," he reassured.

I swallowed the lump in my throat and forced down the flutters in my stomach that appeared out of nowhere. Why was I so freaking nervous? We'd kissed before. Granted, the first time in the flesh was literally only twenty minutes ago, but it still happened. And it was magnificent. So why did now feel so different?

Don't overthink, just do, I told myself.

"Then okay," I said and gave a small smile.

"Okay," he repeated and returned a sly grin of his own.

I began to push myself higher to meet his lips, but before I could move more than an inch, Evander leaned into me, pushing me onto my back so my head pressed into the pillow. I sucked in a breath at the sudden movement as his face hovered just above mine, close enough that our noses almost touched.

Evander brushed strands of hair away from my face, but he didn't kiss me; instead, he just stared. His thumb swept back and forth over my bottom lip in a delicate caress as his grey eyes studied every inch of my face before settling on my gaze. The yearning in his stare was enough to have my heart pounding so loudly that I swore he could hear it. I swore the whole Gods damn house could hear it. He slid his hand around to cup my jaw and gently tilted my chin a fraction higher so that his lips grazed across mine, the gesture a quiet reverence that had me begging for more.

"Evander," I breathed, and he pressed his mouth to mine, devouring his name from my lips and cutting off my broken plea.

His kiss was soft and searching, and as his tongue slipped over mine in the barest of touches, I moaned softly, wanting to lose myself in the feel of him. His grip on my face was gentle yet firm and held an air of possessiveness as if I was his, just for this moment.

And maybe I was.

This kiss was remarkably different than the last. Before was passionate and wild, two people desperate for a physical connection after months of pining. But this wasn't that. It was patience coming to fruition. It was longing and desperation; it was a need so great it went above what our bodies craved. It was my magic reaching out—my *soul* reaching out—wanting to fuse itself to his. A siren's call or a beacon, I wasn't sure which, but I didn't care. I wanted more.

Our embrace was a dance, fluid and beautiful. We moved in time like we had rehearsed the steps for years. Like we had been made to do this together. Every caress of his lips and stroke of his tongue was deliberate and intense and met with eager willingness. It was the kind of kiss that would surely haunt me for days to come.

Evander pressed his chest into mine like he couldn't bare even the slightest distance between us. I snaked my arms around his neck and ran my fingers through his hair, hoping it would stop my hands from shaking as I held back from claiming what I greedily desired. It didn't.

My fingers still trembled as I tried to coax an end to the persistent ache I had for him. He parted my mouth wider, his tongue demanding entry to deepen our kiss and drawing out the sounds from me he so desperately wanted to hear. I wasn't sure there was anything I wouldn't have given him at that moment. He got what he wanted—me completely at his mercy. And I loved every sinful second of it.

Van's mouth began to slow against mine, and his hold on my face tightened like he was trying to savor the taste and feel of me before letting go. He reluctantly pulled back, but I wasn't ready for it to end. I leaned forward, pressing my lips to his again, refusing to let this be over so soon. He grinned against my mouth before kissing me back, and my Gods if I didn't melt more for him right then. His smile tasted like utter perfection, and I couldn't get enough.

I glided my fingers from the back of his neck to his chest, fisting his shirt in my hands to keep him against me as I took more of what I wanted—what I needed. He sighed in pleasure as our lips moved in perfect harmony, and I relished in the noise. I may have been at his complete mercy—my body engulfed in fire at his presence—but I could tell by the tender way he kissed me and how his fingers trembled so lightly against my skin that he was just as lost in the flames, burning right there with me.

I kissed him like he was mine—like he was everything. And for the briefest of moments, I allowed him to be.

Our movements slowed, and the touches became softer, our dance coming to an end. Evander planted two small kisses against me before relinquishing my lips completely, though his hands stayed put. I released a shaky breath as I came down from my high and couldn't help but notice his breathing was also uneven. I tilted my chin up to get a better look at him.

His chest pushed against mine, and his jaw was clenched like his grip on me was the only thing keeping his restraint in check. For the love of the Gods, I wished his control would slip. His brow was furrowed, and the light in his eyes was wild—not with lust or desire but with admiration and wonder. I could feel a deep sense of purpose and belonging emanating from him as his lips lifted in the corner. What was on his mind?

Evander leaned in and slowly flicked my nose up with his before dragging the tip of his nose back and forth across mine. It was something he did often, but for a reason I couldn't explain, the act felt more intimate than anything we had just done. My heart constricted and rather than push him away like I had done every other time he performed that small gesture, I wanted to return it instead.

Evander pressed his forehead to mine as he took a deep breath. My magic began to thrash beneath the surface chaotically and I tensed as I swallowed hard, forcing the darkness to stay within its cage, though it was persistent. Van withdrew at once, no doubt sensing the shift in me, and my fingers curled tighter in the fabric of his shirt.

"It won't hurt me," he promised, tilting my chin to meet his soft gaze.

I wanted to believe him, but something about how it moved felt different. I knew our Gifts were a part of us, but it felt like my magic was directly connected to my soul and begging for a way out—aching for *him*. This wasn't the normal, playful way it had reached for him in the past, desiring nothing more than to swirl around Van's own Gift. No, this was demanding and desperate, violently pushing against me like it needed to surge into him and take whatever it wanted. I didn't know how to trust it.

"Ainsley, it won't hurt me. I promise," Evander said, and his voice pulled my focus just enough that my magic slipped through the cracks, rushing out in full force as it slammed against him. I gasped as I struggled to call it back, but Van's hold on my face tightened as he steadied me. "Just focus, love," he demanded, and my eyes darted around his face, looking for any signs of pain or discomfort I may have caused, but there weren't any.

I closed my eyes in relief and did what he requested, focusing solely on the magic I was expelling. It moved around Van, trying to penetrate whatever internal shield he had up to protect himself from my attack. Though, the more I honed in on the magic, the more I realized it wasn't an attack at all. It pushed against him, not forcefully or violently as it had with me, but rather, it caressed him gently—lovingly. It wasn't taking; it was asking.

"I told you it wouldn't hurt me. Never stop trusting your magic, even when you don't understand it," he instructed, and I nodded as I loosed a breath. Evander's shadows slipped around us, and my own took form, gliding around his. I sighed at the feel of his magic against mine and the pressure that had lifted from my chest at the realization that my magic wasn't trying to harm the man that had meant so much to me.

"Why does it keep doing this?" I huffed, frustrated that I couldn't figure it out or control it.

Van smiled at my irritation like he thought it was the most adorable display in the world, which only annoyed me more.

"Because it *really* likes me," he replied confidently as he tapped me on the nose. I batted his hand away and rolled my eyes at his arrogance, though I couldn't deny his claim. My magic did seem to be drawn to him.

"Clearly, it doesn't know any better," I jabbed, pushing him back so he turned onto his side. I curled into him just as I had this afternoon and rested my forehead against his as I inhaled his scent. Van cradled my jaw, letting his fingers twine into my hair as he adjusted his position to get us as close as possible.

"I think you're just mad because it gives away how much *you* like me," he answered, rubbing his nose along mine.

"You're delusional," I replied, pushing my lips to his, needing to taste him again. Evander hummed against me, pointing out that my words and actions at the moment were two very different things.

He wrapped his arms around me, rolling onto his back and bringing me to lay on top of him, all without breaking our embrace. I moved my hands to his hair as mine fell around us, creating our own private curtain. His fingers trailed over my spine and down my arms, causing goosebumps to spread over each searing pass of his touch. I smiled against his mouth.

"What?" Evander asked, pulling back to meet my eyes, and I shrugged.

"I just never thought you'd be like this." He quirked a brow in a request for me to elaborate. I shifted from atop him to curl into his side once more, taking his hand in mine and playing with his fingers. "You're always like, 'Love, I know you want me and—"

"That's a shit impression of me," Evander interrupted as he chuckled.

"No, it wasn't. Now be quiet so I can finish." Evander's smile became wicked as he opened his mouth to respond. "And don't you dare make a sexual joke," I warned, and he promptly clamped his lips shut tight. I cleared my throat before dropping my voice lower to mock him again. "You can deny all you'd like about how much you want me, but one day I'll have you in my bed and screaming my name from pleasure," I imitated.

Evander's laugh was boisterous, and I couldn't help but match it as he came undone. His smile was beautiful, and I leaned in to kiss each of his dimples, unable to stop myself. He twined his fingers through my hair and directed my lips to his, still laughing against my mouth.

"Tell me something, love," he began. "Did I lie?"

I opened my mouth to reply and quickly shut it as I remembered I was doing just that, not more than thirty minutes ago. I groaned as he laughed.

"I think you're remembering the events wrong," I tried, but Van shook his head, pulling my body tight against him as his lips molded to mine, moving like he owned them. He was relentless in his demand, and I met his tongue stroke for stroke as I let my mind drift back to how good it felt to have him move against me.

"Nice try, but I'll never forget the taste of my name on your lips."

My mind became foggy, and every inch of me tingled at that confession. What were we even talking about a moment ago?

"My point was," I said, pulling away from his branding kiss as I tried to get my bearings straight. "You're normally arrogant and confident like that, but today you've been like Onyx."

"What is that supposed to mean?" he asked with a breathy laugh.

"It means that you're being sweet and cuddly... And extremely needy," I answered, angling my chin towards the sleeping wolves in the corner. Evander's eyes followed the gesture, and together we looked at Onyx, fast asleep entirely on top of Nova, his chin resting firmly on her head and flattening her ears. They really were adorable.

"I see," Van said, giving me his attention again. He brushed the loose strands of hair from my face before dragging his knuckles up and down my arm, feeling the soft flesh there. "When you came here, you were so standoffish—and rightfully so. You refused to let anyone in. Even those nights at the tavern, I knew it was only about physical desires and you trying to mend yourself. There wasn't intimacy in your motives," he explained.

His fingers trailed down over mine and back up to my shoulders. I shivered at the movement, and he smiled softly as he bit his lip. I let my thoughts travel to the moments he was referring to and how, even as I was pressed against a wall with my mouth moving against someone else's, it meant nothing. My aim was not to feel, but to replace the memories of Dashiell with others—though it hadn't worked at the time.

"And then last night and today, you let me do this," Evander continued, moving his knuckles to brush over my cheek before traveling down my neck and back to my arm. "You've never let anyone hold you or touch you like this, and I know that it's only for today, but I promised myself I was going to soak up every second of it."

I closed my eyes and let myself get lost in his touch. He was right, of course. This was the only time I had allowed anyone to get this close. For the first time since Dashiell, I let myself want to be held and touched the way Evander had done all day.

"It may not have been intentional, but getting to have you like this has been the best present I could have asked for, Ainsley," Evander said, and my brown eyes fluttered open to stare deep into his grey ones, watching the honesty within them shine bright. "So, yes. With you, I will sometimes be a cuddly, attention-seeking, overbearing, and fluffy wolf," he added, pressing his mouth to mine, and I smiled wide.

"And other times?" I questioned, and a crooked and devilish grin formed on his lips.

"Other times, I will be the asshole who whispers very filthy promises into your ear," he admitted shamelessly. "Because, one—I like to see you squirm and very much enjoy getting under your skin. And two, because it always seems to take your mind out of whatever dark place it's in at the time. I like knowing that I can bring you out."

I snaked my arms around his neck as I let the weight of his words sink into me. Every time I thought he flirted with me to piss me off, it had been for some deeper meaning.

"And which are you now?" I asked, brushing his dark hair from his forehead.

"Which do you want me to be?"

I thought about that for a moment. There was no denying that I wanted him to fulfill every dirty vow he had made to me, but more than that, I wanted to be with him in the way we had been today. There had always been chemistry between us. But the gentle stroke of his fingers on my skin and how his lips tenderly pressed against mine meant so much more than any sexual desire. I needed him in *this* way.

"The fluffy wolf," I decided.

"Good choice," he responded, smiling as he placed his mouth to mine.

His hands dragged along my spine as I kissed him repeatedly, never wanting this moment to be over, though I knew it would eventually end. But not tonight. Tonight I would hold him and steal the kisses I was desperate for. Tonight I would let myself *feel*.

54.

I had both the best and worst sleep of my life. The best because being in his arms gave me a sense of home I couldn't put into words. And the worst, because every time I drifted off, I'd wake up in a panic, thinking it was time to let him go again. I knew what we shared yesterday wasn't going to last forever. I had agreed to allow myself just that one day with him, but it couldn't be more than that.

The only thing I could ever offer him was the friendship we had created. I felt such a deep and resounding trust in him and what we had together that I couldn't bear the thought of that being ripped away. Evander had the power to hurt me past the point of no return if I continued to give him what he wanted, so I needed to create distance. I wouldn't ever push him away fully, but I needed to reestablish the boundaries that had blurred between us.

After everything that happened with Dashiell, I didn't have it in me to go through it again. But what terrified me the most was how right it felt with Evander. Every instinct in my body screamed at me to give him all of myself, but I was no longer whole. I didn't have anything left to give. I couldn't risk my heart like that ever again. I couldn't be what Evander wanted—what he deserved.

I thought over our time together, from when I first met him in Caelum up until now. He had gotten under my skin so thoroughly, pissing me off at every possible moment, yet I always craved more of him. It had taken me a long time to realize what those little games between us were really about. I had been so convinced he thrived off my anger, and though I was sure part of him did, causing my wrath had never been the point of them all.

He had done it for me.

The games weren't only meant to distract me from my heartache but also to showcase my strength. They were designed for me to struggle and force myself to push through. To learn just how strong and capable I was, even when I felt like nothing more than fractured glass.

He had this way of coaxing the darkness from my bones and making me learn to love it. Because of him, I never gave up, even when I wanted to. I kept pushing through and embraced the magic that once terrified me because he forced me to recognize the power in myself. He had kept me alive and fighting when I was so convinced he was determined to break me. Each smirk, insult, and game stoked the fire within me, keeping the embers hot and primed for the flames he knew still lived.

Tears pricked the back of my eyes as I clung to him and the memory of our day together. I could still taste him on my lips and feel his fingers through my hair as we kissed throughout the night. I should have never let it happen. I shouldn't have given myself a single day with him because now I was being shredded apart by the loss of someone who was never mine to begin with. A lump formed in my throat, and it felt like all of the air had been stolen from my lungs as I realized the one emotion that could cause me to feel agony so great.

"Your silence has never been so loud, Ainsley," Evander whispered, and I startled in his arms, not realizing he had awoken. "What are you thinking?" My eyes drifted to the windows to find dawn's light pouring in between the curtains as a cold winter breeze drifted in, chilling my bare arms. He stroked the skin there, bringing warmth to them once more.

"I'm thinking about how cold it is and how much I don't want to get out of bed," I told him. It wasn't a lie. If I could lay in bed with him forever, I would. But I couldn't, and now that the sun had risen, it was time to back away.

"Likewise," he said as his fingers swept up and down my arms. I took a deep breath, steeling myself before I sat up.

"So I was thinking..." I began, trying to figure out how best to go about this.

"When are you not?" he quipped, and a sleepy smile spread across his face. I rolled my eyes at his sass, trying to seem as normal as possible, and pulled myself up to my knees beside him.

"I was thinking that it's been a while since I stayed in my own room," I told him, already regretting the suggestion. He sat up and shifted himself so his back rested against the headboard before shrugging.

"We can move into your room if you'd prefer," he said like the idea didn't bother him. I pulled on my fingers and averted my eyes. This was already so much harder than I expected.

"I meant alone," I whispered, hating the way the words tasted on my tongue. They were rotten and vile—wrong but necessary. When he didn't respond, I glanced to find him observing me carefully. "It's just that I've been staying here for my safety, but Ministro hasn't made a move against me," I explained, hoping it would have been a good enough excuse. He nodded thoughtfully, though concern flooded his features.

"It's true that there hasn't been another attack orchestrated, but that doesn't mean there won't be one. I would prefer you stay in someone's company, but the choice is yours," he explained. It was a reasonable request and one I agreed with.

"Okay," I told him. "I'm sure I can have Felix and Lia take turns staying with me."

"Am I really such bad company?" Evander teased though I didn't miss the edge of hurt in his voice. My stomach dropped at the sound, and I wanted nothing more than to erase his pain. My heart was breaking to cause him any sort of hurt, but what was I supposed to do? I was trying to create distance the best way I knew how.

"No, of course not," I said at once. "It's just that I've been staying with you for the past month, and you must want your space back. You have to be sick of me by now. Plus, don't you want the opportunity to take someone home without worrying about the woman you're sharing a room with?"

The words were like vomit, coming up all at once. I don't know even why I uttered that last sentence. I knew full well he never intended to bring someone home, so maybe it was just some shallow attempt at showing that it didn't bother me if he wanted to.

"I don't, I'm not, and I won't be doing that," he countered flatly, clearly offended that I would even suggest such an idea. "I enjoy spending time with you, love, and you know that, so just tell me what's going on."

"Nothing," I said, climbing off of the bed. Evander slid from his side of the mattress and walked around to meet me, his gaze hard and unyielding.

"Bullshit."

"Maybe I just want my own space," I argued weakly, knowing the only thing I wanted was him. Evander stepped back and observed me in the exact way he did all those months ago when we first met in Caelum.

"This is because we kissed," he pointed out, and my eyes widened. He smiled, knowing he was right, but the gesture was anything but friendly. It was filled with frustration and anger.

"No, it isn't," I said, shaking my head.

"Oh, yes, it is. We kissed, and now you're freaking out."

"I am not freaking out," I told him, and Evander dropped a pointed stare at the hands that were balled into fists at my sides to stop them from shaking. "Maybe I'm just trying not to punch you right now," I countered.

"If we didn't kiss last night, I would have believed that. Now tell me why you're running."

"I'm not run—"

"Cut the shit, love. We both know you are, and I want to know why. You've never had an issue telling me what's on your mind, so what's stopping you this time?" He knew he was right, and his arrogant tone proved it.

"It's not because we kissed," I replied, and he rolled his eyes, not believing a word from my mouth though it was the truth.

The reason was so much more than just a simple kiss. It was the way we held one another and the unspoken declarations that slipped through with each press of our lips. It was the way I never wanted to stop—to never let him go.

"I told you it doesn't have to mean anything. We can go back to exactly how things were before," he said, but there was just enough edge of doubt in his tone that told me he was questioning if that was a possibility.

As nice as it would have been to act like last night didn't mean anything, it did. It meant everything. And as his grey eyes poured into mine, I knew he knew it too.

"What if I don't want it to go back to how it was?" he asked, and the air from my lungs disappeared like smoke on the wind. A single tear slipped free, and Evander's hands were on me a heartbeat later, cradling my face. "I know you feel this just as strongly as I do, Ainsley," he whispered, and I shook my head with a desire to argue. "Don't pull away. Don't run."

"I can't, Evander."

"You can," he urged softly, and my chest ached even more with his plea.

"I don't want this. Not with you," I said, my voice breaking with each word.

Evander meant everything to me, and I couldn't risk what we had built. I couldn't lose him. I wouldn't survive it. Hurt flashed across his features, shattering my heart like glass. I was subtly aware of a door opening and footsteps sounding in the distance, but my focus was wholly on the man in front of me.

"Let's go, you two. Get your asses outside," Olivier commanded, not seeming to realize what he had walked in on.

"Not now, Olivier," Evander responded, not taking his eyes from mine.

"Yes, now. Neither of you has trained in days and—"

"Oli," Evander pleaded, turning towards his friend. "Please."

I turned my gaze to Olivier as he took in Evander's disheveled appearance and the tears in my eyes. He made to back away, but I spoke up, not wanting to be left alone with Van any longer. If I was, I knew my resolve would disappear, and I'd be in his arms once more.

"It's fine. Olivier is right, we need to go," I announced. "Just give me ten minutes to bathe, and I'll be down." I twisted, angling to flee to the bathing room.

"We aren't done here," Evander cut in, grabbing my arm to stop me from retreating.

"Yes, Evander, we are," I said, eyeing his grip on me, and he followed my stare before releasing me at once. I swallowed hard at the hurt in his eyes and backed away from him slowly. "Can you have my things sent back to my room?"

Evander's throat bobbed, and he turned his head to the side as he blinked away the tears that had formed in his eyes. His jaw was tight, and his chest rose heavily as he fought to overcome the heartache I knew he was experiencing.

"Is that what you truly want?" he asked, unable to look at me.

"Yes," I whispered, and he raised his chin higher, accepting our fate.

"Then consider it done, Ainsley."

I hurried into the bathing room and shut the door as Olivier's voice filled the space.

"Van, what's going on?" he asked softly, though I could hear every word.

I walked over to the sink and turned the water on to drown out his questioning. I could have just thrown up a silencing shield, but the selfish, nosy part of me wanted to hear the exchange.

"We kissed last night," I heard him quietly say. "And now she's running."

Muffled footfalls echoed, and I assumed Olivier was moving closer to comfort his friend.

"Maybe she just needs some time," he offered, and Evander scoffed.

"I don't think *time* had anything to do with her decision."

"What do you mean?" Oli asked, and Evander was quiet for a moment before finally responding.

"I think Ainsley finally realized who I am, or rather who I'm not," he said, the words coming out a perfect blend of bitter and hurt. I waited with bated breath for him to elaborate and explain what he meant. "She's finally realized I'm not who she wants. I'm not *him*."

"Van, I don't think—"

"It is," Evander interrupted, and I crumbled. Did he think I rejected him because he wasn't Dashiell? I was going to be sick. "I just need to get the fuck out of here," he said at once, and then the space was filled with the swooshing sound of wind before being replaced with retreating footsteps.

I fell to the ground, clutching my knees to my chest. I did more than just hurt him. I broke the heart of the one who had supported and been there for me through all my mishaps and mistakes. The person who saw the truth through every lie I threw at him and never left my side. I couldn't let him misunderstand my reasoning and think that it was because he wasn't enough.

I quickly dressed and headed downstairs, but there was no one in sight. I made it outside to the training area to find everyone there—everyone except Evander. Felix's eyes located me the second I stepped into view, like he could feel the pain and guilt from a mile away. I shook my head without meeting his stare, knowing he'd know the gesture was meant for him, and headed to Olivier.

"Where is he?" I asked as Oli organized a row of throwing daggers.

"He had a meeting—"

"We both know he didn't. Where is he, Olivier?" I pleaded. He turned to me and shrugged.

"I honestly don't know, Ainsley. I've never seen him like that." Great, now I was bringing out a broken side no one had ever witnessed from their king. I bit my lip as I looked around, trying desperately to keep the tears that burned the back of my eyes at bay. "He'll be back," Olivier said gently, placing a hand on my shoulder.

"Does he hate me?" I croaked, unable to stop myself. His turquoise eyes grew soft and sad. I didn't know what he thought of me for hurting his best friend.

"Of course not. I don't think he could hate you if he tried."

I nodded as a single tear slipped down my cheek. Familiar arms wrapped around me from behind, and I closed my eyes as I inhaled his comforting leather and spice scent.

"Let's take today off," Felix offered, but I shook my head. I didn't want to let this feeling break me.

"Felix is right," Olivier replied. "Your head isn't going to be in it today, no matter how hard you try to focus. Spend the day with your friend." I opened my mouth to object, but he moved closer, and his face grew serious. "And I need to go and find mine."

I couldn't argue with that. I wanted him to find Evander and be there for him like Felix always was for me. The sooner Oli could find him, the sooner he could bring him home, and I could set the record straight about why I needed space.

"Okay," I agreed, letting Felix tug me from the ring and towards the stables.

55.

I saddled myself on Nox as Felix led us on his mare down the dirt path behind the house. We didn't speak for over an hour until we reached the opposite end of the lake. We dismounted and strode for the edge before sitting shoulder to shoulder to look out at the view.

"Are you ready to tell me what happened with Evander?" he asked gently. I nodded, pulling my knees tight to my chest. I felt slightly guilty that Felix and I would be talking about my feelings for Evander before I had a chance to discuss Dashiell, but there was nothing I could do about that anymore.

"We kissed last night," I told him, bracing myself for a lecture.

"And it was… bad?" he guessed when I didn't elaborate, and I released a breath in relief.

"No, Felix, it wasn't bad. It was perfect and everything I could have hoped for," I sighed. I thought about how it felt to have him holding me close as he kissed me deeply. The feel of his body pressed against mine, and how I felt like there wasn't anywhere else I belonged more than in that moment with him. "But then I remembered everything with Dashiell, and I ran."

Felix was quiet for a few minutes. "You have nothing to feel guilty over, Ainsley. I know it hasn't been that long, but—" His words had me sitting up straighter and facing him fully. Did he think I felt remorse about moving on?

"I don't feel guilty, Felix," I interrupted. "Dashiell made his choices, and that led to losing me. I have every right to move on from him, and I won't apologize or feel ashamed for having feelings for someone else. I don't have a reason to be sorry."

"You're right," Felix said, smiling at the strength in my words. "And I'm proud of you for realizing that. But if you're not feeling guilty about moving on from him, then why did you run?"

Because I'm a pathetic coward, terrified of what being in love will do to me. Because I'm an idiot who accidentally makes the man she's crazy about think she still has feelings for someone else. Because I'm too fucking afraid to admit what I feel for him aloud. The list goes on and on.

"What if it's all a lie again?" I whispered, trying to keep my voice even, though it broke with every word. "What if I get shattered so completely again that there's no hope of putting the pieces back together? I don't think I can survive it a second time."

Felix twisted to give me his full attention, his hands coming up to cup my cheeks as I stared into his amber eyes.

"That will never happen, Ainsley. You are strong and capable, and you have people here who love you unconditionally. You'll never have to go through anything alone ever again."

There was comfort in his claim and truth in it as well. I couldn't imagine Lia, of all people, letting me suffer by myself. Even if I demanded to be left alone, I didn't doubt she'd break down the door and refuse to go until I smiled again.

"Evander has taught me so much. He's helped me grow and be strong, but what if being together is a disaster, and he takes away everything I've worked so hard to become?" I said.

"Evander may have given you the skills to build a ladder and climb out of the hole you were in, but *you* were the one who did the work. You did what you had to do to make your way out of that pit you were stuck in. He could never take that away. You would never let him."

Felix was right. Evander was the one who supported me, but I had to do it on my own. I had to learn to love myself and who I was without the crutch of the two people I had leaned on so hard. No one could ever diminish that, not even Evander.

Felix stood to his feet and pulled off his shirt before reaching his hand out behind him.

"Are you insane? It's winter, and that water is cold as hell."

"You don't have to join if you're too afraid," Felix teased.

He was baiting me with a lure he knew I would bite. I unbuttoned my shirt and pants before kicking off my shoes. Once we were both undressed, save for our underwear, we sprinted into the freezing lake.

Holy fucking hell.

My shivering limbs slowed as we made our way to the middle of the lake for our frozen swim, going where my feet could no longer touch. Goosebumps covered every square inch of my body and my teeth chattered so hard I felt the vibrations in my bones.

"What's wrong, Ainsley? Cold?" Felix questioned, his voice shaky and barely getting out the words.

"I hate you," I said as I treaded water, determined not to be the first to demand our return to shore.

"No, you don't."

"No, I don't," I admitted, rolling my eyes.

He smiled widely, but there was a soft sadness to his expression that told me that no matter how happy he seemed, there was something on his mind. Something he was missing, and I knew exactly what it was.

"I'm sorry you're not with him," I told Felix, and he shrugged just barely to brush off the comment though I knew he was hurting. "You don't have to pretend with me, Felix. It's okay to miss him. I know Dashiell and I have our history, but I don't want you to think you can't mention him around me. He's your brother."

Felix closed his eyes as my words washed over him.

"Thank you," he responded before dipping his head below the surface. He wasn't ready, and I wouldn't push him on it. He seemed to be relatively okay with the idea of me moving on with Evander, but I wasn't naive enough to believe the notion didn't hurt him. I knew how much he loved our little trio family, and once upon a time, I had too. I thought it would be the three of us forever, and I was happy with that. Knowing that beautiful image was gone couldn't have been easy for him.

Felix breached the water with a painful yelp.

"What is it!" I exclaimed, and I glanced around in panic. Felix's eyes were glued to the surface as he frantically moved about, splashing the freezing water around.

"A FISH BIT MY DICK!" he yelled, and I blinked several times, not sure I heard him correctly.

"What?"

"A FISH BIT MY FUCKING DICK!" he repeated, and I burst with laughter before clasping my mouth shut. Felix shot me a death glare and held up the underwear he had been wearing. "It's not funny! It was trapped in these and fucking *bit me*," he explained with a scowl.

I ducked the lower half of my face beneath the water so he wouldn't see my smile, and he reached forward, pressing his fingers against the sides of my ribs and tickling me. I choked on the lake water as I struggled to breathe and laugh simultaneously.

"I'm sorry! I can't help but find it hilarious," I yelled through the bouts of hysterics. Felix broke into laughter as well, unable to hold it back any longer, and for a moment, I forgot about all the bullshit back home and how much I had screwed things up with Evander.

"Let's go back to the shore before my entire cock becomes a snack for these asshole fish," he implored as he began to swim backward.

"Thank the gods," I said, following his lead and happy to escape the cold water.

My legs barely made it to my clothes before I collapsed on the snowy ground, thoroughly frozen. We quickly dressed and wrapped ourselves in the blankets Felix had brought before he started a roaring fire, and the two of us watched the flickering flames in comforting silence.

"I miss him so much, Ainsley," Felix breathed, and I felt his body loosen as if this truth had been weighing him down for months, and the relief of letting it out brought him peace. I set down the warm drink I had been holding and wrapped my arms around his middle.

"I know you do," I whispered back.

I held my best friend as the tears silently rolled down his cheeks. I didn't dare try to calm him, knowing he needed to feel this and mourn his friendship. What

Dashiell and Felix had was like nothing I had ever seen before, and I couldn't imagine the pain my best friend was going through.

"This is my favorite time of day," Felix said, breaking the silence and I looked up to see the sky had turned a gorgeous shade of amber, as a deep chill had set in around us.

"You only think that because the sky matches your eyes," I countered, and he smiled, nodding along. "Are you ready to head back?"

"I think so. Are you?" he asked.

I wasn't sure what I would say to Evander when I saw him this evening, but I knew I had to talk to him. Even though I wasn't sure I could ever be with him in the way he wanted, I had to at least tell him that it wasn't because I still harbored feelings for Dashiell.

I complained the entire way home, and Felix laughed at every insult I threw at him. I whined that I was cold and we had traveled too far out. I blamed him for us missing dinner and it growing dark. I said it was his fault that I was miserable because he tricked me into swimming in a frozen lake. All he did was laugh and address me as Angsty Ainsley for the entire trip, and I couldn't even blame him for it.

When we arrived back at the house, everyone was sitting around the dining room table, finishing their meals—everyone except for Evander. I looked towards Olivier, and as his stare met mine, he gave a subtle shake of his head meant only for me. My insides knotted, knowing I wouldn't have a chance to speak with Evander.

"Where the hell have you two been all day? You look like shit," Cal commented as Felix and I took our seats at the table and began piling our plates high.

"Ainsley had the brilliant idea to go swimming," Felix explained, and I gave him a sidelong look at his blatant lie.

"You're both insane. You couldn't pay me all the gold in the realm to jump in that lake this time of year," he said as he took a swig from his beer.

"That's because you're weak and clearly not as brave as either of us," I offered, giving him a wry smile.

"That's not true at all," he argued, and I knew I was about to get what I wanted. I shrugged as I took a large bite of steaming chicken.

"Not from the evidence I've seen. A little cold water is enough to send you running," I said around my mouthful. He pushed back from his chair and stood with fierce determination in his eyes.

Mission accomplished.

"Let's go. Right now!" he demanded, stalking towards the front door as he shrugged off his jacket and shirt.

Lia sighed dramatically, and Oli rolled his eyes but stood as well. I grabbed my plate and hurried after him with the rest of our friends. We all followed Cal to the pier's edge, watching as he kicked off his boots and stripped off his underwear. He turned to face us and we shielded our eyes, except for Lia, who only looked at him hungrily.

"How long do I have to stay in there?" he asked.

"Just swim out far enough to where you can no longer touch the bottom," I told him.

It was now dark and significantly colder than when Felix and I jumped in, so I wasn't expecting him to last long. Cal turned around and jumped into the water, swearing loudly as he submerged himself. The ice surrounding the pier had melted significantly now that the blizzard was over, which made it easier for Cal to swim out. Once he was far enough away, I handed my plate to Felix and hurried over to grab the clothes he had tossed onto the dock.

"Let's go back inside," I told everyone as I walked past them with the pile of Cal's attire. Olivier and Felix snickered at my joke. Even Lia seemed pleased at our shenanigans.

"Don't you dare!" Cal called, and furious splashing echoed around us as he swam desperately to shore.

"You shouldn't have called me insane!" I yelled over my shoulder but didn't stop my retreat. The run back to the house would only take a minute, so he wouldn't have to suffer long.

By the time he returned inside, I was halfway done with dinner and not bothering to hide the smug look of satisfaction on my face.

"That was for interrupting my breakfast yesterday," I told him unashamed. Cal scowled at me but redressed in the fresh clothes and warm blanket I had left for him in the hallway without saying another word.

"Will he be home this afternoon?" I asked, batting away an attack as I ran through my training exercises with Oli. Evander never returned home yesterday and I was annoyed with him for evading me. It's not what we did with each other—we didn't run. Okay, I technically *did* run, but it wasn't the same thing. I was avoiding the way I felt; Evander was avoiding confrontation. Totally different.

"He'll be gone most of the day, but you'll probably see him tonight," Oli answered, and I blew out a frustrated breath. "I know you two are going through some shit, but I'm sure you'll work it out, and everything will return to normal by the time we go to the Solum festival tonight." I may have been having a shitty couple of days but I couldn't deny that I was excited to experience the event that celebrated Nova and Onyx's bond.

I felt a little easier—a little more hopeful that things would be okay between Evander and me. We went from hating one another to being someone the other relied on and needed in our lives. If we could overcome those differences in the beginning, then I didn't think anything could get in the way of our friendship now. This was just a setback, another test for us to push through.

Every shop along the street was decorated with branches of holly and thousands of twinkling lights connecting each building. Children ran and played along the cobblestone paths, holding sugary pastries and wooden toy swords as their laughter carried through the crowds. Hundreds of people conversed in the streets and danced in the village square as music roared through the open space, submerging everyone in its melody. Snow fell lightly all around—just enough to dust our hair and melt when it touched the ground.

Smiles were bright, and eyes lit with wonder as Nova and Onyx pranced around, donned in flowery wreaths people had made and taking every scrap of food offered. They walked through the area looking more regal than Evander and I ever did.

"It's their favorite time of year because everyone gives them whatever they want," Lia said, rolling her eyes at Onyx, who was now flat on his back and enjoying belly rubs from the children while Nova was being fed entire portions of chicken like a queen.

The whole celebration was to honor their species and the bond they shared, so of course, they would be treated extra special tonight, though something told me they got the same amount of attention year-round.

I observed the space, taking in the view of my people as they enjoyed the festivities, and my chest ached with the feeling of belonging. I couldn't imagine being anywhere else, happy I had finally made it home. Finding my way in this new life was worth the decades of loneliness.

Lia and I strode for the small bakery packed with people waiting inside and along the sidewalk for one of the many treats they had on display. The owners and villagers insisted that we go ahead of them and order, but we both refused. I didn't mind the wait and enjoyed watching everyone else have fun at the celebration. Cal, Olivier, Marce, and Felix eventually found us right as it was our turn, and the six of us made our way over to one of the large tables set up beneath the stars to enjoy our treats. Marce had made it home safely late this afternoon with dozens of Vorsutos soldiers who were now being tended to by our best healers. Thank the Gods.

Everyone had chosen the same dessert—fried dough encased in sugar, but I opted for something different. I wrapped the two portions of cream cheese cinnamon cake with streusel in a cloth and then tucked it into my pocket. It was Van's favorite dessert and something I wanted to wait to enjoy until we were together.

I tried to laugh and pay attention to the conversation, but my eyes kept darting around in search of a tall man with dark black hair and haunting grey eyes. I couldn't focus on anything but the thought of finally seeing him after days of going without. I hated how things ended the other morning after having the most amazing time with him the night before. The more time we spent apart, the more insignificant my fears began to feel. Being away and having this rift between us was worse than anything he could have done to my heart. I was starting to think that maybe being with him was worth the risk—that having and losing him might be better than never getting to have him at all. But nothing was going to change if he kept avoiding me.

Olivier nudged me with his elbow as the conversation flowed around us, and I glanced over to find him giving me a knowing smile. Despite my best efforts, where my mind had wandered off was obvious. He pointed above us, and I squinted through the darkness to see a black shadow drifting through the dark clouds. What was he doing up there? *How* was he up there? I returned my stare to Oli, and he jerked his chin to the tree line where Nox was grazing in the grass.

"Tell her to take you to him. She knows the way," he whispered before bringing his attention back to our friends, too lost in their laughter to notice our exchange.

My feet moved before my mind could catch up with me, and I half walked, half ran to my horse. She perked up when she saw me and then immediately huffed air through her nose when she realized I didn't come bearing any treats for her. I rolled my eyes as I rubbed my hand down her face.

"I need you to take me to Evander. Can you do that?" I asked as I pulled myself into the saddle. Nox huffed again in agitation, and I couldn't tell if she was more insulted that I questioned her ability or that I didn't have any payment for the fare. She at least waited until I had her reigns before trotting away from the festival and along a dark and twisting path through the trees.

56.

It took about twenty minutes going uphill at a brisk gallop before we entered a large snowy clearing, the air thin and frigid. I immediately spotted him on the other side of the cliff as if standing on air, with nothing but his swirling shadows beneath his feet and a trail of them leading back to the cliffside to safety. I dismounted and slowly walked across the field to get to him.

"Hello, love," Evander said quietly. He somehow knew I was here, and I found my heart fluttering at the thought that he could sense me just as strongly as I could him.

"What are you doing out there?" I asked as he turned to face me. A wicked smile lit his face and I nearly crumbled at the sight. I hadn't realized just how much I'd missed him.

"Why don't you come and find out?"

I shrugged, stepping over the cliff's edge and onto the shadow's path. I should have been terrified that I would go straight through, but I knew I could trust Evander's magic to keep me steady. The shadows instantly went solid beneath my feet with each step, and his eyes lit up just barely as I made my way closer.

"You've been avoiding me," I said as I reached him. I kept a foot of distance between us out of caution, wanting desperately to be closer but not knowing if he desired the same. He had insinuated not wanting what we shared the day of his birthday to end, but I wasn't sure if that still held true with how he had been staying away from me.

"It seemed like you wanted space," he answered.

"I did, but that didn't mean I wanted you to stay away," I told him, and he narrowed his eyes as if it meant precisely that. "I wanted some space to sort out my thoughts, not to be away from you completely," I clarified.

Evander nodded and looked away uncomfortably, and I didn't like how awkward this was beginning to feel. Yes, we'd fought in the past, and I very much couldn't stand him at first, but everything had always come easy with us. Now, it was like we were strangers, not knowing how to speak to one another.

"You never answered me," I said, wanting to smooth this shaky ground. "What are you doing up here?"

Evander brought his attention back to me, those grey eyes shining brightly in the moonlight. The snowfall began to pick up at once, coating us in thick flakes. I squinted through the sudden downfall and watched as he held his palm up between us, and all at once, the snow slowed again. I looked at him quizzically, knowing he couldn't control the weather. So how the hell was he doing that?

"Every year, I come up here and shield the festival," Evander explained. "I allow just enough through so the villagers can see the fall, but it evaporates as it hits land."

"It's like a snow globe," I said in wonder, and he nodded. "Will you teach me?" His answering grin was dazzling, his dimples on full display, and my insides melted faster than the snow below us. I knew how to form a solid shield, but I wasn't aware of how to control it enough to filter what could pass through. For me, it was all or nothing. Evander lowered his cover so the top was now below our feet, and we were getting pelted with heavy snow while the villagers stayed safe from the onslaught.

"Hold your hand up like this," he instructed, and I mimicked his movements, squinting at him through the thick snowfall. "Now call forth your magic to create a silencing shield." I did, and my shield spread out around us. "Good, love. Now make it malleable. You'll need to create a dome shape. Just like that—good," Evander praised. "Now you just need to visualize it as something solid and—"

"So, a regular shield..." I said sarcastically, and Van cocked a brow at my sass.

"No, smartass," he said as he tried to keep a straight face but failed miserably. "It has to be solid but pliable enough to let snow in. A regular defensive shield wouldn't do that, would it?"

I rolled my eyes before closing them tight in concentration as I worked on following his instructions. With my defensive shields, I had always pictured them as something solid and durable like a boulder, but I would need to come up with a different visualization for this. I pushed my hands up high as I molded the shield into a dome shape and then pictured the exterior as my shadows. They had always been thin yet strong enough to keep me protected as they bent and shifted to my will. If I could just marry the two...

The intense fall around us stopped abruptly, and my eyes snapped open to find just a few glistening snowflakes coming in from above. Evander glanced around with pure pride on his beautiful face.

"Oh, my Gods, I did it. I actually did it!" I exclaimed as I leapt into his arms, unable to contain my excitement. Snowflakes instantly coated us at my slip of concentration, and Evander laughed as he held me tight against him. He flicked his wrist with such ease, and our snow globe appeared once again. "Sorry," I told him as my cheeks flushed.

He shook his head, pushing off my apology as he stared deep into my eyes. Gods, it felt so good to be this close to him again. My gaze drifted to his mouth, and my pulse quickened as I pressed myself further into him. I raised my hand, cupping his cheek as I lifted myself on my toes and pressed my forehead to his, needing to feel his skin on mine.

The music coming from the village was faint as it carried from below, swirling on the wind all around us. Evander's grip on my waist tightened as he began to gently sway us to the melody, and I closed my eyes as I breathed him in. I was filled with joy and longing as we spun round and round, dancing in our little snow globe while the celebration roared beneath us.

"Love," he whispered, his lips hovering just out of reach. I couldn't hold back from him anymore. I didn't want to.

Being with him was what I craved. What my heart, body, and soul needed. I leaned in to press my lips to his and kissed him softly. Evander's body tensed like the fear of me running away was still fresh in his mind, but then he relaxed and let himself have what we both wanted. His hand curled around my neck as his tongue slid over mine, and I moaned into his mouth, unable to stop myself. His kiss was like venom coursing through my veins, and I didn't care if it would kill me; I wanted more.

Our embrace was just as powerful as it had been the other night, fueled by a burning desire for one another. But just as they had the following morning, my intrusive thoughts took hold. I was reminded of how right things between us felt and how it could all end and leave me empty in the blink of an eye.

A war raged inside me as my heart and mind fought for dominance, one terrified and urging me to flee while the other wanted my feet to stay firmly on the ground. I had made up my mind about being with him, but it didn't stop the trauma of what I experienced from trying to uproot my decision. I slowly withdrew my lips from his, but before I could lower myself to my normal height, Evander caught my chin, tilting it back up as he sensed the hesitation in my body.

"Don't pull away, love. Don't run. Please," he begged, his eyes pleading desperately for me not to go. "Tell me what's keeping you from me." Van lifted my fingers and softly kissed them before interlacing our hands and holding them against his chest. "Tell me what's keeping you from *us*."

I swallowed hard as I stared into his piercing gaze, trying and failing to come up with how to word the torment raging in my mind. Even though I knew I was done running from him, I still wanted to be honest about my struggles.

"Is it because of who I am? Is it *me*?" he breathed.

His voice broke on the question, and he sounded so small and fragile. So fucking terrified. I pulled out of his hold and placed his face between my hands, forcing him to meet my eyes and listen to every word I said.

"No, Evander. You are everything anyone could ever hope for. You—"

"Is it because of Dashiell?" he interrupted.

He tensed at his words like it physically pained him to ask that question. A part of me broke to see the fear in his eyes as he looked back at me. I glanced around as I tried to figure out how best to answer him. I needed to be honest, but I also didn't want him to hurt any more than he was, and Dashiell seemed to be a challenging topic for him.

"Yes," I started, and he began to pull away before I had a moment to finish. It wasn't like he was angry; rather, he was accepting my choice and distancing himself to respect it. I tightened my hold immediately, not wanting him to get the wrong idea. "But not because of the reason you're thinking."

Evander cocked his head, his eyes darting across my face like the answers to his questions were written in my flesh. His shadows swirled along his neck, and I knew he wasn't bothering to hide the deep emotion he was feeling.

Fear.

Fear of losing me, of losing *us*.

"When I came here to Tenebrae, I was so broken, Van. So, so incredibly broken. I don't know how much you remember, but—"

"Everything," he said flatly, and the pain in his eyes was almost too much for me to bear. "I remember everything, Ainsley. Every tear that fell, every wave of pain you felt, every time the light in your eyes went out. I remember it all."

He had been there when I crumbled and broke. He watched me retreat into myself, unable to eat or sleep. Hell, the whole house felt my pain for weeks because I couldn't control my Gift and emotions back then. I had always thought he looked at me with disgust and judgment for my weakness, but now I realized that might not have been what he was thinking at all.

"Then you know how hard it was for me to pick up the pieces. I didn't think I'd ever get back to a point where I could truly laugh again, but the first time I did, it was because of you," I told him, reliving the moment. "It was because of that stupid letter you wrote and how well you knew me. It was the first time my heart didn't hurt as much as the day before. You helped me put myself together and taught me to realize my strength."

His lips twitched in the corners in a display of both happiness and relief. I didn't think he'd ever truly know the extent of what he did for me. I pressed my mouth to his and kissed him gently, knowing words wouldn't be able to express my gratitude. The embrace was sweet and short, just enough for me to show him that I wasn't going anywhere.

"I ran from you that morning because it's exactly what I should have done," I explained. "After everything I went through with Dashiell, I should be terrified to feel again. I should be smart enough never to put myself in that situation a second time. I don't want to be that naive girl that came here ever again."

Evander inhaled deeply before nodding in understanding, though he didn't try to retreat. He seemed to grasp that this was me talking through my emotions rather than saying goodbye, and I felt more at ease knowing the fear in him was subsiding.

"But what terrifies me the most is not that you'll hurt me—it's that I want this anyway. I have worked hard to be the person I was always meant to be. I have taken my heart and my autonomy back. I have unapologetically gone after everything that I've wanted. Everything except for you, Evander. I want you. I want *us*, and I don't want to fight it anymore. I want—"

Evander cut off my declaration with a searing kiss that set my entire body aflame. I wrapped my arms around his neck as he gripped my waist, pulling me flush against him. His hands moved up and fisted in my hair, holding my mouth to his and refusing to relinquish me for longer than it took for me to gasp for breath before claiming me again. Our kiss was brutal and burning and threatened to consume me entirely.

I jumped up, wrapping my legs around his middle as he moved his hands to hold me, squeezing tightly as his tongue did wicked and delightful things to mine. He groaned into my mouth as I gently bit his bottom lip, savoring how he tasted and wanting even more. Heavy snowfall dumped upon us, and I yelped from the sudden cold.

"Fuck!" Evander swore and held out his hand to form our shield again. "Sorry, love," he said, stifling his laughter as he set me down and brushed the white powder from my hair. "Maybe we should wait to do that until we're indoors," he offered, and I whined, already wanting his lips back on me.

"Fine," I pouted, dragging out the word and interlacing my hand with his. "What now?" Evander looked around the space as if searching for something.

"Come here," he said, leading me further out.

A twirl of his fingers later, a blanket and pillows had formed on our floating shadowed platform. He knelt, positioning them how he wanted before sitting down and pulling me with him. I crawled between his legs, shifting my back to his chest and resting my head against his shoulder as he covered us with the blanket.

"Does this mean you want me, too?" I teased, getting comfortable. I reached into my pocket and pulled out the wrapped pieces of cake. Evander grinned and tried to grab his portion, but I held it just out of reach. "Answer my question first."

"I've never not wanted you, love," he replied. I smiled and handed him his cake. "I've never been afraid of my feelings for you. The only thought that has ever terrified me was knowing there was a possibility you wouldn't ever feel the same."

Evander pressed a light kiss to my temple, and I basked in the feel of him, my heart content for the first time in months. I leaned back to look into his brilliant eyes before he bent forward and pressed his forehead against mine. We sat like that for hours, happy to finally just be together. For the first time since arriving, I wasn't afraid of my future because I knew he would be by my side. Whatever storm appeared, we'd weather it together.

Soft lips pressed against my cheek, stirring me. I was warm now, and the ground was no longer hard and freezing. By the heated air and smell of cedar and parchment, I knew we were back in Evander's room, and I settled into the bed. The mattress shifted, and I could feel Evander pull away from where he was wrapped around me.

"Where are you going?" I whined as I clutched his arm to prevent him from fully retreating.

"I have a meeting," he explained before kissing my lips.

"This late?" I objected as my eyes fluttered open to find grey light pouring in through the open window.

"This early," he corrected. "I was supposed to meet with Sirona after the festival last night, but I selfishly didn't want to leave you."

We laughed and talked as the celebration continued through the late hours of the night, and I must have fallen asleep at some point because I definitely didn't remember coming back home. Knowing Evander, he would have just traversed us so as not to wake me.

"And now you do?" I teased, snaking my arms around his neck as I clung to him. He rolled his eyes at my sass, and I smiled brightly at riling him up this early in the morning. I had just gotten him back and wasn't ready to be apart from him so soon.

"You know that's not true," he said, pressing his lips to my throat, and I shivered at the touch despite being wrapped in heavy blankets. His tongue dragged across my skin, and I made it my personal mission not to let him out of this bed before finally having him the way I wanted.

"So stay," I offered, running my hands through his hair. "I'll make it worth your while."

I wrapped my legs around him, drawing out a groan and feeling just how much he wanted me. I grabbed his chin, pulling his lips to mine as my tongue demanded entrance. Evander's hand gripped my hip as I ground myself against him, needing that delicious friction just as I had the other night.

"You're a terrible influence, love," he said, rolling on top and pressing me into the bed as he devoured my kiss.

There were far too many clothes between us right now, and we needed to fix that. I reached for the hem of his shirt, ready to rip it to shreds from his body, when his hand grabbed my wrist, stopping my attempt.

"Sirona will kill me if I cancel again," he said, trying to pull out of my hold. I clutched my thighs around his middle, refusing to let him loose.

"I'd like to see her try," I replied with a playful grin, and Evander's eyes sparkled at my demand. He wanted me just as much, and I could see him struggling with what to do.

"I promise, I'll make it up to you," he said after a moment of his internal back and forth, and I could see in his face there was no changing his mind.

I threw my head back and groaned in frustration. We had spent time apart, both feeling miserable, and now had to be apart again. I knew it was just a stupid little meeting, but I wasn't ready get back to our day-to-day lives before we actually got to celebrate the decision we made to be together.

"I'll come with you, then," I offered as I worked to shimmy out from underneath him.

"No," he said, gripping my chin between his fingers before planting more kisses on my face. "Stay here and rest. I'll be back in a few hours."

"If it's important, then shouldn't I be there?" I argued half-heartedly. The idea of going back to sleep and not having to attend a boring meeting was admittedly appealing. Van smiled wide as he must've read the thoughts written on my face.

"Yes, but I can handle it on my own," he reasoned, pulling away from me and adjusting the blankets to tuck me in again.

The way he said the words left a sour taste in my mouth, and I began to worry about how serious that meeting actually was.

"It's fine, love," he said, sensing the shift in my thoughts. "But the moment I get back, I'll fill you in on everything, I swear."

I nodded, though now I was seriously contemplating just getting out of bed and following him to Sirona's. But Evander had always been honest with me and never held back because he didn't think I could handle a situation. There was no reason for me to believe that's what he was doing now. I trusted his word.

"I'll be back in a few hours," he said, kissing me one last time before traversing out of our room.

I stretched my arms above my head as I stared at the ceiling and tried to calm the intrusive, worrying thoughts in my mind. Onyx took Evander's departure as permission to leave his spot next to Nova on the floor and climb into bed with me.

"I take it the mean king didn't let you up here while I was gone?" I cooed, scratching behind his ears as he curled into me and rested his head on my chest. Evander really needed to be nicer to his wolf, or I was going to claim him as my own too.

57.

The mattress dipped next to me, and I rolled over to my side, facing that direction as Onyx huffed in irritation at being jostled.

"He'll kill you if he catches you here—and in his spot, no less," I said through a yawn.

"Where is he, anyway?" Felix asked, fluffing Evander's pillows behind his back as he wiggled back and forth to get comfortable. Oh, Van was *definitely* going to murder him for that. Onyx growled as he heard Felix's voice and opened an eye to find him in the bed of his master. I pressed my hand to his head and mussed his black fur as I shushed him.

"Go lay with Nova, boy," I instructed, and Onyx leapt from the bed and padded over to my grey wolf sleeping across the room on her usual pile of pillows.

"That wolf hates me," he mused, and I nodded noncommittally.

"Nah, he's just particular about who gets to lay in the bed. And to answer your earlier question, Van said he had a meeting this morning but would be back in a few hours." I peered past my friend to see that the sun had risen, and excitement bubbled to know Evander would be back at any moment. I needed to get Felix out of this bed because the second Van walked into our room, he was *mine*.

"So I take it things between the two of you worked out?" Felix questioned, and I couldn't help but smile as I nodded.

I pictured the moment I chose him and how good it felt to finally admit it out loud rather than continuing to deny it. My cheeks flushed, and I bit my lip as I remembered how I had been in his arms last night and the tender kisses he peppered me with this morning. My Gods, I was so giddy it was sickening.

"I'm terrified, Felix, but I can't help how I feel about him, and I don't want to anymore. There's this connection between us; I can't explain exactly what it is, but I don't want to keep running from it," I told him, and Felix offered a smile, though it seemed unnatural—forced. Was he not happy for me? Maybe this was the final nail in the coffin for his hopes that Dashiell and I would reconcile.

"Did you talk about anything else last night?" he asked, and I furrowed my brows, not understanding what he was getting at.

"We talked about why I pulled away that morning, and I addressed his worries about Dashiell, but other than that, I'm not sure what you mean."

Felix took a deep breath as he nodded to himself, though he didn't offer any more explanation. I suddenly felt annoyed with my friend for his cryptic questions and lack of general joy at my happiness. I had finally chosen to move forward with my life and allow someone in again, and here he was, putting a damper on my mood. And for what reason?

I slid from the bed and headed for the dresser, needing to put my fingers to work so they weren't moving toward Felix's neck to strangle him. I angrily opened and closed drawers as I changed out of the clothes I had slept in.

"Why are you mad?" Felix asked, coming over to stand next to me.

"Because you're being a secretive dick," I announced, sliding a pair of thick wool socks over my feet. "Days ago, you told me to go for it. You said I couldn't live in fear of getting hurt, and as soon as I do just that, you're acting like it was the worst thing in the world. I know you hate Evander, but—"

"It's not that," Felix interrupted as he scrubbed a hand over his face.

"Then what is it?" I demanded, crossing my arms over my chest now that I was fully dressed and thoroughly pissed off. Felix looked around, completely lost for words as he battled with himself. He stepped back and began pacing before me as he rubbed the back of his neck. What the fuck was going on? "Felix," I demanded, snapping him out of his daze.

He stopped and turned back to face me—his mind finally made up.

"You said that you feel a connection to him, right? Do you know why that is?" he asked, and I looked at him curiously.

"Are you asking me if I'm in love with Evander?" I questioned, and Felix shook his head.

"No, because we both already know the answer to that," he replied.

"Then what the fuck are you trying to ask me, Felix?" I demanded, my patience for these games wholly gone. Onyx and Nova both walked to my side as they sensed my anger; their hackles raised, and teeth bared at the source of it. He looked at me for another long minute as he struggled to grasp the words. "Just fucking tell me!"

"You were made for each other!" he blurted, and my eyes narrowed at the outburst. Was he trying to say he approved of us in some roundabout way? But if so, why was he being so secretive?

"Okay?" I said, drawing out the word. "Thank you, I guess?"

"No, Ainsley," he said, shaking his head as he stepped closer to me. "You two were quite literally designed and created for one another by magic."

My eyes widened, and a giggle escaped from between my lips. Felix looked at me confused, as the small giggles turned into full-blown laughter. I threw my head back, unable to stop at the ridiculous nonsense he was spewing.

"What?" I asked through the hysterics.

"The connection you've felt since the beginning—the one you can't explain— it's because you each have one half of a soul."

"You're insane," I said, coming down from the high. "Who told you this? Whoever did was probably just messing with you," I reasoned.

"Evander," Felix replied, and I felt my body relax a bit. Of course, Van would say something like that to Felix. The man would do absolutely anything to watch my best friend spiral. I opened my mouth to say just that when Felix spoke again. "And Sirona."

My heart stopped as the smile on my face fell. Evander might be perfectly okay with making Felix believe some insane untruth, but Sirona wouldn't be.

"Explain," I demanded, my voice suddenly serious and panicked. "Right now."

Felix began pacing again, and it would have normally pissed me off and made me nervous, but I realized it was the only way he could calm himself down enough to talk through the events. My arms tightened around myself as if I could hold the pieces together. Evander and I were made by magic? Did he know? He had to have if he was the one who informed Felix.

"The other day, I headed into town to pick up a few things Lia had asked me to get—one of which was at Sirona's shop. When I arrived, she wasn't at the counter, so I browsed through the aisles as I waited, and that's when I heard voices coming from the back room. I recognized one as hers and the other I could make out as Evander's when I got closer. That's when I heard it.

"Evander was furious about how long something was taking and then started talking about his *Soul Bond*. I didn't understand what he meant until he mentioned your name. As soon as I heard him talk about you, I barged in and demanded to know what the fuck was going on," Felix explained.

"And?" I asked, my chest moving rapidly as my world came crashing down once more.

"I don't know exactly how it works, Ainsley. Sirona would be better at explaining it, but from what I *could* understand, your and Evander's parents sought her help long before either of you were born. They wanted their future children bonded, but I'm unsure why."

"Does he know?" I asked, already aware of the answer. Felix nodded, and I clenched my jaw, fighting the tears that pricked the back of my eyes.

"After I found out, he asked me to give him only one day so he could tell you on his own. That deadline passed last night."

Of course it fucking did. Oh, the irony. The day I was finally honest about my feelings for him was the day he chose to continue lying to me. I wiped my eyes with the back of my hand before a single tear could drop as I turned and stormed out of the room. Felix called after me, but I didn't turn or stop, too furious that I was once again kept in the dark by someone I had given my trust to. I made it to the living room before Felix grabbed hold of my arm, spinning me around to face him.

"I know you're furious, Ainsley, but slow down for a second," Felix implored.

"Why should I?" I demanded angrily.

My magic swirled, and every tiny piece of fractured heart Evander had helped stitch back together threatened to rip apart at the seams. Every memory of the two of us together flashed in my mind, threatening to bury me into the pit of darkness I had been so lost in before. I had been a trusting idiot yet again, and it was my own fault that I found myself in the same predicament as before.

"Because I don't think he meant to hurt you, Ainsley. I think there's more to the story and—"

"He *lied*, Felix! He knew what Dashiell had put me through, and he made a conscious choice to do the same."

We stared at one another for a long moment, and I did the only thing I could think of to get through to my friend. I let down my defenses, allowing his Gift in so he could experience firsthand how much I was breaking inside. His eyes softened as he caressed each bloody and bruised part of me, and movement from the corner of my eye caught my attention.

I twisted to see Evander and Oli entering from the front door as they joked about something I couldn't have cared less about. Van's eyes found mine instantly. The devastatingly beautiful smile on his face as he looked at the other half of his soul sent me completely over the edge.

A tear slid from my eye, and his brow furrowed as he watched it fall. Everything felt like it unfolded in slow motion as Evander looked between Felix and me as the realization of what had happened hit him. His face fell, and I could make out my name on his lips as I rushed for him, screaming as my shadows slammed him into the living room wall.

"You fucking *liar!*" I bellowed as the angry tears fell.

Oli ran for me, but I was too quick, using my free hand to slam him into the opposite wall hard enough that the foundation cracked at the impact. Oli crashed to the ground as my magic disappeared around him. Lia, Calidore, and Marceline sprinted in from the other room, probably wondering what the fuck was going on.

"Everyone stay back!" Evander commanded, though his voice was strained from the pressing weight of my shadows. I squeezed tighter, and Evander coughed as he gasped for air. He wasn't even trying to fight back—he was letting me hurt him.

My magic pulled against me in protest, but I kept my control firm, forcing it to do as I commanded, though it wrecked my heart even more to cause him pain.

"How could you?" I cried as I loosened the restraint around his neck so he could speak. "All this time, you knew who I was to you—what *we* were—and you kept it from me."

I looked around the room and curious eyes met my harsh stare. Each one of the people that I considered family watched me cautiously, not daring to move in fear of my wrath.

"Did all of you know too? Did you help him keep this secret day in and day out?!" I demanded, and Lia stepped forward, arms placating and brows pinched as she looked between Evander and me.

"What is she talking about, Van?" Lia asked, but he shook his head.

"Oh, you didn't hear?" I asked through an incredulous laugh. "The king and I were made for one another. And not in the sweet romantic way you may be thinking. No, I mean in the literal sense." I dragged a hand through my hair as I paced in front of everyone, no doubt looking insane. "As in, we were designed and created by magic. As in, we share a single soul."

"Ainsley," Olivier said, and I looked up at the man who had been like a brother to me. His face was serious and his eyes pleading as he spoke like he thought his soft tone would be enough to dissipate the rage building within me. I exhaled loudly as I stared at him and shook my head in disbelief.

"You knew," I claimed, and he squeezed his eyes shut like it could block my anger and his own guilt. "They all may not have," I yelled, pointing to the others in the room. "But *you* did."

The walls were closing in on me, boxing me in and stealing my breath. My lungs screamed in pain as I fought to clear my frantic mind. I was drowning—suffocating—under the rubble of lies and deception. Each lungful of air I breathed was tainted, rotten soil, seeping into my bloodstream and killing me from the inside out. This wasn't happening. Not again.

"Love, please—" Evander tried, but I cut him off before realizing I was speaking. My rage had taken form and seized control of my body, extracting the words from my broken heart that my mind couldn't form.

"You didn't think I deserved to know? I let you in, Evander," I said as tears spilled down my cheeks in full force. "I gave you my trust, and you lied. You manipulated me into falling in love with you—" I stopped myself quickly as the truth I had been too afraid to admit—even to myself—tumbled from my lips. Panic surged forward as quickly as my magic had. I dared a glance at Evander to find his eyes wide and his face soft as my confession filled the space around us.

"Ainsley," he tried again, but I didn't stop him this time. "I didn't manipulate you; I swear on everything we have built and what we are—"

"That means nothing!" I yelled.

"It means *everything*, and you know it!" he countered. "I know you feel it just as strongly as I do. I love you, Ainsley. Soul Bond or not, I love you."

"No," I croaked, shaking my head as I denied his claim. "It's just the bond; it's not real. None of this has been real."

"Bullshit. You know magic can't create love," he said forcefully as he pulled against his shadowed restraints for the first time, but they held firm, not letting him free until I gave the order. "Use your Empathi Gift if you don't believe me. You can hate me, Ainsley, but don't you dare tell me I don't fucking love you."

I covered my ears as I fell to the floor, not wanting to hear anymore. Dashiell had claimed to love me. Evander had claimed to love me. But from where I stood, the only thing both men had done was lie and break my heart.

"No," I managed to say as my nails dug into the soft strands of the rug beneath, begging it to keep me steady. My friends were quiet, and the room was so silent that all that could be detected were uneven, shuddering breaths.

Slowly, I stood on shaking legs and faced the man who I had given myself to. The man who convinced me to trust and to feel—to open myself up and to be willing to let others in again. I stared at the man who my soul knew as its own.

"You don't get to claim that you love me, Evander," I declared as I slowly approached him, each step more sure than the last. "You knew how much honesty meant to me, and you purposely kept the truth from me,"

"Because—"

"I don't give a shit about your reasons," I interrupted as I held up a hand to stop him from speaking. "You made it well known how much you hated Dashiell for what he did to me, but from where I'm standing, you're no better than he is, Evander."

His lips wobbled, and his face fell as a gentle trickle of tears streamed from his eyes at my accusation. It killed me to see him hurt, but it would destroy me if I didn't hold him accountable. His eyes searched mine fervently as he opened his mouth and closed it several times, unable to come up with anything to say. He knew he had no defense.

I stopped a foot away from him and straightened as I lifted my chin in a display of false composure. I was falling apart bit by bit, but I couldn't let him see it. Even though we both knew what was truly happening.

"What can I do?" he begged, his voice thick with emotion. "What do you want? Anything, Ainsley. Please, just let me try."

I held his gaze as I leaned in, my eyes darting across his face like I could find the answer to what I needed written within his flesh. His charcoal eyes were dark and dim as they glassed over from the tears welling before they fell. I pondered the question though I already knew the answer. I had to get away.

"I want..." I began slowly, fighting the lump in my throat and the pull of my heart and soul begging me to reconsider. "Nothing to do with you." His eyes widened, and he shook his head, refusing to accept my request. "I want to leave and for you to not look for me," I added as I released my magic, and Evander slumped down as a sob broke through his throat.

"You have a duty to your kingdom and—"

"Shut the fuck up, Olivier," Calidore said, cutting off his friend. "You don't get to hold that over her fucking head, not after you and Evander lied to her—to all of us—this entire time. If she wants to go, she gets that choice."

I didn't turn in the direction of the argument, but I was grateful Calidore was in my corner. I watched as Evander rested his forearms on his knees and hung his head as he cried. Every piece of me wanted to go to him and wrap my arms around him. I wanted to kiss and comfort him until I took the pain away, but I couldn't. He had fractured the foundation we had built, and I had to get out of there before I was lost to my heartache forever.

I backed away as Evander pleaded for me to stay, but I didn't stop. I tugged on my boots and slid on my jacket as warm arms wrapped around me. I spun and embraced Lia as she wept and moved her hands to hold my cheeks.

"I didn't know about any of this, I swear," she said quickly, and I nodded, knowing full well that she would have informed me the moment she found out. Lia was an amazing friend in that way. She wouldn't have accepted bullshit excuses; she would have done the right thing.

"I know, Lia," I said back, and she hugged me tighter.

"Where will you go?"

"I don't know," I replied honestly.

I hadn't given any thought to that; I just knew I couldn't stay here any longer. Not while the sting of betrayal was fresh. Marceline came to stand next to us, holding the emergency bag of supplies she always kept with her.

"Keep up with your training," Marce said in her commanding tone. "If I find out you've been slacking, I'll come and kick your ass myself."

I laughed under my breath through the tears as I nodded and took the leather strap from her. Marce snaked her arms around my neck in a rare hug as she pulled me close to whisper in my ear.

"Tell Nox to take you to the lake house. She knows the way, and you can make it by nightfall if you leave now. It's fully stocked, and you can stay there as long as you need until you figure out your next move. There's a pile of transfer paper that comes directly to me, so write if you need anything."

"Thank you, Marce," I whispered as I pulled away, and my attention drifted to the soft whimpers across the room and the padding of paws that had approached.

Onyx lay at his master's feet, licking Evander's fingers as he whined like he could sense the hurt radiating from him. Nova was at my side, a black stuffed Onyx in her mouth as she waited patiently for me to take it. I removed the wolf from between her teeth, and she moved to sit next to the door like she was ready to leave.

"No, Nova," I said, walking over to my wolf and kneeling before her. "You're staying here." She responded by backing out of my touch and pawing at the door in demand to be let out. "No," I said again, though it was a command this time.

She whined but scratched at the wood again, this time hard enough to leave claw marks.

"She won't stay," Marce announced, and I rose to my feet before turning to my friend. "She belongs to you, Ainsley. She's bonded to you in a deep way. She won't stay any more than Onyx will leave Evander."

"I don't want to take her from Onyx," I admitted, looking at my sad black wolf lying on the floor, trying to comfort the man I loved.

"They've been apart for long periods before," Lia added, and though it didn't make me love the idea of taking her from him, I relaxed a little. "Once you're settled, we can bring Onyx to you so they can reunite for a bit." I loosed a deep breath but nodded. It would have to be enough for now.

Calidore appeared and hugged me quickly before pulling back and striding across the room without so much as a goodbye.

"Cal?" I said, unable to hide the hurt in my voice. We had grown close over my time here, and he couldn't bother to utter a single word to me.

"He's not mad at *you*," Lia whispered, glancing sidelong at the disheveled Evander on the floor and Oli standing beside him. It was a relief that I wasn't the cause of his anger, but it still hurt that he couldn't even say goodbye to me.

"You need to get going," Marceline declared, and I took a deep breath as I looked around my home for one last time. It was a place that held memories—a place where I had fallen in love. Somewhere friendships blossomed, and laughs were shared. It was more of a home than anything I had ever felt, and now I was leaving.

"I love you all," I said through the thick lump in my throat and the tears that poured. "So very much."

And then I pushed through the door with Nova on my heels.

Felix was already outside and getting Nox saddled for me. With everything going on, I hadn't noticed he'd left the house.

"I'll be a few hours behind you," he said, and I opened my mouth to protest. "It's you and me, Ainsley. Always."

"But Olivier—"

"Needs to comfort his friend," Felix answered. "You're my priority, and I may care for that man, but I'm not going to pretend I'm happy he kept this from me too."

"Thank you, Felix," I whispered as I reached for his hand so he could help me mount Nox. Felix shoved the stuffed Onyx inside the bag Marce had given me before attaching it to the saddle while Nova batted at my horse's tail, ready for our adventure.

"I'm going to pack some things for you, fight with Oli, and then I'll be on my way," he announced, shoving an apple in Nox's face in payment for letting him near her.

I gripped the reins and threw one last look at my home as I fought the soul-crushing pain that was swirling within. My heart was shattering. My magic hated that I was leaving Evander and my family behind, but I needed space to regroup. I needed to clear my head and try to make sense of everything I had learned.

"Ready, girls?" I asked, running my hand along Nox's side. She huffed in response, and Nova took that as permission to take the lead, prancing to the front. I whispered our location into Nox's ear, and then we were off, leaving my once-intact world behind.

58.

The sun had just barely set by the time we reached our destination. The house was old and beautiful, with smoke plumbing from the chimney on the roof. The inside was illuminated, and I wondered if I would be the only one here or if some other family had taken up residence. Marce didn't mention any other occupants, but to be fair, I didn't ask.

I jumped down from Nox, and the moment I unstrapped my supplies, she hurried to the large stables at the side of the property, apparently familiar with every aspect of the grounds. Nova bounced and rolled in the snow like she was having the time of her life.

Well, at least *she* was happy.

I knocked cautiously on the door several times, but there was no answer. I tried the handle, and sure enough, it was unlocked. Warm air greeted me, and I hurried inside, shutting the door behind me as I quickly stripped off my snow-covered clothes.

I was about to call out to any unsuspecting occupants when a large piece of parchment on the entryway table caught my attention.

I informed nearby residents of your stay and instructed them to ready the house for you. If you need anything at all, the transfer paper is on the desk in the study. It comes to me and only me. Stay safe, and Felix should be arriving shortly. I know you won't ask, but I'll tell you anyway: Evander won't be told where you are. He's broken, Ainsley, but he won't come looking for you.

— Marceline

P.S. Keep your wolf off my bed.

I read through the letter four times before setting it back down. The part where she said Evander was broken sent shards of glass plunging into my heart. I could feel his pain—his suffering. I didn't know what this Soul Bond was, but it was evident that our connection ran deeper than I would have thought possible. In addition to my own pain, I was also experiencing his, and I didn't know how I would get through it.

Unsure of what to do, I strode for the large fire in the living room and sat down on the hearth to watch the twisting flames. Heat licked over my skin, and I sank forward, not fighting the tears that began to form as I looked around the space and realized how alone I was now. This room was void of the love and laughter I had been lucky enough to experience for these past months, and with my family gone, I felt lower than I had in a long time.

Nova appeared beside me with the stuffed Onyx she must have stolen from the bag. She set it down on the hearth and pushed herself up, resting her paws in my lap as her forehead found mine, and I instantly sobbed at her comforting gesture. Everything had been so perfect one second and then so horrible the next. I didn't see how I would recover.

I wasn't sure how long we had been sitting like that when the sound of the door unlocking rang out, and I turned to find Felix striding over the threshold with a large bag in hand. One look at me had him crossing the space in seconds and wrapping me tightly in his arms. He pulled back, wiping the tears that fell from my cheeks as I took several deep breaths until I was relatively composed again.

"I don't want to know," I said before he could tell me anything about Evander or what happened once I left. Felix nodded in acknowledgment before handing me the clothes he had brought.

"Go take a bath, and I'll start on dinner," he said, kissing my cheek and heading to the fully stocked kitchen.

I found no comfort in the hot water like I usually did and instead, my mind was filled with the times Evander had complained about how scalding the pool was when he'd bathe after me. He always joked about changing the water out for fire, seeing as my baths were the same temperature, according to him.

After climbing out of the tub, I quickly changed into soft pants and an oversized sweater before my fingers froze over a pair of thick, knit socks shoved in the bag. They were cream-colored with black stripes along the top—my favorite pair. The socks Evander had made sure were fully stocked at all times. He had even gotten me the pants I was wearing now after he noticed how I shivered every time I wore my silk night clothes. Was I doomed to be reminded of him at all times over the most mundane things? I took a deep breath and slid the socks over my feet before padding to the kitchen to meet Felix.

"At least the one that likes me came along," he said, pointing to Nova sitting patiently at his side with her tail sweeping quickly across the floor. I leaned over the marble island, stole a piece of chicken he was cutting, and popped it into my mouth.

"She's only here because she's begging," I said as I chewed. "She likes food, not you."

Felix gasped in mock outrage, and Nova lifted onto her hind legs and rested her paws on the island countertop.

"You would never use me like that, would you?" he cooed, scratching behind her ears as she gave him the biggest, saddest puppy eyes I had ever seen and whimpered as if calling me out on a lie I hadn't told. "I didn't think so," Felix added as she nuzzled into him, playing him for a fool. He pulled back and grabbed two large chicken breasts before handing them each to her. Nova took his offering, jumped down, and pranced to her spot by the fire as she devoured her meal.

"You know she just played you, right?" I pointed out as Felix headed to the sink to wash his hands and prepare the rest of our dinner. He shrugged as he dried his hands off and then tended to whatever sauce he had simmering on the stove.

"They were always meant for her anyway. I'm trying to buy her love, so I'm pretty sure *I* just played *her*," he replied as he dumped pasta into the white sauce and then tossed the contents to blend it all. "If I can get her to like me, then maybe the black one won't be such an asshole all the time."

"Onyx isn't an asshole," I said defensively, and Felix cocked a brow.

Onyx was absolutely an asshole. I rolled my eyes in defeat as I stole another piece of chicken.

"Stop that!" Felix demanded, smacking a wooden spoon against the marble in the exact spot my fingers had just been.

"I'm hungry, and you're taking too long," I snapped back, grabbing another piece of chicken and sprinting to the couch before he could reprimand me again.

"I hate you," Felix called as he turned back to his work, dishing out the pasta into two large bowls and adding what was left of the chicken on top.

"No, you don't."

Felix tucked a bottle of wine under his arm and filled his hands with our dinner and a warm loaf of bread before joining me on the couch. The smell of our food permeated the air, and my stomach audibly growled. During our journey, I hadn't bothered to eat. My mind was too focused on Evander and everything that had happened. I didn't even realize we had arrived until Nox stopped abruptly, causing me to jerk out of my haunting thoughts.

"No, I don't," Felix admitted as he handed me my dinner and gave me a wry smile.

I dug in immediately, not bothering to blow on the hot food and severely suffering my way through the first bite. My mouth was on fire, and my throat burned as I swallowed, but *fuck* did it taste good.

"Since when do you know how to cook?" I asked, twirling the pasta around my fork and spearing a piece of chicken.

"I've watched Oli do it every night and just kind of picked it up along the way," he answered, and I couldn't help but feel a sting of anger at the mention of that man.

Felix picked up on the sudden shift in my mood and opened his mouth to apologize, but I shook my head before he could. We hadn't discussed what had happened when he left, so we might as well do it now.

"How did the fight with him go?" I asked, taking another bite to hide my uneven tone.

"As you'd expect: lots of yelling and apologizing on his part. I understand why he didn't tell me. Evander is his best friend, and Oli and I have only recently established something. I was more upset that he kept it from you."

"As you said, Evander is his best friend," I mused, pushing my food around the bowl.

"That doesn't make it right."

I nodded because Felix had a point. Olivier and Evander had torn into Felix over his decision to keep King Perceval's plan from me, and here they were, doing the same thing.

"Will you two be okay?" I asked. Felix was falling for Olivier, and I didn't want what happened to me to get in the way of his chance at happiness. He smiled softly and nodded, and I felt the tension over the subject ease from my body.

"He knows you're my priority, and I need to be with you right now. He has his own friend to worry about."

"He wasn't mad?"

"Nope. He kissed me goodbye and told me to stay safe and take care of you," Felix said before taking a bite of his food.

My head perked up at the mention of a kiss, but Felix just focused on his dinner. It wasn't like him not to divulge more information about something big like that happening, but knowing him, he wanted to make sure I was okay before discussing his own happiness.

I was glad Olivier wasn't angry at Felix though I knew he had no reason to be. It wasn't a secret how close Felix and I were, and to expect us not to stick together was idiocy. I couldn't think of any situation where we would volunteer to be apart from one another.

"We happened after the Solum celebration," he said, answering my unasked question about their relationship. "But we'll talk about it later."

"Okay," I agreed, happy that he found his happiness but also that he could recognize that I wasn't in the right headspace to appreciate it.

"To be completely honest, I couldn't get out of that house quick enough," Felix added, and I arched a brow at the confession. Had something else happened to make him want to leave? "That damn black wolf wouldn't stop whining and howling. He was driving everyone crazy."

I snorted, and Nova lifted her head at the mention of him—her Solum bond. I still hated that they were apart.

"Onyx can be a lot," I said, watching my wolf as she tilted her head in question. I wasn't sure if she knew what I was saying, though it seemed she could most of the time. Perhaps it was whatever magic the wolves possessed that allowed them to understand humans. "But I'm sure he's just being overdramatic as usual," I said, more to Nova than to Felix.

I didn't want her to worry about him or whatever emotional pain he could potentially be in. Onyx was loyal and loving and seemed like he could empathize with Evander and me. If his master was hurting, I didn't doubt he was too.

"Thank you for telling me about the Soul Bond," I said quietly. It wasn't a subject I wanted to discuss, but I needed Felix to know I was grateful he had told me the truth.

"I thought about not saying anything until after he had gotten back," Felix admitted quietly, almost like he was ashamed he had been the one to break the news to me. "I could sense how important it was to him that he be the one to tell you, but he missed the deadline I gave, and after everything that happened in Caelum, you didn't deserve to be kept in the dark for a minute longer. I couldn't risk our friendship and your trust again. As much as I wanted to give him grace, I made a vow to never lie to you again, and that was more important to me."

"Thank you," I said, unable to come up with more than that.

"How are *you* doing?" Felix asked, breaking my train of thought. "You seem... better."

I thought about that observation for a moment as I checked over myself inch by inch. My magic was slumbering soundly, and though I could sense it was pissed off at me, it didn't stir or jostle inside. My heart was aching but still intact. I felt sadness but also strength.

"I think I'm okay," I admitted, setting my empty bowl down and reaching for the wine. I uncorked it with my teeth and took a small sip before extending the bottle to Felix. "I just needed some space. I couldn't breathe in that house with everyone watching me as Evander's lies surfaced."

"And being here is helping you cope?"

"Yes. My mind is less cloudy, and I don't have this crushing weight over me. I'm still hurt and furious, but it's not as consuming as before."

I could think and see clearer. I could replay each moment with Evander, and the times I felt a stronger connection to him than usual without breaking into pieces. My heart was fragile, but my will was strong as I focused on each deceitful moment, finally seeing them for what they were—a manipulation.

"And your feelings about Evander?" Felix asked, and I shuddered as I took a deep breath, gathering the strength to talk about him.

"I fell in love with him even when I swore I wouldn't let myself. Everyone knew how hard it was for me to trust after what happened in Caelum, but I offered that to him. I gave him that piece of my heart, not knowing he already possessed half of my soul. And now I feel like a fucking idiot all over again. How is it any different than Dashiell and me?" I demanded, anger filling my tone, not at Felix but at my own stupid trusting heart.

My friend set his bowl on the coffee table and twisted on the couch to face me, grabbing my hands to hold as he did. His amber eyes were soft yet urgent like he held a vital piece of information I needed to know.

"Your relationship with Evander is night and day to what you had with Dash," Felix announced, and I snorted in disbelief. It didn't feel any different. In fact, it felt identical. "You forget I was there to watch both relationships unfold, Ainsley. I've seen and felt more than you realize."

I stiffened. I knew he had witnessed Dashiell and me, but he had always seemed to distance himself from anything that had to do with Evander, so what exactly did he think he knew?

"You and Dash were like flame and ice—complete opposites in a beautiful way. He centered you, calmed you, and grounded you. And you pushed him—forced him to open up and think with emotions rather than logic. Whether you realize it or not, you both complement one another. You made each other better."

"How can you say that?" I demanded, pulling back from my friend. "Nothing about what happened between us made me a better person. I was weak and pathetic and allowed decisions to be made for me without speaking up. I lost who I was *because* I loved Dashiell."

Felix shook his head and huffed in frustration. How long had he been holding this inside? Maybe my fury towards that prince blinded me, but I couldn't see how anything Felix claimed could hold merit. The evidence of the disaster we were outweighed any good.

"You're still filled with such anger towards him."

"I have reason to be!" I exclaimed. Were we seriously debating this right now?

"I'm not saying you don't, Ainsley. But you're the most stubborn person I know, and more often than not, you hurt yourself because of it," Felix accused, and I gritted my jaw hard enough to crack a tooth. "You and Dash both made so many mistakes regarding your relationship, but it doesn't change who you became around each other. It doesn't evaporate that love you gave. You wanted friendship and someone to trust. You wanted to feel safe and protected, and Dashiell gave that to you. It's not *his* fault you lost your voice because of it, so stop blaming him, Ainsley. If you don't, you're never going to move on."

I stood from my spot on the couch as tears pricked the back of my eyes. I didn't want to listen to or acknowledge anything he was saying, and I guessed that was exactly what he meant by my being stubborn. I stalked for the fireplace, gripping the mantle hard as I worked to control my rage. I was ready to spit fire, but I knew that wouldn't get me anywhere, not with Felix. The only good it would do was prove that everything he said about me was correct.

"With Evander, it's different," Felix declared, not giving me a second to gather myself before diving in again. "You two are exactly the same, and that shouldn't work, but for some reason it does. You don't complement or balance one another. You're fire on fire, and that *should* mean destruction. But rather than feed that chaos and burn everything you touch, leaving disaster in your wake, you tend to it. You stoke each other's flames just enough that you both burn brighter. There isn't a line either of you wouldn't cross for one another, and that's a beautiful and dangerous kind of love."

I closed my eyes as his words burrowed under my skin, sinking deep and refusing to let go. I didn't want to admit the truth of what he was saying because it made the pain of Evander's lies cut that much deeper. It was *because* of the connection we shared and the love I felt for him that this hurt so much.

"I'm not telling you to forgive Evander," Felix said quietly as his approaching footsteps rang in my ears. He placed a soft hand on my back as he guided me around to face him, though all I could see was his blurry silhouette through my tears. "But I am asking you to consider hearing him out before you throw away what the two of you have."

Felix's hands cupped my face, and his thumbs swept over my cheeks, catching each fallen bead of moisture from my eyes. A shuddering breath escaped from my lips as I nodded. I didn't know if listening to Evander's side would change anything, but I at least owed it to myself to find out. Perhaps it wouldn't make a difference, but I would get the closure I needed—the kind I had never gotten with Dashiell.

59.

Nova and I stared at one another, unable to fall asleep. Usually, she loved to lay along the foot of the bed and use my legs as a pillow, but tonight she opted to stretch out across from me. Perhaps she sensed that I needed the comfort. Her brown eyes searched mine as her chin rested on her stuffed Onyx, and I ached to see her love for him.

"I miss him too," I whispered as I petted her. "Both of them."

Sleeping without Evander was harder than I could have imagined. My fury with him had started to dwindle and transform into something more like curiosity. I began to focus less on the fact that he lied and more on why he chose to keep the truth hidden. He knew how much honesty meant to me, so his reasoning had to have been important, right? I knew him well enough to know he wouldn't have hurt me just for his own selfish gain. He wasn't that type of man—not when it came to me.

By the time I managed to give up on the prospect of sleep altogether, the sun had crested the mountains, and the light of dawn crept through the wide windows. During the night, Nova had pushed her stuffed Onyx against me, relinquishing her favorite toy like it would help heal the pain in my heart. I returned the gesture by crafting a larger one double the size, which she dragged around with her as we made our way to the kitchen, where the scent of fresh coffee wafted through the air.

"Good morning," Felix said, piling eggs onto a plate as he sipped from his mug.

I padded over, kissed his cheek, stole the cup from his hands, and hurried away before he could object. He sighed dramatically as he went to fix himself another cup, putting his plate down on the island to free his hands... A plate that I snatched up the moment he turned away.

"You could just ask," he said, knowing exactly what I had done without looking.

"But this is much more fun," I replied, shoving the eggs into my mouth. "Plus, you always steal my food, so consider this my retribution." Felix chuckled under his breath and came over to refill my coffee.

"I take it you didn't sleep," he said, looking me over. What a pleasant way to say I looked like shit. I shook my head, focusing on the cup between my hands like it offered more than just a warm drink. "Have you decided what you want to do about him?"

Again, I shook my head.

"The more I think about it, the more confused I am," I admitted.

"Is it really that bad that your soul is connected to another?" Felix asked, and I looked up at him, my brows furrowed in question. "It's just that it could be nice to know you always have someone—"

"Felix, I'm not mad that Evander and I share a soul. In fact, I'm relieved to finally know why this unexplainable connection has existed between us since the beginning. The only reason I'm upset is that he kept it from me," I explained, placing my mug down so I could give my friend my full attention. I didn't want there to be any mistake regarding why I was angry or hesitant with the man I loved. "Evander didn't have a choice in this either. He's just as much a victim in it as I am, and I would never hold him responsible for whatever this Soul Bond is. The blame for that is solely on our parents."

If I felt confident in anything, it was that Evander didn't deserve to be punished for what was decided for us long before we were born. I just hoped he didn't believe I would hold that against him or think he had any part in that decision when it was clear he didn't. My eyes drifted to the open door of the study. I could write to Marce and ask her to talk to him for me. I could have her say that I knew it wasn't his fault. I could—

A knock on the door, in time with the lock turning, had me jumping back from the island and curling my shadows around my hands on instinct. I breathed a sigh of relief as a gorgeous woman with flowing red hair ran at me, throwing her arms around me tightly. My back slammed hard against the marble countertop as Lia hugged me, but I didn't care about the bruise that would no doubt appear momentarily. She was here.

"Let her breathe, Lia," Marce called as she carried their bags through the door. Lia released me, and I strode quickly for Marce and pulled her in for an equally long hug, which Lia decided to also join by wrapping herself around my back.

"What are you both doing here?!" I asked, crushed between those two amazing women.

"You're in pain," Lia answered, squeezing me tighter.

"You didn't honestly think we'd let you go through this alone?" Marce added as we all broke away.

My jaw dropped as I looked between my friends, not sure how to thank them for coming out here for me. For wanting to be in this house instead of the place we called home just because I was upset. Felix joined us and draped his arm across my shoulder as I looked at him with misted eyes.

"We're your family," Felix said softly. "And we'll always be here for you whenever you need us—whether you realize you do or not."

Before another word could be said, a sob broke through my throat, and the three wrapped their arms around me again. No matter how hard I tried, I couldn't stop the tears from flowing. They weren't from sadness but rather from the overwhelming love and support I had been given.

When I arrived in Tenebrae, I went through my heartbreak alone. Even though Felix had tried to comfort me after a time, I didn't fully let myself trust him or indulge in what he was attempting to offer me. I was determined to push through on my own, but that would never happen again. Not because I couldn't do it but because my family wouldn't ever allow it. They would never let me break alone again.

When I managed to slow the stream of tears enough to form a coherent statement of gratitude, Felix led us to the kitchen, where he promptly cracked open a bottle of wine and served us all. It was still early morning, but feeling like shit and having your world turned upside down made it an appropriate beverage. Not to mention, it paired well with the pancakes Felix was cooking for us.

"How is he?" I asked, needing to get that question out of the way first. Lia and Marce shared a concerned look before addressing me.

"Not good," Lia said under her breath. "He's a lot like how you were when you first came here. He won't talk to anyone. It took Marce most of yesterday just to get him to move from the living room floor."

"I've never seen him like that before. It's like he's just a shell," Marce added, and I sucked in a breath as I nodded.

"I know," I said as my voice trembled. "I can feel him. I was just hoping I was wrong."

What I could feel from Evander was pain that was near cataclysmic. It was hopelessness and fear, rage and regret. It was excruciating sadness and an over-whelming feeling of being lost and alone. It was the kind of hurt I wouldn't wish upon anyone, and it took everything inside me to stay strong and not go to him.

I had no idea about the ins and outs of the Soul Bond or what it truly meant to possess it. The only thing I knew was that I could feel Evander's pain so strongly that it was like it was my own. Was there more we could do, or was feeling each other's emotions the extent of it?

"Cal will be here tomorrow with Sirona," Lia announced, and my eyes snapped to hers as curiosity flooded my face. "We all thought you had a right to know as much about this bond as possible."

Relief filled every ounce of my body as I processed what Lia was saying. I would get answers to the questions that had plagued my mind and kept me awake throughout the night. I knew that no bond could force love, but what was our parents' hope when they decided to create us in such a way? Was Sirona the one who produced the bond, or did she simply just know about it?

"You asshole!" Marce yelled and jerked me from my thoughts in time to see her scold Nova for stealing the meat from her breakfast plate. "I've always liked Onyx more!" she called as my wolf chomped down on her stolen food in front of the fire. At some point, she had dragged both of her stuffed wolves to accompany her while she curled up on the wooden floor.

"Leave my new best friend alone," Felix declared, jogging to Nova and presenting her with her own overflowing plate of breakfast. She licked his face incessantly in gratitude before digging into her food. "Buttercup, will you craft something I can use to make her a bed?"

"She doesn't deserve a bed," Marce said, fixing herself a new plate.

I chuckled at my friend's hostility towards my wolf and strode to Felix. My shadow magic dripped from my hands, and I watched as it twisted and bent to my will. I was almost done with a large cushion when an idea sparked in my mind, so I quickly let my creation dissipate and started again. Nova whimpered at the loss of her new bed, and I rolled my eyes at her dramatics.

"You'll like this better," I told her, flexing my fingers and molding my shadow magic into the perfect bed for her.

"It's so cute!" Lia yelled as she ran over just as I dropped the life-size stuffed Onyx onto the floor. Nova's tail wagged happily as she picked up the smallest stuffed toy before padding to her new bed and curling up next to the fluffy black wolf just as she would have if he were really here. I was keeping her from her Solum, so the least I could do was give her as many reminders of him as possible. Though I knew nothing would be as good as seeing his adorable face in real life.

"Pathetic," Marce drawled, but there was a ghost of a smile on her lips.

"At least this one doesn't whimper and howl nonstop," Felix added, and Marceline raised her glass in cheers.

"Was it really that bad?" I questioned, and the three of them groaned loudly in unison. Even Lia, who never once complained about the wolves, seemed annoyed by Onyx's behavior. "What exactly happened after I left?" I asked, coming to sit at the kitchen island next to Marce.

"We confronted Van and demanded answers," she said.

"And?"

"He told us everything. He was transparent about anything we wanted to know," Marceline replied. "It's... A lot, Ainsley."

"Why do I feel like if I ask you to tell me what was said, you won't?" I said, reading the stern expression on her face. I didn't like the idea of anything else being kept from me. I wanted answers, and I didn't care who gave them to me.

"Because it's his story to tell," she finished, and I rolled my eyes in irritation.

I didn't give a shit if it was *his* story. It seemed like everyone except for me knew it, and I felt my anger rise again. Why was it so hard to be granted a bit of honesty?

"I'm not saying that to be evasive," Marceline added. "I'm saying it because there's just so much that I know I won't be able to relay properly. There was so much happening for so long that none of us knew about."

I threw my head back as I closed my eyes and willed my body to calm. As much as I was desperate to know the truth, I couldn't deny that Marceline was right. This was between Evander and me; only he could tell me what I wanted to know.

The whole story.

"Oh, and Marceline beat the shit out of Olivier," Lia said, and my eyes flew open at once, finding Marce grinning proudly. "I mean, I've seen them go at it through the years, but damn—that was definitely one for the books."

I stared at Marce, my brows shooting to my hairline and a look on my face that implored her to elaborate. She gave me a devilish smile as she refilled her wine glass, completely satisfied with the outcome of the fight with her brother.

"He shouldn't have been an asshole and kept that Soul Bond shit from all of us—especially *you*," she said like it was the most obvious fact in existence. I got where she was coming from, but I wasn't sure violence was the best course of action.

"She broke his arm in four different places," Lia chirped as she skipped into the kitchen. "It took me over three hours to heal, and it was the reason we got here so late."

"I would have cut off his dick too if it wasn't for that one stopping me," Marce said, angling her wine glass in Felix's direction.

"I happen to enjoy that part of him," Felix mused from the couch, and Marce made a dramatic show of gagging.

I couldn't help but laugh at how ridiculous this whole situation was. Yesterday I felt like I was suffocating, and today I was laughing about my friend wanting to cut a piece of her brother from his body. It didn't seem real.

I should have been crying—breaking on the bathing room floor, too in my head to function and comprehend anything around me, not sitting there listening to jokes and making stuffed animals. Was this what it was like to go through hardship with friends at your side? People who would keep your mind off the bad and carry a lantern to light your way through the darkness. People who would hold your hand and pull you back from the cliff's edge. People who would stop at nothing to make sure you survived the worst.

I felt both joy and guilt all at once. I was happy that I had them here to keep my thoughts at bay and my will from shattering, but at the same time, I knew they couldn't be in two places at once. They had been at Evander's side nearly his whole life, and now he was utterly alone, save for Oli. For every smile that formed and laugh that surfaced, it was one less that Evander would experience. He had no one, and I hated that.

The four of us spent the day discussing anything that wasn't Evander or the strange-as-hell Soul Bond. My friends did everything to keep my mind off of my own shit and instead talked about the problems they were dealing with. Lia and Cal were desperately trying to find a third person for their relationship, but there wasn't anyone they enjoyed enough. Felix was blissfully happy with Oli—who happened to be on the strict 'do not mention' list—so instead, he complained about how no one in Tenebrae appreciated his sense of humor. However, that didn't seem like very much of a problem. Marceline claimed she had no issues, and even if she did, they were no one else's business except for hers. But then she managed to complain for over an hour about how Cal constantly steals her shampoo and that the wolves keep sneaking into her room when she isn't home so they can sleep on her bed.

I was grateful to have them there, and though I wasn't sure what my next step would be, I wanted to enjoy the time I had left with them. If I chose to leave Tenebrae, I wasn't sure when I would see them all again, including Felix. I knew he said that it was him and I together always, but he had Olivier now, and I would never take him from the love he found. He deserved that happiness, and I would ensure he got it.

A knock at the door interrupted our quiet dinner, and Lia leapt from her seat, excited that Cal and Sirona had arrived earlier than expected. I should have been happy to finally get my answers, but after the long day of feeling his heartache through the connection between us, I was overwhelmed and exhausted.

"Ainsley, it's for you," Lia said in a deadly calm, and everyone in the room tensed.

I slipped off my chair and strode for the door to find Olivier standing there, looking forlorn and disheveled. He was at the top of my list of people I didn't want to see, yet the world just wanted to fuck with me some more tonight.

"Can we talk?" he asked under his breath, and I nodded before following him outside and shutting the door behind me. I stood on the porch, gripping the wooden railing as I scanned the dark horizon and waited for Olivier to say his peace. "I want to start by saying I'm sorry for allowing you to be in the dark for so long."

I inhaled deeply through my nose and clenched my jaw tight to keep the sarcasm from spilling from my lips. Biting his head off wouldn't do any good, even though he deserved far more than that. My eye caught a bandage wrapped around his wrist, and I suppressed a smirk at seeing Marce's work still not fully healed. She must have done some serious damage for him to be still hurting a day later and after Lia's exceptional Medicus skills. I didn't think violence between the siblings would solve anything, but I could admit that I was a bit pissed that I missed watching it unfold.

"I still believe it's Evander's right to explain everything because it involves the two of you. But I should have given him a deadline and ensured he told you."

"So why didn't you?" I questioned, not disguising the hurt in my voice. I considered him like a brother and wouldn't pretend that his lies didn't add to my pain. "You told me you swore to my parents to always be there for me. This kind of seems like the opposite of that, Oli."

He dropped his head in shame at the reminder and gripped the railing in a move that mimicked mine. That little sentence cut him deep, and though it wasn't my intention to hurt him, I had to speak up and say my truth for my own well-being. I knew he was Evander's best friend, but I thought I meant something to him too.

"I know," he whispered. "And I could give you my reasons, but it doesn't change the fact that I was wrong in how I handled everything. I have no defense, Ainsley. There isn't anything I could say that would make how I went about everything right. There isn't anything I can do except apologize to you and ensure that nothing like that ever happens again. I know that requires a second chance and trust, and after what I did, you—"

I cut him off by throwing my arms around him tight and forcing us into an embrace. I didn't want to be mad at Olivier. I only wanted him to realize that what he did hurt me, and for him to have come all this way to apologize let me know he had.

Olivier squeezed me tighter until I struggled for air and had to push myself away. He quickly dabbed his eyes like he could cover up the emotion he had displayed, but it was too late. I saw the tear that gently trickled and arched a brow in his direction.

"You didn't see that," he said in his serious, no-nonsense way. I smiled wide as I looked at my friend.

"Oh, I definitely did," I joked, backing away slowly toward the front door. He groaned as he rolled his eyes, and I laughed at the sight. He lunged for me, but I twisted the handle in time to push open the door... Promptly knocking over three people who had their ears pressed to it. They looked up from the floor shamelessly after being caught eavesdropping, and I sighed with disappointment at their antics.

"Oh, shut up," Felix said, rising from the floor. "In what world were we not going to listen?"

He dusted off his pants before walking over to Oli and planting a kiss against his lips. It was nice to see my friend so happy and comfortable. I half expected Oli to push him away and not want the audience. To my surprise, he pulled Felix in closer as he tangled his fingers through my friend's silver hair and deepened their embrace.

Though it was far from it, things started to feel right again. I was glad that Olivier and I made up, and soon I would have the answers about this Soul Bond from Sirona. The only thing that still felt out of place was the lack of Evander. He had become a permanent fixture in my life, and I struggled to picture one without him. Depending on what I learned tomorrow, there was a real possibility that I would be leaving Tenebrae and not returning.

Everything about that choice felt wrong. My instincts and magic urged me to not even consider leaving my home, and my heart and soul ached at the prospect of never being with the man I had fallen in love with. But I'd trusted my heart before, and it had left me broken and lost. As Evander had pointed out when I arrived in Tenebrae, I made choices based on the love and trust I felt and not on logic. And it cost me. Who's to say that if I stayed, it wouldn't be because I was blinded by love yet again? Even though Van had always told me to trust my magic, I couldn't. It was tainted—biased because it wanted him. How did I know it wasn't steering me wrong because of its desire to be near him?

60.

"Ainsley?" Cal said, gently jostling me awake, and I cracked open an eye to see him smiling down at me. I sat up quickly and wrapped my arms around his neck before pulling him onto the couch with me.

"It's too early," Marce whined from the other end as she covered her head with a pillow.

Last night, we had all been up late and decided we were too tired to go to our rooms, so instead, we had each claimed a spot and fallen asleep sprawled out across the living room.

Marce and I had settled on the couch while Lia curled beside Nova after I made additional stuffed wolves. Lia had requested one twice the size of my wolf with an additional tiny one she could hold through the night. I obliged, of course, and also made Nova a grey one that looked just like her, but rather than sleep with it, she set it on the fireplace hearth and then placed her small black wolf directly on top so its head was resting on the grey one's—the same position she and Onyx slept in nearly every day. Oli and Felix opted for the floor, holding each other through the night, and I audibly cooed at the sight of their entangled limbs.

"Did I miss out on an orgy?" Calidore joked, and I nodded enthusiastically.

"It was one for the books," I replied. "I'm quite sad you had to miss it."

Cal sighed dramatically as he shrugged.

"Just my luck," he said.

A laugh escaped me, and I stretched my arms above my head as I adjusted from being curled into a ball all night. I missed sleeping in my bed at home. I missed Nova lying on my feet while Onyx wormed between his master and me. And more than anything, I missed the man I loved.

"If you carry me to bed, I'll give you a replay," Lia offered as she held her arms in the air from the comfort of the fluffy wolf bed. Cal was up instantly, striding across the room and lifting her into his arms. "We'll be back later," she said, smiling wickedly as Cal carried her to one of the four empty bedrooms in the house. I bit my lip and prayed they would remember to throw up a silencing shield before going at it.

"Hello, darling," Sirona said as she approached, and I gave a warm but tight smile. I still wasn't sure how I felt about her after learning she had known about the Soul Bond, but I couldn't let my weariness get in the way of my mission for answers. "Would you like to talk now or later?"

"Now, please," I said, gesturing for her to sit on the couch with me. My friends took that as their cue to leave and promptly made themselves scarce, giving Sirona and me total privacy, minus the snoring wolf in the corner.

I pulled at my fingers, feeling awkward and unable to figure out where to start. Did I demand why she kept it a secret? Did I ask if she was the one who created the Soul Bond in the first place? Something told me a simple '*Hey Sirona, what the fuck were you thinking?*' probably wasn't the best way to go about things, no matter how much I wanted to ask it.

"I take it you have several questions?" she noted, and I nodded, keeping my eyes glued to my fidgeting fingers. "Why don't I start, and you can feel free to interrupt at any time."

I loosed a breath and agreed. That sounded like a much better plan than just bombarding her with questions in hopes I covered everything I wanted to know.

"Your and Evander's parents came to me long ago and asked me to find a way to create a strong bond."

"Why?" I interrupted immediately, and Sirona smiled at the fact it took less than five seconds for me to do so. "Sorry."

"Don't be," she assured. "They wanted me to create a bond to ensure their children would never be alone. Everyone knew the risk of your mother and father producing children, as they were from two different kingdoms. Evander's late father came up with the idea in hopes that this connection would be strong enough to keep everyone safe."

"How exactly would we keep each other safe?" I asked. "The most I can do is feel him."

Sirona nodded like she was already aware of that fact. Of course, she was—she made the damn bond.

"You can't," she said simply, and I opened my mouth to inquire more, but she beat me to it, already sensing that I would ask about every aspect of her story. "It was a good idea in theory, but I couldn't execute it. Magic is tricky, and a bond like yours has never existed. The closest we have ever gotten was the Entwining. But I could make a connection bond by using magic to create two lives from one soul, so that's what I did."

"But Evander and I are years apart in age. It didn't have to be conducted at the same time?" I asked, trying to wrap my head around the magic.

"The magic was cast upon your mothers. Whatever child they produced first—whenever they produced it—would possess one half of the soul. You and Evander could have potentially been hundreds of years apart, but your mothers wanted you close in age," Sirona explained.

I reached for my wine on the table, taking a long sip before daring to face the woman next to me again. There was still so much I wanted to know and even more that I was confused about. There were questions I had about our parents' motives and how the whole process worked, but more than that, I wanted to know about Evander's involvement. However, I wouldn't ask her why he chose to keep the truth from me as I realized I wanted to hear that answer from him.

"How long has Van known?" I asked tentatively.

"His entire life."

For some reason, that answer made me feel pity for him. He had grown up knowing the other half of his soul was somewhere out there, and there was a chance he'd never be near it. Maybe he hadn't cared? Knowing Van and how important family was to him, I was positive that wasn't the case.

"Is there any way to undo the Soul Bond?" I inquired.

Sirona was quiet for a long moment as she looked around the room, delaying her answer. Did she not know or just not want to tell me? I thought it would have been as simple as a yes or no answer, but the tension I could feel radiating from her told me that wasn't the case.

"Since you arrived back in Tenebrae, I have been trying to figure out a way to do just that," she explained, and I straightened with piqued interest. "But unfortunately, the only way to undo a Soul Bond is through death."

I inhaled a shaky breath as I took in the weight of her words and what that would mean for one of us. The only way to escape would be to die, and there was no way that I would ever willingly allow that to happen. That couldn't have been our only option. Would our parents really have forced this bond upon us without giving us a way out? Since returning home, everyone I met told stories of our parents' love and generosity. They were said to be good and honest people, but tying their children together for eternity without another option seemed like a real asshole move on their part.

"I did find a potential workaround, though," Sirona said quickly, reading the panic on my blood-drained face. My heart thumped quickly as I pushed images of Evander's lifeless grey eyes out of my mind. "Entwining also creates a bond, though it's nowhere near as powerful as what you and Evander share. However, Entwining yourself to someone else could potentially lessen the desire and need to be around your Soul Bonded. It may direct those urges to your Entwined instead. It's all hypothetical, and you both would need to do it for it to have a chance at working," she explained.

I must have looked like a gaping fool as I stared at her with an open mouth and no words emanating from it. Was I seriously being told that after leaving Caelum to avoid being Entwined to someone, I would have to Entwine with someone to avoid a Soul Bond placed on me since before birth? How was this my fucking life?

The irony of the situation had me laughing uncontrollably, and Sirona observed every cackle that escaped me without saying a word. At one point, she even sipped her drink and left me to my inappropriate hysterics, as if it was completely normal behavior I was exhibiting.

"I'm sorry," I said, clasping a hand over my mouth to muffle the giggles. "It's not funny; it really isn't. But at the same time, it kind of is. But it doesn't matter because Evander would never agree to—"

"He already has," Sirona said, and my heart stopped dead in my chest.

My face fell, and all laughing stopped as her words replayed once, twice, three times in my head. Evander despised the Entwining Ceremony. He said it was an outdated practice that deserved to be banned from existence. There was no way he would ever agree to it. Unless...

"When?" I demanded. "When did he agree?"

"I presented him my theory about it the day Felix interrupted us. After your friend left, Evander said he would do it but gave me twenty-four hours to try and find another way. I was supposed to meet him when he finished the Solum celebration, but he never showed up," she said, and I released a shaky breath.

He hadn't met with her that night because he was with me. That was the night of the clifftop and when I told him I wanted him. It was the night I chose him to be mine. Would things have been different if I had never gone to find him?

"And then he showed up the next morning," she continued. "I informed him that I couldn't find another way, though I truly tried to. Evander was as gracious as he's always been and thanked me for everything I had done to help. I thought he would leave it at that and accept the Soul Bond as it was, but instead, he said he was willing to Entwine with someone."

I shook my head as a tear slid down my cheek. He had made that decision after we agreed to be together.

"I don't understand," I croaked. "How could he say he'd be with me while knowing he might tie himself to someone else?" It didn't make sense.

"He never wanted to Entwine himself to anyone, my darling. He was only willing to do it to give you a *choice*. All he has ever wanted for you since he showed up at my door days after your arrival was to give you the option of keeping the Soul Bond or removing it. He's fought tirelessly over these past months trying to research and find a way out of this for you, Ainsley."

I wasn't breathing. There was no air in the room, nothing to fill my lungs except her confession. Every time we went into the village, he made it a point to stop at her shop. I remembered always being annoyed at how long he took there and how I thought he did it just to piss me off. When lo and behold, he was fighting for my freedom—my choice.

I breathed heavily as I gripped the sides of the couch, my shadows spilling between my fingers as the weight of her words pressed into me like a boulder. I hadn't planned on asking her why Evander didn't tell me the truth, but I didn't have to. She divulged enough information for me to understand why.

"Ainsley?" Felix asked, and I looked up to find every one of my friends watching me cautiously, the look of concern written on their faces.

My Gift must have pushed my emotions through the house, alerting everyone of my feelings. I should have calmed their worried expressions, but I couldn't find the words as I stared at them. All I knew was I needed to get out of there and find Evander.

I stood, and without a word, all of my friends scattered. Lia and Marce helped me into my coat and boots, and Felix and Cal ran outside to get Nox saddled and ready. Without me saying a word, they knew the only thing I needed was *him*.

"Is he home?" I asked, mounting my mare and grabbing the reigns.

"No. At least he hasn't been," Olivier said, and I nodded.

It would have been easier if I knew where he was, but that wouldn't stop me from finding him.

"Be safe," Marce said. "We'll head home tomorrow, but write if you need to return. The transfer paper is on the desk in my room."

I thanked her and met the eager eyes of all my family—all of whom had smiles of hope on their beautiful faces.

"Go get him," Felix said, and I nodded before urging Nox forward and taking off at full speed down the path that would lead me home.

61.

The sun had long since set when I made it back. Our house was dark and quiet, not a single light on or sign of Evander to be found. I called out for Onyx, but he didn't seem to be there either. I wracked my brain around where he would have gone. The palace was an option, but he wouldn't have chosen it if he was hurting—and the soul-crushing pain in my chest told me he was—he wouldn't have gone there. If he was an empty shell as I had once been, then he would have desired to be left alone to his suffering.

I mounted Nox again and instructed her on where to bring me. The night air nipped along my cheeks and burned my eyes as we sped through the forest without slowing. My hands were so numb I couldn't feel the reins beneath my grip, and my body trembled from the cold. In my haste to leave Marce's house, I hadn't properly dressed. I was wearing my thin sleeping clothes with my boots and coat.

Nox slowed her pace to a walk as we reached the edge of the trees surrounding the clearing. I squinted through the now steady snowfall and loosed a shaky breath of relief as I found Evander sitting at the clifftop's edge with Onyx stoically planted at his side. I dismounted my mare and walked towards him on frozen legs, though I wasn't sure if I was shaking more from the cold or because he was there.

The snow crunched beneath my boots as the wind whistled through the trees, whipping my hair all around as I approached the center of the clearing. My magic rumbled and purred in my chest the closer I got, seeming finally satisfied to be in his presence again. As if he could sense me near, Evander spun, and his gaze widened as he saw me. *Love*, he mouthed, barely more than a movement of his lips, but I knew what he was saying. He scrambled to his feet but didn't make an effort to move to me, even though he was obviously fighting the desire to do so. Onyx, however, wasted no time sprinting to me, his black fur dark and bold against the pure white powder. He leapt at me, knocking me on my ass as his body pressed me into the wet snow while he whimpered and licked every inch of my face.

I smiled, scratching him behind his ears and giving my boy the love he deserved. After a moment, he picked his muzzle up from the crook of my neck and looked eagerly in the direction of Nox, undoubtedly searching for his mate.

"She's not here," I told him sadly, wishing I had brought her along.

The black wolf huffed like he was annoyed at my answer and buried his face against me once more. I hugged him tight before working to shove him away as melting snow slid beneath my coat and onto my skin. In pure Onyx fashion, he refused to move, and I was pinned down while he got more comfortable.

"Onyx, you have to get up," I said, shoving harder this time, but to no avail. "I promise to give you cookies." Nothing.

He stayed put like if he didn't move, I could never leave him again. Knowing how needy this wolf was, I was pretty positive that was his goal. I yipped as more snow traveled under my shirt and stung my flesh, the cold becoming increasingly more painful.

"Get up now!" Evander commanded with firm authority, and Onyx shifted from above me, allowing enough space for me to wiggle free.

I stood and quickly shook out my coat and shirt as thick globs of ice fell beneath them. I really should have changed into something more appropriate before venturing into the mountains, but I wasn't thinking about anything but seeing Evander again.

"May I?" he asked, and I looked up from my task to find him holding a thick fur blanket he had crafted.

I nodded my permission, and he tentatively stepped towards me before wrapping the fabric around my shoulders. I grabbed the ends, clamping them together tightly to avoid any chilled air getting through. Van stepped back and surveyed me before shaking his head, unsatisfied at whatever he observed. He crafted another blanket and then another, bundling me up before running his hands up and down where my arms were hidden beneath.

We stared at each other as he worked to spread warmth into my body. My eyes were glued to his, and my heart fractured as I studied just how terrible he looked. His hair was disheveled, and his eyes dull and glassy. They were red-rimmed with purpling beneath, and the stubble along his jaw was thicker than I'd ever seen it. It reminded me so much of the girl I saw in the mirror days after I had arrived in Tenebrae—the girl who had lost the only thing she loved and suffered for it.

Evander swallowed, and his throat bobbed like he wanted to speak but wasn't sure where to start. I couldn't blame him for that because I was standing there wondering the same thing. After a minute of trying, he sighed, lowering his hands and stepping back to give me space. Before I could stop myself, my hands shot out from beneath the blanket and grasped his coat as I refused to allow him to retreat another inch. Van's eyes widened with awe and hope as he closed the gap between us again and adjusted my blankets. When he realized I wouldn't let go of him, he pushed himself against me so my hands could stay out of the elements.

"Tell me everything," I breathed, and Evander nodded at once, eager to spill the truth in the hopes of not losing me. I didn't need my Empathi Gifts or our Soul Bond to sense the desperation within him or his willingness to do whatever it took to prevent that from happening.

He frantically looked around the space as he struggled with what to say. His mouth opened and closed several times before his eyes met mine, and I saw the fear brewing there. His tattoo slithered across the skin that was exposed beneath his coat, and his hands began to tremble as they held my blanket closed. He didn't know where to start, and the panic had fully set in. I reached up quickly and rested my hand on his cheek to keep him from being lost in that darkness.

"Breathe," I told him, and Evander's chest rose and fell in heavy movements. "Good." I removed my free hand from his shirt and placed it against his other cheek, not caring that I could barely feel my fingers from the cold. The most important thing was getting Van to calm down and understand that I wasn't leaving him at that moment.

"You've known about the Soul Bond your entire life," I stated, deciding that starting with what I already knew would be the best choice. He nodded immediately as his breathing began to come more evenly. "Did you resent it?"

"No," he whispered, and I felt the tension in my body slowly ease now that he seemed to be getting a handle on himself. "At least not right away. When I was a teenager, I was mad about it for a while, but eventually Olivier helped me get my head out of my ass. I loved that I had a connection with you—that I wasn't alone. That there was an invisible string tying us together. I cherished it every day when I wasn't being an idiot."

His words were rushed and shaky, but at least he could get them out. I offered a smile, hoping it would further bring him back down from the edge he was standing on, but instead, it only seemed to make things worse. His body shook, and I tightened my grip on his face as he squeezed his eyes shut. I could feel the guilt pouring from him the moment he saw me smile.

"Did you ever try to find me?" I quickly asked in an attempt to direct his focus back on our conversation.

"Yes and no," he breathed, letting his eyes flutter open again. "After you had been taken, no one could locate you. We tried for years, but there was no sign of where you were. Sirona thought that our best chance was to wait until you turned twenty-one. We hoped that once you had gotten your Gifts, our Soul Bond would also get stronger, and we could somehow find you that way—though that was just a theory she had. The other possibility was that *you* would come find us when your Gifts manifested and you learned where you came from if you hadn't already been told. We didn't know if you were simply hidden or being held captive," Evander explained. "Either way, once you turned twenty-one, I was coming after you."

I rubbed my frozen thumbs across his cheeks as I nodded along to his story. Evander flinched beneath my touch, and suddenly my fingers were encased in his shadows to keep out of the cold. My magic hummed with contentment as he took care of me.

"And that's why you came to Caelum," I deduced, but Evander shook his head before taking a deep breath in preparation for whatever else he was about to share. Whatever it was, he didn't seem to want to divulge it.

"I was ready to track you down for the rest of my life if that's what it took. I was willing to do whatever was needed to find you and bring you home, Ainsley, but..." he trailed off as he blinked back the tears that had formed. "But I changed my mind," he said regretfully. Evander tried to pull out of my hold as shame radiated from him, but I refused to allow it.

"Why?" I asked, and his eyes darted across my face as his own filled with fear.

"I need you to know that I regret that decision," he croaked, and his hands squeezed my arms beneath the blankets. "If I could go back and change it, I would. I need you to know that, Ainsley. I need you to—"

"I know," I replied at once.

He was unraveling before me, breaking with each spoken word, and all I knew was that I had to calm him down. I had to show him I wasn't leaving because that was the idea that was causing him to get lost in his terror. No matter how hard he was trying to stay present, he couldn't cope. I lifted myself onto my toes and pressed my lips to his in the briefest of touches. Evander's grip on my arms tightened as he held me still like he was terrified that even now, I would disappear.

"I know," I repeated against his mouth before lowering myself again. "I know you would do things differently, but I need to understand what happened and why. We can't move forward if I don't, Evander."

He inhaled a deep breath and nodded before trying once again to compose himself. I released my hold on his face and instead threaded our hands together, wanting to give him space to work through his thoughts while remaining close.

"Our Soul Bond," he began, and his voice still held an edge of uncertainty. "Allows us to feel one another when our emotions, whatever they may be, are strongest."

I had gathered as much from the agony I'd felt these past few days. Though my own heart was breaking, it clearly wasn't just my feelings I was experiencing. The moment I learned about our bond, it was as if that knowledge solidified his presence within my soul. He, of course, had always been there, but now that I knew what to look for, it was unmistakable. How many times had I experienced his fear, pain, or heartbreak and mistook it for my own?

"For your entire life, the only thing I've ever been able to feel from you was sadness and an overwhelming sense of being completely alone. It broke me every time because I knew those feelings had to be intense for me to experience them from you. I was so angry every time I got a glimpse of you because I had no idea how to help. I didn't know how to stop your pain, and I wanted nothing more than to find you and bring you home to our family—to me," Evander explained. My thoughts drifted to my terrible upbringing.

That life seemed so distant, that it didn't feel like mine anymore. So much had changed and evolved since my time with my Caregivers, and I was grateful that I could barely recall it. It held nothing but miserable memories for me and apparently Evander too.

"But then this summer, things started to change," he said quietly, shifting his gaze to the distance like he was watching images play out in the air around us. "For the first time ever, I felt happiness from you. An immense sense of joy and belonging radiated from you every day, and I basked in it."

I remembered how good it felt to be with Felix and Dashiell; how they made me feel wanted and cherished each day. Imogen was always a safe place for me and gave me the love of the parent I never had. Those people were my home and the only happiness I had ever known at the time.

"And eventually," Evander continued, turning his eyes to me. "I felt you fall in love."

My heart thudded rapidly at the realization that Van had experienced it all. I had only assumed it was tragedy he felt, but love was possibly the most intense emotion of them all, so of course he'd be able to sense it from me.

"It was then that I realized you weren't coming home. I couldn't bring myself to take you from the only thing that ever brought you peace. I couldn't rip you away from the person you loved more than anything."

I swallowed hard at his confession and the fact that he was willing to give me up and let me go simply because of the happiness he felt from me. He gave up everything he had planned because he didn't want me to lose the love I had found. A tear slid down my cheek as I stared at the selfless man I had fallen in love with.

"Olivier and I fought for a while about it, but my mind was firmly made up. If you were ever to return home, it would be because *you* came to find us. I hoped you would one day, and if that was the case, I planned on telling you everything, but I wouldn't just force this life on you. I knew it was the right thing to do, but it was still a struggle to remind myself of that whenever I felt you, so I put up a barrier and—"

"A barrier?" I asked, and he nodded.

"Sirona helped me learn to do it as a teenager when I was rebelling against what we were," he explained.

Though I wanted to know what he meant, there would be time for that later. We had a lot of history to uncover, so I needed to prioritize the order in which I learned it. His fighting against our Soul Bond as a kid wasn't a story that I needed to know at that moment.

"You have to visualize the connection between us like a wall of clear glass. The barrier makes the glass appear frosted, causing the images on each side to look blurry or distorted. You can still make out the silhouettes; it's just not as clear as when the barrier is dropped. I could still feel your emotions when they were strong, but it dulled them just enough for me to focus on something other than you."

I squeezed his fingers tighter as I learned of his struggles. He was heartbroken and still had to feel me every day, even though it had dulled. I couldn't imagine the pain he had to go through alone. The only one of our family members he could talk to about it was Olivier, and they weren't on the best terms once Evander had chosen to give me up.

"Then, one night, I was reviewing information about Pravus with Oli in the study when I felt you again. Ainsley, the pain was so intense I fell to the ground screaming as I tried to catch my breath. It was like the soul was being shredded from my body, and I had no idea what the fuck was going on. Olivier was yelling, trying to reach me, but all I could focus on was the agony in my chest and the feel of you slipping away like the wind between my fingers. I realized you were dying.

You were being taken from this world—from me—and I could do nothing to stop it. And then my world went dark, and I passed out from the pain.

"When I woke again, I was in my bed while Sirona and Oli were discussing what the cause of my episode could have been. I didn't bother to answer them at first. I was too busy reaching out to try and find you. Luckily, my soul still sensed yours in this world, and I breathed the biggest fucking sigh of relief to know you were still with me. I told Oli and Sirona what had caused it, and that's when I learned about the hell that night had been."

It didn't take long for me to realize he had experienced what I was going through when I had been attacked at the orchard. I had nearly died that night, and I surely would have if it weren't for Dashiell finding me in time. I was so terrified that my attackers would drag me off to Tenebrae, and I couldn't help but wonder what their actual plans for me had been.

At the time, I thought the orders they were given to keep me alive had come directly from King Evander, but now I was starting to suspect it was Oberon behind the attacks. If women were being sold to him to carry out Conjoining experiments, then I was positive he wanted me for the same.

"Attacks took place throughout Disparya that evening. Some of our villages had been plundered, and even Tallis had dealt with them. We had no idea what was happening until hours later when I received a summons from Prince Dashiell. He was demanding my presence at a meeting to be formally accused of the attempted kidnapping of his bride. Someone had orchestrated the assault and tried to set me up to take the fall. I was furious at the accusation but even more so at the fact that you had been a victim of one of the attacks," Evander said, releasing me to drag a hand through his hair. The cool breeze blew between us as I shivered at both the temperature and his story.

"King Perceval didn't want those summons to go out," I said absentmindedly as I recalled the conversation I had overheard during my recovery.

"Of course he didn't," he said bitterly, raising his hand to cup my cheek. "Because he had you and didn't want anyone to know."

"You really didn't know who I was when we met?" I asked, and Evander's face softened as he recounted that moment and shook his head.

His lip tilted up in the corner, resembling the cocky grin I loved. My heart fluttered to see the first sign of a smile, and I unlocked my fingers from his and wrapped both arms around his middle, needing to get close to him and cherish that small moment of peace.

"The moment I stepped over the boundary into Caelum, I felt you stronger than I ever had, and it knocked the breath from my lungs. For the first time, we were in the same place, and it took every ounce of willpower I had to force myself to keep going and not skip the meeting in lieu of finding you. I said I wouldn't go after you, but knowing you were so close, made the temptation that much harder. I finally managed to clear my head and focus on the reason we were in Caelum in the first place.

"Once I arrived at the palace, Tallis greeted us at the door, which I thought was odd as we always kept our friendship secret from the other kings. But then he hugged me and whispered, '*She's here,*' and my whole fucking world spun out of control."

"How did Tallis know I was there or even who I was if you didn't?" I asked, trying to follow along, but certain aspects weren't apparent.

I was never given a name at birth, nor did Dashiell or Felix provide the name my Caregivers had bestowed upon me to the kings, so how could Tallis have possibly put together who I was? I had never even seen that man until the meeting was over.

"Tallis spotted you hurrying through the courtyard and followed you. He's always known of our Soul Bond and tried to help our parents to locate you. So, the moment he saw you, he instantly knew exactly who you were. He had you secretly trailed to locate where you went and relayed the information to me moments later when I arrived."

"And that's when you cast an illusion on me?" I questioned as I followed along.

"Yes and no," he answered. "I told Olivier what was going on and that he would have to run point on the meeting because there was no way in hell I was going to miss an opportunity to speak to you in person. When we arrived at the meeting room, I said my pleasantries to everyone, though they all knew it was fake as fuck. Felix had shown up a few minutes after I had, and for a moment, I thought he knew exactly what I was planning because he wouldn't stop staring at me. Now I realize it was probably because he knew about your Gift and was debating whether to tell me.

"When he left to retrieve Dashiell, I cast an illusion on everyone in the room and slipped out. Then I followed Felix to where you were being held and hid in the adjoining room as I waited for the meeting to start. It was torture to sit there and do nothing, knowing you were just on the other side of the wall, but I had to make sure I did my part for our kingdom. The second Oli's note appeared on my transfer paper to let me know they were starting, I sliced even further into everyone's mind, digging my claws so deep there was no way they could tell I wasn't with them. My illusion performed my defense, and when I was finished, I wrote Oli back so he could take over the rest of the meeting for me. The only illusion I cast on you was to make you think those men were coming into your room."

My breath caught in my throat hearing that day from his point of view. I had always wondered why he had been in that room, and now I knew. Evander had been waiting for me—waiting for the opportunity for us to see each other for the first time.

"I knew it would be doing me more harm than good, but I couldn't give up the chance to see you. I needed to meet you, to hear your voice, to know your name—just once," Evander admitted as he leaned down and pressed his forehead to mine.

I inhaled deeply, drinking in his comforting scent and savoring his proximity. The fear in his voice from earlier had started to disappear, leaving him to speak calmly and confidently. He seemed to believe I wouldn't run from him, which only fueled his desire to share as much with me as possible.

"I knew who you were to me, but I had no idea who you were to Dashiell. It never crossed my mind that you were the subject of our meeting and why I was in Caelum," he added.

"But you knew I had been attacked."

"Villages were plundered in Tenebrae and Agnitio. Many people had gotten hurt, and I assumed it was the same in Caelum. You said you were the future princess's maiden, so I concluded that you must have been attacked due to your proximity to her at the time. If I had known you were Dashiell's bride, our conversation in that room would have gone very differently."

"You would have told me the truth?" I asked, though I already sensed the answer. Van nodded, and I let out a breath, expecting as much. "So what happened next?"

Evander pulled back, and there was a half-smile on his face as he looked at me. Even while sad and flustered, he was stunning.

"Next," he began, his tone light for the first time tonight. "You entered that room, and I felt my heart stop beating. For twenty-one years, I wanted nothing but you, and there you finally were, standing before me, breathtakingly beautiful and *mine*—my soul's other half. Then you asked why I was there with this glint in your eyes, and I thought you might have known who I was, but you didn't. I only allowed myself to be disappointed for a moment before enjoying the time I had left with you. And fuck, did I enjoy it," he said, and a breathy laugh escaped him.

I couldn't help but smile as I recalled our first encounter and how much I hated him. He was so arrogant and full of himself and had this way of getting under my skin. He was only a stranger to me then, but I should have known it was more. There was an odd connection between us that I picked up on, and never once did I fear he'd hurt me, though I should have. I had chosen not to tell Dashiell or Felix the full extent of our conversation, and at the time, I told myself it was because I didn't want to upset them. Now I realized it was because there was some part hidden inside me that wanted to keep him safe and secret.

"The hardest thing I've ever had to do was let you walk out of that room, but I made a promise when I was a child always to protect and take care of you, and that included your happiness," he admitted as he brushed a knuckle down my rosy cheek. The temperature around us continued to drop, but I wasn't about to leave this spot on our cliff until I knew every ounce of the truth. "I returned to the meeting room just in time to see a fight break out. After deflecting a few attacks, I gathered our family and got us the hell out of there and back to Agnitio, where I waited for Tallis.

"Once he showed up, we talked about the attacks, Pravus' whereabouts, and of course, you. I couldn't stop fucking talking about you like I was a lovestruck teenager. I want to say that you consumed my every thought from the moment I laid eyes on you, but I think it was really when you threatened to turn me over to Perceval that made me fall for you," he claimed, and I rolled my eyes as I shook my head. Evander bit his lip to stop his wide grin from spreading, but it didn't help, and my Gods, his smile was beautiful.

"And that's where Felix comes in," I stated, and he confirmed.

"The moment he said your name, everything inside me snapped, and I had to force myself to stay there and not go rip Perceval's head from his body," he said, his tone cold and malicious.

Knowing Van as well as I did, I had no doubt he would have done just that. Mishal's death would be nothing compared to the brutality of what Evander would dish out to Perceval for keeping me from him for decades. It was killing Van that he couldn't enact his revenge for the countless crimes the King of Caelum committed. Evander's parents had been taken from him. My parents had been taken from him. *I* had been taken from him, and now his kingdom was under the threat of being taken from him. And the man behind it all was sitting pretty on his golden throne in Caelum.

"I knew I had promised to let you be happy, but I had to get you out of there," he added, and I agreed with his decision. I wasn't safe in that kingdom and belonged in Tenebrae—I belonged with *him*.

We stared at each other for a quiet moment, and I knew he could read the unspoken question on my face. It was the entire reason we had fought, and I fled. It was the reason I was standing there before him now. Evander nodded to himself as he swallowed hard, preparing to explain why he chose to keep such a secret from me.

"I was so excited that you were home, love," he said with a shaky breath. "I wanted to tell you about our Soul Bond immediately, but you..."

Evander looked away, unable to hold my gaze as his mind traveled back to my first nights in Tenebrae. I let my thoughts do the same and was plunged into the darkness and despair I had felt so intensely all those months ago. I squeezed my eyes shut as I swallowed the familiar hurt of Dashiell's betrayal and instead focused on what Evander was saying.

"You were so broken and lost," he croaked, choking on a sob as he relived those first moments with me. "I wanted to make that agony stop for you, but I didn't know how or what to do."

"You were always so angry with me," I pointed out, remembering his cruel words every time we had spoken.

"No," he said, shaking his head vehemently. "I was never mad at *you*. I was furious with myself for everything that happened to you. Things might have ended up differently if I had just told you who you were when we met in Caelum. You wouldn't have been blindsided by betrayal and might have still been with Dashiell. It was *my* fault you were broken, and I took my anger and insecurities out on you."

"You were right about everything you said, though," I replied quietly, still ashamed of my complacency.

It was Evander pointing out I had given up who I was and stopped fighting that made me decide to stay in Tenebrae. It was those claims that fueled my body and mind each training session as I pushed myself so I would never be that naive and scared girl again.

"No, I wasn't," he replied, his deep eyes searching mine like he could burn the truth into my mind that way. "What happened to you wasn't your fault. You had love and happiness for the first time in your life. You wouldn't have seen the signs that something was off because you had no reason to suspect they would cause you harm. You gave yourself to them completely, Ainsley. The betrayal wasn't your fault, and I should have never inferred that it was. You were a victim, and I'm so sorry I made you feel like anything less.

"I was such a dick to you those first few weeks because I was angry at myself, but also, it was so hard to have you with me, but not in the way I wanted. It killed me each time I saw you with Felix and the friendship you shared because that was supposed to be *us*. He lied and hurt you, and still, you wanted his company and hated mine. Those little games we played were just as much for me as they were for you. I craved your presence and cherished the moments when you finally started to let me in. I even paid Lia in expensive bottles of wine and a week straight of being allowed to use my bathing pool to just be allowed to sit with you while you were on your cycle. I just wanted to be close to you in any way I could. I was insecure and immature, and I'm so very sorry, love."

A weight I hadn't been aware of lifted from my chest, and I felt like I could finally breathe more easily. His apology wasn't one I knew I needed, but it filled my heart to hear him acknowledge how he treated me and made me feel those first days was wrong. I fell in love with him even more for his admitting it.

"Thank you," I whispered, pulling Evander closer. Just an inch between us felt like a chasm, and I was determined to fill it. He nodded before preparing himself to continue his story.

"You were in so much pain for days, and I felt every second of it. You had just discovered that the people you loved lied to you and that Dashiell was planning to steal your Gifts. I couldn't look at you and tell you we shared a soul. I couldn't have you know that yet another choice had been stripped from you, and you were tied to me forever. I couldn't watch you break anymore. So I went to Sirona and demanded she find a way to end our bond," he explained, letting out a deep and shuddering breath as he stared into my eyes. "I swear I was going to tell you about us, Ainsley. I just wanted to be able to give you the option of getting rid of our bond when I did. I didn't want you to have this with me if it's not what you wanted."

He cherished that our souls were bonded as one and loved our connection, yet he was willing to give that up just to give me a choice. When I initially learned of our Soul Bond, I thought he had kept the truth from me for some twisted game he was playing, but the moment I took a breath and calmed down, I knew how wrong I'd been. I wasn't sure of his reasoning, but I knew *him*. I knew his soul because it was mine.

"Sirona told me that death was the only way to release us from the Soul Bond, which was clearly not an option. She and I spent months researching every type of bond and magic out there, but we are the only two people in existence who share a soul, so the information was limited. You and I were developing a close friendship, and I wanted to tell you the truth every single day, love. It tore me up not to, but I knew the look on your face when I told you there was no way out would annihilate me. So I kept quiet and kept hunting for an answer. I needed to give you back the choice that had been stolen from you before you were ever born," Evander said.

"I spoke to Sirona, and she told me it isn't possible to release us from it," I confirmed, and Van's face grew somber. "She told me about the idea she came up with and that you are willing to Entwine with someone."

"Yes," he said immediately as he nodded. "If your choice would have been to end our Soul Bond, I will do whatever I can to help lessen the connection it grants. The moment you find the person you desire to Entwine with, I'll pick someone, and we'll conduct the ceremony—without the transfer of magic, of course."

Without hesitation, he would Entwine himself to someone, give his life to them and be forever bonded—if I only said the words. I was overcome by how much he loved me.

"None of my reasons were a good enough excuse to keep you in the dark. I should have told you."

"Yes, you should have," I interjected, and Evander's head hung in shame. "But I understand why you didn't. I was a ghost of a person when I arrived in Tenebrae, and as much as I wish I would have known, I don't think I could have handled the truth."

"You could have," he said with unwavering resilience. "You are so much stronger than you give yourself credit for, love. You have overcome trials and trauma over and over again, and I should have never doubted you for a second."

I couldn't argue with him because he was right. Time and again, I'd been knocked on my ass only to return to my feet stronger and wiser than before. I had pushed through my fears and heartache when the world seemed too dark to go on, and because of that, I found a family and let people in again. I gave my heart away after swearing never to again, and I was better for it.

"Is that everything?" I asked, and Evander confirmed it was, as hope and fear diluted his grey eyes. I opened my mouth, ready to say my peace, but he cut in.

"Wait, no," he said as if remembering another critical detail he had left out. "I love you, Ainsley."

The air was stripped from my lungs as the weight of his words settled into my chest. He had said them before, but I denied his claim, too lost in my anger and fear to recognize the truth embedded within. But there was no denying it now.

"I need you to know that what I feel for you has nothing to do with our Soul Bond, and I would never manipulate you into loving me," he said, and I nodded because I knew that was the indisputable truth.

Magic couldn't create love, and now that I was aware of our bond, I could detect the difference between the connection it granted and the love I felt for him. They weren't the same in any way, and as I stared into Evander's eyes, I could see his relief that I believed him. He took a deep breath and cleared his throat before continuing.

"You are my everything—my reason for being. You are what holds me to this world. I don't want you to go and leave the home you found. I don't want you to leave *me*," he said, his voice heavy with emotion as he choked out the words. "I want what's best for you, and if that's being apart, I'll respect your decision. But please, let me be the one to go. I'll move to the palace so you won't have to see me. You deserve to stay in that house with our family. You deserve to be surrounded by the people who love you. Please don't let my decision prevent you from having that."

His gaze darted around momentarily as if checking his mind to see if there was anything else he had left out. Evander placed his hands on either side of my face as he leaned down and pressed his forehead to mine.

"I love you. That's everything," he announced, swiping his thumbs across my reddened cheeks.

I inhaled, drinking in his intoxicating scent and the feel of his hands on me. Now that it was my turn to speak, I wasn't sure where to begin. My mind was a jumbled mess of thoughts, and only his touch on my skin kept me focused. I basked in his warmth and love for a moment longer before I decided it was time to finally speak.

"First, I need you to know I don't blame you for our Soul Bond, Evander. I don't hold you responsible for me not having a choice in it. You are just as much a victim as I am," I said, pulling back so I could look him in the eyes.

His hands dropped from my face as he sucked in a shaky breath of relief, and my stomach twisted with nausea at the thought of him worrying I would think he was the one at fault. There was no scenario where that would ever be the case. I pressed my hand to his cheek as I watched his dark eyes glisten in the moonlight.

"You hurt me," I said slowly, feeling him tense beneath my touch. "Though I understand it, I don't like that you kept me in the dark. I hate that you weren't truthful when you knew how important honesty was to me. When I found out, it felt like I was back in that throne room learning about Dashiell's deceit and betrayal. At that moment, you fractured my heart."

A tear escaped and rolled down his cheek, but I quickly wiped it away as I kept my eyes on his. I half expected him to turn away as the pain and guilt I sensed devoured him, but he didn't. His gaze stayed pinned firmly on mine even though I knew how much he was hurting.

"But despite all that, it doesn't change how much I love you, Evander. It doesn't change that *you* are my home, and I ache for you every second we're apart," I breathed, and his lips wobbled as more tears fell. "And there is no way in hell you're Entwining yourself to another person because you are *mine*. You belong to me and no one else. Do you understand me?"

"Yes, my love," he said, and I cut off his endearment for me with a scorching kiss.

Evander's hand fisted in my hair as he kept my face firmly against him, and his tongue explored my mouth like he owned it—which he did. Desire rushed through me as I savored the taste of the man I was in love with. I jumped up, and Evander caught me as I wrapped my legs around his middle and my arms around his neck, dragging my fingers through his black hair.

I kissed him with everything I had, relinquishing the final hold on my heart and surrendering it to him completely. He was the other half of my soul. He was the man I loved. And tonight, he would be the one I Claimed.

"Evander," I said as I gasped down air before returning my lips to his.

"Love," he replied, just as out of breath as I was but refusing to stop our kiss.

"Take me to our bed."

62.

A moment later, my back slammed into a wall as I was enveloped in dissipating shadows and the familiar scent of our room. Evander kissed me brutally as he ripped open the front of my coat, not bothering to waste time with the buttons, and I smiled against his mouth at his feral need for me. I shrugged out of my coat while I worked to remove his. There were far too many layers between us, and the longer it took us to strip out of them the more my frustration built.

Evander ripped my nightshirt off next, pushing me harder against the wall as he pinned me in place with his hips, letting me feel every inch of how much he wanted me. His mouth found my neck, and I tilted my head back and moaned as I rocked my hips forward, trying to create that familiar friction. He cursed at my movements as his fingers pressed into my flesh hard enough to bruise, which only made me want more.

This act wasn't just about physicality—it meant so much more than that. It was us freely giving ourselves to each other. It was accepting what we were destined to be from the moment I first arrived in Tenebrae. It was me taking the only thing I wanted—*him*.

I fisted his shirt and yanked it hard over his head, needing to feel his bare skin against mine, but it still wasn't enough. My fingers dug through his soft hair as I gathered a handful and pulled it back so he was forced to remove his lips from my neck. I captured his mouth once more, desperate to taste him again as my tongue demanded entrance and my hips rocked forward. My nails pressed into his shoulder, marking his skin and eliciting a groan of determination from him.

Evander spun us away from the wall before carrying me across the room in heady, purposeful strides, never once breaking our passionate embrace. I kissed him harder as the anticipation of what we were about to do grew more potent by the second.

We stopped, and Evander leaned forward, carefully placing me on the bed before kneeling and removing my shoes. I watched him with hooded eyes, silently demanding for him to hurry up, but I knew he was taking his damn sweet time to rile me up as much as he could before finally letting me have what I wanted. It was no different than what he did every single day.

He stood again, seizing my mouth with his as he forced me to scoot backward on the bed. Evander reached for my hips, grabbing my pants and peeling them off my body until I was in nothing more than my underwear. I bit my lip as I watched his dark eyes rake over me hungrily, and his stare shot toward the movement. He leaned down, capturing my bottom lip and tugging it with his teeth like he was jealous I had done it first.

"Mine," he whispered against my mouth, releasing my lip and kissing me deeply. I wound my arms around his neck as his fingers trailed down my body until something sharp pressed against my flesh. I dropped my gaze to see Van had crafted a knife he was angling between my skin and bra.

"Don't you dare," I warned, but Evander smiled wickedly.

"Mine," he said again, angling the knife so it cut straight through the center of my bra, freeing my breasts.

He grasped one with his hand, and his mouth found the other, flicking over my nipple with his tongue. I moaned in pleasure, immediately forgetting that I was annoyed at him for destroying my clothes a moment prior. Van licked and sucked his way across my flesh, and I gave in to the delicious feeling of his mouth on me. Felix was right, we were fire on fire, and my Gods, it felt so good when we burned together.

Evander pulled the remaining scraps of fabric from around my chest before lowering his mouth to mine again. My thighs tightened, and my core pounded with need as I felt the wetness pooling between my legs. He kissed slowly down my body as if savoring the feel of my skin against his mouth. My fingers ran through his hair as he went, pulling roughly when he landed on sensitive parts of my flesh, and I could feel him smile against me every time it happened.

He dropped lower and lower until he was finally nestled between my thighs. He crafted a dagger again and dragged it slowly along the inside of my thigh, making me ache for him. I knew he'd never hurt me, but the blade against my delicate skin added a sense of danger that only made me want him more. We were always chaos and passion, and this embodied that.

I raised a brow in challenge, and he grinned before sliding the dagger beneath my underwear. I sucked in a breath at the feel of the cold metal against my hot flesh and bucked my hips forward. He twisted the blade and pulled it up, slicing through my underwear and leaving it to fall around me in shreds.

"You have to stop destroying my clothes, or else I'll have nothing to wear," I said as he removed the fabric scraps from my hips.

"Maybe that's the point," he answered, settling back down so his mouth hovered right above where I wanted.

I swallowed hard, my chest rising and falling quickly as I waited for Evander to give me what I needed. He leaned even closer, and I wet my lips as I felt the heat of his breath caress my oversensitive skin. I waited... And waited... And waited, but nothing ever came—including me. I propped myself on my elbows and stared at him with pinched brows.

Evander looked back with a sparkle in his grey eyes and a patient look on his face. He stroked my inner thigh idly, but his mouth stayed put, never lowering himself to me. I tilted my head as I tried to figure out what was going on, but then I saw a slight twitch of his lips, and realization dawned on me.

"You have got to be fucking kidding me," I said, and Evander's grin grew wide and arrogant as he gazed at me from his spot between my legs. I shook my head defiantly and he shrugged, planting a soft kiss on the spot where I'd much rather have had his tongue.

"That's fine, love," he said, still running his fingers along my leg.

It absolutely was not fine, and he was being a complete ass.

"You're being a complete ass."

"I know," he replied, flashing his dazzling teeth. "That doesn't change what needs to happen. I told you, I want to *hear* you say the words."

I huffed in irritation and then moaned as he placed another kiss on me. He was teasing me, and he knew it, but by the Gods I didn't care.

"Fine," I gritted. "I want you, Evander. I want you right now."

The very cocky and annoying love of my life smiled victoriously, and I lowered my head to the bed once more, not so patiently waiting for him to finally give me what I wanted.

"See? Was that so hard?" he asked, and I reached down, grabbed a fistful of his black hair, and shoved his face down as I bucked my hips forward. Evander laughed against me before pulling back again. "If you really want it this badly, maybe I should make you beg for it some more," he suggested wickedly, and I propped myself on my elbows again.

"Evander, I swear to the fucking Gods, if you don't use that tongue for something other than running your damn mouth, I'll find someone who will."

He immediately lowered his mouth to me, flicking out his tongue and swirling it around the spot I was so desperate for. I moaned loudly as one hand gripped his hair and the other fisted in the sheets to my side.

"Mine," he growled in warning, and I rolled my eyes.

"Then act like it," I shot back, and his tongue started up a relentless pace, bringing me closer and closer to the edge.

I gasped for breath, and Evander licked and sucked, working me so hard my body felt like it didn't belong to me anymore. It was his to use as he pleased, and my fucking Gods, was he doing it. I was teetering on the brim of ecstasy, but I didn't want to fall yet.

"Van," I said breathlessly, and he hummed against me, never letting up. "Van," I tried again.

"What?" he replied as his tongue dragged up my center, and he groaned in pleasure before doing it again.

"I need you."

"I'm busy."

"Evander," I demanded, pulling his hair hard and forcing him to remove his mouth from me. He glowered at me, and I met his gaze, clearly not happy I made him stop. "I need you right now."

He seemed to sense the desperation in my voice before he pulled back, albeit reluctantly. Evander stood at the edge of the bed and slowly pulled off his pants. My mouth went dry as I watched him stroke himself, and every inch of me clenched with need.

"Please," I rasped, and he dove forward, kissing up my body before reaching my lips.

He positioned himself at my entrance, and my hips bucked on instinctual need. Rather than give me what I wanted, he kept himself just out of reach, teasing me. I groaned in irritation as I tried to thrust forward again, though this time, he placed his palm on my hip to keep me pressed to the bed.

"You're so impatient," Evander said, smiling against my mouth.

"And you enjoy torturing me," I snapped, and his grin grew wider as he nodded unabashedly.

Before I could offer a retort, his free hand brushed loose strands of hair from my face, and something shifted in his gaze. I lost all thought of what my body desired as I focused on the tenderness in his eyes and how he stared at me with a love so deep I couldn't believe I hadn't noticed it before. There was no missing it now.

Evander leaned forward and pressed his forehead to mine. I ran my fingers over the hard muscles of his back, savoring the feel of his skin beneath my touch. We breathed each other in, not caring about anything but this small moment of quiet between us. Everything we had built over the past several months—the friendship, trust, *love*—it had all come to this.

Van pulled back slightly, a crooked smile on his lips. Slowly, he dragged the tip of my nose up with his like he had done so many times. A gesture that had become *ours*. I smiled up at the man I loved before kissing him with all I had to offer.

Van smiled as he kissed me back and finally sank himself deep inside me. I moaned into his mouth and clawed at his back as I rocked my hips forward, meeting him in time with each thrust. Unable to contain my magic, my shadows spilled from my skin as I burned with pleasure and longing. His own Gift caressed over me in gentle strokes, and I basked in the way it felt on my flesh. My heart was full and happy, and everything about us felt right. He had watched me pick up the broken pieces of myself and was there to help me put them back together when I was ready. And this was no different.

Being with him in this way was something I didn't think I'd ever be ready for, but now there was nothing I wanted more. Every movement of his body was patient and loving; it was passionate and tender. It was fierce and desperate. It was everything we were together, and I felt safe and secure in his arms.

"I love you," he whispered as he drove my body past the point of no return.

"I love you," I repeated weakly as I fell over the edge and screamed his name with my release, unable to last any longer. Van quickly followed, letting my name spill from his lips, and I devoured the sound on my tongue, loving how it tasted.

His head fell to my chest, and I stroked his hair as we worked to catch our breath. I closed my eyes, exhausted from the past few days and the emotional stress I'd been under. But it was all worth it because it led me to this moment. It led me to holding the man I loved in our bed as he pressed kisses delicately to my flesh and spoke of his love for me. It led me to choosing to trust and seize control of my life and what I wanted.

"I want to Claim you," I whispered sleepily, and Evander shifted off me and rolled to his side before pulling me to his chest. He smiled down at me as he brushed the hair from my face and nodded.

"Only if you let me Claim you too."

"I thought you already had with all that *'mine'* nonsense," I told him, and he chuckled under his breath.

"That was just me reminding you of who you belong to, but the Claiming will make it official."

"So you're telling me that I can forgo the Claiming, and other people can call me theirs since we aren't *official*," I teased with a hint of excitement in my voice.

"They could," Evander replied seriously. "As long as they draw breath, that is. And I can tell you the moment they try to stake a claim on you, their days are numbered."

I bit my lip as I smiled before pressing my mouth to his.

"You're the only one I want," I said, stifling a yawn.

"No," Evander stated, and I looked at him confused. "You are not going to sleep, love. I am nowhere near done with you."

"But—"

"No," he said again. "I gave you what you wanted, and now it's my turn. And it starts with me taking my time with you."

Evander slipped his tongue between my lips, and I opened for him, drowning in his intoxicating kiss as my body pulsed with need all over again. I arched my back as his hand traveled down my spine and cupped my ass to pull me closer.

"How do I do it?" I asked.

"By spreading your legs," he replied like the asshole he was. I hit his chest, and he snickered, knowing full well I wasn't asking about the mechanics of sex as I was pretty sure we had already covered that. "You have to let your magic out so it can come to me."

"But we both know I can't control it when it does," I argued, and Evander smiled knowingly, but I didn't understand why.

"Your magic has been trying to Claim me for weeks, love," he said, and I furrowed my brows. "After that night in Agnitio, I wondered why our magic kept trying to go to one another. I figured it was our Soul Bond, but when I mentioned it to Sirona, she explained it was the Claiming trying to take place. Our magic chose each other, so there was nothing we could do to change its mind, but she taught me how to stop it from taking place by reinforcing my internal shield."

"So that's why my magic kept trying to get to you? It was trying to Claim you?" I asked to ensure I understood correctly, and Evander nodded.

"Apparently, your magic wanted me as badly as you did," he said smugly, and I shoved him.

"Your magic wanted me too," I pointed out.

"Yes, but I've never kept it a secret that I wanted you. You're the one that's spent months denying it to anyone that would listen."

"I changed my mind. I don't want to Claim you."

"Too bad," Van said, rolling to his back and pulling me over him. His hands traveled down to my waist, squeezing tight and making me lose all sense of reality. "Let your magic out, and I'll accept it before doing the same to you."

I nodded, kissing him again as I leaned down, letting my hair curtain around us as I called to my magic. His tongue skated over mine, and I forgot what I was supposed to be doing as I shifted my hips forward against him. Evander groaned as his fingers dug into my side, but he shook his head, reminding me we had another task at hand.

I called to my magic again, this time not letting myself get distracted by the gorgeous man beneath me. My skin prickled, and I placed my hands on his chest as I released my magic into the world. It surged out of me like a force of nature and went straight for Evander, but instead of hitting a wall like usual, it passed through him. I gasped and moaned at the pleasure I felt as my magic wrapped itself around him, mixing with his darkness and Claiming it for my own.

Evander's head hit the pillow, and a sound of pleasure left his lips as my power dominated his, pushing it down and making it bend to its will. It curved around a small piece of his magic and then severed it from the rest before bringing it to me and planting it near my heart.

He took a deep breath, and before I could ask what to do next, his magic slammed into me, Claiming me just as mine had done to him. I threw my head back as I reached down, needing to feel him inside me in every possible way. Van had once told me that the Claiming could be sealed with an act as simple as a kiss, but I wanted more than that.

My fingers grazed over him to find that he was hard and ready. He positioned me higher, knowing exactly what I wanted without asking. I lowered myself down on him slowly, letting him fill me as thoroughly as his magic had.

His darkness began to retreat, and I could sense a little part of mine missing. It wasn't stolen but exchanged, and sitting where it used to be was now a tiny piece of Evander's magic. I wrapped myself around it, loving how it felt to own a part of him and knowing I belonged to him too.

"Evander," I breathed, rocking my hips against him, wanting to seal this Claiming as soon as possible. I needed to know he was officially mine and that he'd never belong to anyone else.

"Fuck, love," he groaned, and I took that as my cue to go faster, riding him hard until sweat was dripping down my back, and he was yelling my name as he began to come undone.

Before I could push him as far as I wanted, Evander pulled me off of him and flipped me over so my chest was firmly pressed into the bed. In the blink of an eye, his fingers dug into my hips as he slammed himself into me from behind with relentless force. I cried out, and my hands gripped the sheets beneath me as I tightened around him, needing even more than what he was giving. His magic surged into me again, trying to beat mine into submission as he Claimed me and took exactly what he wanted from my body.

His hand fisted into my hair, pulling my head back as he leaned forward and dragged his tongue along my spine. I moaned loudly with each thrust he gave and the feel of his magic wrapping around mine as he brought me closer and closer to climax. But this was just as much about me Claiming *him*, and I wasn't going to lay there and be submissive—even though it felt really fucking good to have him take control.

I shifted my hips forward as I tried to move out of his hold, but Evander growled, tightening his grip on my body and pushing himself in faster and harder. He wasn't willing to relinquish his control as he Claimed me. If I wanted dominance, I would have to fight him for it.

As he dragged himself out to the tip, I took that as my opportunity to get away. I spun, kicking my foot out hard and landing a hit square in his chest as I freed myself from his hold. Evander stumbled back but quickly recovered as he dove on me, capturing my wrists and pinning them above my head. His teeth grazed over my nipple roughly and he nipped at my sensitive skin as punishment for that little stunt.

'I moaned, bucking my hips forward on instinct. I continued to fight my way free as the desire to have him inside me again built. His hold on my hands tightened hard enough to bruise as he pushed his weight onto me, keeping me from going anywhere.

Even more of his magic poured into me, sedating mine and making it bend to his will as he took complete control of my body and my magic. A groan escaped him as he Claimed even more of me, and my back arched as I began to come undone at the feel of that alone. But I wasn't ready. I wanted to be the one to seal our Claiming by owning *him*.

I forced my magic to fight his, twisting it around his darkness as it struggled to take back power over the situation. As my magic handled his, I wrapped my legs around his middle and elicited a groan of desire from his lips. I took his distraction to squeeze my thighs tight as I rocked them to the side and flipped us over so I was now straddling him. I rotated my wrists, freeing them from his hold and grabbing his in return to pin them above his head.

Evander grinned as he took in what had just happened. Before he could even consider trying to regain control, I shoved more of my magic into him. My power dominated his until it was entirely at my mercy, and we both moaned in pleasure at the intense feelings provided by the Claiming. I released my grasp on his hands, knowing my magic was rendering him useless.

My stare held Evander's as I lifted my hips and sank back down onto him hard and demanding. He was mine, and I was going to take what I wanted. I threw my head back and shifted forward as Van's hands found my waist, gripping hard as I picked up the pace. My body clenched around him and he lifted his hips, driving deeper into me and making me swear loudly as I climbed higher toward my release.

Our magic collided in passion and longing as we Claimed one another with the brutal, burning desire we had always had. He was my everything—my light and my dark, my joy and my fury. And every Gods damn thing in between. He was my beginning and end, my salvation and destruction. He was *mine.*

Evander's eyes darkened as he watched me, and I could see the restraint he was struggling to hold on to as I drove him right where I wanted. His grip constricted, and my body began to tremble as we both fought to hold on and not be the first to fall. I slowed my movements, and Evander's eyes narrowed as I brought him back down before picking up my pace again, pushing him to the edge just to pull him away from it.

"That isn't very nice," he commented as I rolled my hips forward, and a tingle went down my spine at the friction I felt.

"I think it's *very* nice," I told him, leaning down to take his bottom lip between my teeth and tugging gently as I continued to move on him. "You're mine now, so I can do as I please with you."

"Is that right?" He thrust his hips higher, hitting a spot so deep I nearly unraveled with that one movement.

"Yes," I whispered breathlessly.

Evander curled his hand around the back of my head, weaving his fingers through my hair and drawing down my forehead to press to his as our breath mingled.

"If I belong to you, then fuck me like it. Stop holding back and take what's yours."

His command broke the last restraint I had placed on myself, and I rode him harder and faster than before. He kept his hold on my head firm, and his other hand guided my movements as I did as he instructed—sealing our Claiming and making him mine.

I moaned as I rocked my hips, the pressure in my core building higher and higher. My whole body was shaking, and I knew I wouldn't last much longer, but I kept moving.

"Take what's yours, love," Evander commanded, moving his hand from my waist to press my clit as I rode him. I tilted my head back and screamed as that one touch sent me hurdling over the edge so hard my head swam with dizziness and I saw stars. "Good girl," he whispered before thrusting deep twice and climaxing with more praise for me on his lips.

I collapsed on top of him, unable to move or think after the events of our Claiming. As I closed my eyes and tried to catch my breath, a hand wrapped around me, and I was vaguely aware of being picked up and carried away from the bed.

"What are you doing?" I mumbled, completely blissed out and drunk on my love for him.

"Taking care of you," he replied, lowering me into the hot bath before climbing behind me.

Evander adjusted us so my back was pressed to his chest, and I let my head fall to his shoulder as I enjoyed the comforting feel of him against me. A warm, soapy cloth spread over my skin as he cleaned the sweat from my body, planting soft kisses across my flesh as he worked, and I couldn't help but smile at his display of love.

"You don't have to do this," I said, extending my hand to grab the cloth, but he held it just out of reach.

"I want to," he replied, wringing the cloth out on my neck so warm suds ran down my back. He bent forward and pressed a kiss to my tattoo. "You are my Soul Bonded, the love of my life, and my Claimed. It's not just a desire to take care of you; it's a *need*."

"Mmmm," I mumbled, too lost in the feel of his soft lips.

"Yes, mmmm. So shut up and just let me take care of you."

I smiled to myself as I closed my eyes again, content to let him do what he wanted. I was reminded of the last time we were in a tub like this. He was helping me to come down from my panic attack and sharing a piece of his soul he hadn't with anyone before. I felt a question surface on my lips, and before I could fight to shove it back down, Evander spoke.

"Just say it, love. I can always tell when you're fighting yourself."

"Does what I'm capable of ever scare you? The brutality of my Gifts and the way I've wielded them?" I asked hesitantly. I was sure I knew the answer, but I needed to hear him say the words.

He released his shadows, and mine came forth, slipping from my fingers and twisting around the magic of the man I had Claimed. I sighed contently as I watched our shadows play gingerly with each other, and I couldn't help but feel peace and belonging at that moment.

"No," he answered. "You're my favorite shade of darkness, love."

I smiled, knowing I felt precisely the same way. Nothing Evander could say or do would ever frighten me. The power of his Gift and the way he was willing to wield it for those he loved was beautiful.

"Do you think they expected this to happen with us?" I asked, knowing Evander would understand who I meant. He was quiet for a moment before finally answering.

"I think our mothers hoped it would, but I don't believe anyone would have forced what we are now on us."

Van didn't have long with either of our parents, but he still spent more time with them than I did, so I figured he was the better judge of character. I grabbed one of his hands and brought it to my lips, kissing the tips of his fingers lightly as I snuggled into him.

"I wish they were here to see us now," I said, and I could sense the same yearning and desire coming from him. "I think they would have been proud of the man you've become."

He squeezed me tighter, burying his face in the crook of my neck as he held me close. He had gone through so many trials and tribulations after losing his family at the young age of five. He had persevered through every difficulty life had thrown at him and now ruled over a prosperous kingdom filled with people who loved him. I needed him to know he was someone worth being proud of.

"Thank you, love," he whispered, and I nodded. "For the record, I think your parents would have been proud of the woman you are today."

"I think so too," I admitted, meaning every word.

My entire life had been difficult, and through it all, I managed to rise above and pull myself out of the darkest caves I was in. I learned to come into my own and trust myself—but not only that, I learned to love and embrace who I truly was.

"Will you tell me a memory you have of your parents?" I asked as Evander began to work the shampoo into my hair. It wasn't necessary, but there was something about him tending to me in this way that was more intimate than sex, and I didn't want him to stop.

"I can remember the last time I saw them clear as day," he said, and I swallowed hard.

"If it's a sad memory or hard to talk about, you don't—"

"It's not sad," he replied, massaging my hair until it was covered in soap suds. "It's one of the happier memories I can recall."

Evander tilted my head back as he poured water over my scalp, removing all traces of the shampoo that had previously been there. I inhaled, noting that the scent was his and not my usual choice. I arched a brow and twisted around to look at him skeptically as I held a piece of hair between my fingers. He smiled wide before mouthing the word *mine* and spinning me around to face him. I crawled into his lap, wrapping my legs around his middle as I stared into his charcoal eyes.

"We were sitting around the dinner table, and I was throwing a tantrum," he started smiling.

"That doesn't sound like you," I said, and Evander rolled his eyes before tapping a finger to my nose playfully, even though he knew I hated it.

"Anyway," he replied, giving me a look that said, *interrupt me again with your smartass remarks, and you will regret it.*

I bit my lip, hoping his punishment would involve a lot less talking. By how his gaze heated as he glanced at my mouth, I knew that would absolutely be the case. Evander cleared his throat to regain control of himself, and I smiled, loving the effect I had on him. He squeezed me tighter and arched a brow.

"Do you want to hear the story or not?" he asked. I nodded and mimed locking my lips and throwing away the key, though we both knew my silence wouldn't last long, seeing as it never did. "I sat there pouting the entire time as my mother and father exchanged amused glances at one another. After giving them the silent treatment throughout the whole meal, my father finally asked what was bothering me, and I told him it had to do with you. They had gotten word about where you were possibly taken and were heading out the next day to find you. I was furious my father didn't mention the plans to me, and instead, I found out by overhearing the guards talking about the trip. When he asked why I was so upset, I told him you were mine. You were my Soul Bonded, and I should be the one to have brought you home."

A grin split my face from ear to ear as I pictured a little Evander sitting at the dining table, making demands and wanting to rescue me despite his age and lack of experience. Even then, he was trying to take care of me.

"Five-year-old Evander sounds adorable," I commented.

"And how about twenty-five-year-old Evander?"

"He's alright, I guess," I told him as I pressed my lips to his.

"Noted," he said against my mouth before continuing his story. "My father said he understood my desire to be the one to bring you home, but explained he made a death vow to your father and wanted to see it through. As a child, I didn't grasp what that meant, but I remember sensing his dire need to bring you back, so I let it go. I made him promise that I would be the first person to see you when he got home, and he agreed, squeezing me tight before he and my mother tucked me into bed. That was the last time I ever saw them. When I woke the next morning, they were gone but left a note that said: '*Van, we left before dawn to get LL. We'll be back as soon as we can. We love you.*' I remember reading that note forward and backward for years after I lost them. It was all that I had left."

I wanted to comfort him, but I had no idea how to. I had never known the love of my parents, so I didn't know what it was like to lose them. Evander did, and it was a pain I hated that he had to feel, though at least he had some happy memories to hold on to. I kissed him gently, hoping to take some of the hurt that way, though I wasn't sure it did much.

"What's LL?"

Evander smiled and shook his head.

"Well," he began looking a bit nervous at whatever this story entailed. "Apparently, three-year-old Evander was *very* curious about how babies were made."

I laughed as I tried to visualize my king as a curious toddler.

"So when your mother was pregnant with you, I decided to ask. Oli tells me they laughed about it for an hour before trying to figure out how they would explain it to me. Finally, your mother told me the way you were made was with love. It was a simple and honest answer that I accepted."

My heart filled to the brim to know my parents loved one another and that I was a product of that. It wasn't a political arrangement for power; it was two people falling desperately in love and wanting to have a family of their own. It was a beautiful piece of information I would hold on to forever.

"As you know, in Tenebrae, it's a tradition not to announce the child's name until the ceremony following their birth. Because of that, I had no idea what to call you while you were still in your mother, so... I called you Love. Little Love, to be exact, but as we got older, I dropped the Little," he explained. "You've always been Love to me."

I stopped breathing as the air was sucked from my lungs. Evander watched me intently as I struggled to process the information he had just shared. *Love.* I thought it was just a pet name he used to get under my skin, but it wasn't. It held a meaning far more significant than anything I could have known. Tears welled in my eyes before spilling over as Evander wiped them away. I pulled him closer, slamming his lips to mine in a passionate kiss as I let my mind journey back to every instance he used the pet name.

"I love you," I said against his mouth as the pressure of his love and patience crashed into me. I was his love. I had *always* been his love.

63.

"You need to eat something," Evander whispered, kissing me awake. I opened an eye to see it was still dark, the sun still hidden beneath the horizon. My Gods, I wasn't complaining, but this had been the longest night of my life. After he carried me back to bed, we were intimate several more times, and I learned Van knew how to do things with his tongue that no one should be able to do. It gave him far too much power and only fed into his already too-large ego.

"I'll eat in the morning," I whined, shutting my eye again and burying my face in the pillow.

"You missed the morning, my love," he said, and I perked up at that. I glanced toward the window to see the moon still high and the sky dark. Dawn was still several hours off, though I wasn't sure how.

"Liar," I accused. Evander smiled before ripping the blankets from my body so I yelped from the cold.

"You slept through the day," he said, and I looked at him skeptically. There was no way that was possible.

I opened my mouth to argue, but he held a finger to his lips before pointing to his ear. I listened intently as he instructed, only to hear the sound of our family's gentle laughter from the floor below. Holy Gods, he was right. Somehow I had slept through an entire day.

"How?" I demanded, looking toward the window as if the sun would pop up at any moment.

"For one, we participated in several activities that exerted a lot of energy," he said, and a blush rose to my cheeks as I thought about each of them. "And for two, you were emotionally exhausted, and so was I. I slept most of the day with you and only left our bed to ensure you had food when you woke up."

I twisted to see an entire buffet of every food I could think of sitting on several long tables throughout the room. It seemed Evander had gone above and beyond in his efforts to care for me.

"A spread fit for a queen," I joked.

"Well, you are one, so it works."

"I am not," I said, rolling my eyes and padding over to the food.

I picked a strawberry from a plate and plopped it into my mouth as his arms wrapped around me from behind.

"Maybe not technically," he said, moving the shirt I had slipped on before falling asleep away from my neck as he kissed me tenderly against the sensitive skin there. "But you are *my* queen, and you always have been. Even our family will treat you as such whether you take the vows or not."

I nodded, picking at the food to evade what Evander was saying. The last time I was supposed to marry someone, it turned out he was just using me to gain my Gifts, and while I didn't think Evander would ever do something like that, it still brought up terrible memories. Sensing my distress, he moved around me and made me face him, cupping my cheeks between his hands.

"Listen," he said, looking deep into my eyes. "I love you, Ainsley. I want to marry you and for you to be at my side as queen. It's okay if you're not ready for that yet, but you need to understand my intentions. You need to know where I stand. I want everything with you."

I knew he loved me, but agreeing to marry him meant far more than just making him mine. Evander wasn't just a random man; he was a king.

"Do you think I'm ready?" I asked and he smiled as he nodded softly, knowing exactly what I was referring to.

"I think you will be a wonderful queen when you decide you're ready for the role." I reached up on my toes and kissed him deeply, my tongue demanding entrance that he willingly gave.

"Eat," he demanded, but I shook my head.

"I'm not hungry for food."

"As your Claimed, it's my job to take care of you," he countered, though he didn't stop himself from taking control of my mouth.

"So then take care of me, Evander," I baited, walking back toward the bed.

He spun me around, and his mouth found my neck as he ran his lips across it. His hand traveled greedily down my body and slipped beneath my shirt. I gasped as soon as his fingers dragged over me, and he groaned as he found the wetness there waiting for him. He swept his fingers back and forth slowly, and I whimpered as he circled my clit, teasing me just enough to drive me insane. Given our relationship, that fact didn't surprise me in the least.

"Please," I begged, arching again to direct his hand where I wanted. He moved his fingers away, and I was left feeling empty and wanting.

"Get on the bed," he commanded, and I did, sliding back to the pillows as I watched him climb over me.

He peeled the shirt from my head before lowering his mouth to my body and kissing his way down. His tongue flicked over me, making me cry out, but he refused to give me more, instead pulling back again. I huffed in irritation as I bucked my hips in need, and Evander chuckled at my attempts.

"I'll give you want you want, love, but I'm enjoying seeing you struggle too much right now," he whispered. He flicked his tongue lightly again before withdrawing as I writhed beneath him.

I let out a frustrated groan and extended my hand down to take my own pleasure. I surely didn't need him to do it if he wasn't going to, but before I could reach myself, shadows wrapped around my wrist. They pulled my arm up above my head as the tendrils solidified into a satin ribbon and tied themselves to the headboard.

"I don't think so, love. It's my turn now to have you as I want," he said as he kissed my inner thigh.

My breathing came in tortured gasps as he slipped a finger inside me—just barely. It wasn't nearly enough. So this was what I got for Claiming him? Note to self: pick a more willing partner in the future.

"How about we play a game?" Evander asked seductively. If this game prolonged his edging of me, there was no way I was agreeing to it.

"How about you just make me come? Or are you too worried that you won't be able to?" I asked, grinding my hips against him, but the bastard pulled his fingers away like he knew exactly what I was trying to do.

"Nice try, love," Evander said as he laughed lightly. "But given that I've already done so several times, I'm confident in my abilities." He pushed his finger back inside me, and I threw my head back as my body tingled with the promise of pleasure.

"Fine," I ground out. "Tell me your stupid game."

My compliance was rewarded with a second finger slipping inside me, followed by the stroke of his tongue. I fisted his hair and rocked my hips against him just as he withdrew once again, edging me like the asshole he was.

"I'll give you exactly what you want," he whispered as he kissed my inner thigh, his tongue sweeping over my skin and leaving a trail of fire in its wake. "But you can't make a sound."

"You're assuming I'll enjoy this enough to do so," I shot back bitterly and moved my free hand down in an attempt to touch myself, but once again, Evander was ready with his fucking shadow pleasure blockers.

He used his magic to move my other arm above my head. With both arms raised, I felt even more vulnerable and exposed than I had just a moment earlier. Like I was a toy for him to play with as he chose fit. Maybe I was. And maybe I really liked the idea of that.

Fuck.

"You could be enjoying yourself as much as I am if you stopped being so stubborn," he teased as he looked into my eyes while his fingers circled my clit once again. "What do you say, love? Want to play?"

My eyes flicked to his full lips as I was instantly transported to the moment they were between my teeth as he fucked me senseless with his hand during one of our many *activities* last night. I nodded before I realized I was doing it.

"Good," he said as he plunged two fingers deep inside me, and I bit my lip hard as I moaned my relief at the feel of him. "Remember; not a sound," he reminded me as his thumb pressed against my clit, drawing even more pleasure from me.

I twisted in an attempt to bury my face against the pillow to stifle the sounds crawling their way free from my lips. Evander rolled his tongue against me, forcing my legs to spread wider as he worked me and created a sense of ecstasy I was sure to shatter from. I whimpered as I climbed higher and higher towards my climax, now heightened from his incessant edging. There was no way I would be able to stay quiet, and soon the whole house would hear me screaming this God damned man's name as I came undone for him. Breakfast was going to be awkward as fuck tomorrow.

Evander withdrew his mouth, and I grunted in frustration. Every time I got closer to my release, he took it away. I stared daggers at him but the cocky smile he wore on his lips told me he was enjoying himself far too much to care.

"I told you to be quiet. If you can't do that, then I can't do this," he declared before dragging his tongue up my center again. My head fell back to the pillow as I moaned as quietly as I could.

"I hate this game," I said breathlessly and I didn't have to look to know he was smiling like a Gods damn asshole. He lowered himself to me once more and tortured me relentlessly with his tongue. This time, I turned my face and pressed my mouth against my shoulder, occasionally biting down on my flesh to prevent the screams of pleasure from ripping from my body. But it was all too much. My body shook as Van worked me so hard I was begging for him to give me what I wanted. I didn't give a fuck who heard.

"Please," I whimpered.

At my plea, Evander flicked his wrist, and a shadow slithered across my mouth and turned into a binding as the sounds became too intense to contain.

"Take what you want, love. Don't hold back," he whispered against me, his voice strained like he was getting off on watching me unravel.

It was all I needed to hear. I rocked my hips faster as his expert fingers and tongue worked me so hard I screamed into the binding a moment later as my body shook with pleasure. But Evander wasn't done. He kept pumping me through my orgasm until I was primed on the edge of another. My hands reached down as I grabbed his shoulders, needing to feel his skin beneath my touch. My nails dug into him hard enough to draw blood as I came again, even harder than the first time.

He slowed his movements until the last of my climax washed over me. The binding was still covering my mouth as my wide eyes found his. They were dark and hungry, making me ache for even more of him. His breathing was just as heavy as mine, his face just as flushed as he withdrew his fingers from me. The sudden absence of them felt wrong. He flicked his wrist, and the binding disappeared from my mouth.

"I'm proud of you," he said after a moment, and I gave him a confused look as he climbed up the bed to lay next to me.

"For having an orgasm?" I asked incredulously. "I feel like I should be saying that to you, as I'm sure the past twenty-four hours is the first time you've managed to ever give one." Evander rolled his eyes at my smart mouth before shaking his head.

"Because you broke out of my hold. My magic couldn't contain you," he explained. I knew I was able to reach down to grab him, but I thought his shadows had released me from the tie. I wasn't aware that I had managed to break free on my own, and I bit my lip to stifle my prideful smile. "Keep doing that, and we're never leaving this bed," he replied, removing my lip from between my teeth.

That didn't sound like the worst thing, so I bit my lip again and watched as Evander climbed on top of me and enveloped us both in darkness.

My back pressed into the wood as I stood there in the open doorframe while Evander kissed me like I was the air he needed to breathe. We were never leaving this damn room. This was our third attempt and the farthest we'd gotten—making it all the way to the door and opening it up.

My ears faintly picked up on the creaking of wood from across the hall, indicating we weren't alone, but with Evander's tongue sweeping over mine and his body holding me firmly in place, I couldn't find a part of me that cared.

"Go get dressed," I said breathlessly as my hands roamed over his bare chest and along each rippling muscle. Wait, why the hell was I telling him to put clothes on?

"It would be easier to do if someone wasn't stealing my shirts all the time," he replied, giving a pointed look to the shirt I was wearing. I flashed a taunting smile.

"Mine," I mocked, and Evander rolled his eyes playfully before giving me a swift kiss and retreating into the room.

I released a longing sigh as I watched him stride away, desperate for him to come back already. The wood creaked again, and I twisted my head to find Felix standing there, leaning against the doorframe opposite mine with his arms crossed over his chest and a wide grin on his face.

I fought my smile as I widened my eyes as if to say, *'what.'* Felix shrugged with one shoulder before pushing off from the doorframe. I watched curiously as he moved his hands straight in front of him as if holding the sides of a tiny box. All at once his hands slowly started to part, making it seem as if the invisible box was growing in size. My gaze moved to his to see a cocky smirk on his lips and curiosity in his eyes.

Finally, I understood what he was asking and shook my head as a breathy laugh escaped me. Felix didn't let up though, making the invisible box as large as possible before starting again. I rolled my eyes but gave in, deciding to play his little game.

Excitement bubbled over as he realized I was going to answer the question. He brought his hands as close as he could together before moving them apart even slower than before. He stopped and raised a questioning brow, but I shook my head, indicating for him to keep going. Felix's hands continued their journey, slowly pulling away from each other until he stopped again. I shook my head once more, and he perked up with wide eyes and a look of joy. I shrugged like it was no big deal and jerked my chin for him to continue his game. He moved his hands apart, and when he stopped, I finally nodded.

Felix smiled wide before mimicking a slow clap. I rolled my eyes at my best friend when movement over his shoulder snagged my attention. I stood on tiptoes to look past him and found Olivier's bare back rising and falling gently as he slept … next to a long thin stick. What the fuck did he use that thing for? My mouth dropped in mock surprise, and my eyes traveled back to my friend's face, where he was grinning from ear to ear with pure joy.

I knew it was killing him not to share the details of their newfound relationship, and I appreciated that his priority was making sure I was okay first. But this was the first time Felix had ever been truly happy, and he was owed the chance to boast about it as much as he wanted. I need to plan a Delicious Duo day where he could do just that.

I held my hands up, reciprocating his movement as if holding a tiny box before moving them farther apart. Felix smirked and shook his head.

"Trust me, buttercup, you don't have the arm span for this game," he teased. There was no way anyone could be *that* big. Arms wrapped around my middle and lips pressed to the side of my neck as I was enveloped in the scent of cedar and fresh snow.

I twisted to look up at Evander, who was trying to peer past Felix's shoulder, though with his height, it came easier for him than it did for me. His features flashed with interest, and he nodded to himself as if what he saw didn't surprise him. I wondered if they talked about Felix and me the same way we did them.

Van stepped from around me, interlacing our fingers and pulling me down the hall before I could object. I waved to Felix as I mouthed, *'lunch?'* and he nodded enthusiastically. I was desperate to know how everything had transpired between him and Oli, but I guessed I could wait a few more hours.

We found Marce, Lia, and Calidore in the library, and the three of them came bounding for us, wrapping us in their arms and offering their congratulations. I didn't miss the few times the term *'Majesties'* was thrown about, and each time, Evander looked at me with a smug, I-told-you-so expression.

We spent an hour laughing with our friends and enjoying being in each other's arms as we listened to the story of their day-long journey and all the small fights they had along the way. Our wolves were sleeping happily in the corner of the room, with Onyx lying firmly on top of Nova like usual, but there was something different about it this time. Something possessive about him that suggested he wasn't ever letting her part from him again.

Marce's head jerked to the desk, and she got up from her spot on the couch and strode for it. I should have known nothing pleasant would last because it never did with us. There was always something in the way of us being truly at peace and happy. Her face filled with frustration as she scribbled a message back and watched it disappear.

"More problems?" I asked, and she nodded, though there was a look of hopefulness in her features.

"Another attack along our western border," she explained as she straightened her posture. "But there's a lead this time."

Evander and I sat up, prepared and ready to hear whatever news she brought. We'd never gotten a lead through battle. It had always been fighting to survive and hoping we could come across something that could help us from books or word of mouth.

"An Ignisian was spotted during the attack," Marce said, and I looked to Van knowingly. Fire wielders hailed from Caelum, not Pravus, and if he was fighting alongside our enemy, it indicated that King Perceval was involved. "That's not all," she said, and the king and I drifted our attention back to Marce. "He also vanished into thin air."

I breathed a sigh of relief, knowing we were on the right track with the stones. Perceval had them, and his soldiers were using them to get in and out of places undetected. There was no longer any need to hunt Disparya for them because we knew at least one place that housed the stones.

"If he has one, he probably has all three," I said, and Evander nodded. "We need to get them."

"I agree, but we need to be smart about it," he replied.

For another hour, we discussed different tactics to retrieve a stone. Cal wanted to try and capture enemy soldiers and steal it from them, but we never knew when or where they were going to strike, and it was too risky to go out hunting them. We also weren't sure if every soldier had a stone or if it was only a select amount. Perhaps the stone's magic encompassed all who were around it. This was the first and only time someone from Caelum had been spotted among the fighting, and I doubted we'd be lucky enough for it to happen again.

When our family drifted to bed, Evander and I sat quietly in the library, curling up in each other's arms as we watched our wolves sleeping contently. An idea had been eating at my mind since the moment Marce shared the news, and I knew that was part of why we were still here in this room. He was giving me time to sort through my thoughts before questioning me on them.

"Send me to Caelum," I said, and Evander's hold tightened.

"As I said before, we need to be smart about it," he answered. "And that is a very dumb thing to suggest."

"It isn't," I countered. "It makes the most sense."

I twisted in his arms to face him, needing to look at him during this conversation so he could tell how serious I was. Me going to Caelum was our best bet, and I had been working on a plan in my mind as soon as my former kingdom was mentioned.

"The answer is no," he said.

"If Oli or Marce volunteered to go, would you let them?"

"That's different."

"No, it isn't," I argued. "I may not be at the same experience level as them, but I know Caelum better than any of you. I have what Perceval wants, and that makes me the perfect bait."

"I'm not sending the woman I love to the piece of shit that killed her parents, stole her from her home, and tried to drain her of her magic. I'm not sending my Soul Bonded—my *Claimed*—to the doorstep of someone that wishes her harm," he snarled.

"Then don't," I replied, and Evander's brows pinched, not expecting me to give in so quickly. "Send the Heir to Tenebrae."

He shook his head, furious at me for giving him hope just to take it away, but I wasn't going to back down on this. I knew my going was our best chance and the right call to make. It's not that I wanted to be away from him and in the presence of someone we hated, but it's what needed to be done.

"They're the same person," he snarled.

"No, they're not," I said just as forcefully. "You can't treat me solely as the person you love, Evander, and you know it. I was the heir before I ever called you mine. I swore to protect our kingdom and people before I ever gave my heart to you." He ran a frustrated hand through his black hair and looked around the room frantically like he could find a solution that didn't involve sending me to our enemy. "I know you hate this, but right now, it's our only choice. We don't know if there is only one of each stone or if there are many. All we know is that Caelum is in possession of at least one of the three we need."

A muscle in his jaw ticked as he fought against doing what he wanted and what he knew was right. No part of me wanted to leave him, but something had to be done, and he knew it.

"You're the king, Evander," I said slowly, gripping his chin and directing his stare back to me. "You can order me to stay if that's what you think is best, and I'll listen. But promise me you'll decide based on what's best for our people and not your heart."

Evander closed his eyes as the battle raged on inside. I hated what this choice was doing to him, but that's what came with the territory. Being rulers wasn't easy, and we'd have to make hard calls regarding our people—and we were no exception. As much as we wanted to keep those we loved safe, there would be times when putting them or ourselves in danger would be the choice that saved the most.

"Give me three weeks to find another way," he requested as his eyes fluttered open. "Three weeks, and if we can't come up with a different solution, we'll do it your way."

I released a deep breath as I nodded, granting his deadline and accepting my order. We had three weeks to figure this out, or I was heading back into the one place I swore I'd never step foot in again.

64.

The mattress beneath me dipped and arms enclosed around me, pulling me into a muscled chest. I sighed sleepily as Evander's lips placed delicate kisses along the sensitive skin on my neck, reminding me who I belonged to.

"Where have you been?" I asked. I let my eyes flutter open as I ran my fingers through his slightly damp hair, undoubtedly from the shower he had taken before climbing into bed.

Ever since Van and I made the deal about me returning to Caelum, he had been working tirelessly to prevent it from happening. Now that we only had one week left until his deadline, he had been relentlessly running himself into the ground. I barely saw him during the day while he journeyed around Disparya in hopes of discovering information that could solve our problem, and I spent most nights alone in our bed before he stumbled through the door at late hours.

His eyes met mine for the briefest of seconds, and they were dark and haunted, swirling with unspoken demons. Before I could question him, he pressed his mouth to mine, kissing me greedily and stealing the words from my lips. I wrapped my arms around his neck and pulled him on top of me, tasting his desire through each stroke of his tongue. I desperately wanted to get lost in him, but my magic screamed that something was wrong. He was withdrawn and desperate, displaying a need so great it was as if he were saying goodbye rather than just enjoying a night with me.

"Van, what's wrong?" I asked against his mouth, but he shook his head as he held my face between his hands and kissed me again. "Evander," I tried again, pushing on his chest to get him to pull back.

He reluctantly relinquished my lips and rolled off me as his gaze locked on the ceiling above. I shifted to my side as I reached a hand to cup his cheek and force his eyes to me. He did as directed, and the pain etched within his features had my heart splintering and my body moving over him. His hands wrapped around my back, and I could feel his heart beating wildly against my chest as I lowered my forehead to his and let my Empathi Gift soak into him. I was grateful that he now trusted me enough to allow me to freely use my Gift on him when I felt it was needed.

I wrapped my magic around him, exploring each aching inch of his heart as he held me against him. There were traces of pain, longing, frustration, and fear—so much fear. I pressed my lips to his in a gentle kiss, letting him know I was there and he wasn't alone. But I couldn't do much more than that unless he opened up and let me know what was tormenting him.

"Talk to me," I begged, my voice catching in my throat.

Evander's fingers caressed my skin as he brushed back the hair from my face, and his eyes bore straight into my soul—*our* soul. The serious look on his face had me worrying even more than I already was.

"Give me two more weeks," he finally said, his brows furrowing with the request. "Please, love."

I stared at him for a moment, noting the heaviness in his voice. It was tearing him apart to have to ask, and I hated seeing him so dejected, but I couldn't give him what he wanted. We didn't have the luxury of time. The longer we waited, the more chance Oberon had to strike at our people, our land, and our home. I shook my head slowly, and Evander shut his eyes as he swallowed thickly and accepted his defeat.

"I'm sorry," I told him, genuinely meaning the words. I didn't want to part from him any more than he wanted to from me. "We can't continue to wait and risk more of our people's lives.

"I know," he whispered, opening his eyes again.

I knew he didn't want me to go, but his reaction told me more was happening in his mind than I understood. My decision was hurting him, and that pain was evident from the look on his face and how his fingers dug into my back to keep me from retreating.

"What's going on? You aren't acting like yourself," I said.

Van's gaze softened as he read the concern on my face and the fear sparking in my eyes. He hated seeing me distressed, but that wouldn't stop unless he talked to me about what else was troubling him. He released a deep breath as he stared into my eyes and relinquished whatever hold he had on himself.

"I'm scared to lose you," he admitted, and I nodded in response, finally understanding his worry.

"I'll be okay," I told him confidently. "Perceval can't steal my magic anymore, and you all trained me perfectly. I won't let him hurt me, and if he so much as tries, I'll get out of there. There's nothing for you to worry—"

"I know, love," Evander interrupted as a lopsided grin began to form. "I know that you are more than capable of handling yourself, and I desperately wish I could be there to see you hand Perceval his ass." He dragged a knuckle down my cheek, and I shivered at the intimate touch, missing him already. His face fell, and his eyes filled with sorrow as he spoke again. "That's not what I meant."

I tilted my head, and my brows pinched together as I tried to understand his meaning. What was he referring to if he wasn't concerned for my safety? My brown eyes implored him to elaborate so I could grasp the worrisome thoughts in his mind and ease them away as quickly as they entered.

Evander opened and closed his mouth several times as if the words were on the tip of his tongue, yet something was preventing him from voicing them. I stayed there on top of him, running my fingers through his hair as I waited patiently for the man I loved to return to me. Finally, he opened his eyes, and I could see they had lightened slightly, and his face was less tense than it had been moments prior. He took a deep breath to steady himself before addressing me once more.

"This will be the first time you've seen him since you left," he whispered.

"Perceval?" I clarified, but Evander shook his head and clenched his jaw like he was fighting to spit the answer out.

"Dashiell," he replied, nearly breathless. My eyes widened a fraction as the name poured from his lips as if he were ashamed of saying it. "I know you love me, and I hate that this has festered in my mind, but what if..." he started, breaking his stare with me to search around the room like he could find the rest of his question embedded in the walls. "What if when you see him, all those feelings you had come rushing back? What if you decide that *he* is the one you want?" Evander finished, bringing his fierce grey eyes back to me.

My mouth hung open as the weight of his words pressed into me. That was what he was worried about? He thought I would see Dashiell and run back to him with open arms as if the betrayal that occurred had never taken place. As if all of these months in Tenebrae and the love I built with him had never taken place. He thought I would throw him away like that? I tried not to be upset, but I couldn't deny the sting I felt at his lack of belief in me—in *us*.

"Van," I tried, but he cut in before I could say more than his name.

"I know how much you loved him, Ainsley. I *felt* it," he said, pressing a hand to his heart. "I felt it every Gods damn day, and a love like that doesn't just disappear. It doesn't just go away like it never happened."

I closed my mouth, unable to respond because what the hell could I say? He wasn't wrong. I had loved Dashiell deeply—endlessly. There was no denying that, so I wasn't going to try. Any attempt to do so would be a lie that Evander would see straight through.

Silence passed between us for entirely too long when Evander finally spoke again.

"You know I'd let you go, right?" he whispered, and I swear my heart plummeted deep into my chest as his declaration rang in my ears. "If he's the one you want, I'd let you go. I just need you to be happy, even if it's not with me, Ainsley."

I shuddered a breath and felt a tear roll down my cheek. I knew he was saying it because he loved me, but I still despised the idea of us not being together. A future that didn't consist of me being by his side wasn't one I wanted to entertain.

"Just because I'd be willing to give you up doesn't mean I want to," he explained, emotion thick in his voice. "It doesn't mean I'm not fucking terrified that it will happen. But until that time, I'm not beneath begging for you to choose me."

"You don't have to," I swore, pressing my lips to his so he could taste the truth of my words.

There wasn't a chance in this life that I would choose someone over him, and he needed to understand the depth of my love and what I wanted for myself. But I also needed to be transparent with him about what still lingered in my heart for another, even if that truth hurt.

"But you aren't wrong about Dashiell," I admitted, and the fear that had been dissipating in his eyes returned once more. "I loved him with every piece of myself, and what we had was a beautiful and tragic love affair. Our love was young and free. It was passion and joy, excitement and longing. It was... pure magic," I breathed, thinking over the times Dashiell and I had shared.

Since leaving Caelum, anytime I thought of him, the pain and betrayal always forced their way into my mind, seizing control of every good memory and infecting it like a virus. But now, I found the strength to look past the hurt and see what was once good. It wasn't the man with deep blue eyes that I thought of; it was how he made me feel. The way I had been put together and made whole after spending my life broken and alone. The way I had been wanted and cherished for weeks before it came to a gut-wrenching end.

"Dashiell gave me the courage to open myself up and offer my heart for the first time in my life. Because of that, there will always be a piece of me that loves him and what we were," I explained, and Evander nodded, though it was a somber motion. "I could never regret what we had—because it led me to you, Evander."

His eyes sparkled with hope, and his chest began to rise and fall faster, making me move with it. I brushed my lips over his as I smiled and melted into the man designed for me. He was everything I wanted—everything I *needed*—and we weren't leaving this room until he grasped that reality.

"The love you've always given me is the only one I want. Through every mishap and mistake I've made, you've been there, loving me fiercely through it all. You've angered me, challenged me, pushed me to be the best version of myself, and never once has your love wavered as I changed. It simply evolved, twisting around me and growing as I did without boxing me in or making me conform to it. You let me find my way and stood at my side every moment. Our love is fierce and strong; it's chaotic, angry, passionate, and tender. It's everything, Evander."

His charcoal eyes were wild with life and hunger, unlike anything I'd seen from him before. He looked at me with all the love I had just spoken of, and I felt the tension ease from his body as he accepted my declaration. I held his face in my hands as I leaned down and gently dragged his nose up with the tip of mine.

"*You* are the one I choose. *You* are my Claimed," I said, placing a kiss between each statement. "And when you stop being so damn stubborn and just finally ask me, *you* will be my husband."

Evander stilled beneath my mouth before pulling back to meet my stare, and his eyes went wide as he digested what I had just said. I bit my lip to try and stifle the smile forming at his shocked expression, though I didn't bother to say anything more about it. He cocked his head to the side and looked at me skeptically, clearly not believing what he had heard.

"I'm waiting for the punchline, love," he said slowly, and I shook my head to indicate there wouldn't be one.

He let out a long breath as if all the air had been dragged from his lungs, and his hands traveled up my body to cup my face. His eyes grew glossy as he searched my features for any hint of this being a joke, but I knew he wouldn't find one.

"If this is your decision because of tonight—"

"It's not," I said, immediately interjecting. "I want you in every possible way, Evander. I want to be your wife. I want to be your queen and rule our people side by side like we were always meant to. I've wanted that for a while now, but you've been so busy, and I couldn't find the perfect time to tell you."

He interrupted me with a brutal kiss that made me lose all sense of reason. His tongue slipped over mine, claiming me as if I weren't already his, and I finally let myself get lost in him and the burning love that was so evident between us. He was all I wanted in this world, and I was glad he finally realized that.

"Marry me, love," he said, smiling wide against my mouth. Every part of me wanted to reply with a snide retort, but even I knew it wasn't the time for jokes.

"Yes," I told him, and Van kissed me before pulling my face back to let me see his dazzling smile.

"How difficult was it not to be a smartass just now?"

"Impossibly," I told him, loving how well he knew me.

Evander chuckled under his breath before gently kissing every inch of my face as his hands stroked up and down my back. He was blissfully happy, which meant I was getting Evander in full Onyx-mode this evening, though I didn't mind one bit.

"We could do this tonight," he said as his lips traveled down my neck, burning a trail in my flesh. "We could gather our family, have Sirona conduct the ceremony, and by morning, Tenebrae could officially have a queen."

I thought about objecting to his rash suggestion, but for what reason? I didn't want a large wedding, though I was positive Felix would lose his shit if I didn't have one. The only thing I desired was to be tied to the man I loved in the presence of our family. There was no reason we couldn't go through with it tonight, and the more I thought about it, the more I wanted to.

"Are you sure you don't want to do it the traditional way with our people surrounding us in the palace?" I asked.

Evander and I had never discussed weddings, but I was sure there was a royal protocol for us to follow, and maybe that's what he wanted. Perhaps he only suggested the idea of it being just our family as a way to make me more comfortable.

"The only thing I want is you. We can celebrate with our people later, but I want this ceremony to be about us," he said, and I fell even more in love with him.

"Do you think everyone is still up?" I asked, my decision made.

Evander grinned from ear to ear as he nodded.

"They were all hanging out in the study when I got home. There were liquor bottles on the table, so I'm more than positive they're still up and drinking the night away."

My heart fluttered, and my blood heated with excitement as the knowledge of what we were about to do set in. He was about to be my husband, and in hours I would sit on a throne with a crown on my head as the world learned who he belonged to. He was mine, and the magic of the Claiming thrummed in my veins at the thought.

"I want to be the one to tell them," I demanded, shifting myself off Evander and climbing out of the bed.

"Of course, love," he said as he slid from the mattress and came to stand next to me. He leaned down and kissed the tip of my nose as he stared deep into my eyes. "If you can get to them first."

And then he took off running.

That asshole.

I sprinted after him, shooting out my shadows and solidifying them into ropes the second they wrapped around his waist. I grabbed hold of one end and yanked hard. Van was pulled back and fell on his ass as I leapt over him and continued running down the hall.

Just as I was about to round the corner that led to the stairs, I felt the familiar tingle of his magic and glanced down to see his Gift snaking around my ankles. Before I could do anything, Evander's shadows solidified, and I fell forward, slamming my face into the hard wooden floor.

Fuck.

"I love you," he singsonged as he passed, and I threw up my middle finger as I rolled to my back and worked to untie the dark knot around my ankles.

I heard his feet hit the steps just as I slithered out of the bindings, and I knew I was running out of time. I got to my feet and took off after him again, but there was no way my shadows would reach him before he got to the study. I had to try something else. I closed my eyes as I called to my Illusio Gift, hoping to penetrate Evander's mind even though it was near impossible and I had only managed it a few times.

"What the hell!" I heard him yell just as I made it halfway down the stairs, and I picked up my pace, knowing that even though my illusion snared its target, I wouldn't be able to hold him long.

Evander came into view as I skipped the last three steps and landed hard on the ground. He carefully stepped in between furniture that wasn't there as he struggled to make it through the corridor. As soon as I got close enough, I dropped the illusion and called my shadows to wrap around him and pin him against the wall.

"I don't know whether to be impressed or annoyed," he admitted as I stepped before him.

"How about both?" I offered, pushing up on my toes to kiss his lips as he struggled to break free of the shadowed ties that held him in place. "Better luck next time," I said triumphantly as I ran the short distance to the study doors.

A split second before I could reach them, Evander appeared in front of me in a puff of shadows and pushed the doors open wide.

"You cheated!" I said, smacking him in the chest as he smiled victoriously.

"I don't know what you're talking about," he replied cooly, and I couldn't help but throw my arms around his neck as I basked in the arrogance I had once sworn to hate. It had been too long since we laughed and played like this, and I didn't want it to ever end.

But as I smiled up at the man I loved, his face began to pale.

I turned my attention to our five family members who looked at us with grave expressions. Something was seriously wrong, and I had a feeling it would be our worst news yet.

65.

"What happened?" Evander commanded, and we both slipped into our roles as rulers with ease, vanishing our once carefree and happy smiles in exchange for the hard masks we had to wear.

The room was silent, and everyone looked at one another as if unable to decide who would have to deliver the news. Lia's eyes were wide and teary, and Felix silently stared at the ground beside her. My heart began to pound thunderously as I watched Olivier step forward from his position across the room.

"There have been more attacks," he said solemnly.

"Where?" our king demanded, pulling me further into the room.

I squeezed his hand reassuringly even though I felt like we were about to be delivered a vicious blow. Things were getting worse by the day, but by the looks on each of our family members' faces, I knew what we had gone through was nothing compared to whatever news we were about to be told.

"Everywhere," Marceline announced from behind the desk. She didn't look at us as she spoke, instead keeping her eyes on the parchments of paper strewn across the top as she scribbled quickly. "Every single kingdom's camps were hit tonight... except for us," she continued, and I stumbled backward as the air was knocked from my lungs.

The numbers Oberon would need to issue an attack of that magnitude didn't seem possible. We should have been able to catch wind of their movements, but it appeared the stones were keeping their soldiers hidden until they deemed it was time to attack.

A soft whimper left Lia's lips as gentle tears streamed down her face. Calidore kissed them away, but I knew it wouldn't erase the pain for her. She was the kindest soul I'd ever met, and she loved her Gift of being able to help those in need. She loved fixing what was broken and healing the wounds left by traumatic events in hopes it would help those people move on and find peace. And right now, she was stuck here with us as the people of Disparya died, and there was nothing she could offer them.

Those soldiers were mothers and fathers; they were brothers and sisters. They were someone's husband or wife. And now they were nothing. They were lost to the brutality of a war we weren't prepared for.

"Why would Oberon strike everyone except for *us*? We're his biggest adversary," I pointed out, looking toward Van who seemed just as confused as I was by the decision.

"Because..." Oli said, and I shifted my attention to him. "The intel we're receiving doesn't report Pravus soldiers among the attackers. Every one of the enemy soldiers possessed Tenebraen Gifts."

Evander stiffened at my side, and I felt the blood drain completely from my face. That wasn't possible. Our soldiers wouldn't betray us and start attacking innocent people, which meant...

"Some of those soldiers had a Gift from another kingdom as well," Olivier added.

"Conjoining?" I breathed, and he nodded.

"It looks like Oberon's been planning his army for a very long time," Calidore said, rising from his spot next to Lia on the couch.

I shuddered to think that if Perceval hadn't been greedy, I might have been in that army, wielding my Gifts with destruction as I took innocent lives. I wanted to think I would have fought against the idea, but there was no way to be sure that was the case. They would have brainwashed me my entire life to think of Disparya as the enemy, and I would have never been the wiser.

"We're being fucking set up!" Marce growled, and a low rumble reverberated in the base of my throat.

She was right. Oberon was making it look like Tenebrae was behind the attacks. He wanted the other Kingdoms of Disparya to turn on us and declare war. He wanted them to finish us off so he could swoop in and scavenge the pieces of what was left. We couldn't let him. We had run out of time, and there was only one option left for us.

"Tallis has been hit too. More forcefully than Venator or Ministro, it seems," Marce announced, and I turned in time to see words finish appearing on one of the papers just as ink rippled across another. "Fuck," she breathed, and I swallowed the rising bile. "Declan too." Marce slammed her fists into the desk over and over again until the wood splintered and caved in under her force.

Darkness slithered over Van's skin, a look of fury and a promise of vengeance in his eyes. Our closest alliances were being targeted. The room began to spin beneath my feet as my world came crashing down. Evander caught me by the elbow to keep me steady.

"Why attack Declan? Vorsutos isn't part of Disparya," I pointed out.

"Because it's no secret that Tenebrae and Vorsutos are friendly. He wants to cripple us in every way he can. So far, he's hurt our allies and turned the rest of the continent against us," Van answered, his voice flat and distant.

"We'll go to the other kings and convince them that we had nothing to do with this," I tried. Evander shook his head.

"King Harbin's guard tried to kill you and I snapped King Arden's most trusted advisor's neck right before his eyes. Do you honestly think either of them will hear us out?" Van quipped. I hated his icy tone, but he was terrified—we all were.

Murmurs broke out in the study as our family discussed our next course of action, but my eyes were firmly locked on Evander's as we held a private conversation. We knew what had to be done next, and though neither of us liked it, it was our only hope.

If I couldn't locate the stones, then I could at least try and gather intel on Perceval's alliance with Oberon. Even the smallest bit of information could potentially save thousands of lives and that was a cause worth putting my life at risk for. It may not have been the best plan, but we were running out of ideas and losing this war because of it. Sitting around was getting us nowhere.

"I can give you one week but no more than that. And if things start to go wrong, I'm pulling you out immediately," Evander said, and I nodded, accepting the mission. "You go in, get what we need, and get the fuck out of there. Do you understand me?"

"Yes. I can do this," I said confidently.

"Do what?" Oli interrupted, and we both turned to see him striding for us as his features twisted in rage. He knew exactly what was going on, and he was furious. "No. She's not going anywhere."

"Oli," I tried, but he ignored me and directed his rage at his king.

"We are not fucking sending her to his doorstep. We aren't risking her life after finally getting her back," he exclaimed, coming chest to chest with Evander, who very much didn't like being called out like this.

"Do you think I want to do this? That I didn't try to talk her out of it while searching for a solution for weeks?" Van demanded, pushing Olivier so he stumbled back.

Cal and Marce hurried to the center of the room, ready to break up the pending physical altercation. They had argued about how to handle things before when Evander told Oli he wouldn't pursue finding me all those months ago. They greatly differed on it, and now they seemed to be at a crossroads again when it came to me.

"I promised her parents to keep her safe. I'm not going to let you send her to the men that will try and hurt her," Oli argued, pushing Van back. Cal and Marce stepped closer, though still far enough to let the men try and sort through it on their own.

"*Let* me?" Evander shot back. "She makes her own decisions."

"And you are a king who commands us all, including *her*. You could easily order her to stay back, and you fucking know it."

Olivier lunged, knocking Van over as he landed a blow to his side. I rushed for them, but Calidore stepped in front of me and shook his head.

"They need to get through this on their own," he said. I knew he was right.

The men rolled on the floor, dishing blow after blow to one another, with no clear victor. Oli cursed furiously as Evander defended his decision to send me to our enemy. There was no changing his mind because there was no changing mine. Evander could have pulled rank and demanded I stay, but we both knew it would only be done out of fear and not what was best for Tenebrae and the rest of Disparya.

"If you need someone to go, send me instead," Olivier gritted, landing a hard fist to his king's jaw. Evander spat blood before locking his legs around his friend and flipping him over as he dealt the same deafening blow.

"Perceval wouldn't let you within fifty feet of the palace before he slit your throat. What the fuck makes you think you're better suited for this mission than *her*?" Van demanded, punching Oli one more time before rising to his feet. "She possesses what he wants, along with the knowledge and training we have ingrained in her. She's the only one who can do this mission successfully, and you know it."

Olivier got to his feet and spit the blood coating his teeth before wiping the back of his hand across his mouth. He paced in place, looking between Van and me like he was trying to devise his next tactic.

"She can't go back to Caelum alone," Olivier argued, and I understood his worry, but there was no other way around it.

"She won't be," Felix replied, and I twisted to find him rising from the couch as he looked at me. "I'll go with her."

"No!" Oli and I both said in unison.

Felix was out of his damn mind if he thought that was an option. He stole me from Caelum, thwarting the king's plans to drain me of my magic. There was no way Perceval would let him live for that betrayal. He would put an arrow in my best friend's heart the moment he crossed into that kingdom, and I wouldn't let it happen.

"He'll kill you," I told Felix as I shook my head, not allowing him to make this choice. "I can do it on my own."

"No, you can't," Felix argued. "I know the palace better than you, and we'd cover more ground if both of us go. I'm our best chance at locating those stones, and I can protect you. You know this is the only way."

I shook my head again, but I knew it was no use. He was right, and though I didn't want to risk his life, he was essential to this mission. I had to believe that

Dashiell's love for his best friend would be enough to spare his life should Perceval try to end it.

"Send me with her," Felix said, directing his request to the only person in the room who could grant it.

Evander considered him for a moment as if trying to decide whether or not he could trust Felix with this particular mission due to his soft spot for the Prince of Caelum. He looked at Oli, who shook his head, silently begging his king. When his eyes finally drifted to me, I nodded, and that was all the confirmation Evander needed.

"You are there for no other reason than to aid our mission and your future queen," Evander replied in the cold voice of a ruler who had everything at stake. Olivier released a defeated breath as he rested his hands on the top of his head and paced the room, clearly distraught from losing this battle. "You will always choose *her* above all others, and if it comes down to it, Empathi..." he said carefully, taking a slow, deliberate step toward Felix. "You will protect her with your life. Is that understood?"

"Yes. I accept," Felix replied, dipping his head in a bow to the king before him.

Evander nodded and then turned to direct his attention to me. At that moment, he wasn't the man I laughed and played games with. He wasn't the love of my life. He was the King of Tenebrae, and I was the heir, ready to accept whatever instructions he gave.

"You will be quick, discreet, and not stray from your mission. You have one week to locate the stones and bring them back. If you cannot complete your task in that time, or the danger to your safety becomes too great, you are to end the mission and get out of there," Evander commanded, and I bowed in acceptance. "One week, and then you get your ass back home so I can marry you."

I smiled wide at the last command before reaching up on my toes to place a kiss against his lips. The fact that I agreed to be his queen was the only light in this dark night, and we both clung to the happiness we felt earlier in our room.

"What?" Lia asked, standing from the couch. I broke Evander's stare to find the rest of our family looking back at us with hopeful expressions. Even Olivier seemed to be interested in the conversation.

"She wouldn't stop begging, so I finally agreed to marry her," Evander replied, brushing the hair away from my face as he gave me that cocky grin he had perfected.

I rolled my eyes at his response just as Lia and Felix collided with me, knocking me down as they half laughed and half sobbed tears of joy. I hugged them both back before insisting they let me up and made my way back to Evander, who was getting congratulatory hugs from Marce and Cal.

"When did all of this happen?" Lia asked excitedly, and my chest ached at the lightness returning to her voice. Tonight had been miserable for all of us, but if this small news about Evander and I could bring them any sort of solace, I'd gladly take it.

"Tonight," Evander answered, wrapping his arms around my shoulders from behind as he rested his chin atop my head. "We were coming here to tell you all and then have Sirona perform the ceremony this evening."

"No," Felix responded just as I figured he would. "You're having a wedding, so don't try to get out of it."

"I just want it to be the seven of us," I responded, and Felix huffed in irritation. "You can throw a big party and invite everyone you want after the ceremony." After a second of consideration, he nodded his head in acceptance.

"There's still time before you have to leave," Lia suggested hopefully. "We can marry you right now, and it could be the one good thing to come out of tonight."

Evander looked down at me intently, clearly curious about my answer. I wanted to say yes and hold on to that happiness while away in another kingdom. Whenever I felt lost and uncertain, I could close my eyes and remember the night I gained everything I wanted. But there was something significant that was preventing me from agreeing.

"We can't tonight," I announced, still staring at Evander.

Our friends took that as their cue to give us some space. I twisted in Van's arms, and his brow furrowed as he tried to read what was on in my mind. I had been so set on marrying him tonight, but when the time came, I couldn't, and he needed to hear why.

"We need to talk," I told him.

66.

"Remember what I told you," Evander instructed as he clipped my bag onto Nox's saddle.

The last hour was spent in the study, devising the plan for how Felix and I would tackle our mission in Caelum. We had only one week to find the stones; if we couldn't, we would leave empty-handed. Van made me promise five times that I wouldn't stray from the mission we discussed, though he knew me coming home without what we needed wouldn't be acceptable to me.

"I know," I told him seriously.

Evander caught my chin between his fingers and leaned down to kiss me. My magic stirred awake and began clawing against me as it tried to free itself to Claim what already belonged to it. Van sighed into my mouth as if his magic was doing the same.

"If you don't go now, I don't think our magic will let you leave at all," he said, and I nodded, kissing him once more before pulling back.

"Promise me you'll be careful," I begged as worry for his safety began to seep into my veins.

After figuring out my and Felix's mission, we discussed what everyone else in our family would do over the next week. Van would be heading to Vorsutos to help Declan, while Olivier, Cal, and Lia would be helping the soldiers who survived the attacks any way they could. Marce was tasked with keeping the lines of communication open between Vorsutos, Tenebrae, and Agnitio as they picked up the broken pieces of their armies. She had also slipped Felix and me both transfer paper should we need to contact her. We couldn't risk anyone intercepting our correspondence, so it was only to be used in case of emergency.

"I promise, love," he said, but it did nothing to ease my stress. "You do what you must, and then you get out of there. Sirona opened the portal that will lead to Caelum, so it should only be a short ride to the palace once you're through."

Evander jerked his chin to the saddle, and I complied, climbing onto Nox and grabbing the reins. I twisted behind me to see Felix doing the same with his mare as Oli stood by and watched with a look of fear and frustration embedded on his face. He hadn't spoken to me the entire hour we plotted, and I hated how we were leaving things, but I wasn't going to give in to what he wanted. Our people needed me, and it was my job to help keep them safe, even if I had to risk my life to do so.

"When the week ends, be at the meeting spot by midnight. Our contacts will be there and waiting. If you get done before your deadline, send word, and we'll get you out quicker," Evander explained for the twentieth time.

Our escape had been planned down to the final second, and I was well-versed in what needed to happen. Elenora would be the one to retrieve Felix and me and get us safely to Agnitio where Van would be waiting. Since Caelum and Agnitio were on good terms, she had less chance of being questioned if caught. Oli demanded he come to the rescue mission, so Evander arranged for him to go disguised as one of Elenora's soldiers to evade suspicion. We were ready.

"I will," I told him, taking a deep breath as Felix's mare stopped beside me.

Evander nodded and then took a step back with his chin held high. This was it. This was our goodbye until I returned home to him. We both had our missions to accomplish, and I prayed to the Gods we'd be successful. We couldn't afford any more losses.

"I love you," I whispered, and Evander's hard eyes softened as he spoke the declaration back. I replayed his words in my mind on repeat as I fought the ache in my chest at leaving him. With one last glance at my family, Felix and I rode into the dark, racing the pending light of dawn.

"You haven't said a word since we left the house," I told Felix as we trod down the path toward the portal.

We had left hours ago, and the late morning sun was beating down on our backs while we crept closer to the destination. In just a few more minutes, we'd be at the caves Evander told us housed the portal to get to Caelum.

According to him, all of the magic passageways had been kept sealed ever since the outcome of the Second Great War, as none of the rulers trusted each other. They were only ever used during extenuating circumstances, like when the kings conducted their meeting in Caelum. They didn't want to leave their kingdoms vacant of their rulers for the length it would have taken to travel to and from. The only exception was the portal that stayed open between Agnitio and Tenebrae. Our two kingdoms had maintained a friendly relationship through the centuries and trusted one another explicitly.

"I just have a lot on my mind," Felix answered, and I could feel the tension surging from him.

He was about to return to the place he'd once called home, though now I wasn't sure if he still considered it as such. I knew he was concerned about King Perceval and the lies he'd have to weave to keep from being killed, but it was nothing compared to the fear of seeing his best friend again. He and Dashiell were once brothers, and I could tell he was questioning if that bond still stood in place for the prince.

It wasn't going to be easy for Felix to see Dashiell again, especially after he stole me from Caelum. We also learned that the prince had journeyed to our enemy's land and that his father was working closely with Oberon. Felix always wanted to see the best in his friend, but the longer we went on, the more I was convinced he was just blinded by his loyalty to him. I couldn't trust Felix's judgment when it came to Dashiell, and although I was worried that would hinder the success of our mission, I had to hold onto faith that Felix would do the right thing when it came down to it. I had to believe he would put millions of lives above just one.

"I'm sorry you have to be away from Oli," I said, deciding that Dashiell wasn't the best topic for us to discuss. "Especially since you finally got him wrapped around your finger."

The corner of Felix's lips twitched as he worked to keep his smile hidden, and I could instantly feel another emotion radiating from him at the mention of Olivier's name—love. He deserved every happiness available in this world, and I felt such joy to know my friend had found it.

I slowed my pace, wanting to savor this conversation together before we reached the caves and began our mission. Talking about our lives in Tenebrae once we passed through to Caelum wasn't an option. We couldn't risk someone overhearing and ruining our plans before we could enact them.

"I love seeing you this happy," I told him, and his face broke into a fully formed smile as he looked at me.

"I am, Ainsley. I'm so fucking happy that it hurts sometimes," he replied, and I nodded because I knew exactly what he meant. "I've never been able to have someone of my own, and now... Now I get to love freely and deeply with no restrictions because of a Gift I was born with. I got to give my heart away, and it feels like my chest will cave in every time I look at him, knowing he holds it. For the first time in my life, I get to have a love of my own. I get to call someone *mine*."

A joyful tear trickled down his cheek, and I couldn't help my own from flowing as I watched the love and happiness swirl in his bright amber eyes. Felix was owed this slice of paradise he found. He was owed the love King Perceval prevented him from having for nearly his entire life, all because of the magic that ran through his veins.

"You deserve every blissful moment, Felix."

"So do you, cupcake," he replied as we reached the entrance to the caves.

There was nothing except a dark tunnel peeking out at us, but that was to be expected. Evander explained that the portal lay farther inside and would only take a few moments to reach it once we entered. I took a deep breath and straightened my posture, preparing myself for the weeklong task.

"Are you ready?" Felix asked.

I twisted my head to take one last glance at my homeland. I took in the mountainous grey landscape and inhaled the fresh scent of snow on the ground as I committed it to memory. Where we were going was nothing like this place, and I knew I would feel homesick for my kingdom only moments after we arrived in the green hills of Caelum.

"Yes," I said, nudging Nox forward. "Let's get this over with."

The cave was dark and damp, but it only took a few minutes to reach the portal. Against one of the stone walls was a shimmering light that looked like a brighter version of the shields I had created so often.

"We just walk through?" Felix asked.

"That's what Evander said to do."

I removed a piece of the transfer paper from my pocket before scribbling a message to let him know we had arrived. After a moment, ink spread across the parchment, and I smiled at the note.

I love you. Come home to me soon.
- Van
His Royal Majesty - King of Tenebrae - Master of Orgasms - Winner of All Games - Future Husband of Ainsley

"Come on," I said, pocketing the paper once the ink disappeared.

We needed to get through quickly so Van could close the portal since we wouldn't be taking it to return home. Once I completed my tasks and we fled, there was no doubt Caelum's soldiers would head to the portal that led home in hopes of trapping us. That's why we planned to have Elenora smuggle us to Agnitio instead.

I held my breath as we urged our horses forward, half expecting to slam straight into the wall, but instead, we passed through. My skin tingled as the portal's magic swept over me, and blinding sunlight filled my vision. I squinted, throwing a hand up to shield myself as I took in the sprawling green hills of Caelum.

My magic stirred as it sensed the land I had once called home and the danger it possessed to me. I had been drugged to keep my Gifts hidden as they were plotted to be stolen away, and it seemed like my magic hadn't forgotten that fact.

"They can't hurt us," I whispered to myself as a reminder. My magic couldn't be taken unless I gave it freely, and I would sooner die than do so.

A faint humming sound came from behind us, and I turned in time to see the shimmering portal disappear and transform into the face of a cliff. Well, there was no turning back now. I reached into my bag before leaning down to offer Nox an apple for her trouble as I gazed at the land ahead.

"We can do this, right?" Felix questioned, uncertainty coating his words. I had a feeling he was speaking more to himself than to me, but I answered nonetheless.

"We don't have a choice," I replied, letting command and unwavering confidence drift around my tone.

Felix needed to know I wasn't going to mess around regarding this mission. He needed to understand that there wouldn't be anything or anyone who would stop me from completing it, including him. I didn't come here as his friend; I came as the future Queen of Tenebrae, and Gods help anyone who stood in my way.

"How far are we from the palace?" I asked, knowing Felix knew these lands better than I did.

"Maybe an hour, but we can cut the time in half if we hurry."

"And how long until they spot us?"

"Any minute now," he replied as we rode away from the portal's entrance and toward the palace.

My heart thundered as quickly as Nox's hooves as we sprinted toward our destination, not wanting to waste a single minute. As we went, I ran through my plans even though I had them memorized down to the last detail. I could do this.

"Stop right there!" a deep voice commanded from somewhere behind the trees ahead. Felix and I did as instructed, slowing our pace to a walk before halting our movements altogether. "Who..." he started before going completely silent as he stepped around the oak he was hiding behind. "Lord Felix?" he breathed as recognition filled his features. Perhaps my best friend wasn't a dead man after all.

"Edward," Felix replied in a friendly tone as he moved forward once more.

"Stop! Don't come any closer," Edward commanded, and Felix froze.

Or perhaps not.

Edward twisted his head to the side as he whistled through his teeth, never once taking his eyes from us. Two more guards appeared at his side a few moments later, looking just as shocked when they saw us.

"Alert the palace that we have Lord Felix and Lady Ainsley in our company and are bringing them in. King Perceval will want to know immediately," Edward commanded, and one of the guards tipped his head in acceptance of the order before hurrying away.

Felix and I looked at one another, and I knew he was sensing the clear tension. I raised a brow in question, and Felix shook his head, letting me know that manipulating their emotions into something calmer wasn't the best idea.

Another twenty minutes passed before the guard returned, whispered something in Edward's ear, and then left again. I closed my eyes, letting my mind flood with thoughts of Evander one last time before I had to banish the distraction. The private conversation we had earlier this morning flashed before me, and I held on to the words I said before kissing him deeply.

'For everything we lost and for everything we have yet to gain.'

"Dismount," Edward commanded, stirring me out of my thoughts. I let my eyes flutter open as I took a steadying breath.

It was time.

Felix and I did as instructed, and I kissed Nox lightly on her muzzle before giving her the order to go home. She took off running in the opposite direction with Felix's mare close behind. The guards looked curiously at one another but didn't question our decision to rid ourselves of our horses. Instead, they drew their weapons and directed us to lead the way on the path.

The guards didn't frighten me, as I knew I could kill them with half a thought, but it still made me uneasy to have a blade this close to me while unarmed. I could have crafted my own weapon, but I had no idea if King Perceval had told his guards about the dark magic I possessed. For now, it was an advantage to keep my shadows hidden until the perfect moment.

67.

We pushed through the final thicket of trees along the path and were met with a clear view of the large palace, wholly surrounded by a shimmering shield. The guards halted us, and Felix and I glanced at one another as we noted the change in scenery, wondering if it was because of our disappearance or if more had gone on in our absence. As we stood there, waiting for permission to enter, my eyes scanned the grounds, noticing they were empty. Not a single resident could be found lounging in the sun or strolling the gardens. The only people that could be seen were guards stationed at random points and one man pacing frantically along the border of the shield.

Dashiell.

My heart stopped at the sight of him, and I inhaled a shuddering, panicked breath. Felix's hand gripped mine, keeping me steady as my eyes locked on the man I once loved. My friend's Gift pushed against me, and I let it in immediately. Not entirely by choice but because I was too out of my mind to stop him. His warmth spread through me, wrapping around my heart and calming my senses. I closed my eyes and focused on what Felix was doing as I breathed in and out slowly.

I couldn't lose my bearings now. We had a mission to accomplish, and it relied on me being able to think straight and not let my emotions get to me. My family—my kingdom—was counting on me. I inhaled one deep breath before my eyes fluttered open, and I looked up at Felix, indicating I was okay and ready. He nodded before slowly withdrawing his Gift, and together we focused straight ahead as we prepared ourselves for our most challenging battle yet.

One of the guards in the distance signaled, and ours motioned for us to continue. The moment we fully passed through the trees, Dashiell's head snapped up, and his eyes widened as he stopped and fully faced us. His fist banged against the shield surrounding the palace, causing shimmering ripples to form but doing nothing to take it down. He yelled at the guards positioned next to him, and though we couldn't hear what he was saying, I had a guess it was to lower the shield. They did nothing but keep their gazes firmly on us, and Dashiell dragged a frustrated hand through his hair and bounced on the balls of his feet as he watched us slowly approach.

Once we were halfway to the shield, our guards halted us again, and I swallowed thickly as I readied myself. This was it. This was what I had volunteered for. I could do this.

The shimmering forcefield dropped, and Dashiell took off the second it did, sprinting straight for Felix and me. I stiffened as he drew closer, and my magic thrashed against me in a violent demand to be let loose. I jerked back and clutched my chest from the sudden surge of strength it was displaying. I sank my claws into my magic, pinning it down as I struggled to keep it beneath my flesh.

My mind flashed over images of us happy together and then to the depression he had caused as I was forced to relive the times he had given me my drugged tea, knowing it would suppress the Gifts he was set to steal. The Gifts that were now demanding to enact revenge for his treacherous lies. Felix gripped my arm as he pushed his magic through me once more.

My magic didn't like that.

It fought Felix for dominance, demanding that it would not be sedated as the man who caused us so much pain was now inching closer by the second. I understood its need for blood. My magic was part of me, so that thirst came from something deep inside. But I wasn't ready to take Dashiell's life. At least not yet.

Not until I had to.

Together, Felix and I worked quickly to seal my vengeful magic inside me, locking it away as I regained control of myself. It banged against the iron box I shoved it in, but it couldn't break through. Not until I allowed it to do so.

I straightened, giving Felix a grateful nod as he released me, and we faced forward again. Dashiell was getting closer, and soon, we would be face-to-face for the first time in months. His pace slowed as he approached, and before he could get within twenty feet, Felix cut in, putting himself in front of me like a loyal soldier. He wasn't protecting his friend from the heartache of seeing her ex-fiancé and the man she loved. He was protecting his queen from a potential threat. His decision was all I needed to finally pull myself together and step into the role I was here to play.

Dashiell skidded to a stop as he clocked his childhood friend's choice. The hurt in his brilliant deep blue eyes told me he knew it for what it was—Felix protecting me from *him*.

"We're fine. Leave." Dashiell said to our two guards, and his voice sent my chest aching again as I remembered how each lie he had ever told me had sounded on his lips. A siren's call, luring me in with its beauty, knowing all along that I would be sacrificed.

"Your Highness, we were ordered to take—" one guard tried.

"I said, *fucking leave us,*" Dashiell ordered as he turned to the man, his voice dark and dangerous. Thunder rumbled overhead, and the two guards quickly bowed before scurrying away to the palace.

Dashiell brought his attention back to us, his eyes darting from Felix to me, standing safely behind my friend. I studied him, noticing how different he looked since the last time I had seen him. He looked older, though I knew that wasn't possible. His eyes seemed darker—haunted and frenzied. His hair was slightly longer, curling at the ends, and stubble was spread along his jaw. There was purpling beneath his eyes like he hadn't known a moment of peace in all these months.

I hoped he hadn't.

His eyes misted over as he took a tentative step forward and extended his hand to us.

"That's close enough," Felix demanded, holding a hand to halt the prince.

At that moment, that's all Dashiell was to us—the prince of Caelum. The man who had tricked me into loving him and planned on draining me of my magic at his father's command.

Dashiell stopped at once, and his chest heaved as he struggled with Felix's order. He closed his eyes as tears spilled and took several deep breaths before returning his gaze to us, though this time, he set his eyes only on me.

"Please, Ainsley," he croaked, his voice breaking on my name.

My gaze dragged over the man standing before me, shattered by his own actions. I couldn't help but feel pity for him. He was broken and destroyed and had no one to blame but himself. I checked over myself, making sure my magic was still locked away before stepping out from behind Felix. Dashiell's stare widened, and his hands trembled with anticipation. Did he think I would go to him? Was he under the impression that I would ever forgive him for what he'd done to me?

"Move aside," I told him, and he loosed a shuddering breath as more tears fell from his eyes. He shook his head as his lips quivered. He was unraveling, his own crushing heartbreak seeping into me thanks to my Empathi Gifts. I couldn't afford to feel empathy for him or fall for any more of his lies. "I won't ask you again."

Dashiell moved for me, his hands reaching out like if he held me, none of this would be happening. Like if I were in his arms, then all the bad and hurt that I had felt would somehow disappear. But I was too far gone for that.

Before Dashiell could reach me, I crafted a long dagger from my shadows and pressed the side into his throat, stopping him immediately. He swallowed hard against my blade, and I could see guards rushing back toward us out of the corner of my eye. Maybe a knife to their prince's throat wasn't the most brilliant move to make with witnesses, but I wasn't thinking. All I knew was that I couldn't let him touch me again—not ever.

Our faces were inches apart and I could vaguely hear Felix trying to talk me down, but I didn't care. I wasn't planning on killing Dashiell, but I couldn't deny the desire to do so while I had him this close. My magic banged against its iron cage in a desperate plea to get out, but that wasn't going to happen. My blood sang as my cold stare seeped into his.

Dashiell glanced down at the dagger, his eyes wide as I held it firm. But the panic wasn't from me holding a weapon to his throat—it was because of the magic I had expelled.

The guards approached, and I could feel the flames of the Ignisians hot on my flesh, ready to burn me alive for attacking their prince.

"It's fine," Dashiell whispered, careful not to move too much as a drop of blood trickled slowly down his neck. His brow furrowed as he studied me and then the blade once more. I tilted my head as I observed the odd response until realization hit me, and my lips lifted in the corner.

"You didn't know," I mused, and Dashiell gave a slight shake of his head, careful not to cut himself any deeper. Oh, the irony. "Well, now you do."

He straightened, and more blood spilled from beneath my blade. I drew back slightly, just enough to stop from slitting his throat completely but still keeping contact with his flesh.

"I don't care about your Gifts, Ainsley. I never did," he replied, and I huffed an incredulous laugh.

"You seemed to care enough to try and steal them," I seethed, and he flinched as if I had struck him. How could he possibly claim not to have cared? He knew how much the possibility of magic meant to me and kept me in the dark about it anyway.

"You're not going to hurt him, Ainsley. Put the dagger down," Felix said gently, and I could tell he said it more to calm the guards now surrounding us than to me. But they needed to know that I was not only deadly... I was done fucking around.

"He schemed his way between my legs and lied to my fucking face for weeks. There isn't anything I wouldn't do," I growled, letting everyone hear just how serious I was.

Dashiell swallowed, and his eyes softened as my words pierced him deeper than my blade could have. Slowly, he raised his hand and gently clasped it around the wrist holding a weapon to his throat. My skin was like fire beneath his touch, and I fought the urge to jerk it away and back down. His eyes darted back and forth over mine as a single tear escaped.

"Do it," Dashiell said, and the guards shifted around us, clearly unhappy with that request. I tightened my grip around the hilt, not taking my eyes off him as he nodded slowly. "It's okay, Ainsley. Do it."

My magic thrashed again, faster and harder, making the iron cage shake in fury as I held his life in my hands. Just one flick of my wrist, and I could claim my revenge. I could take the debt he owed me for the false promises he made and the pain he caused. I swallowed before inching my face even closer to Dashiell's, feeling the heat of his breath brush over my skin. As much as I wanted to take what I was owed, it wasn't the time.

"Maybe later," I told him before letting the dagger dissolve into shadows that drifted aimlessly through my fingers. I pulled my hand back, causing him to release his hold on me as I held his stare.

"Ainsley," he whispered, emotion thick in his voice. His gaze was intense, his eyes begging me to let him in. But that would never happen. Gone were the days when I would give him the time of day to spew his bullshit.

"And don't you ever fucking touch me again," I growled, backing away from him. Dashiell closed his eyes and fell to his knees, his body shuddering as I stepped around him and past the guards.

"Felix," I commanded over my shoulder. I knew he wanted to comfort his friend, but we were here for a mission—not to make amends. Felix's footsteps grew closer until he was beside me, and within moments we were entering the palace with new guards flanking us on all sides.

I kept my chin high as they led us through the corridors while the residents watched with eager eyes and hushed conversations. I let my shadows drift from me, flowing behind like a train of spilled ink and suppressed my smirk as our onlookers gasped.

"Trying to give them a show?" Felix asked under his breath.

"Better they know what I'm capable of now," I answered.

We hadn't discussed whether we would showcase my Gifts or keep them secret, but I wanted to control the narrative. If I knew King Perceval, he would want to keep me hidden, and I wasn't about to let him have the upper hand.

As we walked, a familiar face with dark black hair and warm hazel eyes caught my attention, and it took everything in me not to sprint to her—the maiden I loved like a mother. I kept my eyes glued on our path ahead, refusing myself even a tilt of my head in Imogen's direction. Out of the corner of my eye, I saw her nodding her approval as we passed and was filled with a new sense of purpose. She loved me and got me out of this damn place when I needed it. She had protected me repeatedly, and I was honored to be making her proud.

We halted in front of the large doors that led to the throne room and I was reminded of the first time I stood there. I was a scared girl then, unsure who I was or where I belonged. That wasn't who I was now, and I would ensure the king beyond those walls knew it. After a moment, the leading guards pulled the doors open, and we entered.

The guards slowed our pace in an attempt to stir fear within us. It was meant to give us the sense that we were walking to our death—prey to be slaughtered. Except I wasn't afraid. I was to be the queen of my own kingdom and wouldn't bow to men lesser than me. He may have technically outranked me, but I held four Gifts, and he was a lying, manipulative coward.

I looked around the throne room as we slowly walked to the dais. Unlike the last time I had been formally brought here, there wasn't a soul present. Not even King Perceval's trusted advisors seemed to be making an appearance for this presentation of bullshit. Perceval's eyes drifted to me and the shadows that flowed behind effortlessly. His grip on his throne tightened infinitesimally, and I smirked in response, loving how much my Gift pissed him off. Was it because I possessed the Dark Kingdom's magic, or that he couldn't take it for himself now that I knew it existed in my veins?

We stopped feet away from the dais, and the king jerked his chin to dismiss the guards, clearly not wanting witnesses for whatever was about to happen. Boots on marble echoed around the space, and the moment the door slammed shut, a familiar serpentine smile crept up King Perceval's face. His eyes were the same cold emerald from my memories but didn't hold the element of fear they once possessed over me.

"Ainsley," the king said with a false sense of sincerity.

"Your Majesty," I replied, not deeming to give him the respect of a bow, though Felix did. Perceval clocked my choice, and his smile grew wider as he descended the dais. Felix tensed beside me, caught between displaying his loyalty to the King of Caelum and his friendship with me.

"I'm so glad you are safe and back with us. We were all so very worried about you—Dashiell especially," the king replied, stopping a foot away. I swallowed as I broke eye contact the moment he mentioned his son.

"I'm happy I made it home," I told him, choosing my words carefully. "Though I'm not going to pretend I'm okay with being fed lies for months by you and the prince."

King Perceval shook his head and placed his hand over his heart as a sign of remorse—a display I saw right through. My magic stirred within its cage, though it was a different sense of demand than before. It was a snake, coiling itself up, ready to strike in a calculated and deadly way. Whereas with Dashiell, it was a violent demand that I feared would tear him to shreds when it made contact. Why wouldn't it direct that rage to the man before me now?

"My dear, it was done to protect you—you must know that. I had a promise to fulfill to your father and did what I thought was right at the time. Though now I realize I should have gone about it a different way, and for that, I'm sorry. Please forgive me," King Perceval said, grabbing my hand to place in his. I bit my sharp tongue and swallowed the bile that crept up my throat at his unwelcome touch. I could feel Felix's heart beat anxiously in his chest as he watched the encounter.

Closing my eyes, I breathed deeply and forced myself to think of the man I loved instead, focusing on his grey eyes and the unwavering faith he always had in me.

"Thank you for the apology, Your Majesty, but I'm afraid it's not as simple as forgiving and moving on," I replied. The king nodded.

"Of course, it isn't, my dear, and I don't expect you to forget what was done to you. You're hurt, and I can see that. Trust has been broken, and I know only time will mend it. I just hope you're open to the possibility of reestablishing that trust," he said.

I pulled my hand from him, careful not to yank it away quickly though there was nothing I desired more at that moment. He let my fingers slip from between his hands as his gaze stayed firmly locked on mine, neither of us willing to be the first to look away.

"We'll see," I finally said, raising my chin.

King Perceval chuckled under his breath as he stepped back, creating much-needed distance between us. Felix relaxed his shoulders slightly at the move, and I shot my Empathi Gifts toward my friend, wrapping myself around him to show that I was okay.

"Still as stubborn as you've always been, I see," Perceval joked, the statement meant to be lighthearted but instead sounding irritable.

"Months apart wasn't going to change that, Your Majesty," I replied, fixing a sweet smile on my face.

"Clearly not," he said, his mask of sincerity slipping slightly before he forced another smile. "We have much to discuss, but I'm sure you're exhausted from your journey."

The king snapped his fingers, and the sound rang loudly around us, amplified by magic. The door creaked open and a set of guards pushed their way through and headed for us.

"Why don't you retire, and we can talk more over dinner? Your room is the same as before," he said, taking control of the situation. I didn't want to put off the conversation for hours, but I couldn't deny that a part of me needed to get my head together and regroup. I hadn't expected being back in Caelum to affect me the way it had, and after the moment with Dashiell earlier, I needed some space.

I nodded before turning on my heel to follow the guards out with Felix at my side when the king's voice cut through.

"Felix," he said, his voice thick with command. "A word." I tensed at the request.

"I need him to assist me," I interjected, reaching for Felix's hand to pull him along.

"No," King Perceval said forcefully. "You don't."

My friend tugged out of my grip and returned to the king, following his order.

"Felix," I said, letting the command of a queen drip into my tone, but my friend didn't move. He stood at King Perceval's side, refusing to budge an inch. I shook my head as I turned and stormed out, leaving the two men alone.

The door shut, and the lock clicked behind me the moment I was dumped inside my room. So, I guess I was being kept as a prisoner then, though I couldn't fault them on that decision. I *had* held a dagger to their prince's throat not even an hour ago. I scanned the room slowly, noting that everything was the same as the last morning I had been in here.

Empty vials of Felix and Dashiell's hangover tonic sat on the night table next to a pile of dried-up rose petals. The only thing that seemed to be different was the bed. It was unmade, the sheets lying in a messy heap, though I could have sworn Imogen had made it the morning I had left.

I ventured to the vanity and reached into my pocket, running my thumb over the deep orange gemstone just as I used to. The peridot necklace Dashiell had given me lay delicately next to the pair of amethyst earrings I'd loved so much. They weren't put away with care but rather positioned haphazardly as if I'd set them down in haste. Taking a deep breath, I pulled the flame bracelet from my pocket and laid it beside the necklace that had belonged to Dashiell's mother. I had no use for it anymore and hadn't since I found out who I truly was. As I released the bracelet, my fingers brushed over a small velvet box. My pulse quickened as I remembered the contents. Slowly, I flipped open the lid, revealing the delicate ring that lay inside. Before I could stop myself, I plucked the ring from the box and closed my eyes as my thoughts drifted back to when Dashiell had given it to me.

It was the middle of the night—our last one together—and Dashiell had woken me by gently kissing along my spine. I rolled onto my side to find him holding a blue velvet box as deep in color as his eyes. He smiled softly at me before opening the lid and removing a small ring. On the top of the thin gold band sat a round sapphire stone with tiny diamonds that created a halo surrounding it.

Dashiell grabbed my left hand and slid the ring into place on my finger as he explained the significance of the piece. Like the necklace he had given me, this too had belonged to his mother, but not in the same sense. This ring wasn't just an ordinary item of jewelry she owned but rather an heirloom passed down through the generations of her family. It was something Dashiell explained she had never taken off except to give it to him once she had gotten sick. Her instructions had been clear. This ring was to be given only to the person who held his heart. Not his *betrothed* and not his *wife*. Those titles didn't equal love, and his mother knew that.

The sapphire ring wasn't what I would be given the day we were married. That ring was a strategically chosen item to signify Caelum's wealth and my new status as royalty. The dainty blue stoned ring that sat delicately on my finger meant more than that wedding ring ever would. It symbolized my love for the man kneeling beside me and the unspoken promise I'd make to his mother by wearing it. It wasn't oversized and gaudy like the emerald King Perceval selected for the ceremony. It was modest and timeless, elegant and pure. It was perfect.

I hated taking it off, but I wanted to have our own private ceremony in the comfort of our room after the formal celebration. I wanted the chance to ex-change rings and our own vows rather than only declare our commitment to each other using a prewritten script meant to appease our audience.

A lump formed in my throat as I remembered how his mother's request had brought me to tears. As I remembered how I accepted the ring and the responsi-bility of caring for the man who had given it to me. As I accepted the ownership of Dashiell's heart.

I placed the ring back in its box and shut the lid with an audible snap. I didn't want to think about how much I had loved him. There was no going back to how we were, so there was no point in remembering the feelings I once held. He had betrayed me, and that's all I needed to focus on.

The latch to the door clicked, and I spun around in time to see Imogen scold two guards for being *ridiculous* with their choice to lock me up. Little did she know just how wise they were for it. Our eyes met, but rather than give in to the impulse of rushing toward one another, we held strong, waiting until the door fully shut before sprinting.

We wrapped our arms around each other and slid to the floor as we wept. I inhaled her cinnamon and honey scent as I held her close, feeling like I was about to burst from happiness. Imogen pulled back, cupping my face in her hands as her tears streamed down her cheeks.

"My sweet girl," she said, brushing away the moisture from my eyes. "I've missed having your pain in the ass around here." I laughed through the sobs as I shook my head.

"You've just missed having someone to gossip to," I told her, and she smiled wide.

"That's all you were ever good for, anyway."

We laughed through the tears, hugging each other like we feared the other would be ripped away too soon. This moment with her made every second spent in Caelum again worth it. Once we had settled enough to form coherent sentences without the tears, she stood and led us to the bed to sit.

"Tell me everything," she said, squeezing my hand in hers, and I nodded.

"I will," I replied, holding her gaze in my own. "But first, I want to say this: thank you. Thank you so much for what you did to save me." Imogen reached forward, placing my cheeks between her hands.

"Always, my girl. I'm so proud of you."

68.

I sat uncomfortably at a table too long for just the four of us. The settings were exquisite gold, and the florals were too outlandish for such an informal occasion. Imogen and I had spent hours in my room, going over what happened from the moment I left Caelum until the second I left the throne room today. I told her what I had learned about my parents and each of my Gifts before rambling about my new family and the man that I loved. She seemed intrigued by Evander. My stomach had tightened over whether or not she would approve of him, though I knew she would.

When a servant interrupted our conversation to inform us that dinner would begin shortly, I left immediately, wanting to be the first to arrive. As I made it to the doors, it seemed Felix had the same idea, already waiting outside them. He didn't offer to divulge what happened between him and King Perceval, and I didn't ask. It wasn't a safe place to discuss it anyway. That debrief of information would have to take place late at night when we knew we were alone.

The two of us sat quietly at the table while waiting for the other company to join us. The way this conversation flowed would dictate the course of action we needed to take to move forward. We could plan all we wanted—and we had—but nothing was set in stone, and we needed to be flexible and think on our feet if something seemed awry.

The doors opened, and a single set of footsteps approached. I knew without looking that it was Dashiell, his movements more graceful and stoic than that of his boisterous father. Dashiell sat opposite me, though his eyes were firmly on his childhood friend. Felix met his gaze, and I could see the tension as I felt the pain radiating from them. They both opened their mouths to speak, but before they could, King Perceval entered, stomping his way to the table. I rolled my eyes at the obvious power move and straightened in my chair as I prepared myself for the hell this dinner would be.

"Before we get started with the meal," King Perceval began as he walked to the seat across from Felix. I had assumed he would sit at the head of the table, but it seemed like we were keeping up the ruse of familial informality. "I think we should put all of our cards on the table and get through the unpleasantries so we can make an effort to move on."

I briefly wondered how long he had rehearsed those lines but then decided I didn't care. I leaned back in my chair and crossed my arms over my chest as I settled in. The king took that as my acceptance of his terms and pushed on.

"As I told you earlier, I realize how wrong I was to go about things the way I did. I let my loyalty to your father cloud my judgment and made an error," King Perceval said, and I clenched my jaw at his statement. I didn't like that he was using lies about his friendship with my father to try and manipulate me once again. This time though, it wouldn't work. "But I take it you've been told a different story," he guessed, reading my tense posture.

I leaned forward, unraveling my arms and placing them in my lap. I sensed my hostility toward him was wearing his patience thin. I wasn't sure how much more I could push him.

"I was told that you murdered them," I said, reaching for my goblet.

I brought it to my mouth before putting it back down and dropping a small tablet Sirona had supplied me with into the cup. I watched the powder fizzle and then dissolve, keeping the contents the same shade of red it had been before, indicating no poisons were present. Dashiell and King Perceval watched me intently as I smiled.

"Just making sure," I told them before bringing the wine to my lips to drink. Dashiell's jaw clenched, and the king's eyes hardened as I put the cup back down. "And after you murdered them, you took and hid me so you could steal my magic when I came of age."

Dashiell tensed as he looked from me to his father. King Perceval rested his forearms on the table and shook his head in disbelief.

"That's a lie," he warned, seeming offended that I would claim such a thing. "I loved your father as if he were my own flesh and blood."

"They said you once had, but then betrayed him," I added.

"Why would I do that?" the king asked, and I didn't answer because I couldn't. I still hadn't figured out if he had plans for some bigger purpose or if he'd done it simply because he was jealous of my father. "Tell me this, my dear, if I truly wanted to use you for my gain, why wouldn't I have just forced you to marry *me* instead of my son? Why wouldn't I have just Entwined you with myself the moment you turned twenty-one? Their lies do not make sense," he finished as I nodded, taking a deep breath. I looked at Felix, and he gave me a subtle nod, encouraging me to continue.

"And you didn't know I was from Tenebrae?" I asked Dashiell. He shook his head at once, seeming shocked that I was even addressing him.

"I swear to the Gods, Ainsley, I had no idea. All I knew for certain was that you were a product of Conjoining," Dashiell explained, the words coming out rushed like he was afraid I would cut him off at any moment. "I only just found out about your Gift today," he added, throwing a furious glare at his father. For whatever reason, I believed him, though it didn't diminish his schemes to steal my magic to begin with.

"I chose not to tell Dashiell of your parentage because it did not matter where you were from. All that mattered was that your existence was against our laws. I feared that knowing you hailed from Tenebrae would alter his feelings for you, and I couldn't risk him refusing to Entwine with you because of that," King Perceval explained, and Dashiell shifted in his seat.

For the first time, I could see the doubt working in his mind as he listened to his father. Rather than call him out on it, he directed his gaze to Felix, but I didn't dare draw attention to it. If Felix could get a read on whether Dashiell knew where Oberon's army was hiding or what Caelum's involvement was in the war, we were one step closer to stopping him.

"Speaking of parentage," the king began. "We need to discuss yours. I know your Gift as a Shadow Shifter by your blatant display of it when you entered my palace, but I'm curious about your second gift. What did your father bestow upon you, my dear?"

I leaned forward, resting my forearms on the table just as he was, and reached out my Gift. I was met with a dark forest of thorns, prodding and tearing at my magic as it attempted to enter. The king smiled wickedly as he felt me.

"Ah, another Empathi in our court," he said, and I offered a tight smile as Dashiell leaned back in his chair, looking frantically from me to his father. He shook his head to himself as if denying the evidence in front of him before turning to face his father.

"She's not from Caelum at all?" he demanded. "You lied to me. You—"

"I never said she was," the king finished harshly. "And you'll do well to remember who you're calling a liar. I may be your father, but I am also your king."

I watched Dashiell slink into his seat and scrub his hands over his face. He really had no clue about who I truly was. His father had kept him in the dark nearly as much as he had me.

"I'm curious what other lies King Evander has whispered into your ear," King Perceval mused, swirling his wine glass absentmindedly before taking a sip. My heart raced, and I squeezed my hands into fists in my lap at the mere mention of Evander's name. Every instinct in my body screamed that this king meant to do him harm which sent my blood boiling in response.

"Many, I'm sure," I lied, forcing the words to come out as evenly as possible as my magic clawed at its cage. "Why else do you think I came back?"

"I take it by the dagger you held to Dashiell's throat that it wasn't for my son," he replied.

"No," I answered honestly, and Dashiell nodded to himself as his stare stayed fixed on his lap, keeping the hands he was undoubtedly clenching out of view. "I returned to learn the truth, and now that I have, it seems like I have a decision to make. Either I stay here in Caelum or go back to Tenebrae."

"Why would you dare to return to the people who fed you such lies?" King Perceval questioned curiously.

"Revenge," I answered, and the king's smile grew. "If they are responsible for my parents' deaths, then they deserve to pay for that crime—and I won't stop until I collect."

My magic swirled as the bloodlust began to slip into my system, begging me to take what I had come for. Felix reached his Gift out to calm the hungry thoughts, but I struck at him, sharp and quick, before he could infiltrate me. He jerked back and clutched his chest from the internal pain I had inflicted.

"Don't do it again," I said to Felix as the king's eyes sparkled with joy.

"While I applaud your desire to avenge your family, my dear, taking on an entire kingdom by yourself won't accomplish anything, I'm afraid," King Perceval replied.

"It won't be by myself. You'll help me take Tenebrae," I answered, and he laughed loudly as if I had just told him the most amusing joke he'd ever heard. I sat still, keeping my face even and not letting a single emotion slip through.

"Why would I do that?" he asked through deep laughter. "Your father was my best friend, but I can't risk my entire kingdom to take the life of those responsible for his death, however much I may want to."

I leaned back in my chair as I observed the man before me. His arrogance had me envisioning clotting the blood in his body and moving it to his throat so he choked on it. Then I would craft a sword and pierce his heart before severing his head from his body in slow, jagged movements. I wouldn't make it clean. He didn't deserve that.

"You'll do it because Tenebrae is mine," I said simply, and the king tilted his head as the last of his laughter subsided.

"Just because you hail from a kingdom does not make it yours to rule," Perceval answered, and a sly smile formed on my face as I sat straighter and held his intense gaze.

"Maybe not," I replied. "But it does if you're the heir."

Dashiell sat forward, shaking his head in disbelief as Felix shifted uncomfortably. I didn't like that we hadn't discussed dropping this news tonight, but I had to think as we went. It needed to be done to further our plan.

"So, the rumors are true then?" King Perceval marveled as his eyes dragged up and down my body as they always had done. I internally cringed at the gesture, now knowing exactly why he did it. He wasn't drawn to my body, but rather what he'd always known ran through it.

"What rumors?!" Dashiell demanded, slamming his hand down on the table in fury. "What else have you known that you didn't tell me?!"

"What I do and do not choose to inform you is none of your business," his father said.

"It is when it comes to *her*!" Dashiell yelled, pointing across the table to me.

The king and prince rose from their seats in anger, but before either of them could continue the argument, Dashiell stumbled back a step, his movements becoming lethargic and clumsy as if he were drunk or sleepy. I turned my gaze toward Felix to find his hand outstretched towards his friend as he pushed his magic into him to protect the king.

"Sit down, Dash," Felix said gently as Dashiell gripped the chair for support before falling into it, and my friend nodded toward the king before lowering his hand back into his lap. King Perceval straightened his jacket and looked over his only son with such disgust that it had my shadows curling around my fingers under the table. It wasn't because I wanted to defend Dashiell, but rather that I hated the sense of superiority the king held over everyone. He had lied to Dashiell, and because of that, his son had lost everyone he loved.

"I had heard from a source in Venator that King Evander had been flaunting around his newly discovered heir—a woman, no less—by the name of Ainsley. Imagine my surprise when I heard they were looking for reinforcements to help their cause against some supposed threat to Disparya," King Perceval claimed. "If those rumors are true, then it seems that you weren't captured as we were led to believe, and instead of coming home, you traveled far and wide with your new friends."

Felix shifted next to me and reached out his Gift in a gentle brush against me—a silent request. Reluctantly, I let him in because I knew that despite my best efforts, I wouldn't be able to control my anger now that we were getting into the topic of

Evander. My instincts would take over, wanting to defend the man I loved—the other half of my soul.

"I *was* taken from Caelum by a group from Tenebrae, but I chose to stay when they offered to bring me back," I admitted, remembering to keep my lies as close to the truth as possible.

Dashiell stood again, though it didn't seem to be in anger this time. Instead, he backed away from the table and began pacing as he listened, unable to sit still.

"After learning the truth about the tea and possessing magic, I didn't want to return. I was hurt, angry, and confused. I didn't know who I could trust, except for Felix—and even then, our relationship was fractured," I explained, and the king nodded along, fully engrossed in my story. "When I found out that I had a second Gift from Tenebrae, King Evander seemed entirely too pleased by it, and I instantly felt like he had an ulterior motive. I couldn't place what gave me that idea, but something told me there was more going on with the situation than he was willing to divulge."

I forced myself to go back to those first few weeks with him and the lack of trust I had. I was right to suspect that he kept things from me, but it wasn't what I had expected. Little did I know then that he was aware of who I was to him and the bond we shared.

"He wanted me to assist him in his efforts. I agreed because I wanted to figure out what he was playing at and why he needed me to accomplish it. The only way I could learn the truth was to stay as close to him as I could. And I won't pretend I didn't want to learn more about my magic and how to wield it. King Evander was willing to have me taught, and I took him up on that offer," I said, exhaling a deep breath as I finished.

"What is your other Gift?" King Perceval asked, not seeming to care about any of the information I shared besides that fact.

Of course.

"May I?" I asked, holding out my palm. King Perceval nodded and lowered his mental defenses just enough for me to slip into his mind. I held out my palm and twisted my fingers, allowing a large ornate goblet to appear before him. Dashiell sucked in a breath at the illusion as well. I wasn't originally going to let him see this one, but there was no harm in giving him this small taste of what he would have stolen from me.

The king looked over the object, inspecting all of the bright jewels encrusted into the sides of the cup. The image flickered before us, and I pushed more into the illusion, making it clearer again. The king slowly reached out a hand to touch the cup, but his fingers went right through, grasping nothing but air, and he chuckled under his breath.

"Magnificent, my dear. Illusios are quite rare, but it seems the Gods have blessed you," King Perceval said, still marveling at the cup.

"So it would seem," I replied, twisting my fingers once more and releasing the hold on their minds as I pulled my magic back into me. "So, do I have your assistance in taking Tenebrae?"

King Perceval bobbed his head back and forth as he leaned back in his chair, making a show of trying to decide.

"No," he finally said, and I stood at once, done with these games.

"Fine. Then Felix and I will leave in the—" I began but was quickly cut off.

"No," Felix said under his breath, and I twisted to look at him. His eyes were soft and pleading, his voice a gentle plea. "I'm not going back with you, Ainsley."

I narrowed my eyes at my friend as my features filled with confusion. What the hell was he talking about? I opened and closed my mouth several times as I tried to come up with something to say.

"Tenebrae isn't my home—you know this. You know how hard it's been for me there," he reasoned. "I did what I went there to do, and now that's over."

"What is that supposed to mean?" I asked, a cold bite entering my tone.

Felix closed his eyes and took a deep breath before rising from his chair to face me fully. He held his hand out for me to take, but my instincts told me not to touch him. I glanced at his offering before crossing my arms in a clear refusal.

"I went with you to make sure you were safe, but that wasn't the entire reason," he started, and my heart dropped. "We've been kept from Tenebrae for decades, and I saw it as our only opportunity to get inside and learn what had been kept from us—from *all* the kingdoms."

I shook my head, refusing to believe what he was telling me. My attention darted around the room and landed on the three sets of eyes watching my every movement. My breathing came quick as I struggled to keep calm and silence the screaming in my head.

"You used me," I breathed, not hiding the emotion thick in my voice. Felix shook his head as he reached for me just as he had done that first time in Tenebrae, but I recoiled, taking several steps back from him.

"It wasn't like that, Ainsley. You're my best friend, and I love you—of course, I wanted to keep you safe, but..." He stole a glance at the king before setting his eyes on me again. "But I swore an oath long before I met you. I have a duty to this kingdom, and if I can collect information that will keep the people of it safe, then I will do what it takes to ensure that happens."

My control loosened, and my Empathi Gifts surged out of me, reaching the three men in the room and showing them precisely what betrayal felt like. I quickly pulled back, trying to recover from my stumble, but it was too late. They had already witnessed my hurt.

"Ainsley," Felix whispered gently as his eyes misted over. "Please."

"You lied to me—*again*. After promising me you wouldn't. You watched me break and shatter into a million pieces and held me as I cried over *him*!" I yelled, pointing across the table to Dashiell, and Felix jerked back like the verbal blow was worse than any physical attack I could have dealt. I didn't bother to hide the tears that escaped. They already knew how much I was hurting, so there was no point. "What about Oli, Felix?" I croaked, and Felix swallowed as if the thought of the man he claimed to love caused him pain.

"He's King Evander's right hand. Why do you think I had my sights set on him from the beginning?" he admitted quietly as if ashamed by that fact. I wobbled back a step before leaning forward to grip the table for support. I let each confession rock through me, filling my mind and breaking my heart.

"So all I ever was to you was something for you to use as you saw fit—a pawn for your fucking game?!" I growled, letting my shadows spill from my hands.

"No!" he interjected, pushing his magic out to reach me, but I cut it down before he got close. Felix stumbled from the blow but quickly recovered, holding his hands in defense. "You're my friend, Ainsley!"

"Friends don't fucking lie over and over again!" I yelled, aiming my shadows for him just as I had that first night, but fire erupted between us before they could reach him, and I recoiled back from the flames.

"That is enough," King Perceval announced, rising from the table and distinguishing his fire magic with a flick of his wrist. "Felix is a member of my counsel and—"

"Clearly!" I spat, though the words were aimed at the traitor I called my best friend. He made to step towards me again, arms outstretched as a tear streamed down his cheek, his amber eyes glistening with hurt. "Come near me and I won't be stopped this time," I warned, wrapping myself in shadow again. Felix stopped and lowered his hands.

"Felix," King Perceval said. "I think it best you preoccupy yourself somewhere else for the time being."

Felix nodded, though his eyes never left mine like he was still trying to reach me. I clenched my jaw as I broke his stare and found Dashiell watching the exchange intently—his face an unreadable mask. Once Felix had departed the room, King Perceval cleared his throat in irritation as he set his intense glare on me.

"You are a guest in my home, my dear. Though you may be the Heir to Tenebrae, you'll do well to remember that I am a king. You currently cannot wield the power of a kingdom, so I suggest you learn your place amongst mine if you seek my help," the king said. I turned to him.

"So you *will* help me then?"

"Perhaps. I need to know the reward is worth the price of war, and the only way I can see that being the case is if I take over Tenebrae. I'm supplying the forces and the lives that will be spent, so I deserve the largest share of the prize," King Perceval said with a smile.

"No," I ground out. "Tenebrae is mine by birthright. I am set to rule, and it will not be taken from me."

"Then it seems we are at an impasse." King Perceval sighed dramatically as he reached for his wine, taking another long sip.

I swallowed, trying to grasp what my next move could be. What could I give to him that would satisfy his need for power? In no world would I ever offer my magic or full reign of my kingdom. I couldn't even lie to gain what I wanted because he would likely make me sign some magic binding contract. There had to be something else I could dangle in front of him. My eyes drifted to Dashiell, and I took a deep breath before opening my mouth to relay my offer.

"I'll marry Dashiell," I said, raising my chin high. "But he stays in Caelum, and I get to keep Tenebrae to myself. You'll have the alliance you want and, one day, heirs."

Perceval smiled devilishly as he looked back and forth between myself and his son while contemplating my offer.

"Not good enough. How can I trust that you're true to your word in our alliance without having control over Tenebrae?" he asked, and I clenched my jaw.

"Fine. I'll marry Dashiell, and he will come to Tenebrae and rule as my *consort*. Caelum will have a foot in my kingdom, but I maintain primary control over it. The three of us must agree upon any momentous decisions from this moment forward before the plans can be carried out. If we cannot come to a unanimous decision, the majority will rule.

"Deal," King Perceval said immediately, extending his hand for me to take.

"Absolutely not!" Dashiell sneered, rising from his chair before I could shake his father's hand. "I am not marrying you under these fucking circumstances, Ainsley."

"What's wrong, Dashiell? Don't like being the pawn in someone else's game?" I asked sweetly before taking his father's hand in mine.

"I don't agree to this bullshit," Dashiell said under his breath as he leaned over the table to direct his anger at me.

"Too bad. Two out of the three of us do—and that's a majority, dear fiancé."

Dashiell's face twisted in rage, and thunder crashed outside as a storm rolled in from his fury. He shook his head in disbelief, looking between his father and me as if it would somehow erase our deal.

"Don't do this," he whispered, and his eyes filled with the familiar pain they now always seemed to hold, but I didn't respond as I pulled away from his father.

The king rubbed his hands together as his face lit with a bright and devious smile, pure joy emanating from his hateful heart. He looked at me triumphantly, as if he had finally won everything he had sought for so long.

"We will seek our vengeance for their lives together, my dear," he announced like he could make me believe his bullshit excitement wasn't over his power trip. "When I slay King Evander, it will be in your father's name," he added.

"No," I forced between clenched teeth, and the iron cage my magic was sealed in began to crack, creating tiny fissures along the exterior. The king furrowed his brows at my outburst, and I quickly clarified. "Evander is *mine*. If any harm comes to him, it'll be at my own hand."

"Of course," the king replied, and I nodded.

"We can discuss our plans in more detail another night," I said, backing away from the table.

I needed to leave before anything else could be said. King Perceval needed to believe he held all the cards because that was our only chance in hopes he let his guard down. There was still much work to be done, and I needed to desperately find those stones, though with Felix making his loyalties known, it seemed like I would have to hunt them on my own.

"Oh, and Your Majesty?" I called once I reached the threshold of the door. He looked up from his seat with eager anticipation, and I smirked.

One by one, the dinner settings began to disappear before their eyes slowly. Each golden utensil and then plate flickered before fading away into nothing. Dashiell and King Perceval stood at once as they surveyed the area with wide eyes and shocked expressions. Next, the linen tablecloth was gone, followed by the floral arrangements, dissolving from existence one petal at a time. Everything began to disappear until nothing was left except a plain wooden table and four golden goblets.

"Don't ever underestimate what I'm capable of again," I said evenly before slipping from the room and leaving the men to deal with what had occurred.

It was supposed to be an exercise in control to ensure I could do what I set out to, but after King Perceval decided to insult my magic potential, I couldn't pass up the opportunity to see the look on his imperious face when I showed him just what I could do. Doubting me would be the worst decision he would ever make.

69.

I stirred in bed, feeling a presence that caused me to wake. I had loosed my shadows to swirl around my room and detect anyone who may have wished me harm, but they hadn't notified me someone was there. My shadows disappeared, and my Empathi Gift reached out, picking up on subtle emotional changes in the atmosphere. I cracked open an eye and found Dashiell sitting across the room in the armchair he used to frequent so long ago. His forearms rested on his thighs, and his head hung low in dejection. What was he doing here, and why hadn't my Gift alerted me he had come?

I pushed myself to a sitting position and placed beside me the large fluffy black stuffed wolf I had my arms wrapped around. I couldn't create my own life-size Evander, so his overbearing pet was the next obvious choice. I ached as I thought of Onyx and Nova and how I longed for the four of us to be reunited again. But more than anything, I wanted to be wrapped in Evander's arms, safe and home.

"What do you want, Dashiell?" I drawled, rolling my neck before resting my back against the headboard. I twisted my fingers in my lap, letting my shadows spool around them. I should have locked them away for their incompetence, but I loved them too much to keep them hidden for long. I'd have to figure out some other form of security to keep unwelcome guests from entering while I slept.

"It's just Dash," he said under his breath, and I scoffed.

"Maybe to your friends, but that's not what we are."

"No, we're not. We're more than that, Ainsley," he claimed, picking his head up to look at me. His eyes were red-rimmed, and his hair was a mess—his strands disheveled like he'd run his hand through them repeatedly.

"Not anymore. You saw to that," I replied harshly.

It pissed me off that he just assumed I'd hold him in the same regard as before. Things were clearly different, and he needed to let go of the hope that that would change. Instead, he turned his cheek, focusing his gaze out of the open window that overlooked the gardens. The same one I had peered down at him through on my first day in Caelum. A muscle feathered in his jaw as if he remembered the same thing—the moment he had claimed he fell in love with me. Dashiell stood and walked slowly to the window. He kept his back toward me, and I knew it was meant as a way for him to keep his composure.

"I swear I didn't know anything that was disclosed tonight," he said, setting his eyes on the dark horizon. There was deep honesty in his voice, but it wasn't needed. The look on his face at that table told me he was learning everything about me for the first time.

"That doesn't change anything," I told him, and he nodded.

"I know," he whispered and it sounded like the words had caught in his throat. "I just wanted you to know."

He placed his palm flat on the vanity. To anyone else it would look as though he was just switching his position—getting settled, more comfortable—but I knew his tells. I knew the subtle shifts in his body when he was feeling anxious or fearful. I knew that the placement of his hand wasn't one of nonchalance but rather a way to steady himself. He was struggling. And I didn't care. I *couldn't* care.

My shadows changed direction around my hands and instead started making their way toward him. Most likely because they sensed his weakness and knew it was the perfect time to strike and claim our revenge. I called them home, pulling each tendril back beneath the surface of my skin. When I looked back up, Dashiell was no longer staring out the window. His head was slightly angled and his gaze locked on the items strewn across my vanity. I had packed away the amethyst earrings Imogen had given me for my birthday, but I left the presents from Dashiell out.

Taking a deep breath, he turned to leave. But before he could, I called out.

"Take them," I commanded. Dashiell froze on the spot as if paralyzed by my request. His head swiveled to look and me and then his mother's necklace, the flame gemstone bracelet, and the heirloom sapphire ring. He walked back to the vanity and extended his hand toward the items, but a second before he could claim them, he closed his fist around open air and returned his hand to his side. Dashiell shook his head as his stare sought mine.

"They aren't mine," he said quietly.

"I don't want them," I replied, fighting an ache in my chest I didn't understand.

Dashiell's shoulders sagged, and he looked utterly deflated. Exhausted. *Defeated*. His throat worked, and his brow pinched—an expression I knew meant the gears in his mind were turning as he tried to formulate a way to turn thought into spoken words. His hand gestured to the pieces on the vanity table, but his misted-over eyes never tore from mine.

"Those were presents," he said, referring to the necklace and bracelet. "And that..." Dashiell twisted slightly so his focus was on the ring given to him by his mother. He swallowed hard, and I could feel the heartbreak radiating from him in heavy, crushing waves. "I did as she asked." Dashiell's piercing blue eyes bore into me as he spoke his next words. "These items are yours. Keep them, destroy them, let them collect dust. Do with them what you will. They don't belong to me."

"That ring should be kept in your family," I argued. He turned and made his way through the dimly lit room to the exit.

"I honored my mother's request. It no longer belongs to me." Dashiell opened the creaking door slowly, hesitating on the threshold as he took a deep breath. "I'm sorry, Ainsley," he said, looking over his shoulder at me with such hope in his eyes.

I held his gaze for a long moment, trying to decide on how or whether to respond. I could pretend to grant him my forgiveness and then use him for my gain like he tried to do to me. But would that have made me any better than he was if I did that? Did I care? In the end, honesty won, and I spoke with the part of my heart he hadn't tainted.

"Don't come in here again, Dashiell. There isn't anything left for you."

He closed his eyes and left my room. The moment the door clicked shut, I grabbed my stuffed Onyx and rolled back to my side as I closed my eyes and fought the searing pain in my chest. I clutched my soft stuffed wolf and imagined I was home with the man I loved and not in my enemy's house.

Three days had come and gone, and I spent most of that time in my room or the library, though I didn't dare set foot near the Sanctuary. I knew full well I wouldn't be able to handle the emotions of seeing the place that held so many memories for me. Imogen had helped me comb through the books I had smuggled into my room to research without the prying eyes of the residents, all of whom seemed to be deathly afraid of me. Even Rosella had steered clear of my presence though I had caught her watching me with interest as I returned to my room the other day.

Despite our best efforts, we couldn't find even one book that referenced any of the stones my family and I were under the impression King Perceval possessed. The only other place I could think to search was his Council Room, but Perceval was rarely ever not locked away behind its walls, planning his complete domination of our continent. I had four days left and felt no closer to accomplishing our goal, and I couldn't return to Tenebrae empty-handed. I was our one chance to get ahead for once and prevent more lives from being lost, and I refused to fail.

I rounded the corner to the corridor that held the king's Council Room. Perhaps I could knock on his door and come up with an excuse as to why I needed to see him. If he let me enter, I could scope out my surroundings and maybe spy something useful to us—better yet, perhaps I would locate one of the stones.

"What are you doing?" Felix asked from behind before I made it within ten feet of the room. I whirled around to face him, not hiding the disgust that washed over my features.

"It's none of your business," I replied, and Felix shook his head.

"Ainsley, I know you're angry, but—"

"*Angry* doesn't begin to cover what I feel," I snapped, raising my voice a little too loudly and causing bystanders to glance at the scene. Whatever. It was no secret that Felix and I weren't speaking anymore. I hadn't even seen him since our dinner when he announced his own motives for coming with me to Tenebrae.

"You have every right to feel upset, Ainsley, but you won't even try to see things from my point of view. Maybe if you did, you wouldn't be so pissed off," Felix huffed in irritation.

"You think I wouldn't be upset if I heard you out?" I asked incredulously, stepping towards him. I was vaguely aware of the crowd that had begun to form around us and one person in particular who joined in to watch. Dashiell crept closer to Felix and me as I pointed my finger into his best friend's chest. "Did you have other motives for coming to Tenebrae?"

"Yes, but—"

"Did you lie to me?" I continued.

"Yes."

"And did you choose to side with the people who betrayed me rather than the person you swore to always protect and care for?"

"Yes," Felix admitted.

"Then there will never be a world where hearing you out will make you anything less than a pathetic coward to me," I promised before shoving past him and then Dashiell as I hurried to my room. The palace residents whispered and pointed as I walked, much like they had the day I arrived, though now they also cowered in fear at the shadows that curved around my limbs as I went.

The moment I reached my bed, I collapsed onto it as my body shook in frustration. The iron cage had cracked again as soon as I sensed Dashiell's presence in that corridor, and this time, my magic began to slip through. The moment I felt it slink from between the confines of its cage, I knew I had to walk away from my altercation with Felix, or else I'd also have a dead prince to deal with.

I closed my eyes and reached out my arms, letting my magic tear from me in a violent wave I could no longer contain. Shadows surged from my body, enveloping the room in darkness as I screamed my anger at the world. Muffled shouts from scared residents echoed in the pounding silence within my mind. My shadows must have slipped beneath my door and spilled into the hallway as

I came undone, shaking the palace from the force of its brutality. I knew this was the only safe place to let it out since Dashiell had never returned after that first night. I had to be within a reasonable distance for my darkness to reach him, and as long as we were safely apart, my magic was free to grow to its full and dangerous potential—and it felt *so* fucking good.

You're my favorite shade of darkness, love.

Evander's silken words drifted through my mind, caressing my soul and filling me with the confidence and determination I needed. I replayed his sweet whispers and gentle kisses as we let our magic out to play—each of our tendrils twisting around each other lovingly. Gods, I wanted to go home.

"Is this really necessary?" Imogen questioned through the darkness, and I smiled, though I knew she couldn't see it.

"You know I love being dramatic," I quipped, calling my magic back into me until every ounce of visible darkness was gone. She strolled over to the bed with a lunch tray and a new stack of books for us to go through. Since I returned, this had been our routine—banter, food, research, repeat.

"I heard about your and Felix's little outburst in the hall," she chirped as I popped a grape into my mouth and tore a piece of bread from the loaf. "The king isn't too happy about it."

"Good," I said absentmindedly.

He had refused my request for a meeting to discuss the terms of our deal, and according to Imogen, each day he consumed his meals in the Council Room, so there was rarely a chance of me ever bumping into him. I began to wonder if showing my strength with illusions was the right choice after all. Maybe my potential scared him enough to back off, though I doubted it. If anything, I'm sure it made him double down on his plans to ensure he wouldn't ever be fooled by anyone again—let alone the woman he was trying so hard to manipulate.

"Promise me you'll be careful," Imogen warned, and the worry in her voice had me diverting my attention to her. "He isn't above harming you."

Her hands trembled in her lap, and I reached for her, steadying them in my own. Her hazel eyes met mine and misted over as she stared at me. I pushed the tray aside and scooted closer to my maiden, reaching out my Empathi Gift on instinct to comfort her. As my magic pushed through, I could feel the terror and pain in her soul. She must have recently gone through something horrible and traumatic to react this way so suddenly.

"Imogen, what happened?" I whispered, and she closed her eyes as a slow trickle of tears spilled out.

"He killed them," she said under her breath, her voice breaking with each word. "The morning I was supposed to visit my mother with my siblings, King Perceval requested I stay back, giving me some bullshit excuse about Tenebrae soldiers being spotted in our lands and how he didn't want to risk my safety."

Oh, dear Gods, no. I was going to be sick.

"And then, days later, he informed me that mercenaries from Tenebrae had slaughtered my entire family," Imogen said through the tears, and I wrapped my arms around her, pulling her tight against me. "He killed them, Ainsley. My mother, my father, my brothers, and my sisters. Every last one of them, he brutally murdered because he knew I helped get you out of Caelum but couldn't prove it. It was just a fucking reminder of what he could do if anyone crossed him."

My blood heated as white-hot rage filled every crevice of my body. My darkness clawed at my skin, and I didn't bother trying to suppress it. I let it free to slither across the floor and envelop everything as I held the woman who lost so much because she had chosen to help me.

"I will kill him for this," I vowed.

"And I will help you do it."

70.

The sun beat down on me relentlessly as my body glistened with sweat while I worked through each training exercise. With only two days left in Caelum and still no sign of the stones, a positive outcome wasn't looking good. If we couldn't figure it out soon, I would leave tomorrow night empty-handed. Hopefully, Imogen would find something in the next set of books she planned to steal from the library today. I considered requesting Evander give me more time, but I knew that answer would be a resounding *no*. We agreed on one week, and that was all he would allow me to have.

"Can I join you?"

I spun around with my sword, thrusting it into my target before crafting two daggers and throwing them across the ring. They flew through the air with deadly aim and sank deep into the other marks I had set up. I drank the air greedily before wiping the sweat from my brow and turning to address Felix.

"I don't see why not, traitor," I replied, flicking my wrist and making all my weapons and targets turn into shadows before they were carried away on the wind.

I rolled my neck and shook out my arms as I limbered myself for the physical fight. The guards surrounding the ring eyed each other skeptically, debating whether to break this up or let it play out. I had made it clear to everyone that I would do what I wanted while here, so they didn't bother to stop me from training, even though it was against Caelum's rules for women to do so.

"Ainsley," Felix started, but I lunged at him before he could say anything more. He stayed on the defensive, only blocking my attacks and never offering any of his own. "Please," he tried again, but I cut him off.

"If you want to talk, you'll have to fight me. If not, then get the fuck out of the ring."

Felix gritted his jaw, clearly unhappy with my ultimatum, but what did he expect? After everything he said to me at dinner, I wouldn't hear him out under any circumstances other than this. I would throw at him the anger I was so well known for.

"I'll fight you," a voice added, and I pushed back from Felix to find Dashiell strolling toward us.

"Dash, I wouldn't," Felix tried, and I glared at him. If Dashiell wanted to challenge me, he should be able to do so.

"If it's the only way she'll let me speak to her, then I'll take my chances in the ring," he replied, pulling his shirt over his head and tossing it away. I noted the change in his body as his muscles flexed with each movement he made. I assessed him carefully as he reached for Felix's sword—a predator studying its prey.

He was bigger than I remembered, his body even more toned than before, and there was a gracefulness in the way he held his sword that I swore was new. He must have spent the past several months crafting his body into the perfect weapon now that he didn't have the distraction of Felix or the task of manipulating me into falling in love with him.

"Are you ready to talk?" Dashiell asked, tossing the hilt of his sword between his hands as he got familiar with the weight and feel of the weapon.

"I'm ready to fight."

"You always are," he replied, and I got the distinct feeling he wasn't referring to the physical sense.

I called forth my shadows and crafted two daggers of my own. I was more skilled with them than the longsword and wanted to show him I wasn't the same scared and helpless girl he once knew.

Dashiell's eyes went wide as he watched my Gift take form, and I wasn't sure if it was from amazement or fear—probably both. Fear for what I could do to him and wonder at the Gift that would have been running through his body had he been successful in his plans.

We circled each other slowly, carefully, each step a calculated move. I kept my grip firm on my weapons as my eyes stayed locked on the prince. The tension hung thick and heavy in the winter air, and I could taste it on my tongue.

"I didn't know the full truth about you," Dashiell started, taking another step to the right, and for some reason, that simple sentence sent me into an unbridled rage.

"You knew enough!" I bellowed.

I sprinted for him at full speed before dropping low and sliding across the ground as I swiped my daggers, hoping to catch him in the legs. Dashiell leapt over me before I could make contact, and I swore under my breath as I twisted around and got back to my feet.

"Ainsley, I—" he tried, but I lunged for him, swinging my daggers hard until his voice was drowned out by clanging metal. "Just listen to me!"

"No!" I yelled back, offering hit after hit until he was forced to use his brute strength to push me off him. "I don't want to hear anything you have to say."

Dashiell's face fell at my declaration, but I couldn't find it in my heart to care. I was too wrapped up in my anger as I looked at him and was forced to relive every painful memory. My skin burned as I felt the phantom touch of his hands on my flesh while he vowed to love me forever, and my stomach churned as my senses were filled with the smell of fresh white roses. Every memory was like a sickness that I wanted to rid myself of.

"This isn't you," Dashiell whispered, and I laughed bitterly.

"What's wrong, Your Highness? You don't like that I'm not pathetic and useless anymore?"

"You were never... That's not what I meant. I—"

I swung at him again, this time nicking his arm and drawing blood. The guards surrounding us straightened as they clutched the weapons at their side, and Dashiell held up a hand to keep them back. But their reaction was nothing compared to what was happening to me on the inside.

My magic banged against its new reinforced iron box so violently that I stumbled back a step. It was like it could smell his blood and demanded I release it so it could finish off the wounded prince. I had weakened him and my magic seemed to want to take full advantage of that, but I couldn't let it. Not yet.

Dashiell looked down at his cut and back to me with curious eyes as he watched my odd behavior. I took several deep breaths as I regained control of myself and my magic.

"Do you not remember us—what we were to each other?" Dashiell asked softly, and my heart broke all over again. Not for him but for the naive girl who gave all of herself only to be left in pieces.

I bared my teeth in a snarl for that girl and attacked again. Dashiell spun, stopping my blow just before I could land one to his back, but I quickly recovered and punched his side. He grunted and stepped away to create space so I couldn't hit him again.

"How fucking dare you," I sneered, clutching my daggers in a death grip. "I will never forget how my heart splintered when I learned what you planned to do to me. I will never be able to forget how your cruelty shattered me completely. How I was a heap on the floor, lying in a puddle of my own tears because I was too fucking broken to move."

Dashiell's face fell, and his eyes widened as they filled with something that resembled shock. He turned to look at Felix for confirmation, and the decision cost him. I threw out my fist, landing a hard punch to his throat and stealing the air from his lungs. Dashiell coughed and gasped as he clutched his neck, but I wasn't done.

"I remember how I spent the night teaching you how to make tea, only for you to poison me with it later," I yelled, kicking him in the ribs. "I remember how you promised to be open and honest with me only to find out you had been lying to me for weeks." I punched Dashiell in the stomach, making him spit blood, but he didn't try to stop me even though we both knew he could. "I remember everything between us all too fucking well, Dashiell. And I will remember the look on your face when I make you pay for everything you did to me," I vowed, but before I could hit him again, he grabbed my wrist, twisting hard and flipping me to my back.

"So that's why you came back," he said, wiping the blood from his lips as he swung his sword down on me. I rolled in the dirt, narrowly missing the hit, and scrambled to my feet. "It had nothing to do with making a deal with my father and everything to do with getting revenge on me."

Yes, but I couldn't admit that out loud. A slight shimmer of a silencing shield caught my eye, and I wondered who had put it in place, but I still couldn't voice my answers to the open air. The direction this conversation was going was too damn risky, and I couldn't partake in it any longer.

"I don't know what you're talking about," I replied, letting my daggers turn back into drifting shadows as I walked toward the edge of the ring. Dashiell grabbed my wrist, spinning me around and placing his sword at my throat a second later.

"Whatever it is you have planned, you need to stop. You're going to get yourself killed," Dashiell said low and flat—a warning, not a request.

My stare fell not to the weapon aimed to kill but to where he touched me. My magic burst from its cage and sped through me in a rush. Panic surged, and I quickly fortified my internal shield for my magic to slam into instead of breaking free from my flesh. It was wild and angry, wanting to enact revenge as my skin sparked beneath Dashiell's hold like he had used his Gift to send a bolt of lightning straight through to me.

I tried to pull out of his touch, but his grip only tightened, keeping me firmly in place as he studied me with narrowed eyes. He leaned closer, and as I was wrapped in the scent of lemongrass and sea salt, I noted the other changes I hadn't before. There weren't just obvious physical markers like the length of his hair or the shade of his eyes; there were more subtle differences as well.

There was an air of frenzied calm about him. Dashiell held himself at a distance, being more cautious and reserved than ever before, but at the same time, I could feel how desperate he was to shed that skin. He moved more gracefully—regal—and the way he spoke was with careful precision. His eyes flittered across my face as if he were reading every intention I had since coming here, like he could sense every step I would take before my mind knew I wanted to. As if he knew *me*.

"You're done here, Ainsley," he whispered, but it sounded more like a plea than a threat.

I observed him for a moment longer before relinquishing my desire to hold back. I could have ended our fight the second he stepped into the ring, but I decided to drag it out to study his moves and see if I could extract information from him. But Dashiell's only concern was talking about us, so that plan went partially down the drain.

I closed the distance between us, not caring that his sword pressed firmer to my throat, and I felt the familiar sting of a blade as a warm trickle of blood ran down my neck. Dashiell's eyes dropped to the wound, and he pulled his hand back slightly, but I didn't stop until our faces were inches apart. I held his blue stare as I let him see the vicious, hard creature all his lies and betrayal had turned me into. He was delusional if he thought I would hear him out and let him say his piece. Nothing was going to excuse his choice to lie to me for weeks.

"I told you never to touch me again," I said coldly, and Dashiell's eyes softened as his fingers unwrapped from my wrist.

The moment I was free, I bent away from his blade and swept out my leg, catching him off balance and sweeping his legs out from under him. In the same breath, I gathered my shadows in my hand and shoved them to his chest as I drove the strength of my Gift into him, slamming him hard to the ground below. His back hit the dirt with a deafening sound of crunching bone, and fissures of earth spidered all around him from the force of my assault.

Out of my periphery, I could see the guards and Felix rush for us, but they were met with a strong, unbreakable shield. This was between Dashiell and me, and I wouldn't have any outside interference. My shadows disappeared without my permission, and the prince coughed and gasped for breath as he clutched his chest, groaning in pain.

I dropped to a crouch beside him, and his sorrowful eyes found mine as he waited patiently for the death he thought I would bring. I called to my magic but found it was reluctant to serve me, fighting me every step of the way as I pulled it from my flesh.

Tendrils of shadow twisted around my fingers as I stared down at the prince who had broken me for his own cause, but I couldn't get them to form to my will. My shadows spun around themselves in a vague shape of what I was trying to mold but never quite doing as I directed, and I was reminded of what it was like when I first started trying to access my magic. Why was my Gift so limited? Did Perceval manage to slip me more poison after all? I thought I had been careful, always testing my food and drink before consuming, but perhaps I'd missed something.

Dashiell watched me struggle, and I quickly closed my fist, not wanting him to see that something was wrong with my magic and take advantage of my misfortune. His brows pinched in curiosity as he met my frightened gaze. I couldn't lose my magic—I wouldn't.

The prince's eyes flickered to the side, and I followed his stare to find his sword lying in the dirt. When I turned back to face him, his features were soft and kind, so much like the man I remembered falling in love with. But I knew he wasn't that anymore. He was a liar who wished me harm, and I wouldn't be fooled by longing looks and pretty words ever again.

"It's okay," he said, and I lunged for the sword as I heard faint banging and yelling from the other side of our shield.

Gripping the weapon firmly, I pointed the blade's tip down and pressed it to his heart. Angry tears welled in my eyes as I looked at him and saw no fear in his blue gaze. I wanted him scared. I wanted him to be terrified of what I could do, but instead, he looked peaceful and calm as his own silent tears streamed from his eyes and ran down the side of his face.

"It's okay, Ainsley," he whispered again. My jaw flexed, and my chest rose and fell rapidly from anger.

It wasn't okay. None of what was happening was okay. He deserved to suffer and hurt the way I did for so long, but he wasn't. He welcomed death with open arms, and it only infuriated me more.

I screamed my rage at the sky and called for my magic again, but it was completely quiet—not gone, but silent—refusing to partake. Just minutes before, it demanded to be let out so it could finish the job, and I didn't understand what was happening or why I couldn't access it like always.

"It's okay," Dashiell whispered again, and a strangled sound escaped my lips.

"Shut up!" I screamed, pressing the blade harder, and deep red blood began to leak from his skin. He hissed in pain but did nothing to try and stop me.

"It's okay, Ainsley. Do what you need to. It's okay," he said again as his silhouette blurred from the tears that poured from my eyes.

All at once, someone collided with me. I was tackled and pinned in place by several bodies as they yelled their concern for the prince and commanded me not to move a fucking inch. I closed my eyes and buried my face in the dirt, lost to the pain and confusion over what had happened. Why couldn't I access my Gifts? Why couldn't I just *end him*?

"Take her to the dungeons," one of the guards ordered, and I was hauled to my feet.

"No," Dashiell commanded, and I twisted to see him being tended to by a Medicus, the wound I had given him already almost healed. "Return her to her room."

"But, Your Highness—"

"Have more guards stationed outside her door and see that she doesn't leave, but she's not being taken down to the dungeons. Do you understand me?" he replied, and the guards nodded at once.

Dashiell looked at me one last time before directing his attention to Felix, and I didn't miss the way his face changed entirely. His features twisted with rage, and his hands balled into fists at his side. Felix's eyes were firmly on the ground, and I couldn't help but wonder what words would be exchanged between them. Whatever it was, it wouldn't be pleasant.

"Come with us, Lady Ainsley," a guard said as he stood in my doorway.

I had been taken directly to my room just as Dashiell instructed and kept there for hours. They refused to let me leave, and when Imogen came to see me, they sent her away. I enjoyed listening to her yell and threaten to freeze their balls off while they slept before she stomped away loudly, only to return twenty minutes later, demanding entrance again. For whatever reason, they let her pass that time.

After telling her what got me locked up, she handed me a new set of books to look through. She hadn't found anything while she read them, but it was safer to have two sets of eyes roaming over the texts to ensure we weren't missing anything. Shortly after giving me the books, Imogen hurried away to carry out another task she had planned for our cause.

"I'm not a Lady," I singsonged in response to the guard. I flipped through the pages from the comfort of my bed, not bothering to give the guard my attention.

"Apologies, My La— Your Highness," he corrected quickly. "It's a habit."

Not expecting that response, I looked up from my book to see a familiar face looking back at me wearing a guard's uniform.

"Hello, Tomas," I said, sitting up from the bed. I hadn't really gotten to know the man while I was here in Caelum, but whenever we did speak, he was always nice enough. He was one of the kind souls that danced with me at my birthday ball when I was feeling hurt over Dashiell's absence. "So you're a guard now?"

Blush coated his cheeks as he nodded excitedly while the other guard beside him rolled his eyes. It seemed like a position he wanted, but I didn't like knowing it would bring him closer to death when the war inevitably came.

"Good for you," I replied, climbing off the mattress and striding for the door. The guard gripped the hilt of his sword, but Tomas did nothing but offer me a wide smile. "Where to?" I asked, deciding to make this easy on Tomas as he didn't deserve the hostility I was planning on using on the other guards.

"His Majesty would like to speak to you," he answered.

About fucking time.

We walked through the corridor in silence as I was led to the Council Room. The guards outside it nodded to my companions before opening the tall doors and ushering me inside. King Perceval was leaning over the large table in the center of the room that held a model of Disparya, and I walked towards it, making sure not to let my eyes stray too long as I ran my fingers over the pointy mountains of my home kingdom.

"I'm told you tried to kill my son this morning," he said harshly, and I glanced up from the table to meet his cold emerald eyes.

My magic brimmed to the surface as it sensed the impending danger. Sure, *now* it decided to show up when I needed it. I shoved it back down, though I kept it ready and waiting should I call for it.

"That doesn't sound like something I'm capable of," I shrugged.

"I think you're capable of a great many things, Ainsley," he replied, leaning across the table to close the distance between us. A tendril of shadow leaked from my skin and wrapped around my little finger.

"I told you, it wasn't a big deal," Dashiell said, and I twisted my head to find him sitting in a chair at the far end of the room.

I hadn't seen him there, and my magic hadn't alerted me of the potential threat the way it had with King Perceval. Was it Dashiell who was using some kind of magic to bypass mine? Is that how he managed to slip into my room undetected and sedate my magic when I tried to call it forth this morning?

"I did not ask for your opinion!" King Perceval bellowed, banging his fist on the table. I flinched at the sound, and my shadows slithered around my body on instinct, ready to defend or attack as needed.

King Perceval looked at me hungrily, taking in the magic that had almost belonged to him. My Gifts would have gone to Dashiell, but we all knew King Perceval would truly control them. He would have forced Dashiell to do his bidding as he commanded, so I wasn't sure why he was trying to keep up the false pretense that he cared for me because of my father.

For some reason, I broke eye contact with the man who assessed my Gift greedily and turned to look at his son instead. Dashiell's gaze locked on mine, and he rose from his chair, taking long, deliberate strides for where we were.

"Why did you call us here?" the prince demanded, capturing his father's attention and luring it away from me.

I released the breath I was holding and worked to garner control of my Gift once more. I allowed it to stay out but restricted the shadows to swirl only around my arms rather than my entire body.

King Perceval looked between us and then gestured to a table across the room that had been set for dinner. As we approached, I gazed over the spread that had been placed, though I wouldn't be touching anything until I figured out why my magic had been acting so strangely. I considered sending a message to Evander, but if he learned that I couldn't access my Gifts properly, he'd show up and immediately retrieve me, consequences be damned. I was on my own, but I could stick it out for a little while longer.

"Given Ainsley's proclivity for wanting you dead, I figured it was time to solidify our contract," Perceval answered as a long piece of parchment appeared on the table. "Once we find the terms agreeable, we'll sign and bind our deal. If it's broken, the price will be death."

"No," Dashiell demanded, but his father waved him off as he continued to address me.

"My first term is that you stop trying to kill my son."

I smiled innocently as my shadows molded into the silhouette of a dagger in my hand before drifting back into their smokey shape.

"But it's so fun," I pouted, eyeing Dashiell with a look that told him I wanted nothing more than to put him in the ground.

"Regardless of what you find enjoyable, my son stays unharmed by you," Perceval demanded, and I rolled my eyes before agreeing. Ink sprawled over the parchment as our term was made. "Next, you will take the throne to Tenebrae once I have King Evander killed—"

"No," I interrupted forcefully. "Evander is *mine*. If anyone places a hand on him, it will be *me.*"

Dashiell's brows scrunched in skepticism like he didn't believe I could take down someone of that magnitude and skill, but King Perceval only grinned a serpentine smile as he dipped his head.

"My mistake," he said amusedly. "The death of King Evander does not belong to me, so he shall not die by my hands."

The new term was set in ink, but I didn't miss how he meticulously crafted the sentence because I would have done exactly the same. Neither of us trusted the other, and we were choosing our words very carefully for this deal.

"The day he falls, you will marry Dashiell," Perceval added—another clever way to phrase it. Not the day *I* killed him, leaving me to believe Perceval would have someone else do the job. As long as Evander didn't die by his own hands, Perceval wasn't technically breaking the treaty.

"No!" Dashiell said, rising from his seat. "I am not going to marry her."

"It isn't your choice," I spat, glaring at the prince. "I agree."

The new term was written in ink.

"Wonderful," Perceval mused. "And he will become King of Tenebrae set to rule at your side."

"*Consort*," I corrected. "Tenebrae is my birthright, not his. He can be my consort, but I am the primary ruler."

King Perceval's narrowed eyes filled with disdain, clearly unhappy I wouldn't budge from the stance we discussed on my first day back in Caelum. He was sorely mistaken if he thought he would trick me into giving Dashiell complete control over my kingdom.

"As I said before, any momentous decisions to be made will be voted upon by the three of us, and we will do whatever the majority decides," I stated.

King Perceval released a heavy breath as he leaned forward, grabbed an apple from the table, and sat back in his chair. He tossed it in the air a few times as he held my gaze before biting into it deeply. The juice ran down his chin, and I held my tongue as he continued to toy with me.

"I don't agree to this," Dashiell stated, making his stance on the matter clear.

"Well, it's not up to you," I replied, looking at the king. "Your father is the deciding vote."

Perceval took another bite of his apple as he debated what he would do, though we all already knew the answer. He was power-hungry, and I was offering myself up to him. There was no way he was going to refuse it.

"And what happens in the case of *your* death?" he asked. I blinked at him as I sensed Dashiell tense beside me. "If you die before you produce heirs, what will come of Tenebrae? Sure, the Gods would choose another bloodline, but where is the security in my son's role as Consort?"

Holy shit. He was absolutely going to murder me as soon as he got what he wanted. I looked around the space, trying to decide how I would play this. That wasn't a question I thought he would ask, and I had no time to prepare an answer, which I'm pretty sure was his intention all along.

"If I die before Dashiell and I have children," I said slowly, trying to work through this problem. "Then my husband will be left to rule Tenebrae until his death as well."

King Perceval's eyes sparkled with power and the promise of all his dreams coming true.

"Deal," he said, and the final term was etched into the contract.

He scribbled his signature before handing me the pen to do the same. Once finished, I tossed the pen and parchment to Dashiell, who looked like the life had been drained from him. His eyes met mine for the briefest of moments before he scrawled his signature on the paper. The contract glowed bright, locking us into the magical binding before dimming to its normal shade. I had made a deal using my own life as collateral and could only hope that when the time came, it wouldn't cost me.

71.

The hallway was dark as I walked to my room alone. After we signed the contract, King Perceval didn't feel the need to keep me guarded as I would die if I brought any harm to his son. The hour was late, so there weren't many people out, but as I turned the corner, my eyes landed on a familiar figure.

Rosella was sitting on a bench in the corridor that overlooked the gardens below as she pretended to read, mindlessly flipping through her book. I knew she wasn't actually consuming what the pages had said because her brow would arch and her posture would perk up every time the voices from the ground carried on the open breeze. She smiled at the conversation she overheard before scribbling something into her book, pocketing it, and walking away. I may have hated her, but I couldn't deny she would have thrived in the tavern back home.

When I finally reached my door, my body tightened with awareness, and my magic hummed to let me know I wasn't alone. I called forth my shadows, keeping them at my fingertips as I pushed open the door to my room. The space was dimly lit, but I could make out Imogen's silhouette as she sat on the edge of my bed, patiently waiting for me.

Before I took a step inside, another figure caught my attention, and I twisted to see Felix standing against the far wall, his back resting on my dresser as he stared down at his feet. His hair was unkempt and falling out of its usual tie as if he had been dragging his hand threw it several times. His cheeks and eyes were red, and I could feel pain and guilt cascading over him.

I eyed him cautiously before shutting the door behind me and locking it tight. I created a silencing shield a heartbeat later, not wanting anyone to overhear as I made my way for him. He picked his head up as he watched me approach, and a moment later, I threw my arms around him as he buried his face in my neck.

"What happened? I demanded, pulling back to get a better look at him.

"Nothing that has to do with this mission," he answered, and I nodded, understanding that it probably had to do with his and Dashiell's conversation earlier today. "But I don't think Dash bought any of our performances for one second. He knows I wouldn't betray you again, especially for his father."

"He's not the one you had to convince," Imogen offered, and I nodded in agreement before looking at Felix hopefully.

"I think the king believed me," he answered, and I let out a deep breath as the tension I had been holding on to finally left my body.

Felix and I couldn't risk being around one another besides keeping up the front that I hated him, and I was dying for him to fill me in on what had been going on while we were apart.

"Did you find anything in the Council Room?" I asked quickly, stepping away from my friend and going over to the books I had been browsing through today. For the first time, we might have made a breakthrough.

In one of the books was a drawing of a dark emerald sone with text that was in an ancient language I couldn't read, except for one single word—*Solum*. I had no idea if it would lead to anything, but that word meant something sacred to my people and could be our key to finding Inmuto or the stones. All I knew was that I needed to get the book to Agnitio to be translated. It may have led to nothing, but my instincts told me that wouldn't be the case.

"I think so," Felix answered, and my heart pounded at the luck we were finally having after spending a week hitting nothing but dead ends. "Perceval kept glancing at a stack of scrolls every time we were in meetings. I was curious, so I snuck back in and unrolled them when we were done, but they were completely blank. I chalked it up to him being anxious over pending work that needed to be done, but then I remembered the Indico stone. I think he's hiding something on those scrolls."

"Then you'll need to steal them tomorrow night before we leave," I ordered, and Felix dipped his head. "Imogen, how is your task coming along?"

"Good," she answered. "It's almost finished and will be ready in time."

Everything was coming together perfectly, and soon we would be back home in Tenebrae and one step closer to stopping Oberon from taking over Disparya. My chest ached, and my magic swirled inside me as I allowed myself to picture being wrapped in Evander's arms, happy and content, as Nova and Onyx fought for space on our bed.

One more Gods damn day.

I didn't leave my room the following day, not wanting to risk something happening to thwart our plans and ruin the mission. Imogen stopped by, bringing me my meals and only staying long enough to check in before having to tend to her own assignment. We agreed that Felix would spend today with King Perceval, attending meetings and strolling the grounds at his side as he put on his fake persona of the king's favorite pet. I knew he wanted to be with Dashiell during his last day in Caelum, but I didn't trust Felix when it came to him.

Felix had questioned his friend about why he had been in Pravus, and the prince told him he had gone to find me. Dashiell claimed to have no idea that I was in Tenebrae the entire time, and since none of his contacts in the other kingdoms had said anything about my whereabouts, he assumed I was shipped off somewhere far away. He learned of Perceval and Oberon's alliance during one of the meetings he attended as heir to Caelum, but swore he didn't know the extent of what it entailed once Felix shared the truth.

When I asked Felix what Dashiell's response was to learning what his father was doing, he reluctantly told me that Dashiell had difficulty believing it. I wasn't surprised, and when Felix tried to defend his friend, saying that it was a lot of information to digest and that he'd been brainwashed his whole life, I quickly ended the conversation.

Felix's constant loyalty to Dashiell, despite his wrongdoings, was enough to tell me I would never be able to trust him fully when it came to the prince. I would have to pick and choose what I could share with him, and though I hated not being completely honest with my best friend, I couldn't risk my people and their safety because of his inability to let go.

The clock in the room chimed several times, indicating only two hours left until midnight. A knock on my door sounded a minute later, and I opened it to let Felix inside. Another minute passed, and Imogen was next to show up, quietly slipping into my room.

"You need to leave first," I said to Felix, and he looked at me questioningly before shaking his head.

"We go together," he replied.

"We can't. I know it's more dangerous for us to go separately, but it's safer for the mission. If they catch us sneaking out together, then we're screwed. If just one of us makes it, it'll be enough to relay our findings to Evander."

Felix thought about that momentarily, but he knew I was right. We couldn't risk both of us being captured and failing. If one of us got left behind, we would rescue the other once we informed our family of what happened.

"You're going first," I said.

"No," Felix replied. "You're more important."

"Which is why I can't be the one to leave right now. If they come to check on us, they won't give a second thought to you not being in your room, but if they find mine empty, they won't stop until they locate me."

"But they haven't been checking on you," he argued.

"Not lately, no. But they were in the beginning, and I won't jeopardize our mission because I got complacent and comfortable. I have to wait until the last possible second."

Felix dragged a frustrated hand through his silver hair and looked to Imogen for some backup, but she sat quietly on the bed, choosing not to get involved. I don't know why he thought she'd save him. This was *my* mission, and I was calling the shots.

"Did you get the scrolls?" I asked, and he nodded as he tapped the place on his jacket where they were hidden. I reached into my pocket and handed over my book. "Take this with you and keep it safe with the scrolls. We can't split the items up, and if I can't get out, you have to bring them to Evander. We need both."

Felix reluctantly took the book before bringing me into a tight hug. I wrapped my arms around my best friend and prayed this wouldn't be the last time we saw each other. We could do this and get out alive. And soon, we'd be back in the company of our family and in the arms of the men we loved.

Just one more task.

"I'll be right behind you," I promised as I pulled away and wiped the tears from my eyes. Felix strode for Imogen and hugged her just as fiercely before he slipped from the room and headed to our meeting spot.

I straightened my spine and rolled my neck to prepare for my own escape. Everything I had been training and working for had come down to this moment. I couldn't afford to be scared or worried about getting caught or the outcome. When I left, I made a promise to Evander that I swore to keep.

'For everything we lost and for everything we have yet to gain.'

"Why did you lie to him?" Imogen asked as she stood from the bed and came to stand at my side. I looked at her tiny frame in the dark as I tried to come up with an answer.

"Because I don't trust him with the truth."

Imogen nodded before wrapping me in one last hug.

"Come with me," I begged. "If they find out what you did, they'll kill you. You have a home with me in Tenebrae."

Imogen pushed the hair away from my face as she reached on her toes to kiss my forehead. I tried to talk her out of helping with my task, but she refused to sit back and watch, even though it meant risking her life. As soon as she made the decision, I told her she was coming home with me, and she didn't have a choice in the matter because it was a queen's command. She laughed in my face before reminding me that I wasn't a queen yet and then shooed me away.

"Please," I pleaded, and she lowered to her normal height before nodding. I released a shuddering breath, but before I could comment anything more, she spoke.

"But I can't leave right away," she answered, and my eyes widened. Did she not fully grasp the danger she was in? "Just trust me, my sweet girl. I'll be okay, and I'll make my way to you as soon as I can. I promise."

I knew her mind was made up on the subject, and there was nothing I could say to talk her out of it, so I accepted her offer and hoped the Gods would be kind enough to spare her until then. But if she died before that, I would personally bring her back to life just to kill her again for not listening to me to begin with.

"Wait until there is one hour left, and then do what you must," she said, hugging me one last time before exiting the room and leaving me in silence.

I paced the open space in the dark as the moon grew higher in the sky. Any moment now, the clock would indicate it was time for me to leave this place behind once and for all. A faint glistening caught my eye, and I walked over to the vanity to see my flame bracelet shimmering in the moonlight. I ran my fingers over the gemstone for the last time, letting the final piece of me that was attached to it fade away completely.

Evander had once said I was still holding onto my old life when I had chosen another, and he was right. Some part of me had always missed the smell of the Sanctuary and the feel of the lake's water on my skin. I missed the sound of my laugh when my life was carefree and my days were filled with laying in the meadow with the two boys who meant everything to me.

But I wasn't that girl anymore and didn't want to be.

I loved the power and respect I commanded. I loved choosing my own destiny and not having anyone decide what I could and couldn't do. I loved having a family who supported me through my struggles and a love that grew as I did. After months of holding on, I was ready to finally let go.

The clock chimed, and I pulled my hand away from the gemstone flame as I glanced around the room one last time. I took a deep breath and headed for the door, shutting it firmly behind me and leaving my old life in the past for good.

The halls were quiet and dark, with only a few people walking about as they kept a wide birth from me. My shadows were out and billowing behind me to deter anyone from trying to make conversation, though the chances of that weren't likely. Still, I couldn't take the risk of someone stopping me. I turned the last corner, inching closer to my destination by the second and halted abruptly. Dashiell stood at the far end of the hallway, his arms crossed as if he'd been waiting for me.

Fuck.

"We need to talk," he said as I continued my journey toward him.

"I'm busy, but I'll be sure to make time for you tomorrow, dear fiancé," I replied sweetly as I pushed past him.

"Now," he demanded, his voice booming and strong. I stopped my advance. The hall dropped in temperature as ice splintered up the stone walls all around. A shiver crept down my spine, and I knew it had nothing to do with the cold and everything to do with the fierce look in his deep teal-blue eyes.

How the hell was this happening right now? He had all week to corner me like this, and yet he stayed away ever since that first night. Even after our sparring match, he didn't come and find me again. Why did he feel the need to do so now, and how in the world did he know where I was going?

He stepped forward, forcing me to retreat until my back hit the door of the library we were on the other side of. His presence was commanding and intimidating. I wasn't scared of Dashiell, but the set of his strong jaw and the hard look in his eyes told me he wasn't going to back down. My magic caressed my insides as if letting me know he wasn't going to physically hurt me. For some reason, I believed that. He leaned closer, and I could feel the heat of his body rolling off him in waves.

"You're up to something," he whispered. "And I'm not letting you leave until you tell me what it is." He jerked his chin toward the door behind me.

There was only one room beyond those doors where he'd want to have this conversation, but I didn't want to go there. I didn't think I could. I had said goodbye to my old life, and now he was trying to drag me somewhere that held such significance to that. Clenching my fist at my side, I gathered the strength I would need to do this. I closed my eyes and let my mind travel through the library, taking each familiar step to our favorite room.

Everything would be in the same spot because I couldn't see Dashiell changing anything. There would be books stacked on the window bench and coffee table. The fire would be roaring to life as it always was, never once going out, and blankets would be haphazardly thrown across the couches. I could hear the wooden doors creaking open and smell the scent of worn parchment and wine from the full goblets we made a habit of leaving out. It was everything that once felt like home, and when I opened my eyes again, I knew Dashiell would lead me straight to it.

As much as I didn't want to waste my energy on this, I knew he wasn't going to back down. He wasn't going to just let me go without this fight. I could do this. I had to.

'For everything we lost and for everything we have yet to gain.'

72.

I had lost too much time dealing with Dashiell and knew I wouldn't make it to the meeting spot if I didn't hurry. We were allowed five minutes of leeway to be late, but any more than that and Elenora and Oli were to assume we had been caught and abort the mission to regroup. I didn't have much time left, and I couldn't afford any more missteps. Taking a deep and steady breath, I turned the corner to the final corridor, finding it empty except for two guards fast asleep, just as Imogen promised they would be after she slipped them the drugs.

I stepped over their bodies and reached into my pocket to grab the key she had smuggled me. I could do this. I had to. My magic flowed through me and created a silencing shield around the door to quiet the sound of it unlocking. My shadows gathered in my hand before I pushed the door slowly open, preparing for a fight, but it was dark and quiet... And King Perceval was sound asleep.

I shut and locked the door before expanding the silencing shield to encompass the entire bedroom. It was massive and elaborate, decorated in solid gold and emerald green. On silent feet, I crept through the space, hunting for any signs of a stone that could be one of the three we needed, but I was coming up empty. There were jewels and coins, diamonds and gemstones, but nothing felt like it was the one we needed, though something inside me screamed that they were *here*. I wanted to find them before we left, but as I glanced at the clock, I knew I was almost out of time.

I walked to the enormous window that overlooked the back of the palace, checking that the gardens were empty, as that would be my path to freedom. They were, thank the Gods. I sat down for a moment and closed my eyes to muster up my strength and control. I wanted to go home and see Evander, but there was one more thing I had to do first. My eyes squeezed tight, and my fists clenched as I prepared myself for my biggest battle yet. Felix had the book and scrolls, so if something went wrong, at least our efforts weren't for nothing.

I crafted a sword and dagger in my hands and solidified them into sharp steel before throwing everything I had into my magic. I could do this. I could do this. I could do this.

For everything we lost and for everything we have yet to gain.

My eyes fluttered open as I stood and tiptoed to the side of the bed. Perceval was snoring softly, with no idea that his killer loomed over him in the dark. I stood there for several minutes as if committing his sleeping form to memory and picturing every heinous thing he'd ever done to the people I cared about. He was the reason my mother and father were slaughtered. The reason Evander's parents had died. He was responsible for manipulating his son and making him feel worthless his entire life. He kept my best friend from finding true joy. He murdered Imogen's entire family. He killed my Caregivers to cover his tracks. He stole my fucking life. I raised the sword high, angling the tip right over his heart, and plunged it down with all my might.

The blade dug into the mattress as Perceval rolled off the bed, narrowly missing my assault. I swore loudly as he wrapped his hand around my throat and threw me back against the wall with thunderous force. My grip on my weapons slipped, and they dropped to the ground feet away as Perceval continued his attack.

I tried to kick out of his hold, but his muscular body pinned me against the wall, preventing the use of my legs. His fingers on my throat tightened as he squeezed hard, cutting off my air supply as I struggled to get free. My nails clawed at his arms as my eyes went wide with panic, knowing that there was nothing I could do to get away from him. I made a grave mistake thinking I could take him on, and it showed as the panic set in.

Perceval smiled cruelly as he watched me struggle to keep fighting for life. He loved every second of knowing he could snuff out my existence with the mere flick of his wrist. He leaned close to my ear, a vengeful snarl on his face.

"How dare you think you could kill me," he spat before loosening his grip. I opened my mouth wide and greedily sucked down the air before he constricted my windpipe once more, and I was instantly reminded of how those men in Agnitio tried to drown me.

"You deserve to die," I croaked, and he answered with a sinister laugh.

"You're not wrong, but I'm curious as to why you think that, my dear."

He allowed me another mouthful of air, enjoying this conversation far too much to put an end to it just yet. I gulped it down before trying to punch him in the side, but he anticipated the move and slammed me hard into the wall. I screamed in agony at the pain of the assault, and he slapped me across the face for good measure.

"Answer my question," he demanded as he squeezed my neck hard enough that his knuckles went white beneath his skin.

"You killed my parents," I sputtered, spit flying with each word as I struggled to speak. "And Evander's."

Perceval laughed loudly as he nodded, excitement filling his face, and I was filled with such rage as I realized just how much he enjoyed that fact. He was proud to have been the one to betray my father and orchestrate his and my mother's death. I snarled in his face, wanting to make him pay for what he'd done to them all those years ago. I fought in his hold, wiggling my body as best I could to break free—but I was too weak, and he knew it.

"I wondered when you would finally admit you moved on from my son to him. It was obvious you were together, especially with that '*he's mine*' bullshit you were spewing. Don't think for a second that my contacts didn't inform me about that little show the two of you put on in Agnitio," he snarled.

Whatever he was told, he didn't seem to like it and took to slamming my head against the wall several times until blood began to trickle down my nose and from between my lips. I grunted, my body going limp between his hands as he dealt blow after blow. He was getting off on the strength he held over me, and that I was powerless to stop him. He punched me in the gut, and I screamed as the sound of my bones breaking echoed in the otherwise silent room. Perceval only smiled wider.

"Just kill me," I rasped, knowing that was a kinder end than he was ever willing to give me.

"Now, why would I go and do that?" he asked sweetly, and the smug tone of his voice had my stomach churning.

I spat the blood coating my teeth into his face and braced myself for his next hit. His fist collided with my cheek and the noise that left me was feral.

"Because you've already tried... several times," I replied breathlessly, and he chuckled, the sound wicked and demeaning.

"Was the apple at dinner too much?" he taunted. "I was going for subtle, but I couldn't help myself."

The moment Perceval bit into that damn piece of fruit, I knew he was letting me know he had orchestrated my attack in the orchard. However, the reason he gave the order still evaded me.

"Why?" I asked, wanting to hear the truth of what happened from his lips. I knew Perceval was a liar, but I couldn't see him stretching the facts when it came to something he took pride in, and clearly, trying to kill me was one of those times.

"Because I needed to set up Tenebrae for war. You were supposed to be in your room so I could have you kidnapped for a week or so while I pinned it on King Evander, but that maiden Josephine was there instead. I couldn't let her live after that. And then Pecus spotted my man leaving, which needed to be dealt with as well, and it just became one big mess. You've caused a lot of problems for me." I thought back to the kind man that had helped me the night I almost jumped from the roof of the palace from an illusion. His mismatched eyes—one sea foam green, and one brown—would forever be burned into my mind.

"So Cordelia was never attacked?" I asked, wanting to keep him talking for as long as possible so I could understand everything in hopes it could help us with the war.

"Oh, she was, but that was a part of a much bigger plan, as I'm sure you've realized. I know it was no coincidence that you found yourself back in Caelum after the reports of Tenebraen soldiers attacking Venator and Agnitio."

"They're lies."

"Oh, I'm well aware," he said before slamming my body into the wall several more times.

Tears streamed down my cheeks as every inch of my body started to bruise. If he continued his torment, I wasn't sure how much longer I'd be able to last without blacking out from the pain of the injuries. I needed this to be over and soon.

"Anyway, where was I? Oh yes, Dashiell was very set on not going through with the plan of taking your magic once I informed him of his duty, so I had to offer him a little push to show just how much your life was in danger. Even after you were attacked, he still refused, and I thought I was just going to have to cut my losses and ship you to Pravus—but then everything changed. I'm not sure what you said to him, but whatever it was, it made him agree to my plan."

What the hell was he talking about? What could I have possibly said to make Dashiell want to steal my Gifts? The answer was nothing. I said nothing; this was just another mind game he wanted to play with me. He desired nothing more than to fester in my thoughts and make me doubt myself. It's what he's done since the second I first arrived in the palace all those months ago.

"But now we have a problem," he said, as he slapped me across the face. "I can't have you trying to kill me every chance you get. As much as I wanted your power, it looks like I'll have to settle for stealing your kingdom instead."

"I would have never agreed to Entwine with anyone. That power is mine, and I won't give it willingly," I snarled.

"Who said anything about you being willing?" Perceval taunted.

"You can't take it otherwise."

"Can't I?" A twisted smile curved Perceval's lips. "That may have been the case once, but not anymore," he sneered. My blood went cold, and for the first time in a while, I was truly afraid of what he could do.

Perceval's fingers constricted on my throat, cutting off all oxygen to my lungs as he pressed hard against my flesh. I slapped and clawed, but his jaw only tightened as he put more force into his grip.

"Don't worry, I'll send Evander your way soon enough," he whispered, squeezing so hard the blood vessels in my eyes popped, filling what once was white with deep crimson. My mouth opened and closed as I was strangled, the life slowly draining from me at the hands of the man who had taken everything else. "Say hello to your father for me," he added, and tears ran from my eyes.

Perceval smiled victoriously as the fight in me slowly died, my body going limp in his hands. He didn't stop squeezing though. He didn't let up, even knowing that I was nearly gone and the amount of force he was using wasn't necessary. Laughter escaped him as he watched my bright eyes start to dim.

Blood spattered across my face, and Perceval stumbled back a step, though he kept his hold on me tight as his eyes drifted to his chest... Where a deep blade had pierced his heart from behind. His breathing shuddered, and he looked at me with shocked eyes while crimson liquid began to drip from his mouth. Smiling at him, my form slowly dissolved between his fingers as I called my illusion back.

"That's for Julian and Viviette," I sneered in his ear from behind, completely uninjured and untouched. I twisted the blade and he bellowed in pain, but no one would hear him thanks to the silencing shield. "That's for King Uriel and Queen Dahlia." I pulled my sword from his back and rammed it in again, hard and deep. "That's for Felix and Dashiell."

My fingers gripped his brown hair, and I pulled him back so he fell to the ground with a loud thud. I leapt on his chest and watched the blood pour from his mouth with a twisted sort of satisfaction. My time was running out, and I needed to go, but I also couldn't risk the Medicus finding him and saving his pathetic life. He needed to fucking die—thoroughly. I clenched my dagger as I buried it in his chest over and over and over again, screaming my rage as I listed off Josephine, Annette, Pecus, Mouth, Looks, and Imogen.

I called to my Imperium Gift and sank it into him, clotting his blood and bringing it into his throat so he choked on it. Perceval gargled as he drowned, and I was sure he would never recover, but I couldn't stop. I needed more blood, more pain, more vengeance.

'For everything we lost and for everything we have yet to gain.'

I crafted a cestus with claws on the back just as I had in Agnitio and began to shred his flesh from his body with each strike of my fists. His warm blood coated every inch of me until I was completely drenched in my kill, but I still didn't stop. I leaned back on his chest and picked up my sword, aiming the tip at his throat.

"This is for Evander," I said breathlessly as I plunged the metal into his throat repeatedly, not stopping until his neck started to sever from the rest of his body.

I stood then and walked to his side before raising the sword above my head. "And this is for me!" I yelled as I let the blade fall and disconnect his head from his body.

I collapsed to my knees, dropping my weapons and throwing my head back as I cried. I cried for the mother and father I never knew. I cried for the kind king and queen that were taken from the man I loved far too soon. I cried for the life he had stolen from me. And I cried for the utter joy I felt now that I rid the world of such a hateful man. I had fucking done it.

After months of working to master my craft and training to solidify my illusion like Van could, I fucking did it. The clock chimed again, and I gasped for breath at the realization I had to go right now if I had any hopes of getting to our meeting spot on time. Screams of undiluted pain roared through the palace, shaking the walls and causing lightning to strike and thunder to rumble.

It seemed Caelum officially had a new king.

I was a dead woman if I didn't get the hell out of there before the third Gift finished settling in Dashiell's body. I scrambled to my feet as shouts and banging on the door echoed. They were here, and they were ready to seek vengeance for their king's murder. Fuck.

I flung the window wide, looking at the far drop below and praying to the Gods that my Gift would help cushion my fall. Just as I was about to jump, something shiny caught my eye, and I turned to see the former king's crown sitting on his bedside table. Without thinking, I ran for it, and the moment my finger clasped around the metal, the door to the bedroom busted open. I surrounded myself in a shield as two daggers were thrown at me, but they bounced off as I crafted a pack with my shadows, shoved the crown inside, and slung it onto my back. My magic surged, enveloping the room in darkness as I ran for the window, and leapt through it.

It was a long way down, but my shadows solidified beneath my feet for just long enough for me to use them as steps. I jumped the last several feet and rolled in the grass before scrambling up and sprinting for the woods. Several arrows and daggers were shot at me, but my shadows kept me safe as I ran.

"Ainsley!" Dashiell yelled, and I twisted to find him running after me, covered in his father's blood and with a promise of death in his eyes.

I didn't dare stop.

I should have gotten out of there sooner, but I couldn't stop once the bloodlust kicked in. The illusion of me that Dashiell had been speaking to in the Sanctuary drifted away the second the one in the king's room had. I knew that as soon as the third Gift coursed through his veins, he'd know I didn't deceive him just to get out of having a conversation. Dashiell wasn't stupid. He knew I was up to something but just didn't realize it was his father's murder.

A bolt of lightning struck before me, splitting the earth in two. I skid to a halt, trapped on one side of the divide, and called to my shadows. The lightning cost me, and now Dashiell was far too close for me to get away. I had to fight him first.

Tendrils of darkness swirled around me as I turned to face my enemy. Dashiell slowed his pace, stopping less than twenty feet away. His father's blood soaked through his clothes and looked so dark against the ice coating his hands. He was ready for our battle just as much as I was. He wasn't going to let me leave, and I wasn't going to let him take me. I could only see this ending one way. My magic thrashed against me, seeming to love the idea initially but then started to quiet and curl into itself. I dove into myself, gripping my magic forcefully and refusing to let it drift below the surface like it had so many times when I encountered Dashiell this week. He had to have done something to my magic. Something that prevented it from harming him.

"What were you thinking?" Dashiell demanded as he paced back and forth. I wasn't sure why he wasn't coming closer, but I would be ready once he did.

"I did what needed to be done," I replied, forcing my shadows to curl around my hands. We wouldn't be fighting with weapons.

He shook his head, his eyes hollow but bright. Guards began to spill onto the lawn, watching the fight and readying themselves for their new king's orders. Dashiell's posture was rigid as he frantically paced, seeming at a loss for what to do. "I don't want to fight you, Ainsley," he announced. "But I can't just let you walk away after what you did." The ice coating his hands disappeared and was replaced with flames. Now that his father was dead, Dashiell had inherited the third Gift of Caelum, giving him the addition of fire magic.

"Try and stop me," I replied, pulling the shadows into my hands and crafting a dagger within the blink of an eye.

Before Dashiell could fully register what had happened, I flicked my wrist and threw my dagger at him. He dove out of the way, narrowly missing my assault and throwing a ball of flames in retaliation. I spun away from his attack that went wide, only to realize it was a diversion just as the second ball of flames licked over my skin. I expected to feel a burn, but though the flames were hot, it wasn't enough to hurt me. Perhaps Dashiell didn't know how to control his new Gift, and I could somehow use it to my advantage. I could pretend he was weakening me and let me waste his energy on calling magic that wasn't harming me.

"Take the easy way out, Ainsley," Dashiell said, throwing his flames in quick succession. I threw up my shadows to shield myself from the assault but screamed in fake pain as one of the balls hit me in my leg. Several guards cheered at the sight, and I memorized their faces. I'd deal with them later. For now, I needed to get the hell out of here. I was running out of time and had no more to spare.

Another fireball hit my shield, and I yelled before cloaking myself in darkness and crafting as many daggers as possible while Dashiell continued wasting his energy. This was it.

"Ainsley," Dashiell said gently. It was like he was trying to coax me into coming with him rather than just demanding that I do. My shadows began to dissipate without my permission, letting the man I had once loved come into view. Fire curled around his fingers, and his chest heaved with exhaustion. My plan to wear him out had been working, and he had no idea his attacks had done nothing to me. But rather than looking like a man who won his battle, he looked tired—defeated. "Please," he said, and there was something about the way he spoke the word that had my shadows ripping from my body.

The entirety of the palace grounds was enveloped in my darkness. As screams broke out, I threw each dagger I had crafted in the direction of Dashiell and his guards before I turned and sprinted for freedom.

73.

"**W**hat the fuck happened!" Felix demanded as I fell to the ground before him, making our deadline with only minutes to spare. "Ainsley, whose fucking blood is that?!"

I rolled to my back, gasping for breath and wiping the blood mixed with sweat from my eyes. Even though it was winter, Caelum was hot enough for my skin to be sticky and uncomfortable. I rolled and grabbed Felix's bag, digging through it until I retrieved a canteen of water to clean my face.

"Ainsley, you better fucking answer me," he said forcefully, and I finally looked up at him as I poured the last little bit of water into my mouth to drink.

"Caelum has a new king," I said, screwing the lid back on.

Felix stumbled a step and ran a hand through his hair as he looked at me with wide, furious eyes. He opened and closed his mouth several times, seeming wholly lost for words. I stood, wiping my hands on my pants and glancing around the space. It was after midnight now, and there wasn't any sign of Elenora or Oli.

"Where are they?" I asked. Felix grabbed his bag and slung it over his shoulder as he stormed away from me.

"There's been a change of plans. We're meeting closer to the portal because something has set the guards on edge and more alert. I guess I fucking know what it is now," he snarled, pushing past me, and I followed his lead only because I had no idea where the portal was. "Why the hell didn't you tell me!"

"Because you'd try to stop me," I answered simply.

"Of course, I would have!"

"And that's why I didn't tell you. This wasn't about *you*, Felix. This was about *my* vengeance, *my* revenge, *my* justice. You don't get a say in how I enact it."

He shook his head, clearly furious at me for not only going through with it but also keeping him in the dark. I let loose a deep breath as I squared my shoulders and looked him straight in the eyes.

"I don't trust you when it comes to him. I don't trust you'll choose me because you chose him first," I said. "And because of that, I can't tell you everything."

"What can I do, Ainsley?" he asked exasperatedly. "I have tried everything to make up for lying to you, and yet that doesn't fucking matter. You're never going to forgive me fully, are you? Even though I stayed by your side in Tenebrae for months when I was miserable. Even when I returned with you to Caelum, knowing full well I could have easily been killed before ever opening my mouth to spew a bullshit lie. Even when I gave up my brother *again* for you," he said as tears ran down his face. "I love you, and nothing I ever do will be good enough for you, will it?"

My heart constricted as I looked at my friend and saw the obvious distress on his face. I could feel his pain and guilt as he stood there at a loss for what to do. But what was I supposed to say? I knew he did all of that for me, but it didn't change the love and loyalty he still felt for Dashiell, and that was the problem. The prince and I were on separate sides, and Felix couldn't have us both. Before I could answer his question, an arrow flew between us, and we whipped our heads to find a stampede of soldiers sprinting our way.

"Fuck," I breathed. "I thought he would have waited to regroup and come at me in Tenebrae."

"I could have told you he wouldn't have if you just had told me what the fuck you were planning," Felix spat as we turned and ran through the woods.

The shouts and footsteps were closing in, and I wasn't sure how much longer until we reached the portal. More arrows fired, narrowly missing us and hitting the trees beside our heads. Thunder rumbled above us, and I crafted and threw several daggers behind me, thankful as I heard pains of agony cry out as they found their targets.

We picked up our pace and took a new path to our right as we headed for our destination. If we didn't get there soon, we wouldn't make it. I skidded to a halt as a soldier stepped from behind a tree, cutting us off from freedom. He created a fireball in his hand, but my shadow shield blocked it, and I used my Imperium Gift to crush his heart beneath my magic.

More soldiers popped up in front as the others swarmed behind. We were surrounded and had to fight our way free, but I wasn't sure we could with how outnumbered we were. I wrapped us in darkness, feeling the sting each time my magic took a hit from the weapons they threw.

"You have to go," I told Felix. "I can't hold them for long but can cover as you escape."

"No. I'm not leaving you."

"Yes, you are, Felix. Get the book and scrolls to Evander. You have to, or else this was all for nothing."

My shadows began to flicker as I grunted in pain from the force of the weapons. In the attack on the camps, my shield only protected us from arrows and daggers, but now I was taking hits of fire, water, ice, and lightning. Each magical strike was leaving me weak and in pain.

"Please," I begged as my shield began shrinking and flickering around us.

An arrow managed to slip through and slice deep into my thigh. I screamed as my shield went down completely. We were out of time, and now this entire mission was for nothing. The assault stopped, and I looked around to see dozens of watchful eyes on us, waiting for their chance to bring home the kill.

"Ainsley!" Felix yelled, and as I twisted, I was knocked to the ground by my friend as blood sprayed across my shirt, mixing with the red stains of Perceval. I looked up with wide eyes to find an arrow lodged in Felix's chest.

Right where his heart was.

Time slowed around me as I watched his hands clutch the weapon and blood drip from his mouth as he stared at me before collapsing.

"Felix!" I screamed, throwing my head back and letting my magic rip through me in a storm.

Each black tendril that escaped from me was crafted into an arrow and sent in every direction as I yelled my rage to the sky. The area was filled with nothing but the sounds of my fury, shredding flesh, and dripping blood as my magic poured and poured from me, turning into a deadly weapon the moment it parted from my body.

I fell forward, gasping for breath as I crawled to my best friend. All around us, the woods were painted red with my violence and pieces of body parts from my victims, and it still wouldn't be enough if they had taken this pure life from the world.

I reached Felix, pulling his head into my lap as I brushed his silver hair from his face and shoved my Imperium Gift into his body. I wasn't a Medicus but if I could use my Gift to manipulate the flow of blood, then maybe I could stop it from gushing out of him. My magic moved effortlessly as I sought out the injury in hopes of clotting the bleeding until we could reach help, but as I found the wound, my own heart stopped. The damage was too great for the abilities I didn't know how to use and there was nothing I could do for him.

"I'm going to go find help," I declared. Felix clutched my wrist, his eyes imploring me not to move.

"No," he breathed, his voice shallow.

"Felix, I—"

"Please, Ainsley," he begged, and my heart shattered at the desperation in his words. "I don't want to be alone when I go." His eyes welled with tears as he looked up at me. "I'm scared and I don't want to be alone." I nodded, granting him this one request. We both knew this was the end. I couldn't walk or carry him, and I would honor his wish for me to stay at his side. So, I resorted to screaming for help, though I didn't think anyone was around to hear.

I clutched his hand tight as I wracked my brain around what was happening. It didn't seem real—it couldn't be. Losing my best friend wasn't an option, and yet it was going to happen because of me. Because I had chosen to keep a secret from him. If I had just shared my plans, he would have shot them down, knowing exactly how Dashiell would have reacted, and he'd still be alive and unhurt.

"I'm so sorry, Felix," I sobbed, pressing my lips to his forehead. He squeezed my fingers, and I pulled back to keep my gaze locked on his beautiful amber eyes, not ready to see the life drain from them.

"I love you, cupcake," he said. "I swore to protect you with my life and wouldn't have done anything differently."

"It's not supposed to be like this," I croaked, shaking my head to deny the truth unraveling before my eyes. Felix's blood continued to flow between my fingers as I held him to me. "It's supposed to be me and you, always. And what about Olivier? He needs you, Felix. You can't go."

His lips wobbled at the mention of the man he had fallen in love with, and I hated myself for bringing him up, but I wasn't above guilt-tripping him so he'd stay alive. It wasn't fair that he found this love only to lose it a short time later. His eyes began to shut, but I smacked his cheek, forcing him to open them again.

"No. No, no, no, no, please, Felix. Don't go. I need you. I can't do this without you. You have to stay with me. I love you."

"Tell Oli I'm sorry we didn't have more time... but that it was his fault for being a stubborn asshole."

"I'm not going to say that," I replied to his joke, and Felix smirked. Even on death's door, he was still trying to make me laugh.

"Then tell him I love him. Tell him that even though our time together was short, I never felt more alive than I was with him. Tell him I said thank you for showing me what true happiness was," Felix said, his breaths coming shallower and his words slower. His grip on my hand began to go slack, and my heart splintered at knowing this was it. "Tell him I'll be waiting patiently for him in the next life."

"I will," I vowed as my tears fell from my face to his.

"Promise me you'll stay kind and clever. Don't ever wield such power that you forget that—that you forget who you are," he whispered, and I nodded.

"I promise." His life was slipping through my fingers like sand. "Please don't leave me," I begged, though the words were barely coherent.

"I love you, cupcake," he said as his eyes fluttered closed for the final time.

"I love you," I sobbed, falling over my friend as I felt his heart stop beneath my magic.

I pulled my Gift out, not wanting to feel his death so intimately. I clutched his body as I cried and cursed the Gods and Dashiell for taking him from me, though I knew the only person I had to blame was me.

Branches crunched around me as someone's approach filled the space, and I clutched Felix tighter as I crafted a dagger in my hand, ready to defend myself and the body of my best friend.

"Oh Gods, what happened?!" Elenora asked as she and a companion that wasn't Olivier stepped through the trees and rushed us.

"We were attacked, and he was trying to protect me," I answered, and the man placed his hands on Felix's chest. Everything in me grabbed onto the hope I knew I shouldn't have had. "You're a Medicus?" I asked quickly, but the man shook his head.

"An Imperium," he replied, and I watched as he pushed his Gift into my friend. There wasn't anything *I* could do, but I also wasn't skilled in that Gift, never having been trained properly. I held my breath for a painful moment as the man twisted his head to give Elenora a look I couldn't distinguish.

"Keep trying," she instructed, arching a groomed brow. After the briefest of hesitations, the man nodded and concentrated on his task once more.

I continued to harbor hope as I stroked Felix's hair from his face, which was so much paler than when he was alive, undoubtedly from all the blood loss. After another minute, the man fell back to his knees and gasped for breath as if he had just sprinted a mile.

"I'm so sorry. He's gone," he said. Though I already knew it to be the case from when I felt his heart cease beating, it didn't stop the pain I felt from hearing it confirmed from someone else's lips.

Just then, another set of footsteps sounded, and I watched as Olivier stumbled through the trees. He looked distressed and had a large gash on his leg with blood flowing from it. I glanced around at our company and took in their appearance for the first time. They were bloodied and bruised, seeming to have fought in their own battle.

"They're locking down the borders after receiving news that the king had been killed. We had to fight our way here," Elenora said, and I turned away as Olivier came closer, knowing I would have to deliver the news I never wanted to.

"Oli," I began, but he just shook his head as he looked down at the body I held in my lap.

"No," he demanded, refusing to believe his own eyes.

"Oli, I'm so sorry," I cried, feeling the sting of watching him break and knowing it was all my fault.

"NO!" he yelled, but it came out more like a sob. "No, he can't be... No."

Olivier came forward and dropped to his knees as he took Felix from me, clutching his head in his hands, and cried over the love he had lost.

I shuffled away, wanting to give him space, and Elenora and her friend helped pull me up. A yelp of pain escaped me as I realized I couldn't put any pressure on my leg, thanks to the arrow I had been shot with. The man ripped it from my flesh, and I felt the familiar tingling of magic seep into my skin as he used my blood to clot the hole.

"Ainsley, this is Brandle," she said, and I looked up to see one of the Princes of Ministro standing before me. He had tanned skin and dark hair, and I could see why Dashiell and Felix had assumed I was speaking to him the day of the kings' meeting.

"Felix said you were a total prick," I announced weakly, the emotion thick in my voice at the mention of my fallen friend. Brandle smiled sadly and nodded.

"I am," he agreed. For some reason, that made me feel better. "We can discuss all the reasons why later, but for now, we need to go."

"Where?" I asked, knowing that we were going to have a tough time escaping.

"Get down!" Brandle yelled, and I dropped to the ground just as an arrow flew over us. A popping sound echoed, and I stood to see a soldier's body slumped into the grass. His skull was in pieces as if it exploded from his shoulders. I glanced at Brandle, and he shrugged. "Our Gift allows us to control blood flow and the organs. There's a lot we can do, Ainsley," he said carefully, and the seriousness with which he spoke was like a weight on my chest.

"More soldiers are coming," Elenora said, and she looked at Brandle nervously. "We need to split up. Oli, take Ainsley and head to Tenebrae's portal. I'll inform Evander of our change in plans."

"I'm not leaving Felix behind," I replied, and she nodded.

"Brandle will carry him to Agnitio's portal and—"

"No, he belongs in Tenebrae. He stays with me," I commanded, but Elenora shook her head, and I sensed this would turn into a fight.

"Ainsley is the heir, so she pulls rank," Olivier said, placing Felix down softly before coming to my side to defend me.

"You're right, Olivier, she *is* the Heir to Tenebrae, and that's why our priority should be to get *her* to safety. Our best bet is to split up, and you know it. She can't walk, and you can't carry them both," Elenora explained, and I hated that she was making sense. "Get her to safety, and we'll draw them away from you. I'll get Felix to Agnitio, and then once we're there, we can get his body to Tenebrae."

"I can't leave him," I sobbed, looking at my friend's lifeless body in the grass.

"Ainsley, look at me," Elenora said, stepping into my view. "I swear to you, I won't leave his body here. I will ensure Felix makes his way back to Tenebrae, where he belongs."

I looked at Olivier to gauge whether or not he thought it was a good plan, though I knew it was. He nodded subtly, and Eleanora took that as her cue to have Brandle carry my friend before I could give my permission.

"I'll let Evander know to open Tenebrae's portal now. It's right through those trees and should only take ten minutes if you run."

"Fifteen on that leg," Brandle added as they began to leave the area with my friend in his arms. "You might want to hurry," he announced, jerking his chin toward a hill, and I stood on tiptoes to find another group of soldiers running up it.

Gods dammit.

"There's a book in Felix's pocket that we need translated," I instructed, and Elenora nodded.

Olivier scooped me into his arms with a grunt of pain, and we took off in the opposite direction of Elenora and Brandle. Faint popping sounds, followed by horrified screams and Brandle's soft laughter, echoed in my ears as we ran while they diverted the attention to them rather than us.

Oli sprinted hard through the night as we aimed for the portal, both of us quiet as we grieved the loss of Felix. I may have been alive, but I wasn't sure how to survive such a loss. He was my best friend, and I treated him like shit in the end. He risked his life for me time and again and deserved so much more than I gave him.

The portal appeared in the distance, shimmering in the moonlight and ready for our arrival, but before we could get close, Olivier screamed in pain as an arrow pierced his shoulder. I tumbled to the soft grass as he dropped me, only to see him fall when another arrow landed in his leg. I sat up, crafting a dagger and throwing it at one of the soldiers running for us. It landed between his eyes, but not before he shot an arrow that lodged itself in my side.

I screamed in pain as the next soldier ran for us, sinking his arrow into my shoulder before I could release my dagger. I collapsed onto the grass as the pain of my injuries blurred my vision. I was going to pass out from blood loss at any moment, and I couldn't focus enough to call on my magic to try and stop my bleeding. The soldier fell to the ground with a sword embedded into his chest before he could reach us, thanks to Olivier's perfect aim. Oli got to his feet, though one leg dragged behind him as he tried and failed to pick me up.

A scream tore through my throat as agony rippled along my body from wounds that covered me. Oli was too hurt to lift me, and I was too broken to stand on my own. We were so close, yet so far from tasting freedom. Shouts rang out in the distance, indicating more soldiers were on their way, and the dark night sky lit up as lightning struck all around. We were being hunted, and King Dashiell wasn't going to stop until he found his father's murderer.

"We have to hurry," I said, rolling to my side and deciding I would crawl the last stretch. There was no way in hell I was going to be a prisoner in Caelum. I had lost too much tonight, and my freedom wouldn't be taken too.

Arrows landed all around us as we reached the portal. Olivier entered first, grabbing my arm and pulling me through until we were in a dark cave in Tenebrae. I watched as he reached for the transfer paper in his pocket and wrote a command to close the portal. We covered our heads as weapons passed through until finally, a humming noise sounded, and the shimmer disappeared, leaving the rock wall solid again.

A minute passed when the swooshing sound of wind echoed in the cave, followed by thunderous footfalls.

"Ainsley!" Evander bellowed, rushing to my side. "What the fuck happened?!"

"We were attacked," Olivier answered. I screamed from the pain as Evander lifted me and traversed the three of us away.

I was enveloped in the familiar scents of our home, and I stifled a cry to know I was finally safe with him. My body may have been broken, but if I died tonight, I'd do so in the arms of the man I loved and in the place that was my safe haven.

"I've got you, my love," Evander whispered, kissing my forehead as we hurried through the house. "Don't you dare fucking leave me." The agony was overwhelming, and I could feel my grip on the world start to slip. I was being pulled away to wherever we went when we died.

"Felix," I croaked, and Van looked down at me with mournful eyes. Blackness began to cloud my vision as the pain of my injuries became too much for my body to handle.

"I'm so sorry," he said. Though he hated Felix, I knew he meant every word.

"I killed Perceval," I admitted, and Evander nodded as we rushed through the halls. Apparently, he had already heard the news. He didn't offer his opinion, knowing it wasn't the time for that.

I felt such joy tonight at ending the man that had brought so much suffering to me and those I held dear, only to be filled with a grief unlike anything I had ever known. My secrets may have led to Felix's death, but it was King Dashiell's men that shot that fatal arrow. It was *his* order that ended my best friend's life. And that was something I wasn't ever going to forget.

"And now I'm going to kill Dashiell," I promised before darkness invaded my mind and consciousness was stolen from me completely.

74.

Dashiell

Blood dripped, warm and thick, the deep red appearing more like black in the night. I twisted my hands to look at my palms, still unsure why I hadn't bothered to wash the event of what had happened from them. The night was silent, at least for me, as I drowned out the angered commotion with my own fucked up thoughts.

When I saw Felix sneaking through the grounds earlier this evening, I knew without a doubt he was leaving.... Which meant Ainsley would be following right behind him. And I wasn't going to let her go without hearing me out—at least, I thought that would be the case.

Once I realized she had cast an illusion to evade me, I was both impressed and furious. I was angry she was never going to hear my side. Angry that I would never get to see her again. Angry that I didn't get to say goodbye... To either of them. We were a family, and now we were nothing.

"Your Majesty," a voice said with such urgency that I was sure he had been saying my new title several times in an effort to grab my attention.

Majesty—king.

I was the fucking King of Caelum now. Flames licked over my stained skin as if the realization called forth the Gift I was unable to control fully. I quickly recalled the magic, bringing it back into myself. I knew Ainsley was powerful and intelligent—it was evident in the way she effortlessly wielded her Gifts and how she meticulously played my father for a fool. But I didn't ever think she'd be *this* reckless.

Not only did she murder a King of Disparya in his room, she got caught doing it. There was no hiding behind her actions, no covering it up. She murdered the King of Caelum and would have to be held accountable for it. She had to be caught and brought to justice. And my job as the new king was to do just that—even if it broke my heart to make that call.

"What is it?" I demanded, finally looking up from the grass that now contained a small pool of blood from my dripping hands—my father's blood. "Did you find them?"

"Yes, but..." my late father's favorite advisor said. "Well..."

"Fucking spit it out," I commanded, my patience thinning.

"Bring him out," he announced, and my guards escorted a soldier drenched in blood who looked both terrified and furious. I turned from where I had watched Ainsley disappear into the woods and strode to meet him halfway as my instincts urged that something was very fucking wrong.

"Your Majesty," he said with a false confidence given away by his trembling hands. "We found them." Already? Ainsley and I had fought no more than a half hour ago and she had gotten a decent head start thanks to her shadows making it impossible to see for a while after she left.

My pulse picked up, and I glanced over my shoulder as if I'd see them striding through the tree line, but there was no one. My eyes drifted back to the soldier before me, and I arched a brow in a clear demand for an explanation.

"We surrounded them in a clearing not far," he said, and I pushed past him, ready to head there myself. "But..."

I froze at that single word, clenching my fists as flames spread over my flesh. Did they manage to get away?

"I know you said to bring them back unharmed..." he stated, and the air was stolen from my lungs at his insinuation. I was explicitly clear that they were to be returned to me without a scratch on them, and if that weren't the case, I would kill whoever was responsible for it. "But..."

There was that fucking word again.

I turned slowly, waiting for him to finish his report before I ripped his throat out—either for hurting them or for taking too fucking long to tell me what happened out there.

"When one of the arrows injured Lady Ainsley—"

"Princess," I interrupted. She may have been wanted for murder and treason, but she was still royalty. I sucked in a deep and steadying breath as I let his confession of her injury wash over me before making a mental note to destroy the soldier who defied my order and loosed the arrow.

"Princess Ainsley," he corrected quickly. "Well, she murdered our king, and we saw it as our opportunity to take her out."

My magic thrashed in my body in a desperate attempt to get out. It had always felt connected to her, and hearing that she may have been killed was causing it to lose its shit.

"But..."

"Say that fucking word one more Gods damn time," I warned, and the man swallowed hard.

"Lord Felix dove in front to protect her and..."

No. Absolutely fucking not.

"And he was killed, Your Majesty."

I spun and fisted the soldier's uniform, needing to hold on to something tangible. Thunder rumbled as my Aerian Gift surged forth, bringing Caelum a storm as violent as the one occurring within me. There was no fucking way this was happening.

"Are you sure?!" I demanded, tightening my grip.

"Yes, Your Majesty. It pierced his heart."

I dropped the soldier to the ground, stumbling back a step as my world was torn from me in a single night. The pain of my third Gift ripping through my body was nothing compared to the excruciating agony I felt now.

"Bring me the soldier who killed him!" I snarled.

"Which part? There's nothing whole left. She killed them all, and I only barely managed to escape."

My mind flashed to the corpse of my father and the condition he was in. He was... Unrecognizable. His body was nothing more than a bloodied heap of shredded flesh and bone with a severed head next to it.

Our king was killed by the woman I loved, and my kingdom wanted retribution. My soldiers wanted payment for that debt, and I couldn't blame them. I would punish them for disobeying their new king, but I couldn't fault them for being in an uproar. And now my best friend... Felix, who was my brother—my family—was taken from this life because of Ainsley's choice to murder my father. And it couldn't stand. She made her choice, and now she would have to live with the consequences.

I reached into my pocket and clutched the red stone of my father's ring.

"Find her and bring her to me, now."